Julian Rathbone is the author of many books, including *Joseph* and *King Fisher Lives*, both of which were shortlisted for the Booker prize. His most recent novel, *The Last English King*, was widely acclaimed on publication, and is also available in Abacus paperbacks. Julian Rathbone lives in Dorset.

JOSEPH

THE LIFE OF JOSEPH BOSHAM,
SELF–STYLED 3RD VISCOUNT OF BOSHAM,
COVERING THE YEARS FROM 1790 TO 1813,
EDITED WITH A PROLOGUE AND AFTERWORD

JULIAN RATHBONE

'. . . Wellington lived in the grip of a nervous inability to
refrain from answering letters.'

(Philip Guedalla: *The Duke*)

'. . . this work, and others like it tend to corrupt as much as
please. The best one can say for them is that time spent in
their study is time lost to more profitable pursuits.'

(Charles Edward Bosham, 1750–1811)

An *Abacus* Book

First published in Great Britain by Michael Joseph Ltd 1979
This edition published by Abacus 1999

Copyright © Julian Rathbone 1979

A CIP catalogue record for this book
is available from the British Library.

ISBN 0 349 11227 4

Typeset in Bembo by M Rules
Printed and bound in Great Britain by
Clays Ltd, St Ives plc

Abacus
A division of
Little, Brown and Company (UK)
Brettenham House
Lancaster Place
London WC2E 7EN

JOSEPH

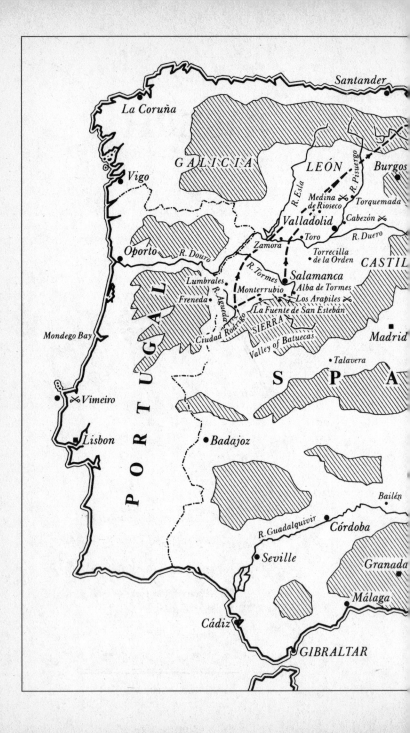

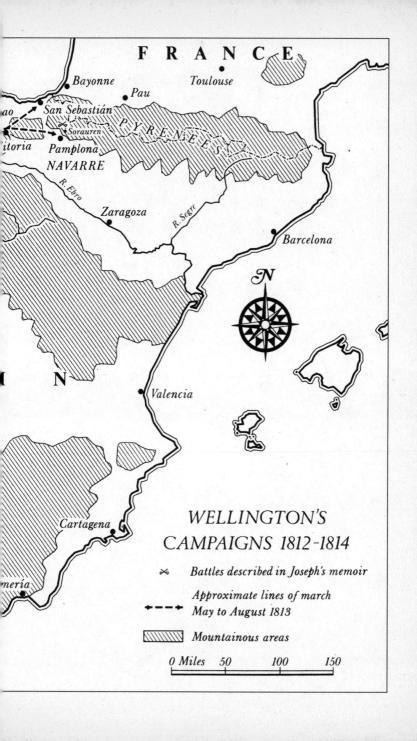

FRANCE

Bayonne
Toulouse
Pau
San Sebastián
~ao
Sorauren
P Y R E N E E S
itoria
Pamplona
NAVARRE
R. Ebro
Zaragoza
R. Segre
Barcelona
N
N
Valencia
Cartagena
mería

WELLINGTON'S
CAMPAIGNS 1812-1814

✄   *Battles described in Joseph's memoir*

- - - ▶   *Approximate lines of march
May to August 1813*

▨   *Mountainous areas*

0 Miles   50   100   150

PROLOGUE

The *Marché à la Brocante* in Pau, in the Atlantic Pyrenees, is an ugly, modern, circular hall in cream-painted concrete. The arrangement of the stalls follows the circular structure – each vendor's segment of the circle narrows from the perimeter towards a concentric passage which takes one round from stall to stall, and each vendor arranges his wares on roughly the same pattern. Thus at the front, at the narrowest part of each segment, are one or two tables with glass-topped boxes of coins and medals, most a century or more old but none in mint or even collectable condition; these are often overshadowed by a coat and umbrella stand hung with Napoleonic sabres rusting away at absurdly high prices and supporting flintlocks and bayonets from the same era. One even has a regimental colour, a *Tricolore* with tarnished tassels and a brass eagle on the top of the pole, but the regimental number has long since been torn from the central white panel.

Immediately behind the coins many stalls have books: almost all modern and all trashy – illustrated histories in several volumes but the last always missing, paper-backed romances, and last year's porn (*Lui* and *Absolu*) gone soft already. Here too, old linen is displayed – petticoats and shifts, clean and pressed though darned and sometimes rust-marked or singed – sought after for the quality of the lace edgings which often would not disgrace an altar.

Next come the finer things, kept under the stall-holder's eye either because he fears they might be lifted or because he knows this is where his turnover is quickest – cases of dissecting instruments brought in by students who have qualified or failed, microscopes, draughtsman's gear, glasses and crocks of real quality though chipped; then, as each segment widens, massive pieces of furniture, wardrobes as big as coaches pushed up against ranges made from what looks like gun-metal, and piled on top of them huge canvases in heavy gilt frames, and gilded statues of Virgins and Saints, some perhaps genuinely Baroque but lacking an arm here and a nose there, the gold leaf flaked and speckled with wood-worm.

Amongst all this, beneath a table covered with lace-edged linen, I found the Branwater Trunk.

It was smaller than a modern trunk, only just over a yard long and about two feet deep, the bottom part made of wicker-work, the vaulted lid of moleskin. Four brass letters on the top – R.F. P. B. – hint at the identity of at least one of its past owners; a faded torn label is more specific: 'Miss Renée Branwater, Steyne Hotel, Harrogate, Angleterre. Not Wanted on the Journey'. After three months in Pau, researching background for a thriller I was planning, I was already familiar with survivals from the town's English Period – the elegant Villa Lawrence with its lawns and cedars, now a public park; Rue Henry Russell, and Rue Alexander Taylor; St Andrew's Church now only in use on the fourth Sunday of every month; and most pathetic of all, the little collection of English books tucked away in a corner of the modern functional library, books whose fly-leaves carry their histories: for example, '*Ex Libris* James Branwater, 1865' in a flowing copperplate, followed by a rubber stamp 'St Andrew's Church Library', then 'Ville de Pau, Bibliothèque de Prêt', all on the inside of *The Ordeal of Richard Feverel*.

And now in that ugly hall filled with the gloom of a November afternoon I had stumbled on the Branwaters again. Most of the stalls were closing; nevertheless I tugged at the cracked dry leather straps and slowly lifted the lid. It groaned and the wicker-work beneath cracked as a long forgotten tension returned to its structure; I know it is fanciful but I felt it was saying 'at last, at last'.

The vendor thought so too. God knows how long he had had the thing on his hands – probably he had inherited it from his father or even grandfather. As I straightened he was standing at my shoulder.

'*Deux cents francs,*' he said. He was a small man, with a thin grey moustache and a black beret.

'For this?' I cried. I was holding one of those folders children used to carry piano music in – two stiff boards with loose flaps at the edges, hinged on one side with a strip of canvas and with ribbon ties on the others. I had found it on the floor of the trunk. It was stuffed with papers.

'No, no of course not. For the trunk, two hundred. It is antique. For that . . . ,' he glanced shrewdly, but I am sure he had never seen it before, 'for that, fifty francs.'

I had only forty on me. I undid the ties and glanced at the top sheets, then I did them up again, rather quickly.

'Forty francs,' I said. 'It's all I have on me.'

He shrugged, muttered a gallic curse or two, and agreed.

The market was not open again until the following Saturday, but I went back then with two hundred francs I could not really afford, for I was in an elated state, and I wanted to do something extravagant, silly. The wicker and moleskin trunk went with the papers it had guarded so well, and before I got properly down to work on them I felt they should be reunited. But the trunk was gone; absurdly the vendor claimed he had no recollection of selling it; had I not had the papers at home I should almost have suspected that I had imagined the whole thing.

The third sheet was an autograph letter from the first Duke of Wellington, and it was this that I had seen when I paid up my forty francs. The rest, apart from two more letters from the Duke appearing later, is the memoir of one Joseph Bosham, third

Viscount Bosham, and it follows this prologue almost exactly as I found it, with only minimal alteration to spelling and punctuation, and no cuts. It appears to have been written between 1816 and 1823, and it recounts the quite extraordinary adventures of Joseph Bosham from his birth in Italy around 1790 to the Battle of Sorauren in the Spanish Pyrenees in 1813. It was written in Pau, while the author was in and out of the service of a retired English officer – Captain Branwater, who must surely have been one of the founders of the English colony there, and presumably an ancestor of Renée.

'In and out of' the Branwaters' service – occasional 'misunderstandings' with his patron and employer, only slyly alluded to in the text, seem to have been the initial inspiration of the memoir, or rather the need to replace an income suddenly cut off as a result; for Joseph seems to have started with the idea of writing his life for publication, with a dedication to the Duke of Wellington. In this respect it will be remembered the Duke considered himself 'much exposed to authors' claiming this privilege. Part of the memoir (notably Chapters II and III in Volume I, Chapter II in Volume II, Chapter I in Volume III) seem to have started life as drafts (presumably here expanded) of letters actually addressed to Wellington in answer to the letters from the Duke that preface each volume. What we do not have are Joseph's original letters to the Duke, but it seems he was not above bothering his august correspondent with begging letters or worse – I doubt if he dared to stoop to actual extortion or blackmail, but he probably hinted.

Thankfully, the hope or need of 'raising the wind' was merely the initial inspiration – the reader will quickly discover that the main motives, as I suppose is always the case with such memoirs, are confession and self-justification, with the borderline between the two constantly, amusingly, and sometimes unwittingly blurred – and all thought of a public, whether ducal or otherwise, is forgotten. Clearly throughout most of what follows Joseph is writing for himself, and we should not allow ourselves to be confused or put off when, just occasionally, he slips back into addressing himself again to 'Your Grace'.

Briefly, I must acknowledge with gratitude the patience of my publishers, the kindness and generosity of Charlotte and John Wolfers, and my wife's help with typing, proof-reading, and correcting Joseph's not always correct accenting of French and Spanish. To her I dedicate (with permission) my share in bringing Joseph Bosham's memoir to light.

Finally, of course, it is his work that is offered here, not mine. I am sure he would not wish to be taken too seriously, at least not as fodder for post-graduate research in his period, but if he is read with something of the pleasure afforded by, say, Cellini's Autobiography or Boswell's Diaries, then he will have had his deserts, and my labour will not have been wasted.

J.R.

Contents

PROLOGUE

VOLUME ONE

Part One

I   An Early Memory of Happy Times in Later Infancy,
Being a Fitting Introduction to Much of What is to
Follow   7

II   A Brief Rehearsal of my Antecedents   20

III   My Domestic Situation in Childhood; the
Eccentricities of my Education   30

IV   My Introduction to the Martial Life, and an Adventure
that Followed, Less Pleasing to the Sensible Reader   39

Part Two

V   My Father makes Provision for my Future, by which I
enter on a Twelvemonth or More of Pleasure   57

VI   A Short Chapter relating my Inglorious Introduction
to the Art of TAUROMACHIA   71

VII   In which Rafael is Betrothed, and I too discover myself
Susceptible to the Tenderest Passion, but fix on an
Object Unworthy of my Attentions   75

VIII   A Disturbing Chapter, not Unconnected with the
Preceding and Perhaps Better NOT Read by Sensible
Readers or the Gentle Sex   93

IX   A Chapter more Edifying than the Last, not entirely free from Error, but this time of a Philosophical Nature, which in these Times, will give little or no Offence   110

X   A Chapter entirely Edifying providing a Fitting Conclusion to the Two preceding it, by showing Justice done to a Wrong-Doer, and thereby Refuting by Experience some of the Errors in the Rational Discourse of the Curate of Los Arapiles   125

XI   A Visit to my Father's Holding for the Grape Harvest leads to a Meeting with a Notable Man, and thence to a Favoured Place at the Bull Fights   133

XII   In Which Town and University Celebrate a Grand Festival of Bulls in Honour of Our Lady   145

PART THREE

XIII   A New Invasion by the French leads to a Strange Reunion with a Close Relation Long Forgot   159

XIV   The Wars Begin. After some Uncertainty as to whose side we are on, we March off to Join Battle with the French   174

XV   My First Experience of Battle; in which my Resolution to Stay Alive does not Fail   187

XVI   We Suffer a Grievous Loss   200

XVII   A Long Chapter including – A Lucky Escape from Certain Death; A Piece of Modern Music, most Affecting; and news of a General not like Those Met Before   208

VOLUME TWO

PART ONE

I   An Account, Prematurely Placed in the Narrative, and not in every detail Accurate, of How I joined the British Army   239

II   Concerning the Vexations that followed a too nice Desire to Spare the Feelings of the Bereaved   251

III   An Instructive Evening with a Very Great Man,
      followed by the Comments of the Curate of Los
      Arapiles. Much Nonsense and some Wisdom – None
      of it Invented by the Author   269

                         Part Two

IV   Carnival under the French, Followed by a most
      Fortunate and Affecting Reunion   313
V   I Enter on a Life of Ease in the Midst of War   335

                        Part Three

VI   I am Forced into a Career Fraught with Dreadful
      Dangers, yet Contrive to Make Shift   351
VII   Of Devious Schemes Resorted to, Necessary for
      Survival in Difficult Times   373
VIII A Visit to Los Arapiles Discovers an Old Man
      Wandering in his Wits   383

                    VOLUME THREE

                         Part One

I   A Short Chapter, Introductory to the Third Volume,
      offering Examples of a Softness that Honours a Noble
      Nature   407
II   Salamanca, so recently the Scene of a Glorious Triumph,
      is Abandoned again to the Mercies of a Rapacious Foe;
      on the Retreat I fall in with Mistress Flora Tweedy, an
      Heroine too late introduced if what I write were
      Fiction merely, but an Heroine nonetheless, in Fact   413
III   A Night Disturbed with Dreams and Illusions, yet
      Important Matters of Fact occur as well   435
IV   In which I carry Two Ladies through Terrible
      Vicissitudes and Perils to a Happy Outcome   446

PART TWO

V   Of the Enchanted Time spent in the Batuecas, a Space for Recollection, to set certain Records Straight   485

VI   The Same, Continued   509

PART THREE

VII   Mistress Reaney Indisposed, Unseasonable Weather, and Paqui gone lame, bring us late to Salamanca, where we learn News – Some Distressing, Some Curious   545

VIII   A Grand Competition for a Cup, Recalled; a Feast; and a Review   573

IX   We Reach the Basque Lands, but Mistake our Way, and, after Dangers Survived, Blunder in amongst the French, who yet provide Us with a Commodity we despaired of – a Mid-Wife, and she an old Friend at that   588

X   A Meditation on Eggs, Yet Another Battle, concluding with Matters that will be of Interest to the Reader who has come with us so far   608

XI   A Long Chapter Recording Amazing Scenes after Battle; How a Villain suffered a Fate Deserved; and How Providence put me in way of a Wet-Nurse, with other Matters too, of almost equal Import   624

VOLUME ONE

Apsley House
London

3rd October, 1816

The Duke acknowledges receipt of Mr Bosham's letter of last month. The Duke does not outright deny the possibility of some obligation to his correspondent since he has no recollection at all of ever making Mr Bosham's acquaintance, and where memory has failed in one respect, it may well have done so in another. The Duke therefore advises Mr Bosham that he cannot entertain Mr Bosham's request for employment at the time of writing; however, if Mr Bosham would be so good as to furnish full details of his antecedents, of his present station in life, of the circumstances under which he met the Duke, and, very specifically, of the exact nature of the obligation he claims, the Duke will reconsider his decision.

Wellington

PART ONE

Chapter I

*An Early Memory of Happy Times in Later Infancy, Being a
Fitting Introduction to Much of What is to Follow.*

I

That I was born in 1790, that I resided in Spain, nay in the very
cockpit of Spain, I mean in Salamanca, between 1796 and 1813,
must evidence to anyone versed at all in the History of the Late
Wars that the tale of my life will in part be the story of those wars.
Indeed it is so. I played my part in many a long campaign, through
tedious sieges, and at more than one glorious battle, not the least
of which was that fought on the Twenty-Second of July, 1812,
round and in the very village where my youth was spent, a league
and a half South of the City – I mean *Los Arapiles* itself.

Yet there were strands in the thread of my life other than the
bloody one of War and it is no easy matter to separate all out, so
closely were they spun together; and to those who find the confusion of matter in what follows a reason for censure I must say –
thus was my life in its entirety, and life is not often nice nor neat,
and if they want their Wars and Heroes unmixed with stuff of a
lower sort, they should lay out their money on Histories, or on
Memoirs of the Great, or on some other kind of *Fiction*.

Beside the bloody strand of War, mentioned above, the *yarn* of
my life is flecked with the green thread of Love and the black one
of private enmity or *vendetta*, and since I knew of both before I
heard the beat of drum or crash of musket; since, though scarcely

ten years old, I had made a mortal enemy and enjoyed the tender caresses of the Other Sex, and this within the space of three days in the Summer of 1800, it is in that time that I choose to begin this truthful account of the years I have so far been blessed with.

This is the manner in which the feud that has shaped my life began. One hot afternoon the three of us, being small boys and no less inclined to vice than small boys usually are, took it into our heads to relieve ourselves against Tía María's back wall; and I can still call to mind how growing comfort was nicely measured by three irregular arches of wet blackness that slowly spread up the pure brilliance of the newly white-washed plaster, and by the three puddles that sank away in the red dust of her yard, but this satisfaction was short-lived.

Hens squawked and the muffled percussion of beating wings heralded the arrival of their Mistress, an ugly stout woman, like a sow, armed with a leather bottle, half-full, swung like an Antique Mace from a raw-hide thong. With this powerful weapon and to the accompaniment of many curses, she sent *Rubén* headlong into her dung-heap, gave *Fernando* a bloody nose, and put me on my back, untrussed as I was. As soon as we could we upped and fled, severally and in different directions, but knowing where we would reassemble once sure the pursuit had failed – that is we made for the angle between the brown stone wall of our village Church, my Father's Church, and the wall of his cottage garden. Here, beneath a pair of stunted cypress trees, we caught our breaths again: Fernando tilted back his head and Rubén rubbed his singing ear. Yet for all our injuries we had had an adventure and the time passed sweetly in the telling of it and re-telling, until gradually the heat and boredom settled over us like blankets, and the steady chirp of the Cricket in the Cypress Tree twisted its way into our ears: three boys – dirty, mop-headed, squatting in the dust and shale, poking our noses, picking at the ground with twigs, at a loss for something to do.

Rubén chucked a stone into the cypress tree but the cricket chirped on. He ran his hand through his coarse red hair – his

Judas hair for everyone knows Judas had red hair – and he turned to me.

'José's thing,' he said.

I looked at him, determined not to let a change of countenance reflect my feelings.

'Pepe's thing,' repeated Fernando, using the familiar form of my name, and he giggled.

There was a note in Rubén's voice that made me wary – micturition in Tía María's yard had been my plan; the result for him had been a stunning blow and a tumble in a heap of dung: would he now seek revenge for his humiliation? He straightened and squared up to me.

'Let's see it,' said Fernando, 'let's see the English thing.'

Rubén spoke slowly: 'It is not an English thing. It is a Jew's, a Moor's.'

The cricket at last bated its vacuous song and the very dust motes in the air ceased their lazy dance beneath the hard blue sky, as Nature awaited what was to come.

I licked dry tongue over cracked lip. Rubén was bigger than I, and though slightly built, a head and more taller. His fists were round and large.

'Jews and Moors,' he went on more quickly, 'have the bit of skin at the end cut off – because God said they should. As a sign they are dirty, dirty like . . .'

I delivered my attack head down, charging his stomach, and he banged my ear as I came. I charged again, this time for his eyes, and he caught my fingers and twisted them until they cracked and I had to scream, then he pushed me into a heap of rubble left by a mason who had repaired the wall maybe a decade before.

'Jew,' he said. 'Moor.'

My hand closed on a large piece of dressed stone, with sharp corners. It must have weighed all of a pound and more but my aim was good and somehow he misjudged its flight: it would have hit his body or his shoulder, but he ducked his head into it. It went across his scalp like a butcher's knife parting the russet hair of a kid;

for a second nothing, then the dusty hair flooded with a deeper scarlet, an awful tide broke across his forehead and ran in streams over eyes and nose.

He was badly dazed. He raised his hand to wipe his face, and then looked at it. Till then he had not realised that the blinding fluid was vital.

'*Jesús María*,' he said, 'You've killed me,' and he fainted away, so that I thought he was dead indeed.

I ran blindly out of the village and uphill into the wheat which was head-high and just turning gold. Flocks of larks and fieldfares rose ahead of me. Soon the slope steepened and the wheat gave up – I was at the foot of a stony hill whose flanks supported scrub oak. Here on the edge of the sea of wheat I paused, shaded my eyes, and looked back at the village, already half a mile away. On the near side was the church, ochre, squat, with its one bronze bell hung beneath a stork's nest, and the houses huddled round – white, brown, grey, red-roofed, just one, my Father's, with a chimbley. I forced my breathing into regularity and strove to listen. A dog barked, but there were no shouts or cries, no chase behind me. I set my face to the hill and continued my escape more calmly, with less terror. Already resentment predominated over shock and fear. What had happened was not my fault. Rubén was a bully, a Judas, everyone knew that. I walked on. A magpie whirred up from the ground twenty yards away and sailed over the scrub, and I looked up to the summit of the Lesser Arapil, the *Arapil Chico*.

This eminence is the smaller of two cliff-like crags that rise from the plain a mile or so away from my village, and to my village they have given a name – *Los Arapiles*. I was approaching the top from the West, the gentler slope, stony but supporting flowers – in Spring tiny blue ones and yellow, star-shaped, in July poppies, cornflowers, daisies and some dried out by the sun before they dropped and for this reason called Everlastings, and everywhere thyme and the smell of thyme. The last twenty feet were more difficult, steeper, strewn with boulders, but I had been here often on my own and could pick my way, small though I was, with ease. At the top I threw myself down in a rocky hollow in which I knew I could hardly be seen, but from which I could survey the country around and be sure I had reached my ayerie unobserved.

A half-mile to the South rose the *Arapil Grande* – a flat-topped rampart, black and shadowed, above the wheat and the distant oak forest where wild boar roamed. Between me and it a red kite floated on a level with my eyes, supported on the limpid element. Then it tipped its wings, the sun illuminated its bold plumage, and it soared up like a huge sheet of coloured, jagged paper.

Beneath, a cloud of red dust progressed, it seemed by inches, along the track towards the village and I could hear the squeak and rumble of a cart and just discern the wide spread of an ox's horns in front. Although I could not see the drover, I could hear his whistle – the only proof that any human other than myself was left to walk the earth.

I shifted. To the North the plain, in gently undulating hills, spread like a huge down bed beneath a quilt of ripening wheat to the City four miles away. Framed between two hills the brown battlements rose to a cluster of honey-coloured towers and domes – the cathedrals, churches, convents and colleges of Salamanca.

2

I was there throughout the long afternoon and experienced during this time a variety of emotion in which loneliness and defiance were most to the fore. Always I sought to justify myself – to excuse the angled rock I had hurled, the swift rush of blood – and to this end I had to pursue lines of logic that would have taxed a brain not precociously tutored in reason as mine had been by a philosophical parent. I had thrown the stone, that much

I had to admit. But why? Because Rubén had called me Jew and Moor and because I could not fight him, and because he was bigger than I. Why was he bigger than I? Because . . . but no, excuse did not lie that way – I could not shift the blame simply because he was bigger.

A stone clinked nearby. A coney scattered pebbles and vanished with a flash of his tail. The villagers snared them, we boys went after them with slings, Rubén's father, the baker, had a fowling piece and he shot them.

Why had he called me Jew, Moor? Because my thing did not have a cap of skin. I giggled at the memory of Tía María and her newly whitened, newly stained wall. The shadow of the kite floated across the rock towards me, swift and dark, and put me in mind of the carp in the deeper pools of the River Tormes, and then I thought again – why was my thing bald? Why was I small?

My shadow lengthened, the sun lost some of its powerful heat. I began to wonder if I was brave enough to see out the night: there would be owls, foxes, a mountain cat perhaps, witches.

Down below a black shape moved away from the Church and into the wheat. Soon I was certain – the black cassock and wide-brimmed hat could belong only to my Father – and he would know where to find me. I watched his progress with divergent feelings – relief entirely at odds with newly awakened apprehension. He reached the lower slopes of the Arapil and was for a moment lost from view. I need not look to be whipped, I told myself. Only once had he whipped me, and that when I had spilled an ink-well on his copy of Ferguson's *Cosmology*. That, it seemed to me, would rank more serious than killing Rubén, for I quite wrongly believed that my Father set more store by his books than by his neighbours.

He reappeared, about an hundred feet below me. He shaded his eyes and called.

'Joseph. Joseph, may I come up?'

It was a good omen that he had used the tongue of our English forbears: it was a sign of intimacy, even tenderness between us. In anger or company we used Spanish or Italian. I stood up and waited and sucked my thumb.

Soon he was squatting beside me, his knees spread beneath his cassock and his black sombrero, decorated with a blue cornflower, dangling in his hands.

'Good place this,' he remarked, when his breath had become easier. 'I'm glad you still come here. Fernando said you headed this way.'

It was my Father who had brought me to my ayerie two years before, and most of the way I had ridden on his shoulders. But age had shortened his country walks and for a year now he had ventured hardly more than a mile from the village unless on his mule and with the weather neither hot nor miry.

'Rubén's all right you know. Scalp wounds always bleed alarmingly, but he'll be up and about in a day or two.'

I wept then and even now I can remember the dry warmth of his black serge as he took me, old though I was for such comfort, on his knee.

'Why did you throw the rock at him?' he asked, after an interval had passed. Since I did not answer, he went on: 'Was it because you are too small to fight him any other way?'

I nodded.

'You must not mind your size. Many lads leave their growing to an age above yours. But why did you want to fight him?'

'He called me a Jew, a Moor.'

'Silly of him. It's unlikely you could be both.' Then he stroked his thin white beard, which was like a goat's, a sure sign that the principle of open-minded rationality by which he endeavoured to regulate his life was about to assert itself. 'But by no means impossible. I have read of Jews who live in Barbary. Further to which young Rubén should know that red hair like his is common in certain Berber tribes . . . but he called you Jew and Moor and you were incensed. You were wrong to be moved. Only the ignorant would find such epithets unworthy. Many very rational men have belonged to those races, which have, in their time, attained . . . never mind. Why did he call you Jew and Moor?'

The tears and rare embrace had loosened restraints and yet it was with some difficulty – I found I did not know the English word for the offending organ – I managed to tell him.

He sat in silence for some moments and breathed two deep sighs – a sign he was preoccupied, as in his last years he was with increasing frequency, with the incorrigible irrationality of the human race.

Then: 'Foreign matter,' he began, 'can be trapped beneath the foreskin, and cause infection, pain and disease. Circumcision is the useful sacrifice that *Venus* may make to *Hygeia*, or, to use a word I only came across yesterday, derived from the same Goddess, it is a matter of *hygiene*. Perhaps one may say it is *hygienate*. Or *hygienic*. The Moorish and Jewish races show themselves more rational than us in many, many ways, not the least in practices hygienic or hygienate. Even their religions, which one may take to be their least rational parts, enjoin frequent bodily cleansing and ritual ablutions. Knowing all this, when you were born, I took you to a Rabbi who was a friend of mine and he performed the excision. I am sorry now that it has led to this misadventure – naturally I believed my action to be a rational one . . .' And he continued in this vein for some time, until, taking me by the hand, he led me down the steep rocky slopes, through the rosy goldness of the gathering dusk, towards the wide valley below, and as he did he was prompted into an exposition of how the *sinking* sun was an illusion, how it was the earth that turned and thus shifted us away from the sun, and this he attempted to demonstrate with two stones, one large and one small, the small one being the earth, which confused me, and he marked it with a dot of chalk taken from his pocket, and turned it to show how the dot turned away from the larger stone he called the sun.

'Father,' I asked, when at last he found no more to say on the subject, 'why did you not have this circumcision done on you?'

He stopped and I could hear the high-pitched, distant cries of swirling, mewling swifts far, far above us. At last he heaved the deepest sigh of all – the one he reserved for the recurrent redis-covery of his own by no means always latent irrationality.

3

Since these notes of mine, prepared towards a memoir, have already trespassed beyond the limits set by taste and decorum, I must now suppose that they will never be perused by eyes other than my own; yet I must acknowledge that setting them down has occasioned me some pleasure, and it seems a harmless thing to continue this solitary exercise and add the postscript to the adven-ture I have just rehearsed, a postscript which I shall find, if I continue to record what has been most important in my life, con-tains a hint of adventures to come and may therefore turn out to be more of a prologue than an afterword.

The three days after breaking open Rubén's head, I was left much to my own devices – Fernando and my other friends were perhaps a little in awe of me, and possibly wanted too to see if Rubén, who was – by virtue of his superior cunning – our leader, should incline to vengeance. And so it was without company that I set out again in the late afternoon of the third day for the Arapil Chico, but this time equipped with a sling. My purpose was a rabbit – a quarry often attempted but never yet achieved.

About half way through the still uncut wheat I realised I was followed by a girl, whom I soon identified as María Victoria – dark, winsome, a year or two older than I, the daughter of the far-rier and therefore born to the village *oligarchy* – those families that owned a little land of their own or carried on some trade essential to the rest of us. She was an hundred or so paces behind me. Puzzled, I gathered an ear of corn, threshed it between my palms, winnowed it by blowing through my cupped and laced up fingers, and then chewed the moist and fragrant grain. When I had spat out the last husk I found she was nearer and I could see she had stuck poppies in her hair, which was bound up above brown shoulders and a grubby white shift or smock. Across the hot swaying sea of corn I could hear she was singing to herself.

However, as I entered the bushy oaks my eye caught a flash of white, and all thought of María Victoria was obliterated as I set myself to get nearer the prey I had come after. I proceeded by inches over hillocks and round gnarled trunks until I could see six rabbits grazing on dried grass and wild lavender.

With bated breath and pounding pulse I fingered out a pebble from the leather pouch at my belt and unwound my sling. Whether to whirl it round my head for added velocity or launch it in one sweep was now a matter of urgent consideration: the first method was wildly inaccurate, the second achieved little more power than I could procure by throwing. My excitement was intense and all thought of the girl had quite gone. I fixed on the largest beast, a doe most likely gravid with young, and even as the leather rasped away with a rippling crack I knew I had it right – but I was lucky too. My projectile missed the doe but pitched with such force that on a rising rebound it bowled over one of the little ones and left it stunned as its uncaring companions vanished into the fastnesses of the warren.

Stunned or paralysed with fear? Perhaps both. At all events very much alive, with palpitating side and liquid brown eye that flickered shut and open as I crept nearer. But it would not move. As I stooped into a crouch above it I noticed a tiny drop of dark blood on its nose. I reached out my hand and caught it at the nape, enclosing its long flat ears. Its fur was dry and warm.

Now its consciousness returned and with it such a fury of motion, of convulsive strength as I would never have imagined. It nearly wriggled free but at the last moment my shifting grip fastened on its kicking back legs, so much longer than they had seemed, and holding it thus I was able to smash it against a rock, not once but again and again, so sometimes its head took the blow, sometimes its back.

I felt dizzy, almost sick at last – but not with revulsion: more out of the weariness that follows fulfilment. Now I could caress the still warm fur, peer into the dulled eye, feel the dead weight of the complete inanimate. Nothing is so dead as a creature that a second before you have felt to be alive – far deader than a stone, or a body in a coffin, or a carcase in the market.

I felt no pity and no guilt, save a sort of savage guilt, the guilt one sees in a cat's eyes when it looks up from a dead mouse, the guilt that makes it look round to see if it too may not now be the prey of something bigger. But there was no-one there, nothing. Never had the world seemed so quiet.

Cradling my baby rabbit in my arms I continued the ascent of the Arapil Chico.

María Victoria was waiting for me in the rocky hollow where my Father had found me. If I shut my eyes and smell a handful of dry thyme I can see her now. She was thin, leggy, very brown, with boyish chest and glossy black hair, braided and pinned above a pert, heart-shaped face. She was just of an age where her elders still considered her a child because there was no detectable swelling of breasts, but in fact she was already a true daughter of Eve. Soon she would be locked away behind barred windows to learn the arts of housewifery, the significance of chastity, and the glories of properly sanctified motherhood, but at the time I found her on the Arapil Chico she was as free as she would ever be, and how she chose to use her freedom supplies a lesson on the natural inclinations of the fair sex. Imagine what a pit the world would be if grown women were allowed the licence enjoyed by this girl!

The surprise I felt when I came upon her was not shared by her – she had been waiting for me, and giggled now at my nervousness.

'Hallo, Pepe.'

'Hallo, María Victoria.'

'Did you expect me here? Don't be frightened. I won't hurt you. Hey, you've caught a baby rabbit – is it still alive?'

'No, I killed it with my sling.' Absently I stroked the fur.

'Let's look, go on, let me look. Brother Jaime can't hit a rabbit with a sling. He can't even hit a dog and he's older than you as well as bigger.'

A little warm now with pride I crouched in front of her. She crouched too and stroked the rabbit in my lap and bent her head to kiss it. I could smell her hair and I marked the fine orange dust of the fields caught in the down along her neck-bone. The papery poppies were already wilted but remained as scarlet splashes in the darkness of her tresses. To steady herself she put her hand on my leg just below the knee, where my breeches ended. She caressed the bare skin on my calf.

'Was it a boy rabbit, or a girl?'

I blushed. 'I'm sure it's too young to tell.'

She giggled. 'Tell me exactly how you caught it.'

I lay back. The deep blue of the hot sky was a pool in which her intent face, dark eyes and thick eyebrows, swam. I rehearsed my adventure and as I did the feelings that went with it returned, but more sweetly.

When I was finished she was silent for a space. The red kite wheeled and soared above us.

Then she curled round and put her head on my stomach, away from my face, so I could not see her expression. Her voice was muffled.

'Pepe?'

'Yes?'

'Let me untruss your breeches.'

A spasm like a burning arrow shot through my chest and seemed to lodge at the root of my throat. It was not terror exactly, but something close to it, though not unpleasant.

'Why?' I asked, though I felt I knew the answer, indeed knew then that this was why she had come.

'The other boys say you are different.' Her hand was already fiddling at the opening.

'All right.'

She shifted her position so her elbows were on my stomach, her face still away from me. I was trapped with her thus.

'You are different, but nice.'

Nimble fingers caressed me so that soon I felt dizzy and the delicious melting sickness I had felt when stalking the rabbits returned, but with a sweeter strength. I began to moan and twist and this perhaps frightened her for she suddenly stopped and turned about to face me.

'You are a dirty little boy to let me do that.'

I felt cheated and falsely accused. 'It was your idea,' I said, 'and you're bigger than me.'

She giggled and leaned forward to kiss me; then, 'You had better truss up again,' she said.

'You can do it. You undid me.'

'He's gone soft and little again, quite shrivelled up,' and her giggle turned to a laugh and her silvery mocking rings in my ears yet.

Thus my first experience of love, of death too perhaps – at least of death brought so nearly home as the bundle of fur that had once been a rabbit; and thus too the reason for which Rubén never ceased in the next thirteen years to do me injury whenever occasion arose, for he bore the scar on his forehead as an everlasting witness of the rock I had hurled at him, and he never forgave me for it.

Chapter II

A Brief Rehearsal of my Antecedents.

I

Your Grace has done me the honour of enquiring into my antecedents, and I shall undertake, Your Grace may be sure, to give as full and proper account of them as I may, and it is my hope that what is curious in my origins will moderate the tedium that might attend a full recital of them.

I am then the *legitimate* son of a *celibate* priest of the *Catholic Faith*; the heir and rightful holder of a noble title in a country I have never seen; no nation claims me, yet by parentage and birthright I belong to three . . .

My father kept a genealogy which he encouraged me to be diligent to study, and though through the exigencies of these troublous times I no longer have it by me, I think I may rehearse without error its chiefest points.

The first *Boshams* (it should be said *Bozzam*) were pastry cooks to the Earls of Arundel in the reign of Edward III of England. By the time of the eighth Henry, him who gave over his people to heresy for the sake of a Protestant Whore, they held land for the Dukes of Norfolk and though not armigerous lived in the style of gentlefolk and were considered such by their neighbours. They remained firm in the Catholic Faith suffering persecution, confiscation of land

and moveables, and like misfortunes up to the time of the last Rebellion.

In the months preceding that Glorious Attempt my Grandfather *Joseph*, whom I am named for, entered into a plan by which the Castle at Arundel would be delivered up to the Stuart cause to provide a *tête de pont* for French troops who might land at Littlehampton. Nothing came of this at all – perhaps because the French lacked stomach for it, perhaps because it was realised the ancient castle would not withstand above a day the pair of battalion guns at the barracks in the neighbouring town of Chichester; the consequence was Joseph fled North and joined his Prince somewhere near Carlisle.

The History of the Campaigns that followed is well-known, and I need not recount it here; what is material to my story is that my Grandfather lost a leg at Culloden, and gained a place amongst many similarly deprived gentlemen in the Royal Bedchamber.

Charles Edward could not long support a large establishment and many of my Grandfather's companions had to find employment or other means to keep body and soul together. Some, my Grandfather amongst them, found their way to Rome where our Prince's father, known by them as James III of England, Scotland and Ireland, still maintained a sort of dignity, though as short of chinks as his son. He yet commanded some respect in the World (an asset the Bonnie Prince soon lost in drunkenness and whoring) and by letters addressed to Christian Sovereigns still happily in possession of their Realms was able to obtain commissions in the Armies of the Faithful throughout Europe. Others, through his second son Henry, Cardinal and Duke of York, found placement in the bosom of our Mother, the Church. My Grandfather, however, had lost with his leg a taste for War but had not acquired a desire to be celibate. With his Monarch's blessing he addressed himself to the task of finding an adequately dowered bride.

Don Ramón Graciliano y Pérez, Conde de Monterrubio de la Sierra, lived in Rome, a member of the large Mission to the Holy See maintained by the Spanish King. As a Lord of Castille, belonging to the second rank of Spanish noblemen and giving place to the Grandees only, Don Ramón would never have entertained the prospect of an English commoner as son-in-law had he not had six daughters – to find six dowries as rich as his peers would demand was beyond his means; moreover, all six were high-spirited and passionate and had declared a united resolution not to be nuns, the usual stratagem employed by Spanish families in this case. Don Ramón had long been a widower and had little control over his brood; *Eugenia*, the second, declared she would have my Grandfather, and hinted that a Clandestine Marriage had already been contracted if not consummated.

In despair Don Ramón made urgent petition to my Ancestor's Liege Lord and was shortly gratified to learn that the Fount of Honour had been pleased to raise Joseph Bosham to the Peerage with the style of *Viscount Bosham of Bosham in the County of Sussex*, and thus he was quickly possessed of a beautiful and adoring Bride together with an income of a thousand pounds a year deriving from rents on land in the neighbourhood of Salamanca in the Kingdom of León.

Salamanca. The world's pulse quickens at those tuneable syllables and every breast must glow with gratitude at remembrance of that glorious field, at the thought of the Great Architect of Victory who presided, Jove-like, on the heights of the *Arapil* where as a child I picked flowers I would bring to my Father's knee, so that he might name them for me. Your Grace will perhaps recall my dear friend Fernando who was your guide and lost a leg at your side on that Glorious Day. Well, poor Fernando still dwells at Los Arapiles, and I have heard that he makes a sort of livelihood show-ing travellers over the scene of Your Grace's greatest triumph. He waits for a pension from the Ingrate Monarch of that land, for other nations are less generous than ours, less punctilious to acknowledge and meet the obligations due to those who have deserved well in their country's cause . . .

2

My Father, saintly man, was born in 1750 and christened Charles Edward, with the Monarch's permission, who also stood, by proxy, Godfather to the child. His early years were clouded by successive tragedies of a domestic kind. In '52, '53, '54, and '56 his mother, the passionate María Eugenia, gave birth to siblings for him, and all died in infancy. In '58 she was brought to bed again, this time the child was still-born and she expired soon after of the puerperal fever. From these occurrences my Father derived his contemplative and melancholic disposition. The sadness that afflicted him my Grandfather sought to alleviate by the employment of a tutor, Doctor Shinall, who had studied the *Mathematicks* and was also well-versed in the *Philosophers* of the time, especially those who looked forward to a *Millennium* when the Human Kind would be guided by Reason alone – in short, he was an Optimist. Thus to my Father's already melancholic turn of mind was grafted the belief that all the ills that afflict us arise from our failure to exercise properly the Rational Faculty.

My Grandfather died in 1767, the year after James III his Patron, and left my Father a modest but apparently secure income by means of which he was able to afford an apartment not far from the Spanish Steps where he pursued his studies in Philosophy, Mathematicks, Opticks, and Astronomy. He went out little into Society though he attended Spanish *tertulias* and Italian *conversaziones* when he felt sure that the talk would be earnest and rewarding; he corresponded much, and had a love of music, especially that of Scarlatti.

He kept up his religious duties, nor did he find this practice unreasonable: he argued that most of our kind lack the leisure, ability or taste for Reason that he was blest with, but all alike require some prop or shield against the general misery of life; that religion provides such a succour, and so long as absurd superstition is discouraged and the worser excesses of devotional enthusiasm, it is the duty of the Rational Man to support the Established Forms for the sake of those who need them, and as a means of preserving decent order in the Commonwealth.

His main preoccupation was Astronomy. Through application of his ability with the Mathematicks to what he knew of the movements of Planets and Heavenly Bodies he was able to predict a partial eclipse of the Planet Venus and was only a day, or a night, wrong in his prediction. This won him esteem in the small circle of *dilettanti* who knew him, and even some notice in the wider world. He showed me more than once a congratulatory letter from the Astronomer Royal, and all this encouraged him to venture, after some months more of labour, a second prediction – that a visible comet would pass across the skies.

The comet did not arrive. For three months my Father dissipated all his energies in recondite researches and calculations. The outcome was a nervous prostration, not, he told me, the consequence of his exertions, but because his travail had led him to be sensible of an immensity, a complexity in the mechanism of the Heavens which defied, he supposed, and always would defy human understanding. This appalled him – that something in Nature should be beyond our power to comprehend; but the more he thought about it the more it was clear that it was not only the mechanism of the heavens that lay beyond the grasp of Human Reason, but every observable phenomenon, right down to a grain of sand or a drop of dew. This being so, by what light can a man who would be wise regulate his life? All that remained was Divine Revelation interpreted by the Authority of the Church to which he now turned for the consolation he had prescribed for souls less illumined by the light of Reason than his. He embarked on a programme of intense mortification; he fasted; he prayed; he wept; he whipped himself and wore a hair-shirt – but all without effect, visionary understanding failed to come; the only consequence was he began to ail in his body as sorely as he did in his mind.

Fortunately his Confessor was a truly good man, a man of wise moderation, who managed to persuade my Father that a settled life with the worldly but sanctified cares and responsibilities, as well as pleasures, of Matrimony might save him: the cure worked; in time content returned and some of his lost faith in Reason with it.

For the next six years my Father was a tolerably happy man. His union with Elisabetta Granacci, a devout girl of a contemplative turn of mind, a Florentine to whose city he removed, was blessed – your humble servant being the first born – but in 1796 all was upset again, though this time by the consequences of reason rather than its failure. A Republican, Jacobin mob, inflamed by the success of the rational French at Lodi, rose, burned and looted the houses of all but the Great, these being guarded by police and militia, who would have been better employed dispersing the Mob. From the holocaust my Father was able to save only my Mother and me. My Mother died shortly after, but not before begging my Father to promise that he would enter Holy Orders as soon as he might and devote what remained to him of life to the service of Christ and His Church.

'I gave my word,' he once told me, 'and she died with a smile on her lips which Reason forbids me to say was sanctified, but which was, at least, an happy one.'

Now I would crave Your Grace's indulgence while I refute a vile fabrication which has been directed at me at least twice in the course of a life less tolerable than most, a fabrication which calls in question much of what I have just set down concerning my birth and the History of my family.

That the holy Elisabetta Granacci had a sister three years her junior, and as different from her in character as may be imagined, I do not deny. My Father spoke of her with quiet distaste on two or three occasions. That this Annabella, for such was her name, was brought to bed of a boy at much the same time as her Holy sister was, and she being unmarried, is also not to be disputed; nor is the fact that she was a healthy girl of strong physique while my Mother had a sickly constitution weakened by her devotions and frugal way of life and so both boys were set to nurse together at

the same dishonoured breast. In fact it is a matter of pride to me
that my noble and generous Father continued to allow the presence of this girl and the natural fruit of her disgrace in our
household where she continued as nurse and as a companion to
my Mother. My Father's kindness was such too that this bastard,
whose name I do not recollect, was brought up with me without
difference made between us. What is not true, and yet has been
said, is that the child plucked from the inferno was the child of the
said Annabella, and that I am he. This is a slander that has been
cast at me by Evil Men.

I have no recollection at all of my Mother, and only vague inti-
mations of my life before her decease. The flames which destroyed
her removed from my Infant Soul all consciousness of what passed
before that date and have cost me therefore the first six years of my
life. I count this not the least of the injuries done me by the
Victor of Lodi – may he rot in his Island prison – and not the least
of the reasons why I am happy to remain the obedient servant of
the Victor of Waterloo.

3

Your Grace will now be satisfied as to my birth. On the male side
I am English, as English, if I may make so bold, as Your Grace is;
my ancestors were Yeoman, Gentry, and, though I should be the
last to insist upon the *currency* of this or even the form, ennobled.
My Grandmother was Spanish and of high birth, my Mother
Italian, and if not so well-born, then of a Saintly Disposition.

What remains is that I should now recount the brief acquaintance I shared with Your Grace and the nature of the more
weighty obligation I undertook for Your Grace, which I now
humbly invite Your Grace to share with me.

However, neither the Connexion nor the Obligation would
have occurred had not my Father removed, with me, to Salamanca,

and so I conceive the story of my arrival and early years in that town are part and parcel of the antecedents Your Grace has been so good as to ask me to furnish.

It was not possible for us to remain in Florence – the Granacci family were picture framers and picture frames are not bespoken much in times of trouble – moreover, our income, derived from lands left by my Grandmother, had become uncertain with the Wars, indeed in one year just previous no monies arrived at all; and so my Father judged it expedient that we should come to the source of our little wealth and oversee the collection of our rents in person. We travelled by land to Naples, by sea to Valencia, and by land again to Salamanca, and there started a new life in a Town which my Father was happy to see had been given the *sobriquet Roma la Chica*, or, to English it, Little Rome.

Our connexion with the Graciliano family and the Count of Monterrubio de la Sierra, who, although quite a distant cousin and never coming into the country at all, preferring to reside in Madrid at the Court, was nevertheless a considerable person, having added to his title by marriage and become a Marquess and Grandee, procured my Father immediate *entrée* to the very best Salamantine Society. Here, though he found much that irritated by way of frivolity and a distasteful preoccupation with rank, was enough to please and make him believe our removal to this new sphere had been well-judged.

Above all he found much congenial company amongst the doctors and professors of the University, particularly amongst those who were engaged at that time in shoving off the lumber of two hundred years of stagnation and dull floundering in sloth and luxury, and especially in the four *Colegios Mayores*, now closed by Royal Decree for these reasons. He joined an *Economic Society* whose purpose was to improve the lot of the poor and the state of the nation by debating ways in which agriculture and industry might be advanced on truly modern lines, *viz.* – Should sugar *beet* be grown in the Castilian Campo or sugar *cane* in Andalucie? Tobacco: would the prosperity arising from the production of a cash crop outweigh the ill effects of increased drinking of the sot-weed? and so on. Here were Lawyers like *Ramón Salas*, Clinicians like *Antonio Zepa* who approved *Brunonism* as my Father did, and many more, not least *Bishop Trevira* who discreetly encouraged all who strove to light dark corners with the candle-flame of Reason.

He rented a pleasant set of rooms in the Great Plaza and before a twelve month had passed fullfilled his vow to my Saintly Mother and was accepted into Orders at the hands of that same Bishop. Moreover his income now increased to double what it had been once a scoundrelly bailiff had been sent packing, and all in all things seemed set fine for a while.

But Fortune's Wheel is ever turning, and by the end of a further year we had once more fallen on bad times.

The Bishop of Salamanca was a man of Liberal Tendencies, his gaze turned not to the *hills* for help but to the *Pyrenees*, and thus he was an offence to the Holy Office, and though he was under Royal Protection and that of Godoy, the Chief Minister and the Queen's Lover, his *protégés* were not.

My Father's simple trust in the rationality of his fellows prevented the most ordinary precautions; consequently when the Familiars of the Holy Office burst into his study one evening they found there volumes by *Locke* and *Hobbes*, *Voltaire* and *Descartes*, and books that showed how the earth moves round the sun, and much other mischief, all on the open shelves that lined the walls.

He now faced interminable questions which he submitted to with dignity and an intransigent honesty of reply which did little to help his case. For a time it seemed things would go very hard with him – confiscation of property, family disinherited for five generations, myself committed to the care of Franciscans in an asylum for the offspring of common criminals, and more. His health, ever precarious, took worse, for a time even his life was despaired of. In this weakened state the Bishop, acting in his interest, prevailed on him to make the confession the Inquisition desired, and after they had moderated their demands a little, he at last gave in. He was permitted to make this confession, which had to be in the form of a sermon, in one of the side-chapels of the Cathedral, and at an early hour without publick advertisement of it beforehand; the content was reduced to an itemisation of the books he was possessed of with an acknowledgement that there might be danger of Mortal Sin to anyone who perused them. All this, though not much, was something more than he could happily do and he left the chapel a saddened man, broken even.

Followed from all this a desire to withdraw from publick view; moreover he now declared that he had been somewhat in error though not exactly how the Office had accused him. He said he had a duty to his neighbour which all his life he had neglected, a duty which Reason imposes as surely as it is commanded by Holy Writ and Holy Church. And so he removed for the last time, to the village of Los Arapiles, a league and a half from the town, where the Cure was vacant and which the Bishop had in his gift.

Your Grace knows the village well, it being the site of one of Your Grace's most celebrated Triumphs, as noted above.

Here my Father lived out his days occupied with saying Mass and administering the Sacrament in decent form, supporting the Poor amongst his Parishioners with discreet Charity, and devoting himself to my education – alas that I was such a sorry pupil.

Chapter III

My Domestic Situation in Childhood; the Eccentricities of my Education.

I

Before passing on to the history of my acquaintance with Your Grace, and of the Obligation due from us both to *another*, an obligation which has been a Pride and a Blessing for me to undertake and which I know Your Grace will find to be a reward rather than a burden once Your Grace is in possession of all the circumstances that attend it, I must complete the task you have put upon me and turn now to my boyhood and education, and so these will be more properly understood, I shall begin by describing the situation in which they took place.

My Father's cottage in Los Arapiles, where I resided from 1799 to 1809, that is from age nine to nineteen, was small but decent, with three rooms, the arrangement of which deserves notice since it exemplifies the application of the rational principles that characterised most of my Father's actions. As Your Grace will doubtless remember, having travelled the length and breadth of the *Peninsula*, and lodged humbly enough on many an occasion, the common arrangement of such cottages is thus and thus: the ground floor serves as stable for a mule, a pig, poultry, and possibly a cow; the two rooms on the first floor as bedchamber and dining room for the Tenant and his family, while the attic above serves as kitchen and living quarters for the *domestics*. Not so with my Father.

He reasoned as follows: *item*, there is no large stock of animals, only a mule and poultry which can share a lean-to beside the house; *item*, it is a waste of labour to carry fuel and food to an attic, if the meals are then to be brought down to the first floor for consumption; *item*, hot air rises – a cooking fire at the top of the house heats only the rafters, but one lit at the bottom of the house will also warm the rooms above. And so he determined to make the ground floor room, the largest in the house, a commodious and pleasant kitchen. There was only one impediment to this plan – the lack, in common with all other cottages in the village, of a chimbley, our neighbours evacuating the fumes from their attic kitchens through holes in their roofs. This did not deter my Father: he called in masons and bricklayers who constructed a chimbley according to plans he put before them, and so well was it planned and made that it fell down only once before a French round-shot knocked it down, and was the envy and wonder of all our neighbours.

Thus our ground floor was our kitchen, a warm and fragrant cavern. Along one side was a range including a sort of raised trench in which wood and charcoal smouldered beneath a deep layer of white ash. Across this trench a stew-pot simmered and provided the basis of our simple diet. On Feast Days the charcoal would be made to glow and a rabbit, a chicken, or a brace of partridges would be set across a grill to spit and hiss beside the stew-pot. From the blackened ceiling hung long, hard sausages stuffed with smoked pork and hot red pepper, a flitch of rustic ham, a string of onions and another of garlic, and a bundle of dried herbs – thyme, wild lavender, a bunch of bay, and sage. Between the back-door and the unglazed window were a heavy table whose top was gashed into steep hills and valleys like a butcher's block, and a dresser with earthenware platters, bone-handled knives, copper saucepans, ewers, ladles and the like.

This kitchen was the domain of *Tía Teresa*, a widow of some forty and odd years who looked after us, and she was a mother to me who had none, her own brood all being grown and gone from home. She was not a native of Los Arapiles, having been born in Zamora some ten leagues to the North.

Opposite the range in the kitchen was a curtained alcove, and this is where I slept beneath quilts and cloaks, on a palliasse of straw and lavender. So big was this bed, and so malleable its elements, I could fancy myself there a King and Emperor or Captain of a ship or Grand Mogul of the Indies. Once I had three mice for pets there and kept them above a week, but one night I forgot them and woke to find them crushed.

Above, reached by a narrow flight of wooden steps, were my Father's rooms, occupying the whole of the first floor, or *Piano Nobile*. The first of these was where he dined if there was company, received visitors, carried on the business of his Cure that could not be done in the vestry of his church, as dispensing Charity or advice of a worldly sort, and tutored me. This room had a dark oak table in the English style, six upright chairs to match, a settle, and a large tallboy. On the table was a brass candelabra to hold six tapers, though I never saw more than three lit at a time, and then only in company. One of the few glazed windows in the village looked across the street; during lessons when my mind wandered more than it should I would move my head and make the warped glass distort the baker's shop on the other side of the road. A *clavichord* on which usually rested the bound sonatas of Scarlatti, and bookshelves against all the walls completed the furnishings of this room.

The second, at the back, was my Father's study, bedchamber, and *den*. It was very crowded. First, all the walls here too were lined with book-cases, then there were the *apparati* of his various fields of study – telescope, new-fangled *microscope*, cases of specimen rocks, old coins, and pressed flowers and grasses. The table was always littered with papers, more books, pens, and pen-knives – for he always used a quill, never a steel nib – sander, inkwell, and such of his findings as he had not yet sorted, classified, and put away. An oil-lamp, an *Argand* with a glass funnel above a circular wick, allowed him to study far into the night.

Amongst all this was a cot or truckle-bed concealed beneath a quilt Tía Teresa had patched up from scraps; my Father was always one to encourage such economies. Above this bed was a simple brass Crucifix, a concession to the memory of his dear wife, my Sainted Mother, not a stimulus to devotion.

When I remember this room I remember the smell – a dry, dusty, leathery smell, lightened and spiced by the fragrances that emanated from a blue and white china *pot-pourri* which my Father replenished with aromatic spices and fresh petals each succeeding Spring.

Finally, I should make mention of the garden plot that lay behind the kitchen, enclosed by a five foot wall of white-washed stone. Here my Father cultivated vegetables and salads, including the *tomatl* from *New Spain* to which he was very partial, although his neighbours disdained or even abhorred it as the *love-apple* offered by Eve to Adam; and the related *batata* which he believed would do much to alleviate the lot of his poorer parishioners, if only he could persuade them to cultivate it, since it would relieve them from excessive reliance on wheat, subject to poor harvests and fluctuating price. There were also a pear-tree and almond tree and a covered well, not deep, so no winding gear was needed, yet neither was it ever dry. Against one wall four bee-skeps, of which he often said: 'There is nothing I love so dearly as these bees; it is one of my delights to sit watching them, and listening to their murmur.'

2

Shortly after our arrival in Salamanca, and nearly three years before our removal to Los Arapiles, my Father began to concern himself with my education, I having mastered the *abecedarian* stage with my nurse. For many months, tedious months, right up until his confrontation with the Holy Office, he attempted to force on me a strict regimen of Greek, Latin and the Mathematicks, with

Musick, and a grounding in Natural Philosophy, including the Physicks of the *Divine Isaac*, by which he signified Sir Isaac Newton. As a pupil I lacked application and by every evening had forgot what he had taught me in the forenoon. At the same time, and with more success, he ensured through daily discourse that I was ready-tongued in Spanish, Italian, and English, the language he favoured when we were alone. Further to this, seeing I had a facility with tongues, we did some French which I perfected later and even started in on *Román*, the tongue of the *Zin-cali*, or Spanish gypsies, among whom my Father cultivated a small acquaintance, for sake of Charity.

Now all this was done with oft-repeated doubts that he was flying against the most advanced theorising of our time, derived from Jean-Jacques Rousseau, that grounding in number and letter is all that a lively and enquiring mind needs to tutor itself in accordance with the Principles of Nature. Sometimes he attributed my failures to an idle and shallow mind, sometimes to a lack of *Rousseau-ism* on his part.

Much to my relief, though not to my lasting benefit, this second approach to education gained ascendancy following his confrontation with the Holy Office: it seems that throughout this disagreeable episode My Father retained – such was his generous spirit – a respect and even a liking for his Inquisitors, with some of whom he was already acquainted, and who remained pleasant and urbane in manner even when most tiresome (fortunate it was that the days of *strappado* and *rack* had long departed), and when all was done he was led to ask himself and others how such persons as these honest, decent clergy could be so blind and superstitious.

An *American Theoretician*, with whom my Father corresponded, a student of Jean-Jacques, provided an answer in the form of a long letter, the gist of which was as follows: the Inquisitors were the victims of a Jesuitical Education which repressed, restrained, and stifled not only the generous impulses implanted by Nature, but also a desire for genuine Knowledge. Societies were, the American

from Harvard argued, happier in inverse proportion to the amount
of education they forced upon their Young – witness the paradisial
existence enjoyed by Amazonian and Patagonian Indians and
Polynesians in their pre-Columban innocence, none of whom
presumed to teach their children more than Nature indicated.

All this in the aftermath of the burning of half his library by too
rigorously educated priests led to a relaxation of the regimen I
laboured under; from then on my Father concerned himself only
with keeping up my proficiency in languages and occasionally
attempting to improve my penmanship. Indeed in those first years
at Los Arapiles he withdrew into his inner sanctum and thus
deprived of his company and his example I sought those of others,
namely those of children of an age with me, and following the
instincts of our Race became in all outer manners indistinguish-
able from them; indeed I slavishly aped them – this, I believe, in
response to a natural instinct to be uncritically like one's fellows
that Rousseau and his followers take too little note of.

3

Only once was I whipped during my education; and oddly
enough this was under the Rousseau-istic phase.

It was shortly after our removal to Los Arapiles, on a bright day
in our first Spring in that country. We had been out collecting
flowers to press between the leaves of a large plain book bought
for the purpose. My Father proposed that I should write the
names of the flowers at the bottom of each page at his direction,
hoping thereby to profit from my interest in the flowers by
improving my penmanship, all this in accord with the most
modern principles of education.

But my interest in the flowers was now dissipated – in truth it
had been assumed to please him and keep him in my company –
and now I could hear my new friends Fernando and Rubén a-
whistling and a-calling out of doors.

'Periwinkle,' murmured my Father, cradling the blue, five-pointed star in his palm. 'P-e-r-i-w-i-n-k-l-e. In Spanish *vincapervinca*. A flower round which many Pagan superstitions still cluster . . .'

My hand moved towards the pewter ink-pot.

'It seems the Ancient Victims of Old Sacrifice were bound with its . . .'

And over I tipped it.

It spilled on a prized copy of Ferguson's *Cosmology*. To hand was a switch of cat-kinned hazel we had garnered and he struck me thrice with this across the back of the legs before either of us was fully sensible of what he was doing. Horrified by this sudden lapse into a refinement of educational procedure unheard of amongst the Patagonians or Polynesians he flung the switch away from him as if it was he had suffered the sting, whilst I, more frightened than smarting from the blows, scampered below stairs to bury my face in Tía Teresa's very ample skirts.

'Poor lad, poor boy,' she crooned. 'Poor little *Lazarillo*.'

All was soon mended between us, and a day later I asked my Father: 'Sir, what is a *Lazarillo*?' and had to recall for him the circumstances under which I had heard the word.

He mused for a while resting one side of his face in his palm, elbow on the table, or twiddling a strand of his unfashionable beard between long fingers. Already his face was hollow-cheeked, his eyes deep-sunk, but always kind in expression. He spoke, as always, gently and carefully.

'I suppose Tía Teresa made comparison between you and Lazarillo in the book *Lazarillo de Tormes*. It is a book well-loved in Salamanca, though little read.'

Hoping for a story I encouraged him to proceed.

'It is the tale of a boy, much of an age with you, whose widowed mother pushes him into the world to fend for himself. First he serves a Salamantine beggar, a blind man, such as today you'll see selling lottery tickets in the Grand Square. Next he is

the servant of a priest, a mean and miserly man . . . Good
Gracious. It cannot be Tía Teresa thinks I'm mean, can it? If she
does, then it must be so, for she is an honest woman . . .'

I tried to reassure him that he was not mean, but I could not say
enough and he had to ring for Tía Teresa with a small hand-bell
he kept for the purpose. Followed a long and most confused conversation, for the poor woman had no idea of why she had been
summoned, and, not yet being used to my Father (later she was
better acquainted), feared she was being rebuked for calling me
names, which distressed us all for it seemed to call in question the
trust that had begun to grow between us, but all at last was settled.
Often my Father's generosity and self-doubt led to like confusions.

When Teresa had been smoothed down and returned happy to
her kitchen I asked my Father to continue with the story of the
boy Lazarillo.

But story-telling was not a skill my Father practised – scholarly
exegesis was more his line. He opened the book (he had found it
high on a shelf) and placed it in front of him by a bowl of Spring
flowers.

'*Lazarillo de Tormes* is the first modern example of a style of tale
imitated from late Antiquity and now known as the *Picaresque*,' he
began. 'For the most part it is a low sort of literature, about low
life, and not one I would recommend to youthful attention,
though it enjoyed some esteem in England in the last century. A
pícaro, as you know, is a rogue, and who can read about rogues
with profit? But there is charm in this work, considerable charm,
arising from a nice use of comic irony, not always recognised by
later readers who see only absurd incidents and grotesque characters. This is how the irony works. Lazarillo at eight years old is a
delightful, lively, but wily youngster – at the end of the story he is
grown-up, a cuckold, a scoundrel, a fool. The skill of the writing
lies in the way in which he himself, as supposed narrator, appears
to present this development or decline without being aware of it,
although the perceptive reader is. Part of the machinery employed
to achieve this comic effect is a device whereby the whole fiction

is presented in the form of an *apologia* to a Grandee or Lord whom the elder Lazarillo wishes to influence in his favour. But such subtilities are not, as I said, evident to every reader and on the whole I think this work and others like it tend to corrupt as much as please. The best one can say for them is that time spent in their study is time lost to more profitable pursuits.'

He returned the volume to a shelf beyond my reach.

So ended the incident of the spilled inkwell; one of the many memories I cherish of the good, kind, if confused, gentleman who was my Father. It has always been my aim to emulate his better qualities, to be worthy of his memory; how far I have succeeded I leave your Grace to judge, if Your Grace will only do me the honour of continuing to turn these worthless pages.

CHAPTER IV

*My Introduction to the Martial Life, and an Adventure that
Followed, Less Pleasing to the Sensible Reader.*

I

Your Grace does not need to be told by me that the youthful pulse
quickens to the rat-a-tat of the drum and the squeal of the martial
fife. It cannot be otherwise than that Your Grace as a child felt
some inkling of Honour and Glory beyond compare when first
the sounds and sights of soldiers on parade or on the march
impressed themselves upon Your Grace's senses. So too it was
with me. Oh that the coats the soldiers wore could have been red
not blue, and their orders of command in a language native to my
ear, but it was not to be: the fault is History's not mine. The first
army that I ever did see was not *Britannia's*, nor was it even that of
Spain – it was FRENCH. How my childish soul would have
recoiled in unsupportable horror had I had the powers of Prophet
or Sybil; alas, I had no such gifts. I was but ten or eleven years old,
and ignorant of the World as well as of the Future. Your Grace, I
confess it, my blood marched with their feet, my soul rose up
when they lifted their golden eagles.

It happened thus, in July of 1801. Rubén, Fernando and I were
searching for crayfish in the Tormes, near the Santa Marta ford
rather less than a league above the City. Your Grace will bring the
spot to mind, I make no doubt. Eleven years later Fernando, the
same Fernando, marked the limits of the ford for Your Grace, the

very day before the Glorious and never to be Forgotten Battle of Los Arapiles, or Salamanca, a full account of my part in which will appear at its proper place in this present History according to due chronology.

In 1801 Rubén and I pretended to friendship again, but his forehead bore a crimson scar, close to the hairline, which witnessed that it had not always been so. On my part there was now no ill-will for the childish insult he had hurled at me; but I now truly believe that he continued to harbour an abiding grudge for the rock I had launched in reply, for as this History will show, he has ever been a Mortal Enemy to me. Even that very day, before the last gleams of sunset had faded behind our City's spires, he gave an evidence of this, not so clear or so vicious as was yet to come, but harm enough in its childish way.

For most of that afternoon then the three of us paddled about the shallow pools beneath the poplars, lifting stones and peeping into deeper eddies for the elusive shellfish. Rubén's father, the baker, relished them greatly and had promised us two *cuartos* for each one found. In more than an hour we had caught but two and these were now in a keepnet improvised from one of Fernando's stockings and fixed in a pool, where it still may be for all I know, because we most surely forgot it, and the fish too.

But for all our failure as fishermen, I remember it as a pleasant afternoon, peaceful and untroubled. Fernando had more or less given up and was amusing himself building dams, creating pools, canals, and waterways on which he guided twigs and other flotsam. There were big jewelled dragonflies, and swifts skimmed low after midges. The flies were not a bother except near the mire where the cattle came to water; we could hear the monotonous chime of their bells and the girl who looked after them sang a gypsy song. The little church of Santa Marta marked off the Angelus and we stood a moment to make our duties.

Rubén was the first to lift his head, ear cocked to the East.

'What is it?'

'Can't you hear?'

'The Angelus.'

'Fool.'

'Rooks?' suggested Fernando.

'No. Horses, and a trumpet.'

'Rooks,' said Fernando, and returned with more certainty to his dam.

'Fool,' repeated Rubén, and kicked a shower of pebbles in his direction.

'*Hostia!* What did you do that for? You could have put out my eye . . .'

'Shut up,' I called, for now I had heard it – not the trot of a distant traveller's mount, nor even the multiple beat of mules dragging a cart or diligence, but a low distant rumble, made up of many different noises – hooves, jangling harness, raucous shouts, and then sharp and clear, high and bright, the silvery call of a bugle.

We scrambled up out of the pools, up over the banks, and on to the High Road, the road to Avila and Madrid. Long and flat, it curved white and stony away towards the ford at Huerta a couple of leagues away and out of sight – out of sight at any time, but certainly out of sight then, for a great cloud of orange dust hung across the road, two miles or more off, perhaps a quarter of a mile wide and an hundred feet high, which, as we watched, discernibly grew closer.

Now distinct forms were taking shape – first a dark blur, then nodding plumes, glittering harness, horses' heads, breasts, legs, hooves; one sound became detached from the rest – a rhythmical clopping of may be an hundred sets of hooves, a steady jingling of harness at a trot. The advance guard, a century of horse, was almost upon us. Suddenly my insides were caught by a wild excitement, a contrary mixture of exultation and terror as I sensed the unity of all that movement, caught the feeling that here were not an hundred men, an hundred horses, but one thing, one composite, inexorable force moving not swiftly but steadily, irreversibly, down the road towards us.

The bugle again. Four figures – they were now only half a mile away, perhaps less – drew away from the main body at a steady canter; soon they were on us, past us, and then – how can the sudden thrill of horror be recaptured? – one of them wheeled his horse sharply about, sending stone and grit scattering under the trees, coming right round so that he towered above us.

For only five seconds he stayed there, horse quivering and snorting with its grey head reined in, before he pulled it round again, touched spurs and was off down the road after his companions, no doubt satisfied that we were but three boys and no ambuscade; but the image offered in that five seconds is stamped on my mind as if with a brand.

He had a tall round black hat swathed with a yellow scarf beneath a small black plume; his coat was dark green with silver frogging, black shoulder straps, and wide white sash; his breeches were red above black boots, and his horse, a large heavy grey with sweat lathering around the reins and foam at its bit, was caparisoned with a black saddle-cloth edged with yellow. But what I most remember were the Hussar's sword, and his face. The former was a heavy, long sabre, slightly curved, sheathed in what looked like silver, with a large silver basket hilt with tight black tassels – I had never seen such a weapon: the Spanish horse soldiers I had seen carried much lighter affairs with more pronounced curves, graceful weapons that look pretty at parades. This one would cleave you from the top of your head to your crutch and leave you in two halves like a sucking pig at Epiphany. And the Hussar's face suited it – lean, bronzed, narrow-eyed beneath curling eyebrows that sneered, with moustaches waxed and turned up, and white powdered hair tied back in a knot like a bull-fighter's pigtail – it was the face of a man who could do just that: slice a child from skull to privates if the fancy took him. He was the first French Hussar I had ever seen, though of course at the time I had no idea that that was what he was; he was also the first *real* soldier, and that was something I recognised.

I felt a tug at my breeches – Fernando was in the shallow dry ditch behind me; I looked back and saw Rubén pale, with bottom lip quivering, a yard or so further back.

'Come out of the way,' he called, but I shook my head.

The rest of the advance guard, a squadron of Hussars like the fellow just gone by, were now drawing level – they clattered by in column of four, file by file, in perfect order even though at the end of a long hot day and a march of seven or eight leagues, and every man was upright, every pair of eyes faced the front.

How can I describe the next hour? There was so much, so many, such noise, such variety, such life. There were foot soldiers in tall black hats with peaks, blue tailed coats, and baggy white trousers; there were men in drum-shaped bearskins like Russians, carrying long muskets with glittering bayonets; there were more cavalry on even bigger horses, whose riders wore shining breast-plates and huge gilded helmets; and there were the guns. Twenty, thirty perhaps – huge, studded wheels higher than my head, black tooled barrels, each drawn by six plumed mules, each with its limber cart of powder and shot – they added a deep bass note, like a roll on the kettle-drums, to the orchestra of noise around us.

There was a baggage train, huge wagons and carriages, and women walking alongside them in stocking hats, some with blue, white and red rosettes, some nursing babies in tight-wrapped shawls. For the most part these women were tall, thin, brown with lank black hair, and they sang, and jeered, and tweaked my cheek painfully as they passed.

And best of all there were the officers: in their high-waisted, dark blue tail coats, their tight white breeches, their high tasselled boots, the facings of red and the epaulettes of gold, they came and they went up and down the column, wheeling and turning on large thoroughbreds, shouting in that strange nasal womanish tongue. Right in the middle of it all was the General – his horse was bigger, his moustaches wider, and his hat, a huge hat with white plumes, was enormous. How firm he seemed, how confi-dent, how set apart, scribbling a note on his *sabretache*, the sun glinting off his huge epaulettes, so weighty with bullion, and from the stars on his chest. This, though of course I did not know it, was General Leclerc, brother-in-law to Napoleon Buenoparte, then First Consul of France and the Author of all our Woes to come . . .

In spite of our initial fright from the Hussar, confidence and excitement quickly returned to us. At first we stood and gaped – I remember I had my arm round Fernando's shoulder and Rubén on my other side gripped my elbow. Whenever some sight seemed nobler or more enthralling than the rest, or the noise achieved yet more *crescendo*, or a bullock cart threatened to push us into the ditch, he pinched my arm until it hurt and I squeezed Fernando. Then after the baggage train, when behind everything we could at last see the very end of the column and nearly ten thousand men had passed us, we turned and marched along with them and the big men with their big moustaches and their high hats, their tall muskets and white straps and packs, glanced down at us and smiles creased the corners of their eyes though relentlessly their feet continued to march one-two, one-two, one-two in time with the steady beat of the drums.

We scampered on, for short bursts faster than that inexorable one-two, one-two, one-two, then paused out of breath, chests heaving as one-two, one-two, one-two the same giants came up to us, passed us and we had to scamper on again.

Now the front of the column had reached the Southern end of the Roman Bridge whose twenty-five arches span the Tormes beneath the towers and domes of Salamanca's twin cathedrals. On a small plain just by the Arrabal water-mill a scene even more stirring was being enacted. That vast concourse of men, women and animals had ceased its dreadful forward progress and like some *gargantuan* serpent was winding its tail coil upon coil into itself. All seemed confusion, the dust rose higher and higher, the bugle calls became more frantic, men shouted, women screamed, horses neighed, booted feet stamped, the butts of muskets crashed to the ground.

Quite suddenly the noise and movement diminished, though

there was still plenty of both, but we could now see that the whole column had come to an halt in something like a square each side of which was at least an hundred yards long, and in one corner of which we were standing. The sun threw long bars of light and shadow through the serried ranks, each beam caught in the swirling settling dust; a horse neighed, harness jingled, an officer trotted across from one side to the other. The men rested at ease, their hands folded across the muzzles of their long fusees.

Then over on the far side we caught the glitter of the sun on burnished brass, on frogging, braiding, epaulettes more heavy with silver and gold than any we had yet seen; near this group of resplendent uniforms I could make out long bulky objects from which soldiers were stripping leather casing, and five gold eagles were raised above five billowing banners of blue, white and red. In front of all this there now appeared the most gorgeously arrayed creature of all – seven feet tall he seemed, with huge brown moustaches, a great hat plumed with blue, white and red, a coat paler blue than the others and encrusted with gold – there were even splashes of gold down his white breeches – and he carried a long gold staff, heavily carved, almost as high as his shoulder. This he now lifted high, high above his head so the dying sun caught it and turned it to fire, and then down it came in one swift movement. The band crashed out – bugles, fifes, sackbuts, drums, and great brassy cymbals, and all the men around, ten thousand of them, began to sing –

> *Allons enfants de la patrie*
> *Le Jour de Gloire est arrivé . . .*

I looked at the eagles and some memory of something I had seen among my father's books was stirred.

'Hey, Rubén, those eagles,' I whispered, 'they must be *Romans*.'

He looked at me and his lip curled.

'Stupid, they're *French*. My Dad said they would come in a day or two, but I forgot.'

'Why are they here?'

'To fight the Portuguese, of course.'

'Oh.'

Now the square of men was breaking up; one side was forming into columns of three again and was moving off after the band, others were turning away – to bivouac, as we later learnt, on the banks of the river. Just by us five cannons began to trundle after the first column, and suddenly one of the men broke free and grabbed me round the waist; for a moment I struggled and kicked, but before I could break loose I realised what he was doing – he perched me astride the barrel of the first gun, and placed my hands over the chasing round the touch-hole where I was able to take a sure grip.

'*Sois tranquille, m'p'tit, sois tranquille,*' he cried, and patted my cheek, then he caught up the other two and placed them on the gun behind. All the soldiers around cheered, whips cracked, the traces took the strain, the mules heaved, and we were off after the drums and fifes and the eagles across the Roman Bridge, up through the winding streets, right into the centre of the town, the *Plaza Mayor.*

2

It was about dark when we reached the Great Square. The soldiers lifted us from the guns and placed us on our feet – large hands in my armpits, a gust of garlic, tobacco, and sweat in my face, and there we were huddled against one of the pillars while flambeaus flared and hissed above us and spat hot tar on our heads and long shadows raced around the colonnades. The soldiers marched off in sections to quarters in the Town, save for a guard on the cannon now marshalled in batteries beneath the carved splendour of the Town Hall.

What to do? Rubén would not walk back to Los Arapiles, not

through ten thousand French men, and then a league of darkness, bulls, witches, and may be wolves; while poor Fernando on his part looked to be whipped if we did not return. I was very hungry, and thinking first to satisfy that need I recalled a friend of my Father, a Mr Curtis of the Irish College, lately come to teach the Irish Deacons newly installed in the now defunct *Colegio Mayor*, previously known as the *Arzobispo* after its founder, archbishop Fonseca. I was sure this Mr Curtis would give us food and lodging or help us home in company. But I had not been in Town for upwards of two years, our arrival in the square had been distracting, and somehow I entirely mistook the way, leading my friends off into a warren of back streets crowded with gypsies, French soldiers and young Spaniards wrapped in brown cloaks and smoking *cigarillos*.

Shortly it was plain I was lost; Fernando began to blubber, and Rubén cursed. We came at last to a stop outside a large tavern filled with French, and we gazed in, mouths watering, on the animated scene. Mutton and Pork cuts, and whole Chickens were skewered and set to hiss over the big wood fire; leather bottles, bulging like udders, were slung from mouth to mouth, from table to table; bayonets and jack-knives hacked at hard sausage and white bread. Smells wafted out at us – acrid wood-smoke, the sharpness of spilled wine, the salivant richness of dripping burning meat; and the noise – a steady babbling of voices in that nasal, twanging tongue, punctuated with shouts and laughter as serving girls in long flounced dresses passed between the tables banging down platters of loaves or ladling out of black cauldrons steaming helpings of thick chick-pea stew.

At length one of these girls took notice of us, came out and sank on her haunches to look up into our grubby, tear-stained faces.

'What's this then? Shouldn't you be at home, this time of night?'

She had thick moist lips, snub nose, heavy black eyebrows, and her black hair was already adrift from the wooden comb she wore.

The string of her once white chemise had loosened and I could see the swell of creamy mounds and the purple shadows in the gap.

'Cheeky thing!' She drew the string tighter, but grinned.

'We're lost,' said Rubén. 'Pepe here lost us.'

'Came to town on an errand and stayed to watch the soldiers, did you then?'

'I'm hungry,' cried Fernando, first taking his fist from his mouth.

'Come on then. There's plenty here for little ones like you.'

She took us in, each in turn, and squeezed us on to the ends of separate benches.

The soldier she put me by – a dark, wizened little man with deep-set eyes that twinkled – thrust a wineskin at me and jabbered in his comic language, all pushed out lips and spittle. I drank and spluttered – never had I had wine undilute before. Then he hacked off a chicken wing and thrust it at me with a round of bread for trencher; the chicken was redolent with wood-smoke, herbs, and garlic, and soon I felt much recovered. By the light of candles and the flickering fire I could discern Rubén and Fernando; they grinned and waved, and seemed as comfortably fixed as I.

After a time the platters were cleared away but the bottles continued to circulate. My friend pressed more upon me and soon I began to giggle and belch. His companion across the board had bushy eyebrows and large ears which he caused to move in independent fashion – this first set me to helpless laughter, then to a fit of hiccoughs. Finally they urged upon me the fuming mouthpiece of a clay pipe; I had not drunk the weed before; the room swayed; blood roared in my ears; a tertian perspiration broke out along my limbs and down my back; and, just as I was about to vomit, I found myself briskly hoisted by the waist and carried into the yard behind the tavern.

It was the girl who had understood my condition and its likely consequence. She held my forehead and scolded me gently for my indulgence, reserving her riper scorn for the thoughtlessness of the soldiers who had so reduced me; all this while I evacuated my stomach of most of what I had had. Miserable and shivering I was when she led me back to the main room, and in no state to discover, as I now did, that my friends had deserted me; at Rubén's insistence I later learnt. This was all together in excess of what I could support and I gave way to yet more sobbing, clutching at my wench's apron and refusing to be parted from her. She took me to the street and tried to disembarrass herself of me, but one glance that took in orange moon, three brawling soldiers, and no sign at all of my friends was enough to fasten me more tightly than ever to the comfort and warmth of her sturdy waist.

'There, there,' and 'all will be well,' and 'don't take on so,' she crooned, and then what all along I had longed to hear, 'all will be well in the morning, and you can bed with me till then,' and she stooped to wipe my nose.

3

Back through the main room, the kitchens, and into the yard again she pushed me before her, and then up three flights of rickety outside stairs, right up to the roof itself above the guest rooms now filled with drunken soldiery, and into a tiny attic below the sloping rafters. It was barely ten feet by ten feet and only under the roof-tree or in a sort of alcove made by a narrow dormer window was it possible for her to stand upright. She blew on the wick of the taper she had carried up with us and by its dull flame discovered a floor covered with a large palliasse, some covers, clothes, rags and so on, and that was all, save for an image of Our Lady as the Immaculate Conception. She set the taper in front of this, blessed herself, and turned to me.

'You'll be all right here till morning,' she murmured, 'warm and cosy, and when it's day you'll find your way home again.'

She sat me on the palliasse and pulled at my shoes, and then, as I rubbed my eyes – I had stopped crying and was almost asleep – she pulled at my breeches too.

'You'd best keep your shirt . . . Gracious, what's this then?'

She cradled the *little monster* in her palm and shifted so the light fell better on it.

'Well I never . . . that's a funny little thing. How did he come to be like that?'

At which I began to cry again.

'There, there, there, never mind. It's a pretty little thing. Neat.' And suddenly her head came down and she pecked a kiss on him, her lips cool where her hand had been warm. Then she pulled the covers round me tight and kissed my forehead too.

'You go to sleep now, there's a love. I'll be back soon and mind you're asleep by then,' and she was gone, taking the light with her.

I heard the click of the latch, the creak of the steps, and then her progress was lost in the noises of the night. Two cats wailed, there was shouting and singing down the street, a file of soldiers tramped by; down by the river a bugle called and was answered by a distant picket. Something rustled in the straw, a mouse perhaps, I was used to them. A sliver of moonlight grew down the side of the dormer, and when it had spread to a hand's breath I heard footsteps on the stairs again, but heavy this time, and the grunting rasping breath of a large, drunk man. Terrified I pressed myself in under the eaves, as far from the door as I could go.

The latch lifted and in he came, a French Sergeant, a huge Grenadier with white pantaloons and bushy moustache, helped by a push from behind which caused him to crack his head on the lintel. Half cursing, half laughing he tumbled into the palliasses pulling my girl after him and she fell across him, but managed to stay on her knees, and by the light of the moon I watched as she pulled at his boots in much the way she had tugged at mine. Soon they had most of their clothes off and he rolled her on to her back and began the *animal act*. I could see his enormous arse rising and falling above her, hear his breath dragged in and out, and smell the rising odours of sweat stale and fresh, human dung, and other sweeter odours too. I knew what they were doing. I had seen animals, I and my friends had speculated and guessed at it, once we had spied on a couple from the village hard at it on the side of the *Arapil Chico*, but they had been a long way off. This was fiercer, went on longer.

After the time you might take to tell an hundred twice he began to grunt and gasp like a stranded whale and she was moaning too with urgent pleasure at the thrust of his heavy rump, and then he gave a great sigh that came echoing out of the cave of his chest; she cried out with sudden longing or despair, and he rolled off her, disengaging. A pause, then she uttered a curse, beneath her breath.

'*Hijo de puta!*'

Then she giggled a little and he snored.

Some minutes passed. Knowing she was not asleep I remained still, crouched under the rafters. To move would have been to show that I had been awake all the time and I guessed she would not be pleased to discover that. At last she pushed back the covers, gently so as not to disturb her monstrous companion, though not even the *Final Trump* would have roused him then, I'm sure, and moved on all fours across the mattresses until she was under the casement.

She stood up in the moonlight. She was wearing a shift that reached her knees and which she now used to wipe her crotch. Wittingly or not she thereby induced a pleasurable warmth which rekindled unsatiated desire – alas, she now lacked the *natural* means for its satisfaction. Suddenly she raised her arms and pulled the shift over her head, leaving herself as naked as *Eve*. Thus, she leant against the wall, full in the light of the Summer Moon, with her eyes fixed on it, and she continued the same movement with her bare fingers as she had started through the shift.

It was the first time I had seen a woman so.

She had a thick neck, heavy shoulders. Her breasts were large and creamy with small coral nipples, and, like her shoulders, glazed with perspiration; her long black hair looped and fell about them. Her waist was short, her stomach round, her legs which were set apart, were strong pillars of yellow ivory in the moonlight, and the stubby fingers of both hands now rummaged in the thick black hair between them.

Soon her head went back and I could see her throat arched against the dark frame of the casement, her knees flexed and I could hear her breath again. The movements became more urgent, she began to croon and rock, and then at last she clenched herself into a spasm – breath held, face twisted to hold back the cry of extasie, a moment thus, and then the tension leaked slowly away from her face and body in a long sigh that ended in another giggle.

The moonlight spread into most of the room and as she turned from the window she saw me, eyes starting, a blanket stuck in my mouth.

'Why you . . . little monkey.'

She knelt down above me. I could sense the weight of her breasts, smell the odours of venery.

'Were you awake all the time?'

Dumbly I nodded.

'And you never stirred or made a noise.'

She giggled again and I realised she was not after all angry.

'I was frightened of the man.'

'Don't be afraid of the likes of him. Harmless drunken brute.' She pushed, quite viciously, at the Sergeant's head. He grumbled on a snore, grunted, and then recaptured the broken rhythm of his slumbers.

'Time we were asleep as well.'

She wriggled herself under the covers between me and the Soldier, found my hand with hers and drew me out from under the rafters until my head was cradled on her warm soft breast.

My lips settled on the nipple. Her hand moved up between my thighs.

'Funny little thing,' she murmured; and thus entwined, we both slipped into sleep.

So ended my childhood.

PART TWO

CHAPTER V

*My Father makes Provision for my Future, by which I enter
on a Twelvemonth or More of Pleasure.*

I

It is a strange thing to sit here, in a small, ill-lit room, at a plain
deal table, with these papers spread before me, and reflect how the
fortunes and misfortunes of the Late Wars rapt me like a piece of
flotsam from the town I called my own, carried me will I or will
I not through countless calamities and perils and finally dropped
me in this strange country where, perforce through lack of funds
or will to move, I must remain. Strange, and to tell truth, sad: for
although this is a very pretty country with wide champains and
rolling hills with forest clad beneath the awful mist-enshrouded
crags which sometimes fill the mind with thoughts sublime and
more often daunt the heart with terror, it is not to my taste,
and the people are not my people. My only consolation is that
here the Darling Boy who was put in my charge can grow up in
the company of children of his own age and nation, and that too
in France where I had despaired of ever hearing the tongue of our
Fathers. Moreover I must count myself fortunate that the excellent
Branwaters can give me useful employment as tutor to their children in the Italian and Spanish tongues, though I fear they do so
more out of Charity and Pity for the Boy mentioned above than
out of any real interest in what I am supposed to be doing for
them.

Enough of this. If I continue in this vein I shall become down-right maudlin. It is not my purpose to dwell on the humilities of the present but to recapture the pleasures of the past. To continue my story, then . . .

During the five years following General Leclerc's passage through our City little of note occurred to disturb the even tenor of our lives. The news were brought to us no doubt of *Austerlitz, Jena,* and *Ulm,* and perhaps they had significance for my Father. To me they meant nothing, and I doubt I even connected them with the mighty host I had seen on the banks of the Tormes. Now, as I write this, I have an History of the Late Wars before me and I can say that Portugal duly fell to that army, which was then taken across the seas to the Indies where all, or almost all, perished in San Domingo of the Yellow Fever and the like, General Leclerc himself not spared, nor the lusty Sergeant whose drunken coupling I had unwillingly observed, for all I know.

The action fought at sea off the Cape of Trafalgar made some mark. Until then it had not been a point worth comment that my Father and I were English by blood and that the Nation we were in was at war with that of our Ancestors. Few of our adoptive countrymen (that is in Los Arapiles, there were plenty of Salamanca) cared much for the French whose war it was, and most would as soon have been on the other side, as indeed they would be in a year or two; but the destruction of their Fleet, in which they took some pride, came home to them a little more nearly, and for a day or two my Father kept me close behind doors. Rubén with some friends, not Fernando, threw stones at his windows and broke two panes before the Village Constable chased them away and that was the nearest the Wars came to us, until they burst about our ears and brought all down around us, the full story of which you may be sure I shall relate in due course.

The year after Trafalgar, however, marked the beginning of a period of happiness I look back on with pleasure almost unalloyed by feelings of guilt or remorse. True it is I did much that was wrong or even, unless I believe my dear but confused Father, downright wicked, but I did all in a state of thoughtless innocence that must excuse much of the offence. If the sins of youth are nought against the conscious wrong-doing of maturer years, then also I suppose one must say that green delights are trivial in comparison with the Extasies of Later Years, but unconsidered pleasures shall not lack their champion in me, not when the choice is between them and a Painful Joy. So, I dwell on this period, from Autumn 1806 to Summer 1808, with less reluctance than I shall approach withal the *climacteric* years of my history.

In September 1806 my dear Father suffered a slight apoplexy which left him with a palsy on the left side and especially in his left hand which had the tremors for some months. This put him in mind of his own mortality and his responsibilities to those who would survive him. First he settled a sum of money on Tía Teresa; then he sent word to Mr Curtis in Salamanca that he would seek his advice and two days later that good man arrived on a fine glossy mule as big as an horse.

Mr Curtis needed a strong and sturdy mount for he was above six foot, of a handsome mien and strong figure for all his sixty and six years; he had a fine head of long white hair that fluffed out from beneath his old-fashioned tricorn, large deep-set eyes, and big high-arched nose. His hands were strong and quite unarthritical and he was a great player on the *fortepiano*, having a *grand* one by Stoddart of London, brought over at huge expense, in his rooms at the Irish College. Patrick Curtis was a great friend of my Father's, being a scholar and a gentleman, who had taken his first degrees at Salamanca University before returning to Ireland to serve for a decade or so as Parish Priest; thence back to Spain where he was a Chaplain on a Man-of-War and was taken by the British at the Battle of Cape St Vincent; turned scholar, especially of Astronomy and Natural History and corresponded with my Father; finally returned to the University where he now held the Chair of Astronomy, had refurbished the Observatory, and was Rector of the Irish College. It was his custom to come over at least once a month to report to my Father the latest proceedings of the Economic Society as – Should the Eucalyptus be introduced from the Antipodes? Could a Modern Iron Manufactory or Mill rely on Charcoal for Smelting or must it always be sited near where *Fossil Coals* were available? or to seek my Parent's advice on some problem of *Astrogeny* or the like.

However, on this occasion he was closeted with my Father upstairs for half a day while I sat with Tía Teresa below and chafed and fidgeted knowing what was toward and not too happy at it for I liked my way of life well enough and change seemed an uncomfortable thing to have thrust upon me. At last the door at the top of the stairs was opened and Mr Curtis, tall and filling it, stood there.

'Joseph,' he called, 'you must come up now, and hear what your Father has to say,' and with heart beating a little quicker than usual I did as he said.

He led me through the first room and into my Father's den where the good old man lay in his cot, his face pale, his hand shaking, and I sat on a stool beside him for his voice was still weak and he quickly became breathless. Mr Curtis remained standing at the end of the bed.

'Joseph,' my Father began, 'we have been talking of your future, and Mr Curtis is to be thanked for helping me to see how it should be, for I doubt I should have managed it on my own, poorly as I am.'

Here I bent my head towards the Ancient Irishman who hemmed and waved his hand as if to disclaim any credit, but as my Father proceeded he nodded and grunted approval.

'The thing is this then. We believe you should be brought up to a profession which may keep you in the sort of style you seem settled on, for I fear you show no frugal traits, but which will also make you useful to your fellows. I would not have you enter the Church, though many of laxer habits even than yours have done so, for such bring disrepute on Religion. I would not have you a soldier, for we live in time of war and I fear you would be called upon to fight – and that is an ugly business. There are left the Law and Medicine, both with Faculties reformed and flourishing at Salamanca. Mr Curtis favours the Law as being more fitting a gentleman, and because the students of medicine are much given to rowdiness and riot and we think you peculiarly susceptible to evil example. However he is not fixed about this . . .'

'Not in the least, not at all,' said Mr Curtis, and took snuff which produced an explosive sneeze that shook the air of the room, stirred the papers on the table, and set the dust motes dancing.

'. . . and I favour Medicine,' my Father continued, when all was still again, 'for it is a science that has done much in the last fifty years or so and is now pursued more rationally than hitherto, and no-one can doubt the usefulness of the Profession when it is carried forward with skill and sense. Whereas I doubt the usefulness of lawyers: they have many opportunities for roguery that I fear would tempt you, and I would rather see you debauched as a student than a parasite on the commonwealth later. So, Joseph, what it comes to is this – can you find it in yourself to go along with my wishes and allow Mr Curtis to see to your enrolment at the University, with a view finally to becoming a surgeon or physician?'

There was nothing to say but acquiesce, for how could I hold out against the good old man with him so poorly, and, as I thought, like to die?

He smiled and nodded at my undertaking to follow his wishes in everything and put his head back on the pillow so his beard stuck up in the air, and for a time was silent save for the wheezing of his breath.

Mr Curtis took up the tale. 'Joseph,' he said, 'let me outline for you now the procedure to be followed. On St Luke's Day, the eighteenth of October next, you will be presented to the Schools for the Matriculation, and undergo a brief and elementary examination in Greek and Latin. Charles assures me you are sufficiently proficient in these tongues and indeed the standard required is not high. You will then embark on three years study for the Baccalaureate before entering the Medical School. Three more years there, if you are diligent and apt, will procure a Licentiate and the right to practise your profession – a good and early start, for you will be then scarce twenty-three.'

Six years of study seemed a great spell, but I kept the thought to myself. Instead I asked what courses were followed for the *Baccalaureatus Philosophiae.*

'A student seeking eventual entry in to the Medical School will be examined in the Mathematicks, Logic, Metaphysicks, and Experimental Physicks including Anatomy. The course is not arduous to anyone of moderate ability and application, requiring not more than four hours a day in the Schools and four of Study . . .'

If I blenched at the thought of eight hours a day working he did not notice it for he went on at some length describing these courses, rattling off the names of pedants, doctors, and professors, at which my Father nodded and smiled with his eyes closed, relishing this catalogue of those numbered in the Groves of Academe as if they were Heroes in the ranks of Ilium or Achaea.

When Mr Curtis was done he opened his eyes and continued thus: 'It remains, Joseph, to decide where you should lodge. I had hoped Mr Curtis would have taken you in, but of course the rule of his foundation forbad it: you are neither Irish nor set for Holy Orders, but he has recommended to me the household of one Don Jorge Martín . . .'

Here at last were good news. 'Why, Sir, I know the family. Don Jorge's son, Rafael, is one of my dearest friends.'

'I have heard you speak of them. Don Jorge is a lawyer, I believe, and Rafael studies to be one too, but both honest, Mr Curtis assures me, and a home with this family will surely remove the temptations attendant on living in a hostel or College of Residence. Now. I shall see you are paid a regular allowance of eight gold duros a month, nay there is no need to go on your knees to thank me, I pray you get up, you will convince me Mr Curtis was right to say it was too much if you go on so . . .'

And so I removed to Don Jorge's apartment in the Plaza de Santo Tomé, opposite the fountain.

In all this, as in so many other cases when my Father sought the guidance of Reason in managing the affairs of others, he sadly mistook the inclinations and abilities of those he sought to help. In the event study for the Baccalaureate was never more than occasional with me, and was soon perfunctory. Don Jorge was a genial man and saw no reason to disturb my Father, who remained poorly for some months, with ill reports of my lack of application, and Mr Curtis, who had also promised to keep an eye on me, lived the other side of Town; once he had seen to my Matriculation he restricted his care of me to asking me to share a dish of tea with him once every two months, when he would ask me a question or two about my studies and then play his *fortepiano* at me – usually sonatas of the London School, or nocturnes of Field, though he also played my namesake Haydn.

I took with me to Don Jorge's my dear friend Fernando who shared my room with me and who also enrolled at my Father's expense (such was the good old man's generosity). I waived his share of the rent, paying it all myself out of the allowance above, and in return he performed the occasional tasks our tutors asked of us, prepared my exercises for me, dissertations and so on when they were called for.

2

Don Jorge's apartment was on the first floor of what had once been a palace: the rooms were large, the ceilings high, the passages wide, but there was no ostentation or luxury in the furnishings or appointments save in the three reception rooms. The first of these was where Don Jorge carried out most of his business and was dominated by a large and heavy desk in the latest Imperial Style. The walls were lined with glazed bookcases of leather-bound law books, and there were three very large and well-cushioned chairs for Don Jorge and his clients. Next came two rooms reserved for *tertulias* and feasts, also done out in the modern style with ormolu ornaments, porcelain and crystal chandeliers, but neither opened above once a month.

These three rooms opened off a wide hall-way fitted out with a fine white and gilt table with a marble top whose front and legs were elegantly bowed in the French mode of the last century. From this hallway branched another passage, concealed from the curious by a heavy curtain, which led past eight more rooms to the kitchen and offices beyond. Here all was simplicity. The walls were not hung with painted paper but whitewashed; the floors not polished marble but slate and tile, and the furnitures were plain, strong and sufficient in the good old Spanish style. Our room was the first on the left and had two truckle beds, a table, and a press for clothes. The floor was covered with a rush mat and shutters at the small window served for drapes. The other rooms were the same, save for the kitchen which was bright and airy; this was where the household normally took its meals off a heavy scrubbed table big enough for ten or a dozen to draw up to together.

So large a board was needed, for Don Jorge and his wife Doña Regina had four daughters and a son and besides them a cook and a maid who, as is the custom in Spain where the domestics are considered family, sat down together, not to mention his Clerk who often stayed to dine though he had lodgings elsewhere.

Don Jorge was tall and elegant; a genial, kind soul much adored by all his daughters, though of course he favoured his son above them, the fifth and last of the brood. Doña Regina was cast in a severer mould – small with sharp eyes and aquiline features, she must, some twenty years before, have possessed a fine and striking beauty. Indeed it is only the convention that denies an ageing woman who has had five children the right to that quality that prevents me from ascribing beauty to her now. I confess I held her in some awe.

The girls were lively, pretty, small in figure, fine in feature, and more than is usual in a Nation which brings up its daughters for marriage, child-bearing or the Convent, they were talented in drawing, conversation and especially music. The oldest was just married (hence the vacant room) and lived beyond doors in Ciudad Rodrigo; the three who remained were *Violeta*, *Jara*, and *Margarita*, and they were truly flowers, their names in English being Violet, Rock-rose, and Daisy. Violeta was betrothed to a Lieutenant of Foot called Tebaldo Zúñiga.

Rafael remains, who was truly an *Angel*. Two years older than I, and already a Bachelor for he had matriculated at fifteen, he was tall, slender, not gawky, fresh-complexioned with yellow hair and pale brown eyes. He moved with grace, spoke quietly, was kind and generous to a fault, fond of merriment and laughter and yet in repose had a dignity much like his Father's. Our whole acquaintance prophecied a glorious future for him – alas, at the time I moved into his Father's household he had less than two years to live.

I soon discovered that the eight hours a day in study promised by Mr Curtis were an exaggerated estimate: as above, Fernando took notes for me at those lectures I found tedious, I aped his work done at home, but as well as this there were many High Days and Holy Days so I did not find the programme too irksome. Indeed some of it had its entertaining side, most especially that connected with the new Science of Nature whose appliances and devices seemed like nothing so much as toys for grown men to play with, *viz*: *item*, a solar microscope that projected an image on a screen; *item*, a *gravesande* or *heliostat* which, by an ingenious arrangement of clockwork, kept the sun's rays focussed through a lens on one stationary point where it would boil water in a vessel though the earth moved and shifted the sun's light; *item*, an *hydraulic* apparatus by which a man might lift a weight three times his own. There were demonstrations too, as one by Dr Juan Manuel Pérez who proved by inverting a glass in water so that a chamber of air remained locked within that Matter is Impenetrable – all could see how glass, water, and air remained separate; then proved us mistaken, or so we thought, by putting silver in *aqua fortis*, which caused the silver to disappear in much frothing and fizzing to be replaced by black particles suspended in the liquid. 'But no,' the worthy Doctor insisted, 'this does not prove the first hypothesis wrong – for the explanation is simple: all matter is impenetrable, but some is *porous*.' I sometimes think I might have had a gift for Natural Philosophy of this sort had not the Wars so cruelly interrupted my studies.

Occasional visits to the Anatomy Theatre, by the Civil Hospital, in the poorest part of the town which provided specimens enough, also helped to pass the time once curiosity was allowed to supersede revulsion. First the exhibits were displayed to us, in glass jars, brought down from locked cupboards – a human foetus, the vessels which carry the blood, including the heart, all ingeniously separated out, mounted and embalmed, and other organs too including those male and female which I will not name vulgarly and whose Latin I shall pretend to have forgot. A Doctor Zunzúñegui, a Biscayan I suppose from his name, was in charge here, and once I was privileged to watch him at work (for normally only those already bachelor-ed attended his performances – my Father's name procured me the entrée). I still recall the finess of his movements and incisions as he handled his scalpel, saw, needle and probe, and most wonderful of all fine jets of water fired through glass tubes whose force he used to separate tissues as light and transparent as gossamer.

When on an occasional visit I reported this to my Father, he grew solemn and pulled his beard; I asked him the matter and he declared that it misgave him, such pulling about of cadavers, not, of course, out of superstition relating to the Day of Judgement and Resurrection, but because he thought such practices bred up in the young a Contempt for what was after all Human, where only Reverence was due, since, as he always averred, Man was the nearest thing we could know to the Divine.

Logick and *Metaphysicks* were beyond me and I left the unravelling of them to Fernando; what of the Mathematicks I could not learn by rote I contrived to dispense with or cribbed off my neighbour; and so one way and another, and by means no more devious than those employed by many a young scholar before me and doubtless since, I contrived to get by the eighteen months of University study that fell to me before the wars came on us, and that without too much *ennui*, without being dismissed, and without learning anything at all worth remembering.

3

But it is not my studies in that period I look back on as on a paradise of innocence departed, but on those days when no work was done on account of Holy Days, High Days, and Sundays and a month in the Summer so that all in all I calculate of three hundred and sixty five days in the year two hundred were free. These were the paradisial times when Rafael, Fernando and I issued forth with carefree hearts and dressed up in the *Majo* style we affected at festival time. We grew our hair long and contained it in silk hair nets, wore high two-cornered hats with silken tassles, waistcoats laced up loosely to show our fine white shirts; round our necks we knotted bright scarves while broad belts supported our velvet breeches worn very tight; below our knees came stockings, green or pink, and shoes buckled with silver; likewise there were silver buttons and fastenings wherever they could be worn. We carried brown cloaks and smoked small black *cigarillos*, and we cultivated a proper look of boredom and disdain for everyone except *Maja* ladies, and everything except the *corridas de toros*.

Most disdained of all were those Salamantines who aped the French Fashions, who wore *trousers* or *pantalons* and high hats with brims, who lisped or warbled but did not speak, who could not eat but *fed on honey-dew*, and never drank but *sipped at elixirs*, the *Petimetres* we called them from the French for Little Master.

Rubén, employed now as a clerk at the Town-Hall, was one of those and if we found him or one of his ilk alone and unattended, it would be our sport to jostle him a little, mimic his gait and his sugary speech, and if the ways were miry spatter his fine trousers. We meant no harm yet he continued to harbour a grudge against me and in time took disproportionate revenge.

And what were the pleasures and delights we sampled in that Golden Age? We would rise at nine to hear Mass in whatever church the Ladies of our choice would most likely be, would break our fast with chocolate and cinnamon-flavoured sippets; then we would take the air for an hour or so to hear the news and show off our fine clothes. Wherever we began we always ended in the *Plaza Mayor* of Salamanca, that most harmonious yet sublime construction which takes the heart with beauty yet does not oppress the spirit, rather it stimulates the mind to joy and wit and provokes discourse and thus amity. Only yesterday I recalled its excellence to Captain Branwater and he remembered it well with a smile and a little thoughtfulness: then he remarked that he dared say he would as soon live in a world without the Comedies of Shakespeare as in a world without the Grand Square at Salamanca, and he added, 'The Truest Delight of the Mind that I can conceive is to read the one while sitting in the other.'

I have no time for those who exalt the Works of Nature above those of Man, for what work of nature can surpass Man who is the Crown of Nature? The Pyrenean Peaks I can see now from my window, the very *Pic du Midi d'Ossau* itself, are a set of broken teeth beside the Grand Square of Salamanca, ay and its churches and convents, colleges and cathedrals too – or such as these French about me left standing.

At about the hour of two we would take a glass of wine in each of the three taverns which lie below and behind the Plaza, and our custom was that the last of these should be Antonio's. Antonio was a broad, thick-waisted man, with a heavy face, long-nosed, and lugubrious of expression. But his appearance belied his impish nature, for by years of industry he had mastered various *prestidigitatorial* arts, and would amuse us all by making small change fly from his tray to his pockets unaided, by discovering an egg in one's ear, or a frog in one's pocket.

From *La Covachuela*, for that was the name of the Tavern, back to the Plaza de Santo Tomé was only a step, and at about three in the afternoon we would take it to pull up our stools at Doña Regina's table and dine off good Spanish stew or *olla*, a piece of fish, and since it was a feast day, a chicken or partridge. We would dine quietly in spite of wine already taken for that good lady, though no scold, would not tolerate rowdiness at table, nor anywhere else in her house.

And then to rest, from four to six.

Rafael and Fernando would study away the hours from six to nine, even on these days when the schools were closed – the first at his Law, the second at his Logick or Physicks. They attended the Tutor – I complained of the head-ache, remained in bed and read Romances; they pored over their text-books – I practised the art of dice-throwing; they took messages for Don Jorge – and I would accompany them just to the point where the strumming of a guitar caught my ear, or the flutter of a fan in a passing chair caught my eye – then I would beg off and arrange to meet them again for the *paseo* at nine.

From nine till ten, in company with the entire population but the very old and infirm, we would parade about the Town but chiefly in or near the Grand Square which would be illuminated, parade at that stately pace which combines dignity with ease and which is not to be emulated by any Nation other than the Spanish, passing the time of day with all our numerous acquaintance, stopping at one of the stalls for a confection of *mazapán* with sugared water in Summer or hot chocolate in Winter. And if some girls came by in *Maja* costume with white *mantilla*, tight waist, flounced skirt with ribbons and lace, bows and tassles, spangles and jet, we would pause and offer the compliments we had polished all day, *viz*: *item*, 'I never knew that flowers could walk'; *item*, 'Blessed is the Womb from which such Beauty danced'; *item*,

'Turn your face to the West and make the Sun return'. To which they answered not with the simpering coyness of your *Petimetras* or French Misses but with tart riposte, enticing sharpness.

At ten we would return to Doña Regina's table for a supper of eggs or salads, then out again to the theatre if it was Summer and a company from Madrid or Barcelona was in Town, especially if it was that from the *Teatro del Príncipe* of Madrid which presented such grand and tragical spectacles as *The Prodigious Piety of Leopold the Great* and *Everything Lost for Love or the False Czar of Muscovy*. In Winter we would most likely be invited forth to a *tertulia* in the house of one of Don Jorge's friends or to a *Publick Ball*.

The day would end in a tavern where the *Toreros* resorted, for Rafael especially was ever keen to search out their company. And what better company could there be than that of these young and not so young men dedicated to bravery, artistry, and passion between the horns of a giant Fighting Bull? For hours we sat with them, buying them chocolate, lemonade, whatever they called for, listening to their stoickal conversation uttered almost entirely in single words, or playing dice while a gypsy strummed on a guitar. Then when Dawn first stroked the Golden Domes of Salamanca with her rosy finger tips we would stagger back through the dewy streets to the Plaza de Santo Tomé, climb the long dark stairs and throw ourselves on our truckle beds for a few hours of fitful sleep.

CHAPTER VI

*A Short Chapter relating my Inglorious Introduction to the
Art of TAUROMACHIA.*

I

Toreo, Tauromachia (for I shall not call thee *bullfighting*, since the bull
is not fought, but tamed, dominated, and sacrificed – with art and
valour if he is a courageous bull, with satire and ridicule if he is
not) what hours, nay days of happiness have I spent in thy Round
Temples? Perhaps more than in the Temples of the Faith, I shame
to record, for a Mass may be heard in twenty minutes but a *corrida*
of twelve bulls will last a day.

It was Rafael's ambition to *torear* himself, an ambition which his
doting Father from whom he might ask all else in his power to
offer was ever resolute to discourage, although the good man
enjoyed the Fiesta as much as any of us, but he saw in it too well
the dangers that his only son exposed himself to, and also perhaps,
as Lawyer and Gentleman, bore in mind the law of the land which
said no *Hidalgo* may course with bulls on foot; however, this law,
like most relating to *toreo*, was more honoured in the Breach than
in the Observance – to use a favourite phrase of my Patron,
Captain Branwater. I too found it an ambition difficult to share,
though remaining addicted to the *spectacle*, as above, after my first,
last and only taste of it.

It happened thus, in October 1806, just after I had first removed
to Don Jorge's house, at the time of the *ferias* for Santa Teresa de

Avila, celebrated throughout the Province, but most especially in *Alba*, three and a half leagues from Salamanca, where the Saint is buried.

I well remember the setting out of our expedition – Rafael and I on mules, Fernando on a donkey borrowed for the occasion, taking our place in a long line of youths bent on the same purpose and similarly mounted or on foot. Early in the morning we made our way down the steep cobbles to the Gate of St Paul, along the avenue of acacia trees to the Roman Bridge, and thence on to the Alba Road, winding its way easily over the stubbled downs, out into the forested hills. It was a clear, cold, crisp day with larks and finches fluttering in flocks about us, a kite or two above us, and the rich smell of wild lavender and thyme beneath the oaks.

We left early, for the journey would take three hours and there were to be three bulls before dinner, and six more in the afternoon, but we could not forbear making a halt at the Fountain of Teresa, just half the way. Fernando plucked some flowers there and garlanded the image of Our Lady Adored by the Saint that stands upon the spot, whilst I refreshed myself from a leather bottle brought with us lest we should be thirsty on the way. And perhaps I had recourse to that bottle more than once on the road down through the hills and back to the river where it bends round the Castle and palace of the Dukes of Alba (to whom I make no doubt I am distantly related through my connexion the Marquis of Monterrubio) and the little town it shelters beneath its lofty walls.

2

At all events, by the time we had found ourselves a good position on an upended bullock cart that formed part of the improvised ring, and watched the first young bull *caped*, *banderilla-ed*, and put to the sword (there were no *Picadors* – so small a town could not afford the horses), I found myself possessed of a different kind of courage to that I normally own, which is *rational* if nothing else.

(I do not lack rational courage – I heard the mines blown at Ciudad Rodrigo, saw the charge of Le Marchant's Brigade at Los Arapiles, and watched the French Lines break at Vitoria – but these do not compare with a charging fighting bull.) I seized my cloak as the fifes announced the second beast, and before any could restrain my *spontaneous* urge dropped to the sand beneath.

Slowly I made the *Torero's* salute to my friends who roared with laughter, save Rafael whose face now had a pensive look; slowly I shook out my cloak, conscious that the laughter and cheers had changed their tone, but not too conscious why, and then as I turned to face the gap in the compound whence I expected my adversary to come . . . the world performed a summerset.

My escape was a miracle, and I thank Santa Teresa for it each year that brings October back again. At the last second the bull followed the cape as I shook it out and his horn caught my broad majo belt when it should have taken me in the stomach. What a shaking, and a tumbling and a drubbing I suffered then! At last the belt broke and I crashed to the ground so winded I could not stir, and with my eyes and mouth full of sand. The bull wheeled, turned, sighted me, and nostrils snorting fury, eyes red with rage, came on . . . but my gallant friends – did man ever have such comrades? – had joined me in the ring: Rafael drew off the beast with a series of dexterous passes while Fernando pulled me up and away back to the carts. I got one leg over the side, he pushed me the rest of the way, and I fell in a heap on the other side.

3

My troubles were not over. Before I had scarce recovered senses or breath the youths of the town I had fallen amongst began to beat me with sticks, a courtesy they extended to my friends when they rejoined me. The Constable appeared, a huge man whose moustaches were echoed by the droop of his enormous black hat, but to my astonishment it was not for our relief that he came, but for our arrest. With the aid of the youths who were beating us he haled the three of us to the house of the Mayor of Alba and all the way a jeering crowd flung cabbages and even rocks at us.

Rafael explained.

'He will fine us at least, you know,' he said as we waited in the Mayor's parlour and listened to the hooting crowd outside. 'And may hap worse. He could have us ridden out of town with our faces turned backwards over our animals' tails, while these friends you have made throw what they like at us. But I doubt it'll come to that. He is acquainted with my Father.'

'But why?'

'Because we saved you. We should have allowed the bull at least two more charges. That is the rule when a man takes on a bull one to one. No-one should interfere until the bull has completed his first attack of three charges, for that is his inalienable right.'

And so it turned out. At dinner time when the Chief Magistrate of the town returned from the *corrida* where he had presided and had therefore witnessed our intervention, respecting Rafael's family he merely fined both him and Fernando, though I of course paid – two dollars each, no less – and after asking us to dine with him, which we refused, not wishing to embarrass him further, asked us to leave Alba quietly and by the back streets – which thankfully we did, being mindful of what he might have decreed had he thought to be harsh.

Such was Rafael's goodness of heart that he never once on the journey home complained that the day's sport was ruined, and the bulls we had missed the last of the season, but indeed contrived to cheer us on the way with songs and glees.

CHAPTER VII

*In which Rafael is Betrothed, and I too discover myself
Susceptible to the Tenderest Passion, but fix on an Object
Unworthy of my Attentions.*

I

I have already said that Violeta, Rafael's eldest unmarried sister,
was betrothed to Tebaldo Zúñiga; and it is time now for me to say
something of this Zúñiga family. *Don Lorenzo de Zúñiga y Castro*
was a prominent banker in Salamanca, perhaps the most prosperous there, being a Galician by birth, and a Catalan by breeding
(both races being noted, like the Jews, for their ability to make
money *grow*), his Grandfather having come from Barcelona and
settled in Vigo and made a fortune from owning a fishing fleet.
Much of this fortune had been turned to banking and an increase
in prosperity and wealth in the latter half of the last century in
Salamanca had brought Don Lorenzo to the Town with some of
this fortune, where no bank had been needed before.

He also brought his Galician wife and cousin by marriage Doña
Elvira Castro, and before many years she bore him Sebastián, his
heir; two daughters – Isabella and Marisa; Tebaldo; and a last
daughter Angelica, some fourteen years old and only just returned
from a convent in Madrid much patronised by the Nobility, where
she had been sent to complete her education.

The betrothal of Don Jorge's daughter to Don Lorenzo's second
son Tebaldo had been a business of not very much importance,
there being little to it except to arrange that the couple would

have enough to live on in comfort without ostentation, Tebaldo
having no inclination to banking, but preferring to be a soldier, to
which end he had already attended the Academy at Toledo. But in
the Winter of 1806 and 7 Don Jorge proposed a match between
Rafael and Isabella for on the following Day of St John, in June,
it was expected Rafael would take his Licenciate and be ready to
set up home and practise Law like his Father before him. This
match involved long and protracted negotiations (since Rafael
was Don Jorge's heir), of which, for the most part, the *Principals*
remained ignorant. However, by the middle of April, all was settled, the young people were approached, and having met already
and having conversed frequently at *tertulias* and the like following
the earlier betrothal of Violeta and Tebaldo, both expressed themselves severally willing to enter into the proposed match. All that
was needed now was that they should fall in love.

The third of May, being the Feast of St Philip and St James the
Less, marks the beginning of the Temperate Season, and is, in that
country as elsewhere in Spain, celebrated with a grand *romería* or
pilgrimage, in this case to a hermitage some four or five leagues
from the Town, at a delightful spot on the banks of the River
Tormes. Since it is also the day of the first great *corrida* of the year
I was surprised when Rafael asked me to accompany him not to
the *corrida* but on the *romería*. When I exclaimed at this he was
good enough to take me into his confidence and tell me what I
have just sketched out – namely, his imminent betrothal to Isabella.

The form of their falling in love was to be thus and thus,
making use of a charming custom then current whereby at times
of Festival, at *romerías*, during the *paseo* on a Great Day, girls would
throw small darts – too slight to cause pain or damage unless to the
Recipient's heart – these darts being decorated with streamers of
coloured paper, by which the Recipient could identify the family
of the thrower, if not the actual she who had thrown it. The possession of this dart with its streamers entitled the 'wounded' youth
to present himself to the family with whom he would remain for
the rest of the day, sharing whatever entertainment was provided,

and seeking to find out who was the cause of his presence, whether by stealth or playful questioning or simply by the burning looks which would be directed at him from behind an agitated fan. If then he was a proper gallant he would in secret engage himself to be the lady's *novio* or sweetheart, would send her messages, follow her to Church, and sing lovesongs beneath the grill of her bedchamber.

The forenoon of that May morning, just a year before that fateful May when all Spain rose against the French Invader, provided then a scene of gentle beauty. I call to mind a long line of carriages and gigs – all dressed with flowers and drawn by glossy mules with nodding plumes – each adorned with nymphs dressed for delight beneath gay parasols, the gentlemen riding beside them and servants following with paniered asses, loaded with provisions. The morning air was balmy, the roadside jewelled with the flowers of Spring, the wheat in the *campo* already a foot high and a deep luxuriant green. Swallows skimmed around us and larks sang.

First Rafael saw his own family properly attended by Tebaldo and Sebastián Zúñiga in the characters of *novios* to his sisters, then he and I cantered together up the line of slowly moving carriages until we approached that of the Zúñiga family. It was not one of the largest, but much the most elegant, being mounted on steel springs in the English fashion, indeed it was a product of the workshops of *Felton* in London, and as such a tribute to the Zúñiga fortune and an evidence of the inefficiency of the Corsican Tyrant's blockade of the Nation of Shopkeepers.

The game was that we should approach this remarkable equipage slowly and make as if to pass it unaware of the Fair Nymphs within, but then discover on Rafael's coat the dart or snare which Isabella was to fix as we passed. Alas, the plan went awry. As we trotted by we heard a gasp of horror drowned in a cascade of light laughter. Rafael, his face already colouring slightly, first examined as much of his person as he could see then hissed at me: 'Is it there? In my back perhaps, or on my harness?' But I could not discover the toy. We were now in front of the carriage, but even above the clopping of the mules we could still hear the peals of silvery mirth. Just then Jaime, the mule-driver who rode on the leading beast, touched my shoulder with his whip.

'Your honour,' he said as quietly as may be, 'My Lady would not wish you to ride on without offering to return her daughter's favour,' and he gave me a broad wink, and placed his finger on the side of his large and pitted nose. Now at last we located the errant dart – not on Rafael, but in the thick folds of my cloak which I was carrying over my shoulder.

'God's Wounds,' cried Rafael. 'Here's a pretty business. What shall we do?'

'Take the favour,' I suggested, 'and carry it off as if it had found its proper target.'

'Give me your cloak then, and you spur on a little.'

I was of a mind to bargain with him for it, but he was dreadfully in earnest, bothered perhaps that the outset of his wooing should pass off well, so I did as he said.

For a space of about three minutes I was able to look around me, undistracted by a companion, and enjoy the loveliness of the hills in all their Springtime freshness and colour, mark the playful antics of amorous sparrows and the deadly swoop of a distant hawk, and savour the softness of a zephyr on my cheek; then hooves at a brisk canter and a sharp *halloo* from Rafael caused me to look back and rein in as he came up with me.

'It will not do,' he said, and his expression was more flustered than ever, 'our stratagem was observed and it is you who are to be the guest, since you received the dart.'

'But what about you?'

'Oh doubtless I shall be invited to remain, as a friend of yours.'

And so it turned out. We rode back; the carriage halted; and Doña Elvira, a handsome, silver-haired woman of forty-five dressed in dove-grey silks, invited me up to sit between her and her eldest daughter, Isabella. Unfortunately there was not room for Rafael who had to trot behind, and moreover lead my pony as if he were a groom, all the way to the Hermitage, while Isabella

alternately blushed and paled at recollection of her faulty aim, and
cast such pleading looks of remorse over her shoulder at him that
he had quite recovered his spirits by the time we reached our destination. Meanwhile Doña Elvira prattled on to me in the most
delightful way.

'Don José Bozzam – well, I do declare. Let me see, we might I
think be distantly connected. Your Father is the eccentric Curate
of Los Arapiles – is that not so?'

I agreed.

'Then there is a connection. Your great Grandfather was the
Conde de Monterrubio de la Sierra and his first cousin was my
Grandfather. Isabella, you are to be congratulated in your aim, I'm
sure that *clown* behind us is not so nearly related to a *Grandee* as
Don José.'

'Oh, *Mama*, how can you be so cruel? I am quite mortified,
cannot you see?'

'La, child, it's of no consequence. We shall laugh at this for
many years yet, I don't doubt. Now, Don José, let me present
Isabella's sisters whom I do not think you have met since they are
only just returned from the care of the Sisters of the Holy Trinity
in Madrid. The quiet one in the corner is Marisa, she is fifteen
years old and performs well on the guitar, in the Italian style of
course, she is no gypsy I promise you; and opposite is Angelica,
my youngest pet. Forgive her outlandish clothes, I am sure if her
Father had seen her he would have sent her indoors to change, but
he is in Avila on business, and when he is away they do as they
please . . . it was her fantasy to come as Isabella's page boy, and
nought we could say would restrain her.'

I made my courtesies to each in turn as well as I might seated
so close to all in that swaying carriage. Almost my knees touched
Angelica's and I found it difficult to keep my eyes off her. She was
dressed in a brown velvet suit, jacket and breeches, like a boy, with
red waistcoat, white shirt, black scarf, and silk cummerbund
striped in turquoise and red. She wore a turquoise turban. Like her
sisters she had a heart-shaped face with thick dark brown hair

pulled back beneath the turban, wide-spaced eyes very dark, a broad nose and a full mouth; but there was a liveliness in her glance, a pertness in her mouth, a delicacy in her air which the others lacked.

'Do you play the guitar as well?' I asked, not for want of anything better to say – I could have offered her my heart, my soul, my life – but these were the only words my tongue and lips seemed capable of.

A slip of pink, like a cat's, passed across her top lip.

'A little,' she murmured. Her voice was deeper than I had expected.

'She is in a good way to becoming accomplished,' her Mother asserted, 'for she has her first *novio*, Don Julio Sorrello his name is, a theological student. He serenades her most plaintively in the Galician style which I favour, for he comes from Oviedo. But I fear he has deserted us today.'

A slight heat rose in Angelica's cheeks, which made her even more divine.

'Oh *Mama*, how can you be so silly? You know I pay him no attention at all, for what use is there in a *novio* who is like to become a priest?'

'La, girl, what a thing to say! You are too young to be looking for *use* in a *novio*, and if you are not then we shall have to find you a husband . . . pardon me Don José, I say more than I should, look yonder, what bird is that?'

It was cinnamon coloured with black and white striped wings and crest and long beak.

'A hoopoe, madam.'

'Is it indeed? I am sure it's very pretty, very pretty indeed. And an uncommon talent in a boy to be able to name birds unless they be game.'

'It was my Father, Madam, who taught me to name most wild things,' and I continued by pointing out and designating others of the feathered kind that could be seen together with what I could remember of their Natural Histories. In this way I entertained the

company, and I flatter myself with more profit than even Rafael
might have managed, until our caravan achieved the object of the
romería, which was not so much the Hermitage – a tiny chapel, no
bigger than a shepherd's croft – as the surrounding country.

This was on the banks of the Tormes, near a watermill. Across
the wide lake poplars and alders shimmered in their new foliage
above the placid stream; coots and moorhens – their young like
sooty balls of fluff – cut arrows of light across the surface. Behind
us gentle hills swelled and subsided beneath the grateful shade of
scattered oaks, and through the verdant landscape a gentle rivulet
meandered between rushy verges to join the greater river below
the weir.

Over this smiling terrain the coaches of the townsfolk wandered, each searching out a dell or shady tree, and yet such is the
spaciousness of the place all were accommodated with ease. Rugs
and carpets now were spread, the Ladies handed down, paniers
and baskets unstrapped and unloaded, and soon the sun glittered
over fine napery, cristal and silver; and cold meats and early fruits,
cheeses, sausages, crisp loaves and salads added their beauties to the
scene.

As she supervised the disposition of comestibles and wines,
Doña Elvira returned to the subject of my Father.

'Your Father is a most ingenious man from all accounts.
I declare when he was first among us, and still mixed in Society, I
met him on several occasions, some twelve or eleven years ago.
I remember him well for he came to me for a housekeeper who
would mother his boy for him – goodness, how foolish of me –
the boy in question must have been you, Don José.' And she
crowed with laughter at the recollection. 'What a pretty thing
you were then, so shy, of course you hardly spoke Spanish at all,
just Italian and English. For a short time you had a poor cousin of
mine, Doña Simoneta, recently widowed and in difficult circumstances, to look after you, but quite soon she married again, and
left you. Dear Simoneta. I recall once . . .' and here her tone
became confiding or conspiratorial, 'she begged me to come and

see while she bathed and washed you, she wanted particularly that
I should see you because already I had Sebastián and Tebaldo,
who is much of an age with you, and she, poor innocent, for
though widowed she was only eighteen, thought there was something, something not right, *missing* . . . oh, la, what am I saying?'
and here my hostess coloured more than ever either of her daughters had, and fell to a coughing fit, which caused her much distress,
and such restoratives as *hartshorn* and sugared water were called for,
which her three daughters were quick to administer. This left me
time to recover too for I was not a little discomposed, which
might have been Madam's intention, having surmised the *lack*
about my person to which she had been on the point of referring.

When all were settled again Marisa fell to strumming her guitar,
in the Italian Style, while on a knoll nearby Isabella spread herself
like a Queen, albeit still a little shy from the maladroitness of her
aim, to receive Rafael's hommage; Angelica assumed her role as
page-boy, and stood behind shading her sister's face with a parasol
of fine green silk. Isabella was dressed in a golden yellow satin with
pale blue bodice, with her hair in a scarlet snood that matched
Angelica's waistcoat, all set off by a plain fur-trimmed cape
brought against the uncertainties of the Springtime weather. On
her white apron her black pug *Frolic* rested, and in her hand she
held a fan to cool the blushes called forth by Rafael's gallantries.

But more lovely to me was Angelica. Her eyes more deeply set
beneath brows more delicately arched, held still that playful know-
ingness that first enchanted me and all my resolve was to find
occasion to converse more fully with them, unobserved and away
from all the world.

2

The brightness of the morning expanded into the glory of Noon
and settled on the torpor of the after dinner hours. Fathers undid
their coat buttons, pushed back their wigs, and spread kerchiefs

over their now rubicund foreheads. Their spouses yawned behind their fans or gossiped with diminishing *brio*; small children squabbled.

Our dinner had been long and sumptuous. Two cold duck had succeeded a large bream in mayonnaise; conserves, almond comfits, fruits and candies had followed the duck. To help things on for Isabella and Rafael, Doña Elvira had brought two bottles of prized Galician wine – thin stuff I thought it, but it added to the enervation of the hour, especially since Rafael, who was by nature abstemious, had covertly filled my glass from his. Now, with all cleared away, Doña Elvira scandalised for a time with her gossip from a neighbouring party, then when this friend departed she allowed herself to nod beneath a parasol; Rafael and Isabella murmured together, making each other rings and necklaces from daisies; Marisa continued to strum, in the Italian style. Her *E* string was flat. Angelica fidgeted – she was bored: occasionally she would catch my eye with hers and in hers I saw a depth, a darkness for a moment, then she'd grin and look away, and leave my pulse beating a little quicker. Behind us all, Jaime the mule-driver snored beneath a cloud of flies, nor did his posture conceal the empty wine-skin he had tried to hide beneath his cloak. Only Frolic was active, sniffing out the grass, yapping at passing dogs, making as much as he could of the lead attached to a string that tethered him to our carriage wheel.

A smile more mischievous lifted the corners of Angelica's mouth; a butterfly flew by her head and settled near the lap dog's lead. She aimed to catch it in cupped hands, it fluttered free; she paused where she was, and again her eyes held mine.

It was a moment or two before Frolic realised the completeness of his freedom, for Angelica had slipped the string from his lead. At first he continued to sniff about, with the button of his tiny tail wagging more feverishly as he penetrated new zones hitherto beyond his reach. I offered to speak, but Angelica laid her finger to her lips, and I kept mum. She picked at the petals of a buttercup and waited.

A *Majo* went by with two sleek *coursers* at his heel; Frolic pricked ears and scampered up to them, cocked head, and yapped. The coursers looked down their long noses and paused. Frolic yapped again, one courser barked, Frolic leaped back a foot, the other courser snapped, and Frolic was off trailing his short lead behind him, scampering over tussocks, and through the remains of people's picnics; he yapped and the coursers snapped in pursuit. Happily they were well trained and came to heel as soon as their master whistled them up, else surely they would have torn the pug to pieces in no time for Frolic lacked the pace of their natural prey, the fleet-footed hare.

But Frolic had gone and all was consternation in our party. Rafael and Isabella had started up but knew not which direction the pug had taken, Marisa swore he had gone one way, Angelica was strong that he had gone another, Doña Elvira belaboured Jaime with her reticule, and Jaime yawned and spluttered, and called upon the Virgin and All the Saints to witness he had shut his eye for no more than a wink, or a minute at most. Isabella burst into tears and offered her fan, a very pretty one, to whoever would recover her pet.

Angelica took command.

'Isabella and Rafael, do you go that way,' pointing towards the river, 'José, see that copse of willows by the brook, see if he's amongst those trees. I shall look this way, up the hill, under the oaks.'

'I shall accompany Angelica,' said Marisa laying aside her instrument, 'for she has chosen the way he went and she shall thus gain the promised reward.'

Angelica looked down at her elder sister with flashing eyes.

'You'll do no such thing, you must stay here with Mama, else she'll lack company.'

'Yes indeed, Marisa, you must stay with me, I beg you.'

'Very well. But I'll wager Angelica finds him, for I last saw him but an hundred paces off, up under the oak trees.'

Thus commanded we set off severally, I alone towards the copse of willows indicated, which marked the boundary of the area

used by the picnickers, and after skirting three or four groups
similar to ours, all dozing off the effects of dinner, found myself
entering the wood along the grassy banks of the stream. Here all
was cool and quiet, save for the purling of the waters round
gnarled roots and mossy stones. The trees were aspens, not willows
(again my Father's lore came to my aid) as I knew by the charming shimmer of their leaves in every air however light, which
added a sibilant rustling to the sound of water once one's ear was
tuned to catch it. I cast about for Frolic but with little hope of
seeing him – I shared Marisa's conviction as to the direction he
had taken, but I marked with pleasure the flight of a yellow and
glossy brown dragonfly and the tiny constellation made by a clump
of wild strawberry flowers, and then, to my surprise, I heard
him – his yap, over to my left, up the slope, and coming towards
me. And then there *she* was – Angelica, carrying the errant hound
securely tucked under her arm. Her cheeks were flushed, her eyes
sparkled, her hair was coming adrift from her scarf. She placed the
cool soft fingers of her free hand on my wrist and looked round
breathlessly.

'What an adventure!' she gasped. 'We have five minutes, Frolic
is excuse enough for that,' and without more ado she set him on
the ground, tied his lead securely to a branch, and set off further
into the wood, nor heeded the dog's whining lament, nor whether
or not I followed her.

She already knew well the power she had over me, but I doubt
she knew its full extent – my blood pounded, an almost sick
excitement had me by the throat, I feared that after all my legs
would fail us both.

She did not go far – just to a shady dingle hidden alike from the
slopes above and the path near the stream – then she stopped,
turned and put her arms around my neck.

'Kiss me,' she commanded. Indeed I should not have needed
telling.

I kissed her and after a moment she put her tongue between my
lips.

Her brown velvet jacket was short. My hand slipped beneath the sash.

'Go on.' She wriggled herself against me. Soon I could feel the coolness of bare skin beneath her breeches, the soft roundness of her buttocks.

'This is pleasant,' she said, and stood on tiptoe to bite my ear; then she sank to the mossy ground, pulling me after her.

Distantly Frolic continued his complaint.

'Pay no attention.' She caught my hand and put it on her breast. 'Kiss me again. Harder.'

For a time the world seemed very far away and all there was was in her lips and her hair and the warmth of her small body beneath mine. Then she pushed me away again and her hand moved down over my stomach towards the hard protuberance beneath my breeches.

And Frolic barked.

'*Hostia*, there's someone coming. You go the way we came, back to Frolic, I'll find my way out at the top of the wood. Quickly now. We'll find another time, I promise,' and she pecked one last kiss on my cheek and was gone, scrambling through brackens and up the mossy slope.

I found Marisa holding the lap-dog. On her insistence her Mother had released her, and she had followed Angelica into the wood, and discovered Frolic by his whining. I was hard put to explain how I had not seen him myself and confessed I could not imagine how it was he had come to be tied up. But when I asserted I had seen no sign of Angelica I strained her credulity too far.

'You may kiss me too,' she said.

I did but with less relish than her sister, and shortly she put an end to our embrace.

'Well, at all events,' she said, ''twas I found Frolic, and I make no doubt that neither you nor Angelica will dispute my claim to Isabella's fan.'

3

Angelica had promised *another time* but a week went by with only one sight of her, and that at Mass on Sunday, when, with her veil and in the gloom, she looked scarce different from her sisters. I languished dreadfully, sighed, moaned at nights, began definitely to sicken until Fernando insisted that I tell him what the matter was. I described my case and it was his suggestion that I should present myself at my Beloved's window in the formal pose of a *novio*.

I misgave the venture from the start – the style of *novio* had always appeared to me an unseemly one, inviting scorn from the Mistress, ridicule from passers-by, and a talent with voice and guitar I lack. However, Violeta, Rafael's sister, betrothed to Angelica's brother and already an intimate of the Zúñiga family, came to my aid and told me which grill of the Zúñiga house (for they owned not just an apartment, but a whole villa, much as if they were nobility, which they were not, merely bankers) I should make my offerings at; I conned some verses, apt ones I hope, including one by *Luis de Góngora*, which actually had this to its first stanza:

> *There is no green Ash without its inscription*
> *No white Poplar without its motto*
> *If one Valley resounds with ANGELICA*
> *The other replies: ANGELICA.*

Thus fortified, and with my passion which, swollen by dreams and fancy for a week, had grown prodigious, I took myself off one midnight, and when I saw the lamp lit in the room signifying that my Beloved was about to retire, I began my addresses by calling her as loudly as I dared.

At this a cloaked figure in a nearby doorway, of whom I had taken only passing notice, moved into the dim light cast from the casement and disclosed himself as Don Julio Sorrello, the Galician novice with whom Doña Elvira had twitted Angelica on the *romería*. I knew him slightly, and indeed had seen him only two days before when he had been *acolyte* at Sunday Mass.

He was above three years older than I, very well built, with large heavy hands. He had thick black glossy hair and there was a sort of manliness in his figure which women like and which ill became the cloth he was preparing for, as did his actions which followed.

He was very angry. As well as the guitar which was slung across his back, he carried a cudgel, which, as I backed off, intending to withdraw, he dextrously interposed between my ankles and brought me to the cobbles.

Then he belaboured me with it, about the back and head, bloodying my nose, chipping one of my front teeth, and setting my ears to ring; all this preceded by a hearty kick in the stomach which so winded me that I could not cry out, and with no word at all from him all was accomplished in a sort of hideous silence. At last he stopped, stood back, and let me struggle to my feet. He turned me round so I was facing the way I had come and gave me one more kick, in the fundament this time, to set me on my way. As I reached the end of the alley I heard the first chord struck on his guitar, followed by a mellifluous arpeggio, and I fancy the casement window above him may have opened. I did not stay to see.

There perhaps the matter would have ended, for on returning home I found my ardour to be much less. Fernando, though peeved at the loss of his guitar which I had borrowed and which had suffered almost more than I from The Novice's blows, offered to send for a barber to dress my wounds, which, when I refused, he washed for me with much sympathy and some self-blame since it had been his plan that I should turn *novio*. When Morning came and disclosed with its pearly beams that I had two black eyes and a very swollen lip, what feeling I had left for the *jennet* turned to anger and despair, for I would not venture forth to brave the ridicule of my friends while I was in that state, and I was now like to miss the Grand *Corrida* of Bulls promised for Ascension Day. Giving myself up to misery, I requested Fernando to put it about that I had fallen sick of an unseasonable ague.

I have already said that the room Fernando and I shared was the first of the private chambers in the Martín apartment, and so all that morning I could hear the comings and goings of the household as I lay abed: *viz.* the sober tones of Don Jorge welcoming a client; Doña Regina off to market with the maid; Rafael going forth with one of his sisters, I was not sure which; and so on. But at about two in the afternoon my attention was suddenly caught by a different sort of noise, one which had stealth in it – footsteps barely audible on the stone floors, the rustle of a dress, whispering, and suppressed but silvery laughter. I sat up in bed, cursing the mattress as it creaked, and strained my ears towards the door, and even as I did so the handle tipped and it opened slowly, six inches, a foot, and there – my head could not credit it but my heart leaped with sudden delight – was Angelica and Violeta just behind.

As soon as she saw me her hand went to her mouth as she tried to convert a peal of laughter into a sympathetic cry.

'Oh José, you poor thing. Violeta, look at his darling eyes. Oh isn't it a shame, no but *really*?'

'They are worse than they were this morning,' said Violeta, who had brought me a cup of chocolate and heard some of the tale from Fernando. She kept her voice low and held on to her friend's arm.

'Oh you poor, poor thing,' went on Angelica, 'do they hurt terribly? I vow I've told Julio Sorrello that I never want to hear his songs again, and I'm sure I shall go to St Mark's for Mass as long as he remains at our Church; I can't bear to think of ever seeing him again. If I'd known who it was he was fighting I should have called the Watch, you may be certain.'

She made to come towards me but Violeta held her back saying: 'That's enough, Angelica, we must go now or someone will surely find us here.' At which my Darling shrugged her off and said, 'Look Violeta, I must speak with him a little more, ten minutes, there'll be no harm. Darling Violeta, please wait outside, keep the door for me, and tell me when I call, if the way out is clear.'

Violeta's little face with her huge eyes now lit up – first shocked, then puzzled, then delighted to be party to an intrigue.

'All right then, but never call out, Angelica, or you'll surely be lost. Tap three times on the door, I'll hear it, and then I'll open up to you when I've seen there is no-one to observe you,' and picking up her skirts she was gone.

Angelica now came across to my bed and in the dim light, for the shutters were closed, sat beside me and kissed me feather light on my swollen lip, and passed her soft forefinger over my face. She paused, then seemed to make a decision, for I could discern a subtle smile playing at the corners of her mouth.

'Are you glad I came?' she crooned.

I could only nod, bereft of all powers of speech since her first appearance.

'Will you do something for me?'

Again I nodded, though wondering what she thought me able for in my condition then.

'Well José, I want to see your . . . you know, your *little man*, José.'

The light was too dim to see if she blushed; but without waiting for a reply she was already drawing back the covers, which she did as far as my knees. Then she caressed him through the linen of my night-shirt.

'Holy Mary,' she said, 'how he grows!'

Perhaps her oath put her in mind of her sinfulness, for now she glanced up and saw the image of Our Lady on the wall some feet away. She rose, found a handkerchief about her person, and draped it over the little statue. The bed dipped beneath her weight again and I felt the cool air play about me as she pushed back the night-shirt.

'He's prettier than I expected. He's not like others is he? No. I'd heard. This is like a *Jew's*, but you're not a Jew. Or a *Moor*. You're English. I think he's nice.'

She shaped the fingers of her hand so that their tips formed a circle, like the petals of a long flower. Then she circled him so that the bald end of him rested in her palm, like a bumble bee inside a honeysuckle, and slowly she began to move her hand up and down so that her finger-tips just teased the ridge. Pleasure blossomed like flowers in the first warmth of Spring.

'Is it good?' she asked.

I nodded again.

She also nodded, almost briskly.

'They told me it would be.'

I did not ask who *they* were. The caress continued. I could not restrain a moan.

She bent her head towards me. The same pert smile played around her mouth, but her eyes – dark and liquid – held no expression save perhaps a sort of searching curiosity. Occasionally she looked back to where her fingers teased and soon she began to increase the speed of their movement.

Although, like all boys of my age, I had played with myself in similar fashion as often as I felt moved to do so, this was the first occasion since the onset of puberty that anyone else had performed the service for me. The delight was increased ten fold: first because it was my Beloved who was doing it and not some drab picked up off the street, and secondly because the pleasure was now beyond my control, and I had perforce to make a delicious surrender to a lingering out of an experience, which, left to myself, I would have brought to a too swift and abrupt conclusion.

Soon I felt constrained to squeeze my eyelids tight in spite of their bruised condition and lights began to explode behind them. I tightened my buttocks, relaxed and squeezed again. Willy-nilly my hands flew down to the burning parts to clutch at the root of my delight. Now, I could feel the warmth of her breath on my cheek, as she leaned closer to me I could feel her breast on my shoulder; and then I could feel nothing but pleasure, searing, striving, explosive.

'Ugh!'

The inevitable had happened. I kept my eyes shut.

'Ugh!' she repeated. 'I never realised that there would be so much. It's all over my hand. What can I wipe it on?'

Still with my eyes closed I pulled my night-shirt over my head and offered it. I did not feel that after everything else she would object to complete nakedness.

'It's all up my arm, on my dress.' She rubbed away. 'There, I don't think it'll notice now. What a comic little thing he has become! Dribbling too. I think you should cover yourself.'

I pulled up the bedclothes and, as if she was a nun in an hospital, she straightened them and tucked them in.

'There. That was good. I feel I know a lot more about it all now,' she continued. 'Thank you, José. You are really quite sweet, and I shan't entirely forget you,' with which words, curious then but later all too intelligible, she kissed me once on the forehead and glided away to the door. She tapped as arranged, Violeta appeared, and without more ado they were gone.

Her handkerchief remained on the image of Our Lady. Fernando found it there when he returned: I was hard put to it to convince him that I had not debauched one of Rafael's sisters, which he would have considered a terrible thing. As indeed it would have been.

CHAPTER VIII

A Disturbing Chapter, Not Unconnected with the Preceding and Perhaps Better NOT Read by Sensible Readers or the Gentle Sex.

I

Although I must feel sure that no eyes other than mine will ever see these pages, and indeed the very thought fills me with cold dismay, I find the writing of them easier if I suppose myself to be address-ing a Reader. Thus I can apostrophise him, stir him into recollection of earlier scenes, direct his attentions to moments apparently lacking in significance whose meaning will be enlarged by later events, and so on. But who is this Reader? He can only be *ME*, some future *ME* who will one day scan these pages to live again days and memories already faded, to see again faces already half-forgotten and which – say in twenty years time, supposing I am spared so long – will be even dimmer, will, without the aid of these *Memoirs*, have become dull shadows of their former shadowy selves.

For these former selves, the ones I have now before me, are already shadows, and yet even more shadowy on these pages than in my eye, I mean my Soul's eye. For if I close my body's eyes I can yet conjure up the fragrant swags of Angelica's hair, the supple slightness of her waist, and the coolness of her finger-tips; and at night I have started suddenly awake knowing that if I had woken but a blink before I should have heard her laugh and the rustle of her dress, marked the door of my chamber closing, and counted her footsteps on the stairs.

And so the Angelica on these pages is but a ghost of the Angelica that haunts my brain – yet when all is done this ghost of a ghost, this Angelica of ink and paper, may yet be the longest lived. Certain it is the real Angelica, the flesh and blood Angelica, was raped by eight French Hussars who had previously quartered her baby son before her eyes; she survived and took to murdering for revenge, but took few pains to conceal her crimes which were done with the knife after she had enticed her Enemies to her home in the guise of a compliant courtesan; she was soon discovered and garrotted in the public square at Oviedo.

And the Angelica of my mind, who like the real one brought me the delights described in the last chapter, is a slowly dissolving spectre who will be quite gone when I am dead.

But the Angelica on these pages will last as long as paper and ink may last, which I believe is a long time. I have heard of books still readable after upwards of five hundred years if the damp and vermin were kept from them, and so this Angelica may live that long too – a sort of spiritual *chrysalis* even ready to become a butterfly for a time in the mind of some other he or she who may read these pages. But I forget; I must not allow myself to consider such a reader; again I must recall that I write for no-one's eyes but my own, and when they cease to read – then, good-bye Angelica. From now till then perhaps these marks on paper will serve to give that spectre a colour and a glow, in my mind alone, but that is all: she'll not live again in the consciousness of another.

To tell truth, if I thought otherwise I should not be able to continue. I call to mind again my Father's complaints against the *Lazarillo de Tormes* and other similar works, *viz.* – there is little profit to be gained from reading tales of vice, and none when the vicious remain unpunished. I could claim that what I write is no idle tale, no erring fiction; I could claim that the sufferings of my manhood were the just retribution of a Divine Providence for the sins of my youth: but on the one hand memory plays false tricks and a truth gilded with flattering ornamentations may be more deceptive than unvarnished lies; and on the other – well, let the reader judge, the reader who can only be some future *Me*, whether or not my sufferings have really been enough to purge away the very devilishness of what I stooped to in the next episode of my life.

For ten days I nursed my face and duly missed the Ascension-tide *Corrida* – it took that long before the bruises had faded to what would pass as shadows left by a sleepless night – and every day I looked for the return of my Beloved, but she never came. I thought of enlisting Violeta's help, but that was not easy: I rarely saw her on her own for more than a moment about that crowded apartment, and then a shyness of talking about it always seemed to freeze my tongue.

On the eleventh day we were all called forth to the Zúñiga house itself – for a grand *tertulia* to celebrate the betrothal of Rafael to Isabella which, they having obliged their parents and themselves by falling in love, could now be announced to an expectant world.

The Zúñiga house was one of the largest and most lavishly appointed in Salamanca at that time, being of three floors set round a patio garden in the Andalusian style – though this was affectation: as I have said, they came from Galicia and Catalonia. Since the occasion was a Betrothal, the celebration was of the most formal sort. This meant that on arrival, at about a quarter of ten in the evening, men and women were separated into two vestibules on either side of the entrance. The men stood around admiring the furnishings in their room – there was a lot of gilt I remember – and particularly the paintings which were in the French taste of fifty years ago: courtesans, goddesses, and the like. The guests vied with each other to show off their knowledge of the style and brushwork, but in truth they were admiring the rosy buttocks and creamy breasts of the ladies depicted. Amongst these *connoisseurs* I discovered the bullish figure of Don Julio Sorrello – I gave him a smiling bow to show I bore no grudge for his ill usage of me (all's fair in love and war, I thought, and besides

I believed I had received more of our Mistress's favours through the beating he gave me than he had won on his guitar), but he saw fit to ignore me.

At last, when all who had been invited were assembled, some fifty or sixty all told, a *Major Domo* appeared with a staff and led us ceremoniously through the patio which was lit with *flambeaux* and decorated with orange trees, geraniums and fuschias, and up a wide stair in the *plateresque* style, and so into the main reception room. Here, at one end, Don Lorenzo and Doña Elvira presided in gilt chairs set on a low daïs with Isabella and Rafael standing beside them. We all passed in turn before them, kissing the ladies' hands and making our bows to the gentlemen. Don Lorenzo twiddled with an eye-glass, nodded, occasionally yawned. He was an oldish man, red-faced, bewigged and beribboned, with a fat stomach; Doña Elvira found too much to say to everyone and thus prolonged the ceremony to a tedious length; Rafael and Isabella stood quiet and almost dull, each with an expression of pained embarrassment. Isabella wore a dress with a black bodice and a skirt of bronze satin, with a black lace shawl and a high *mantilla*. She looked, in my eye, rather severe for the occasion, as if she was already the wife and mistress of a household.

There was no sign of Angelica.

At last the presentations were completed and liveried servants appeared with refreshments: sugared water, chocolate in water flavoured with cinnamon, lemonade; preserves, dragees, pralines and *mazapáns*; and a small consort of fiddles set behind a curtain struck up in the French style – minuets, gavottes, and the like. The Zúñigas and Rafael now left the daïs, moving among us, and the conversation became more general. Cards and dancing were promised for later.

A disturbance at the door and Angelica was at last arrived. She looked like a Goddess, and since I must believe it was the last time I ever saw her, I must dwell on her appearance. Her dress was pale blue velvet with a huge pink silk flower between her breasts and her hair piled up high and fastened with another silk flower. But for all her grandeur she was still a girl, just returned from Convent and lacking the assurance her finery demanded, and she moved quickly across the room to stand with her Mother, rather than take her chance with the guests, yet it seemed to me that her Mother was not entirely welcoming. I joined them in less than a moment, having knocked over a bowl of geraniums in my passage.

'My dear,' cried Doña Elvira, 'here is Don José, recovered from the *grippe* at last. I declare he caught it on our *romería* but he says not. So polite. Don José, is not my daughter the truest vixen, staying away so long and then appearing like this, as if she was the *Duchess of Benavente*? I'm sure Isabella will be furious, and rightly too.'

'Isabella is never furious,' my Darling pouted, 'she is far too good-natured.'

'But your dress, my dear. I hope Don José does not think I suggested you should wear that gown tonight.'

'Angelica looks very beautiful,' I managed to stutter.

Her Mother looked at me sharply.

'Come, come. She's not old enough for that sort of public gallantry, you will only turn her head.'

Angelica fluttered her fan with impatience; her lips smiled but her eyes retained their wariness.

'It would not be right for Isabella to look too striking on this occasion,' she said. 'She has her man now, and I do her a good turn to make her seem modest. By seeming plain on her side she does well for me, who have yet to catch one.'

'Angelica, I despair of you. I declare of all my brood you cause me most concern – at times you are just too sharp for your age. At all events it doesn't do for me to stand chattering with you in front of all our guests. Don José, pray escort her for a while: it seems you bear with her more easily than I,' and she sailed away.

'Oh Angelica, Angelica,' I murmured, as soon as her Mother was out of hearing, 'when shall we be alone together again?'

'José, behave yourself. Someone will hear.'

I looked round and thought her mistaken – the whole throng was now chattering like a flock of starlings, and no-one, as far as I could tell, marked the person who talked to him, let alone anyone else.

'Oh my Love, no-one is close enough to understand, and my heart is too full . . .'

'José, I declare you are being absurd. And you look far too earnest to be up to any good. Please let me pass. Or at least walk round with me and try to look more cheerful.'

I took her hand. She rapped my knuckles with her fan.

'Angelica. Once you came to my room. Why only once? I stayed indoors for ten days . . .'

'Silly, everyone knows you hid yourself away on account of your poor face, not because of me . . .'

'But it was because of you that I was beaten. Please come again – alibis can be fixed upon, servants bribed, whatever is needed I will perform . . .'

'La! You have been reading *novels*, I'm sure. *Santa María*, José, leave go!' She took a step closer to me, her face now flushed and her eyes no longer wary, but truly enraged. 'Now listen, José, I came because I liked you, and I'd heard about your . . .' here her expression softened and she giggled, 'your funny you-know-what, and I was curious. But also I came because I was a little frightened of things to do with all that, and for my own reasons I wanted to find out. You seemed a gentle person, and fun on the picnic, and I didn't mean you to get all silly and serious. Now that's all I can say. Please don't try to see me again. Look, people are distracted by us.'

She stepped back, opened her fan, and emitted a cascade of silvery laughter, the last time I heard it.

'La, Don José,' she cried in a loud voice, 'what a funny story – do please tell my Mother, it will make her laugh so – look, she's over yonder,' and with that she swept away to join her sister Marisa who seemed to be in earnest conversation with Don Julio Sorrello.

As shortly after as I could I made my respects to my hosts, and to Rafael and Isabella, and found my way to Don Antonio's tavern beneath the *Plaza*.

2

At that late hour *La Covachuela* was almost deserted, there being just three gypsies who sat in the low window. I took my place not far from them and ordered a small bottle of sack and a glass, and I began to drink. At first the effect was cheering. For a time the gypsies seemed fine fellows – the guitarist was a small impish-looking man with gaps between his teeth; his friends, who accompanied him with fast rhythmical clapping, were taller – one bald, the other younger and with long hair to his shoulders. All wore Andalusian gypsy gear, but shabby and old, and all had tips of horn mounted in silver hung from the braided hair of a black mare's tail round their necks to ward off the evil eye. Their songs were about the pains of love and often denounced women for their deceptions while proclaiming the singer as a faithful servant – they fitted my mood exactly and by the time the bottle was finished I was nodding my head in exaggerated agreement. Antonio came over to me and asked me for money for them.

'How much?' I asked.

'A silver duro for each of them.'

This was too much, but they were all three now standing in front of the low doorway with the moonlit night behind them, looking at me from dark, cold eyes. I put the three coins on Antonio's tray and he made them jump into his hand. The three gypsies bowed and were gone.

I ordered a second bottle of sack and soon my mood changed to one of maudlin despair; my head sank to the table, cushioned on my arms, and I only lifted it to drink. At the third glass, or rather tenth, I discovered a companion across the board from me. At first I did not recognise him.

At last he spoke.

'Do you not know me, Don José?'

I looked up, moved the candle, and its light fell on the red hair of Rubén. He wore it longer now and cut in disorderly locks so that his head looked as if it were on fire – this being, I realised later, the newest fashion in Europe – together with a high white collar that framed his cheeks and a tight stock beneath, and a pale blue frock coat. The hair was brushed back off his forehead and livid white in the red rawness of the rest of his face I could still make out the scar I had given him seven years before.

'I know you, Rubén,' I said. 'Drink with me?'

'All right.'

Antonio brought another glass, and, at my suggestion, another bottle. Rubén filled his glass and mine.

'Your health, José. Though I must say you look wretched. Whatever can be the matter?'

I looked up to see if he was mocking me, but his eyes, now very close to mine, were blankly serious, though their sharp blueness seemed compelling and held my gaze for a moment or two.

'Nothing really.' I muttered. 'Woman. Girl. Own fault, I suppose.'

'Poor man,' he murmured, and I felt his fingers tightening on my wrist. 'Tell me about it.'

''S simple really. She bewitched me. Came to my room once. Doesn't want t'any more. Rubén. I think there's another man.'

'Tell me about her.'

Little by little he had the whole story of me, though I suspect I omitted the beating Sorrello gave me.

'. . . she has lovely hair, gentle fingers . . .' I concluded, giving way to despair.

Deftly he caught the bottle I had toppled and set it upright; then he wiped his cuff with a clean handkerchief.

'This won't do, José. You must win her back.'

'Can't make her love me if she doesn't want to.'

He looked into his glass, which he revolved slowly between white fingers.

'There are ways to make a girl love a fellow, you know,' he said at last.

'What sort of ways?'

'Charms. Spells. Spirits and Familiars. That sort of thing.'

'Don't believe all tha'.'

'Don't you?' His voice sank to a hiss. He took my hands and held them firmly on the table between us. 'Don't you? Look, José. Look at me. Look at these clothes. Look at this ring. Yes, it's a real diamond. None of this came from clerking in the Town Hall, you may be sure. I'm rich now, José. I didn't want girls, I wanted money. But I can get you your girl, the same way I got gold.'

I felt frightened, but it was true he seemed very well dressed.

'I expect you robbed someone. Robbed your Father's cash box.'

'José, that's not kind. Why say a thing like that? We've always been friends, haven't we? Would I lie to you?'

His hand released mine, and passed across his forehead, lingered for an eye-blink on his scar.

'Yes,' I said, still unaccountably frightened, 'we've always been friends.'

'José. What would you give for a night with this Angelica, what would you pay?'

'What would I give? If she came willingly, stayed all night, and really loved me? I'd give a gold ounce. No. Two.'

I began to weep again.

'At dusk tomorrow bring me two gold ounces and before midnight Angelica will be in your arms. Come to the *Calle de los Moros*. I have rooms above the Roper's there. Just ask for me. Here, to show my good faith I'll pay your account, for since the gypsies took your last duros, your purse is empty,' and he placed a gold duro on the table.

He was right. My purse was empty. Without his help I should not have been able to settle with Antonio.

Next day I did not awake until five o'clock in the afternoon. I found the good Fernando at my bedside.

'Thank the Saints,' he said, as I came to, 'I thought you would never waken.'

I felt very ill, but he helped me to the Jerusalem pot in which I vomited and then to the jakes where I evacuated my bowels, at which I felt better. Meanwhile he fetched me several jars of cold water which also served to restore me.

Soon I felt more composed.

'Fernando,' I said, 'I must have two gold ounces by nightfall. Take all but my cleanest clothes, take my sword, my ring, every-thing to the pawn-broker's behind St Mark's and see what you can get.'

'You won't get two gold ounces.'

'What can you lend me?'

'A gold duro. That's all.'

'It will help. Now do as I say and take the things.'

When he was gone I struggled into the things he had left and then ventured out into the passageway, crossed it and knocked on Rafael's door. No answer. Thinking he might not have heard, and not wishing to disturb the household by calling louder, I lifted the latch and went in. There was no-one there. In a small *éscritoire* beneath the window I found five gold doubloons which I took, knowing he would have lent them to me had he been there to assist me – such are the privileges of having true, noble friends.

At seven Fernando returned with two more doubloons which left me now short of three duros to make up the two ounces I needed. With a little persuasion Fernando allowed he could add these to the duro he had already promised.

The blue of the sky was deepening and it was time I set off to keep my dread appointment. As Fernando helped me into my jacket he asked at what hour he could expect my return.

I paused and fear clutched at my heart.

'My return, my good Fernando?' I said. 'Don't look for my return. You were best to forget me now for it may be that the name of José Bos'am is one you will learn to curse.'

'I'm learning to do that already,' he muttered, as he brushed my collar.

'At all events,' I continued, 'I am embarking on a perilous adventure. If I do not come back, I pray you make application to my dear Father, who will discharge what I owe you, but try to hide from him the nature of my dread end.'

'I doubt not I shall be able to do that,' he said, 'since I have no notion of the fate Your Worship is setting forth to meet.'

3

The Roper's was not hard to find: for a sign Pepe Clemente had displayed above the street one of his more ill-famed productions – a hangman's noose. I entered and found the small shop filled with ropes of all sorts – some thick, and strong enough to moor a first-rater with, and coiled like bee-skeps; others of the sort used by bull-ranchers, hanging in skeins; and from the ceiling yet more nooses like the one outside. The place reeked of the dry, nose-prickling, sour stench of unbent rope.

A large barrel-chested man with beetling eye-brows stirred as I entered. I took him to be the proprietor, and asked if Don Rubén García lodged with him.

'It's possible.'

'Don Rubén, son of the baker at Los Arapiles.'

'Where he comes from is no concern of mine. Where he ends may turn out to be, for I think they'll come to me for one of these,' and he touched the nearest noose above his head, 'when his time comes. He has the attic – at the top of the stairs,' and he drew back a sacking curtain.

I climbed the narrow steps until there were no more and found myself facing a low door. The only light up there came from gaps between the roof tiles an inch or so above my head. I knocked, and a voice bid me enter.

Rubén lay stretched on a cot in his shirt and vest; his blue coat hung over the back of a chair. Behind him a small window admitted the twilight of summer with balmy airs and the twittering of swifts.

'So you came,' he murmured. 'And with the chinks.'

'What earnest can you give me that you will perform what you promised?' I asked, as I passed over the coin.

'No earnest at all,' he said with a smile. 'But we shall leave your gold here and if you are unsatisfied at dawn you may reclaim some or all of it. But first allow me to give you a taste of the powers I command.'

He stood up and ran his fingers through his copper-coloured hair; then from a shelf above the bed took down a stoppered vessel and glass. The liquor he poured was clear like spring water but seemed heavy in the glass though neither oily nor viscous.

'Drink this. It won't harm you, man.'

It was fiery but not in the way of brandy or *aguardiente*.

In a moment or two I felt warmer, slightly dizzy, but more at ease.

'It gives you courage, I think,' said Rubén. 'But that's not all. Now look in this candle flame while your pulse tells seventy-two.'

I did as he said. The dark corners of the room receded, and the cot on which I was now sitting seemed to float with a pleasant and easy motion.

'Take this mirror. Breathe on it until it is quite misted. Now wipe off the mist. Look in the mirror.'

First there was only darkness, like that of a deep mill-pond, then there slowly formed the watchful eyes, the delicate brows, the slightly too broad nose, the blushing cheeks, the lips that curled in a knowing smile, in short the face of Angelica, framed in her loose dark tresses that swirled like waterweed at the edges of

the glass. A wave of heat swept over my body, bringing an out-
break of perspiration with it, which seemed to emanate from
those parts that are root and spring of all that is evil in our mortal
natures, and indeed I found my member had risen hard in a state
of extreme excitement.

'She's there, is she not?' Rubén's voice had thickened, as if he
too was touched with ecstasy. 'Good, we can go further. First you
must drink off the rest of this potion.'

I did and a rushing filled my ears like the passing of a mighty
wind. As if from a distance I heard Rubén's voice continue, com-
manding me to follow him. He was standing on a chair and had
opened a trap in the sloping ceiling, his legs swung, he was gone.
Then framed against the indigo of the evening sky his face
appeared, a long white arm descended, and after a short struggle
I was with him on the roof.

How beautiful was Salamanca in the fast falling twilight of that
Summer night, seen from this eminence! How majestic her towers
and domes, how elegant her spires, how soft and mellow the rose
and gold of her stone!

Rubén stood by a chimbley which looked like a pile of bricks
stacked by a wanton child.

'Come close. Look in my eyes.'

I did so. A breeze stirred his full shirt sleeves, now glowing
luminously white, and ruffled his flaming hair. His eyes, blue like
glass, held mine and slowly we descended, I know not how, to the
street, or rather it seemed to a height a foot or so above the street,
which was deserted and unfamiliar, but which soon rushed by in
steep perspective until we were in the *Plaza* itself. This was
deserted too, but illuminated as if for a fiesta. We were in the
corner which faces the baroque gateway in the North side and the
smaller less ornate one to the East, the *Arco del Toro*.

And now a figure appeared in one of the arches of the Main Gate
and began to cross in front of us – a hag it seemed, bent double and
wrapped in an old black cloak, but even as I watched the figure
straightened, the hood fell back, and there she was – Angelica

without a doubt. The breeze stirred her hair and pulled back the gown to reveal those breasts I'd never seen – they were small, white like chalk, widely spaced. She turned and was gone, through the Arco del Toro.

'Was that she?' Rubén asked, by my side.

'Of course it was she,' I moaned, in despair at thus losing her again.

'Have no fear, we shall find her.'

Now again memory will not unfold to me just how or where we did come up with her, for the next thing I remember is a room, completely dark and yet a room in which I could see, could see Angelica, if nothing else at all. I remember embracing her, and the feel of her breath hot in my ear, and her body hot against mine; I remember the pure whiteness of her unblemished flesh, glowing in that *Stygian* darkness, I remember the ardour of our embraces, the swooning ecstasy of fulfillment, and then the complete, royal, darkness of the very deepest sleep.

Had that been the end of the experience, all in my mind would have been well, brief though those moments of wild passion had been, but that sleep I now entered into was plagued by dreams, or succeeded by them, of an unutterable foulness, only two of which I dare relate.

I was, it seemed now to me, stretched out on a cold stone slab, entirely naked, and in what seemed to be broad daylight, in a room, quite empty and with white-washed walls. There was a window, large and unglazed, but all I could see through it was an entirely featureless blue sky. Although I was not bound I found I could not move any of my limbs, not even raise my littlest finger. Imagine my fear when, in this predicament, I realised I was not alone but had been joined by a foul and misshapen hag. Her hair was dishevelled, her cheeks hollow, and her neck shrunken. Her lips were black, she had no teeth, and her nose was hooked like an owl's but broken and crooked too. She was seven feet tall it seemed. As I watched her she stripped off her shift, her only garment, and began to smear an evil-smelling unguent all over her body from the top of her head to the soles of her yellow feet. She was terribly thin and her bones stuck out from her at all angles through skin that was dark, hairy, cracked and leathery. Her female parts were almost entirely obscured by the folds of her stomach which was like a sheepskin hung halfway down her thighs, and her breasts were like the dried-up udders of an ancient she-goat.

When she had finished anointing herself she stepped towards me, and to my horror began to anoint me too, and I was power-less to resist. The ointment was greasy and clammy, and very, very cold, and my first dream ended then, for this coldness deprived me of my senses, and yet before I quite lost consciousness it seemed to me that that dreadful hag gave place to no other than the object of all my desires and the cause of my frightful situation, the lovely Angelica herself.

The second dream was yet more awful. It began with flying through the night sky again but not this time in my own shape but in the form and substance of a *bat*. I found that most of the sky around was thronged with similar beasts and birds of ill-omen – kites, barn owls and more bats. Soon we, those creatures and I, were caught in a *maelstrom* or whirlwind that span us down corkscrew fashion towards the ground, and each one of us, as we alighted, resumed the shape of a human being. Gathering myself to my feet I now saw that I was a member of a group smaller than I had imagined when we were in the air: there were perhaps six or seven of us with perhaps five or six still thronging the air above with the beat of black wings about our heads. It was difficult at first to be sure for everything was very dark, a confused *mêlée* of bodies, mostly as naked as I. Then a fire of red coals was kindled by the action of someone blowing on it, and its light revealed the most hideous sight of all.

In our midst was a Monster, very large, so that although he was sitting on his haunches, his head was well above those of us who were standing. And what a head! – it was a goat's but huge, with great horns that curved up against the night sky to hold the cres-cent moon between them. They were wreathed with ivy leaves;

beneath them his eyes glowed orange tawny with a hateful malevolence; his grey lips, pulled back, revealed yellow grinders above a shaggy matted beard. The body was equally foul, being entirely covered with matted hair, black and yellowish-white and, this was the awful thing, the shape of that body was human though gigantic, the chest and torso were wide and square, not those of a beast of the field but of a creature that would walk upon two legs, and between those legs he had the parts of a man, the member enormous and always upright Yet, withal, the hands and feet were those of a goat – hooved and cloven.

Round this Being and the fire that lit it, the group of which I was a part went slowly circling hand in hand in an enchanted dance; wordless cries broke from our lips; we stamped the ground in time to the dull throb of a distant drum, and pipes, not unlike a shepherd's, could be heard, but always echoingly as from a distance. And who were we – this shadowy group of naked dancers of which I speak? I must confess I have no very clear recollection – in that meagre light, constantly flickering and casting elusive shadows, all was changing, indistinct. Sometimes I fancied I saw Angelica, sometimes Rubén. Once, I thought I could discern above pitifully stick-like hams the visage of my dear Father, but in this at least I know I must have been mistaken. Who else? The hag who had anointed me – to be sure, she was there, and often closest to me: always it seemed in the dance that either she was leading me on or else I was pursuing Angelica.

One other face there was in that ghastly crew that filled me with deeper terror than all the rest, a female face dragged from the recesses of my *Italian* past, a past that in the daytime I have forgot. She was beautiful and young, almost as young as Angelica, but fairer coloured and heavier built, and in this dance it seemed to me she smiled on me with tender sweetness that wrung my heart. I did not recognise her then, but before the year was out I saw a face much like hers, but it could not have been the same – a difference in age and a thousand leagues preclude it.

The Beast at last raised both cloven hooves of its front legs or arms and the dance came to a halt, each body sinking to the ground, but sinking slowly, with a floating motion, much as a sheet of finest paper stirred from a table top will settle to the floor. For a moment we remained in a loose coil of bodies, then some began to stir and two or three left the group and returned with baskets filled with food, with meat, and began to offer round the choicer morsels. Angelica, and the second Lady I have just described, stooped in front of me, both naked in the flickering light, and both wearing expressions of kindest affection; they offered me food from the basket they carried between them.

I now discovered in my hand the foot and lower leg of a new or still-born babe, so small it scarce filled my palm. The skin was blistered and in places blackened, as if by fire.

There was a great rushing in my ears and I heard as from a great distance a long-drawn howl, the howl of a small child lost but issuing with the strength of adult lungs, my lungs. A look of doubt, then anger, then fear crossed the face of Angelica and she rose to her feet above me. The second Lady had melted away into the darkness at my cry. And now the face, the breasts of Angelica became confused, and below them appeared the flopping stomach and spindly legs of the hag. I howled again and again, and then my head exploded, and the flames and stars and suns which blossomed out of it enveloped and overcame the horrors around me, till all was consumed, and swiftly dilating darkness flooded back, utter darkness.

CHAPTER IX

A Chapter more Edifying than the Last, not entirely free from Error, but this time of a Philosophical Nature, which in these Times, will give little or no Offence.

I

My recovery was slow and my recollections of its early stages confused and dim. Many times I was despaired of and twice the Sacrament was brought to my bedside.

My first memory is of Fernando and Rafael carrying me up the stairs to the Martín apartment. It seems they found me in the doorway to the street the third morning after my venturing forth; my head was bloodied, and my clothes torn and insecurely fastened – they thought I had been set upon by thieves, though I now judge the state of my dress to have arisen from the careless hands who reclothed my naked and comatose body before carrying me from whatever place those foul ceremonies had taken place in.

Next I have dim recollections of voices talking at my bedside, hushed and serious; then of hands, gentle and kind, which washed and soothed my fouled and feverish body. These I later learned belonged to Doña Regina and her large-eyed daughter Violeta.

At first they thought I would make a slow but steady recovery from what they still took to be an excessive but conventional debauch followed by an attack by thieves, but on the second day I was seized by terrible cramps and aches, which caused me to toss and scream and tear the bed linen, and which were accompanied by fits of terrible vomiting of black bile and blood. From this I fell into a deep sleep from which nothing could shift me, a *coma* which, apart from a very shallow respiration barely more frequent than five or six breaths a minute and a pulse that could hardly be felt, had all the appearances of Death itself.

Doña Regina sent forth for the parish priest of St Julian's and Fernando borrowed a mule off Rafael's Father to ride with all haste to Los Arapiles. The priest came first, performed what rites he could, and instructed that he should be called again if I came to my senses, so that he might confess and shrive me.

Fernando returned with my Father some four hours later. First the good old man examined me, then he questioned Fernando most carefully on all that had led up to my going forth that fatal Summer's evening, eliciting the news of my love passion for Angelica, my need for gold, and other details, and thus came from all these occurrences, more and less, to a correct opinion of the causes of my condition – such was the wideness and depth of his learning in all branches of knowledge. At which he went forth to the markets returning with a small parcel of herbs from which he brewed an infusion which he held beneath my nose so I inhaled the vapours. I stirred, sneezed, moaned and mumbled, and my Father, much encouraged, begged Fernando to remain at my bedside while he went forth for further help.

After he was gone I became quite conscious and lucid for a spell, at which devout Doña Regina, remembering the parish priest's instructions, sent forth for that person, so that he might come and shrive me. But by the time he was come the beneficient effects of the potion had worn off and I had returned to my former coma, at which he began the Last Rites, anointing the orifices of my body and blessing them with his Crucifix, and at this moment my Father returned, accompanied by the cloaked and cowled figure of a Nun.

He seized the priest, and feeble and weak though he was, spun the cleric round in such a way that some of the Holy Oil was spilled.

'Has this boy's body not been sufficiently abused,' he cried, 'but that you must come and defile it further with your useless unguents?'

A furious altercation followed, which might have gone ill for my Father for the Priest was a member of the Holy Office and well remembered my Father's earlier trial before that Court, but the Nun now intervened.

She was, Fernando said, a person of extraordinary presence, tall, of an age with my Father, with a face soft and gentle and clear, calm eyes. Her habit was austere white with a black cowl and she wore no shoes, but on her finger was an amethyst, and her silver cross bore similar jewels. In short he took her to be the Abbess of the *Barefoot Carmelites* whose Convent lies just beyond the City walls on the road to Villamayor. Not the least of the mysteries of the business is that such a person should break the Rule of her enclosed order at my Father's bidding.

At all events she called the brawling Priests to order and he of St Julian's on discovering who she was, prevailed upon her to let him kiss her ring. She then examined me, turned to a small box she carried with her, and disclosed within it certain stoppered vials in blue and white ceramic, one or two of which she passed beneath my nose. At this I stirred again and sneezed violently several times, and this sneezing fit is the first event I clearheadedly remember since drinking the draught in Rubén's attic. The Abbess now mixed up further potions, which, when I drank them, filled me with a delicious warmth and relaxed all my limbs which hitherto had remained convulsed in cramps.

The Priest of St Julian's picked up his vessels and departed, his two boys with bell and candle preceding him, leaving my Father in consultation with the Abbess. For a short time I watched and listened. I cannot recall a word of what was said, but the scene has left engraven in my mind a memory of tranquil love and happiness that moves me to tears whenever I recall it and which must surely be the heavenly lot of Saints in Holy Converse.

2

My continuing recovery was sure, though slow. Within three days my Father, who at Doña Regina's invitation had lodged in the apartment, declared me fit enough to be moved and hired a farm cart for that purpose; and thus ignominiously, though well-pillowed and cushioned, I was brought home to Los Arapiles and the kind care of Tía Teresa. Through the last days of June and through the first of July I lay in my wide old bed while a yard or so from me that good lady busied herself in the kitchen, shooed the chickens back into the yard, and fetched me cool *gazpachos*, buttermilk, and coddled eggs.

Although my body remained weak for upwards of a month it was in my mind that I suffered more, being plagued with nightmares, memories, and even daylight delusions as of a giant spider where a breath of air stirred a feather, or the slithering of a serpent where the sunlight played on a runnel of spilled water.

To rid me of these fantasies my Father drew from me a full history of all that had happened and strove then to set all to rights by using Reason as a purge of guilt, by which I mean he sought to show me that I should not blame myself for the ills that had befallen me. In one particular alone was he severe and that the borrowing of gold from Rafael's room, and no matter how I protested that it was but a loan that I would discharge he insisted that if it was as a loan that I had taken the money I should have left a note excusing the liberty, and as for discharging the debt he had already done so. What most vexed him in all this was that the money had been missed and Doña Regina's maid questioned – it was known she had a spendthrift brother – and the girl had suffered much until the truth of the matter came to light. But I think my Father was wrong to make so much of it – this *Abigail* was an idle wench though well-favoured, and anyway Fernando had guessed the truth and revealed it shortly after she was first accused. In all a *peccadillo*, in my estimation, compared with whoring, drunkenness, consorting with the Devil and *anthropophagy*.

Now I shall set out my Father's reasons that I should not blame myself – first in a general way, then in the matter of whoring, finally in the last two abominations as above. I present this as the discourse of a single day, though the telling, much of it repeated for greater reassurance, took four or five times as long.

First he sought to excuse me on the grounds of my character and education of which he had this to say.

'You are a lad,' he began, 'of sudden desires, impetuous whims, a lad used to early satisfaction of your wants. Partly it is in your nature to be thus, partly it is the result of your upbringing which included too few restraints, which left you like a badly or partly broken colt, resentful of curbs. For this I am more to blame than you, though it's hard to see how I should have done other than I did. Perhaps I did not interest myself in your upbringing until too late, for by the time I began to teach you it was already clear that you were not of a ratiocinative or meditative turn of mind. Reading you found irksome, writing you hardly attempted after you had passed the abecedarian stage, and number, when you had mastered simple multiplication, you were content to leave as a mystery. Now I believe it is idle to force a young mind to accept what it cannot understand, for I believe it will reject all such forced teaching once the force is removed (whether it be the *ferule* of the *pedant*, or a Father's more tender insistence), and what is true of the teaching of knowledge is true of moral teaching too. That this is so is witnessed in the Annals of our Kind for who can deny that the generality of our race possesses no real sense of right and wrong at all? And this is because what it might have learnt by Reason is denied by its disability in reasoning, and what is taught by the rod is rejected when the rod is no longer feared.

'One class of person does behave tolerably better than others but it is the class least likely to affect the course of History, although the most numerous, namely the poorest and simplest. And how do the poor and simple achieve this tinsel goodness? What makes the peasant in the field, the serving woman in the

yard more saintly than their betters? Why, nothing but the rankest superstition, the hope of Heaven and the fear of Hell (two rods
whose power to those who never knew a schoolmaster is greater
far than any teacher's birch), and all the frippery that attends it, no
more worthy of veneration than that old idol *Mumbo-Jumbo*, ven-
erated by the negro heathen. Now this sort of belief, this sort of
teaching, I denied you, save that I asked of you a gentleman's
respect for the purer forms of worship – the Mass said simply and
the Sacraments of Baptism, and Absolution, none of which may
be offensive to the Benevolent Deity which Reason tells us
exists – until such time that Reason and Experience would reveal
to you the healing qualities these Rites, solemnly and decently
performed, can bring.

'And yet your present suffering shows that superstition still
flourished like a foetid and pestilential weed, an infection I suppose breathed in on the air from your playmates in the village,
from wiseacres and grandams, from Tía Teresa herself, good soul
though she is, else you would not have been so susceptible in these
matters of witchery, flying, and the Devil. But more of all that
later.

'So how did I expect you to learn proper conduct in this Life
since Nature had not gifted you with more than ordinary powers
of Reason and I denied you the force of Superstition? Well, I
hoped you would learn by experience tempered with good sense,
and the example of the best philosophers which I put before you;
I knew Experience could be a hard master, but I always thought
here was a home and shelter for you should its lessons prove too
hard. Poor boy, I little thought you would suffer so much so soon;
yet I rejoice you have come through unscathed and I hope with
good lessons well learned which will guide your future in this
confusing world.

'But very chiefly you must cease to blame yourself, and for this
reason, that you were led into all this mischief by one of the most
powerful forces of Unreason that can undo a man, namely the
obsessive desire to mate with one very particular person which

philosophers call *Eros*, poets label passion, and common people call *love*, which most certainly it is not.'

At this point in his discourse he became somewhat disturbed, gripping my hand tightly in his and emphasising words by raising and sharply lowering our entangled fingers, while his thin face and ill-kempt beard nodded up and down with increased agitation.

'What is this *Eros*? Ordinary appetite called Lust, it is not – a man, under the influence of appetite, may lust with some niceness after fat women, or young girls, or black-haired beauties, or even members of his own sex – but still this appetite is never over nice, is never unbendingly particular even as to *types*, let alone individuals; for a reasonable man who hankers after a leg of pork will not lightly refuse a saddle of lamb, if that is all there is, even if he has dined off mutton for a month. But Eros is always particular and always obsessive, and leaves the man he has assailed without resource or escape, so he can think of nought but the object of his desire, so filling his mind that all other preoccupations are driven out, even those arising from hunger and thirst on which bodily survival depends. Poor boy, under this malignant influence I can find it almost in me to excuse the theft of your friend's purse . . . no matter, we'll not discuss it again, I'm sorry I returned to it.

'Great Captains have thrown armies away for this passion; old men respected for their wisdom have become the butts of their acquaintance; merchants have lost their fortunes; statesmen and princes have cast away kingdoms; all manner of woe and misery has followed in its train. And what is it for? What does it achieve? Always we should seek a reason in Nature for Nature is Reason, but no reason has been found for Eros. It is an aberration pertaining to man alone . . .'

Perhaps at this point I intervened – truth to say I felt cured of my love for Angelica, but at the same time a part of me regretted the cure itself as well as its manner. Love had been a fine thing in its way, and life seemed a little flat, a little dull now that it was over.

'No, no,' my Father cried out when I put this to him as Nature's reason, 'it cannot be. Was Anthony bored with half a world to rule? Did Phaedra languish for want of amusement in the court of mighty Theseus? Did Socrates seek the arms of degenerate Alcibiades because the ratiocinations of his mind filled him with *ennui*? Surely not.

'I repeat. What is it for? All things in Nature have a purpose if we can but fathom them, but there is no purpose in Eros. The procreation of children? No. Simple lust will see to that, simple lust we share with beasts and birds. And this Lust is no mean thing: just as mankind has raised other bestial instincts to something nobler – this is the gift our consciousness bestows on us – so it is with lust. We admire the courage of a Bull, but how more admirable is courage in a Man who knows the odds he contends with? What then is the Lust of a Bull in Rut compared with that of a Man and a Woman who know what they are about, who can with art and skill and mutual well-wishing prolong and refine the pleasure and thereby find estimable gifts of affection, bodily companionship, banishment of loneliness, and all sorts of other goodness in the warmth of their connubial bed? These are not the gifts of Eros, oh no my boy. This is Venus, Aphrodite, and a far better business altogether!'

At last he broke off, not this time with a feverish anger and a shaking of his hands and head, but with a sort of coyness that led me to speculate when he had gone on how his relations with Teresa might have progressed in the few months of my absence.

3

Thus far much sense, although not necessarily such as will recommend itself to the young in love. What follows has foolishness in it: for now the good old man's Guide and Light, namely Reason, led the way, deaf to considerations of Faith or Custom or Experience. *Don Quixote* it was said was wise at all times except on the subject of chivalric gests – my Father too was wise except when he followed Reason alone unbridled by Authority or Tradition.

This time I think of us in the room where he used to tutor me upstairs, where he had just played a Scarlatti Sonata, though missing something in the bass on account of his still weak left hand. The decorous yet colourful progression of each succeeding theme to its sweet resolution had brought a moment or two of peace to my still troubled soul.

'It seems, Joseph,' he began, his eyes compassionate beneath their drooping lids, 'that when Rubén and the Mistress of his coven besmeared you with their unguents and filled you with their potions you believed you had immersed yourself in a very cesspool of vice and evil, to the irremediable confusion of your soul, and that even now you are troubled that your immortal part may have taken some indelible taint.'

With tears pricking I nodded dumb assent.

'Well, the worst mischief that you have suffered is that you believe it for there was no great evil in what you did that night, once you had left Rafael's chamber, and not much in the practices of those poor people . . .'

'Poor people . . . !' I was at a loss. 'Sir, Abominations were practised, the Lord of Evil held sway over us, we partook of the most ghastly sacrament of all . . .' and again recollection overtook me and it was some moments before my Father had comforted me sufficiently – much as a Mother does her Child – for him to continue.

'Let us consider as clearly as we can what happened that night, and only then test it for wickedness. Let us start by separating illusion from reality, for there can be little to blame in illusion. That you flew through the air was illusion, provoked by possets and ointments. It is well attested by sound authority that witches have the power to make such nostrums, but that they fly in actual truth and practice is evidenced only in the confessions of poor creatures broken on the wheel and rack and in terror of the fire. Who would not confess to anything in like circumstances? No sir, you thought you flew, but in truth you did not.'

'How can you be so sure?' I muttered.

'There are many proofs – not the least that shown by the Mathematicks and the Natural Philosophy of Isaac Newton, since supported by experiment, namely that the human body, equipped with the best wings in the world, cannot find in itself alone the strength to lift itself into the air.'

'But when I flew I was a bat; I swear it.'

'My boy, when you were a child did you never dream, in the darkness of your bed, that you were a great thinker, or a philosopher, or a benign ruler handing down Laws of perfect Justice to his People . . .'

'Oft I was Captain of an Army, like Tamerlaine, or Commander of a Man-of-War. When I was very small I made out I was a Giant . . .'

'And so, alone and unaided your imagination or phantasy could translate you: how much easier is such translation when aided by potions and the arts of Mesmer?'

He was now pleased to believe that I was satisfied I had not flown.

'Next. The actual presence of Satan, Baal, Beelzebub, call him what you will. You would have it that what you saw was an incarnation of the Evil Principle of our Universe?'

Perhaps not understanding too well, I nodded, merely.

'This is not rational. How can a philosophical abstraction, for that is what a *principle* must be, said to be the sum or essence of what we judge to be bad (which often is simply what we do not like) in all the physical phenomena of the Universe, an abstraction whose existence cannot be demonstrated by Reason or Natural Philosophy to have a concrete reality save when it manifests itself phenomenologically, that is in part, specifically as an instance or example and never wholly, how can we believe that such an abstraction can manifest itself *completely*, and as a Horned Beast?'

I shrugged.

'Joseph, let me be plain. It was not Satan. It was a man, cunningly dressed in skins, with the mask and hooves of a goat.'

I had already guessed as much.

'Nor was Angelica Zúñiga there, of that I can be sure.'

'How, sure?'

'I have incontestable proof that that night she was in Toro in the arms of a runaway novice called Julio Sorrello of Oviedo, to which city they have since made their way.'

This I had not guessed, and it was some time before we could return to our discussion, my Father first protesting that he had believed me cured of Cupid's sting, then reprimanding me for cursing the runaways, since he believed they deserved compassion more than censure: firstly they were obviously victims of that Eros that had afflicted me, secondly it would be a year before the necessary patents were drawn up to release Sorrello from his novitiate vows, and meanwhile he would be hard put to it to find gainful employment, and she would be shunned by Society as a Whore.

When I was recovered from these news he returned to the subject of the orgiastic sabbath I had attended.

'What are we then left with?' he resumed. 'Under the baleful influence of possets and whilst in a Mesmeric catalepsy, you copulated with a poor old woman, perhaps long widowed, despised and neglected by her family. You did not suffer by it, because you thought she was young and fair. Presumably she was equally gratified. Where is the harm in that? If you shudder now you dishonour the poor old soul and show a wholly false squeamishness . . .'

With my conscience already eased a little we broke off, for Tía Teresa had called us to table. Unfortunately, she being a native of Zamora, as mentioned above, and it being the last day of the *patronal feria* of that town in honour of SS. Peter and Paul, she had pot-roasted a large leg of *goat* for us, heavily seasoned with fresh *garlic*, for it is also the garlic fair at that time, when thousands of ropes of fresh garlic are brought in from the country and the streets and markets reek of it for a week. This leg, still with its cloven foot, lay in a long platter, swimming in its juices and redolent with the pungent herb, and I had perforce to leap up and make for the garden with my hand at my face, but whether it put me in mind of the *Macho Cabrío*, or the baby's haunch I had been offered at His Feast, or whether because some infernal infection still lingered in my soul which was troubled by garlic, a sovereign nostrum against all things hellish, I do not know.

When I returned Tía Teresa offered to scold me but – 'Leave the boy be,' my Father cried. 'Bring him an omelette, that will be just as nourishing,' and she did so, grumbling that no egg could match the restorative power of good, red, freshly-killed meat.

Which left me time to wonder at what a changeabout we had here – Father relishing the juices from the creature's thigh as he thrust in the carver, while it was I who was content with eggs and a salad of herbs. Truly Tía Teresa had worked more than one miracle in my absence.

'And now,' said my Father, wiping his beard with his napkin as Tía Teresa cleared away the remains, 'we come to *Anthropophagy* – to you no doubt the worst that occurred and a truly terrible experience I make no doubt, though less terrible when studied in the light of Reason rather than in the Stygian gloom of Superstition.'

'Sir,' I cried in protest, 'an hour since, I felt sure you would instruct me that this too, like the Devil and flying, would be illusion; you cannot now mean . . .'

'Joseph,' he interrupted, 'we must follow courageously where Reason and Truth lead us. First, have you asked yourself whence came those poor corpses that were served up to you at that abominable feast?'

Dumbly I shook my head.

'I believe,' he ventured, 'that they were the bodies of babes miscarried either through disease or the willing contrivance of their dams, aided perhaps by your companions at that dreadful meal – in either case as the result of Nature acting in Her own interest against her unnatural enemies, *viz*. – poverty, pestilence, starvation *etcetera*, such as can be discovered in the crowded hovels to the west of our City.'

When I protested that contrived miscarrying could not be congruent with Nature's Laws he found me many instances to prove me wrong – rats and mice, he averred, ate their young when food was short or conditions crowded, cattle slip their calves if the pasture is bad or meagre, and many more similar examples he found – how the first-hatched chickens will smash the eggs of their unborn siblings or make their first labour the toppling of them from the nest.

I protested that such practices or their like done by Men or Women were contrary to Law, to Decency, and to the teaching of Our Holy Mother the Church.

He waxed peevish, asked me, who scarce went to Church save to gawk at some girl and who had stolen my best friend's purse, to refrain from quoting Church or Scripture at him who was Pastor and Scholar, and he demanded of me if I knew not the texts 'Judge not; lest ye be judged,' and 'Vengeance is mine, saith the Lord, I will repay.'

Now, and I scarce believe this as I write it but it is true, I do the silly man's memory no wrong by repeating it, he digressed from anthropophagy for a while and delivered a canting sermon on these texts which was as follows – that the poor and ignorant who murder, whether by procuring miscarriages or in the course of theft, so be it the theft of necessaries they would otherwise be without, were less likely to be called in question on the Last Day (supposing such an event to be in the future, which he privately doubted) than Hangmen who kill at the command of the Law, and the hangmen less than the sentence-giving Judge, and the judge less than the Ministers who framed the law that guided the judge.

'Indeed,' he said at this point, 'judicial homicide I account the most wicked of all murders for several reasons – *item*, it is against Reason, yet its apologists justify it by appeals to what they call Reason, and thereby defiles doubly that Noble Function; *item*, it fails in what it sets out to do, for the crimes punished by Death are no less frequent than those punished in other ways; *item*, by making a holiday show of it, it invites coarse and lewd enjoyment of another's suffering which degrades the onlooker and debases the decent majesty of the Law; *item* . . .' but enough items – he had many more all much in the same fashion, and all, it seems to me now, who have seen so many horrors where the rule of Law has failed, of an alarming and *anarchistical* nature.

Likewise he included in his crazy list of unjustifiable homicides the soldier in battle, the Captain who directs his aim and gives the order, the General who commands the Captain; and found less offence in a husband who in a passion dashes out the brains of his wife's lover, who acts according to a sort of warped Natural impulse . . .

'Why warped?' I asked, wondering what further absurdity lay concealed behind the qualification.

'Warped by Society whose instruction encourages such revenge with all our foolish beliefs about Honour and such like frippery. A Rational Society might insist upon surrender to a more generous impulse whereby a husband might freely offer his wife to his friend, so be it his wife was willing . . .'

Another passage of all this *fustian* I recall *verbatim*.

'The vulture on the battlefield, tearing the liver from the breast of a still-living soldier, is nobler far than the man who fired the ball that laid his fellow low,' and again, 'it is commonly held that few evils surpass the bestiality of the lonely shepherd who *rogers* one of his ewes,' (at which I nodded vigorous agreement) 'but I ask you, may not that shepherd later cut her throat for market? If the ewe is sensible of either act, which do you think she most resents?'

At this the labyrinthine logic of his discourse brought him back to anthropophagy. I recall now the horror that overcame me as I heard him say that he could see no distinction in Nature or Reason between one sort of meat and another, provided that they were the equal of each other in flavour and wholesome nourishment, and since a wolf would eat with equal ease the flesh of a dead man, or a dead sheep, or even of another wolf, without taking harm, he could not see why a man should not do likewise.

'But,' he concluded, 'the reason for this is that the dead flesh is insensible – the crime in flesh-eating, when crime there is, arises from the manner of the creature's death – let it be dispatched with dignity and without undue suffering, that is all I ask, and in the case of human flesh let it not be killed to provide food, though it may be ate following death from a cause unrelated to the table it finally graces . . .'

One thing became clear to me that day – and that is that Nature and Reason are poor guides for a man's conscience, and I am happy to be able to say that I have only rarely followed either in my life, but have allowed myself for the most part to be patiently directed by the properly constituted Authorities of the Church and State in all things. This has not always been as easy as one might expect: I have lived amongst Catholics, amongst Protestants, and amongst those who professed to have done away with God and have trumped up first a Revolution and then an Emperor in His Place; I have lived under the English, hated the French, and affected to despise the Spanish; under the French and hated the English and the Spanish; and under the Spanish and both loved and hated, by turns, the English and the French, and have managed so well as to give only a minimum of offence to those above me, to which I attribute, in part, my fortune in still being alive.

My Father was less happy. As I shall unfold, in its due place, he later turned Bedlam and finally died in most miserable circumstances.

CHAPTER X

*A Chapter entirely Edifying providing a Fitting Conclusion to
the Two preceding it, by showing Justice done to a Wrong-
Doer, and thereby Refuting by Experience some of the Errors
in the Rational Discourse of the Curate of Los Arapiles.*

I

By August I was well-recovered and able to share again with
Fernando our room in Don Jorge's apartment and there followed
then two months of untroubled pleasure. But before I describe
these I must briefly rehearse what happened to the protagonists of
my Spring adventures. The Zúñiga family felt the disgrace of
Angelica's conduct most hard and withdrew from Society until such
time as the girl could be married or lodged safely in a Convent. The
weddings of Rafael and Isabella, and Violeta and Tebaldo, were
postponed *sine die*, much to the chagrin of all – though Rafael was
able to return to the bull-ring with a clearer conscience.

And what of Rubén, that red-headed Judas? He disappeared –
but whether into the backstreets and hovels, the shacks and attics
of Salamanca where perhaps some hag of his coven gave him
secret shelter, or further afield, I cannot tell, but that he narrowly
escaped a fearful end (though one no more fearful than that which
he finally suffered) will be seen from this following anecdote, the
concluding footnote to the story of my obsession with Angelica.

Apparently Rubén left his lodging above the Roper's in the
Calle de los Moros about the middle of July and no doubt he did
so forearmed with knowledge of imminent betrayal, a knowledge
he chose not to share with his accomplice the Roper himself.

At the end of the month constables sworn by the Justices of the town entered the premises and in a thorough search uncovered gold, clothes, snuff boxes, trinkets, and other valuables, some of which were positively identified by the pitiable widow of a traveller in textiles from Barcelona. This Catalan Merchant had last been heard of in *Medina del Campo*, some twelve leagues distant, though the landlord of the *Parador de los Toros* in Salamanca, with some equivocation, admitted that a man who might have been the traveller in question had booked a room with him some two days after he was presumed to have left Medina, had gone out for supper and had not returned – his baggage being later collected by a boy who bore an instruction that it should be released. On these and other evidences the Roper, Pepe Clemente, was condemned to death for the robbery and murder of this Catalan and other lonely travellers as yet unknown.

You may be sure I followed all these proceedings with much interest; indeed I thought at one point in the trial a leather purse examined and rejected by the Catalan widow bore a close resemblance to that which I had borrowed from Rafael, but I remained silent – there being no point in implicating in other crimes a man already sure of death for murder.

But strangest of all in the trial was the silence of Pepe Clemente who never once mentioned an accomplice or companion although he was put to the Question on this and other points which remained obscure. But it was only at the moment of extremity itself that he tried to implicate his red-headed lodger – perhaps up to that moment he retained a simpleton's belief in Rubén's supernatural powers to bring him succour or reprieve.

One fine morning then at the end of August, in the early hours when the sun was just gilding the golden domes of the Cathedrals and the Clerecía and there was that stilly peaceful freshness that hangs like a garment on trees and buildings, lawns and gardens, the bells of the City began an unwonted lugubrious tolling that was to continue for six hours throughout the forenoon. Then, starting in the *Plaza Mayor*, came the Town-Crier with hand-bell and preceded by his bugle. At each of the seven entrances to the Square he stopped and made the solemn declaration, enforced with all the authority of Justice and the Municipality, that on that day, at the hour of noon, in the *Plazuela de la Yerba*, would die by the garrotte, for the heinous and most atrocious murder of travellers and strangers to the City – one *Pepe Clemente*, lately Roper of the *Calle de los Moros*, for whose soul on whom Justice was to be done our prayers were called.

2

A public execution was a rarity in the City and indeed I had never seen one before – there were, I believe, never more than one a year and, in many years, none at all: this proceeding from the clemency of the Magistrates, the corruptibility of Lawyers, the subornation of Witnesses, and, perhaps, the disposition of the Citizens to avoid the most extreme of crimes. However, none of these availed poor Pepe who, it was said, had brought into disrepute the town's reputation as a good place to carry on trade.

Most of the City, and not a few of the Clerecy and the University judging from the black gowns that mingled with the crowd, were up betimes to witness Pepe's last moments on this earth, and soon all began to collect in the main squares through which the wretched victim of his greed would be taken, the rout being thickest of course in the Plazuela de la Yerba itself. It was to this point I hied with Fernando at an unwontedly early hour.

There then passed an uncomfortable interval during which we were deafened by street sellers purveying *churros*, melon-seeds, and, as the sun grew hotter, cold water, sherbets, lemonade; we were trampled on by merchants in their curled wigs and black coats; we were prodded by their matrons' parasols; we were jostled by *Majos* and *Petimetres* in long cloaks who threatened to burn holes in our garments with their *cigarillos*; in fact generally we were constrained, the two of us, to defend our few square inches of pavement near the scaffold with every means we could muster.

But at last, when Noon wanted but twenty minutes, there was
a further stir and commotion in the throng, a wave of animation
this time focused on the North side of the Plazuela and the street
of St Paul down which Pepe would come in his final progress.
There was the rat-a-tat of drums and then above the heads of the
crowd we could see the steely glitter of bayonets, and the red
plumes of a company of foot soldiers who forced a passage
through to the scaffold and lined it at five pace intervals. By them
we were pushed further back and all were forced to surrender
those few square yards of paving and all one could hope to do was
stand on tip-toe to peer above the mantilla of the woman in front
and restrain oneself from committing a capital offence on the
Petimetre behind and thereby giving cause for another spectacle of
the same kind in six weeks' time.

Now came the protagonist of this brief but awful drama – Pepe
riding on an ass, his arms bound before him, his legs beneath the
ass's belly bound perhaps with ropes his own hands had twisted.
He was dressed in a sulphurous yellow robe, with head shaved
beneath a tall crimson conical hat. His heavy face was pale beneath
his beetling eyebrows, but his thick lips were set firm as though no
word of hope or penitence would be torn from him albeit two
Fathers of the Brotherhood of Peace and Charity walked backwards in front of him with Crucifixes, and chanted the Litany.

And now this tiny procession had reached the foot of the scaffold and it was on that stage that all eyes were fixed – a long
wooden platform, not more than five feet from the ground, but
high enough for everyone in the square to witness the last
moments of Pepe's brutish life. Not for him the carpeted boards
that attend the death of a Noble, not even the noose hung from a
beam above his head such as he had prophesied for Rubén, his
partner in deeds of darkness – but a low wooden chair set against
a stake, and the cold iron collar of the garrotte.

At the foot of the scaffold Pepe seemed to become aware of
what was to happen, and that nothing could forestall his fate.
With the rope beneath the ass cut he began to shout and kick,

lashing out with heavy boots at all around him. The chant of the priests rose in volume and intensity as they sensed the presence of a soul not truly penitent, one incompletely resigned to earthly justice, one not after all content to stand at the throne of Divine Mercy with worldly sin expiated. It took three soldiers to carry and drag Pepe up on to the scaffold and still he struggled. The crowd, now deprived of the moving purgation of a dignified death, began to jeer and howl, and the lady in the front of me spat out a shower of melon-seed cases and – 'No balls,' she cried, 'no balls,' and turned to her neighbour. 'The ones who kill in the dark never die well,' she said, and her gossip agreed.

At last he was securely on the chair and his feet again bound. For a moment Pepe was silent and the Priests began to intone, in a loud voice, the Creed. The crowd grew still; hoarse and cracked we heard Pepe's voice stumbling behind the Priests'; and at this moment the last actor in this grim scene stepped out from the shadows behind – Suero, the gypsy, he who had played the guitar that fateful night at Antonio's Tavern. His spaced white teeth beneath snub nose and narrow grinning eyes flashed against the duskiness of his brown skin; the drums began to beat again, and the bells of the Cathedrals rolled out their bronze notes, bleeding noise across the roofs of the City. With practised fingers Suero clasped the iron collar round Pepe's neck and at this final moment the Roper writhed and screamed again – words, but what words none but Suero could hear, for as he span the screw behind the stake the dying man's voice was strangled away into a choking cry, his face empurpled, eyes now horribly staring, tongue forced between his teeth by that sudden pressure, and the Priest cried with a mighty shout.

'*Pax et misericordia et tranquillitas*',

and the crowd blessed itself and echoed '*misericordia misericordia*'.

I was never so excited in my life. Indeed I found I was clasping the matron in front of me so that her buttocks were pushed against my groin: yet also I felt a most terrible awe, a dreadful fear. How wrong my Father was! What majesty, what tremendous affect such moments have, how much can we learn from them of the supreme finality of justice!

I released the matron – who had been unaware or at any rate had not protested at my involuntary embrace, and looked around.

Fernando was on his knees, supported still by the press – for a moment I thought he had been moved to devotion by the scene, but then from his extreme pallor and the whites of his eyes I saw that he had fainted clear away.

On the way back to our room (he recovered quickly) I mused again on the absurdity of my Father's beliefs: aside from all else, as I contemplated Pepe Clemente's last moments I was moved to say:

'– Never, no never, will I ever put myself at the risk of such an end; no temptation could ever exist strong enough to bring me to the Shadow of the Scaffold.'

3

One evening a few days later I gave my friends the slip and made my way to Antonio's Tavern, hoping to find the gypsies there, nor was I disappointed in this expectation. I sat as near to them as I could and being in a less agitated frame of mind than the previous time I had seen them I was able to study them with attention while they played. Suero, the executioner, had a lissomness about him, a puckish merriment that betokened devilry and mischief. The essence of this lay in his grin which was twisted a little, and revealed small teeth, evenly spaced with wide gaps. Of his two friends Pedro (as I discovered his name to be) was the older, perhaps ten or more years older than the others who were not above twenty, with a bald pate tanned to bronze, and, what was remarkable considering his talent at the percussive clapping, the index finger of his right hand was twisted like a mark of interrogation – following a break clumsily set, I surmised. Luís, the third, had very long dark hair, like a girl's, large brown eyes and a receding chin.

Antonio tolerated this ill-omened trio because they attracted custom – partly by reason of their music, but also because the execution of Pepe was yet fresh in the townsfolk's minds and Suero was a wonder to be gaped at: the street sellers and stallholders from the market came in for a wine before supper and stayed for three or four more, and a couple of girls from the *barrio* of *St Julián* swirled their flounced skirts on the pavement outside, fingers clicking, and eyes scanning the crowd for a drunk whose purse was not yet empty.

For an hour I stayed there, smoking *cigarillos* and buying Suero wine when he seemed to need it. At last he realised it was not his nimble-fingered music that kept me there: he passed his guitar to the bald-headed Pedro, leant forward, and spoke to me in the lisping whine of his tribe.

'What is it, *O Busné*, that thou want'st of me?'

'*Calo*,' I replied, for through consorting with *Toreros* and singers of *flamenco* I had improved my mastery of the *Egyptian* dialect, 'a week since you tightened the screw on the neck of Pepe the Roper.'

He looked wary now, perhaps suspecting I was a relation come to avenge Pepe's death.

'All here know that. It is my trade and the *Busnés* pay me *sonacai* for it.'

'I will give you *sonacai* too, in return for a favour.'

'What favour, *O Busné*, can a poor *Calo* like me do for a little Lord like yourself?' His grin widened as he offered this mild insolence.

'*Calo*, when you placed the collar round Pepe's neck he cried out, and none could hear the words but you, for the Priest was hollering his benedictions. What was this cry?'

Suero shrugged.

'There was no value in his words – no clue for hidden treasure, nothing worth your gold.'

'*O Calo*, I said nothing about gold.'

He paused, and then began to clap to Pedro's strumming.

I sighed and slid a gold duro on to the table, by his glass.

He shrugged again and leaned towards me. I placed my ear by his mouth and felt his breath hot across my cheek.

'The last words of Pepe the Roper,' he hissed, 'were an invocation to his Master. "Adonaï, Adonaï," he cried, "Lord Satan come for me now." And then: "Rubén, Rubén," which I take to be another name or title of the Lord of Mischief. I span the screw gladly for I reckoned he was sure of Hell with that name on his lips.'

CHAPTER XI

*A Visit to my Father's Holding for the Grape Harvest leads to
a Meeting with a Notable Man, and thence to a Favoured
Place at the Bull Fights.*

I

One parcel of the land which was my Father's inheritance and
from which our income (apart from his beggarly stipend as Curate
of Los Arapiles) derived, lay in the oak forest towards Monterrubio
de la Sierra, some three leagues South of Los Arapiles. Most of the
land about there belonged to our connexion the Marquis and was
leased to a bull-breeder called Don Eusebio Camacho, and, as pasture for a herd of fighting bulls, remained open, the bulls feeding
off the mast and aromatics beneath the oaks, and roaming freely;
however my Father's patch had been fenced off by a wall of finely
split granite, set in upright posts, proof even against bulls, and the
enclosure thus created ploughed over, though the oaks left standing. On this land, some six or seven years before the time of
which I write, my Father had caused to be set five hundred vines,
the rest being given over to wheat – and, the position of this little
vineyard being sheltered and on a warm southern slope, the grapes
ripened early, a week or so before the September *feria*, the grand
festival of Salamanca, which celebrates the Nativity of Our Lady.

At the end of August my Father sent for me, and ever dutiful I
gave up an engagement to play at dice with some of my acquaintance, and borrowing a mule of Rafael's Father, Don Jorge, rode
out to Los Arapiles, arriving shortly before dinner. The matter on

whose account I had been summoned was thus and thus – my Father, sensible again of the natural presentiments arising from fee-bleness of limb and uncertainty of thought, had decided that it was time that I more directly interested myself in the source of the money I spent beyond what had hitherto been my custom – namely simply drawing my allowance from the Zúñiga bank on the first of each month – and proposed that I should visit this vineyard and supervise the picking of the grapes, he having been advised by the old couple whom he employed to overlook the land and tend it, that the harvest or *vendimia* had come.

At first I felt a sort of resentment at this proposal but after thinking it over a little further saw that it had its appeal, and finally I willingly consented, engaging to be at the vineyard two days later at ten of the morning at which time four or five day labourers hired by my Father, with a couple of ox-carts, would be in attendance there, ready to bring in the crop. And what had pro-cured my willing assent was a notion to make of the occasion a fine and private *fiesta*, a *romería* or picnic for myself and my friends.

So it fell out. Rafael and his three unmarried sisters – Violeta, Jara and Margarita – Fernando and I, the men mounted on mules, and the girls on asses, all of us tricked out in our finest *Majo* style, and with an extra ass loaded with provisions, arrived at the vineyard, not at ten o'clock, but shortly before noon on the day appointed.

That we were late was not so much the fault of tardy setting out, as of the distractions we met with along our way. Of the five leagues we had to cover the first two and a half were dull enough, through corn land reduced to dusty stubble a month or more before, and with no interest save for the wheeling kites and soar-ing buzzards. But once we had gone half a league beyond Los Arapiles (which we passed on our left since we were following the Royal Road to Béjar, Cáceres and Sevilla) we began to pass through the oak forest – and now all was enchantment.

The land here is softly rolling (Captain Branwater compares it to the Downs in Sussex, the Land of my Forebears) with gentle slopes, sheltered valleys, and winding brooks, deliciously carpeted with lavender and thyme, poppies and ox-eye daisies, which last prompted our first delay: it was our conceit to garland Margarita and her ass with these flowers for whom she is named; but the main feature of this country is the vast concourse of massy giants – by which I mean the proud and sturdy holm-oaks.

Through the operation of nature almost unaided by man each of these spreading trees stands like a king in his own ground, separate from his fellows, thus imparting to the landscape an open and park-like aspect that is easy on the eye and lifts the spirits. The lowest boughs are high enough for a man on a mule to pass under with ease if he but tilts his head a little to one side, and the highest are yet not so high as to impede the view or fill the mind with notions of oppressiveness – a feeling I suffer in this town of Pau when I contemplate the giant beeches on the hill near the Castle – no, the grandeur of these Salamantine oaks comes from the spread or extent of their horizontal boughs, which provide wide circles of grateful shade, and which shed a carpet of rich mast, and support in their superabundant foliage whole villages of birds.

In the sparser areas near the crests of the Downs coveys of red-legged partridges chuck-chuck-chucked away out of the scrub, lower down pigeons clattered away from our approach and then wheeled above us, wings winking in the sun, and ring doves coo-coo-cooed endlessly, somnolent in the late morning heat. There were magpies too, crested hoopoes, blue, green and russet bee-eaters, and rollers in two shades of blue with their comical lolloping flight.

And on the ground there were conies, and hares which set Rafael's two braches in a frenzy of excitement, snuffling and yapping, bounding and baying on a view; fine bitches they were, grey mottled with maroon, named Ula and Zela. Once we passed an encampment of charcoal burners – the men small with dark faces, the children naked, the womenfolk sullen and in rags round their turfed-over kilns and turfed-over hovels – one could not easily say which was which – with banks of oak logs on one side and piles of carbon, like coal heaps in the Asturias, on the other:

for the oaks provided a harvest of wood as well as mast, each tree being topped out perhaps once every four or five years in the dead of winter. Near the charcoal burners we passed a grove of topped out trees and they cast a gloom for a time – thus pruned and shortened so that only three or four boughs, almost horizontal, remained, they had a gallows look about them, an air of *Golgotha*.

Twice we saw herds of pigs, snuffling in the mast, fine red porkers, long haired, the boars of each herd with tusks (the swineherd's dog was a fearsome brute as well he might be with such brutes in his charge) and once, on a hill that lay in our way, some five and ten or twenty bulls, huge black giants with crescent horns, the true and only Dukes or Princes of the region, of whom more later – I mention them now only to say that despite Rafael's experience in the Ring, despite our knowing that they rarely fought unless separated from their companions, but because of the insistence of the three fair and gentle ones amongst us, we made a detour and added perhaps half a league to our journey.

And thus it was that the grape harvest was well under way before we arrived, but it would be a peevish soul, I say, who would find fault in us for being late.

2

The old man who tended my Father's land was called Francisco, 'Paco', and by coincidence his wife was Francisca, 'Paqui', and Paco and Paqui now came running and stumbling up the path from their little cottage to welcome us, to ask forgiveness on Paco's side, for allowing the men to proceed with the picking, but they would need five hours of daylight at the end of the day to bring the harvest back to Los Arapiles in the ox carts, and, on Paqui's, to express a hope that my friends, whom she had not been expecting, would join her and the men in an afternoon repast she was preparing – she had another hen she could kill and pluck and add to the pot that was already simmering.

They were a round, comfortable pair, as alike as brother and sister, whose life was clearly an easy one, thanks to my Father's benignness. Paco had a round red face – Paqui likewise: the difference was that Paco's was covered by an even layer of white bristle half an inch long, and half of one ear was missing, taken he said, but none believed him, by a wild cat of which there were a few thereabouts.

Paqui was not at all discomposed to hear we were amply provisioned for, and begged leave only to bring us some fresh-picked salads from their little garden, to which we readily assented.

The spot we were come to was a Garden of Eden recreated small in the midst of the paradise we had come through. The Southern slope of the valley was given over to vines planted in neat rows that formed lines whichever way one looked at them, that is obliquely as well as up and across, so carefully had Paco set them, this geometry not broken but interrupted by the oaks, most of which had been left standing but trimmed somewhat so their shade would not impede the ripening of the grapes. Up and down these rows the men my Father had appointed now moved like slow somnambulists, bent double over the plants that reached to just below their waists, dragging along on the ground the wicker baskets they had brought with them. Two robust and handsome girls, their daughters, wives or *novias*, worked with them, carrying the full baskets on their heads like stately schooners, across the slopes to the ox-carts where they emptied out their load of soft jewels, for such the grapes seemed like pale topazes or deep-hued sapphires. One of these girls sang a gay *charro* air of the country.

Below the vineyard the valley flattened out into a wide and grassy plain, watered by a tiny rivulet which even now in late Summer still ran, for its source was a spring scarcely a mile away, and the grass grew to a foot or more though one crop of hay had already been took from it, and it would be mowed again before September was out – this grass filled with flowers of all sorts as daisies, tansies, marigolds, poppies, chervil, and fennel.

In one corner, set against the stone fence of my Father's land, stood Paco's and Paqui's cottage, just two rooms beneath a turf roof, but decent and comfortable as may be, cool in Summer, snug in Winter, and with a plot for vegetables and salads, one milch cow with a calf, three sheep, poultry and white ducks.

We found a shady spot beneath an oak and spread out rugs and cloaks over the fragrant carpet of lavender, thyme, basil and sweet marjoram. Fernando took the stone bottles of lemonade and the leather ones of wine to the stream and set them in the water to cool; the girls sank on to the cloaks and spread their skirts around them so they looked like flowers; Rafael followed Fernando to the stream with the beasts and his dogs to water them, and then he tethered them in the shade, the while I mused on the beauty of it all, savouring the decency and wholesomeness of this country life after the stench and noise, the unruly passions and feverish pleasures of the Town.

A pleasing fancy then came to me as I looked at Violeta, Jara, and Margarita, in the shape of a verse of a song I had picked up in some tavern.

> *Tres serranas he encontrado*
> *Al pie de una gran montaña*
> *Que, según su gesta y maña*
> *No debén guardar ganado**

And Rafael returning and remembering the song better than I, laughed and went on with verses about how these girls were dressed up richly in veils and silks and ropes of fine pearls, adorned with laurel and trimmed with diamonds and emeralds, and how each one carried an ivory crook.

Then Fernando came and completed the song with:

---

* I met three girls from the high places, at the foot of a great mountain, who, by their gestures and their manner, were certainly not shepherdesses.

Ruecas de oro en su cintura
Traían y prendederos
De aljófar los rocaderos
Los busos de plata pura
Seda hilando con mesura
Y cantando esta canción:
¿Dónde está mi corazón?
Por un valle se han entrado★

At which we all laughed, and our spirits thus lifted after our long ride, Jara fetched out her guitar and began to sing another song — *Soy garridica, y viva penada, por ser mal casada* — 'I am a pretty girl and lead a sad life since I'm ill married', at which Violeta turned down her mouth since she was a pretty girl and led a sad life because following the scandal of Angelica's elopement, she wasn't married at all, when perhaps by now she would have been, and we had to tease her back into a good humour.

And thus we passed a happy hour or so, singing songs or listening *al son dulce acordado de plectro sabiamente menado* 'to the sweet and harmonious sound of the plectrum cunningly used'.

Towards two o'clock, when the heat had become oppressive and the harvest was nearly complete, one of the village girls came across with her basket on her head, a comely wench she was, dressed in yellow green with an orange kerchief, and asked if she and her workmates could pause a while since Paqui had called them to dinner. I of course agreed whereupon she gave a courtesy and left some grapes as dessert to our own meal.

Violeta and her sisters now unpacked our paniers — there were slices of sausage, cold chicken and duck, fresh cheeses, peaches, apricocks and melons, almond comfits and *deliciosas* flavoured with cinnamon, and I know not what all, and Fernando fetched up the

★ They had gold distaffs stuck in their belts, with brooches, and the knobs on the distaffs were pearl, the spindles silver. They span and sang in time to this song 'Where is my Heart?' as they went into a Valley.

lemonades and wines from the stream. The only bother was the flies and other insects, but the smoke from our cigarillos kept the worst of these away.

As our feast came to an end we heard the plaintive chaunt of a fife and the rattle of a country drum, and over by Paco's cottage what should we see but the men and the girls performing a *charro* dance, while old Paco played both drum and fife together, rattling the drum beneath with a cane held in his left hand, while the fingers of his right governed the stops. On the insistence of the girls we left our oak tree and joined them, the girls and Fernando joining in for they knew the steps, while I and Rafael looked on. The dances were neat and courtly, not the passionate stomping and clapping of Andalucie or the Gypsies, but required sharp foot-work, and a fluttering of handkerchieves, and much bowing and courtesying and changing of partners up and down the line.

At last old Paco declared himself exhausted and doffed his wide-brimmed sombrero, which had little tassels all round the brim. The gesture required little interpretation and I doubt I needed Rafael's prompting to make the man a present of a silver duro.

The worst heat of the day being gone the men and their girls now returned to the vines where there was yet an hour's work to be done, and Violeta and her sisters moved into the meadow to pick posies and weave garlands, while Rafael, Fernando and I stretched out beneath our oak to finish our cigarillos and let digestion take its course.

3

We were suddenly and soon awakened by an extraordinary noise, as of bulls roaring in the distance and closer to us the screams of the girls whom we – once we were upright – perceived to be running across the meadow towards us with skirts lifted high and no attempt to keep modest so frightened were they, with their flowers and garlands streaming and falling apart behind them. To all this frenzy was now added the wild barking of Rafael's tethered bitches. Fernando grasped my arm and pointed up the valley – 'Look yonder,' he cried, and coming down through the oaks, and stirring up dust and flocks of birds as they came, were a herd of black bulls moving at a fast trot and behind them and on their flanks five horsemen carrying *garrochas*, stout lances each armed with a sharp nail-like point, and bull-roarers, horns through which they blew in imitation of the noble beasts they drove ahead of them.

Now Rafael gathered up a cloak or cape and charged with huge strides down the slope towards the cattle, interposing himself between his sisters and the leader of the herd, a giant snorting beast with sharp upturned horns and long glossy back, an animal of some six or seven years, in the very prime of its male glory. But my brave friend need not have feared for his sisters' safety for one of the horsemen had seen the girls, and spurring his steed – a fine large bay gelding with white flash and socks – came galloping round so close to the bull he was able to strike it across the muzzle with his pike or lance and then spur away as the beast lowered his weapons and charged in fury after this newer and closer target.

For a space of three or four minutes we watched the bull make successive charges at this *Centaur:* for truly that is what he was, so perfectly did man and horse work as one, always keeping just out of reach of those scything points, but never so far that the bull lost sight or interest, until at last he came to a standstill, with sides heaving, tongue swollen, tail swishing, up to his knees in the grass and flowers. At this the horseman rode past once more, this time doffing his plumed hat and sweeping it across the bull's muzzle, and then with a laugh we could hear he turned his back on his dominated foe and came towards us at a slow trot. The bull began to graze as did the rest of the herd behind him.

'¡*Hola!*' cried the *Garrochista*, reining in in front of Rafael, 'You've taken up a brave position there.'

Rafael blushed and shrugged. 'Had I known *Don Julián Sánchez* was with the bulls I should not have troubled myself.'

At this the horseman raised his brows at finding himself thus named, perhaps suspecting irony too, and then, leaning forward to pat the neck of his gelding who was somewhat lathered by its recent exertions, he took a closer look at our friend.

'You are Rafael Martín, are you not?'

Rafael agreed that he was.

'Then perhaps it is I who should have held back for I saw you at a *tienta* of Don Eusebio Camacho last year, did I not? Young though you are you handled the cape well and with great bravery, and that to an *herrero* that was *bronco*.'

It was Rafael's turn to suspect irony.

'An *herrero* however *bronco* is a small thing to yon full-grown *toro*. I'm glad you came, and honoured too to have seen such fine horsemanship.'

'Well, you're a likely lad and in a moment you shall see some more. And these are your friends?'

Rafael now named us and Fernando and I came forward to shake the Garrochista's hand and the girls courtesied. Truth to say I felt a shade put out that this Julián Sánchez did not see fit to dismount, but he was a fine looking man, some thirty and odd years old, with sun-bronzed face, clear blue eyes, a noble brow, a large and eagle-like nose, huge black moustaches and bushy sideburns, which indicated he had been for a soldier, for in that Nation amongst the commonalty only those who have are allowed to wear them. In figure he was large, but well-made, and his hand was strong and dry.

'Now, if you care to remain here, where you will be quite safe if you make no sudden movement or noise,' he continued, 'you will see us performing the *suerte de garrocha* on four *herreros* in that herd, and if they prove as good as we hope it will be some sport for you.'

And he pulled his bay around from us and cantered out into the sunlit meadow where his companions were waiting for him.

'He is a proud man for a *Garrochista*,' I said as soon as he was out of hearing.

'It is not a calling to be ashamed of,' said Rafael, 'requiring as it does great skill and bravery. Julián Sánchez is the best in the province, nay the best in all Spain I dare say.'

'Did he not go for soldier?' asked Fernando.

'Ay,' said Rafael, 'and such is the arsy-versy nature of our times he fought first against the French with the English as Allies at the siege of Toulon and was wounded by cannon fire when the guns were directed by Buenoparte himself; then was at Cadiz when the English Fleet under Lord Nelson bombarded the town, and was wounded there too. They say he carries nine scars on his body from these Wars. But look, the *suerte* is about to begin.'

Three of the *Garrochistas* now cantered off towards the herd which had fallen to grazing behind their leader and with much hallooing and fine manoeuvring cut out one of the younger bulls and drove him back across the plain towards where Don Julián (for now I was convinced he merited the title) sat waiting stiff behind the high pommel of his saddle, *garrocha* or lance at the ready. When the bull was at a certain distance from him, his men wheeled away so only Don Julián was in the bull's territory, at which the *Caballero* cited him with a shout of '*Toro, toro, toro.*'

The bull charged, Don Julián touched heels to the gelding at exactly the right moment, and with the movement of both beasts cunningly played against each other, he was able to use his lance as a lever and tip the hurtling bull over on to its side. It tumbled in a cloud of dust and grass seed, hooves kicking in the air.

'This is the meaning of this *suerte*,' said Rafael. 'It is a test of courage. If the bull now seeks to charge again and again . . . yes, here he comes, and over he goes . . . if he charges three times and thereby shows he has *cojones*, he will be returned to the herd to grow until he is big enough and strong enough for the last *suerte* of all, in the Plaza . . . There, that is the third charge. He will be reprieved.'

On a signal from Don Julián the first bull was now trotted back to his companions and a second one brought out.

'And if he does not charge after being so cruelly tipped?' asked Violeta, large eyes serious and wide.

'Why then there is no point in fattening him up on good pasture to grow more cowardly than before; he will be driven off this very day, back to the ranch, and either butchered there or sent to market.'

'Oh, how can they be so cruel!'

''Tis not they who are cruel. 'Tis Nature. See, this one did not like the tumble Don Julián gave him. He is confused and winded by the fall. He lowers his head, but he paws at the ground, a bad sign, he lacks determination for a second charge. Nay, do not weep for him, sister. Or if you must, save your salt tears to season your beef stew withal tomorrow or the day after.'

This, I mused, is not the same Nature my Father speaks of. But the subtlety of this consideration was too much to pursue then, and has remained so since.

So the *suerte de garrocha* continued, and, as I remember it, Violeta had no more call for tears, for the remaining two bulls did as well as the first. The second was roped by a skilful throw of a noose and led off, but before all went Don Julián returned to us.

'Don Rafael,' he said after he had received our praise on his skill and courage and a sprig of wild lavender from Jara which he put in his hat, 'a week today I am *Picador* to Pepe Hillo in the Plaza. If you present yourself at the Torero's lodging early that day and ask for me, I doubt not but that I shall fetch you a place in his troop.'

With that he saluted us once more, and rode away across the meadow leaving Rafael in an ecstasy of joy and his sisters equally moved by horrid fears of what would befall when the day came and their brother faced a full-grown *toro bravo* in the Plaza.

Chapter XII

*In Which Town and University Celebrate a Grand Festival of
Bulls in Honour of Our Lady.*

I

It is not difficult to call to mind the beauty of the Great Square in
Salamanca, tricked out for the *fiesta* in September that honours
Our Lady's Birth, and with a square arena erected in it and scaf-
folding supporting terraced seats, almost enough for the whole
population, right up to the balconies on the first storey – not difficult, but the emotions Memory brings in her train box the
compass, from aching regret that I shall never see its like again, to
warm delight that once I did.

Every balcony, for three storeys right to the cornice and even
including the attic lights beyond, has its drape – a Manila shawl, a
carpet, an embroidered image of Our Lady, or a tapestry hanging,
and any gaps are filled with wreathed flowers, laurels and palms;
from the string course of the principal gallery of the Town Hall
hang three rich banners – the arms of the City, the arms of the
University, and the third and middle one a fine tapestry of the
Immaculate Conception taken from the Ribera that hangs in the
Agustinas' Convent. Above these sit or stand the chief func-
tionaries of Church, Town and University, Bishop, Dean, Rector,
Maestre Scuela, *Bedel Mayor*, *Corregidor*, all in the robes of their
several offices, scarlet, carmine, cerise, white, gold, black, among
them the man appointed *Presidente* for the day, he who presides

over the Grand Course of Bulls to be run, baited, pic-ed, banderilla-ed, and put to the sword.

At an early hour the terraced seats begin to fill with people of the humbler sort – farmers and labourers from the villages; artisans such as wheel-wrights, shoemakers, coopers, smiths, bottle-makers, ropers, and the like; Franciscans and Curates; tradesmen – as families who hire market-stalls, shop-keepers, water-carriers, and muleteers who may have paid their entrance by bringing, the day before, gleaming snow in a special cold wagon at a full gallop from the heights of the Gredos Mountains twenty leagues away, right to the Town Hall where now, flavoured with juice of peach, pomegranate and apricock, it melts away as icy sherbet in the glasses of those dignitaries aforesaid; and all is racket and noise as ticket touts argue for the price of a bench; sellers of pistachio and cashew nuts, cold water, melon seeds hawk their wares together with favours in the colours of the *Espadas*; and groups of *charro* dancers with tambourines, fifes and drums, no doubt Paco amongst them, foot it out in the sand of the arena in honour of Our Lady, who may be watching, though I doubt if any others are, for all the tinsel and spangles on the women's bodices, and the posturing of the men, all having seen them many times before.

Towards noon the balconies begin to fill with people of the richer sort, who, if they were not acquainted with an owner of one of the apartments and often even if they were, will have paid an inordinate sum to be there, perhaps as much as a gold Dollar, and all tricked out in their finest clothes as silks and satins, fine lace and furbelows, high mantillas and gorgeous shawls; the men if they affected the French style in high crowned hats of silk or beaver, and waisted coats, and high stiff collars pushing up beyond their ears and white, yellow, or grey trousers; or if not, then in gaudy *Majo* style and carrying for the *corrida* special sticks, the bark peeled in rings, with a lump at one end and a fork at the other.

But not Rafael, Fernando and I – not on the occasion I have particularly in mind, which was the day Don Julián Sánchez had appointed. All the town knew where Pepe Hillo lodged, that he was given an apartment, and his rival Pedro Romero with him, in the Monterrey Palace just down the hill to the west of the Grand Square, for his use and that of his following for the week. Thither we went at nine o' clock in the morning, and already all was bustle although there were still three hours before the first course of bulls – lacqueys and servants came and went, messengers from the Town Hall, gifts of flowers and other presents for the two great *Espadas*, and, just as we arrived, the waiters from a nearby pastry-shop came in carrying trays with large cups of steaming chocolate, cinnamon sippets, fresh bread, and even, so close to the ways of noblemen had the style of the greatest *Toreros* come, *butter*, in the English fashion. And all set out on fine porcelain with silver utensils.

Just as we gawped at these a *Major Domo* came down the steps and into the yard where we were waiting (we knew he was *Major Domo* by the silver-knobbed staff he carried) and asked our business, at which Rafael spoke up to the effect that we were sent for by Don Julián Sánchez, who was to be Pepe Hillo's chief picador that day.

'And every day if Pepe could command it,' replied this elegant youth, for he was but our age, and a nephew of the Espada, we later discovered. 'You had best come up then, though I'll have you cudgelled and turned out if Don Julián denies you. We have too many like you, and most dressed in your *Majo* style, who try all sorts of wiles to gain admittance.'

He took us up wide stairs carved in the old but tricksy style of the Catholic Kings, and through an oak-lined ante-chamber where more servants and hangers-on lounged about, and thence into the bedchamber.

Here at last was some sense of what was toward, for, although the room was spacious and had some fine furnishings, and although Pepe himself in bed-gown, dressing gown and turban was sat up like a monarch on the pillows and tasselled bolsters of the largest bed I ever did see, the people around him, some four or five in number, were no longer fops or loungers but bull-fighters all, and the room held an air of tension, purposeful and reined in. These men – all brown, wiry, somehow older in their faces than their trim figures suggested – were conversing quietly and slowly, almost as if reciting a lesson by rote (I have since seen men talk thus when they knew a battle was coming), meanwhile sipping at the chocolate and nibbling at the hot bread, and it was a moment or two before we were able to understand what it was they were saying.

There were two principal speakers, one of whom we now recognised by his moustaches (for the room was almost dark, lit only by a candle, by an oil-lamp before an image of Our Lady, and by the sun that filtered through the slats of the closed shutters) as Don Julián. He and his colleagues were carefully itemising the characteristics of one of the bulls Pepe would fight that morning, speaking in turn as aspects of the creature (whom they had studied together in the pens at dawn while Pepe still slept) came to mind. Occasionally they would differ on a detail, occasionally Pepe or one of the others would volunteer a suggestion or a query. At last they were finished and Pepe lay back on the bed with eyes closed as if committing to memory what had passed. Then one eye opened and he called more loudly than we had yet heard him speak: 'Well Jaime, what have you got there hiding in the shadows?'

'Friends of Don Julián, Maestro. They say they were sent for.'

Don Julián looked up, saw us, murmured to the *Espada* and came over to us. Seeing him for the first time off a horse, his height and figure impressed even more than expected.

'Don Rafael alone I asked for,' he said.

'The Lawyer's son who is good with a cape?' asked Pepe.

'The same,' answered Don Julián, 'but he's brought along his friends too, which are two more than I bespoke.'

'Rafael's not to blame,' blurted out Fernando, 'we followed him and for old friendship's sake would not let him turn us off.'

'Ay,' said Pepe, a little wearily, 'let'm all stay – bring yon Rafael over, he's a good looking lad and the crowd will take to him if he's known in the town, as I'm sure he is, and let him hear what you have to say on the fourth bull which I hope will better the others. The other two stay by the door and if we find a use for them let them jump to it, otherwise let'm pretend, as we shall, that they are to be found elsewhere.'

This 'Pepe Hillo' whose real name was José Delgado was, with Pedro Romero and Gáspar Romero, one of the three great *Espadas* of our age. I know not why I say 'was'. For aught I know he is still alive, though he will be getting on in years if he has been spared. I should dearly like to see him fight a course of bulls again if 'twere possible. He had a fine figure and a serious face, and though he never offended by lack of dignity or self glorification, he brought a touch of fire, of *gracia* to the *fiesta*, which owed a little to the School of Seville which he adorned and much to his own artistry.

The next two hours or so went quickly and were full of interest. After Pepe had heard all there was to know about the Bulls he was likely to meet that morning, his breakfast things were carried back to the pastry shop and his toilet was begun. In this he was aided by the old man who was his dresser. After washing and emptying his bowels in a commode brought for the purpose he had his waist and thighs bound round with clean linen – not so much to protect him from the bull's horns as to provide a sort of ready-made dressing against a goring, an awful event, not uncommon as witnessed by the puckered scars on his pale thighs; then he was helped into a pale white shirt, a little old-fashioned as to cut, for *Toreros* affect in the ring the styles of thirty years or so ago, with lace at wrist and neck, and then a pair of leather breeches, soft chamois leather from the Pyrenees, flesh-coloured stockings and supple leather slippers.

At last his dresser made him sit before a mirror, and combed back the dark hair from his forehead and plaited the longer strands behind into a short queue tied with a ribbon, this done to ensure it could not obscure his vision, and finally gave this *coiffure* a sprinkling of powder which added to the Hero's dignity. All that remained now were his cloak or cape, which was turquoise embroidered with silver and gold and sewn with spangles to catch the light and the attention of the bull, and his sword, tool of his trade and emblem of his pre-eminence.

Meanwhile the rest of his following completed their preparations, which had been more advanced before we came, for the most part now being only a matter of collecting cloaks, hats, and so forth. Don Julián and the two other *Picadors*, holding their wide-brimmed white sombreros, left early to harness their horses and collect their lances; and thus, by half past eleven, or even a little later, all was ready for the *paseo* or procession up into the Great Square.

In the palace yard, now lit stark by the blazing light of noon and warm with the breath of an oven, Pepe met and saluted his friend and rival Pedro Romero and all their trains saluted likewise their counterparts *viz*. *Chulos* or *Peons* (of whom Rafael was one); *Picadors* on horses, muleteers with their beasts to drag off the corpses whether of hacks or bulls; dressers, barbers, surgeons and the rest; and when all was done with sober ceremony and a Franciscan had led us through the Rosary in which we all made devout response, we set off at last, preceded by two mounted constables, up the hill and into the Square, and to our delight, and not in the least to our shame, Fernando and I were given a long heavy case filled with spare cloaks, and swords, and so forth to carry between us, and thus had our credentials to remain part of our Hero's following.

The streets up to the Square were narrow and steep and shady and quite deserted, though maid servants, cooks and the like thronged to the windows to see us pass and some threw posies, carnations, pinks and sweet williams. Since all was quiet and a little solemn between us, save for the clatter of hooves and the jingle of harness, we could hear the steady roar or boom of the crowd, like the Atlantic surf I've heard since from a distance at Biarritz. This roar reached the level of *Pan-demonium*, the City of Devils, when we wheeled out into the sunlight, felt the drag of the hot sand at our ankles, and blinked at the glare, and paraded across the arena to make our salutes to the dignitaries in the Town Hall and especially the *Presidente*, who gave a little bow to every rank of us, from the *Espadas* themselves through to Fernando and myself, still clutching our cumbersome bag right at the end of the procession, and sweating with the weight of it.

Since immediately in front of us the mules were driven out again at a gallop with whips cracking, I felt we too should look lively and I set out for the *barrera* at a smart trot which made Fernando at the other end of the bag, trip and sprawl. This caused many of the lighter sort in the crowd to laugh, which laughter was increased when Fernando took off his hat and beat me about the ears with it for all the world as if we were clowns, which mortified me, the more because I suspected the hilarity depended in part on the disparity between heights, Fernando being a foot taller than I.

2

There were six bulls to be fought in the morning and six more in the evening, and it would be tedious to tell all, so I shall content myself with the fourth in the morning, since I remember it best.

By the time the fourth bull came the crowd were near Tumult, already hurling abuse and insults and even more dangerous missiles as vegetables and eggs – and all with some reason since the first two bulls had been sway-backed and weak-kneed and had not been well-killed; worse still the third had been *manso*, that is coward, and still the odour of gunpowder and burnt flesh (so horridly familiar to me in later years when I have seen and smelled it like a pall over battlefields and cities) was in the air, from the banderillas furnished with firecrackers and made to explode as close to the bull's flesh as possible, used on coward bulls to stir them up to fight. But even these had failed, Sir Ox refused to charge, but stood still in the ring near the gate he had come in by, and bellowed pitifully. So Pedro

Romero refused to dishonour his sword on him and the dogs
were let loose instead. They had their sport, brought the creature
fainting to its knees, when the senior *Chulo* come forth, whipped
them off, and stabbed the sorry creature to death with a heavy
dagger blow in the back of the neck.

Thus the first three bulls and the reason for the crowd's dis-
temper.

The fourth was a grand animal, a noble beast, and the tenor of
the crowd's fervour changed on sight of him. He was full seven
years old, and very large, nigh on a ton, yet lively, alert, and fast.
His weapons were like crescent moons or like one crescent
obscured by a passing cloud in the middle, and coming to points
of poniard sharpness at the extremities which were tinged with
ebony against the ivory of the rest. In colour he was uniformly
black – velvet as to his coat and ebony again at his hooves; his eyes
were glistening beads of jet. Only his nostrils flared scarlet in his
silken muzzle. You may be sure that while this monster was in the
ring I kept safe behind the barrier and even there I felt none too
secure: beasts of that sort have been known to smash up oak
planks in their rage.

His first charge into the arena brought him straight into the
middle, where he paused, and the dust settled about his feet which
he set apart in the front and closed behind, and he held his head
right up, as alert and alive as a whippet, and his tail thrashed the air
like an angry cat's.

The leading *Chulo* flapped a cloak to his side, he turned tightly
as a dancing horse and shot like a bolt towards it, slicing the air and
snatching the cloak right out of the peon's hands, which rag he
now carried on his horn like a knight at a joust, carrying his standard or his lady's favour on his lance (the Branwaters require me
to read of such stuff from the latest novels to their children) and
thus he trotted down two sides of the square in all his glory.

Pepe came out behind him and cited with voice, high, much as
a falconer calls his hawk, '*Toro, toro, toro*,' and round he swung, ears
pricking, eyes searching, till he found this new quarry and again

he charged, yet more furiously than before, but Pepe handled his
cloak like the *maestro* he was, and drew it aside just in time, so the
beast stuck hooves to the sand to halt and wheel and come back
for his elusive prey. Thus Pepe, three times and more.

Enter, to sound of cornets and drums, three picadors, the first
well-mounted, the latter two on foundered nags, the well-
mounted one being Julián Sánchez. Pepe now brought the giant
in three sweeping charges at the cloak to sight and smell of Don
Julián's horse, an old but still sound and strong dapple grey, whereupon he attacked with even more fury than before, but by a skilful
manoeuvre Don Julián avoided the horns yet thrust with his lance
firmly into the bull's neck, at which the crowd roared, seeing the
crimson flood burst forth. The bull paid no heed to this wound
but pushed and lunged and sought again and again to get at Don
Julián's mount, but every time Don Julián escaped unhurt though
leaving further wounds in his adversary, until at last one of the
Chulos lured the *Toro* away with his cloak. And now some of the
crowd cheered the *Garrochista* but others booed and whistled,
because they did not value his horsemanship, nor his skill with the
garrocha, but only wanted to see the horse upset and disembow-
elled – indeed some said it was the Bull's Right, these no doubt
being gypsies who trade in old horses and like to see their stock
used up.

Nor was this satisfaction denied them, for the bull now caught
sight and smell of one of the other horses, forty paces away, and,
seemingly unweakened by the wounds he had suffered, delivered
a most terrible attack on it. The force of the charge tore the lance
from the *Picador's* hand, the raking horns gathered his horse, like
the arms of a child scooping into a basket of nuts, and lifted it clear
from the ground and dumped it on its side, nor did he fear the
threshing hooves but went straight in again and again; the horse
screamed; its crimson blood and purple gut fountained into the
air; and mercifully it expired.

Again Pepe was at hand to bring him off and lure him into a
third attack on the third picador, and now it was the Toro took a

brief revenge: for the chief *Chulo*, seeing Pepe's design, and fearing there would not be sufficient capes to cover the third *Picador* should he too be dismounted, shouted for another to station himself in readiness, and he, an apprentice, moving too quickly took the Bull's eye from Pepe's cloak. The *Toro* went for him; he could have turned and vaulted the barrier; but no, he stood his ground and took the Bull's charge in his cloak; again the cloak caught on the point of the horn, but this youth held on, was dragged into the sand; the Bull feeling the weight on his horn turned quick and raked at the recumbent figure, once . . . and a second time would have done for him there and then, but Rafael, who had played little part so far, came forward and drew him off with a *quite* as neat as any of Pepe's, and led him back to his charge on the third horse.

The youthful *Chulo* was carried to the side, his face dead white, and blood issuing through a rent in his shirt. The wound was not much however, and would have mended, but it took infection, as three out of five do, and the boy expired three days later, but not before thanking Rafael for saving him for long enough to be properly shrived and houseled, which was a consolation to us all, and not least to the youth himself.

3

Meanwhile the noble beast took the pic three more times before overturning and dispatching the third horse in like manner to the second and now Fernando remarked to me that he understood why Pepe Hillo valued Don Julián as *Picador*: he paid his wage in horse flesh alone, which is usually a charge on the *Espada*. 'More sound wood in a sound tree than three rotten ones,' was the proverb he found on this occasion.

But it was at the *banderillas* that Don Julián most distinguished himself, and won back the crowd's favour entire, for having decided the *Toro* was truly frank and honest in his charges, he made petition first to Pepe and then to the *Presidente* to place the barbed darts from horse back, a thing rarely seen these days, since the Nobility no longer *torear*, but Don Julián though a plebeian rode a horse like the *Duke of Albuquerque* himself, as many a Frenchman was to find to his cost.

So, at a signal, Don Julián's bay gelding was released into the ring, and at a whistle from its master trotted to him, whereat the *Garrochista* mounted and took the darts even as, at the other end of the arena, the *Chulos* drew aside and let the *Toro* have a sight of his latest foe. Three times he charged, three times Don Julián wheeled away, lifted his mount off the very points of the horns, and planted as he did so the *banderillas* and at the end all six were fixed within the circumference of a gold *onza*, and all this with no recourse to reins but guiding and spurring the bay by pressure of thighs and heels.

And now at last our foe had been brought to that dread moment of the *lidia* when wild beauty has been tamed, brute strength humbled, and nought remains of that glossy pride he came with but the courage that first said, 'Let all die but I', and now pleads, 'There is nothing left but Death'. This brief moment belongs to the *Toro* and the *Espada* alone, and Pepe Hillo, armed with only a rag and a sword, walks out into the sunlit square and all is still, even the crying of a child is hushed. They pause, the two of them, facing each other; the man fixes the dying creature's gaze upon the rag and then both move towards each other like parted lovers into an embrace; the sword slides deep into the *Toro's* vitals, he staggers, his knees subside, and all is gone the way all good things go, which is what I take the figure of the *lidia* to be – an emblem of our common fate.

PART THREE

Chapter XIII

A New Invasion by the French leads to a Strange Reunion with a Close Relation Long Forgot.

I

That was the *feria* of September 1807, the last before the Wars, the last real *feria* I saw for before the Wars were done I was beached on this foreign strand, where now I pen the annals of those glorious times.

Before the Year was out we felt the first tremors heralding the convulsions that were to come, though it would be false of me to suggest that I understood then the Chain of Events that led up to our Occupation, brief in this next instance but not without significance for me, with the History of the Late Wars in front of me I can make shift to patch together what was happening in the great world with what took place in Salamanca and its Province.

That my country was knit by Alliance to France and therefore was at war with the Nation of my Ancestors I knew; but it hardly touched me at all; indeed, the Wars meant very little then to any of our Nation, save the one fifth or *quinta* of able-bodied peasants conscripted into Armies, which, however, never marched beyond their parade grounds, and not often as far as that. That Spain was a reluctant ally to the Corsican was clear – all knew that this Corsican was an atheist who had humiliated the Holy Father in Rome, and that the alliance only continued at the insistence of our King's Chief Minister, Prince Godoy – a jumped-up sausage

maker who had debauched the Queen and most of the Court
Ladies as well and who hoped to benefit from the alliance to the
extent of a crown for himself in Portugal.

At the age of seventeen five years is a long time and since matters had stood thus for so long it seemed reasonable to suppose
they would remain so for another hundred, and the continuing
tale of Imperial Conquests in remote places the other side of
Europe soon ceased to be of any interest to us; for the Church
bells had not been rung nor the Great Square illuminated for a
French victory since Austerlitz two years before, though there
had been plenty.

One piece of news was remarkable though, and it reached us
during the *feria*, remarkable only at the time for its singularity –
none could see it as the start of what ruined all our lives. I doubt
not Your Grace apprehends the event I mean – the invasion by the
British of Denmark, the capture of the Danish Fleet, and the
Firing of Copenhagen, all of which took place in August; and its
singularity lay in the fact that here the Imperial Design for an
United or Common Europe was dealt a buffet on dry land – the
first since Egypt. Your Grace will pardon me – the sheets that
brought these news no doubt made mention of an English
General named Sir Arthur Wellesley who played an illustrious
part in that campaign – but the Capture of a Fleet and the
Burning of a Town in a country whose place in an atlas I would
be hard put to find was not so great a matter after all, and the
name of the architect of those Triumphs was even less likely to
remain fast in the memory; almost a year was to pass before I
heard it again.

What I now discover, in this History aforementioned, is that
the rape of Denmark provoked a terrible fit of Imperial Rage, that
the Corsican decided there and then that no friend would remain
to perfidious Albion throughout the length and breadth of a
Continent, that all doors should be shut to her, all harbours closed;
that the Tyrant enquired what harbours there were that still traded
with her, and discovered two, and both in Portugal – *Lisbon*, the

Capital of that country, and *Oporto*. Forthwith he raised an army, appointed a Marshal – Andoche Junot, the Duke of Abrantes – and sent it off to conquer a second time that incorrigible land.

Salamanca was on the Noble Marshal's route and he arrived there with his army on the tenth day of November, 1807, and there he stayed for a week or more, making our City his General Head Quarters.

The weather had been fine – a fortnight of unbroken clear skies and hot sunlight, but with a seasonal chill in the purple shadows and an iciness at night – when out of the North, down the Great Road from Bayonne, Burgos, and Valladolid, came the Grand Army, crunching through frosty stubble at Dawn, stirring the orange dust of the highway at Noon, and foraging across a terrified countryside at Evening. For this army was different from Leclerc's of six years before. It was five times larger; it was part of the machine that had conquered Europe; it moved seven leagues a day; and it lived off the land. It had come the one hundred and twenty leagues from Bayonne in less than a fortnight when a single traveller in a hurry might allow himself so much.

They came so quickly that we knew they were upon us only an hour before the first of the cavalry screen came clattering and jangling up the Calle de Zamora and into the Square, yet several of us were there to see the spectacle. For all we had given little heed to campaigns a thousand miles to the East, now these soldiers were upon us (bronzed, tough lancers who wheeled and strutted and struck sparks from the flags as, obedient to words of command, detachments trotted off to all the main gates and squares) we felt a glamour and a glory about them which stirred an enthusiasm in our breasts that had had nothing to arouse them since the September *corridas*. Young boys cheered; Rafael, Fernando and I smoked our cigarillos and watched, wrapped in our brown cloaks, and agreed with each other that these were *soldiers* and that with such efficiency, such *éclat* and *élan*, it was no wonder that save Portugal (and Portugal's turn was evidently on the way) all Europe was either allied, as we believed we were, or subject to the Modern Rational Rule of the Benevolent Dictator.

In short, for a day or two, we were like to become true *Afrancesados* or *Frenchifiers*.

But bit by bit, tittle by tattle, the true character of the invasion of our country (I mean Province) became known. At first they were small things – the vast tricolour flying alone from the Town Hall with no banner of the City or of our King beside it; the way the *Corregidor* on his official visit, made in his gilded coach drawn by six white mules, passed into the Town Hall unsaluted by the tall grim Grenadiers, though the most junior subaltern in blue frock coat and white pantaloons was welcomed with the *Present*; the sudden heat we felt, Fernando and I, when, brusquely challenged at night on our round of taverns, we were sent home because we could show no good reason for being abroad after nightfall. Yet a week later there were still a few of us to give a short *huzza* when the Marshal, a man not yet middle-aged but showing the coarseness in his face and round his waist that accompanies good living and success, swung into the saddle of his large grey mare, reached down for his heavily plumed hat, and with a flourish sent the Grand Army on its way to Ciudad Rodrigo and Lisbon.

And soon the city buzzed with more serious complaints. The three principal corn merchants had been forced to empty their granaries and the Army had taken five hundred head of cattle; the price of bread and beef remained doubled until Christmas; in Pedrosillo de Ralo, a league to the North, a swineherd and his whole family had been bayoneted to death when he drew a knife on the Sergeant who had come to drive off his hogs; the bodies of two girls, their bellies ripped open, were found in a garbage pile near the market; and an abbess had to part with all the plate of her convent before a billeting officer consented to annul an order made to house an hundred men amongst her nuns and novices. Some students, for the most part *religious* as Agustinians and Franciscans, rioted at these news and were fired on.

And I too suffered a strange and frightening confrontation.

2

This came a clear week after the main army had moved on, leaving behind a garrison or rearguard, or army of occupation, of about two thousand men under an old General called Calvinet. This force caused resentment in the town since if we were trusted as allies it could not conceivably serve any military purpose. More disturbing, there were rumours of dawn arrests, of interrogations, even of beatings and executions, though nothing certain known, and none of our acquaintance ever heard of such things at closer than fourth or fifth hand. Yet the Tricolour continued to hang outside the Town Hall and the sentinels continued to smash their butts to the paving as they marched and counter-marched outside.

This General Calvinet was an old man who had served Buenoparte well in Italy some fifteen years before, where he had remained as a garrison commander, being fit, by reason of his years, for little else. There he had acquired a fortune and a Mistress: he had now run through the former while the latter remained a charge on his person, so he had come campaigning again in the hopes of another, and the Mistress with him too.

In that week we saw her a couple of times, but always at a distance, stepping out of her carriage and mounting the stairs into the Town Hall. From afar she was a statuesque woman of very splendid figure, dressed in black, with black furs. She was known, so a French Chasseur who spoke a little Spanish informed us, as Anna La Granace – though he believed her Italian; and many wild stories were current about her, as that she kept a bordello in Naples where Orgies were had, but the details either reticence or inability with the language prevented him from telling us.

Such was the way things were then when one morning early, before nine o'clock, there came a pounding on the street door below, followed by a pounding on Don Jorge's door, accompanied by the voice of Don Jorge's *Portero* informing us that two French soldiers had come to fetch Don José Bos'am to the Town Hall where he was to be asked some questions.

'Quick,' cried Fernando, who had leaped from his bed and torn the covers from mine, 'the casement. I can lower you to the area on a rope of sheets.'

Rubbing the sleep from my eyes I followed him across the icy floor and stood behind him as he flung open the shutters. A wall of frozen air moved in on us – frozen, for a freezing fog had settled on the Town in the night, and we could barely see the pump in the little quadrangle below. A dark shadow now separated itself from a doorway, came over to the pump, and took on the form, still blurred at the edges, of a huge Grenadier, who grinned horribly at us, yellow teeth against the frosted blackness of his whiskers.

Fernando shrugged. 'The wise dog stays at the rabbit's bolt-hole', he muttered, and together we withdrew – I to my bed where I began to pull on my breeches.

They were rough with me and they frightened me as they hustled me up the ghostly Calle de Zamora and into the Town Hall. Their brown hands, cracked and scarred with powder burns, bruised my arms; they laughed when I stumbled; and one of them let me feel the cold steel of his bayonet point on my buttock as they chased me up the long wide stairs.

I was pushed into a large room on the top floor which was used in better times by the Inspector of Water and Drains, and there found three people waiting for me, whose presence surprised me the more, the better I was already acquainted with them.

First was a French officer, whom I did not know at all, and whose presence occasioned no alarm beyond what I was already feeling. He had a blue coat with red cuffs and facings and one gold epaulette, and he was sat behind a table covered with papers, pens, inkwells and so on. He was not much above my age but his face was weather-beaten and he had black moustaches.

In a large arm-chair, padded and covered with leather, sat Anna La Granace, the General's Mistress; my first thought was that the Grenadiers had brought me to the wrong room; but before this thought had properly taken shape the third person, so far a figure silhouetted against the window, turned and provoked the worst shock so far – it was none other than Rubén.

'Is it really you?' I cried, struggling with conflicting feelings – hatred for the beastliness he had tricked me into in the Summer gone, relief to find a face I knew among those I took to be my enemies.

''Tis really I, José,' said he and his sandy eyebrows rose a little and his pale lips cracked in a sort of smile.

A rustle of heavy silk from the arm-chair and a sweet but spicy fragrance drifted across the room as the woman stirred and leaned towards us.

'Is this the boy?' she asked.

'This is he, José Bozzam,' said Rubén.

She looked at me and for the first time I looked properly at her, and as I did a wave of heat and then of cold passed through and over me, for the face I was looking into was, for a moment, that of the girl then unknown to me that had moved me with such sensations of tenderness and loss at the Abominable Feast of Witches. That it should appear now, and in the presence of Rubén again, filled me with feelings of awe at the supernatural. But even as I looked the magic retreated – the face in that dreadful dream had been that of a girl of sixteen or less, the woman in front of me was over thirty, though at this moment she seemed to have shrunk away a little and looked even older. Her head was sunk back between her shoulders and her large reddish-brown eyes peered up at me with an odd expression that combined wariness, curiosity, and some deeper anxiety whose meaning I could not guess at.

'Your Father is the Curate at Los Arapiles?' She spoke Spanish, but not perfectly.

'Yes, Madame,' I replied.

'Then you can speak Italian?'

'I have not spoken it much for several years,' I replied in that tongue.

'But I think we should speak it together,' she said, 'for it is our Native language, is it not?'

I shrugged – to me English is my first language for all I learned Italian at my Mother's knee.

And now a suspicion as to who this woman was began to grow upon me. *La Granace* must be, I thought, the Frankish for *Granacci*, Anna short for Annabella, and this strange lady my Aunt and wet-nurse, the fallen sister of my sainted Mother, Elisabetta. These discoveries brought back the fainting fear, which, however, I still managed to disguise. I also resolved not to allow my awareness of this relationship to show until she acknowledged it herself: and, for that she never did, it remained unspoken between us; she must have decided that my Father had never told me of her, and so, preferring not to reveal her first descent into whoring, she kept mum about it all. Nevertheless, then, and during the strange before dinner-time that followed, my eye wandered with curios-ity yet discreetly as may be over this strange figure from my long forgotten infancy.

'I knew your Father when he lived in Tuscany,' she went on. Her voice was husky and deep. 'You too. Though of course you do not remember me?'

There was an upward lilt on this last question which seemed to express a touching hope. It was not difficult to deny her, for I could scarce admit that the only recollection I had of her, or rather of her face, was at a witches' Sabbath only months, not years, since.

'Well, well, it was not to be expected.' She sighed and lowered her gaze at a fur muff which concealed her hands in her lap, and she sat like that for perhaps a minute. Her darkish hair had cop-pery lights in it, no doubt placed there by art rather than Nature, though her eyebrows too were coppery rather than black. She painted much, especially round her eyes. The dress she wore was a travelling one and buttoned to the neck, but did not conceal the promise of a bosom *en bon point* (which I confess I felt a sort of warm curiosity about), and it fitted a touch too tightly over her round belly. I did not of course take all this in at once, but most of it – as I have said I was curious about this Aunt of mine from the past, and this was the first opportunity I had had of observing her without meeting her gaze.

Rubén coughed and she looked up, withdrawing as she did so a black-gloved hand from the muff. Between the fingers was a handkerchief of lace with which she dabbed a drop of moisture that had formed in the corner of one eye.

'Well,' she said, looking now at my acquaintance, 'you do seem to have performed what you promised, and I must do the same,' and she nodded to the Lieutenant, who had been pretending to busy himself with his papers. 'Give him the money, Charles.'

The Lieutenant looked up, muttered something in French, found a key, and unlocked a small strong-box in front of him. He counted out three gold napoleons and left them on the edge of the desk. Rubén pocketed them, directed an awkward bow to La Granace, and his twisted smile at me, turned and was gone. We listened to the clatter of his boots on the stairs.

'I presume he will share it with you later,' said La Granace. Again I shook my head, 'No? Then you were not in this together?' And she fell to looking at me again most intently, so that I felt my colour rise.

'I declare I'm making the poor boy confused,' and suddenly she leaned forward and took my hand between her gloved fingers – the silkiness set my teeth on edge. 'Giuseppe, I should like you to be my escort this morning on a little excursion I have in mind.'

I muttered something that must have sounded polite.

'Good, that's a good boy.' And she stood up, all her silks rustling together, like the leaves of a grove of aspens. 'Charles, my cloak, please.'

She was taller than I, and the cloak was black like the rest of her clothes, black, glossy fur that reached to an inch from the floor.

The French Lieutenant led us down the stairs into the Calle de Zamora along an alley or two, and into a yard where we discovered a handsome closed landaulet with two fine white mules whose breath filled the icy grey air with warm droplets. Charles handed *Madame* or *Madonna* up into this fine vehicle and motioned that I should mount too.

'We are going to Los Arapiles,' she said, pulling a rug across her knees as I settled myself on the seat facing her, 'pray direct the coachman for me.'

I did, telling him to cross the Roman Bridge and take the Royal Road for Béjar, but I did so with difficulty for my heart had begun to pound at the thought of this . . . witch was the word that came unbidden to my mind, arriving unannounced on my Father's doorstep. He could not but be much disturbed to meet again the harlot sister of the saintly woman he loved, would perhaps, despite the difference in character, discern something of the dead in the living. Indeed, I too wondered if this woman resembled the Mother I had forgotten. Perhaps something of my agitation was understood by my companion, but for a long time she said nothing.

The mules slithered on the icy cobbles as we dropped through the misty, almost empty streets, but they could do little to make our ride uncomfortable, so well sprung was the little carriage. Both hoods were up, and neat windows that could be raised or lowered also protected us from the icy fog. Soon I became aware of hooves behind us, and found two hussars were doing duty for us as outriders.

We clattered across the Roman Bridge and so foggy was it we could scarce see the Cathedrals, and the River was frozen almost right across, and that near the weir where it runs most briskly.

The landaulet climbed slowly into the hills through the greyness and whiteness that surrounded us, whiteness because the fog left snow-like crystals on every stalk of stubble in the still unploughed fields, and on every clod where the earth had been turned. It glittered on the twigs and branches of the occasional trees and hardly a streak of ochre or dun or red showed through anywhere. Suddenly a dark shape loomed through the air to our right, huge wings rowing slowly through the fog, then tilting and gliding away from us to be swallowed in the vapour again. I do not know if my companion had remarked it; the hussars behind must have done: I presume they recognised the beast for it was none other than the *Imperial Eagle*, a not infrequent visitor to our plains in Winter, and the emblem of their Tyrannical Master.

I had no coat and soon I began to shiver, so much that my teeth chattered.

'You are cold.' As far as I recollect these were the first words the Lady whom I was beginning to think of as my Aunt had uttered since we left town.

I agreed that I was.

'Come and sit by me. We can share this rug.'

Obediently I moved across. She tucked up the rug so that it covered both of us and soon I felt a little better, especially those parts of me that were close to her. I became yet more conscious of the perfumes that clung about her – there was a richness in these fragrances I had never experienced before and they chimed well with the soft opulence of her fur cloak.

'Is it much further?'

I looked about me trying to find in the fog a landmark, a sign. The road was familiar and I was not nonplussed for long.

'In five minutes we must take a byway on the left. There is a small farmhouse at the corner. Then a mile up the road we come to Los Arapiles.'

I felt sick now with anguish at the thought of our arrival there, and stiffened and perhaps shrank from her welcome warmth.

'What is the matter, Giuseppe? Do you not want me to see your Father?'

I made no reply.

'Well, I do not expect to see him. It is not my intention. At least . . . I would not speak with him.'

She sighed and then began to catechise me on the subject of the good man – how he lived, what were his circumstances, how he came to occupy so lowly a position. I answered as well as I could, and I hope truthfully. Then we came to the turning and she fell silent again, partly at least because the road was now ridged with frozen ruts and the coach swayed and rattled and occasionally stuck. As we passed the first squat hovels she pulled down a heavy veil that had been furled up above the brim of her small hat.

'Perhaps that will make you feel easier. Now direct the driver to your Father's dwelling.'

I did so, and the unexplained feeling of anguish swelled between my heart and stomach like a rising hysteria. I really thought I should have to ask leave to get down and vomit.

The familiar cottages slowly flowed by; from this coach, small though it was, they seemed mean and poor, which I doubt not they were: it simply had not occurred to me before that such was the case. The roof of the coach was above their eaves from which icicles hung; the street – alley or passage would be better words – wound round them and in and out amongst them, and was scarce wide enough for our small equipage. At least we were not thrown about anymore – most of the village is built on an outcrop of shaly, friable rock, thereby not occupying farmable land, and the paths are stony, not muddy and churned up by the animals or men who dwell there, or the ox carts that pass through.

We saw no-one; though doubtless we were seen. The cracks at the edges of the stuff that covered doors or window holes must have been filled with peeping eyes. I shrank back, not wishing to be recognised by any of the numerous acquaintance I had there. Even the dogs that lurched away from us up the side alleys into the mist I knew by name. At last we came to the Church and my Father's square stone cottage. How familiar, yet alien it looked to me, how dream-like the whole experience had become!

'This is it,' I croaked, and pulled myself in even further behind that strange woman's furs in a vain attempt to keep out of sight of the window of my Father's study, which was now three scant yards from the window of the landaulet and only a foot or so higher.

It happened. His gaunt face, beneath a white wool cap and above his black cassock, appeared behind the thick, distorting glass.

'Is that he?' she whispered.

I would not look any more for fear I should be seen, but acknowledged that it was.

Ghostly each must have seemed to each, like apparitions, separated by two panes, by my Lady's veil, by the mist, and by the years; they gazed at each other for an eternity, but not for so long that I could not hold back my breath for the whole span of our stay there, releasing it only when she called to the coachman to move on.

3

When we were clear of the village on our way back my Lady threw off her pensive mood and was soon in fine high spirits. First she remarked my pallor and my returning fit of teeth chattering, and drew me in closer to her, pulling the cloak up and around so it enclosed us both above as well as the rug did below, and then undoing all again to find a small flask in her reticule which she made me drink from – it was a fiery cordial flavoured I think with bitter cherries – and she had some too, and then tucked us in again all round.

'Zeppo,' she cried, when all was settled to her liking, 'this is a dull, forbidding sort of place, and I'm heartily glad it's not mine.'

I protested she had not seen it at its best; that in Summer, or at least in Spring, it was a pleasant enough little hamlet.

'Nay, Zeppo – is there company here, are there Assemblies, card-playing, beaux? Is there coming and going and intrigue? Are there *affaires* of great moment? Indeed is there anything toward at all?'

I said yes there was – at all events in Salamanca – and would have gone on to tell her of *romerías* and *corridas* in Summer, and balls and *tertulias* in Winter, but she was in no mood to listen, but rattled on for a time about Italy and especially Joseph the King of Naples, and the fine court he had there, and all the fine ladies, and

the opera, and I began a little to like her, for now she seemed to
be herself, a gay miss, if old enough to be my mother, with some
life and fun about her.

For a time she held my hand in hers, beneath the rug, and
pressed it hard against her, so I could feel the warm firmness of her
thigh, even through all the crisp and rustling silks she wore.

But then as the coach dropped down the hill-side towards the
River, and the poplars rose up through the fog and the shadows of
the Cathedrals beyond, a little of that first solemnity returned and
she heaved a deep sigh or two, and glancing up at her, for by now
my head was on her shoulder, I caught sight of a tear like that I
had surprised on her in the Lieutenant's office. And she fell to
asking me about my future and plans and learned of my studies
(on which I put a prettier gloss than they deserved) and my assured
(I then thought) if limited means.

At last she squeezed my hand, and withdrew her fingers, bringing them gloveless on to the rug in front of us.

'Come, Zeppo,' she said, 'we must soon part. God knows if we
shall ever meet again. I knew you well when you were little, and
your Father even better I dare say, and it's been something for me
to see you a grown lad, quite a man, though small, and to see that
crusty old fogey up there in his stony village, with all his dull old
books about him, and God knows I must forgive him. Aye, look
puzzled if you like, but I'll say no more. Now Zeppo, I'm going
to put you down here as I dare say you know your way back to
your lodgings. But first give me one kiss – for your Father's sake,
for old times' sake.'

I did as I was bid and offered to kiss her cheek but she put her
arms around me and kissed me firm upon the lips, which provoked a strange heat in me, and a yet more pleasant sensation of
comfort. Then she released me and took a ring from her finger.

'Here, Zeppo, take this. Now promise me not to go sell it for
trifles though it will buy a deal of them; nor use it to get out of a
gaming scrape at dice or cards; nor keep it unused and unviolable
for nothing is worth that sort of Jack-do-not-touch-me sanctity.

But keep it for a day when you really need it, to get out of the worst sort of business imaginable. And if such a time comes use it wisely, and when you're free and out of it, spare a thought for me. Now be off with you, for I feel a fit of the dumps coming upon me and I would not have you see me weep.'

I got down into the road and scarcely had I done so when the coachman whipped up the mules and the whole equipage, Hussars behind and all, clattered away at a brisker lick than it had achieved the whole time I was with her.

The ring had a large white stone, and at the first opportunity I tried it on a pane of glass, which it scratched, and so I concluded it was a true diamond.

Thus my Aunt. I own I was at first surprised at both her affection and her generosity; but later I reflected that a whore's life must be, in all respects but the most abjectly mundane, a miserable one; and that she must look back on the time spent in my Father's household with warmth and gratitude as a brief if golden period of virtue in an otherwise vicious life.

Chapter XIV

*The Wars Begin. After some Uncertainty as to whose side we
are on, we March off to Join Battle with the French.*

I

Three days later General Calvinet marched on into Portugal, news
having arrived that Marshal Junot and his army had fetched up safe
at Lisbon – the Regent of that country having fled to his Colonies
in the Americas.

The next five months, from December 1807 to April 1808,
were like the slow removal of vain decorations and worthless
ornaments from the façade of some monstrous Charnel House in
the way they revealed to our sorely abused nation the true Nature
of the Tyrant's strategy. First, King Carlos and Godoy signed a
cheating treaty at Fontainebleau which gave French troops the
right of passage over our land – and so their armies flooded in, but
not to pass through, rather to occupy the principal fortresses the
length and breadth. By February Pampeluna, San Sebastián, and
Barcelona were garrisoned by these so-called allies, and then
Valladolid, only four days' march from Salamanca. Soon, whipped
up by the priests and friars, the people began to murmur against
these intruders and the government that had let them in – pam-
phlets were published, broadsheets distributed all calling for the
abdication of the King in favour of *Fernando*, his son, who now
came to be known as the *Desired One*, and an armed resistance
came to be thought of.

In Salamanca a group of men engaged in Trade and the Higher
Kind of Commerce, with some from the Professions amongst
them, Don Jorge Martín and Don Lorenzo Zúñiga in the front,
put up the money to raise a Militia, and since it was Winter, and
there was little to do on the land, they soon had a fine Battalion of
Peasants at a Peseta a day, tricked out in an handsome uniform
designed by Doña Regina and Doña Elvira, and in this Militia
Rafael and I were Ensigns, and Fernando a Corporal. Under the
direction of a retired Captain called back to the Colours we drilled
on the *Campo* to the North of the Town, though most of the men
made do with broom-handles and staves, since muskets were in
short supply. The University too raised like militias recruited
mainly from those in minor vows, the Friars and the like, for all
the religious were hot against the French whom they knew to be
atheists and notorious closers of Convents.

Then in March we heard how a *Tumult* at *Aranjuez*, stirred up
by the many Grandees and Clergy who hated Godoy, had brought
about first the fall of that Minister and then of the King whose servant he was, and Fernando ruled in their stead. But hardly had we
cheered at this when news came that both Princes and their
Minister had been dragged off to Bayonne to attend the Emperor
there; that Madrid itself was now occupied by a French Army; and
finally that our brave Monarchs had signed away their birthrights
and that a new era was born with the accession of Joseph, that
erstwhile King of Naples my Aunt had talked of, the brother of
the Corsican.

For several days a dull confusion reigned in Salamanca, for
there were several there, including the Bishop, who had been
infected with French thought, and who welcomed a French rule,
while the Friars continued to preach insurrection and riot against
all liberals and atheists. But although there were some noise and
perhaps some blows at street corners and in the lower sort of
tavern, nothing else – until the fifth of May when a Friar who had
ridden pell-mell from Avila brought news-sheets and third-hand
reports of how the people of Madrid had risen on the second,

how they had dared the cannon's mouth and the whirling sabres of the troopers, and massacred the French Army of Occupation.

Now nought could restrain us. True we had no French soldiers to kill but we had what was better: the *Frenchifiers*, the traitors amongst us. Several hundred of the most public spirited gathered in the Great Square, animated by a desire to defend the honour of our Town and Country. A Friar began to preach, we gathered round, and soon his message became clear. Our Land had been betrayed by Liberals, Frenchifiers, Atheists, and Freemasons. They should be wrenched out like the foul weeds they were and cast upon the eternal bonfire, just as the Jews and Moors had been in the days of the Catholic Monarchs. Some Jews, he continued, had escaped then, had pretended to be good Catholics but had continued in secret their foul practices of crucifying baby girls and all manner of filth and obscenity, waiting till now to declare themselves, to bring in the Rule of Anti-Christ and Rationality. But Our Lady and Our Mother the Church had foreseen the danger and now was the time to destroy the Jews, the Frenchifiers and the Freemasons in our midst.

'How?' we shouted. 'Lead us, Father, tell us what to do.'

'Destroy the Anti-Christ,' he cried, 'destroy the Frenchifiers.'

'Destroy the Frenchifiers,' we echoed.

The most prominent Frenchifier in our midst was the Bishop, as above, but we found the narrow entrance to the square in front of his palace, opposite the old Cathedral, held by a company of regular infantry, whose Captain offered to fire on us if we did not go away.

Someone then remembered that the Abbot Marchena, who was so much a Frenchifier that he had gone to live in France rather than answer to the Inquisition some twenty years before, had a cousin, a candlemaker in the Street of Candlemakers, down by the old Church of San Benito, so off we went there, led by our Friar, a dark, fanatical sort of man with black hair and red face, though now there were only fifty of us.

When we reached the street no-one was sure which of the

several candlemakers was the one we were after, but soon a shutter was thrown open above a sign that read *José Luís Sánchez* and a round little man stuck his head out of the window.

'It's Juan Iglesias you want,' he shouted in a comically high-pitched voice and pointed to the shop at the other end of the row and on the other side. 'He has the contract to supply the Basilica from his cousin the canon, and his son married a Marchena six years ago.' By *Basilica* he meant the Old Cathedral.

We flocked down the Alley and our Friar hammered on the shuttered doors and windows of the Iglesias shop, and of course received no answer, whereat he appealed to us to help him break down the door. When this was done he plucked a torch from one of us and with the words *In Nomine Patris, Filii, et Spiritus Sancti* hurled it in. I had a brief glimpse of a room filled with candles, most hanging from the ceiling by their wicks, then several confusing things happened almost at once.

Straight way we were driven back by the heat and the cloud of foul noxious smoke as if a thousand candles had been snuffed at once, then a woman and child, a girl, appeared at a window on the first floor.

'Jump,' called some of us; 'Climb to the roof,' called others, while some just screamed at the horror of the poor woman's predicament. At that moment I heard three percussions, unmistakeably fire-arms, and a ball chipped the cornice above my head. To my astonishment what should I see coming through the smoke but the tall, fair figure of Rafael, in his Militia uniform, smoking pistol in one hand, drawn sword in the other, eyes dark with anger, and about ten of our men behind him.

'What can I do to help?' I cried, rushing over to stand by his side.

'Why, get this fire out, of course,' and with his men and ten or so of the mob whose retreat had been cut off by the smoke and flames he organised a chain of leather buckets between the well by the church and the shop. As soon as this was properly under way he entered the house next door, broke out on to the roof, and thence down to the woman and child whom he led back to safety. Soon the fire was damped down with little damage done except on the ground floor.

Rafael now told me to go home, put on my Ensign's uniform, and so to the Town Hall where I should learn of terrible doings in Madrid and would be told what to do to preserve our City from a tragic fate.

Well, to cut a long and confused tale short – this is how things stood. The Rising in Madrid had failed; the French Marshal Murad had his army intact after all and thousands of the citizens had been executed in a terrible proscription the day after the Tumult; consequently the Notable of our own Town, from the *Corregidor* down to the poorest shop-keeper, and of our University from the Master of the Schools to the Minor Beadle, were in mortal fear for their safety and the safety of their property – on the one side they feared the Mob, mostly students, and on the other the French troops at Valladolid who, they felt sure, would descend on us if we showed any sign of emulating the Madrileños, and so they were determined to restore order, to arrest preaching Friars, shoot arsonists, put sentries on the houses of Frenchifiers, close the University, disperse the students and so on. And all this they did in the name of the abdicated Kings who had issued a proclamation which said, amongst other things, 'all those who speak to you against France thirst for your blood; they are either the enemies of your nation or agents of England,' and went on to call for obedience and loyalty to our new Monarch, King Joseph the First.

Thus it was I started the day an *agent of England*, and ended it a *Frenchifier*, and wearing a uniform which had been given to me so that I might fight the French.

2

Things went differently in other cities. In Bádajoz, an important fortress to the South on the border with Portugal, the Mob dragged out the *Corregidor* and hanged him in the Square. He was a Frenchifier and Junot's man, protecting the rear of the French Army in Portugal. Similar incidents happened throughout May in Cartagena, Cádiz, Sevilla, Valencia, in fact in all the major towns not occupied by the French. Early in May Murad ordered Dupont to withdraw from Valladolid and fall back on Madrid – as soon as he had gone the students of that town rose and erected a gallows on the courtyard of the house of the Captain General of Castille – *Don Gregorio de la Cuesta*, and under its threat he promised them that he would raise an army and march upon the French. They would have served their cause better by hanging him, as will appear in due course.

And so it was that less than a fortnight after our Militia had been called out to defend the lives and properties of those who loved the French or feared them too much to fight them we were ordered to march to Valladolid and join this army the Captain General was raising.

But before we set out other events, more happy it seemed at that time, took place – namely the marriages at last of Rafael to Isabella and Violeta to Tebaldo which immediately followed on the news that Don Julio Sorrello had at last got leave to marry Angelica in Oviedo, and thus the stain on the honour of the Zúñiga family was removed. These nuptials were put in train with a sort of urgent swiftness which I was soon to recognise was a feature of these new times: in Peace the preparations would have lasted a month or so, the joint feasts of two families outdoing each other in friendly rivalry would have remained in the memories of guests numbered in hundreds for half a century; afterwards there would have been much splendour as of balls, *tertulias*, illuminations, new clothes and ribbons for all the connexions and servants, and I know not what, and perhaps even a course of Bulls paid for by the Lawyer and the Banker.

But Tebaldo was called to be with his regiment at Bádajoz by the end of the month and Rafael was to march with the Militia and so all was done in two or three days. Nevertheless it was a

happy occasion, the climax of which was the Nuptial Mass in the
Old Cathedral conducted by the Dean – the Bishop not venturing out of his palace at that time – and I carry in my mind a sort
of picture of the four of them in the porch of the Cathedral, lit by
the kind sun of May, as my last recollection of the happiness of
Peace though, by reason of the fact that both Grooms were in
their soldiers' uniforms, the shadow of Mars darkened the
Hymeneal Scene.

Here is my picture: first Rafael – tall, thin, and fair with wavy
hair cut long in the new fashion, with a smile of love playing on
his lips, but his pale brown eyes always a little solemn as he looked
down at Isabella on his arm. She, also a little solemn, looking up
at him, her wide-spaced eyes, darker than his, brilliant with an
unshed tear. Then her brother Tebaldo, the oldest of the four,
being turned twenty and already a Captain in the Army, a large-
boned man, a little fierce, but now laughing down at Violeta, the
smallest, youngest, liveliest of the quartet, with long brown hair
done up on her head with a mantilla, and huge eyes that always
seemed to promise some jest.

Thus the wedding of the best friend a man ever did have, and
afterwards there was a feast, and the poor came to the door to be
fed, and the gypsies filled the warm moonlit street with sound of
guitars and love songs till Dawn. I could write more of it all but
my heart is heavy at the thought of what came so soon after, and
besides, the Nuptials of Others are not part of my Tale.

Three days later, all doubts now resolved as to whose side we were
to fight on, I rode out on a mule of Don Jorge's with Rafael at my
side at the head of the Salamantine Militia, *en route* for Valladolid,
and my only care was that Isabella had secretly made me promise
that if aught mortal befell Rafael I should return with some last
token of her husband's love, as his wedding ring. I say I was at the
head of our Militia – but harvest time was not far off; indeed in
the hills the first hay was already being mown, and we had been
hard put to it to muster more than fifty of our two hundred: in

fact we were now one Captain, two Ensigns (Rafael and I), a Sergeant, and forty-eight men, including Corporal Fernando. This adjustment in our numbers had eased the problem of arms – only eighteen men were now without muskets, all had uniforms, and all had a spare pair of boots, though these last were mostly sold off cheap in the villages we passed through in exchange for wine, chickens and eggs. For this the men must not be blamed – our quarter-master had decamped the day before with the funds Don Lorenzo had given him to buy our rations withal.

Our Militia was not the only force in our column. The University had raised and equipped three hundred, mostly seminarists, and the line ended with three families of gypsies, another of muleteers, and some seven or eight of the ladies of the town, all of whom foresaw profit in the vicinity of the large army we were on our way to join. Thus I thought we were a fine sight as I turned at the top of the first hill on the road (San Cristóbal and this Down will figure again in my story) and looked back at the golden domes and towers that now seemed to nestle beneath us by the river, and my spirit lifted, not only at the sight of our little power but also because I felt myself at last to have an honourable calling – that of a soldier. A large bird of prey floated through the limpid element above us, and, not without difficulty for it was new, I drew my sword from its scabbard and directed it at that omen of good fortune to Conquerors and Emperors.

'I feel like *Alexander*,' I cried, 'at the head of his host marching through the Cilician Gates and on to the Plain of Orontes.'

'*Dios*,' said Rafael, 'sheath your weapon before you do yourself or your beast an injury. And if yon bird put you in mind of Alexander, I should have thought you to have known better since you brag always of your knowledge of birds. That is no eagle. 'Tis a vulture.'

'You can't be sure at that height.'

'When there are four or five, as there are if you look back there, you can be certain. Eagles hunt singly or in pairs.'

We rode on in silence for half a mile.

'Pepe,' he said at last, 'if we beat the French we shall be the first army in Europe to do so for half a century.'

'You sound like my Father,' I replied.

That worthy man had indeed taken a mournful view of my new occupation when I called to make my adieus. I found him drawing water from the well while Tía Teresa busied herself with pork cutlets in the cool kitchen behind him, and he had looked uncommonly hale: his cheeks pink with the peachy bloom some old people get if they are content and well-cared for, and the palsy in his hand so much improved as almost to be gone. So well was it under control that he claimed he could now play on his clavichord the full score of the most difficult of his Scarlatti Sonatas, which he had not done since his apoplexy. But his countenance clouded at my news.

'Ah well, Joseph,' he said, 'so be it. I have never gainsaid you in anything. Ah well. I suppose you may return but we cannot pretend to be sure of it.'

'Come, Sir,' I protested, 'this is surely idle talk. Not everyone who goes for a soldier dies of it.'

'Most do. Only the more fortunate return, but rarely whole. Most, like my own Father, leave at least a limb in the battlefield. Joseph, it's a very ugly, savage, brutish business. I lost my dear wife, as you know, when these tedious wars first started, and now I should much rather you stayed behind.'

'Oh Sir, enough. Pray give me your blessing and I will be gone.'

'I doubt my blessing will help you – but a good dinner cooked by Tía Teresa and some advice from me might.'

At dinner my Father ate two chops, drank a glass of wine, and finished up with a salad and a goat cheese. Tía Teresa looked on, her round shiny face, her strong bare arms akimbo, and I fancy she was possessed of some secret thought that delighted her as she watched my Father dine so well, though she said nothing.

I dined well too, of course, but the advice my Father offered when we were done seemed poor stuff – full of much fustian about how a good soldier keeps alive; how a good officer looks after his men and never risks them without necessity; how there is more honour in seeing them well-fed and well-shod than dying in the breach with them. At last he grew repetitive and tiresome, and when I left his last words were yet again: 'Survive, good Joseph, survive. A good soldier survives.'

Well, I did survive – seven or eight battles, three or four sieges, five campaigns, and perhaps my poor Father, were he still alive, would say I had been a good soldier; but I cannot find it in myself to claim that title. Perhaps Your Grace, if you ever read these memoirs to the end, will be able to settle the point, Your Grace being the greatest soldier of our age, perhaps of any age.

3

By nightfall on that first day I felt a shade less pleased with my new trade. The rest of the forenoon was hot, dry and dusty. At two o'clock we paused for dinner and after dinner the men determined on having a *siesta*. Our Captain stormed among them, lashing out with his cane, but all to no avail – in the end the Sergeant promised him an early start on the morrow if the men were allowed their *siesta*, and perforce he had to agree. At Castellano de Moriscos, the first village of any consequence, three men deserted: they had relations there and searching for them would have been a waste of time. In all that day we travelled scarce three leagues. If only we had continued in that leisurely fashion we would have missed a battle or two, which would have been no bad thing, but unfortunately the Sergeant was as good as his word and we were on the road by nine in the morning next day and most days thereafter. The consequence was we were at Valladolid by the End of May.

In and around that city extreme confusion reigned. The Army was bivouacked on a dry hot plain outside the city walls amidst fields of unripe corn, the cause of much trouble. The Commissariat seemed as ineffectual as our Quartermaster decamped: it might just as well not have been there; it followed that the men began to harvest the fields first on behalf of their cattle and even in extremity on their own behalfs where the corn was in ear; soon both men and beasts were swelled with the wind and many beasts died of it, so when we came to move just over a week later there were guns without mules, troopers without horses, and wagons without oxen. To say truth most of these animals had died of butchery, not flatulence: the grain was the pretext the men gave while they dined off fresh meat cooked on their bayonets in the white ash of their fires.

Every forenoon there was a parade or Review, and my first duty was to go amongst the ten or twelve men who were my special care and kick or cajole some life into the drunken stupor left from the night before; often there would be a girl or two amongst them who would spend an hour combing out their hair and alternately wheedling or scolding the while for more money than they had already procured or filched, not from the peasants in our ranks, who had none, but from the students. By ten o'clock, if I was lucky, I had my charges in place with the rest of our Militia, which was now attached to a regiment of Castilian Foot, more or less in uniform, the front file with muskets, the rear without, and the middle about half and half, with straps and belts freshly pipe-clayed, hair powdered and tied back, shakoes on straight. At this point our Captain General might, or might not, make his inspection.

Don Gregorio García de la Cuesta was in his sixties, nearly blind, very deaf, and three parts mad, one part senile. One did not have to serve under him to come to these conclusions – merely to see him was enough; however, service invariably provided proof infallible of the judgement.

Dressed in a dazzling uniform covered in as many stars, ribbons and bows as King Carlos himself and with a huge cocked hat whose ends fell below his shoulders, he rode past us on a mule supported on either side by *Aides-de-Camp* who steadied him when he looked ready to fall off. Occasionally he would manage to shift his hat in answer to the *huzzas*, perfunctorily given, that rose up as he passed each regiment, and then he revealed untidy white hair, a grey complexion, arched brows, a long nose with a bump at the end, and a mouth whose bottom lip drooped help-lessly but whose top lip curled with a grandee's disdain. He never took advice, listened to intelligence, allowed for the strength of his enemy, or the lie of the land; such was his arrogance. His ability in martial arts was limited to two points: he knew how to march his men towards the enemy; then he would bid them stand still to be killed. Had they obeyed him in the last as well as they did in the first he would have been done for soon enough – however, most of them usually ran and lived to fight under his command another day.

After the morning parade we practised drill and manoeuvres for so long as the men would tolerate such a tiresome matter: no two regiments followed the same system of orders and everything went awry; companies would march into each other or split up into two halves heading away from each other; when they were asked to deploy from column of march into open column of companies, chaos would reign for twenty minutes or more before all were properly dressed and facing the same way. The dust rose thicker, tempers were lost, and such is the native pride of the Iberian Peasant it only needed one Ensign to strike a man with his cane for a whole regiment to leave the field and return to bivouac where they would sulk until their Sergeants could assure them that an apology had been made. But if the cooking pots had begun to simmer, the joints of mule flesh to brown over the fires, then not an apology from San Pedro himself would have brought them back.

The after dinner times and evenings passed pleasantly enough; the army took its *siesta*, its officers played dice and smoked. In the cool of the evening we would apply for *furlough* to go into Valladolid where the townspeople of the better sort were glad to receive us: picnics were arranged, *tertulias*, balls, all was *fiesta*, and more than one of us was captivated for a time by the dark and sparkling eyes of the burghers' daughters peeping shyly but with admiration from behind their fluttering fans. Rafael of course rarely came on these jaunts – he remained in camp and penned endless epistles to patient Isabella.

Indeed such was the entertainment and flattery we received that we almost believed ourselves heroes when at nightfall and slightly tipsy we picked our way back to our lines past glowing camp-fires where fresh meat once more hissed and spat, and the large-eyed, gap-toothed, dusky peasants who passed for soldiers, sent the wineskins round, guitars tinkled, and the Ladies of the Camp spun their skirts and sent the dust swirling over their bare feet to the staccato clapping of their gypsy *Pandars*.

CHAPTER XV

My First Experience of Battle; in which my Resolution to
Stay Alive does not Fail.

I

On the first of June we celebrated a victory. According to the Orders of the Day published over Don Gregorio's signature the presence of a large and well-equipped army at Valladolid had caused the precipitous withdrawal of units of the French Army numerically superior to ours to lines North of Madrid, towards Rioja and Santander, which town was held by patriots who would doubtless destroy the retreating invader as soon as he arrived. We were promised the honour of being the first troops to re-enter Madrid and this before the end of the month, though it was not expected we should have to fight for it. When our numbers were complete – reinforcements from Estremadura were assembling at Ciudad Rodrigo to the South of Salamanca where there was already a regiment of Lancers – we would move East and Murad would retire in confusion before us.

However there were French troops much nearer than any of these places – namely in Burgos twenty or so leagues to the North-East, and these, instead of retiring towards France as quickly as they could, embarked on a terrible swift advance at us on the fifth of June, and this despite the fact that they numbered scarce four thousand, while we, as far as anyone could be sure of anything at all, were at least ten thousand. Our Leader saw no reason to panic. He expected the French to be halted at the walled village of Torquemada where four hundred peasants armed with blunderbusses and fowling pieces stood behind upturned ox carts; there were, moreover, four thousand patriots in Palencia. Consequently our preparations went ahead with careful deliberation, without undue haste, and indeed without any real expectation that an encounter would take place at all.

On the sixth of June Lassalle stormed Torquemada, massacred the defenders, and allowed his men a brief carousal during which all the women were ravished several times over and many of the children butchered. Finally the village was fired. These crimes against humanity produced a profound effect on the good people of Palencia who expelled their General by the servant's door while sending their Bishop to the front entrance to answer when the Frenchman knocked, which he duly did next day. The church bells were rung, the people cheered, and scarce a hair on their heads was hurt. The French were now less than a day's march away and we were still in bivouac.

However, our General now decided that the French had advanced enough and to call a halt to them he ordered all those units of his army that were properly equipped to go out to the town of *Cabezón*, some three leagues distant and to the right of the Invader's line of march. Now it had been a matter of Salamantine pride that our Militia should always present an immaculate front of muskets at morning parade and so it was presumed we could be numbered amongst those in a fit state to fight. With a couple of thousand others we marched off, with two muskets to every three men, and ten rounds of cartridge to each musket. Near us in the column were five hundred students from the Valladolid seminaries who sang patriotic songs and songs in honour of Our Lady which put heart into our half century of *charro* peasants.

By an extraordinary and uncharacteristic feat of good judgement Don Gregorio had nominated a spot which it was possible for us to reach in advance of the French, but it was a near run thing. Cabezón is a small village whose cottages cling to the steep sides of a skull or head shaped hill – hence the name which Englished means *big-head*. This hill is almost circled by a river, the *Pisuerga*, which is spanned by a Roman bridge of fifteen arches. Now, with the bridge covered by cannon, two thousand men behind the river and in the houses could have held this position for several days against forces two, three times as strong. At the same time such a substantial force on the flank or across the supply lines could not be ignored; and thus our Militia Captain expounded the position to us when we came in sight of the village, and he seemed to cheer up. Truly, he surmised, we would halt the French advance and without heroism or sacrifice on our part.

He grew glum again when we were ordered to cross the bridge and take up a position on the North bank of the river with the river between us and the village, and with the enemy, when he should appear, with a long slope in his favour, at our front. It was about three in the afternoon when we reached this station, and our men promptly unpacked their cooking gear and sat down to dine off what they had brought with them. A ten mile walk in the morning sun does much for the appetite.

Indeed, to the unpractised eye the scene was attractive. In front of us and to our right two squadrons of the Queen's Light Dragoons, the most professional elements in our battle, trotted and wheeled through the corn carrying out with parade ground care the manoeuvre their drill books described as *Providing a Screen for an Army Assembling on the Field*. They looked splendid and the sun flashed from their helmets and their accoutrements and the steady jingle of their harness took the edge off our uneasiness.

At about six of the clock in the evening there was a sudden flurry and commotion in their midst; some broke line, all fell back a furlong towards us. A young Subaltern came back at full gallop heading for General Head Quarters at the bridge. Dust rose beyond the crest above us and a distant bugle sounded. The French had arrived. With hearts racing we stood to arms and beat our drums; and, with many an anxious glance at the river behind us, and at the road curving back to Valladolid down which we hourly expected reinforcements, we awaited the assault.

It did not come. It did not come that evening nor that night, nor the next day, a Saturday. At night the fires of the enemy twinkled along the low crest ahead of us, at day we could see the thin columns of blue smoke ascending into the deeper blue of the Empyrean, and hear their bugles, and even the squeak and rumble of their train. At noon a message came from their General to ours under flag of truce. We saw the party go by at fast trot. Their horses were larger than ours, their officer in spite of the plainness of his gear smarter than ours, and his file of Dragoons – moustached, stern-faced, bronzed – well, simply they looked like soldiers. Their offer of honourable terms to a force they saw to be trapped was haughtily rejected, and in the afternoon a thousand more men from Valladolid crossed the bridge with seven pieces of cannon, and sat down beside us.

Still no attack. Perhaps Lassalle could not credit that our General was putting more and more troops into an impossible position and suspected a trick. It was the only time I know of when a Frenchman paused in front of Don Gregorio – excepting when he had the British Army alongside him at Talavera. After Cabezón they came on at him as soon as he stood still long enough for them to do so.

The second night their camp-fires were more numerous and their forward pickets so close we could hear laughter, the rattle of equipment, a burst or two of song, and in that hot darkness I was moved to recall the first French Army we ever saw down under the poplars at the Santa Marta Ford, and brought the occasion up with Fernando who was wrapped in his blanket nearby.

'Do you remember how they rode by us, and we marched along with them?' I asked. 'How they paraded and sang their National Hymn? And took us into town astride their cannon?'

But he was in a dull mood, and would only remark it would be a foolish man who'd pick a quarrel with such soldiers as we saw that day, and added laconically, 'To every pig its San Martín, eh Pepe? and I fear for us St Martin's Day is here.' St Martin's Day being the day in November when the country pigs are killed after fattening on the acorns. So I fell silent again like most of those around me and listened to the monotonous croaking of the frogs in the reeds. The moon silvered the shallow pools and the hill behind looked more like a skull than ever. It was a sad place after the camp at Valladolid – there were no gypsies here, no dancing girls, no smell of freshly roasted meat. The loneliness of fear had settled over us and each man communed with his own soul since none could find a word which would put spirit in his neighbour.

A summer dawn, by a river, with trees, is a lovely thing. There is mist and freshness. The frogs at last are quiet, birds sing, a stork rows by above the poplars. This dawn was of that sort, the dawn of Sunday the Tenth of June, and Friars went amongst us and many of us took the Sacrament.

We discovered our Militia Captain had gone. Rafael and I whispered this over and then put it out to the men that he had been promoted to the General's staff – Rafael was to be Captain in his stead. The men did not seem to care. Perhaps they already doubted the usefulness of officers.

2

But still the long morning wore on, losing its dewy freshness and thickening into a sultry noon; and nothing happened. Ahead of us, amongst the scattered pines and oaks that lay beyond the nodding corn, the hundred spirals of blue smoke drifted up again as the French got out their cook-pots and settled no doubt to a hearty meal. Amongst us some porters from Valladolid came with bags of dry weevily biscuit some merchant had sold off dear to the army and a wine-cart with an allowance of half a tepid canister for each man.

Shortly after noon our vigil was enlivened by a sight scarcely to be credited. Round the side of the skull-like hill, down the track from Valladolid, and on to the further bank of the river came a stately procession of carriages and landaus, coaches and *barrochios*, perhaps thirty in all, drawn by glossy mules, with gay gallants as outriders and servants on asses in attendance, all bright with parasols and shawls, mantillas and high hats: a *romería* no less, just like that we *Salamantinos* make in May, and all the well-to-do of Valladolid were there to take their dinner *al fresco* and watch us beat the French.

Don Gregorio was led back across the bridge to greet the first coach. From where we were we could see him doff his huge hat and it was not difficult to guess the matter of what he said, for now this convoy of all that was noble and fair in that country halted, the men dismounted, the ladies were handed down, the mules turned loose to graze or brought to the river's edge for water, rugs were spread and the sun glittered on glass, silver, fine napery. Our General had assured these good people a fine afternoon's entertainment for shortly, he must have said, he would march his men up the slope and drive the French from the field.

At half-past one a single cannon shot, only a four pounder, cracked on the ridge above us. Before its puff-ball of white smoke had dispersed in the limpid sky, the cannonade it heralded began.

There seem to be current at this time two modes which are thought proper to be used when describing the tumultuous collision of contending armies, and I am a little at a loss as to which I should employ in these memoirs of mine. Following the example of the History of the Late Wars I have in front of me I could make a dry and practical discourse of it – list the elements of the contending powers; the names and degrees of the Commanders; and report with cool objectification the several movements and manoeuvres of the different brigades, corps, or divisions; concluding with an assessment or totting up of accounts, *viz.* – numbers dead, wounded, missing, taken prisoner on both sides, according to which arithmetic the palm or Victor's Laurels are awarded.

For example: at Cabezón the French cannonaded the Spanish, sabred them with cavalry, and drove the remnant from the field with infantry charging in columns. Five hundred students made a gallant stand, were all slaughtered, but behind them the Spanish General was able to make his escape. The French lost twenty-two men including two officers; no account was kept of Spanish losses, but since none remained alive on the field at the end of the affair we may safely award the crown to the French.

Thus the cool or English mode. The other or French mode is the *heroic* – full of the roar and smoke of battle, the flash of guns and steel, the cheers of the Victors, the despairing cries of the Vanquished, the whole spiced by one or two modestly told instances of valour on the part of the Narrator if he happened to be present.

Myself, I never acted once, in all the battles, sieges, skirmishes I witnessed in the coming years, and least of all in this my first engagement, with anything but the most abject cowardice; to which fact I ascribe my continuing presence on this Earth. It is patent therefore that the second mode is not for me. And since the first mode depends upon knowing after the event exactly what happened, and at the time I was totally at a loss about it all, I must bodge up a third mode all of my own. Thus . . .

Almost the first ball the Frenchmen fired took off the head of the soldier next to me and, after plashing his brains about my tunic, passed through the shoulder of the man behind, doing it no good at all, and ended in the stomach of a third. All three died, but only the headless man died quick; he remained upright for a count of five while his still beating heart fountained gobbets of blood out of the mess where his head had been, and then he fell over. The other two soon joined him on the ground but screamed lustily since their power of speech had not been so drastically reduced as their silent friend's.

The second shot I knew aught of fell short, almost in front of Rafael, and sent a shower of gravelly soil into his face, before bounding over his head and into the men behind him. He staggered about, calling for help, with his hands over his eyes and nose and blood issuing between his fingers. It seemed idle to stay where I was, the river was only fifty yards or so to the rear, and I soon found myself a comfortable *niche* in a bed of reeds well protected by the bank above, which I managed to keep to myself in spite of the efforts of several of my men to wrest it from me. My drawn sword and pistol no doubt convinced them that they should look elsewhere for shelter. However the claims of Ancient Friendship are not to be denied and when Fernando appeared some moments later, leading the blinded Rafael, I made room for them both.

At last the cannonade ceased — I say at last but I doubt its duration was more than five minutes — and in the comparative stillness the screams of our wounded were pitiful to hear, especially those of the soldier whose stomach had become the last resting place of an eight pound shot. His guts were spread about him like those of a well-gored *Picador's* horse, and occasionally he left off screaming to examine them with a sort of sad wonder. One or two of the braver of our men now ventured back out on to the plain to bring in these wounded, an ill-judged move for the earth began to shake again — not with the thunder of the guns but with the hooves of five hundred or so sabres who came amongst us. I stayed long enough to see one poor fellow sliced obliquely from the point where his neck joined his shoulder to a place somewhere near his navel, at which I set out to cross the river; nor did I allow the efforts of those around me to do the same to impede my progress. Indeed, although I had to wade thigh deep through muddy water and twice as I recalled fell into it, although I was often pushed and shoved from behind, I was one of the first to reach the furthest shore. Admittedly I was no longer encumbered with my sword and pistols, and many of my rivals in this race not only obstinately clung to their weapons but, being common soldiers, also had knapsacks and so forth as well.

Now another foe had to be faced – the picnickers of Valladolid.
Old men with sticks and pretty girls with parasols poked at us and
even beat us about the shoulders and tried to shoo us back as if we
were a flock of geese that had strayed into the wrong field – no
doubt we were muddying up their fine clothes and table linen,
perhaps even in a few cases bleeding on them – however, not even
the scorn of the fair could have made me recross that river to
where giants on horseback were now spurring down into the
reed beds we had left, trampling with iron hooves and smashing
with their sabres all who remained.

I then cast about to see if I could not borrow a mule or ass from
amongst the carriages, but quickly saw that a mount would not
serve where I was. By now even the picnickers had realised that
they were in some danger and were making efforts to get themselves off – but the road, with river on one side and hill on the
other, was narrow, and up near the end of the line a coach had
spilled and all was jammed up so none could move. It was obvious
to me that I must place this congelation of beasts, carriages, old
men, and girls between me and the French, before seeking a
mount, and to this end I scrambled along, sometimes in the river,
sometimes out, until I could see the road clear ahead of me.

About now I heard the second most fearful noise I know on
earth – the drub-a-drub-drubbing of the drums of a French
Infantry Corps at a *pas-de-charge*, but I did not turn to look. (The
most fearful noise of all is the continuous rolling volley of a line of
English muskets, but many a month was to pass before I heard
that.) Casting about I discovered a good strong mule that had no
doubt got loose when its carriage tipped, and was now quietly
nibbling at a bush of broom or gorse by the roadside; with my
spirits much restored at this sight I climbed up on the road and ran
towards the beast.

I had scarce secured its broken trace in my hand when an ostler,
from his livery, who was struggling to get the three mules that
went with mine back between the poles of his master's chariot
with a view to getting all out of the ditch where it was stuck,

espied me and came at me with his long muleteer's whip. How bitterly I now regretted that I had cast away my weapons. I was on the very point of surrendering the beast when, miraculously it seemed, the situation was redeemed. A pistol went off, so close to my ear I could hear the report above the noise of battle, and the ball took away the jaw of the ostler who was so grieved at this loss that he gave up all interest in his mule.

Looking behind me I discovered none other than the faithful Fernando, with poor Rafael on his arm and a smoking weapon in his free hand. I put Rafael on the mule, mounted behind him, looked round to be sure Fernando was following, and discovered the silly fellow at the side of the ostler whose smashed up face he was trying to dress with the pink sash from round his waist.

'I did not mean to hit him,' the good man kept crying, 'I did not mean the pistol to go off. I only meant to frighten him,' but he allowed himself to be pulled away when I showed him that the owner of the carriage, a bald-pated old fool who had lost his wig in the upset, was coming at us with his sword, a short dress rapier, more gilded ornament than weapon, but a real sharp for all that.

And so off I spurred, up the almost clear road ahead, and Fernando jogged along behind holding the mule's tail, and Rafael clutched the beast's big ears.

We got clear away by these means; the French were held up first by the gallant five hundred seminarists who kept the bridge in true *Spartan* or *Horatian* style, and then by the picnickers who blocked their way and provided irresistible opportunity for plunder and rape.

The wonder is we did not come across Don Gregorio García de la Cuesta – for he got off in much the same fashion as us.

3

After we had gone a mile or so I became aware that Fernando wanted to stop, and thinking the poor man was blown I managed to slow the mule's trot to a walk, but it transpired that he wanted to get Rafael down so he could bathe and soothe our friend's face.

This was indeed a pitiful sight – a mask of drying blood and mud, pitted with scarlet craters, and no certain feature in it save his mouth which, though bruised and split and with teeth broken, was still able to emit strange wordless groans and cries. He did not seem to be losing much blood save from the corner of his left eye socket – the eye itself was gone – where a tiny pulse continued to pump a slow flow of the Sanguinary Fluid. I glanced back down the road, and though there was still no sign of pursuit it seemed to me our friend was in greater danger from the sabres of the French than from lack of a dressing.

'First, good Fernando,' I said, 'let us be sure we have escaped, that we have conducted him to a safe place. Then let us tend his wounds.'

'Just as you say, Pepe. By all means let us find safety.'

We continued down the track for a league or so without further incident and reached the Great Road that links Burgos and Valladolid. Fernando was now leading the mule and without pausing he took the left turn for the latter town.

'But it is the way to Salamanca,' he insisted, when I remonstrated. 'Surely, Pepe, we may now go home, may we not?'

'Indeed we may, you wooden head, and perhaps borrow a carriage for Rafael from the French, who will, I make no doubt, be knocking on the gates of Valladolid long before we get there.'

'Mother of God,' he cried, 'you're right. Better to go alone than in bad company, as they say. Which way shall we go then?'

I thought.

'This road we are on continues as a track across the *campo* to the North-West, does it not? That were the best direction I am sure, for North-East to Burgos and South-West to Valladolid there will be the French, and we know they are behind us.'

Thus we hit upon the direction taken by the five thousand or so of our troops who had not reached Cabezón in time to be butchered, and who had been ordered to retreat upon *Medina le Rioseca* which lay to the North-West, but of course by the main road, so at that time we did not see them.

As evening fell we came to a village. Here the Priest, on seeing Rafael's face, called out the Barber, who found in his stock soothing unguents which he smeared over our poor friend's wounds, then bound all up in a long white bandage leaving nothing uncovered save the hole that was his mouth. While he was thus employed we entertained the priest and other Notables of the village with an account of the day's doings at Cabezón, and in this we were ill-advised; we had hoped for food and shelter; for which when we asked they withdrew a space from us and consulted solemnly together. At length they all nodded and the priest came forward as spokesman.

'Honoured Sirs,' he said, 'you must be gone and God speed you on your way. Forgive us, but we are a poor village and defenceless, and we do not think it right the French should find us harbouring their foes; however, we trust you will accept this sausage and some wine, which will sustain you on your way.'

I was for refusing food so churlishly offered, but Fernando took it up and later I must say I had my share, though it was from the hands of knaves and cowards.

By now it was time to be off, for a couple of stout staves and even a blunderbuss were to be seen amongst those kind people, and the faces of those that held them showed a determination to use them, if need be.

It was almost dark when we left this village and for a time I walked in front of the mule, giving Fernando my place behind Rafael. No doubt we were a strange sight in the dreamy unreality of the twilight, following the track across the *campo* through grain shoulder high, while a near full moon rose orange behind us and the little owls swooped round, and in our midst Rafael with the featureless white disc on his bandaged head. At all events three labourers coming out of the fields dropped rakes and sickles and scurried away through the wheat, blessing themselves and calling upon Our Lady to deliver them from the figure of Death who had come among them on a mule.

A short time later we bivouacked beneath the moon and stars, supped off the sausage and wine, and slept with Rafael propped up between us against a rock, sure that his appearance would frighten off the bravest of footpads or highwaymen.

Chapter XVI

We Suffer a Grievous Loss.

I

Early in the forenoon of the following day we reached the carriage road that joins León to Valladolid, and straightway saw signs that a host had passed not long before us as – an ass, starved, galled, and dead, already food for crows and magpies; an occasional litter of discarded baggage, worn-out boots and the like; an abandoned wagon with a broken wheel; and overhead the vultures soared, but Rafael could not now see them to name them.

Ahead of us at the top of a long and gentle incline two men hobbled together like a pair in a three-legged race such as we have in villages at *fiesta*; as we drew closer we could see both were lame and helped each other along. They were soldiers, and they paused to let us come up with them.

'Ah Masters,' cried one, a thin evil-looking wretch, 'stay with us, for left to ourselves the French will surely catch us.'

I asked them who they were and how far ahead they reckoned the main body of the Army to be, and what news they had.

'Your honour,' said the second, who looked even more villainous than his comrade, 'we are of the Fifth Estremaduran Foot and the Army will be no more than a league off though they are going as fast as they are able. They say the French cavalry are coming and we'll all be sabred if we fail to make as much speed as we can. Yesterday we marched East and heard the noise of a battle, then came officers on horses in a lather and right about we faced and have marched North and West ever since, as fast as may be until the sole of my shoe came off.'

The first one now spoke again and his voice took on a sort of gypsy whine. 'Your Worships have a fine mule there: surely we can take turns on him and thus we'll catch the army again and be safe.'

'My friend here is hurt and needs attention,' I replied, and set the mule, which I was then leading, into a brisk trot, Fernando kicked at his flanks, and Rafael swayed back and forth clutching at the mane, but hardly had we gone ten yards before a pistol popped off behind us and a ball whistled over our heads.

'Run faster, Pepe,' cried Fernando, 'those sons of whores are ready to kill us for our mule.'

I took a glance behind and saw the thin villain levelling a second pistol at Fernando's broad back. Quick as thought I jerked the mule's head to the side and thus upset his aim. The second ball followed the first and did no harm, though but for my prompt action, which had tumbled me into the ditch, it was like to have taken the top of Fernando's head off.

'Get out of the ditch,' Fernando shouted, 'you will be safer from the rogues running with us, for they are lame, than lying there waiting for them to reload.'

Cursing his stupidity – for it seemed he thought my fall had arisen from a desire to save myself – I picked myself up and together we went pell-mell up and over the crest of the hill.

Now the road led down and away ahead of us, straight across an enormous, flat and featureless plain filled with ripening corn until it disappeared in a barren range of hills beyond; in the midst of this panorama was a great cloud of dust and from it we could hear, though the nearest edge was still a league or more away, the hum or buzz that is the commixture of all the noises of a great host on the march. Cheered by this sight, which spelled some sort of safety, we hurried eagerly on, reaching the end of the column a little after noon after passing many more stragglers and more than one carcase for the birds.

There were no further attempts to rob us of our mule, but a Captain of Artillery took it from us as soon as we came up with his battery, for one of his guns was pulled by ten men and a donkey, and the men were for cutting the traces and leaving it.

This was a bad business for Rafael who now had to walk for a time, and it may be that this added strain on top of all his other afflictions brought on a fever whose heat promoted the putrefaction of his face.

2

At about two o'clock the army paused for an half hour, and the men near us began to look about their persons and their baggage for odd scraps of food or potable liquor: alas, there was little enough of either, and no sign of any commissariat to supply our wants. Good Fernando now discovered a little of the sausage secreted in his pocket and half an onion and the two of us dined off that. Even then a poor soul near us begged for a mouthful which Fernando, against my counsel, gave him.

We did not know what to do for Rafael. It was clear he had lost the power of speech – through the gap in the bandage only gurgles, croaks, and groans came forth which neither of us could interpret. Moreover when I placed my ear close to his mouth I could not but be conscious of a most sickening and putrid breath about the orifice not overlayed but mixed with the aromatic odours of the barber's ointments.

'He must need water,' Fernando suggested, 'it cannot be but he wants water.' Then he raised his voice putting his lips to where he judged our friend's ear to be. 'Rafael, sir, if you want water raise your right hand.'

And this Rafael did, feebly but plainly.

Fernando had to buy water – tepid, stagnant stuff – of a

Sergeant who had a full canteen. A peseta for half a cupful he charged and Rafael wasted most of it, for it dribbled back out of his mouth bringing with it a yellow slime streaked with blood.

'Water and patience remove all griefs,' said Fernando, and tried again. This time Rafael kept some down.

The halt was soon over – no-one had the means for a proper repast and all still feared the French cavalry too much to take *siesta*, though the heat of the day and the dryness of the land were almost unbearable. Not a bird sang, nothing moved at all over the great calm sea of blue-green corn, only vultures and kites kept up their effortless cruise above us. Fernando and I supported Rafael between us, his arms slung round our shoulders our arms linked round his waist, which was awkward and clumsy on account of the disparity in our sizes, so his monstrous head lolled and his feet dragged.

'Look at this,' a fool nearby cried out, 'here's a *paso* for Holy Week – Christ between two thieves,' and this brought such laughter from the others around that Fernando, who liked not blasphemy, cursed them, at which the original wag remarked that doubtless the round large one was the unrepentant thief, while the small stunted one, meaning me, would go to Heaven. Others now took up the sport for a while and said they were the Penitents in the procession – for they had no shoes and carried crosses, by which they meant their muskets – and their friends offered to whip them like the flagellants, but no, came the reply, we have certain *Ultrapirineos* engaged for that task, if only they would keep the engagement they had made. But it was too hot and dry to keep up this sort of bantering for long.

Towards the evening there was another halt and officers on mules and horses came up from behind, pushing us over and to one side into the corn so a heavy carriage could get by, and in this carriage was none other than Don Gregorio himself, who had taken so long to track down the whereabouts of the Army he was meant to command. I confess my heart sank to see him again, though those about us, who had not been at Cabezón, were cheered at his presence, saying that now surely we would be safe, and like to beat the French as well.

When night fell we bivouacked and Fernando sought out a Surgeon Major and, persuading him to leave his table, brought him to Rafael, at which the Surgeon became angry.

'Why, this man's wounds have been dressed already,' he cried. 'I had supposed him still to be bleeding.'

'But Sir,' Fernando pleaded, 'can you not see he is ill, perhaps mortally, and in much pain and distress?'

'To be sure he may be, and it is not my art to prevent it if he is. A surgeon can stop bleeding by dressings and amputation; he can remove a ball by aid of probes and set a broken limb; but thereafter Nature is the Physician, not Science. If God wills, your master will get better: I have known many a man wounded in battle to make a fair recovery,' and with that, no matter how we pleaded, he was done and went back to his supper which looked, Fernando said who had seen it, much better than ours was like to be.

3

Through the night Rafael's distress waxed more and more pitiful. At times he tossed his huge white globe of a head back and forth and clawed at it with his hands until we had to restrain him for fear he would loosen the bandages. This tossing of the head put me in mind of a fretful bull who sought to dislodge the barbs of the *banderillas*. At other times he seemed to utter soundless screams dragged from the bottom of his heaving chest, but such was his affliction only hoarse exhalations emerged and not much noise. The stench upon these exhalations made them yet more difficult for us to bear. On one occasion when both Fernando and I had fallen into a doze he stumbled away from us over the recumbent forms of our neighbours, fell, and woke one of them who gave out a horrid scream of fear at the deathly figure on all fours above him. This brought us back to wakefulness and a more careful watch on our charge.

In the first grey light of dawn the Sergeant who had sold us the water the day before discovered us.

'Your Worships,' he said, 'you'll have to do something about him,' and he gestured at our friend. 'It's unsettling the men; they'll not stay together with him around. There's the smell, then his grunts and groans, and then his appearance which would frighten off the Devil himself.'

He was a large fellow with bushy orange whiskers and he carried, besides his Sergeant's small club, a brace of pistols stuck in the red cummerbund that swathed his stout waist.

'Where is there to go?' asked Fernando. 'Anywhere else in the army the same objections will be brought.'

'That's your affair,' the oaf replied, 'my only concern is this file in my charge, and they want yon *Cabezudo* elsewhere,' using the word for a Carnival Big Head. 'You must be off, I say.'

Fernando turned to me: 'We could leave the Army and search out a village until his face is healed.'

'And be sabred by the scouting French?' I objected, 'or hanged for desertion by our own people?'

'What then?' cried Fernando, in despair.

'Put a bullet through his monstrous head,' said the Sergeant, 'and end the poor fellow's miseries.'

The white globe of bandages seemed to nod in grateful accord, but this could have been illusion.

We stood there, nonplussed, and the Dawn spread like a stain over the waking host. Camp fires were lit or stirred to life, a faint cheer arose some way off where a water cart appeared and some porters with biscuit too. The Planet of Morning glowed above the hills and high above us a pale streak of cloud took fire like molten gold as it caught the beams of the sun not yet risen. A bugle called, an ass brayed, a cock crew: at this last someone nearby muttered he would give a lot to get his hands upon the bird.

The stench of putrescence was suddenly unbearable. Peering over the muffled folds of our cloaks, which we thrust into our

mouths and over our nostrils, we gazed again with horror at our
friend.

Rafael was sitting where we had left him, propped against the
wheel of a cart, and had unbound the bandage and was now tearing at the pad of lint beneath.

Fernando caught at his wrists and called for me to help, but
before I could overcome the nausea that rose in me at the fumes
Rafael had managed with one last burst of expiring strength to
place his knee in Fernando's stomach and heave him over and on
to his back. And in the second of freedom he'd won he pulled off
the remaining gauzes which came together in a lump the size of a
plate.

The flesh on his face came with it, like the mask that represents
Vanity in some old devout pictures I have seen, leaving a mess of
pus, blood, sinew, and white bone. One eye remained, lidless
now, and clouded like that in the head of a sheep newly flayed. He
croaked three words – the only distinct ones we had heard since he
received his wound – 'Isabella, my Heart,' and then he fell back
just as Fernando recovered enough to catch him.

'He's dead,' said the Sergeant. 'And it must be for the best that
he is.'

He went off but was back soon with two long-handled spades.
'You'd best bury him. You'll not want to leave him as he is, and for
sure you can't take him any further.'

The sun was hot on our backs before we'd scraped a trench deep
enough in the dry stony earth, and the army was already on the
move. Around us bugles called, drums beat, and Sergeants bellowed,
but all was lost on me as we laboured. Instead of the squeal of carts
I heard the flutes and violins in the Zúñiga house when Rafael
danced with Isabella on his arm, and the bugles were the cornets of
the fiesta announcing the turn of the *banderillas* in the Plaza. When
the General Staff rode by with mad old Cuesta in their midst the
clop, clop of hooves put me in mind of *romerías* and picnics beneath
the poplars of the Tormes or the oaks of our country.

I picked up his feet, and Fernando slid his hands beneath his shoulders, and a thousand seething flies rose from the head of our friend as we lowered him in. Fernando then went for a Priest or Friar, but in all that host could find none, or none at least that would risk being left behind by the Army. Meanwhile I performed the service enjoined on me by Isabella and slid off his ring; then, hoping thereby to discourage pillaging of the shallow grave, took his other valuables too.

Fernando returned with a handful of blue cornflowers, daisies, and poppies that had somehow survived the presence of so many men and animals; by the time we had filled in the trench they had wilted, but we left them there, poor signatories of a good man's grave.

CHAPTER XVII

*A Long Chapter including – A Lucky Escape from Certain
Death; A Piece of Modern Music, most Affecting; and News
of a General not like Those Met Before.*

I

I find it a tedious and even a nauseating business recording the history of the rest of that campaign. Your Grace, a year later, had cause to curse the arrogant stupidity of our General when Your Worship sat down beside him at *Talavera*, and I make no doubt you will excuse a brisk summary of the events that followed Rafael's demise, especially as they have no great bearing on the matter of how I came to be what I am, which is the purpose of these Memoirs.

The Army moved on to *Medina de Rioseco*, where, our purses being replenished by a small fund of gold coin I had found in Rafael's pockets, put there against a time he might need it by his poor wife, already a widow, and with my assurance to Fernando we would make full restitution on our return, we managed to buy meat and a skinful of wine from certain provisioners who came into the camp. The meat was old dried out stuff and we gave most of it to our hungry companions, but the wine was good and rich from Nava del Rey some miles to the South, and it restored our spirits as much as could be expected after the loss we had suffered.

Rafael's store of gold was far from exhausted and next day I put half of what remained to yet more profitable use when we came upon a Militia of Volunteers from Béjar, a town in our own

Province of Salamanca, whose Colonel was happy to sell me a commission as Ensign, thus regulating our position in the army. This had become necessary because the Sergeant we had fallen in with earlier was on the way to thinking of us as a *file* of his *platoon*, and had already drawn rations for us and would probably have taken our pay too, had there been any possibility at all of any of the troops being paid. Fernando remained with me as my servant but was denied his Corporal's chevron there being already a superfluity of Corporals in this new Militia.

A few days later we came to Villalpando, on the road to Zamora, and there our army joined an even larger one from Galicia, under Colonel Blake – a soldier of the Irish Race but born in Málaga – and we had here a few days' respite since this Blake brought with him provisions, clothes, guns, and munitions, most manufactured in and sent from England, which country was now our ally. There also came news that an English power was to be landed – not in Spain, our Generals being confident they would beat the French without the aid of foreigners; but in Portugal. If the name of the Commander of this English power was mentioned Your Grace will forgive me if it did not stick in my mind at the time.

All this led me to reveal my English antecedents to my fellow officers and word soon reached the General Staff of this; the day we left Villalpando I was sent for by Don Gregorio García de la Cuesta himself, and I duly presented myself at his lodgings in the Mayor's house. After a long wait I was ushered upstairs into a small room – but the largest in the house, and possibly the largest the town could afford – which was almost filled by a four-poster covered in quilts and sheets which were dirty and torn.

In the midst of this sat the Captain General himself, propped up on the pillows, dressed in a gold embroidered night-shirt, which was as soiled as the rest. Two Secretaries or *Aides-de-Camp* sat on the giant bed beside him. With difficulty one of these managed to convey to the deaf old man who I was and remind him for what purpose I had been sent, at which I made my bow.

He then spluttered and hummed a good deal and one of his aides wiped the phlegm from his lower lip, and at last, with much rhodomontade and circumlocutory rhetoric communicated to me his instructions, which were that I was to attach myself to the staff; that in two or three days I should see the French routed at Medina de Rioseco whither the army was even then preparing to return; that I should then ride to *La Coruña* in Galicia where I should find the English Agent, and perhaps even the English Captain General who was daily expected to land at La Coruña on his way to Lisbon, to either of whom I should communicate the news of the battle, being sure to make clear that it was the *Castillians* under Don Gregorio that had won it and not the Galicians under Blake.

The reasons for this flummery were clear: Don Gregorio hoped thereby to attract to his own army a supply of arms, powder, coin and the rest the like of that furnished by the English to Blake and his Galicians.

I begged leave to take Fernando with me, which was granted when I explained that from childhood he had learned some English of me and was not unable in that tongue, and now the necessary orders were made and signed and I was given a copy to authorise my transfer to the staff.

The only thing I lacked was a horse, and one cannot be on the staff without a horse; besides, if there was to be a battle again I was determined to be properly provided for at the outset – picnicers with mules were not to be expected again. I applied to the Commissariat and was laughed at for my pains so I went to the gypsies instead. There were always gypsies near the army, and even at the worst times they always had a horse or two for sale, though where or how they concealed them no-one ever knew. I struck my bargain, my way made easier by my skill with the gypsy tongue (never was horse flesh bought so dear, but needs must, as they say) and appointed to meet this gypsy three hours later at a certain place in the country thereabout, where I conveyed to him the rest of Rafael's gold together with the silver buttons that I had

cut from my good friend's coat while Fernando had been searching out a Priest and picking flowers.

Although old and knocked up this horse, a knobbly-kneed
dun mare, had never been properly broken either, doubtless this
was why it had been refused even by the *Picadors*. However, for the
moment it sufficed – there was no need to ride it faster than a
walk, and with Fernando at its head it got me to Medina de
Rioseco without a fall.

Would that it had not.

A gentle incline from this Medina carries one to a command-
ing height or Down perhaps a league or so to the South, which
overlooks and commands most of the Plain or *Campo* thereabouts.
The French Army, now increased in numbers and under the
command of Marshal Bessières, approaching fast from the East,
Don Gregorio drew up his line of battle between this hill and the
town to wait the assault. On top of the Down he put Blake and
the Galicians, this being his Left. He placed his own force on the
Right, just outside the town. He thus fulfilled an important rule
of the Position Defensive – to have flanks difficult or impossible to
turn. However, he now had no troops left to put in his centre, a
circumstance whose significance was more apparent to the French
Marshal than to him.

The battle commenced with a brisk cannonade which caused
Blake's Galicians to withdraw a little from the front of their position – a manoeuvre on their part full of sense; however, when the
cannonade drew off and the French at a *pas-de-charge* came a-
drub-a-drub-drubbing up the hill nothing would persuade them
to come forward again. Thus the French gained an equal footing
and the Galicians had lost their only advantage – that of height.
They were soon being cannonaded again and finally were routed
by Lassalle's sabres, the same that had done such fearful execution
at Cabezón.

Meanwhile Cuesta had been prevented from aiding Blake by an
attack on his front which, it seemed to him and his staff amongst
whom I was now numbered, perched on our nags on a knoll

above the town, his troops were withstanding well. But the French were not yet pressing home, content to wait until the work on the hill was complete. About two of the afternoon we received word from Blake that he wanted reinforcing and our General sent him a couple of squadrons – not enough to make any difference; a little later the Galicians broke – some went off to the West and South, some sought safety with us and were caught on the slopes first by cannon and then by cavalry in the unoccupied centre of our line.

Followed a brief respite while Generals Lassalle and Merle reformed their divisions on the hill; and our General took counsel what to do. It was suggested to him that a planned withdrawal was in order since he was now threatened by superior forces on two fronts at once, one of them having an advantage of height. Our *Hidalgo* General would have none of this but ordered his best infantry to march up the hill and retake it from the French, and that was the last I knew of the manoeuvres or tactics of the battle; indeed that was the last planned movement made by our troops at all.

Soon the French were coming at us from all sides with shouts of *Vive l'Empereur*, *Pas de Bourbons*, and so forth, at which my nag took fright and bounded away with me holding on its mane; Fernando was lost to me, so were the Staff and the Captain General, all was noise and jolting confusion, I had just time enough to realise my steed had brought me to the outskirts of the village when it was shot from under me, throwing me, head and shoulders first, against the baked mud wall of a cottage, which fall bereft me of consciousness.

This was as well, for had I shown any sign of life the French Lancers who came scouting down the street some half hour later would have surely finished what was so well begun. As it was, the first or second of the troop found all the sport he wanted in sticking his lance two inches or more into my right buttock.

Thus I received the wound whose scar I still carry and which occasioned me much discomfort for many days to come: my other evidence of the narrowness of my escape was the body of an old man, similarly wounded but in front, which lay near me – he being at his doorway to preserve his wife and daughters from rape. Their screams, and the pain of my wound, were the first signs of returning consciousness and both warned me to proceed with care.

Since my face was raised by a low dung-heap into which I had fallen I was able to see by opening one eye only the whole length of the street. What I saw disposed me to shut that eye and remain where I was, offering silent prayers to Our Lady that my wound would not drain off all the vital fluid from my veins, and that nothing about my appearance would attract further notice from the devils around me.

Why the *Virgén Purísima* should have heeded my supplication and not those offered to her with even more fervour from all the poor women and girls of the neighbourhood, I shall never understand, for the day being the Fourteenth of July, and the Marshal being well pleased with his victory, he allowed his army to do what it liked until first light the next morning. The screams continued all evening and well into the hours of darkness, shots continued to be fired, the smell of burning, sometimes of burning flesh, came more and more to my nostrils, and the raucous singing and shouts of brutes on the carouse became increasingly confused as the night wore on.

One thought recurred to me at every spell of consciousness that was allowed to me and that in the form of a question: how did these French find so much wine when our army had had to pay gold for a skinful in the same town only the week before?

First light discovered a sort of sick fog lying between the houses through which dark figures staggered, often arm in arm, with trousers unbraced and stains of wine and vomit in their beards and down their coats. Outside the town a bugle blew and these figures became a hurrying procession, big men, bleary-eyed, mouthing their uncouth language, like the Damned returning to Hades at cock crow, many carrying plate, ornaments, candle-sticks, gold and silver chains, and such like, filched from the few houses of any note, and all the sacred vessels from the Church together with altar hangings and vestments. One Corporal was dressed in the gold and white kept for Easter, and it was his device to mimic the Interment of the Dead over every corpse he saw. Thus it was he heaved me over with his booted foot, kicked dung in my face, and intoned these words:

> *Cendres à cendres, merde à merde*
> *Requiescat in Pace.*

I remained very still and he passed on his way after performing a similar service for the old man who still lay beside me with the lance hole in his chest.

With the sun up and dispersing the fog another group came by, and these, from the regularity of their step and the measured tone of their voices, were sober – perhaps a sort of Police kept back to round up the looters, rapists, drunks and pillagers who had not heard the bugle. One of these, and I could not distinguish him clearly for I kept my eyes all but closed, and anyway such was my state it could have been illusion, had red hair which glowed in the first shafts of sunlight as he came and stood over me.

'Is it you, José?' I swear I heard the Judas say, 'is it really you? Dead on a dung-heap?' and he kicked me on the shin, but I did not wince, and so he went on, and the French soldiers with him.

2

I was a month on my way home and such were the privations I suffered, what with the heat, lack of food and drink, my wound, and not knowing my way, and shamming dead on more than one occasion as French Cavalry went by, I was in a sorry state when I arrived at my Father's cottage one day in the middle of August. I doubt I should have survived on this horrid journey but for Rafael's wedding ring that I had taken from his finger before we buried him, he having no further need of it, and with Isabella's instruction in mind. It saved me from starvation scarce five leagues from home, for the countryside had been ravaged by the successive hosts that had gone through it and the poor peasants would part with bread, some eggs, a salad and some wine, which saved my life, only for gold, and I rested up there a day or two as well. By this ring I preserved the one given me by Anna La Granace – the one with the diamond, which in those days I kept secret about my person though later I hid it at my Father's cottage. I judge I was right in this – such simple fare and lodging was scarce worth gold, let alone a Jewel as well.

Two days later I arrived in Los Arapiles, fainting away on the very threshold; Tía Teresa took me up, put me to bed in my old place and there I fell into a fever that lasted for many days, and for all my Father's knowledge of simples and Tía Teresa's kind nursing, my life was despaired of. However, these and God's Grace not lacking, I pulled through, and by the end of the month was sufficiently recovered, though very weak, for them to move me to my Father's cot on the first floor, that is in his inner room or study.

The two good old souls did this, they said, because I should be cooler away from the kitchen and the hot weather still upon us, but also, I realised, 'twas so they could reoccupy the big bed, for it was now their custom to cohabit there comforting each other in their old age with the warmth of carnal affection, though I doubt there was much carnality in it, and no harm at all that I could see, Tía Teresa being well past the age of child-bearing.

There had already been good news at the time of my return though I had been too sick to heed them, namely that a great victory had been won in the South, that a French Army had capitulated at *Bailén*, and twenty thousand men taken there; that because of this the rest of the French had fallen back North and East and were like to leave the country by the end of the season; and now, the day I was moved upstairs, we heard all the bells of Salamanca ringing and we wondered what new victories they foretold.

We did not have long to wait. Before dinner the clop-clop of hooves on the cobbles signified the arrival of a visitor and my Father and I heard the voice of Mr Curtis of the Irish College answering Tía Teresa's welcome, and presently he came bustling up the stairs with a bundle of papers, the latest dispatches, and other sheets of which more anon.

Proud he was, he said, to be Irish on that day for, he proclaimed, an Army from Ireland, from Cork itself, had fallen upon the coast of Portugal and there, under an Irish General or – to be fair – a General born in Ireland, had so completely defeated Junot and the Frenchmen who had passed through our town the last November that all had surrendered and would be taken off in British boats so, as he put it, 'There'll not be a *Johnny Crahppo* left in the whole of that country to the West of us, at all,' which were mighty good news, because the town folk had been fearful that with the earlier French defeat, as above, Junot would return the way he had come, and no doubt looting and pillaging as he came.

'And how was it done then, how was it done?' cried my Father.

'Ay, it was a simple enough matter,' said Mr Curtis, spinning on his heel and clicking his fingers, 'from these accounts the French came on in columns, the Irish stood fast in lines at a place called *Vimeiro*, and gave them volley after volley till they would come on no more, then fix bayonets, down the slope, and all was done. But it was a matter too of discipline, cool heads, and right timing I make no doubt, and this General must be a very fine man.'

'And what's his name then?' asked my Father.

'Why these sheets say *Don Arturo Velsee Caballero del Baño* is his name, but that's your Spanish version to be sure – we can guess he is *Sir Arthur, a Knight of the Bath*, but what *Velsee* is we shall have to wait on. But that he's a man to beat the French is certain, and we'll hear of him again, you'll see.'

My Father now took up the dispatches and discovered that the Army was British, not specially Irish, to which Mr Curtis replied had he ever heard of an English regiment that was not two thirds

Irish, leave alone the Irish ones, as the Connaught Rangers, which were Irish all through, and thus cheerfully disputing the point they went downstairs whither Tía Teresa had called them for dinner.

She brought me my broth and sitting up in bed I reflected as I supped, on this line of Irish or British that had turned the French *pas-de-charge* I had twice seen, and wondered what manner of men these could be who stood fast in the face of such an onslaught – for the Spanish victory at Bailén, mentioned above, was not a matter of facing the French in battle: the case was that the French had blundered into the presence of a host three times their number, a stroke of fortune we could not expect to have repeated whenever it fell out we needed it.

After dining Mr Curtis and my Father returned upstairs, not to bear me company as I had hoped, but to play on the clavichord in the front room from some sheets of music Mr Curtis had brought, but as soon as he struck the first notes I forgave them for neglecting me, for the music stirred me mightily. It began with a sort of drumming in the bass, echoed by a trilling phrase in the treble, bugle-like, which seemed the very picture of a gallant army, but pure and noble, not cruel and bloody as I had learnt them to be.

My Father was not so pleased.

'What is this?' he cried.

'Your first subject,' shouted Mr Curtis, over the din, pounding vigorously.

'And what is the key?'

'C major.'

'How can it be? You have there an E flat.'

But then it changed – a new phrase, five notes down, four notes up and the fifth sliding back again, so it seemed to me in my enervated state, like a caught breath or sigh.

'And that I suppose is the second subject,' my Father remarked with sarcasm in his voice.

'Indeed yes,' called Mr Curtis, 'and now see what he makes of these two tunes.'

'Tunes?' cried my Father, 'Chanticleer in my yard is more tuneful.'

'Sequences then,' said Mr Curtis and fell to a regular pounding and showering of notes such as I'd never heard, nor that poor clavichord supported, and indeed shortly a string broke with a great jangling and twangling, and perforce silence of a sort returned while my Father hunted out a replacement and fixed it, all the time expostulating about what he'd heard so far, how it was an offence against good taste, a barbarism, a neglect, no, a deliberate destruction of all the laws of harmony and tonality, the while Mr Curtis tried to show that such was not the case but that the composer had developed those laws and pushed them further, and found new powers of expression in music such as had never before been heard, at which my Father gave his 'pshaw!' and doubted whether music was meant to be expressive, unless of the harmony and reason that rule the Universe and would rule our souls an we would let them.

At which Mr Curtis drily remarked that the sufferings of our adopted land in the last three months and of Europe in the last two decades gave little hope of the dawn of an age of reason and harmony, and meanwhile this new music seemed better to fit the present time.

'I do not like the age and I see no cause to like its music,' my Father grumbled, but Mr Curtis now resumed, though with a little more moderation in his playing, so no more strings were burst.

And out of all this chaos and cascading I heard again and again echoes of those drums and bugles, and then that other phrase that sank then rose with hope only to break on a sigh, until quite suddenly this second came out clear again, but noble and majestic this time it seemed to me, and then yet once more but quieter and resigned, to be swept away by a final flurry of drums and bugles.

There was a moment's silence then came my Father's voice, heavy with tears in it like the strong wind from the Ocean that carries clouds and scatters drops of rain.

'Ay, ay,' he said, 'you're right. The age is in it. There's nobility and sacrifice, but a deal of warring and chaos too, and no proper resolution. Oh ay, at the end he returns to the laws of harmony, but it's not in the spirit of what the music said, a grammatical resolution merely, for the sake of form and manners, but no meaning to it, peremptory, dismissive.'

'A gesture of farewell?' suggested Mr Curtis.

'Ay. Just a gesture.'

There was another pause.

'But there's more,' said Mr Curtis.

'More?'

'Two more movements. But you must be still though the next will try you very sorely, indeed with its restless shifts in key, and then again there is no break. The next finds its way into the last, or perhaps one should say the last grows out of the . . . no, that is not quite right neither, the second is a sort of labour out of which the last is born, already complete.'

'Enough,' cried my Father. 'This will never do. You put too much that seems errant and fanciful in my head which will colour my reception of it. If your modern needs this sort of phantasising commentary, then it fails. Get back to the score, Master Curtis – and I hope for your sake it won't crack your finger joints and bruise their ends like the last.'

But there was none of that fiery energy in the second movement, which was quiet and slower. However, there was no peace in it at all and indeed to my feverish brain it was yet more unsettling than what we had already heard. On a phrase of only three notes, and the first two of these the same repeated, the music led me on into a strange, shifting, insecure, mysterious world – always restless, always changing, though never noisy or violent, simply unsteady, and out of this I was transported as if in a vision to my childhood, to the age of six, when my Father and I set sail in a bark from Naples, to come at last to Valencia, and what I now remembered of this voyage, clearly re-experienced as if in a dream, was the sea – deep blue and sunlit with an uneven swell, but not rough, and porpoises rushing alongside the boat or diving beneath the keel, blowing clear the water from their vents and diving again; and always there was motion, but not quick, always heaving motion and sighing in the rigging and restless rattling of blocks and spars. All this the music brought back, and, with the vision of the boat, and the sea, and the porpoises also came an unsupportable feeling of anxiety, even of dread, which no doubt I first felt on that boat, uprooted as I was at that time, with Mother, Aunt and family lost, *en route* for a foreign strand, with the newly sombre and saddened man who was my Father all that remained of the old world, and the emotions came back with the memory of that time.

And then just as the tears were beginning to flow freely down my cheeks and were like to damp the pillow the music worked its way through to one single note held, and out of it, with a feeling of unaccountable sweetness and gentleness, came the most firm, settled and harmonious tune of all, and we were thus launched into the third movement with a wonderful sense that we had arrived, or more truly that something had arrived for us, and the strange thing was that this tune somehow recalled the second tune of the first movement, the one that rose with hope to fall back in doubt – this new tune though different recalled that one, but was now a complete version of it – all doubt and uncertainty gone, and my spirits rose, and I swear if I had been myself I should have danced.

Indeed I now heard my Father give a huzza and to my amazement saw, through the open door and projected on the sunlit wall of the next room, a whirling shadow which could only have been the skirts of his coat and cassock beneath his coat, swaying as he pointed his toe and turned on it to the sweet joy of the music. And thus he continued, although the second section (for this was a *rondo* and so much my Father's musical proclivities had taught me to recognise) fell to tumultuous drubbing up and down the keyboard, as if the noble hero of the first section had to give a bully a thrashing before returning to the serenity of his natural self, which duly happened with the return of the first section.

This would have been ample, but no, that heroic tune had yet to rise to further nobility, which it now did through a reversion to minor keys in the middle section which brought a return of tension and anxiety, a sense of complexity, a feeling that nothing is ever so perfectly simple, or that if it is, like the simplicity of that tune, then it is a simplicity that has to be won, fought for, it cannot merely be found.

And so section by section the *rondo* achieved its form, its circle of completeness, and it did so with sparkling triumph, in double speed and with *arpeggios* like the church bells signalling the Victory of Vimeiro, though even in the very final bars where all now seemed bright and sure, all doubts gone, all conflicts healed, all battles won, the E flat of the minor key returned to hint that after all it was a mortal glory, that even in this jubilation we should not entirely forget that all things change and move on, that no final statement is possible, that all things hold the seeds of another future, not necessarily their own.

'Well, well,' and 'ay, ay,' I heard my Father say, breaking the warm silence that had rushed back upon us after the last notes had faded. 'Ay, indeed, there is much of the times in that music, and the old times are gone, that much is for sure. Yet I doubt the man is right to be so optimistical; I cannot see things falling out so well.'

'Come now,' cried Mr Curtis, 'things are never so bad as they seem . . .' but before he could continue his argument a new noise, a clamour outside of shouts and donkey's hooves, laughter and I know not what broke in upon us and then the voice of Tía Teresa below stairs calling up at us: 'Masters, masters, come quickly, for here is Fernando Sánchez returned from the wars.'

Such was the commotion that followed that the music was for the time forgotten, and I never after had occasion to ask my Father or Mr Curtis who was its author or what its title, but I do recall Mr Curtis had said earlier that the poor man was reputed deaf when he wrote it; but I cannot think that likely, that a deaf man should pen such music.

3

Fernando was indeed come home, and full of tales of his adventures, more strange and fortunate than my own following the battle at Medina de Rioseco that had separated us, and I would rehearse them all here, but this is my history not his. Yet some I must set down, for he described them so well, and one particular scene, of which more in a moment, that has ever stayed in my mind as if I had seen it myself.

In brief then: when my nag bolted, he offered to follow, but was commanded by a Sergeant to keep his place on pain of instant death for desertion in the face of the enemy; a short time after, though, all broke and ran, each man for himself. Fernando now hid in a ditch beneath a dead mule and thus escaped the sabres and lances of the French cavalry. Later, when all was clear and the French gone, he looked over the field of battle and through the town for me but could not come on me in all that host of dead and wounded, and so concluded that I must have got off. He now bethought him of how we had been instructed to go to La Coruña to tell the English that Don Gregorio had won a great battle, not Colonel Blake, and it seemed to him possible that I had indeed gone on this errand, though perhaps now to report 'twas Blake threw away the contest, not Don Gregorio. In any case, there seemed fewer French on the roads to the West than to the East, and so that was the direction he took, and soon fell in with a party of Galicians who were heading for home. These travelled by night and hid up during the day for fear of French pursuit. In this manner he came to Orense and thence to Vigo on the coast, the whole journey taking some ten days.

At Vigo he discovered an English ship, a frigate, and learnt from the Captain that the British General had left La Coruña some days before, and had gone South towards Oporto in Portugal, and that a British Army was on shipboard, and passing down that coast at that very time.

It now seemed to Fernando that his only course was to go that way too – he supposed that if I had reached La Coruña in time to meet with this general I might then have stayed with him, being English myself; or if I had not got there in time then I too would now head South, and his best chance of fetching up with me again was to do likewise. So he took ship from Vigo to Oporto and was very frightened as soon as the boat got clear of the wide and tranquil bay and came into the swell of the Ocean, for Fernando had never seen the sea and had thought all would be as calm as the bay which was placid like a lake.

Vigo to Oporto is no more than two days' sailing if the wind sits right and the poor man was spared a longer travail on the watery element. Thankfully he staggered ashore in the evening of the next day after he had sailed, resolved for ever after to remain on *terra firma*, a resolution that did not falter, no, not even when he learned that the General he sought had left that very day to join the British Fleet and his Army waiting in transports down the coast at a place called *Mondego Bay* where they were like to disembark.

To cut his story shorter yet, he saw the British land at Mondego Bay and watched them fight at Roliça and Vimeiro, saw the French troops marched on to British transports at Lisbon, and heard of the Capitulation at Bailén, and in all had sought for me everywhere, and failing to come up with me, at last concluded that I was not to be found, and knowing the way home was clear at last of French, turned back for Salamanca and Los Arapiles, being fortunate enough to get a place with the troopers who carried the dispatches, and so had come to town on the very day the news of Vimeiro arrived.

And now to set down the scene that I best remember from his account of his travels and adventures, and 'twas not the battle of Vimeiro itself, for all that was a noble and enlivening scene, but was the Disembarkation of the British Army at Mondego Bay, the very beginning of six years of travail and glory which finally drove the Invader and his barbaric hordes from the land I still most easily think of as my own, and which set the laurels of Supreme

Soldier of the World on the brow of him who on that day regulated, and set right the landing of his troops.

Here then Fernando, sat at the head of the big pine table in our kitchen, and all the notables of the village and many more beside crowded round and me there too, carried downstairs by Mr Curtis and placed beside my friend; so many the room was dark, although it was yet broad daylight, and the doorway filled with faces and even the garden, and silent children on the stair; here then Fernando, his round jolly face burned brown like a nut beneath his heavy eyebrows, his large hands flat on the table save when his tale required an ample gesture of triumph or one to show the chopping down of foes, and as he spoke a couple of wineskins went the rounds and an earthenware vessel of water, and all was quiet save for his voice, by turns grave and animated but always measured, beneath the dark beams hung with garlic, herbs, and a rustic ham. And it's memory, not fancy, that makes me see amongst those faces the dark-eyed beauty of María Victoria, she who had put poppies in her hair before climbing the *Arapil Chito* (married now and with a baby at her breast), and Tía María, unchanged and as sow-like as ever, who had floored us in her yard with a wineskin.

'Masters,' Fernando began, 'the Ocean is . . . the Ocean is a thing . . . I cannot express it. So vast, so huge, so . . . so much everywhere when one is on it, as I had been but three days before; it fills the mind, the soul, one's body rises and falls with its gigantic swell, one cannot escape it; it is the world: a blueness so deep as almost to be black, save where the water breaks translucent green along the sides of the ship or white as pure as the, as the Virgin's milk, along the crests of the waves; and beneath it great whales disport themselves, along the tops of the waves the Flying Fish skim, and in its fathomless depths lies that great Leviathan who will awake only at the Trump of Doom.

'And almost more powerful is it, nay more powerful, more horrid, if seen and heard from the land at a place where its mighty rollers in ceaseless formations surge, unbroken by rocks or reefs, on

to long sandy beaches such as make up much of the coast of
Portugal I saw. Then these rollers, as high as a man, no, as high as
two tall men, say like Don Carlos Bos'am and Señor Curtis standing the one on the shoulders of the other, yes, so high, come
rolling in one after the other, ceaselessly breaking in long lines of
surf swirling up over the white sand and sucking out again, and
the ceaseless barrage of breakers sets up a mighty roar and the sand
trembles beneath your feet as if a thousand kettle-drummers beat
the Tattoo at once.

'Such a spot is Mondego Bay, for although a river has a shallow
estuary there and there is a headland too, it is no harbour; and the
surf breaks still without interruption, especially if the wind is all
from the North. I arrived at the Bay shortly after sunset on the
day before the landings commenced, and having ascertained from
a Sergeant of Soldiers serving at Sea or *Marines* as the British call
them, who were lodged already as garrison in a small fort that
overlooked the estuary, that the Army would come on shore the
next day, I climbed into the sand hills which lie like a long barrier between sea and land, and there found a warm hollow filled
with coarse grass that squeaked when one trod on it, and endeavoured to get as much sleep as the thunder of the surf would
allow. I was excited too at the presence of the mighty fleet which
I had not yet seen properly but whose lights danced on the swell
in such numbers they stretched right across the bay for several
miles, yes miles.

'An hour passed and the moon came up and now I could distinguish the shapes and silhouettes of giant ships, as big as, as big
as *cathedrals* they seemed, far out at sea beneath the towering lacery
of their rigging, black against the molten silver of the moonlit
water. For a long time I gazed at this wondrous sight until at last
fatigue o'ercame me, for I had been travelling for nearly three
weeks, and mostly on foot, in search of Pepe here, and the next
day I hoped to find him.'

Here the good Fernando reached out a hand and grasped mine
across the corner of the table, and the tears that had started when

first I welcomed him were like to start again. 'Old wine and old friends are best, eh Pepe?' he murmured, and then resumed.

'The sun was up an hour and hot on my face when I came to, and rolling on my front I looked over the crest of my sand hill to see what was toward. And now the sight I saw was yet more splendid than any I have yet described. As the sun was yet new risen and shining from my right, so the vast armada in front of me was lit obliquely and brightly, with no mist or heat haze, and every detail, even at a league or more, stood out with unthought-of clarity. In the furthest distance — yet by reason of their size undiminished in stature in comparison with the ships closer in — were the Men-of-War, perhaps twelve in all I could see, hove-to whilst no doubt beyond them sloops and frigates watched the seas below the horizon. So big and majestic were these craft that they lay on the water it seemed, quite undisturbed by that enormous swell, black and yellow with gilded figureheads and sterns, and their masts soared up, yes, to the height of any building in Salamanca, I swear it, and these masts thicker at the deck than the trunks of our broadest spreading oaks, each carrying one or two but by no means all their sails, and decked with coloured pennants, flags and standards, by which, as I understood it, they made signals one to another; and from time to time a puff of white smoke blossomed here and there, and so great was the distance a heart-beat or two would pass before I heard the report, just a sort of *pop* above the noise of the surf; and this occasional discharge of cannon was signals too.

'My eye now turned from these tranquil giants to the fleet of smaller ships nearer the surf; rounder, fatter boats that wallowed in the swell, and here all was hustle and activity, for round their sides clustered flat-bottomed barges — open rowing boats they were but very large, each rowed by fourteen or sixteen oars — and I could clearly make out how soldiers in red coats with white breeches, with packs on their backs and clutching muskets, were clambering down rope nets that had been put over the sides of their ships, and, with the help of the sailors who stood up fearlessly in their tossing craft, were handed down to sit upon the thwarts that ran across each boat. And now four long boats, not these barges, and filled with sailors not with soldiers, drew away from the transports and headed across the heaving water towards me, straight for the long line of thundering surf; and – here was the wonder – they were racing, these madmen, for who would come first to certain upset and likely drowning where the house-high breakers curled and broke in long lines of pure white foam.

'But like four darts or sabre thrusts, and almost together, these long boats cleaved through the waves, cresting the breakers and riding on them so that momentarily keel and oars were clear of the water as if they would take off like the flying fish I had seen on my way by sea to Oporto, and then through they came with the foam boiling along and over them, clear right up on to the sand, and as they touched ten stalwarts from each leaped into the waist high eddies and, seizing the boats by the ropes that looped round their sides, ran them the rest of the way to safety on the beach.

'There were now upwards of eighty sailors on the shore; they were dressed in blue or white sail-cloth trousers and little or nothing else; lean, spare men they were with backs tanned to the colour of red Cordoban leather and hair tied back in pig-tails held in place with knobs of tar. Soon I discovered the purpose of their landing ahead of the troops, for as the flat-bottomed barges approached the edge of the surf these fearless Titans (the Sailors) strode out into the water, where one moment it was at their waists and the next above their heads, and endeavoured to secure the barges at this point so they could be unloaded without being swamped where the waves broke, or driven on to the beach, and this because each barge was to make several journeys during the next four days. And the manner of the disembarking of the soldiers was wonderful too, for most of them climbed out of the barges and on to the shoulders of the sailors who thus carried them, musket, pack and all, through the crashing breakers into safer water where they set them down as carefully as if they were chests of precious china, and went back for more.

'The next wonder was the landing of the horses. It is scarce to be credited, but I now beheld one of the transports had fixed up a sort of running rope from its main yard, whose end was attached to a windlass which many sailors manned and whose other end was a sling or harness, and by means of this device horses were hoisted from their stabling below decks, swung with the yard over the water and above the barge and thus lowered, but with rolling eyes, piteous neighing, and lathered with sweat, on to the flat boards of the boat, but their hooves did not thrash as they might have done, being hobbled.

'But when they came to the shore there was now no derrick for taking them out of the barges, so these barges had to be run through the surf and grounded, and a sort of port or gate was let down in the side of the barge to make a ramp down which the horses could be led – but here was a difficulty, the horses could not come off by the ramp hobbled, and unhobbled they lashed about, kicked and reared (so that more than one sailor was badly bloodied) and having got to the beach there was no holding them and they careered wildly up and down the sands, tossing and neighing and rolling their eyes, and, so constrained had they been in the transports for upwards of a month, and so disturbed by the hoisting and carrying ashore, and so upset by the crash and roar of the surf, there was no catching them for an hour or more, but they galloped up and down the sands like a herd of wild beasts.

'A couple of companies of soldiers were now on the sands, with their officers, and these now advanced in a long single line, each man at ten yards from his neighbours, up off the sands and into the dunes where of course they came upon me and for a time were suspicious I might be some sort of spy, but I parlayed with them in their tongue so that they took me to their officer and to him I gave a digest of how I had gone on since Medina de Rioseco and was now looking for my friend Don José here, whom I thought might have joined their General at La Coruña . . .' (And again the good soul took my hand and his white teeth flashed in the darkness of the kitchen as he smiled.) 'This officer,' he resumed, 'a

young man much about my years, said he knew nought of the
Spanish Gentlemen who had come with their General except
that there were indeed several such and for all he knew my Don
José might be one of them, and he bade me stay on the beach till
the staff were landed when I should see for myself, and he also said
the staff would be grateful to receive first hand news of the campaigns of Don Gregorio and Colonel Blake. Having said this he
left me in the care of a Corporal who would show me the staff
when they came, and he went off with his men beyond the dunes
to do picket duty and watch out for the French.

'Now the sands presented a picture of life, confusion, and bustle
that increased as each new barge came to the shore. In one place
arrivals collected by companies and rolls were called round
grounded muskets; in another stores were piled by the sailors
including biscuit, salt pork, and bales of fodder for the animals,
and men not in uniform checked them off in big leather-bound
ledgers; in another place a party of ten or more men carried
the barrel of a cannon ashore while others behind manhandled the
carriage and wheels through the surf; and most extraordinary of
all, a party of women came off one boat and immediately set to to
build fires on which they boiled water to which they added a
pinch of Indian Tea which my Corporal said was a sovereign
remedy for most ills, and especially brewed on this occasion for
those, not a few, who had been upset in the surf and nearly
drowned.

'At about ten of the clock my friend suddenly caught my arm
and bade me to walk with him, for, he said, the General and his
Staff were come ashore. I looked and looked but saw no carriages, no plumed hats nor splendid gilded uniforms, but just the
same confusion of red coats, with some in green, but mostly red,
as ever, and none of the pomp or ceremony that must surround
the General of such an army; but my Corporal urged me forward
through the throng and sure enough I now discovered a group of
some seven or eight, not much differently dressed from the rest,
who were gathered round a small table that had been set in the

sand and behind which sat a man who, by the attentive sharp way he listened, and then by the brisk but steady tone of his commands, but by no other means, I took to be, if not the General, then someone with more authority than the others; and in this I was only partly right – for it was indeed the General.

'He was a man of middling height, well-built; not much, if at all above forty years of age; and he wore no badges of rank that I could see save one star sewn on his chest, yet his appearance, now I was near him, commanded respect.

'His eyes were blue, clear, and deep-set beneath high brows; his soul seemed to live in them, for always they were fixed and alert on whoever was talking to him, or to whomever he spoke, and they seemed to say either – "Tell me what you have to say quickly and without ceremony, for we are busy today; but mind now – leave nothing of import out," or, "Listen attentively to what I say, and then go quickly and certainly to carry it out, but if you have a doubt about what to do then ask again until you are sure." Thus his eyes. The other feature of his physiognomy was his nose which was large and arched high up near the bridge like the beak of a bird of prey – already, on shipboard I suppose, it had caught the sun and peeled somewhat.

'After a time he took notice of me and the Corporal standing patiently in the rear of his staff, and "Corporal," he says, "You have some business for me?" he says; "Yes Sir," cries the Corporal, and pushes me forward, "Major —— instructed me to bring Fernando here to Your Honour's notice. It seems he was at a battle in the North of Spain and has news of it, and he speaks English a little too." At this the sharp-eyed gentleman fixed me with his steady gaze and briskly asked me the news of Medina de Rioseco and was grateful to have it right, for it seems at La Coruña they told him that there had been an orderly retreat in the face of larger numbers and that the armies of Blake and Cuesta were still intact instead of routed and destroyed as I well knew; then he asked me if I could speak Portuguese and "No, Your Honour," I replied, "but I can make shift to speak my own tongue so Portuguese understand me," and so he asked me to be so good as to go with a gentleman of the Commissariat who was trying to hire or buy draught bullocks and could not make himself understood and was like to be cheated, and so off I went and in this and like ways made myself useful on that day and in the weeks following till the battle had been won and all the French taken off, and the way clear back to Salamanca, and all my friends here.

'I saw much of that General at a distance in the next few days, though the day after the battle he was General in Command no more, two old men (one from England the other from Gibraltar) who were senior to him having come, and they seemed more of the class of Don Gregorio, but the Virgin be praised, by then my young General, whose first name was Arthur and whose second no Spaniard can pronounce, had beat the French and the old men could do no harm. And I tell you this – there was never a man like him. Wherever there was trouble, whether it was Portuguese drovers who refused to move, or a French column that was like to break his line, and shot and ball falling like hail, he was always there, and always calm, and certain, and whatever trouble it was was briskly put right and we went on as if nothing had happened.

'But most of all I remember him on those first days with his troops landing around him, and he sometimes paddling with his shoes and socks off along the edge of the surf in the heat of the day, and even there ordering the affairs of his host, or riding out over the dunes at eventide to inspect the picket lines inland, a figure on a horse cut-out against the flaming sky when the dunes themselves reflected the rosy glow of the heavens, and out at sea those giant Men of War rode the swell behind him, and their dancing lights began to glow like the emergent stars above.'

Thus Fernando at Mondego Bay, and the crowded hot kitchen was silent. Then my Father coughed and said, a little shyly, for sentiments like the one he was about to give tongue to were foreign to his expressed beliefs about rationality and the force of reason, though perhaps more typical of him than he normally allowed, 'It's a wonder, and a good omen, that at times of trouble a man called *Arthur* should come out of the Western Sea to save us.'

'Stuff,' cried Mr Curtis, a little cross at such *Gothick* nonsense, ''tis not in his name the secret of his strength will be found. But come, Fernando, tell us how this General and his Irish Army licked the Johnny Crahppos at Vimeiro . . .'

VOLUME TWO

Apsley House
London

18 September 1820

The Duke has received Mr Bosham's communication dated
the first this month. A diligent search of the Army Lists has
failed to discover Joseph Bosham commissioned in any of
His Britannic Majesty's Regiments or Armies during the
years Mr Bosham claims to have served. Lacking this, or
equally convincing documentary evidence, the Duke regrets
he is unable to support Mr Bosham's claim for a half-pay
pension.

Wellington

PART ONE

Chapter I

An Account, prematurely placed in the Narrative, and not in every detail Accurate, of How I joined the British Army.

I

Your Honour has done me the kindness to enquire how and when I enlisted in the armies of His Britannic Majesty, or rather was commissioned therein, and since I have nothing to hide on this count I will set forth the circumstances as honestly and fully as I may.

In November of the year 1811 it was my fortune to be employed as a courier or clandestine messenger between Mr Curtis, Your Grace's *Correspondent* in the City of Salamanca, and the *Guerrilla* of Don Julián Sánchez, at that time secretly quartered in the *sierra* near the Portuguese border at a village called Lumbrales, some twenty leagues off and an outpost of the Allied Army, then in cantonments with its General Head Quarters at the Portuguese village of Freneda. I say *fortune*, albeit this occupation was prostrating and perilous, since it was yet a way that suited my situation and talents in the cause of bringing about the downfall of the Tyrant, and I had been employed thus and similarly for more than two years.

Such occupations cannot be followed for ever and I had been lucky to escape detection so long – this though several of my colleagues had been caught and garrotted or worse, a fate which I daily expected but which I did not dwell on since to do so would have interfered with the proper execution of my duty.

The news I carried on the occasion of which I wrote was of the removal from our City of a Brigade of Grenadiers whose ultimate destination was believed to be the Steppes of Russia, and intelligence of this I carried stuffed in the saddle of my mule as I jogged across the Plain South and West of Salamanca one cold morning in November, when the frost still clung to the stubble and the breath of the few wretched cattle left to us by the Intrusive Foe hung visible in clouds about their heads.

I had passed the night in the loft of a patriotic peasant in the village of La Fuente de San Esteban, not a stone's throw from the Church of St Stephen itself which (this being, as Your Worship doubtless recalls, the half-way point between Salamanca and Ciudad Rodrigo as well as the junction with the track to Lumbrales) was fortified as a block house and garrisoned with some two hundred French – such posting stations being necessary to them on account of the threat of Don Julián's *Lanceros* to all French or Frenchified travellers on the road.

It had been my intention to rise before dawn and slip away unseen by the sentinels on the roof of the Church, but mine host's good red wine kept hidden in a deep cellarage beneath his house had been uncased once early dusk had settled upon the hamlet, and, I know not why unless it be that the very need to carouse in silence, in the dim light of one tallow candle, lest our libations should attract the attention of the garrison aforesaid, led me to be unsensible of how much I had drunk, I failed to rise at the appointed time, and it was the subdued crowing of a cock that brought me awake at just about that moment before dawn when one can clearly see one's hand before one's face.

Chanticleer's reveillez was subdued perhaps because the wise rooster wished not to advertise too broadly his continued existence amongst the needy, but more probably out of a doubt as to the propriety of crowing at all: his yard, the village, the surrounding plain, and above all the Church with its steeple, now a watch-tower, were all enveloped in a thick and freezing fog – the sort that settles ice on each particular branch and twig and quill of

stubble. Once cognisant of this blanket, as apt, I thought, to mask
deep stratagems as the coverture of night, I decided that all was not
yet lost, that if I stirred myself briskly I could be on my way to
Lumbrales without the watchers on the tower espying me.
Therefore I harnessed up my mule, wrapped cloak about me close
against the cold, and made my adieus to the aforesaid patriotic
peasant.

As I left the village Nature vouchsafed me a sight as fine as any
in her stock – not the most sublime perhaps, but one unmatched
for elegance, refinement, and harmony of parts: the sun cleared
the edge of the distant *sierra* behind me and in a transformation
scene that would, I warrant, have drawn applause at *Drury Lane*,
changed the cold grey mass like freezing cotton waste that clung
about me, into measureless numbers of jewels in which fine rubies
predominated, with diamonds too, emeralds, sapphires, and
amethysts, thereby following faithfully the Laws discovered by the
Sublime Isaac (as my dear Father, by then dead, used to call him) by
prismatifying itself into iridescence. The first moment passed, but
not the beauty, for soon the chief hue shifted into gold, bright
gold, as *Sol* inched further up the sky.

At this point the church bell rang – and not with the steady
beat that once called the simple country folk to Mass before their
Liberators came and hanged their Curate, but with a fast clangour,
a tocsin. I turned in my saddle and saw, imagine my dismay, the
whole tower with rounded spire on top, floating as if some con-
juror had called up *Djinns* to do it for him, above the fog, and
silhouetted, as if cut out by the cunning hands of the Inventor of
that Art himself, against a sky for the moment as immaculately
blue as Our Lady's Cloak.

A moment's consideration was enough for me to conclude that
my appearance to those in the steeple would seem every bit as
magical – especially as they were sure to be watching me through
a glass: my hat with brim pulled down over my ears, my brown
cloak swathed about me to the waist, at which the fog would have
cut me off leaving me floating like an apparition in some tale of

enchanters, and in front of me the ears of my mule. However, the French are a down-to-earth sort of race, *sans* any taste for fancy – how well I know this, having lived amongst them now some six or seven years – and reveries on the magical whims of Nature are not likely to occupy them long. To the sentry on the tower I might have seemed a vision sent from *Faërie*, but I was also a breaker of the Curfew which extended a clear half hour beyond sunrise, and as such *ipso facto* guilty of a capital offence.

Hence, no doubt, the tocsin.

I shook the reins, clapped spurs to the sides of my mount, and without another glance behind careered off at a good lick across the *campo*, with the mist separating and swirling around us, and in this fashion we covered a league, which brought us to the brow of a low eminence, crowned with oak and pine; here I drew rein and turned to see if my fears were grounded.

They were. The mist had by now risen, shed its lustre and its glory and now lay, a gray pall, between the plain and the sky; indeed it was not easy in the distances to distinguish the one from the other by reason of the frost which still lay on the plain obscuring the good red soil and ochre stubble; yet clear enough, two miles or more away, between me and the tower still clearly visible, was a full file of ten Polish Lancers. The time required to draw three breaths was enough to confirm that I was indeed their quarry: their course was directed towards me with the straightness of an arrow's flight; they were coming at a fast canter – far faster than any speed my surly steed could match, the pace of their approach caused the pennons on their lances to stream out stiff though the chill air was still, and the morning light, though dim, gleamed on their helmets and accoutrements.

What was to be done? I could dismount and hide, or spur on into the *campo*, further into the domain of Don Julián's *Guerrilla*, who constantly had out pickets and *Vedettes* with just such prey in mind as a file of horse strayed too far from their fort. The country was open – for the most part stubble, with only low rocks and scattered trees and shrubs on the infrequent rises, so the latter plan seemed proper. I turned, drew my sword, and using the flat of it on my poor beast's rump, stirred him into a gallop. I had, I reckoned, at most another league before my pursuers would catch me, but six miles from La Fuente de San Esteban and the Main Road was well into Don Julián's territory; thus I could hope to find friends before the Polish Troopers caught me, or they would realise their peril and abandon the pursuit.

Yet it was – and I am sure Your Grace will pardon the plagiary of a phrase that has lent lustre to our History if not our Tongue – *a near-run thing*.

2

The rest of the adventure I shall tell shortly lest it seem I include unneedful matters to stimulate the esteem of the reader. Suffice it to say that two more miles brought my pursuers within a couple of furlongs so I could hear their shouts and the conglomerate pounding of their hooves above the racket of my own mount. It was surely time to give up hope of coming upon a *partida* of *Guerrilleros* and instead stir for myself, forlorn hope though it was that I should achieve thereby more than the lengthening of my life-span by a minute or so. However, I was resolved that I should not die alone: to cross that bourne from which no traveller returns is an awesome thing, and the company on the way to Hades of a brace of Polish Lancers, or may be three, would be better than no company at all. Thus, quaintly, my mind reasoned to itself while my eyes swept the terrain for a place where I might make my final stand.

Two giant oaks crowned a knoll in front, their extended branchlets entwined like chaste lovers' fingers who thus keep company though their trunks are far apart, and between them, and a yard or two behind, a long rounded rock broke the thin soil of the *campo* like the back of a great whale. This seemed as good a place as any – with the rock at my rear and the trees on my flanks

I judged it a position which, repeated on a grander scale, might recall the hill-crest at *Busaço*. I urged my mule between the trees, turned, sheathed my sword and drew my pistols. Accoutred thus I attended the onslaught of my enemies. Unhappily they were not unversed in pursuits of this kind and the wild charge I hoped for, through which I might have broke, causing some loss amongst them, and leaving them with the embarrassment of wounded to care for while I made my escape, did not come off.

Instead they checked at two hundred paces and milled about while a man might count an hundred, stirring the powdery frost from the stubble, the breath of their lathered horses clouding up the air above their heads, their harness jingling, and I could make out the guttural accents of their tongue. At last one came away from the rest towards me, but only ten paces or so, still well beyond the range of my pistols, and hallooed a parley. He tried a Spanish so bad I could not follow it, but two crows could for they now took off and flapped away across the stubble; then French which, with my gift for tongues, I had mastered in three years of our Torment, but even his French was poor, he being a Pole or Lithuanian or something of that sort.

'Man, you come here, your pistols dropped, and you die quick. But stay and you die very slow.'

No proper answer could be made, so I made none. He kicked his horse on a further ten yards but drew rein when I raised a pistol.

'You make fool with little pistols,' he tried again, 'which will not hurt us' – here he rapped his polished breast plate, 'and then we will take you. First we cut off your balls, and then we cut you into four pieces for the crows. *Comprenez-moi?*'

This I did indeed *comprends*, the dismemberment described being one commonly practised by French on *Guerrilleros* or spies, and indeed occasionally resorted to by the *Guerrilleros* on straggling French by way of reprisal. I confess I paled at the thought – but death at La Fuente seemed now a certain fate; and surely, I thought to myself, I can contrive matters at least so well that they are forced to kill me in open fight, and thus deprive them of the bestial joys they seem set upon. Consequently I kept mum but watched to see what their next move would be.

The Sergeant pulled round his charger's head and trotted back to his men – more talk followed – clear across the frost, and jingling of harness with it and the occasional snort and whinny from the horses. My own mule shifted a little uneasily beneath me at the proximity of their animals. Then, as if on parade, the ten moved out in column to their right till ten paces separated each from each, turned at a bugle note from the Sergeant, and thus deployed came on at me in line – at a steady trot. Their tactic was clear, and the intention that lay behind it. Clearly, following their chase, they did indeed have a mind to sport with me, to take me alive, for they had carbines in handsome bucket holsters slung from their pommels and with these could soon have picked me off from a distance beyond the range of my pistols. No – they wanted me alive and to that end would come at me from all sides, trusting I would fire too early and too wildly to do much harm, when, having discharged my fire arms, they would overpower me with little trouble and no danger to themselves, being ten against one.

My only hope lay in moving with a suddenness and speed that might upset them and to that end I scanned their line, already within an hundred paces. The fourth from their left, from their Sergeant, was a fattish barrel of a man with black mustachios and a face like uncooked beef – he, I reckoned, would be slow. And in the fifth position a tall youth, very fair, who at this distance seemed no more than seventeen or eighteen years of age – he, I hoped, would lack experience. Having thus marked my spot I gathered up my reins and put them in my mouth, snapped my pistols, and when they were at fifty paces kicked my mule into a fast trot straight for the gap between these two, having left, I hoped, my move so late that the lancers at the extremity would not have time to follow round and flank me or take me from behind before I had discharged my weapons.

Almost this stratagem prevailed.

As I broke their lines I fired off first to left and then to right, and saw the fair youth reel away with face and jaw all bloodied – but on the other side fortune smiled less sweetly for my weapon did not take, the priming powder having been thrown from the pan by the movement. The fat fellow too was quicker than his size portended; as I passed he had his horse's head round far enough to give him room and line to charge me with his lance – their design to take me alive remained in his mind, and it was my poor mule that took the *pic* in its haunch, which caused it first to buck and then to rear, giving out a dreadful sound, half scream, half neigh, and throwing me – my hands still occupied with my pistols – headlong to the ground, where a boulder lay in wait to receive my skull upon its round smooth surface and put all, for the time being, to sleep.

3

I was not long insensible.

I came to to find that two of these ruffians were dragging me by the heels face down in the stubble, back, though I was not immediately aware of it, to the oak trees. They fetched me up against the larger, propping me against its bole, and soon my vision cleared, the rush of blood in my ears caused by the crackling and rough pricking of the stubble across my face abated, and I could take in the altered scene.

The fair haired youth who had taken in his face the ball from my lucky left hand pistol sat on the ground nearby – what of his visage had not been shot away or splashed with his own blood and bone was deathly pale, and he was emitting through the mess harsh croaks of pain. Two of his companions endeavoured to soothe and bandage him, but I did not think they would easily staunch the claret flow. Further off three more, still mounted, stood in the plain, a couple of hundred paces between each, doing duty *en vedette* and amongst them was my mule, now quietly grazing on the stubble, not much the worse for the wound inflicted by the fat, dark, red-faced trooper who had caused my downfall.

He, with the Sergeant, a mean-faced man with pale complexion punctuated with large red boils, were standing nearest, arms akimbo, looking down at me. The Sergeant was, I realised shortly, in an *Hyrcanian* rage, the particular cause of which came to me only slowly as my ear grew tuned to their broken French, and pieced together the mixture of foul abuse and threats that they venomed forth at me. It seems the youth, who was like to die and had certainly lost his good looks, had inspired in their bestial breasts an animal passion the equivalent in such natures of tenderness in rational souls. To be plain – he had been their *bummer-boy*, a circumstance that now prompted them to plan a revenge on my poor person both lingering and apt.

The details of what followed are not necessary to my purpose, which is to recount how I joined the British Army, and so I shall not dwell on them. Suffice it to say, an half hour later, I was bound naked to one of the oak trees, which had, as is the custom in that part, been topped out to encourage a widespread of branches, leaving three main limbs, which from any single point of view, gave the whole the appearance of a living cross. To this, as I say, I was bound, my arms being wrenched up over two of the branches, my legs, forced apart and bent at the knees and my ankles joined by another rope that passed behind the trunk. I was in some pain since they had already done some mischief to me, but numb too with the cold, which I was like to die of before they had done all they wished; for the fair-haired youth had run mad with pain and stealthily found a carbine while the others were busy with me, and, placing the barrel in what was left of his mouth, had blown off his head, thereby finishing the work I had begun. This increased the Sergeant's wrath, and he was resolved to keep me alive as long as possible, and this proved to be his undoing. Had he dispatched me mercifully, he would have got off; had he not exhorted his men to attend closely and study his refined approach to the task in hand, instead of keeping a proper look out, the surprise would not have been so complete.

As it was the first fusillade brought down three of them, including the Sergeant who was killed outright by a ball that broke his neck. Two more fell as they made off for their horses, the remaining four careered off across the plain with ten or a dozen of Don Julián's *Guerrilleros* in their brand new British uniforms, scarlet with gold trimmings, their black fur bonnets and red scarves, in hot and efficacious pursuit.

All four were soon well-skewered on the *Garrochistas'* lances.

But they were not *Guerrilleros*, nor Spanish Lancers who now appeared over the rock from behind which they had let loose their murderous hail of fire, but six stalwart Irish men, Connaught Rangers, and amongst them the two best men I have ever had to do with, Privates Kevin Nolan and Patrick Coffey.

'The poor cratur,' said Kevin Nolan, eyeing me on my tree, 'is he living yet?' and he reached up to cut my thongs.

'Living or not, he's in a state of natur that should not be seen in broad daylight by any Daughter of Eve at all,' said Patrick Coffey, as he lifted me down, big and strong and smelling of baccy as he was, and put me on the ground, 'Give us your great coat Kev, and cover the poor sod.'

'Sure and I will not; yon varmint on the ground that was carving at him with a knife has no more need of his at all, we'll cover him with that and he'll be a sight fit for a Princess,' said Kevin Nolan, and stripped off the dead Sergeant's coat while Patrick Coffey raised my head and found my mouth with the neck of a flask I later learnt he always carried, and which, like the Widow's Cruse, was always full – not with oil but black Jamaican rum.

A third voice in my native tongue now added itself to these; it also had an Irish lilt but not so broad – marvellous to say, it was a woman's.

'Shame on you Kevin, and you too Patrick, that you should think first to cover the poor man's shame from my eyes, when he has hurts to tend, and serious ones I'm sure.'

At this I opened my eyes, and looked up at her as she stood there above me on the back of the whale-like rock.

Against the pearl sky she was a tall figure, cowled with a green shawl about her head; beneath she wore a soldier's coat bleached to the colour of red earth, and then a long woollen skirt of green and red plaid. She came down the rock and Private Nolan held out his hand for her, which she took like the Princess she was.

'Sure, Ma'am, I meant no harm, save only to spare your eyes what no lady should . . .'

'Away with you, Patrick, there's nothing these eyes of mine have seen in the wickedness of these wars that could turn me from an act of charity – now you go make a fire and set a can of water on it: a drop of tea will do this poor soul more good than devil's rum; and you Kevin, wrap him up well for warmth or the cold will starve him first, and not just for dacency – here, take my shawl.'

With her shawl off I could see this Angel's hair was fairish brown but shot with red and gold; it was looped up about her ears and on top of her head but strands ran loose. Her brow was high, wide and white, and her eyes a bluish grey but touched with violet.

She worked with efficacious haste to staunch the flow of blood and when she was done, Kevin holding me round the shoulders the while, and Patrick had brought me tea, I found my tongue at last.

'Madam,' I said, 'my name is Bosham. Joseph Bosham. I am much beholden to you.'

'And mine is Flora Tweedy,' she said, and smiled, and took my hand in hers.

'Faith,' cried Patrick, 'but he has our tongue like a native, and I'm sure he's none of your heathen *Diego* at all.'

Well, that, to conclude all swiftly, was how it fell out. They took me back to Lumbrales where three mixed companies of Connaughts and Portuguese riflemen or *Caçadores* were in cantonments side by side with Don Julián's *Lanceros*, and there I made the acquaintance of Captain James Branwater. He took me up as his personal guide and interpreter for he had not long been posted and had as yet no knowledge of the Spanish tongue, an employment I was glad to take, since now I should be known to the French in Salamanca for what I truly was, and return save as part of a victorious Army would serve no purpose but to put a garrotte around my neck.

In this capacity I hope I served him well – for three years – and I believe I did for before the year was out he made me an Ensign by brevet, thinking such rank befitted my breeding and education. The badge was of little concern to me at the time, I have never valued rank, but now, Your Grace, I wish I had pressed for the commission to be regularised; if it was and I drawing a half-pay pension, I could make shift to get by, I'm sure, even with the Darling Boy who is my care, for I am well used to thrift.

CHAPTER II

Concerning the Vexations that followed a too nice Desire to spare the Feelings of the Bereaved.

I

Having thus set forth in moderate and modest form the means whereby I was recruited to the Britannic Army, and sent off a shorter version to His Grace who owes me perhaps more than he knows, and who I know will now see the justice of my plea for a half-pay pension (for truth to say I am at the moment in very straitened circumstances here in Pau), I now have leisure to fill. And how better to use up hours that lack occupation than by continuing my Memoirs on from where I left them, in the kitchen at Los Arapiles listening to Fernando with his account of His Grace's landing at Mondego Bay and first victory at Vimeiro, on, up to, and beyond the scenes just described which took place three years later?

Certain I am it will be a tale more lively and affecting than the History of the Late Wars just put out and before me now, for what my record lacks in completeness and scope as a History of Our Times, it will make up in having the touch of life upon it – so come *Mnemosyne*, inspire my pen with recollections sweet and horrid, let no detail of vicissitudes survived, of terrors mastered, of invasions, battles and sieges, be forgot; nor let me fail to set down truly lesser stuff, for the past is a rich cloth and plainer strands are woven in with those of brighter hue and set them off, and it is the nature of our times that quotidian matters are spliced with the marvellous so the History that contrives to ravel out one from the other spoils the pattern and lies by omission.

Thus my Muse invoked above prompts me will I or will I not to the Memory of how, not many days after we had heard the news of Mondego and Vimeiro, and while I was still confined to my Father's cottage by reason of the wounds received at Medina de Rioseco, I was much privileged to receive a visit from Doña Isabella Zúñiga y Castro, the widow of my dear friend Rafael Martín, accompanied by her sister Marisa.

Sensible of the honour though I was, the occasion was a painful one, for Doña Isabella had come to hear from my own lips just how her gallant husband, my dear friend, had died.

I received the two sisters in my Father's study where I had been employed with a book from his library – the *Confessions of Jean-Jacques* – my Father being out on business of his Cure, and after requiring of Tía Teresa that she should bring chocolate and sippets (Doña Isabella refused the chocolate but begged if she might put my Father's good companion to the trouble of a glass of water) I bade them be seated.

Both of course were in mourning weeds and Isabella particularly looked very fine and tragickal in black taffetas and mantilla, which last she left over her eyes, though often having to staunch the flow of tears beneath with a delicate lace-edged hand-kerchief. Her only ornament was the plain gold band of her wedding ring. Marisa did not seem so perfect – grief had brought little pallor to her cheeks and she seemed more interested in my Father's bric-a-brac, and particularly his clavichord, than in what I had to say. Occasionally she refreshed herself with a fan spangled with jet and in this I found no fault – it was an afternoon in September and the Autumn chill of the early morning had long gone off beneath a heat like that of Summer.

When we were thus settled I began. First I faithfully recounted how Rafael had taken the place of our renegade Captain at the head of our militia in front of Cabezón, how he had given heart to our men before the onslaught of the French, and how he had been undone in the very first moments of the cannonade.

'Pray tell me the exact nature of his wound,' Isabella softly asked, 'you can give me no greater hurt than that I have already suffered through his death so spare me no detail whatever. In so far as I can I must seek to share his last moments on this Earth.'

In spite of this admonition I paused; news had been brought to me of the nervous prostration she had fallen into on first knowing herself a widow, how she had been despaired of for upward of a week having gone quite out of her mind, even to the extent of declaring the news false and the creation of swindlers and rogues; and so I resolved to myself to make the tale I had to tell as little distressing as may be, which is why I answered the way I did when she pressed me yet again.

'Pray go on, Don José, tell me all just as it happened.'

Marisa ceased her fluttering and silence fell in the warm room – I shifted in my chair which creaked.

'You must understand,' I said, 'he was not directly struck. A shot from a cannon hit the ground in front of him and sent a mass of shale and flint into his face, which blinded him. We, that is Fernando and I, got him off when our line was broke. His hurt did not seem bad, there was even hope in my mind that in a week or so he would see again. A barber-surgeon dressed his eyes in a village nearby and we thought all would be well – but the wounds became infected . . .'

'Was he in much pain?'

'That I am not sure of . . .' and at this moment I determined to equivocate, for the image returned to me of Rafael's head encased in its globe of bandages, of his dull croaks, of the growing stench and his agony – what point was there in adding more to his widow's misery with all this stuff? '. . . as you well know,' I temporised, 'Rafael was ever the bravest, most courteous of men, and the very last to give a moment of unnecessary trouble to another – he spoke not of pain at all, but kept our spirits up with assurances of his faith in Our Lady and Her Son that They would see us, him and us, through whatever vicissitudes might face us . . .' and thus I concealed from them that the poor man was dumb as well as blind.

At this point in my narration Doña Isabella was quite overcome for a time and truth to say I found it difficult to remain composed myself. Marisa alone seemed to feel no touch of pity – or if she did she hid it well. Her grey eyes, less fine than Isabella's, less captivating than those of that jennet her younger sister, held mine above her fan, but quite without expression.

When Isabella was recovered I continued – explained how the next day we had come up with the army in retreat, how as the afternoon wore on Rafael had fallen into a fever – at this point I saw fit to try to draw her off from feeling too keenly her husband's suffering by enlarging on our own, that is Fernando's and mine, how we were short of food and water, and how our mule had been seized. And thus, at each stage seeking to dull her pain without too sharply deviating from the path of truth, I came through to that Dawn when our much loved friend was taken from us.

'And pray, what were his final words?' Isabella bravely asked.

This question, which had I my wits about me I would have prevented, placed me in a quandary – the poor man having been in truth incapable of actual speech at all apart from his last despairing cry. I had to improvise, but what? Clearly I should report my friend in the best light possible – and indeed no taint of deceit could be attached to me if I did, for he truly was a most noble man, and well-known for his liberality.

'His last thoughts were first for his men,' I said, and emotion took me in the throat as I spoke, for surely it was true, Rafael being, as above, the man he was. 'He seemed to know his time had come, for a peace descended on him and his voice, though weak, was calm and rational. He begged us, Fernando and me, to take his money when he was gone and put it to the best use we could devise that would forward our cause, the cause of our King and Country, and that being done begged us to use any that might remain for our own well-being.'

Here I paused, for Marisa had folded up her fan with a click and inadvertently struck a note on my Father's clavier, at which she was sitting; Isabella drew in a sharp breath or sigh, as if in reproof of her sister's clumsiness, and then turned her red-rimmed, wide-spaced eyes back to me. 'Pray continue,' she murmured.

'I shall try,' I answered, 'but it is not easy.'

'I understand, for it is hard for me to bear what I hear, but bear it I must.'

'Of course. Well then. He earnestly begged us to commend him to you, and to your Mother and Father, but particularly to you – Isabella, my heart, were his exact words. Finally his thoughts were of the life to come, and he requested that together we should say the Rosary. Engaged thus, at about the third *Our Father*, good Fernando touched my arm and opening my eyes I saw that Rafael was no more with us, that the noble spirit had fled its tenement of clay.'

At this the conduits of Isabella's eyes again o'er flowed and mine were like to also – however, Marisa, with another brusque movement, spread her fan. 'Was there no Priest,' she asked, 'to offer my sister's husband the Consolations of Religion in Proper Form?'

'Doña Marisa,' I said as solemnly as I might, 'there were Priests and holy Friars with the host but I beg you to recall that two days before a terrible defeat had been inflicted on us. There were many wounded as well as Rafael, little water and no food, and many acts of charity for the religious to perform.'

I then told them how Fernando and I had buried our friend and marked his grave with flowers. 'Thus it was,' I concluded, 'we did what we could – had we had time and strength and means to raise a monument of brass and marble we could not have done enough.'

Silence fell again while Isabella quietly wept. Outside a small dog began to bark – the note was familiar, and I guessed that Frolic, her pug, had been left with the coachman, and indeed similar thoughts must have entered Marisa's mind, for our eyes met again, and this time a touch of pink passed across her cheeks and was gone, lending her a prettiness she did not own. I recalled the kiss she had tricked from me on the picnic over a year before.

She turned to the clavier and picked out note by note a melancholy phrase, no doubt remembered from her repertory of tunes for the guitar in the Italian Style.

'Well,' said Isabella at last and smoothed her skirt, 'so that was all.'

Marisa left off and the phrase hung in the air so my ear felt the lack of the tonic note like a step one expects in the dark and descends before it is there.

'That was all.'

'My sister has in mind I believe an instruction she laid upon you regarding her husband's wedding ring.'

'Marisa, I beg you . . . ,' Isabella turned displacently upon her too blunt companion, while I sought composure behind my kerchief – truth to say I had forgot the ring, though well in mind of the gold, but I never lack invention for long, and quickly saw a way to put all right without causing the poor girl more distress.

'Dear Isabella,' I cried, as she turned back to me, 'would that you had not given me that task. I did indeed remove the ring from his finger and kept it safe about my person. Know then, a fortnight since your Husband passed away we came again to face the French, in the engagement my horse was shot beneath me . . .'

'Horse?' asked Marisa.

'I had been promoted to the General's Staff and it was necessary I should have a mount. It was shot beneath me and in the fall I sustained I was stunned and remained insensible on the field for a night and a day. When I recovered all I had of any value at all was gone – Rafael's gold, his ring, even the silver buttons from my coat. The truth is I had been pillaged – whether by French or Gypsies who were about the place, I cannot say. I beg you to forgive me – I looked on it as the weightiest duty to bring you back his ring and would now give my right hand to have been able to do so . . .'

'Of course dear José, of course poor dear Pepe . . .' and here the distrait widow revealed the generosity of her soul and placed her hand on mine, and thus together we mourned our loss. Marisa repeated her Italian air and this time completed it.

Not much later they took their leave, Isabella kissing me chastely on the cheeks, her sister offering me her hand. I marked the rustle of their skirts upon the stair, and then the yap of Frolic at the sight of his mistress. The casement was ajar and just above their open carriage. Judge my astonishment when I overheard the following exchange as the two sisters settled themselves and their skirts about them.

'Don't ask me how I know, dear Isabella, but our Pepe can tell a lie if need be.'

'I'm sure you're wrong to say so – true, his account differed from Fernando's, and why I have yet to discover. Perhaps only in such matters of detail a man of sense would wish to spare me, perhaps . . .'

'Tut, you were too soft with him. Did you not mark he made no mention of the ring . . .'

What else this meddling virago had to say was lost in the rattle of wheels and hooves as red-faced Jaime, still their coachman, set their equipage in motion. I was peeved a little – I would readily have told the truth about the ring and had only sought, as Isabella surmised, to spare her unnecessary pain, in the gloss and varnish I had put on the facts.

2

The Autumn went on and soon I was much recovered and able again to move in Society and even contemplate a return to Study. For a month or so this seemed possible – reports and news sheets told us how the French were pushed back to the very Pyrenees and it seemed the Tyrant's Iberian Adventure was ended, all would go on as before, save for the gaps left in our ranks by the loss of such good friends as Rafael and others.

At the first opportunity I took the good but plain-spoken Fernando to task for telling Doña Isabella so straight the story of her husband's death. He tried to turn his fault with one of his blessed proverbs – 'He who has good wares to sell tells no lies,' by which he meant to signify there was no dishonour in the truth of Rafael's death – 'No, good Fernando,' cried I, 'but pain to Doña Isabella in an account too blunt: I only sought to lessen her suffering in my neglect of the full horror of his death and your frankness now has put me quite out of countenance.' 'Gesso and gilt conceal the worm,' he replied; by which I feared he meant to impute a less worthy motive to my gloss, and this was the start of a coolness between us which was further aggravated when the Martín household sent out notices of Mourning and Funeral for our lost friend, so all could pay their last respects.

This was at the very end of October – the delay being caused by the fact there was no body to be interred, no remains over which a Requiem Mass might be said or sung. At some expense Don Lorenzo Zúñiga (for to tell truth it was from the Zúñigas came the idea of a ceremony of some ostentation) sent Fernando to search out the grave in the *campo* towards Medina de Rioseco – he asked me to go too, but I declined, being not yet fit for such a journey. Fernando found no trace at all of the shallow pit we had made and was forced to the wretched conclusion that what was earthly of our friend had been devoured by crows and vultures, foxes and the vermin of the Plain.

And so it was that his coffin was provided only with the Franciscan Habit his good mother Doña Regina had paid for at Rafael's birth for just this purpose, and laid up in a closet against the day of his demise, according to the belief (one my Father had taught me was offensive to reason and against the wiser teaching of our Church) that St Francis visits Purgatory once in every three year span and carries off any of the Little Brothers he may find there – as I say, we were called forth to pay our respects to and say our prayers over a coffin containing a Franciscan habit and a lock of Rafael's hair that poor Isabella had been told to give up by

Father Miguel, the Priest of Santo Tomé and Confessor of the Martín family. (He of the Holy Office who had nearly been the cause of my death following the potions Rubén García gave me two Summers gone.) All this was too much for Isabella and her wits began to turn again, the final twist being the interference of a meddling peasant woman, as I shall relate in due course. How perfectly right I was to moderate my account of Rafael's death! Had all concerned showed as much sensibility, the poor girl's wits would surely have remained, unaddled.

We all assembled then at the Martín apartment on All Hallows' Eve – that is Don Jorge Martín, Doña Regina, Rafael's sisters, *viz.* – Violeta, Jara, and Margarita and the other older with her husband come up especially from Ciudad Rodrigo; Fernando, myself, and other friends; and all the Zúñiga household too, *viz.* – Don Lorenzo, Doña Elvira, Sebastián, Tebaldo (that was Violeta's husband, married on the same day as Rafael and Isabella), Marisa, and Rafael's widow Doña Isabella; together with servants, clerks, acolytes, Franciscans, and others – in short a goodly *cortège* and worthy of the deceased.

Thence we processed, all of us suited in black and none carrying or wearing cloaks out of respect of the dead, as was the custom in that country, through the streets to the church of Santo Tomé (this by a longer route than necessary, at Don Lorenzo's request, for he wanted the display – in truth the Church was just the other side the small square); and on the way passers-by and girls on their balconies doffed their hats or crossed themselves out of proper respect, though already in holiday mood and dress for the festival next day.

At the church all was tricked out decently for the occasion, the altar and so forth hung with black, a draped catafalque with the spurious coffin on it and four large wax candles at each corner with chairs on either side for the family; Fernando, I, and the rest not connected by blood or marriage standing in the nave. When all was settled Fr Miguel with choir and a small band of muted sackbuts, hautboys, clarinets and the like performed the Requiem

Mass, and all went off properly enough until right at the end, in the *Requiescat*, Isabella's voice suddenly burst forth high and plaintive in tones that made the blood run cold – 'But he's not there, not there,' she cried, ''tis all a savage farce, he's not there, not there, I tell you,' and was like to carry on thus but Doña Regina and Doña Elvira on either side her caught her in their arms and soothed her down.

And at the end, according to the usual practice, we all processed past both the families, solemnly bowing and making our adieus, and as we did, Doña Isabella still shook her head and wrung her hands, and shook her head with great certainty as if to signify, though silent now, 'he is not there'.

Well, when the service was over I made my way to Antonio's Tavern, La Covachuela, for I felt the need of refreshment and indeed something to lift me out of the dumps – one can mourn even the very best of friends only so long, and Rafael had always been one to promote good cheer and would not, I felt sure, have wanted us to remain sad for him more than a season, but rather feel happy to have known him, and happy, as the good Priest had said in Church, that such a good man's time in Purgatorial fires would be short and soon he would be among the Blessed and in sight of Our Lady's Throne; and thinking this I took a glass or two, and soon felt able to join in the palm clapping to gypsy Suero's guitar.

Anon comes in Fernando, and I called him to me, thinking to refresh him too, and put him back into a good humour in like fashion, but he was well fixed in the dumps indeed and had further bad news to tell of Isabella.

'She will not believe he's dead,' he declared, refusing wine and calling for water, 'she'll not accept the truth.'

'Ay, good Fernando,' I declared, 'it pains me to say so, but I believe the fault lies in your too exact account of how he died. I see it this way – his death was so horrible the way it was, she will not believe it; and not to believe the circumstances leads her not to believe the fact at all.'

'Nay, Pepe, that's not the way of it at all – the trouble lies with you: she was almost over this trick of saying he is not dead, but then hears two separate accounts that don't match up, and so comes to believe all are botched up to some purpose – she knows not what – but if lies there are, then all might be lies, or so she reasons, and Rafael lives.'

'Well, well, an if you're right – which I doubt – it's a passing whim, born of intemperate uxoriousness, and she'll be over it by and by.'

But here Fernando shrugged to signify he was not so sanguine, and went on thus: 'As I came away there was more to do – you know how girls believe if they sit on their balconies on the Eve of All Hallows their future husbands will pass in the streets below . . .'

'I marked many such on the way to Church.'

'Well, even now, as I left, Isabella pushed her way on to the balcony and will not come in, no matter how her family plead with her, and when asked the reason says she is sure she will see Rafael pass by ere long, he will come ere long, she says again and again, and will not budge.'

''Tis all irrational folly,' I replied, 'the custom speaks of husbands not yet won; it makes no case for husbands disappeared.'

'And yet . . .' said Fernando.

'And yet?'

'I think you should go along and tell again the story of his death, and make it chime with the truth.'

'Perhaps,' said I, 'perhaps I will, but let us see if she mends by herself,' and I turned back to Suero, who flashed me his sly grin and struck the opening chords of one of my favourite *malagüeñas*.

3

Two days later I jogged into town to visit the Cemetery, the day now being All Souls' Day, and partly I did this to sprinkle the Martín Tomb with Holy Water (each drop puts out a Purgatorial flame) and partly because it's a sight to see, and not so dismal as you'd think, a Spanish Burial Ground on All Souls' Day, for only in families new bereft is there much in the way of grief – for the rest, such is their faith in the power of Masses said for the Dead, the Intercession of the Saints, and so on, all are convinced that those who have gone before and whose memories they keep green, are happier placed than we who yet remain on earth.

Of course this day starts most solemn – with muffled bells from first light and requiem Masses said in every Church. Then long processions wind through the streets of the town, past the Agustinian Friary and then that of the Franciscans and so to the St Bernard Gate by the Irish College where old Mr Curtis was Rector, and so on to the road to the Cemetery, between an avenue of cypresses. And these processions are very solemn and dignified to watch, all being in black but carrying silver and silver gilt lanterns on ebony staves, and the Dignitaries of the Town and of the University, with all the Doctors in their scarlets and the like, the Bishop too, and may be solemn music from the garrison band with muffled drums and muted brass.

Then as the day wears on the mood begins to lighten – the graves are decked with flowers, braziers are set up for chestnuts and toasted melon seeds and round them gather those who have made their duties and now seek to warm their hands and their spirits too; a blind beggar might strum a guitar and may be a *charro* flute will set the peasant girls in motion, sweets and candies may be bought and more than one gallant will carry a flask of *aguardiente* which he'll not mind sharing.

At early dusk the procession return to town, lone lines of lanterns through the cypresses, and on the graves the night lights twinkle and flicker like the constellations in the frosty sky above.

But that particular All Souls' Day was marred: first I waited an hour or so by the Martín tomb (a simply done affair in the old and decent style – not florid with the *churrigueresque* frills and flounces of modern tombs nearby) expecting the families Martín and

Zúñiga to come forth amongst the other processions, and still they did not come, which puzzled me mightily, and then suddenly came Fernando – breathless and in angry haste, his face suffused with red like a ripe strawberry and his breath issuing in clouds in the frosty air, almost as if he was a horse.

'How did I miss you?' he cried. 'I rode out to Los Arapiles and now back, we must have passed on the road, how did I miss you?'

I shrugged. 'There were many on the road,' I said, 'but why the haste, Fernando, what's the matter?'

'The matter? Why, 'tis this. You're called directly to Don Lorenzo's house where all is in ferment and you are most anxiously awaited.'

I clapped hand to brow. 'Oh, the fault is mine,' I cried, 'no wonder no procession came here; I've been waiting this hour or so and they were waiting on me, knowing how close a friend, the very closest, of Rafael I was and not wanting to leave without me – no doubt it was the good Isabel's wish to stay for me . . .'

'That's not the way of it at all,' said Fernando and a note of dourness I was beginning to find unpleasantly familiar was in his voice as he took my elbow and hurried me off with quite unseemly speed down the straight road through the fields and back to town – unseemly, for processions were still going the other way with decent gait and more than one of the mourners looked askance to see two youths running in the opposite direction.

Presently we reached the Zúñiga house, clattered up the carved stairs out of the tiled patio, and into the long room where once I had bantered and flirted with Angelica at the *tertulia* that marked the engagement of Rafael and Isabella nearly eighteen months before, but now plain with none of the flowers or comfits, gay company or music of that more pleasant time, and a liveried servant who waited for us there turned at a nod from Fernando and went out to give news of our arrival and fetch the family.

'Well now, Fernando,' I gasped, as soon as my breath was back enough to do so, 'you must tell me just what all this is about.'

'Peace,' he said, 'I'm bound by my word to be mum – all will be clear in a moment, I promise you.'

And even as he spoke, a door was opened on the red draped daïs at the far end and silently and in solemn order the families appeared, ranging themselves across the space as if they were to have their picture done.

In the centre was banker Don Lorenzo Zúñiga, in old-fashioned frock coat and breeches with buckled shoes and a small dress sword, all in black beneath his beef-steak face and powdered wig; to his right his wife, Doña Elvira, Marisa, and his eldest son Sebastián; to his left some of the Martín family, to wit Don Jorge and Doña Regina, with Violeta and her husband Tebaldo Zúñiga. I watched all gather, and there were more perhaps than I have mentioned, and as I did my heart began to fail – for all were in black and all so solemn, none offered me a greeting, and those that looked my way did so with cold unfriendly gaze, so I began to feel there was much amiss, and possibly – though I could not guess why for my conscience was clear – possibly amiss for me.

At last when all were standing where they thought they should be, just, as above, as if I was to paint their picture, Don Lorenzo nodded to the door and Doña Isabella with her Dueña came in. She stood a little in front of the rest, paused for a moment, then lifted back her heavy veils. Her face was white yet, like marble, composed and expressionless – indeed she was a statue of herself; and now a stillness fell on the room so I could hear their breathing, a muffled cough, a stir of silks, and the tolling of the distant city bells.

Again Don Lorenzo gave his nod, and I felt Fernando's hand behind my elbow; he urged me firmly forward down the hall till we were standing beneath the daïs, for all the world as if he were a turnkey and I a felon put up from the cells for trial.

Don Lorenzo fished with his white podgy fingers in his weskit, brought out his snuff-box, took a pinch, returned the box and dusted himself, and all the time his protuberant eye remained fixed on me, so I was forced to look at the polished flags beneath my feet. Thus his practice, it was said, with those who came to him for loans and such like.

When this little ceremony was done he cleared his throat and spoke.

'Don José Bozzam,' he said, and his voice was deep and phlegmy, 'you have told my dear daughter how her husband died, and how later you were robbed of his gold, his silver buttons, and his wedding ring when you lay insensible on the field of Medina de Rioseco. This account, and you will forgive me for the moment at least I hope for this, I must ask you now to say was true, or if in any detail it was not, now I beg you to tell us in any particular whatsoever, if it deviated from the truth even by a tiny jot.'

Despite the obscurity of this speech the gist was clear enough – I was being asked to admit myself a liar, and this is something I have never done, nor, I believe, ever had occasion to do. I felt my colour rise, and my voice, when it came, trembled a little with the consternation I felt. 'I'm sure, sir,' I said, 'I never lied in my life and wish I never may, and certainly not to a lady I hold in such esteem as I hold Doña Isabel.'

'I beg you pause a moment,' went on Don Lorenzo, 'often times there is no fault in a lie where the intention is good' (and here I to myself remarked such casuistry may suit a banker or a lawyer but not a gentleman, and took heart at the thought), 'and under such circumstances no-one may scruple to correct such a lie knowing he will lose no reputation thereby, may even gain; the business is this. My daughter, you know, wishes to believe her husband is still alive; she drew hope from the fact that your account of his death differed from the good Fernando's in matter of detail; from these differences she plucked the hope her husband lived and she grew mad in this belief,' (through all this Doña Isabel remained quite still – I don't believe she even blinked), 'and now another circumstance has unfortunately come to light which strengthens her in her error. For her sake we must now get to the truth and banish all doubt. I repeat sir, were you robbed as you said on the field of Medina?'

I doubted now what to say – clearly something I knew nothing of was to be brought forward to throw my story in question but I was too far in, and there were too many people there to witness my discomfiture, to draw back: as I say – there are things a gentleman can do in public and things he can't, and owning a lie is one of the latter.

'Sir,' I said, 'I say it again, to you and all this company, it fell out at Medina just as I said before.'

At this the banker gave a sigh, drew out a huge white kerchief edged with lace from the pocket in his tails, blew his nose as if he were the Archangel on the Last Day, replaced the kerchief, and then gave his nod to the door again.

The flunkey returned, this time leading behind him a large peasant woman, as broad as she was tall, wearing a black gown and a black shawl round her head.

Don Lorenzo turned to me, 'Don José,' he said, 'This woman you see here is *Abuela* María Sánchez and she comes from the *pueblo* of Santiz, some six leagues North of our City. Do you know her?'

I sought in my conscience for an answer.

'I cannot swear I have never seen her.'

A sort of sigh, only just audible, was breathed by all on the daïs above me – but only Isabella moved: she turned her eyes on me for one moment and held my gaze and in her eyes I thought I read a prayer that she might be allowed to live in hope, and out of this I gained the courage I needed – for had not Don Lorenzo argued that a lie can be good? And if this is so then it follows that only the teller can decide whether or not his lie is justified, for he alone knows all the circumstances. It was not for Don Lorenzo to judge my lie, I alone could do so.

I went on: 'Many hundreds of women like this one come to our City for the markets, the fairs and the feasts. So probably I have seen her. That is not to say I know her.'

Don Lorenzo turned to the woman. '*Abuela*,' he said, 'do you know this man?'

She now looked at me, took a step or two towards me and rubbed her eyes, which were rheumy.

'Your Honour, this may be the man.'

'May?'

'Your Honour, this gentleman here is a fine young man, though small; his clothes are clean and fashionable; his face is filled out and bonny. T'other was weak and ill, near starved, his clothes, which were a soldier's in rags, and he was unshaved. It was two months ago and more. No, 'tis almost three. Though t'other was small in stature too, I'll not swear to it.' Then she turned to me. 'I want no trouble . . . I thought I was doing right.'

'Tell Don José why you are here,' Don Lorenzo commanded.

Well, I did not need to listen, for already I had guessed her tale. 'Twas her daughter took me in on my way back from the battle, who fed and cared for me and took Rafael's ring in payment, and she, this Grand-dam, had been around at the time – but always my cot was in a dark corner, and she could not swear to me with any honesty, I'm sure. She now said she had known nought of the ring until I'd gone, indeed until only the week before, when her daughter had asked her how it might be sold. Inscribed on the inside rim were the names – Rafael Martín and Isabella Zúñiga – and these had brought her first to the Martín house and thence to the Zúñiga. For, she said, it seemed wicked to her a man should lose his marriage ring thus and wicked of her daughter to take it for what should have been an act of charity – but I am sure she hoped only to be better rewarded by the owner than she would be selling it off in a pawn-shop.

When she was done, and her tale took some time and gave me opportunity for thought, Don Lorenzo turned to me again and said: 'Don José, you have this good woman's story and now I will ask you once again – were you the wounded soldier her daughter nursed? Were you the man who gave up Rafael's ring in payment for food and lodging for a week? But before you answer I beg you take note – my poor daughter here now believes that wounded man was not you, but Rafael, that this woman's daughter stole the ring, that Rafael may yet be alive, perhaps even a prisoner in this woman's village; albeit Fernando and you have said you took the ring.'

My way was clear – as I have said, only a banker would expect a gentleman to own a lie before his friends, in company of his equals, and I counted the Martín family my equals, though lawyers; it was also now quite clear to me from the one pleading look Isabella cast in my direction where her interest lay: happiness for her was hope her husband lived. There was after all no moral dilemma: I did not fail her.

'I was never, Sir, in Santiz in my life,' I said, and I answered boldly and firmly.

That was the end of the wretched story of the ring. Isabella remained in her madness some two years and died in the cold of 1810 of an ague, still confident of Rafael's return, and so, I suppose, happy. It was some years before I was welcome in either family again, and never in the Zúñiga house – which did not trouble me at all; I had come to think them rather low sort of people. Fernando too was unrelenting, and that pained me and deprived me of support when I needed it, which will appear in my account of the next year.

What pains me even now in all this is that I am quite sure that had Rafael known how I disposed of his ring, he who always had the interest of his friends as his foremost concern, would have warmly commended the use I made of it.

CHAPTER III

*An Instructive Evening with a Very Great Man, followed by
the Comments of the Curate of Los Arapiles. Much Nonsense
and some Wisdom – None of it Invented by the Author.*

I

In December of that year (1808) I underwent a most strange and
marvellous experience, the sort that Providence allows to few
ordinary mortals and then only once or twice in a lifetime; the
occasion I mean was an evening spent *tête-à-tête*, or rather with
only two other people and one of those my dear Father, an
evening that lasted beyond the evening and into the night and so
even to the early hours of the following day, which was the
Nativity of Our Lord, an evening spent without attending ceremony, frippery, or protocol, with a *Very Great Man*.

That this Very Great Man was also a *Very Evil Man* is not something anyone will now deny, least of all myself who has suffered so
much in consequence of his Ambition and his Philosophy; nevertheless I cannot but count myself privileged, as an historian of a
sort, as a student of my race, to have spent some five or six hours
in his company; not every recorder of our times, not those who
have already put pen to paper, nor those who no doubt will in
years to come, has been so privileged as I. And then too I must
add this: to most of Europe now, to all but a few confused and
loyal friends of no great distinction (those who were *Great* albeit
in his shadow have now deserted him and grace the courts of
those he strove to usurp), to most of Europe he is a monster. The

case was not so then – in 1808 Emperors and Monarchs bent the knee, philosophers were pleased to hang on his every word, and armies moved at his command.

As above, the Autumn of that year, following the Spanish victory at Bailén and the British one at Vimeiro in Portugal, saw the withdrawal of the French almost to the Pyrenees and the removal to Vitoria in the Basque Lands of the Intrusive King, who, like me, was named after the Carpenter of Nazareth, I mean Saint Joseph. But in late October the French Armies began to stir, the trumpets called, the drums beat, the Eagle in her mountain fast-nesses shook out her pinions and her unhooded gaze scanned the fertile Plains below; while across the Peninsula, in sea-girt Lisbon where the British Men-of-War swung on the tide in the roads of the Tagus, the British Lion yawned and stretched and flexed his newly bloodied claws; and throughout the land between these two the call to arms again was sounded and our Generals – Cuesta, Blake, and the rest – gathered their scattered armies about them to halt the tide that was about to flow again or, if chance should favour them, complete the cleansing so well begun, and all this at the coldest and most inclement time of year.

Fernando, Tebaldo Zúñiga and others rejoined the Colours – I excused myself on grounds of continuing ill-health arising from wounds so lately inflicted, and soon news came of armies in Aragon, Navarre, and Asturia bloodily defeated, though how our friends had fared remained uncertain for months to come.

The next was the arrival of the British in our town in mid-November. I saw little of them. Their General, the ill-fated John Moore, lodged with Mr Curtis in the Irish College, others of their officers were billeted in the households of the Zúñigas and the Martíns. As above, I no longer visited at either estab-lishment; indeed throughout most of the month they were abroad in our Province I remained mewed up in my Father's house with a seasonable ague; news reached us, however, from

Tía Teresa when she went to town on market day, and from others of the village, as the blacksmith who was called on for farrier's work and those neighbours who had winter fodder in excess of their needs, of parades in the Great Square, the private men all spic and span in red and pipe-clayed white with powdered queues, with bayonets that sparkled in the Winter sun when it shone, of men who smoked tobacco through clay pipes and paid for their drinks and let the Ladies pass on the sidewalks – indeed Tía Teresa had a sack of cabbages and turnips carried across the town for her by one red coat – of wares and services paid for with bills that were promptly honoured with English gold by Germans lodged in the Town Hall, all in all of an Army of likeable lads whose only faults were bad temper and whoring when they were drunk, which was nightly; and even then there was more noise about it than real harm, and when there was harm the culprits were bound over a gun carriage and flogged almost to death by a Sergeant while their mates looked on. A consequence of this punishment was few offences against the Ladies of the Town were brought to book – though whether this was because of the rigour of the penalty or because the compassionate hearts of our *charro* ladies were so touched by the sight of the poor men's bleeding backs that offences went unreported, who is to say? All in all the Army was well-liked during its stay and regretted when it went, though many shook their heads and doubted if such pretty boys could fight, doubted indeed if they were the same who'd come on so well at Roliça and Vimeiro.

The General was extremely handsome with large eyes and a soft expression that bore witness to a soul of great sensibility: he seemed, it was told us by Mr Curtis who visited us during this time, to be more of a poet than a soldier, and all found the news of his death two months later in the moment when he knew he had his army safely off in the presence of a superior force, most affecting.

Before that he kept with us almost a month awaiting news of

the French so he might guess their intentions and numbers and act accordingly, and in the second week of December he had such news: that the French, with no less a person than the Emperor himself at their head had forced the Pass of Somosierra North of Madrid and were now established yet again in the Capital and were there preparing to go South into Andalucie and avenge Bailén. In consequence of this news Sir John struck camp and moved off North by East towards Valladolid and Burgos, his intention being to join with Blake and his Galician Army and cut the Great Road that links Bayonne with Madrid and Lisbon; and those were the last news we had for some three weeks for now the cold set in, rain fell and froze, and then came snow, and few travelled unless they had good reason.

But before I pass on to the extraordinary adventure that befell my Father and me, I must add one footnote to this brief occupation by the British which occasioned me a smile or two when I heard of it, and I nodded my head and tapped my nose as if to say: well, I could tell a thing or two an if I would; and that was this – who should go off with the British, and in wedlock too though the knot tied hastily and at a drum-head by an Irish Chaplain, but Marisa Zúñiga, who had been caught in bed with a Subaltern of the King's German Legion, a Hamburger called Von Schmidt, who was made to marry her by his Colonel since the rules against officers debauching the locals were very strict. At the time it not only occasioned me amusement to hear of this escapade but relief as well that the Town was rid of the minx – and some sympathy for the youth; though three years later the consequence as near as a hair caused my death, and that most vilely, but of that in due time and place.

In spite of the weather, as above, we travelled, my Father and I, for while such matters of great moment as the movements of Armies and the strategies of Generals were spinning one strand in the course of events that was to lead with our meeting with the Great Man, another strand, altogether more sober and more gentle, more quiet and more personal, was also in the making and it was the twisting of the two together that brought us to share a lodging with the Emperor of the French.

On the twenty-third of December my Father's cottage was disturbed by a peremptory rat-a-tat on the door which occasioned me some alarm – I was snug in the fireplace in Tía Teresa's kitchen reading the *New Heloïse*, and I thought Here come the Holy Office, so I put it up and hid it behind a loose brick in the chimbley. But my fears had no ground for it was a traveller whom Tía Teresa admitted and a poor one at that, his head cowled in uncured rabbit skins, his hands in fingerless gloves like bags secured with drawstrings, his feet swathed in coarse sacking. Snow lay on the brown cloak pulled across his mouth and sparkled in his bushy brows which were all that could be seen of his face. In a gruff voice he begged to be admitted to my Father, 'for the sake,' he said, 'of Holy Charity, for that was the sum of his business'.

Teresa led him up the steep stair, for it was my Father's instruction that all should be admitted without question, even strangers, if they claimed a need he could answer, and as he went I marked how he stumbled and almost fell, as if he was near starved for lack of food, or repose, or both, or for the cold he had travelled through.

For a moment or two we sat there, I with my book, Teresa carding wool, then came my Father's voice calling for a bowl of soup with an egg in it for the mysterious traveller, which good Teresa was prompt to supply, and not much later down comes my Father, and in some agitation.

'Come bustle, bustle,' he said, directing himself at me, 'time to be done with such namby-pamby stuff (meaning my book, for recently he had turned against Jean-Jacques), we have a journey to go. Teresa, my dear, put us up some ham and some bread, and whatever else you think fit, young Joseph and I have a trip some fifteen leagues to go. And you, Joseph, come help me saddle up the mule and then you must ask Pepe Sánchez (this was

Fernando's Father) if we may borrow his donkey for . . . you must say for a week.'

It can be imagined this did not suit me at all, and Tía Teresa too thought the good old man had at last taken leave of his senses, but nothing we could say would move him and piece by piece, tittle by tattle we had out of him, as our preparations went forward, what was toward.

In short the matter of it was thus: Some ten years earlier, not long after my Father's ordination, he had been chosen by reason of his learning and his birth to be Confessor to a Community of Barefoot Carmelites amongst whom were numbered several ladies of breeding and education, and pre-eminent was the Abbess herself, Mother María Manuela Rascón. 'Of all the Ladies I have ever conversed with,' remarked my Father when we were left and on our way, 'María Manuela was the one most signally compounded of the virtues of her sex, indeed of our race, with no taint at all of vice unless it was an occasional impatience with the stupidities of others. In this she most worthily followed the example of the Holy Foundress of her Order, St Teresa . . .' and he went on to extol this paragon for wisdom tempered with sense; learning salted with the wit to see the vanity of learning; humility and modesty that yet would not bow to what her conscience told her was not worthy, and I know not what all. 'Twas this Lady who had broke the rule of her order to come at my Father's request to administer what simples and infusions were necessary to remove from my addled brain and knocked-up frame the ill-effects of Rubén's possets and potions, and take off from me too the love-sickness I had fallen into for Angelica Zúñiga . . . 'So,' said my Father, 'you owe her a life and a favour, and you will not scruple to accompany me on this errand of grace and charity.'

And this was the errand: Not long after she had administered to me the Holy Mother had suffered an apoplexy from which her recovery had been slow and incomplete and the Superiors of her Order had determined that the cares of a House so large as that in Salamanca had become a burden to one of her years and in poor health and so they had removed her, with her consent, to a much smaller establishment of only some ten or twelve souls in a tiny village called Torrecilla de la Abadesa, some fifteen leagues to the North in the neighbouring Province of Valladolid. There some three or four days past she had fallen ill again, this time of a fever accompanied by severe pains in the chest ('Doubtless an inflammation of the *pleuritic* cavity and walls,' my Father said) which had gone on so severely that her life was soon despaired of. In this state the sisters had asked if the Priest should be sent for, who was a bigot and illiterate to boot – Mother María Manuela had long since had as little to do with him as may be – and she had called for my Father, doubtless forgetting in the throes of her fever the distance he would have to come, the inclemency of the weather, and possibly even how he had advanced in years. Such was the esteem she was held in in the village, although she had only been there a twelvemonth, that the nuns found no difficulty in finding a man prepared to search out my Father although he had to make the journey on foot, that village having lost all its beasts of burden in the wars of the Summer. This man (Pedro was his name) had reached us, as above, near starved with cold, hunger, and exhaustion, and my Father's last instruction to Tía Teresa as we left was that he should bed up in the warmth of the kitchen until our return or until he was recovered, and be given all that he needed in the way of good hot food and drink that would assist his recovery, and it was this Pedro's incapacity to travel again that necessitated my accompanying my Father to Torrecilla.

With one thing and another, as difficulty with Pepe Sánchez's mule – it lacked a shoe – and Tía Teresa's insistence that we should take with us enough food for five for a week, which caused some bickering between her and my Father, and that he should tie a scarf over his wide-brimmed hat to keep it on and protect his ears, which forced the brim down and made him look absurd, and such like trivia, it was clear past noon before we set off. Father's last thought was to send a lad to Mr Curtis in Salamanca begging a Priest from his acquaintance or Colleagues to say Christ's Mass in the village for it was sure we should not be back in time, and in this, as always, my Father showed the care he had for his flock.

Once off we made good progress. Thanks to the frost the ways were not miry and the snow was only a powder an inch or so deep, but it was bitter cold and well-wrapped up though we were we soon found fingers numb on the reins and eyes and noses sore with the ice in the air. However, my Father cheered and instructed me with his talk, as always, and the time and the miles passed quickly enough.

That night we lodged with the Priest at Villona, a village at near enough the half-way point of our journey.

The next morning we set off early and since more snow had fallen in the night were advised to strike off a little to the East to avoid some hills which report said might be blocked or difficult with drifts and it was this chance that put us across the track of the Grand Army of the Tyrant. But first we fell in with, or rather were overtaken by, at about eleven o'clock, three clerics of whom one was the Vicar of Tordesillas, an important town ten leagues North of Torrecilla, and the other two were young Irish Deacons from Mr Curtis's college, who were hurrying on post haste with their Superior's blessing and encouragement, to join Sir John Moore's army which they knew to be some two or three days' march ahead of us to the North. Though my Father wished to make good speed and would have stayed up with this trio, they were better mounted than us and after exchange of news and civilities they went on ahead.

It was some two hours later we first became aware of a distant buzz on the air which, had I not heard its like before, might have caused some trembling in us, so different was it from any other noise in the world. My experiences of the Summer just gone led me to guess that somewhere, perhaps a league or so off, a mighty Army was passing; and this was a surprise, for all our intelligence had it that both British and French armies were now well to the North save for the Emperor's army at Madrid, which was thought to be preparing to move South against Andalucie if anywhere at all.

A further half hour brought us to a low eminence and a view across the plain.

The day was overcast but no snow was falling and the air was clear and light; from our point of vantage we could see many leagues ahead of us and to either side, leagues of undulating snow-covered stubble interspersed with parks of oak trees whose foliage pricked blackly through what would have been a virgin coverlet had not, across this plain from South-East to North-West, a great host been on the move. It was in three columns, the nearest only a mile or so from us, the most distant at about three leagues. The spine, as it were, of each column was marching men, in dark blue and white with black bearskins and glittering bayonets, and amongst them waggons and carriages, and one of these latter in the first column was the largest carriage I ever did see and surrounded by Lancers with burnished breastplates and plumed helmets; and more cavalry scouted in squadrons up ahead and down the flanks of each column and at the rear; and in the middle of each column came the guns, black and portentous, trundling like monsters across the snow, some fifty of them in each corps. Soon we were nearer; the buzz we had heard before became a roar like the thrumming burden the double-basses and double bassoons make in modern symphonies, and up above the bright bugle calls and rattle of drums giving the marching beat completed the score. All went forward without pause or halt or interruption of any sort at a pace such as I should find difficult to keep to on foot for more than an hour, so that even as we watched for a moment or so the whole host went on and looked like to do so for ever.

I had told my Father how the French did march but he had not seen the like before. I looked at him now. He was sat up straight upon his mule, his gloved hands clutching the reins above the withers, his back like a tree, his scarf still pulling his hat brim about his ears, and his grey patch of beard struck out in front of him and his beak of a nose held high though it was blue and had a drop of rheum upon the tip, and he chewed his lip and shook his head a little from side to side. At last he turned his cool blue eyes upon me, a little blurry with cold and age, and said: 'It's an awesome sight, and it goes with these times and I like it not at all.'

I waited for him to finish.

'That is a machine. Men are men, and ants are ants . . .' he shook his head more vehemently and dislodged the moisture from his nose, '. . . and that is a machine and an impudence.'

Poor man, the grandeur and the terror of the scene had deprived him of coherence.

As he spoke we were spied, for five horsemen trotting with a squadron a quarter of a mile below us now wheeled away from their companions and came up the hill towards us, pennants fluttering from their lances, harness and gear clattering about them, and the powdery snow pumping out behind them for all the world like Summer dust. As they grew near Father reached for his hat to doff it courteously – he was bred up in another Century and supposed they had come to bring their officer's compliments due to one of his cloth, but Teresa's scarf prevented him. Before he could loosen it they were milling around us and without a word their Corporal came alongside and gathered up my Father's rein near the bit, dragged it from his fingers, and led off his mule at such a smart lick that he was near unseated, and had to hold on to the pommel of his saddle for dear life. I quickly fell in behind him and followed, thus forestalling like treatment.

We were conducted thus down through the cavalry screen and right up to the column, where, still without any word being offered us, we were handed over to a colonel of Foot who signified to us to dismount and march along with him while our beasts were led behind us. Through all this my Father was first confused, then angry, but not once I'm sure did he show any sign of fear at all. I, being experienced in the ways of the French, was ready to die of terror.

To cut things short we marched along with them for an hour and this Colonel questioned my Father as to who we were, where we were going, and what was our business, and he answered straightly in the French tongue, though somewhat breathless through the pace we had to keep up, and the necessity to shout above the din around us of tramping feet and jangling harness, and the rumble of gun carriages and waggons and so forth, as above, but now deafening.

And though I did not see it done, being preoccupied with keeping my feet in the snow and my place in the column, this Colonel must have made report on us, and the report reached an higher level than one would dare expect, for about when the said hour was up back came orders that we should remount, that we should proceed as we wished, which was to go straight on with the host since Torrecilla lay in its path, and this with the *congé* of the Emperor himself, which brought some confusion to our Colonel, who now treated us with servile deference, offering us bread and cognac which my Father refused, but which put new heart in me, you may be sure.

Another hour went by during which our Colonel expostulated how curious our treatment was – it seemed only that forenoon the Dragoons had fallen in with three travelling clerics; like us they had been apprehended, questioned, then searched, whereupon it was discovered they were spies carrying messages to Sir John Moore and so would be shot at Dawn the very next day notwithstanding it was the Day of Christ's Nativity. These news put us in a gloom since it was ten to one the three he spoke of were the Vicar of Tordesillas and the Irish Deacons who had passed us on our way.

Our tedious progress continued without break till four or so in the afternoon when dusk with some large snowflakes began to gather round us. About now we became aware of bustle and toing and froing, and occasionally all halted for a space and then moved on but by fits and starts; as far as we could tell the column to our right had headed off through the rack to stations further North, and soon we were entering a small village dominated by a Tower and a Convent that went with it. Our Colonel told us this was our destination, Torrecilla de la Abadesa, that it was the stopping place tonight of the Emperor too, that we were to share lodging with him in the hostel attached to the Convent. Indeed hardly had

these news been given us than we clattered into the courtyard of
the said hostel and found ourselves crowded up against the wall for
the large carriage, and it almost filled the courtyard, the carriage
I had remarked near the head of the column. Such was the press
of Grenadiers stamping about, of plumed Lancers, of braided and
bullioned staff that we could not have dismounted had we wanted
to, and so from the back of Pepe's donkey I had time to scan this
monster conveyance.

It was as big as a dilly but modern in line and sprung like the
coach of an English Lord; it was painted dark green with gold leaf
trimmings and gold leaf spokes to the wheels and the paint shone
with a mirror-like lustre, and on the door panels was painted in
gold a device of three bees enclosed in a laurel wreath. A moment
or two of shoving and pushing now went on and the Grenadiers
formed two lines from the door of the coach to the door of the
hostel, a flunkey threw down the steps that folded up beneath the
door, the door swung open, and there he was, just as expected –
green coat, white breeches, dark hair in quiff above his ivory
brow, and eagle's nose. His huge black hat was handed to him, the
Grenadiers presented arms, and down the steps he came, and was
lost to our view for he was less than five and a half feet and all his
Guard were eight feet tall with their bearskins.

I confess I was moved by this moment, the first time in my life
I looked on such fame, such glory, such achievement. The face, a
little plump, a little shiny, had seemed to me to glow, I had felt a
presence, a power – as it might be I had looked on the face of an
Angelic or Demonic Power.

My Father was less impressed; and when, an half hour later, I
tried to explain some of what I had felt he humphed and pooh-
poohed, and said that Greatness of this sort resided not in the object
of adulation but in the minds of the beholders, and the more so
when the minds are young, or lack discipline and are easily
impressed. As for the *charism* I had felt or seen, that, he said, in so
far as it was there at all, was the rosy sheen that comes from coddled
living, and before now he'd marked it on the brow of certain

Bishops. I retorted that all the world knew the Emperor for an abstemious man, to which my Father testily retorted that all did world knew of his addiction to hot baths.

All this took place in a small cell with a rush mat and two cots to which a turnkey employed by the nuns to look after travellers' wants had brought us; it was a cheerless place but he assured us there was comfort and warmth in the hall though it was not yet decided if we should be admitted there until the Emperor's wishes were known. My Father, not interested in Emperors, questioned this turnkey, and old hunchback with fingers knotted up like oak twigs, about the Abbess's health, if she yet lived at all; the turnkey was a fool and seemed not to know, and this doubt about his old friend's condition doubtless made my Father irritable, that and his age, for surely only the ailing wits of an old man could have left him so insensible of the nature of the Company we kept.

I also learnt from his *sotto voce* mumbling that yet another concern was on his mind – the lives of the three clerics to be shot at dawn; and indeed now I was put in mind of them it did seem a pity – he of Tordesillas had seemed a gallant man, large, red-faced, loud-voiced, but courteous withal, and the two Irish boys were but boys and so a shame if shot. So what with these lads and lack of news of the Abbess, my Father chafed and indeed was poor company – it was cold too, and we were hungry, and thus it was a relief when a knock at last came and the gibbous turnkey led us down the stone corridors to the Hall.

This Hall was no more than a largish room, not more than thirty feet by twenty, plain stone walls with a large Crucifix at one end, a good blazing fire at the other, and a table at which perhaps ten might sit, in the middle.

2

The figure who stood before the fire warming his hands, his back was to us, was unmistakeable even before he turned, which he did on hearing us. I was for a moment quite non-plussed – remember there was no-one else there at all in the room, we were alone with this man. Presently I recollected myself and went down on one knee, my head bowed low, while feeling up at my Father's hand as quietly as may be, to pull him down too. The silly man shook me off and remained straight and only blinked once or twice while his mouth set in a firmer line.

The Emperor, however, took no offence at all, but smiled a most gracious smile, spread his hands, which were white, delicate, even beautiful, and called in the French tongue to us: 'Monsieur Bozz'am, I am delighted to make your acquaintance, quite delighted, and your son too – Joseph, Giuseppe they told me he is called, like my good brother now your King – get up, my boy, get up, we have no ceremony tonight you see, no ceremony at all, just a quiet evening amongst friends. My boy, I should show the respect you have offered me to your dear Father. Believe me, dear Sir,' and here he laid his hand close to the glittering star on his breast, 'I speak sincerely – and only beg you to excuse the outward show of what is deeply felt. And now, sir, come to this fire and warm yourself.'

Mesmerised by these strange words we obeyed his latest command, I at any rate, much as if in a dream.

'We have one more guest before we eat,' our host continued, 'but I do not think we should wait on her before refreshing ourselves. May I offer you a glass of wine?'

Without waiting for an answer the Emperor turned away to a side-table and busied himself with a silver decanter and crystal goblets that had been laid out there; I supposed he travelled with them for never had such furniture graced the hall of that poor hostel before. He handed us a goblet each.

'Your good health, Sir,' he cried, 'and let us say, rational men though we are, for even rational men can play with toys, let us say *Joyeux Noël*, a Happy Christmas.' And he lifted his glass beneath my Father's nose. 'I pray you, Sir, clink glasses with me, stand not on Ceremony.' And now a reedy note entered his voice, a rasp of warning, and my Father lifted his glass and the crystals chimed.

The wine was sweet.

'Later we shall share a bottle of my Chambertin but meanwhile I thought it courteous to ask the Lady Abbess for the best from her cellar, for an *apéritif*, you know? Do you like it?' The Emperor rolled it on his tongue. 'Not bad, eh, for Spanish?'

Later, my Father told me it was the Communion wine, though not of course consecrated, and indeed I had guessed as much since a House of Barefoot Carmelites would have no other – a point the Great Man did not seem to have thought of, for he continued: 'These nuns do themselves well, I dare say, good wine, good food, and what else I wonder?' and he laughed, but then turned quickly serious when he saw my Father was not amused (though I smiled). 'Tell me, M'sieur Bozzam, do you still continue your astronomical studies?'

At last my Father spoke: 'No sir,' he said, 'my eyes, my age, and other preoccupations have cohibited such work for many years.'

'Now that is a pity,' and here the Emperor pushed a finger at my Father's chest, 'for your work on the *Ecliptic of Venus* is, I believe, a classic. At least it is still studied at my *Institut*, you know . . .'

And here my Father blushed a little, just a little, and 'I'm much gratified to hear it, sir,' he said.

'Yes, yes . . . and so when I heard my Dragoons had come on the author of such a work, a scholar, a scientist right out in these wilds – I said, Surely Providence has smiled on me today to send such a man to share my meal tonight . . .'

And so he went on, and my Father melted a little, and offered replies, and seemed a little to enjoy himself. Later, when opportunity arose, and he had drunk another glass, he murmured to me in English: 'Whatever else this fellow is, he is deucedly well up in all sorts of matters, for a soldier.'

Now the reasons for our welcome were made clear I too relaxed somewhat for up to then I had been very much confused, with shaking hand and palpitations, but now, as I say, I relaxed, and, as far as I could without seeming too curious, looked the

Great Man over while he continued his interlocution with my Father.

Since we saw him come down from his carriage he had changed his clothes, perhaps bathed in scalding water, for his face was a little flushed and yet more shiny than before, and now instead of his plain green coat he was got up with some splendour – more than seemed nice for that simple hall. He wore a black velvet coat with scarlet cuffs and scarlet silk lining to the tails, but white facings. This was dressed up with gold buttons, as was his white vest beneath, and on his shoulders heavy epaulettes in solid gold. Beside the silver star – five-pronged, each prong divided against a sun-burst, all set with white gems as they might be, and probably were, diamonds – two small medals hung from short ribbons pinned to his chest; over his shoulder a scarlet sash supported a short dress sword mounted and tasselled with gold. His breeches were white chamois and his black boots, that shone like mirrors and sported silver spurs, came above the knee. Doubtless on account of their wearer's stature these also had raised heels. Well, such dressing up looked loud perhaps in that plain room but splendid it was too – there was dignity and elegance in his appearance and in palaces no doubt, surrounded by kings and dukes, what now seemed ostentation would appear restrained.

One point was a blemish, and would have been so anywhere, and that was that the bottom three buttons on his vest were strained and the material forced into three transversal creases – the Emperor was getting fat and this put me in mind again of my Father's remark about Bishops.

About when I had concluded my careful if surreptitious itemisation of the Great Man's appearance, I became sensible to another presence amongst us though how and when she had appeared I could not say, so quiet and discreet was her arrival, and it was only a gasp and a cry of welcome from my Father that drew my attention. The presence, or personage, of which I write was a tall lady and straight-backed though nearly eighty and twice as old as the

Emperor, and she was dressed in the simple habit of a Carmelite – that is black hood and cape over a pale gray gown, and these in rough worsted. It was to her face that one inevitably looked – this Lady, and she was of course the Abbess María Manuela Rascón whose sick bed my Father had been called to, had a high forehead, very smooth, a long straight nose slightly spread towards the tip, a firm mouth scarce wrinkled for she kept her teeth, and pale eyes of violet hue that were always bright and aware, yet filled one with repose if she looked at you straight for any time at all. Her skin was soft and rosy and lined all over, not deeply, but like an apple kept up the Winter long in straw. Only her hands showed signs of much age, being knotted at the knuckles, which occasionally she rubbed as if they pained her.

The Emperor welcomed her with great effusions, she dipped the slightest of courtesies to him which charmed him, he said, and he insisted on kissing her hand, and then he pressed a glass of wine on her which she sipped and put to one side. My Father, as soon as opportunity arrived, inquired of her health and she murmured that the pain had almost gone from her chest, the fever had abated, and that she would live a while yet – and all this she said to him with every sign of tender affection, as if to a very old friend, and included me in her compliments, protesting we should not have come, nor heeded the delirious vapourings of a silly old woman, too well-served by her nuns and friends in the village, that had she been able, she would the next day have sent after the messenger who had gone for us and called him back.

The Emperor was out of countenance at this which was all in Spanish, and asked me brusquely if I had ever served as a soldier. I thought it best to reply in the negative (my Father's attention being all on the Abbess) fearing an examination as to how and when, and he told me I should, I should, 'twould make a man of me. Then he interrupted the collocution between the two old people, bade them seat themselves at the table, one on each side of him, who, of course, sat at the head with his back to the fire and his face to the Crucifix, and then he clapped his hands.

His own flunkeys now brought in the meal they had been dressing in the convent kitchen, and served it up on his own service: very fine ware in dark blue with gold leaf borders, decorated with gold bees and laurel wreaths and all made in Sèvres – this I knew for the Emperor turned his plate over to show us the mark – and the cutlery was gold and heavy to handle.

There was only one main dish, but that a huge one – a whole fowl each, fried in oil and served on heaps of bread which had also been fried up with a cream sauce and fried eggs served with it: all very rich and oily – indeed the waste of oil seemed a great extravagance and I doubt not Tía Teresa would have thrown up her hands in disgust and despair to see it all soaked into everything instead of carefully drained off and preserved against another using.

'Of course,' the Emperor said, with the air of a man apologising where there is really no need, 'there should be crayfish in the sauce – but when we are campaigning we often travel too fast, not only for our enemies whom we always catch with their trousers round their ankles, but also for our Contractors, who do not always catch us,' and he laughed with charm.

'Crayfish?' murmured my Father.

'For it to be Chicken Marengo as it was first served to me on that glorious field. It is,' the Emperor added simply, 'already an historical dish.' He sat back and looked at us with an air of expectant satisfaction. We murmured that we liked it.

'Of course. It is very good – rich, nourishing, but not too fancy,' and he fell to with a will. A flunkey poured red wine. The Emperor tasted, smacked his lips. 'Chambertin,' he said. 'I always have it: it travels well.'

It seemed thin to me and left an ashy taste at the back of the tongue.

'Tell us, Sire, what signify the star and medals upon your coat?'

It was the Abbess who had spoken and I was so amazed to hear her quizz the Emperor thus, almost as if she were a girl or young wife in worldly society rather than an Ancient and

Reverend Religious, that I missed the beginning of the Emperor's answer through falling into a scrutiny of her face: for this seemed to have undergone a sort of transformation – before it had seemed the face of one who already dwelled half in Heaven but now her eyes were fixed on the Emperor's with a fond smile in them which had a hint of the coquette in it. She maintained this new attitude for the rest of the evening, but had assumed it only after some ten minutes' inward study, as if in that time she had read the part she had to play and conned it too: for now she hung upon the Emperor's words as if the Apostle had come back to Earth to Preach again – and indeed what we now heard was a sort of sermon. With occasional promptings from her, and one or two from my Father, the Great Man relieved himself of much that lay behind his Noble Brow, gave us the gist and kernel of the machinations of his splendid Mind, the Mind that had conceived such great enterprises and carried them forward with such success.

All the time the meal went on – our chickens were removed after an half hour or so, scarcely touched by my Father and the Abbess, mine half gone and the Emperor's reduced to a heap of bones albeit he had talked throughout; sweetmeats came in – still the Emperor talked, and talked, and sometimes he gesticulated with a drum-stick or a wing, picked his teeth, occasionally belched behind his napkin, dabbed the sweat from his forehead with his napkin, leaned forward to make a point, sat back to await the answer to a rhetorical question or listen head on one side and eyes hooded to take in the rare less than rhetorical question (an attitude that flattered the questioner) and then he was off again.

I noted much of what he said when we were back at Los Arapiles and filled out my notes with my Father's recollections, so what I now set down is near enough his own words verbatim, and for convenience of study I leave out most of his actions – picking his teeth and so forth – and most of what my Father or the Abbess interjected (I, for the most part, was silent).

A GREAT MAN'S TABLE TALK

'Reverend Mother asks me what end was served by those high endeavours these stars and medals record. Well, first I must say these three . . . *rattles*, I call 'em, I only wear to please the people, they like to see a little glitter on the Great. They could have been three others, or three more, or yet again three, I have a drawer full of them, no particular distinction is attached to these. So, Reverend Mother, what you really ask is what end is served by my life, and all I have done, and will do to crown achievements the like the world has not seen since Alexander.

'Madam, the cause, the end can be summed up in one word only – CIVILISATION. And what is *civilisation*, you ask? And I reply – civilisation is *Social Unity*. Civilisation, social unity, social happiness (here he smiled with great benevolence) are all words for one and the same thing – and that is ORDER. The greatest possible *order*, that is the harmony of the desires and the pleasures of all. This is a noble end, is it not? Is not this an end one may dedicate a life to, make sacrifices for? I think so.

'First I brought order to France, my adopted nation – though who adopted whom is a question not easily answered, eh? (and he laughed). That country was in a terrible condition, a state almost of anarchy. Well, well, I need not go into all that. It was simply my Destiny to put all to rights, my destiny and the Sovereign Will of the People. At the loss of Liberty, Mr Bozzam? I did not destroy liberty, liberty was not there. There were persecutions, deportations, no proper education. The church was suppressed, Madam, the Armies hopeless, profiteers and so on, and so on. You see these were the fruits of Revolution. Whatever people may say, Revolution is one of the greatest misfortunes with which Divine Anger can punish a nation. It is the scourge of the generation that causes it and for long years, nay for a century perhaps, it brings unhappiness to all, and happiness to only a few.

'So I put a stop to all that, and it was the Will of the People that I did. Listen. The first duty of a Prince is, without doubt, to do what the People wish. That is agreed, right? But let us remember: the common people scarcely ever want what they say they do. See it this way – their will and needs should be less expressed by *them* than *felt* by their Ruler. That is what is wrong in your country now – the people *want* an end to feudalism, they *want* equal rights, they *want* a strong, central, rational government with their best interests at heart: that is what they *want*. But what do they *ask* for? They ask for their Inquisition, for their Church, for that irresponsible, cowardly Ferdinand for King – really he is a malicious idiot, that man – even though I have offered them my brother. Why are they so stupid as to ask for these things? Because the press, unfettered, in the pay of the English Oligarchy, urges them, because the Priests and Monks living in luxury fear to lose their privileges and the people are superstitious and believe their Friars . . .' And here the Great Man, whose face had become a little suffused, gestured wildly at the monastery walls around us and then suddenly pulled himself up short, perhaps aware of a coolness, a stoniness in the expressions of his two interlocutors, a priest and an abbess. At all events he now slumped back and surveyed us broodily for a moment from under his lids.

Then he sighed and sat up again, and continued in tones once more restrained – 'I say – my policy exists in ruling people to the will of the great majority. In this way, I believe, one recognises the Sovereignty of the People. Listen. In order to end the war in La Vendée I made myself a Catholic and signed the Concordat with the Pope who later consecrated me and all my endeavours. Yet as a Mussulman I managed to establish myself in Egypt, and again as an Ultramontanist, a friend of the Pope, I won all hearts in Italy. If I were ruling a Jewish people (here he laughed again) I would restore the Temple of Solomon. In this manner I spoke of liberty in the free part of San Domingo and confirmed slavery in the other half. Oh yes, I reserved the right to improve and limit the conditions of slavery where I allowed it to remain; and in the places where I upheld Liberty I also restored order and discipline, for that is what people really want.'

He drank some wine.

'Order is what people want. Most people. The Majority who silently and decently go about their business every day for the common weal of all. There is no order in Spain. Look how your laws change from city to city, from one Ancient Kingdom to the next. Look how different people have different rights. In France now everyone has the same rights, except those who might broadly be called the Working People – they have to be restrained a little, they have to carry an identity document, the Prefect fixes wages and so on – but these restrictions are necessary and reasonable, and anyway the working people of France are good people, patriotic, and they are well-paid. My Wars ensure that. But here in Spain all is confusion! Why, you even have tariffs between cities, you even have different weights and measures in Aragon to those in Andalucie. How can a modern state function if one town cuts cloth, or weighs corn on a different scale to another?

'Mr Bozzam nods his head and he is right. Listen. All Europe will measure and weigh by one standard, and that will be good. You agree, I can see. What we have done is this: a line from Mont Jany, here in Spain, near Barcelona, is drawn through France to Dunkirk. This is a North-South line and it spans exactly ten degrees. This is the measure from which all else comes, and we call it one thousand kilometres or ten million metres. I am sorry. One million metres – to be wrong by a factor of ten is only a slip. And so we have the Measure, the Metre. From that all else comes. For Measurement by Volume we have the cubic metre. That is too big. Divide by ten, a cube of one tenth of a metre to each side and we call it a *Litre*. Then for weight. Here our unit is the *Gram*, and that is simply the hundredth part of the weight of one litre of water. I am sorry, Signor Bozzam (*Signor*, for occasionally now the Emperor lapsed into Italian, in which language my Father courteously replied) one *thousandth* part. That factor of ten again. You ask at what temperature? The water? It matters? So. Mr Bozzam is a scientist and the answer is at four degrees. Not at nought degrees for then water freezes and there is a problem with the air trapped in the ice, not at one hundred degrees for then it boils and there is a problem with vapourisation. So we take four degrees, the lowest before freezing commences.

'Now is this not all Rational? Is not this an impressive structure with which to sweep away all the irregularities and absurdities, the anarchy and disorder? And it all stems from the metre – one thousandth, I mean one millionth of that line drawn from Dieppe in the North of France to a point in that part of Spain which is now part of France too. Yes, it is reasonable and good and a length or width of cloth will be the same in Paris, in Madrid, in Berlin and one day, yes, in London too. And every peasant from Gibraltar to St Petersburg will weigh his cabbages and cheeses by the gram. That is my aim, my hope, my design, the kernel of all my labours . . .

'You smile, Madam? What I mean is this metrified system is like a symbol for all my labours. Signor Bozzam – you are a scientist, a rationalist, an enlightened man – you will understand this dream of mine. In France there were thirty millions – all at war with each other, now there is one nation. Here is how I achieved this. By the Law of the Twenty-eighth of Pluvoise in the Year Eight I have created the most powerful mechanism of government ever devised. Everything can now respond to the Will which acts, decides, impels, stimulates, disciplines, and, where needed, represses. Everything is connected and moves in unison. This is how. France is now ninety-eight Departments under ninety-eight Prefects. Spain shall be divided into thirty-eight Departments in the same way – I have people in Madrid already working on it. Each Prefect acts according to the government's will – they secure by decrees the execution of all general laws. Under them four hundred and twenty Under-Prefects control thirty-thousand Mayors and municipal councils who can only act with the approval, supervision, and verification of the Under-Prefects and the Prefects. And so by successive transmissions, through channels regularly disposed, the motive power, my Destiny, descends from the top down to the broad foundations, without losing its force.

'All works according to plan. From the Rue de Rivoli and Quai Voltaire in Paris instructions go out and reports come in – all composed to a standard form for easy reading and assimilation, all bound identically in the red tape that has become a holy symbol of order throughout the land; and thus on the same day each Prefect, whether in *Seine et Oise* or *Basses Pyrénées*, whether in *Guyenne et Gascogne* or *Alpes Maritimes*, makes the same inspection, addresses identical schools perhaps with the same speech – and now the same too, not only in Bordeaux and Nice but in Amsterdam and Rome as well, in Bonn and Salzburg, and tomorrow in Madrid, and the day after in Berlin, and one day in London and Moscow.

'For this is my Destiny, my Dream – the fusion, the federation of the Nations, which have been separated and turned one against the other by feudalism, dynastic stupidities, religion, by revolutions and politics. Thirty million Frenchmen, fifteen million Spanish, as many Italians, thirty million Germans, all shall be united into one strong national body. Surely the accomplisher of this work will be awarded posterity's most beautiful wreath? And I feel myself strong enough and called on to undertake this work. And when it is done then all people will be able to devote themselves to the realisation of the ideal at present only a dream of a higher civilisation. Then there will be no more vicissitudes to fear, no more mess, for there will be only one set of laws, one kind of opinion, one view, one interest – the interest of mankind. Is it not, my friends, this plan of mine of bringing about a Union of Nations, the noblest, the most courageous, the highest minded . . . ?' And here he bit off a huge mouthful of leg of chicken which he had first dipped in egg yolk and he flung himself back in his chair chewing savagely and eyeing us from smouldering eyes, the sweat glistening on his ivory temples.

There was silence, only the fire crackled, then the Abbess, her cheeks flushed, sat up straighter than ever, and began to clap her old and knotted hands; my Father, at first astonished, caught her eye and began to do likewise with firm percussive strokes, his head raised, his beard bobbing as 'Bravo,' he cried, 'bravo.' Amazed at the antics of these two old people though I was, I thought it best to join in, and added my plaudits to theirs.

The mask in front of us relaxed and a smile positively that of a flirt spread across those well-shaped lips, the head, the greatest head in Europe, shook from side to side with the delighted modesty of an actor or a bull-fighter who knows he had done well and is pleased with the homage of the crowd, and finally he held up his fingers, long, white, and a little podgy, and nodded his head as if to say 'enough, enough'. In fact he murmured again and again, 'too kind, too kind, you are all too kind.'

When at last we were silent he called and his Moor or Turk or whatever came in, and was sent for another bottle.

'It is almost Christmas,' his Master cried, 'and tonight we may relax a little, may we not?' Then to himself it seemed he muttered: 'It was Hellish Cold, and the day before, damnable; and the snow and ice on those Mountains, those shit mountains, mountains of frozen shit. But I got them over, you know; oh yes, I got them over.' His voice now raised a little – 'I walked with them, you know; got out and marched with them, that's how I got them over.'

I supposed he meant the Guadarramas, North-West of Madrid. Indeed it was truly extraordinary he and his army had gone so far so fast in such weather.

He motioned the Moor to fill our glasses though my Father's and the Abbess's were scarcely touched, then he raised his which slopped a little – 'To a United Europe,' he cried, and we all drank.

'That's why I'm in Spain, you know, that's why I'm in Spain. To make Spain part of this grand design. Listen. In the crisis in which France now finds herself in her fight for new ideas and the Struggle of the Century for Europe we cannot leave out Spain, and abandon her to her enemies. We must bind her to our policy of her own free will – if not, then sacrifices must be made and force used. The Code of Laws for Nations is not the same as that for people. The Spanish people despise their government and demand a return to the old stately, solemn ceremonial. That is the meaning of the Tumult at Aranjuez, of the turning out of that pig Godoy, and Charles with his lewd Queen. Well, since Providence has raised me so high I am the one called on to carry out this renewal. I can carry it out in peace. I want no bloodshed. I do not wish a single drop to smear Castilian independence. I have freed the Spanish Nation from a horrible form of government, I have given you a liberal constitution, and my own brother. All his advisers and ministers are Spaniards. In doing this I have conferred the greatest benefit that has ever been given to a nation. Listen. When Charles and his son Ferdinand came to Bayonne, of their own free will, I was able to judge their complete incapacity and an unspeakable compassion filled me for the fate of a great people. Bayonne was not an ambuscade but a huge and brilliant *coup d'état*. I scorn sordid and low means; I am too powerful to need them. I act like Providence which heals the sufferings of mortal men in her own way, even by violent means, regardless of condemnation no matter where from or on what grounds.

'Yet I am resisted everywhere. And so. Listen. (And here he leaned forward and punctuated each word with a light blow of his gold knife handle on the board in front of him.) If a people decline their own happiness, then they are giving way to anarchical inclinations. They are guilty. The Ruler's first duty is to punish the guilty.'

And again he sat back, as if expecting our applause or at least acquiescence. This time nothing was forthcoming and I began to be fearful that we would displease the Emperor by keeping mum – indeed a most uncomfortable silence fell so that I became aware of my pulse and sweat in my palms, as the Emperor's hooded gaze shifted from face to face of us; and though my Father and the Abbess did not lift their eyes from their plates I contrived a weak sort of smile.

Then just as I was expecting an outburst of rage, which might have ended with our executions, or imprisonment anyhow, my

Father saved all by changing the subject entirely. He bowed his head a little towards the Great Man, and spoke as follows: 'Sir, I have always interested myself in the education of the young, have endeavoured to discover the best foundations on which this noble duty should be established. I believe you have done much for your people in this line, and I should deem it an honour to hear your views on this subject.'

The Emperor seemed much restored by this question, perhaps even relieved that an occasion for sternness had passed, and with some animation set out his views, and I must say I found some sense in what he now said, though next day my Father became most irritable with me when I said so.

'We must start,' he declared, 'as always, from first principles. And these, in the case of education, are clear, whatever the *metaphysicians* and *ideologists* may say. The first principle of education is *Order*, that things should be well regulated throughout the state, so people may get on with their business undisturbed. Everything which disturbs Social Unity is of no value, and most of the ideologue's ideas on education seem directed towards disturbing Social Unity. The second principle is *Efficacy*. After promoting order, education should promote efficacy, should help people to be more productive at work, and if they are in government, then more efficient, so all things can go on at all times smoothly. To these ends I have made, and just this year the work is coming to fruition, my *Université*. This is like my government but on a smaller scale. At the top – Men of Wisdom and Distinction who naturally agree with me about what is needed. From them what should be taught to whom at all levels is handed down, right down to the youngest level, just as government goes through my Prefects, my Under-Prefects, to the Mayors, and so on. But education starts at the bottom and works up, so let us do likewise.

'The very young may be taught by Priests, who have always undertaken this task and who are respected by children and women. They look after reading and writing and elementary number and instil the Catechism. The Catechism has been reformed and is now useful. "Question: What should one think of those who fail in their duties to the Emperor? Answer: According to the Apostle St Paul, they would resist the order established by God himself and would make themselves deserving of eternal damnation." Simple, yes. But effective. At the next stage we go on, leaving behind those who are dull and will work with their hands, and women too. I do not think we need trouble ourselves with any plan of instruction for young females (he smiled his flirt's smile again, and put his white hand over the Abbess's): public education is not suited for them – manners are all in all to them and marriage is all they look to. I was once asked by a clever woman (and clever women are monsters in Nature, are they not?) who is the greatest woman in History. I replied: She who has had the most children. (Again his laugh.) But I digress.

'At the next stage the teacher becomes very important. So long as there is no teaching body with strong convictions there will be no well-defined political state. If one does not learn in childhood whether one is to be a Republican or a Monarchist, whether one is to be a believer or an infidel, the state will never form a Nation. It is at this secondary stage that the principles of belief and conduct that are conducive to a well-regulated state should be instilled. The teachers must be dedicated, celibate until thirty, and above all steady, reliable people, and very well trained. They will be paid highly but subject to instant dismissal and even prosecution under the Code, if they transgress in what they teach. In the State of Athens, he who corrupted the young with metaphysics and ideology could be punished by death, and rightly, for, for good or ill education is a powerful thing.

'At the tertiary stage the aspiring student undergoes courses in Geography, modern History, Mathematics, the Sciences especially those that are practical, which will serve the State and the student's career. Rhetoric, *belles lettres*, and all such other fustian from the Middle Ages, we leave to one side. Literature of course can help a man aspire to what is noble – Racine and Corneille do this, and Ossian as well – but truly it is a matter for the evening, at the theatre or when one relaxes with a book before retiring. I have been told there is no new literature in my Empire. Well, that is the fault of the Minister of the Interior. I shall look into it. But I must say I do not think literature is difficult to produce – and I speak as an expert: I wrote a novel when I was young. It was really rather an easy thing to do.' And here, suddenly, he directed his gaze at me so that my stomach turned to water – 'Young man, you have the look of a reader of novels about you, a sort of milk and water look. I wager you are reading a novel, eh?'

'I have just finished the *New Heloïse*, Sir,' I heard myself reply.

'Well, well. The *New Heloïse* is a work which has been written with much warmth and will always remain the young people's book. I read it when I was nine. It is better than Madame de Staël's book. I have not yet read her book, but I will when I have time . . .'

At this point the Great Man realised that the meal was almost at an end. The comfits and sugared candies – he had shown a preference for crystallised violets – were almost gone and the second bottle of Chambertin almost empty. Yet he showed no sign of wanting to close the meal. Truth to say I fancy he was lonely at that Nativity Tide, he wanted to go on talking and we were an obedient and encouraging audience. Yet he was very tired too and his efforts, *Herculean* is not too great a word, in shifting his huge army from Madrid to Torrecilla in so short a time and in such cold and snow, had no doubt taken their toll. At all events he continued with us a space, indeed for another hour or more, but his speech became a little slurred and its content ceased to keep connection – and this despite the *coffee* he now called for.

'Will you share a pot of coffee with me, Reverend Mother?' he demanded of the Abbess.

'To be sure, Sir, I have never taken it in all my life,' she replied demurely. 'I should like to try, for I have heard it is now drunk instead of chocolate in the cities, and though I am old, or even because I am old, I like to try new things. That is if my Confessor can assure me there is no sin in it.' And she smiled at my Father who briskly replied: 'No, no, my Dear, no sin I assure you,' and he turned his head away from the Emperor to conceal a most surprising grimace, as if he would suppress a laugh. Not for the first time I wondered what these two were at, and feared that if there was disrespect to the Great Man in it they would undo us all.

The Emperor noticed nothing untoward but clapped his hands, and his flunkeys now brought in cups and saucers in the same service of gold and deepest blue, and a silver gilt pot that steamed. There was sugar too, but coarse and grey, and later my Father told me it was manufactured from roots, cane sugar being difficult to obtain on account of the British Fleet between Europe and the Indies. With some ceremony the coffee was poured. The Abbess declared the aroma to be divine, which enchanted the Emperor, but she ill-concealed her dislike of the bitterness in spite of the sugar. 'It's a little hot yet,' she said, and went on quickly before she could be quizzed on it, 'you are, Sir, I can see, a Religious Man. I mean you have mentioned God and Providence in words that must imply a Faith that is Deep and Sincere.'

The Emperor's voice now took on a tone of solemnity, and he spoke in measured style, almost as if he were in chapel or church; he put his folded hands on the table in front of him and looked straight down between us, at the Crucifix on the wall in front of him, with a fixed gaze, eyes slightly narrowed, yet I had the impression that he marked not the Image of Our Lord at all.

'Yes, Madam,' he began, 'I am religious. I have a deep faith in Providence, in the Divine Will, and in Myself as its Instrument. However weak the individual may be when compared with the omnipotence and will of Providence, yet at the moment when he acts as Providence would have him act he becomes immeasurably strong. Then there streams down upon him that force which has marked all greatness in the world's history. And when I look back on the five years that lie behind us, then I feel I am justified in saying: That has not been the work of man alone. But I hope I shall not offend if I insist that one may only believe what one may rationally hold to. Listen. The dogma of Christianity is being worn away before the advances of Science. Gradually the myths crumble. All that is left is to prove that in Nature there is no frontier. The man who lives in communion with nature necessarily finds himself in opposition to the churches.

'What comes naturally to mankind is the sense of Eternity, and this sense is at the bottom of every man. The soul and the mind migrate, just as the body returns to Nature. Thus life is eternally reborn from life. As to the "why" of all that, I feel no need to rack my brains on the subject. The soul is unplumbable. The Man born into the World asks himself: Whence do I come? Where am I? Whither am I going? These are Mysterious questions that urge him to Religion. We believe in God for everything around us proves His Presence. Have not the Greatest Minds believed this? Not only Bossuet, but Newton and Leibniz. Oh yes. Everything points to the Presence of a God, that much is certain.'

He mused now in silence, then drank some coffee.

'But all our religions! That is another matter. Clearly they are the creations of men. Why are there so many? Why has not ours always existed? Why do these religions mutually discredit each other? It comes from this, that men are always men, and priests have always and everywhere introduced lies and fraud. This noble and rational impulse towards the Deity has been debased and degraded by the Churches for the sake of power and luxury and easy lives. But in spite of this when I attained power I restored religion. I made use of it as a fundamental basis, a root: in my eyes it protects good morals, true principles – decency and good order. And then, as I say, men's minds are so constituted that they are in absolute need of the Marvellous, the Unlimited, which religion offers us and it is better for a man to seek this in religion than in soothsayers, adventurers, rogues. And the Story of the Nativity, which we celebrate tonight, is also a very beautiful one, a beautiful story, an emblem of Pure Motherhood . . .' and here I do believe a suspicion of moisture occurred in his eye, '. . . I too would like a Son, indeed I have several, but I should like one I can own.' Then he seemed to pull himself up, drank more coffee, and his tone hardened – 'But, Madam, I am above all a realist. My true religion, as I have said, is Social Order. For my part I do not see in Religion the mystery of Trans-substantiation, but the mystery of Social Order. Society cannot exist without inequality of Property, an inequality that cannot be maintained without Religion. It must be possible to tell the Poor: "It is God's Will there must be rich and poor in this world, but hereafter and for all Eternity, there will be a different distribution."' He put down his coffee cup which he had been holding beneath his chin, and, misjudging the distance to the surface of the table, tumbled the cup so a dreg splashed his vest. '*Je m'emmerde,*' he muttered, dabbing furiously at the stain, then looked up a little wildly. 'With the Concordat came fifty million souls – ten million soldiers,' he cried.

The Abbess I now perceived looked quite out of countenance, indeed near distracted, and again I feared we would not get off without a row – clearly there had been some offence to her in what had just been said, but again my Father came to the rescue. 'Sir,' he said, and spoke quite boldly, 'your ideal of Social Unity is a fine one. I pray you, what do you consider its greatest enemy is in these times we live in?'

The Emperor left off mopping himself and fixed my Father with his clear stare. 'Come, come, Reverend Sir, you are not a fool. It is clear enough surely. All who are opposed to us are our enemies. Who is not for us is against us.'

'Yes, yes,' my Father muttered, 'opposition to Social Unity must be disruptive, but opposition to government . . .'

'I have never yet,' and the tone was reedy, again, irritated, 'I have never yet been able to understand what good there is in opposition. Whatever it may say, its only result is to diminish the prestige of authority in the eyes of the people.'

'But if government . . .' my Father's tone was measured and sweet, and could give no offence, yet the Emperor interrupted.

'Governments are compelled every day to break the law,' he cried, 'it cannot be otherwise, government would be impossible if it was. Listen. There is not a single minister anywhere ever who has not at some time been liable to impeachment. But this is foolish. Laws are not for governments, they are for the governed. If the Emperor acts, then it is not illegal, by definition. If, for example, the Emperor approves an action because of national security, or because of a threat to peace and order, then the Emperor's decision is one that enables those who carry it out to do so without violating the Law. This much is clear. Why then have an opposition? Why have a free Press? What is this Liberty people make a fuss about? Freedom is the need of a class that is not very numerous and is privileged by circumstances; equality, on the other hand, is what pleases the Crowd.

'You asked what is the greatest foe of Social Harmony. I answer: in many places it is the so-called free press. We do not have that problem any more in France. The papers print what I say. This enforced censorship is good, it is the right to prevent the publication of ideas that disturb the peace, the interests, and the good order of the State. It has been proved that a strong force of public opinion produces nothing but confusion and excitement. In England it is all right. There the common people are too rough, and crude, they are always too drunk to let themselves be excited by writings. Even so, one day the English Government will be toppled by the freedom of their press. But in France where the common people have the gift of quick apprehension, are endowed with lively imaginations, and are susceptible of strong impressions, unlimited freedom of the press would be absolutely fatal. Without well-regulated surveillance of the press I would be overthrown in three days.

'It has been said I fear criticism from the press. It is true that the sheets in several countries have criticised me and often very wrongly, inaccurately. This is what creates confusion. They said I massacred the Turks outside Jaffa. Certainly I had a few thousand shot down, but they had already broken the articles of an earlier capitulation. Anyway I could not feed them. And so they were shot. They say I murdered the Duke of Enghien, that he was not concerned in the plot against me, but those who really know

agree that the fault is with those who planned to overthrow the
Republic and murder its highest official . . . I did not do these
things, I did not do them . . . It is my Destiny, my Fate that
works through me . . . The fate, the Destiny of the World that
works through me . . . I am destined to change the face of the
World . . . after the Battle of Lodi I realised I was a superior
being . . . A man like me is hardly concerned with a million
lives.'

And now his face, hitherto flushed, had become shiny white,
like certain soapy marbles, and his pinched lips narrowed to a
thin line, and beads of perspiration stood out on his temples. He
hunched forward over the table and his hands gripped the wooden
arms of his chair. It was obvious that he was in the clutches of
pain, but he gave no sign of what ailed him though he wriggled
slowly on the cushions beneath him as if he could relieve thereby
the discomfort that afflicted him. With some alarm the Abbess and
my Father offered to send for help, poured water for him and so
on; but the help he refused most firmly and the water he barely
sipped; at last he gasped that the attack was a mild one and was
passing, and within a moment he recovered sufficiently to whisper: 'I declare I am the Greatest Slave among Men – my Master
has no Entrails, and that Master is the Nature of Things.'

This strange saying reduced him and us to silence for a space of
perhaps five minutes. The fire, burning low, crackled occasionally;
the candles guttered. The Great Man sat, slumped back in his
chair, his head forward on his chest, his hands still clutching the
armrests. His eyes glittered behind half-shut lids. The next day my
Father speculated on the nature of the attack we had witnessed
and decided that the Emperor suffered grievously from *hemor-
rhoids*, the result of nervous over-stimulation of the blood flow
which could be cured by administering depressants – but this was
the *Brunonian* physiology he favoured and is, I believe, now dis-
counted by the Profession.

The quietness was broken by the tolling of the Convent bell,
and then, distantly, from across the yard, the chanting by the

twelve nuns of the Introit for Compline of the Eve of the Nativity came sweetly across the snow. Against this magical sound the Emperor again began to talk – his fit of illness or pain having passed but leaving him in doleful mood.

'What is a man?' he asked. 'I believe that man has been made from loam, warmed by the sun, and bound together by an electric fluid. What are the animals, an ox, for example, if not organic matter? So far, so good. When we see that we have an almost similar composition are we not justified in believing that man is only matter, somewhat better put together, who almost approaches perfection? Perhaps one day beings will arise whose composition is still more perfect.' His head fell forward on his chest again and the chant of the nuns came frosty clear. 'I remember, when I was a child,' he added, 'I saw a kid's throat cut in the Market, by a butcher, and then, young though I was, these were the ideas that came to me concerning the Nature of Man.'

The Abbess now covered the Emperor's hand with hers, as if to offer some comfort. 'I wonder,' she said softly, 'what was the childhood like of so great a man?'

He lifted his head, his eyes opened a little, fixing hers, and something of his former smile passed like the sun on a cloudy, windy day across his face, and then he spoke very quietly, as if seeing himself again as a very small boy. 'I was quarrelsome,' he said, and chuckled, 'pugnacious. I feared nobody. I struck one person, scratched another, till all were afraid of me. My elder brother Joseph was the chief sufferer. I struck him and bit him. Then it was he who got the scolding, for before he had time to recover from the blow I had complained to Mother. Well. Joseph is extremely mild and good. He possesses intelligence, is cultured, is amiable, and I have made him amends, for now he is your King.

'But Pauline was my favourite. She and I used to tease my Grandmother who was bent like a witch, and gave us sweets. But it was Pauline who was always punished, for it is easier to lift up a little girl's dress than unbutton a boy's breeches.'

He nodded and chuckled at this for a moment more and then at last pushed back his chair and pushed himself up on to his feet. He looked at each of us in turn and nodded to himself as if setting our faces in his mind. 'Madam,' he then said, 'Sir. Young Man. I have had a pleasant evening, most pleasant. You have entertained me . . . well, very well. Your discourse has been charming, charming and witty. In the absence of my Ministers, my men of Science, Philosophers and those I dine with in Paris, I have had the excellent Charles Bosham, Astronomer and Rationalist. Although I have not shared this Christmas tide with my Empress, nor with Madame Mère, I have been with this excellent Reverend Mother, who henceforth may be known by this new title – The Empress-Abbess.'

This pleased him and he chuckled again and then held out his hand to the good old lady who took it and once more bobbed a courtesy.

'What will the Empress-Abbess's first edict be?' my Father now asked. 'Your Majesty could allow her, as if in Faery Tale, just one *ukase*.'

There was a moment's silence then her old voice came clear and sweet like the bell beyond: 'If I were truly an Empress,' she said, 'the prerogative I should exercise with most happiness would be that of mercy. My Lord, I beg you release the three clerics for me, who you have said will be shot in a few hours' time.'

The Emperor frowned, then relaxed, and then, impertinent that he was, reached out and tweaked the old woman's ear, quite sharply, so she gasped. 'All right, my dear Empress-Abbess, you shall have them, you shall have them. But I shall have the ears at least off all monks or priests I catch meddling with politics or war in this country.'

And at last, with one nod more at each of us he stumped away to the door where his flunkeys received him, and conducted him away by candle-light to his chamber.

His walk had a certain ponderosity about it, and now I wonder if my Father's diagnosis of his ailment was not after all a right one.

3

My Father and the Abbess, well-pleased with their night's work, now went off to the Chapel where the small community waited to hear Mass for Christ's Birth. I was a little drunk and very tired and begged off; it was after all almost midnight. I was woken while it was still dark by much toing and froing, by light dancing across the ceiling of our cell cast from huge *flambeaux* in the yard, by the clattering of horses' hooves and the rumbling wheels of the Emperor's huge coach, brought back to receive him. We watched through our window and saw him stump out across the yard, in his green coat again, and mount the steps – then the door was closed, the steps folded under, the team whipped up, and in a moment all was gone. It was very cold and still snowing out of a moonlit sky – large flakes that floated down like blessings. The Great Man could have had no more than three hours sleep – perhaps not so much. The noises continued for an hour, but more distant, as of bugle calls, marching feet, shouted orders and the rumble and squeak of countless waggons. By daybreak only a small detachment of cavalry remained behind as screen and escort for following couriers.

My Father spent some time in the morning with the Abbess and then sent to me to prepare to leave, so I packed up our few things, wrapped up well, and saw to our cattle. By eleven o'clock we were on the road and looked to be in Los Arapiles in time to dine the next day. But we were grievously delayed and it was a week before we were back, and this on account of the fact that the first village we came through had been sacked and fired by the French and my Father insisted we should do what we could there until help should arrive from Valladolid, the Provincial Capital – but this help was long coming, for the Emperor resided there a fortnight, though sending his army on to catch Sir John Moore, and the village had been razed on his order because on the afternoon of Christmas Eve two French Dragoons had been shot dead as they crossed the fields nearby, shot down by peasants who escaped into the narrow streets and alleys, and so all was destroyed.

Every house had been looted and fired; the women raped, some children bayoneted, many of the men shot, but not all shot dead, some hanged and mutilated.

The sights we saw and the work my Father insisted we did there turned his mind, for when we finally set off back, on New Year's Day (1809), we had a strange talk in which I believe he showed signal lack of sense.

It started thus: 'Well, Joseph, what did you think of the Great Man?'

I pondered a little and then answered in this way: 'There is much to be abhorred. The sights we have seen these last few days lead me to condemn the means he has to use. I cannot condone murder, theft and rape, and yet such horrors have always gone with wars. And wars have oft times in history been the means for settlement, for spreading civilisation. Thus Plutarch and Livy have shown us how Greece and Rome used war to ensure the spread of great and glorious benefits to Mankind.'

'Come, come Sir: this is fustian, this is unutterable nonsense.'

I fell silent, hurt at the savagery of his rebuke, and we rode on for a space over the snow. To our left black crows tore and cawed at a shapeless mass on the ground, and since we were still in country through which the French Cavalry passed daily, scouting and patrolling, I prayed to myself that my Father would not take it into his head to investigate it. I had no desire to be scraping up a grave of snow and frozen earth with our bare hands. At least there had been spades for such work in the village we had just left.

But either my Father had not marked the corpse, if that is what it was, or recognised it was beyond his help, for after a space he resumed: 'I am sorry I spoke harshly, you are still young and impressionable, and I should not forget that.' His mule jogged on, then he turned again. 'Pray tell me, Joseph, what of civilised value do you think this man will create?'

'Sir, I found his talk of Social Harmony admirable,' I replied. 'It seemed, as he himself said, a noble, high ideal, one for which sacrifice may properly be made, and one which will confer incalculable benefits on mankind if carried through.'

'I cannot think so, I cannot think so,' the old man replied and shook his head violently from side to side. 'During the last few days,' he went on, 'I have thought much and deeply about all this . . . this Social Unity, this harmony of men's desires . . . such philosophical musing I find alleviates the distress felt when engaged in such pitiful work as had been forced on us, and I recommend it to you if, or rather when, for the times are bad, we are next faced with like horrors. And the result of my musing is this: I cannot call the new state he would create out of old Europe civilised.

'He offers us peace at home but eternal war, or preparation for war, abroad. He offers material welfare – food, clothing, work for all, education of a kind for many, in a word a sort of safety: but he demands blind, unthinking acquiescence – and acquiescence to what? – not to an ideal, not to something noble, or spiritual, or beautiful, or even true, but simply and completely to the machine, the machine he would make us all part of. He has no moral sense, no sense of what is good or fitting, and in the name of efficacy and efficiency he would deprive us too of this sense he lacks. You heard him: to talk of anything but what he could measure with his metre rule brought forth his favourite condemnation:- all such talk, he said, was the stuff of ideologues and metaphysicians. Oh Joseph (and here his voice broke a little), if sublime Isaac, if honest Locke and courageous Hume had seen . . . if they could have known where . . . but no, this is nonsense, it must be. Other forces created this monster, this leviathan – not the ratiocinations of good men . . .' and so he rambled for a time.

At last, feeling irritated on one side and my confidence fortified a little by the clear lack of logic he displayed on the other, I interrupted thus and briskly: 'Come Sir, you talk of morality and such like stuff, of individual conscience and I know not what, as if you were a Saint and the Emperor a Devil – yet that Christmas Eve you were no martyr. You were happy to take his bread, nay you went further, you positively flattered him and your precious Abbess did so too . . .'

'Enough, Joseph,' my Father cried. 'Do you wish to make me angry? You know I do not anger easily, but you are being presumptuous.'

'Nay but . . .'

'Be quiet . . . you – puppy.'

And again, both of us mortified, and suffering no doubt from exhaustion, cold and hunger, we rode on in silence; but all the time my Father's mind was churning over what I had so imprudently said and at last he began again, but this time speaking slowly and carefully, trying not in inflame me or himself.

'Joseph, what we did that night was not for ourselves, our so tame acquiescence to that monster, though even if it had been it would have been justified – survival is always a right, even if it is one that should be waived if occasion or will demand. But we behaved thus for our three friends due to be shot without trial, as spies, and thus we got them off, albeit an ear short each, which, when all's said and done, they could spare. And I believe we were right – in a State where dumb acquiescence to the material welfare of the many is the only morality then true expression of our human needs will be marred by such necessary compromises as I and the Abbess made. We who believe in humanity will need to cover ourselves, will need to cheat the Cheaters – by whom I mean the Ministers and armies of Clerks with their reports and metre rules and red tape who cheat us out of our human birth rights if we let them; we will have to do these things if we are to live and think in their despite.'

'Sir,' I replied, like him endeavouring to moderate my tone, 'you speak of human needs – yet the State he spoke of is designed to . . .'

After all he could not forbear from interrupting: 'To give comfort, work, enough to eat and an education in technics, to provide in short the means of achieving nought but enslaved contentment

such as is enjoyed by cows and horses and hens in a yard. You
heard him say he saw no difference 'twixt an ox and a man.'

'What then Sir, are these so very human needs we do not share
with other beasts?'

He looked at me with a sort of lofty pity I could not but resent.
'The life of the Mind, of the Spirit is not nurtured by warm
clothes and meat dinners. It requires above all else Freedom – freedom to develop and grow and become itself. To go where it is
prompted, not where it is pushed. To dwell with beauty and a
kindness that does not presume to intrude or mould, to . . .'

And on he went with similar transcendental stuff.

As we drew nearer Los Arapiles his wandering mind returned
to what the Great Man had said about the press and about
Literature, and so forth, and all this he now anathematised more
almost than the rest put together for, he said, unfettered communication was the life blood of the intellect. And at last he
concluded thus, shaking his head most woefully.

'If this Grand State that is to be built manages all normal communication, validating or invalidating it only in accordance with
what it sees as social needs, then the values alien to these needs
may perhaps have no other medium of communication than the
abnormal one of fiction.'

This, the idea that in *Novels* one may find a sort of Truth not
available elsewhere and important at that, is surely mad. I waited
until he had finished and then showed my opinion by changing
the subject.

'Sir,' I said, 'you'd best find your scarf and pull it about your ears
before we arrive, to prevent a scolding from Tía Teresa.'

'Ay, ay,' but he did nothing, and blushingly I recalled he had
used the garment to swaddle a squalling and naked infant in the
wretched village we had left.

'Joseph,' he said, as we passed between the two flat topped
eminences who give their name to our village, 'men deprived of
their spiritual side by the Grand State, or by any other means, are
but shadows of men, they lack substance, they are but figures of

men. It is to that the Times are tending and That Man is pushing them along. Imagine. A world of shadows, of men existing in one dimension only. It does not do to dwell on it; it will not do to dwell on it.'

And here I agreed with him. Thinking too much on such things indeed sickens the mind, and I wondered if his was not too far gone to mend.

PART TWO

CHAPTER IV

Carnival under the French, Followed by a most Fortunate and Affecting Reunion.

I

Tedious it would be to rehearse the complete catalogue of defeats, routs, capitulations, and surrenders that followed the Great Man's brief sojourn in our country. Already before that Christmas Eve General Blake had been defeated at *Espinosa* and then again at *Gamonal* to the North of Burgos. At this latter, regiments raised in our Province, including one of Students of the University, were broken with heavy loss, not the least of which was Tebaldo Zúñiga, Violeta Martín's husband, sabred in the front file of his men as he led a forlorn counter-attack though it was not until the New Year (1809) that the news reached us. Thankfully Violeta was, as shall be seen, cast out of a different metal than her sister by marriage Isabella and not many months passed before she found a consolation for her loss which shall be recounted in its due place. But to continue – Castaños in Aragon was broken at *Tudela*, La Romana at *Mansilla* in the Asturias, in Galicia John Moore slain and his army hustled out of *La Coruña* in the first week of the New Year, and in January also General Victor with King Joseph committed most dreadful and hideous slaughter on a rabble of students, Friars, Peasants, and Artisans who, though twice their number, could do nothing against the new King's Imperial Cohorts at *Ucles* to the South of Madrid.

And the worst news of all was the fall of gallant Saragossa in February at the end of a siege where bravery and endurance found limits beyond those yet achieved by our race, but which have been well recorded elsewhere and by more worthy pens than mine.

It seemed then by the middle of February that all resistance to the forces of Enlightened Rationalism were at an end – though true it was a sort of Junta or Regency went on from Seville, and later Cadiz, and a sort of army was maintained by that old fool Cuesta in Estremadura, and a garrison of red coats remained in Lisbon and another in Gibraltar with those wooden castles Fernando had seen at Mondego Bay behind them, but these seemed but shadows or cobwebs, shortly to be swept away, of far less account than any of the hosts already broken up, and many there were who welcomed this – now the bloodshed was over the Rule of Reason would prevail and our country would be properly ordered, for the first time in its existence, according to the best Principles known to Man.

Thus it was that when a regiment or two of French – a detachment from the Army of Marshal Soult who, having seen the English off at La Coruña, as above, was moving South against Lisbon and Portugal with this said detachment holding his left and communication with Madrid – arrived in our town in late January under General Dorsenne who shortly received letters patent from King Joseph nominating him Governor; when, I say, these troops arrived a fair number of us turned out to cheer, especially as Illuminations were promised for Shrovetide and Carnival, and Bulls in the Great Square too, though nothing came of these last. Of course others of us were less than ready to welcome the Intrusive Monarch, letters from the Junta in Seville were circulated in the taverns and at *tertulias* which called for continued resistance to the foe, and newspapers too; in the back-streets and alleyways roistering French would be brained by a falling tile or found face down and smothered in a midden, and when all householders were called to the churches for an Oath of

Loyalty many stayed at home or went with sullen faces. Some priests let it be known at Confession and other like opportunities that the oath, though solemnly sworn, could not bind, being forced and in flat contradiction to Natural Law, which was God's Law, as well.

The Town was well divided, and the University too. In the former the merchants and bankers and many of the artisans, especially those employing others in manufactories, welcomed the new reign and the promised reforms – especially the abolition of tariffs between Towns and Provinces, whilst the poorer sort, pushed on by Priests and Friars (on whom many relied in times of hardship and famine for food and clothing) remained most determinedly against the atheistical French. In the Schools those of Theology and Rhetoric, being peopled mostly by Religious, likewise went against the French; the reformed schools as Medicine, Law, Astronomy split evenly, there being many *Afrancesados* or *Frenchifiers* amongst them, though also there were those who, while hoping for the Dawn of the Age of Reason, remained unresigned to French Rule – perhaps out of fear of atheism, or tyranny, and not a few out of admiration for England and Britain. Most of the young and able of both these groups deserted cloister and lecture hall, anatomy theatre and Observatory, during the next six months, the Frenchifiers to Madrid for civil posts in King Joseph's government (rational rule requiring far more clerks than any other sort), the Loyalists to Seville and Cadiz to work in and for the new *Cortes*, formed to rule until legitimate Sovereign Ferdinand, the Desired One, should be released from incarceration in France.

I was unsensible of the extent to which these divisions had reft our society until the Shrovetide aforesaid, though already stray French soldiers had been murdered, as above, and General Dorsenne had erected two pair of gibbets, one in the small square outside the University, one in the Market Square. The first was hung with two Augustine Friars taken *in flagrante delicto* sermonising that killing French was no sin; on the second the bodies of two cooks believed to have poisoned a Sergeant of Fusiliers were now dressed victuals for the rooks and daws that cackled about the Convents and Churches nearby.

I came in early from Los Arapiles on Shrove Tuesday, across the cold hills, deeply frozen and bleak as they were, carrying my Carnival Stick, a cudgel with a knob on the end and the bark peeled in rings and fancy designs done in hot poker work, and all in my *Majo* Gear, eager to join in the processions and fairs of the morning, to see the bulls in the Great Square in the afternoon, and the Illuminations at dusk. It's true too that I was especially glad to be away from my Father for a day (though as I shall relate it was many months before I saw him again) for he had remained tetchy and poorly after our Christmas-tide Jaunt; also he refused to give me funds to set myself up in town again, as before, on grounds that the University remained closed as far as teaching went, so we had been at loggerheads for some time, and indeed the day before we had downright quarrelled.

So, I took a gold duro from his purse (a mite of what he owed me in unpaid allowance) and set off for a day of pleasure. Alas, it turned out quite otherwise.

First I lacked a friend with whom to share the festivities, so I directed my steps to the Martín Apartment to see if Fernando, who lodged there yet, would come on the streets with me and round the Taverns. I climbed the stairs with a light heart for already fire-crackers were loosed off in the streets and strains of music could be heard, and so was somewhat dashed to find the familiar door, with its brass knocker in the shape of a welcoming hand, hung with a mortuary wreath of bays decked with black ribbon. I knocked and as I waited for an answer read the notice on the wreath and thus discovered the loss of Tebaldo Zúñiga slain at Gamonal, as above. I feared now that a house in mourning so soon again after an earlier and yet more grievous loss, that of dear Rafael their only son, would not provide the company I sought, but I remained where I was, composing condolences rather than invitations to sport.

The door was opened by the maid, the one to whom some blame had been attached after my foolish neglect of telling Rafael I had borrowed money from him, a misfortune long since remedied by apologies and a gift from me and a smile and a courtesy from her. Notwithstanding which her reception of me was cooler than I expected and, to my surprise, she showed me into Don Jorge Martín's booklined study, rather than into the family quarters where I had once been so welcome. This dull formality discomforted me a little, but I put it down to the condition of mourning the house was in, and fell to speculating on how much those old leather tomes were ever read and how much they would fetch in *Angel's*, the Bookshop.

After a space steps in the passage heralded the good Fernando. I moved to embrace him for we had not met since before Christmas, indeed not since the misunderstandings at All Hallows' over Rafael's ring, but he forestalled me with a raised hand which I offered to shake instead in the English style, thinking this may be the fashion he now affected after his sojourn amongst them in Portugal – and then again he had been much in their company I believed during their stay in Salamanca, but that was not his intention either; with a shock of shame I discovered he meant a rebuff.

''Tis really you, José? Whatever brings you here of all places?' he gasped in his voice most unlike his usual gruff, bonhomous tone, being now a cry strangled into a whisper as if he did not wish to be overheard.

I explained that I had come to offer my condolences on this second grievous calamity that had befallen the Martín Family and especially to Violeta who had always been a favourite with me since she had kept the door when Angelica visited my bed of sickness.

'You cannot think this household will take kindly to commiseration from you,' Fernando replied sternly.

'Why ever not?' and I felt myself colour up.

'A cracked bell sounds ill however struck.'

The choler rose at this like the hectic yet I held myself back from striking him and instead demanded of him: 'Is it you who calls me a cracked bell, or your masters here whom you feel obliged to ape?' for I knew Don Jorge continued to employ him on menial errands as carrying messages, copying, and paid him with lodging and tuition in the law and a place at his table.

'Well, well,' he cried, 'I ape no-one. And the length of our acquaintance forbids me to take so hard a view as others may. The fool relishes the bad fish he's bought and I'll love the memory of our childhood until I die . . .'

'Me too, Fernando,' cried I warmly and offered my hand again, but he continued, '. . . but now Rafael's gone there are none here but see in you a history of deceit, if not thieving, of luxury and extravagance if not depravity, of . . .' but here I stopped my ears fast and beat my heels on the floor, for only thus could I restrain myself from taking up my cudgel and beating him about the ears, broader, heavier, and of course taller than I though he was, and thus I remained till he had finished his catalogue of my imagined failings, or I thought he had, for as I unstopped my ears I heard his final shot: '. . . and 'tis even said you favour the French in your reading and may be outside the study too.'

'Fernando,' said I, and I managed to cohibit my voice for I was sensible of being in a house of mourning and had no desire to break the silence, 'now is not the time to go over again how my design in all things contiguous to Rafael's memory or property were done out of respect for his estate, his wishes, and his widow, out of feelings of a most refined and sensible nature, and 'tis not flattery to myself to say my conscience is easy . . .'

'Oh, 'tis not only this . . .'

'What else then?'

'But so much . . .'

'But what? You must say something. Your studies will have instructed you that the accused has a right to know the charges laid.'

And here the good man, for such I still esteem him however

mistaken he could be, slapped hand to forehead, turned on his heel, and then back again, and almost spat his next salvo which clearly he expected would send me down the stairs like a kicked mongrel: 'I was at Gamonal too,' he cried, 'see here,' and he pushed back his sleeve to show a sabre cut on his left arm, the scar still scabbed and livid, and suppurating at one end. 'I was like to lose this arm, and was lucky to get off, and Tebaldo was cut down beside me and José Luis, and Ramón López, and Rafael Portillo and . . .' and he enumerated more of our friends and acquaintances from the Schools, 'and,' cried he, concluding, 'you were not there. Why were you not there?'

I looked at him with all the forgiveness I could express. 'You know I was wounded too, at Medina. I too am not yet recovered . . .'

'Holy Mother of God,' he cried, 'it will not do, it will not do. The world knows you were fit and well at All Hallows. The world knows you for either a coward or a Frenchifier, and Don Jorge has instructed me to tell you that neither are welcome here, and that must be an end of it now. José, the blame lies not with me.'

'Nor with me, I'm sure. Fernando, you are horrid hard on me.'

He shrugged. 'That's as may be. Remember – there is no better mirror than an old friend; but now you really must be gone before Don Jorge finds you still here and sends for the Porter to throw you down stairs.'

2

There was nothing to do but leave with dignity, and so I did, but bitterest mortification flooded my breast like gall, for what injury is more grievous than to be falsely accused of crimes that right-thinking men scorn as fiercely as they damn them? I confess my thoughts, my feelings were neither temperate nor forgiving and I roundly sent the Martín family, the Zúñigas too, and Fernando to

Hell or the Antipodes and resolved henceforth to bodge without them. In this mood (and I swung my Carnival cudgel at hitching posts and stray dogs and threatened any who stood in my way with it) I took myself direct to Antonio's Tavern in its cave beneath the Square, and pushed my way through the tipplers – already crowded up to his counter although it wanted an hour of noon – and drank off a bumper or two as quick as may be. And as I did Antonio himself, he who could make small coins fly through the air from his tray to his pocket, singled me out and said I had been sought for by an old friend – and that none other than Rubén García. At this my blood ran cold, I had no wish to see such a villain, I declared, and took myself off out again into the streets still angry and ready to do an injury to anyone who should cross me.

Unfortunately, inspired by the wine or my Evil Angel, or simply following the slope of the alleys, I headed East from the Great Square, through the market with its horrid gibbet and so down into the poorest quarters – the *barrios* where nine years before Rubén, Fernando, and I had lost ourselves and I ended up bedded with a whore and a drunk French Sergeant – unfortunately for here all was riot and licence already and increasing every moment as the day wore on.

The narrow streets were filled with muleteers, market people, gypsies, water-carriers, sellers of melon-seed and chestnuts, charcoal-burners, and all the riff-raff of the town even meaner than these, and all out on the one rampage of the year when tradition forbad the patrol of constables or the intervention of soldiery. Guitars thrummed everywhere, fifes squealed, drums rattled, skin bottles of cheapest wine were tipped and thrown and splashed and sprayed so within minutes my clothes stank of vinegar or worse. Many were in patched up fancy dress as of skeletons and death heads painted on black robes; others aped their betters as Bishops or Judges but all marred with the crudest obscenity, as a man dressed as a Beadle had a staff carved at the end in the shape of an engorged pudendum; the girls went forth in white dresses that revealed their breasts which they powdered stark white, and their faces whitened too save for circles of carmine upon their cheeks like painted dolls, and they capered in grotesque dances, arms flung up stiffly like marionettes, or whirling and prancing to the fifes, or pelted their neighbours with flour or melon seeds or simply the filth scooped up from the miry cobbles at their feet.

At corners tough women, toothless but with arms thick as gateposts, stood duty over seething cauldrons from which, for a *cuarto*, they would scoop up blood puddings, purple and grey like the guts they were made from, or pigs' feet. In the tiny squares men in tattered breeches with sacking on their feet to serve for shoes, and undone shirts, their faces blotched and swollen with drink and cold (for the day remained overcast with a sky like lead and occasional flurries of snow) occupied themselves with divers barbaric sports as mounting on each others' backs and charging each other down, fighting blindfold with cudgels or sacks filled with saw-dust, or, and this was a bloody game, they hung from the eaves of a house or a shop sign a live cock by its legs and swung at it as it flapped and crowed and so looped about in the air, with swords or knives, and they did this too with blindfolds so not all the blood spilled was from the roosters, and some splashed on me as I passed.

And through all this throng, and mingling with it so it was like a current of water running through an eddying pond only distinguishable from the rest by the direction of its movement, a procession passed, but turning on itself again when it reached the edge of the *barrio* by the market and so never trespassed upon the better part of town, a procession that had at the head fifes and drums and capering women, then a large banner with a leering face painted on it, and then men and women carrying dolls, life-size, stuffed with straw and known as *Uncle Sparky*, *Sister Saucy*, and *Don Bravo*, all of which were tossed in the air in blankets to the accompaniment of much merriment and hoots of joy; and after them a straw giant, bigger than the rest, the *Pelele* from whose coat hung a large sardine, pinned there with a ribbon, which piece of stinking fish would be buried with mock

solemnity at the end of the day to signify the end of Carnival and
the beginning of Lent.

It was when this procession passed me the second time that dis-
aster fell. By now I was, I confess it for who would not be with
the provocations I had suffered that morning, drunk, and my
temper had not mended with it. The doll Don Bravo, which signifies a gallant *Majo*, was dressed in coloured rags in coarse
imitation of the style I affected. Whether I was pushed or stumbled I do not know, but I now fell in the path of the drummers
(there were six of them) at the head of the procession, who beat
such a confounded tattoo about my ears that I was maddened by
it and tore from their midst right into the group of girls who were
carrying and tossing this Don Bravo, and stumbling against them
caused one who held, at the moment, the legs of the doll to fall,
and she, not letting the doll go, pulled it in two.

The commotion was now indescribable as of women screaming, girls crying, children hollering to find out what had
happened, and I helpless jammed up amongst them so I could not
get out but bobbed to and fro like a piece of flotsam, so open
mouths with broken teeth and stinking breath bellowed in my
ears, and elbows hammered my ribs, and fingers dug in my arms
and pinched, and shoulders, breasts and wild hair were flung about
my face, at which fear welled in me with the anger I already felt
and in my panic to get out I began to lay about me with fist and
cudgel as well as I might in so close a press, and as soon as I had
bloodied a nose here and made someone else's ears hum their
claw-like hands fastened more securely on me and fists and sticks
belaboured me in return.

Now out of the clamour came a voice, and what it said taken
up by others till all the throng echoed the sentiment which was
that I, having been the cause of the breaking of the doll Don
Bravo, should take its place, being appropriately dressed for the
office and not much bigger than the original, and, notwithstanding that I kicked and clawed a bit, I was seized on, nor did they
scruple where they seized, and bundled into the blanket. Well, I

weighed more than a straw doll and a moment or two was needed before these viragos could come together with their heaves and hoist me and the blanket all at once, but on the third attempt they did and up I went and the arms, breasts, faces turned over, upside down, and fell away from me then swung out of sight as the sky and snowflakes, black against the bright clouds they were spinning out of, lurched up, then all below spun back to me as I twisted and fell, and then up again, and but for the terror of it I might almost have savoured the sensation, at least as a relief after the pinching and beating, but on the third ascent I went high as the roofs, came down too fast, the blanket split, but not completely, and pulled the girls in on me who almost hit the ground which might have broke my back, or head, or limbs, so I was in mortal fear now and pleading them to stop – which either they listened to or feared for their blanket, for they rolled me out into the gutter where I begged them to leave me, but they were not done yet; they were still without a *Majo* doll, my coat and breeches would serve they cried, with a cushion or two for stuffing, and once again those prying, clawing hands went over me, and blotched, pipeclayed breasts and greasy hair swung over me, as they tore off my clothes down to my drawers, at which I at last broke free from them and ran, and they screamed and some followed hallooing, the crowd giving way to watch the chase; near naked as I was I must have seemed an escaped Bedlamite. Dodging about the alleys and between the stalls I went to earth at last in a Church, the tiny one of San Román, whereat they desisted, for the licence of the day stopped short at profanation.

The Church was empty. I closed the door, it had been open, and crossed the short nave to fling myself on the chancel step and there I swooned. I know not how long I remained in this faint but it must have been some hours, for when I came to the early dusk had begun to gather and the inside of the church was almost dark, save for the Chancel Lamp. For a time I lay without moving, numb and frozen, my head filled with spiritual agonies beyond the telling at all the humiliations and hurts I had suffered through that

Shriving Day, so I wept inwardly and without sound though scalding tears bathed my icy cheeks. At last I contrived some sort of
effort to lift my head and take in my surroundings – the dull glow
of gilt, the gleam of silver, and above the white of an altar cloth a
Christ on his Cross as naked and as humiliated as I, but with
the comfort of the Three Marys at his feet, a comfort I for the
moment lacked though the thought of these Holy Women in
contrast to the hoydens who had tormented me made me cry and
sob again, but this time out loud. The movement this involved
discovered such aches and bruises, such cramps and such biting
cold that my sobs straight turned to cries of pain, and such convulsive shuddering and shivering as I could not, try as I might, for
a space of several minutes master; and thus I was – lying on my
side with my knees pulled up, my filth around me, when through
my pain and misery I discerned a presence above me: because the
figure was white I was paralysed with fear – I took it for a spirit
risen from the vault beneath the floor, then for what it was, one of
the viragos from the Carnival, perhaps one of those very monsters
who had so abused me, and might I thought be back to abuse me
more.

And in this I was only partly right for – 'Poor soul, are you still
here?' she exclaimed, and kneeling beside me contrived to gather
my head and shoulders into a warming embrace in her lap which
gave me the strength I needed, for I feared more mischief and
leapt away, calling on her to keep her distance as if she was a
spirit of damnation sent to torment me, and I clambered over the
furniture in the Choir to be away from her.

She did not follow me but rose and stood where she was –
carmined cheeks, bare whitened breasts, white dress, and so quite
undistinguishable from her companions, and I see it now though
I did not then, but for a heart that still beat with human warmth.

'Poor little fool,' she said, 'I mean no harm. I simply came to
see if you're still here.'

I made no answer, indeed my shivering had returned and my
teeth knocked together like a leper's rattle.

'Well,' she said, 'you need some clothes at least, wait awhile and I shall see what I can find.'

The door at the back of the church opened and she was gone out again into the noise and drumming and squealing and racket of Carnival that was building up again to its final height. While I waited my fears subsided and my feelings of anger and hate for all about me returned, for the Martíns, for Fernando who I saw had brought me to this pass, for the filth and brutality of the Populace who had become the instruments of my degradation, for the gloom and cant and superstition that surrounded me in that church – and especially for that white figure nailed to his cross with the drops of life-like blood on his brow and streaming from the wound in his side; what sort of people can worship such an image on the one hand and devote themselves to such cruelty as I have suffered on the other, I asked myself, itemising the cuts and scratches and bruises and cramps and cold I felt.

After a short space the heavy door creaked ajar again and the girl was back, though more ghost-like than ever for the dusk was almost night.

'Are you still here?' she called. 'Ay, I can see you.' She came forward, but not right up to me and left a bundle on the floor between us. 'These should help you on your way.' Then she took a step over the bundle and faced me, arms akimbo. 'Don't take what happened to heart, little master, 'twas only sport, and if you found it rough sport then take note of it and don't come meddling down here again.' From the way she spoke she took me for a lad much younger than I was, a mistake often made by people who do not know me well on account of my fresh complexion and small stature.

She had not brought much:– an old brown cloak, dirty, frayed, and patched, half a loaf of bread – grimy and one end wet with Lord knows what, a piece of warm sausage, and a small bottle, almost empty, but what was there was *aguardiente* flavoured with *anis*. I wrapped the cloak round me and attacked the vittles and drink, while she sat on a bench and watched me, hugging herself – she was scantily dressed and no doubt almost as cold as I.

'Do you know what?' she asked presently, 'but the news of it is all over the *barrio* – that Julián Sánchez – you recollect him? – the soldier turned *Garrochista* – well, he's turned brigand now, and this very morning they say, out near Vecinos, just a league or so off, fell on a train of French provisions, powder and the like, and carried all off, though he has only ten men and the French were twenty or more. All the town is buzzing with it and they say the French *Corregidor* is in a rage, but nothing to be done for it.' So carried away was she by this tale, she now got up and came into the chancel standing above me. 'They do say there was Paris finery too. Well, we would all have gone on our backs for him after the Bullfights a year and more ago, and most would now I dare say, especially for Paris finery. I tell you what, little master, you should find him and join him, for there's gentlemen with him, they say. He'd make a man of you. And if not him, then there's plenty of us would another way, an you were a brigand with Paris finery in your caves.'

Well, hunger and cold were still uppermost in my mind, not to be easily distracted by tales of brigandage from a chestnut seller's daughter, and presently I thanked her for what she had brought and slipped away, still swathed in the cloak, up through the quietest alleys I could find and back up to Antonio's tavern beneath the Square, for there I hoped to beg more clothes and a supper before going on to seek lodging at Mr Curtis's in the Irish College.

The streets were filled with wilder uproar than ever – firecrackers exploded in the gutters, girls screamed with delighted fear, there were signs of drunkenness and debauchery everywhere. Antonio's was crowded with a rout of young men and women all in Carnival gear and masked, and I despaired of finding anyone who would help me; Antonio and his family were far too occupied to heed me, probably they did not recognise me. At all events I was much relieved to see one face I knew, unmasked and sober, at the back of the room – red hair, pale face, smoking a paper *cigarillo*, and with a glass of wine before him – Rubén García, and my earlier distaste at the thought of his company was quite gone on account of the extremity I was now in.

3

'Well,' called he, as I approached, pushing my way through the heaving throng, 'is it really little Pepe Bozzam? This is well-met indeed for I have a commission to find you and came here believing you would be around some time this evening.' He moved down his bench and contrived thus to give me room to slip between him and a bearded ruffian who smoked and spat and drank in tedious rhythm. Thus close it was no longer necessary for him to shout. 'But first, little Pepe, tell me how you came to be in such a state – that cloak will not on its own keep out the cold and I perceive (here he poked through a rent with his finger) you've nought else on,' and bit by bit I told him most of my day's misadventures, and I did not scorn to vent my choler and spleen on all who had brought me to such dire misery.

He heard me out, and I was aware his interest increased, and he grew by turns curious as to details and thoughtful as I recounted my latter trials in the poor *barrios* behind the market – and at length cut me short with a brisk '*Hostia*, I think it might serve – if nothing else has turned up yet' and to my amazement rose, threw a *cuarto* to a passing serving man and taking me by the elbow positively hustled me out: 'Come Pepe, you must tell this story to the Authorities,' he declared, 'such plundering of Gentlemen by the poorer sort so near the seat of government cannot go unpunished . . . no, no, I insist, 'twill be for the best, for both of us, I assure you,' and round the corner and up the steps into the Square he pushed me.

Though our passage across the familiar flagstones to the Town Hall was accomplished in a matter of seconds and though I scarce had time or inclination to take in what I saw, the scene there nevertheless demands some space. The Square was illuminated as had been promised by the new French Governor, and illuminated with more magnificence than ever I had seen it yet with at least three lights to every window, with lamps along all the corniches and pediments, indeed on every ledge that would support them, and huge *flambeaux*, two to every pilaster of the arcades. But for the smoke and smell of wax and tar one could well have thought the sun had reversed its natural process and returned again. Beside all this every balcony and balustrade was swathed with drapes and swags, with wreaths and ribbons in laurel and oak, and the centre piece below the four great windows in the Chamber of the Town Hall was a portrait of King Joseph represented as Hercules with club and lion skin. Most extraordinary of all was this: whereas with decorations and illuminations on a scale so magnificent one would have expected the place to be filled with a multitude of holiday makers gasping and exclaiming in excited chatter, it was almost empty, that is to say there were so few people one could cross the great Piazza without an excuse or apology or deviating from a straight line.

Yet not entirely empty. In the centre and towards the Town Hall some citizens of the richer sort tricked out in their best finery and carrying dainty masks on sticks for Carnival passed to and fro and bowed to each other with uneasy formality and yet withal a sense of wariness too, though what they should be feared of was a mystery, unless it be the soldiers. These were three companies of Fusiliers drawn up across the South side, with four guns and their teams of horses. There was also a squadron of Dragoons in green with fur caps and red epaulettes which designated them, I later learnt, a *compagnie d'élite*. I wrongly surmised these troops were drawn up thus for some ceremonial purpose, why else should they stand so stiffly to arms in fighting, not marching order so late on a festival evening? Finally there was a band – right in the centre of the Square, and this too was soldiers, and as we passed was playing a March in the Turkish Style, pretty stuff that accorded well with the festive surroundings.

Rubén now directed me firmly up the wide stairs on which, to my surprise, he was saluted by the Guard, and into the Chamber which we discovered to be as brightly lit as the Square and filled with a crowd which hummed and bustled though what was toward was not apparent. He made me wait a moment in an alcove and set off, pausing only to direct a word to a group nearby, to the end of the Chamber where once the Bourbon standard used to hang and now a tricolour, beneath which stood and sat a staff of officers about their General, who kept on his gold trimmed cocked hat with its white plumes and was thus easily distinguished, and to him Rubén directly addressed himself.

Meanwhile, who should detach himself from the group near me but Don Lorenzo Zúñiga, whom I had not seen since he catechised me about his son-in-law's death All Souls' Day just passed, and had had no desire to see since either; yet, he quizzed me now and after an 'ahem' and a 'tush now' delivered himself on this soliloquy (for I made no answer) as follows: 'Bad business, bad business,' and he shook his fat red face that glistened with sweat so the pouches beneath his chins shook like a turkey-cock's, 'bad business. You've come from the *barrios*, young Rubén told me, been treated badly there, yes, I can see you have. Hum. No good will come of it, mark my words. And then there's this Brigand Julián Sánchez robbing a mule train out at Vitigudino. No good will come of that, no good at all. Can't have brigands and robbers making an excuse of the French to pilfer unpunished and two men murdered, they say. The first priority, we're all agreed, is Law and Order. That first. And Law and Order here means these monkeys,' and he nodded towards the French staff, 'and our duty is to them until they're pushed out again. Ah,' he concluded, 'here's young Rubén on his way back, capital lad, knows what's needed. By the way, José, if you see Don Jorge in the next day or two, it would be best not to say you saw me here, difficult to get a chap like that to see both sides of a question, capital fellow though . . .' and here Rubén took me by the elbow again and steered me down the Chamber towards General-Governor Dorsenne, and as I went I wondered who had the story of Julián Sánchez's brigands right, the girl who put the attack a league from the Town or Don Lorenzo who had it some nine times further off.

Before I could come to a conclusion in this I found myself in front of the General who was a small thin man with grey face, dark skin round his eyes, and a thin mouth, and who proceeded to interrogate me thus, in French.

'Monsieur García tells me you were set upon in the *barrio* and robbed. Is this correct?'

'Your Honour, it fell out in . . .'

'Please confine yourself to short, straight answers. We are in a hurry. You were robbed?'

'Yes, Your Honour.'

'Of clothes, shoes . . . money?'

'I had perhaps a duro in change . . .'

'Of money, in silver.'

'There was some silver, I believe . . .'

'You were robbed of silver? Answer.'

'Yes.'

'And beaten, molested, assaulted?'

'Most dreadfully. Your Honour, if Your Honour permits I can show you . . .'

'That will do. Now tell me about how things are proceeding in the *barrios*. Are the men there under arms?'

I thought for a moment.

'Did you see any weapons?'

'Your Honour, it is Carnival . . .'

'Are you quite sure you did not see weapons?'

At this point I realised that this General's staff were now gathered round and listening very intently, as if to a matter of some importance, and indeed that many of the burghers in the room, Don Lorenzo among them, had ceased their chatter and were pushing up behind me. A voice near my ear prompted in a whisper: 'Surely they were carrying arms?'

I was put in mind of the sports I had witnessed earlier as of men with short swords and knives slashing blindfold at a trussed but flapping fowl, of others cudgelling each other.

'Yes,' I said, 'some were armed.'

A general movement as of a breeze in a wood rustling the leaves passed through the company, but the General wished yet to be particular. 'Armed? How armed?'

'With knives. Some with swords. With staves and such.'

'No fusees, pistols, or the like?'

'Sir,' I said, 'I saw none in the forenoon when I was first there, and in the dusk I came up as privily as I might for fear of being attacked again and hid when any came near me . . .' but now I sensed impatience and also vexation on the faces before me, and since it has always been my particular bent, perhaps even it is a failing, but surely a generous one, to give pleasure to those I am nearest to, and that without always reckoning up the consequences, I added, '. . . but there were many percussions and flashes, as they might have been fusees and blunderbusses loosed off into the air . . .' though I knew well that most were firecrackers and any arms had been charged with powder alone, no ball.

But this was enough, for the General directed his gaze to the burghers behind me. 'Gentlemen, I am right to think this man is known to you?' and they nodded and murmured and several said 'ay', no doubt Don Lorenzo among them, 'and tells the truth? Well, you have heard what he has said – that he was robbed, beaten, stripped, barely escaped with his life, and this by an armed mob which is even now raging in the streets below. This with the murderous attack on the convoy this morning constitutes a dangerous situation which must be met with determination and severity if property is to remain safe in this town. Colonel Gérard?' and one of the officers behind him came forward and saluted smartly, 'you know your orders. Be so good as to carry them out,' and the officer saluted again, turned on his heel and marched out briskly, followed by three or four younger men.

Perhaps some intimation of what had been decided now came to me for suddenly I felt faint (though I was cold and hungry too) and was like to have swooned had not Rubén observed my indisposition and helped me to a stool near the big fire that burned behind the General, and there I remained for a few moments, not able to mark too well what went on, though I knew that most of the company had turned away and were leaving as quickly as may be and in silence too.

Presently, when almost all were gone, I heard the sound of a bugle, shouted commands, the rattle of hooves on the paving below, and marching feet. Meanwhile in the Chamber a servant came in, lowered the chandelier, and began to dowse the candles – I looked round and discerned Rubén sitting at the table behind which the General had stood.

'I think,' he murmured, as soon as he had apprised himself that I was now sufficiently recovered to mark him, 'I think you would be advised to lie low for a week or so.'

'Lie low?'

'Some rough work will be done tonight, and there will be those in town who will say you are somewhat to blame.'

I was bewildered by this and said so.

'Never mind,' he replied, 'I'm sure it will pass. Such things are soon confused in people's minds, muddied up by contradictory recollection, and then forgotten. But for a time I would, if I were you, lie low.'

'How can I? The world knows I may be found at my Father's.' Though I was still at a loss to know why he should think me in danger.

'Well, well. That need not be so. You forget that I am already engaged by another to seek you out.'

'I'm sorry . . . ?'

'When first you came to La Covachuela I told you I had a commission from someone to find you.'

'Oh aye. But it's late, good Rubén, and I'm in no state at all to be received . . .'

'I think the Lady in question will be glad to receive you as you are, for I believe she has your health and interests most closely to

heart and will be glad to answer your present wants.' He said this
with a high note of sarcasm that I did not like, although I had no
idea of what or of whom he was speaking, 'no indeed, I doubt if
things could have fallen out much better. She'll lodge you for a
month or more to boot, I warrant. Come, José.'

I followed him – what else could I do? – though I went down
the stairs behind him in considerable fear for my soul as well as my
body, recalling the evil he had done me scarce eighteen months
before. My trepidation increased with the sudden sound of a fusillade and not so very far away at that – as the echo died Rubén
turned his white face up at me and with a smile or leer whispered,
'It starts, you see?'

The Square was now empty and many of the illuminations
extinguished, only pickets of soldiers stood at each entrance and
one of the guns with its team. The sky had cleared, a large moon
hung in it, the paving glistened now with frost and the cold struck
into me like dagger thrusts. From down beyond the market, quite
invisible to us, a tumult could be heard as of more shots, shouting,
screaming, and so forth.

The journey we were on was a short one, just across the Square
and into an entrance that lay, I reckoned, just above La
Covachuela. A large door faced us, lit by a lamp, and Rubén
hammered on a stout brass knocker fashioned like a mermaid at
her toilet, yet hammer as he might some minutes passed during
which I near fainted with the cold before a Judas opened and a
voice, as of an old woman, called: 'Signor García, is it you?'

To which he replied, 'Of course, and open up quickly, for I
must take this lad here up to your mistress, she expressly desired
me to bring him as soon as I found him, no matter what the time
of day or night.'

'Ay, ay, she told me of it,' the woman mumbled as she drew
back bolts and chains, and pulled back the door, revealing a hall-
way and a narrow flight of stairs.

At first sight of this crone who had but two teeth and her hair
in papers, and was dressed in a woollen dressing gown, and carried

a candle, I misgave again for she put me so much in mind of the witches of that earlier Sabbath, but Rubén urged me up after her, pausing only to replace the bolts.

'Come on, you old fustilugs,' he called, for she wheezed and blew and mounted with difficulty, 'cannot you see my poor friend José is nigh starved to death with cold? I warrant you your mistress will put you down at once if he snuffs it before she sees him.' And indeed my teeth were chattering again like dice rattled in a cup. But now the beldame had reached a landing and was fumbling at her chatelaine again for another key.

'What?' cried Rubén, 'are you yet alone here?'

'Ay, there's none come yet but my mistress and I. Others are not expected this fortnight or more. Tell me, young Rubén, there's fires started down in the shanties below. It'll not spread here, will it?'

'No, no, no danger with the market place between.'

'That's what Madame said,' the beldame returned, and at last pushed back this second door.

Who or what I expected I now forget, but that it was not what I saw, I'm sure. At the end of a long room, newly painted in pale, pinkish grays, and white and gold in the rococo style with white and gold furniture to match, stood, robed in fine black silks with low bodice and full skirts and hair dressed high on her head, my mysterious benefactor of the previous winter – Anna La Granace, she I believed to be my Aunt, and as she saw me she came – how shall I say? – floating on a rustle of petticoats down the long thick carpet, a sort of dusty rose colour it was, and breaths of Eastern perfumes like Zephyrs swam in the warm air (for there was a blazing fire in a modern marble fire-place) about her, her arms, long, bare, white, stretched to embrace me, and as she came, and as she enfolded me, pressing my poor, aching, frozen head into the comfort of her breasts, she cooed, 'Giuseppe, Zeppo, is it really you? Oh, you poor boy, what have they been doing to you? Oh *mi' bambino, mi' bambino*, come, let me warm you,' and outside another fusillade and the dark sky beyond the window she had been standing at glowed red.

CHAPTER V

I Enter on a Life of Ease in the Midst of War.

I

I remained at my Aunt's for many months and, I believe, made myself useful to her, she not having the Spanish tongue off with any ease at first, nor her maid either, the beldame called Marinetta who was Italian too. After three days recovering from the privations I had suffered at Carnival, which I spent in my Aunt's large and downy bed, the most *sybaritic* I have ever slept in, I undertook to carry out the provisioning of the household, and I also on her behalf engaged painters and joiners, for she required the whole house to be refurbished from top to bottom in a most lavish style, and these I supervised and instructed for her too. For all this she gave me board and made me presents too, so that anything I needed she provided and often prevented my wants before I had realised them myself; as on the day I pronounced myself fit to be up and abroad again I discovered three complete turnouts of clothes from hats to shoes, and all fitting me, and all in the most becoming and modish styles imaginable, so never before or since have I gone forth so well attired.

As I say I lacked nothing that would aid a quick and complete recovery, for she installed me in her private chamber, this being the only one at that time apart from the chief room of the house, the one in which she had first welcomed me, that was furnished and painted up, and there I was warm and coddled and she brought me soups and jellies and eggs prepared she said by herself, until she was satisfied I was better, and at night she shared the big bed with me too but she was careful there should be no sinfulness between us, neither then nor later, for I bedded there often, and no doubt this was because she was mindful of the relationship between us, that she was my Aunt; and yet she would often embrace me and kiss and hug me and call me her Darling Boy and I derived much pleasure and contentment from these signals of an affection I had sought not nor deserved.

As above, on the third day I was up and having dressed in a fine blue frock coat and white pantalons with a high hat, the first I ever owned, went forth to market with Marinetta whom daylight showed to be not the fright I had first thought, but when up and dressed and painted a most respectable looking sort of body, not much above middle years. It was, as I recall it, with the sun warm and cheerful where it shone, and the chill of the frost still sharp where it could not reach, and I was in high spirits as we went from stall to stall, Marinetta signifying what was needed and I making the purchases for her as two brace of partridges, a piece of porterhouse steak of several pounds *avoirdupois* (no grams or kilograms yet), two dozen of eggs and they should all be white for Marinetta shook her head over the brown ones, and so on and all went well until we reached the pork butcher, for that day my Aunt had a fancy for pork cutlets. But here, as I made the order I realised that a small crowd, perhaps ten souls all told, had begun to close in on us, as of porters, one or two serving women, an Augustine Friar, and so forth and these were pressing on us and jostling us in a most unpleasant fashion. When our purchase was made they followed us on and now I began to feel frightened, for they were quite silent and intent and I realised that they would not let us go until they had done us some mischief, and why all this was I had no idea at the time.

I now tried to make our way out of the market and back to the Square but whichever way I took our way was blocked, and at last a large and uncouth man, a porter I knew him for, for he had worked in the market for many years, put himself before me, took his nose, which was swollen and pitted with blackheads, between his thumb and forefinger, and voided his rheum upon my new trousers. At this the rest around did likewise, either spitting or emptying their noses on us, and the Friar not the least, and the other people around stood and watched with no expressions at all upon their faces, and in the midst of all Marinetta's basket was upset, all our purchases spread upon the floor and kicked and trampled, and of course all the eggs smashed. Seeing the eggs a child, a girl not more than six years old, dabbled her hands in the yellow mess and smeared it over my coat. All was done in a moment and then they melted back in the crowd, becoming undistinguishable from the rest, and looking round I saw the reason why: two Grenadiers were advancing upon us, their bearskins with red cockades and bayoneted fusees clear above all heads. I took Marinetta by her chubby hand, and led her as quickly as may be, blubbering and gasping as she was, back to my Aunt's apartment, or rather house, in the Great Square.

The cause of this vile and foul mishandling was clear enough with only a little reflection: by speaking to Marinetta in Italian and to the stallholders in Castillian, I had shown myself to be a Frenchifier in those poor people's eyes who could not distinguish Italian from the Gallic and supposed all foreigners in the town to be French; the remedy too was plain – my Aunt had friends in the Town Hall and from that day onwards a Grenadier always stood at our door and accompanied us if business or pleasure called us into places where the like or worse could occur.

There were many such, indeed two-thirds of the City remained uncertain and unsafe for all who might be thought to have sided with the French – that is the poor *barrios* where I had strayed during Carnival, and the University with the Convents and Colleges, though the latter soon became almost deserted as the students all went off for soldiers, and the teachers to Madrid or Cadíz, as above. The poor places remained a problem to the end of the War and this despite frequent incursions of Grenadiers and

Dragoons which caused much loss of life and damage to property, but the Populace remained obdurate in spite of correction.

2

My most important task in the next month was to assist my Aunt in the refurbishing of her apartment and this I much enjoyed, not least on account of the extraordinary singularity of her instructions regarding certain of the rooms on the top storey. The floor in question had, like the two others below, just two rooms, one large with a balcony overlooking the Square, the other smaller and at the back, and the first thing was to make four rooms of equal size out of these two, and each with its own door – a scheme which required much alteration, knocking down of walls and building up of new ones – it was all, she said, for four *nieces* who would shortly be coming to join us, four *nieces* who would quarrel like shrews if any felt disadvantaged in comparison with the rest. But yet more uncomfortable were the *decores* and furnitures that went into these rooms, and the more I heard her instructions in this the more astonished I became.

The first was done out with perfect simplicity like a nun's cell, but so much to the life did it have to be, and expense no object at all, that my Aunt ordered the walls to be faced with real stone. When this was done she had the window barred and for the bars I had to cozen a lieutenant she knew who was billeted with his men in a now empty convent (for King Joseph had closed many Religious Houses and expropriated their land, thus to pay his soldiers) for a wrought iron grill that was authentick. Four more furnishings completed this cell, *viz*. – a large Crucifix, two small paintings – one of Our Lady and the Magdalen washing Our Lord's Body, one of St Teresa in her extasie and finally a cot or bed. This last had to be bespoke since it had to appear just like the bare hard pallet of a Carmelite, yet was soft to lie on and broad enough for two.

The second room was furnished in contrast in great luxury, but still there were oddities – the bed again was bespoke and this time large and round, about seven feet across and heaped with pillows and cushions and, instead of blankets, furs. There was no painted paper on the walls, nor pictures neither, but instead mirrors, pier glasses of marvellous clarity which we had to send for to Madrid and were brought at great expense by a team of grumbling carters through troubled country and over wild mountains, without a crack or chip. And one of these was set in the ceiling above the bed, a matter of some difficulty since the glass was heavy and had to be well and safely secured.

The third was done out like the chamber of a Chinese, but a Chinese of marvellous taste and fashion with lacquered cabinets, furnitures in delicate bamboos, tall vases of white and blue, and six paintings such as I have never seen before done on long strips which came rolled up and when let out were seen to depict each one a man and woman, Chinese of course, variously occupied in the Act of Love, which Act they achieved in ways I should not have believed likely had I been told of them, though the artist, who had worked as is the fashion there with soft brush and water paints and inks on paper, had made all seem possible. Down the edge of each picture ran a legend in Chinese characters – 'Lady Secret Rose will no doubt be able to scan these for us,' my Aunt said, 'for I make no doubt they add meaning to what we can already see.' This I doubted to myself, for meaning in these pictures seemed clear enough already.

The last room was done out like a Moorish tent, that is white drapes hung from a point in the centre of the ceiling billowing down to a point where the wall met the floor, with a large black pole, inlaid with silver, set at an angle in the middle of the floor to simulate the support. The floor was covered first with carpets – Persias and Turkeys – and then with brocade and tasselled cushions: there were so many of these there was no need of a bed. There were also many silver lamps, a bowl with incense, dishes filled with scented Delights and a little spirit stove on which an infusion of mint tea could be made; there was also a *hubble-bubble* pipe – an apparatus for smoking which allowed the smoke to be drawn through rose-water – nor was it tobacco that was used but *haschisch* which I later learnt produced an effect on the smoker not unlike that produced by sparkling champagne.

All this took about a month and it was March and Spring weather when the day came that La Granace, Marinetta and I paraded through this suite, I having paid off the workmen that very morning. My Aunt led the way, dressed as usual in her rustling black taffetas, and she seemed mighty pleased with what had been done though her sharp eye was quick to see blemishes, as a workman's thumb-print on a mirror or a chip in the gilded moulding of a frame, but when we were done she nodded two or three times – 'It will do,' she said, 'it will do very well,' and then, 'tell me Zeppo, what do you think of it all?'

"'Tis very fine, Madame,' I said, for I always addressed her thus, our consanguinity never being acknowledged.

'Nay, but what do you really *think* of it?' she insisted, and there was now an archness in her voice.

'Why,' said I and felt myself colour, ''twill make a fine, a fine . . .'

'A fine what, Giuseppe?'

'A fine . . . bordello,' and now my face was surely puce.

'Oh la, Zeppo, never say it, never say it. This is to be an establishment of considerable refinement – call it a bawdy house and the clients will behave as if it is. No, no. Come sit with me and let me explain,' and with her garments rustling about her she placed herself on an ottoman – we were now back on the first floor in what from that day she called the *Publick Rooms* – and taking my hand guided me to sit beside her. 'First, no gentlemen will come unless they have been invited by me or recommended by someone I approve. They will come as if to a supper party and there should always be between eight and twelve of them – this is to promote a spirit of rivalry and gallantry – for I have only my four . . . nieces to accommodate them – after supper, which will always be sumptuous but conducted with the manners of the best society, there will be gaming and cards. How the gentlemen get on with each other in this is not material, but it is understood the girls, my nieces, always win, and by and by one and two and soon four will slip away upstairs while the others go on drinking and gaming, and an hour or so later return, and thus through the night until dawn. At dawn our guests depart – singly if they wish, or together, but, however it is, you will be at the door to hand them their hats and cloaks, and to receive any small gift they should like to leave the house.'

'I, Madame?'

'Indeed yes, Zeppo, and you must make very careful count of what you receive and report to me exactly who gives what, for those who refuse or offer too little shall not come again.'

'Pray, Madame, what will be too little?'

'That is for me to decide, but you may be sure a Lieutenant may pay less than a General, say two napoleons as against five from the General. But most will pay more than that – our last year in Naples, after King Joseph had closed the religious houses there and there was much plate about, brought in a straight twelve thousand. Ay, you may well goop, but there were five of us to live off it, and Marinetta and a boy like yourself, and very considerable expenses; but we'll do well enough, you'll see.'

Now let me turn to the four nieces, or nymphs I should say, who despite the refinement and care and luxury Madame used to make attractive our Place of Trade remained, for all, the principal attractions. They arrived from Madrid the very day after the rooms were ready, having resided there a fortnight and been a week on the way; in February they had come from Naples by boat.

They were: *item*, Brigid from Copenhagen, very tall and very blonde, and she it was who affected the habit of a nun when called away from table or cards, and carried on the business in the cell – if her customer required it a priestly garb could be found for him, as of a Cardinal or an Abbot, whichever he preferred, though most who chose her were happy to remain in their soldier's dress and were often those too old, or too infirm, or even too generous or too much upon their dignity to indulge in the frequent opportunities that occurred for rape of real nuns in the surrounding countryside.

Item, Dolores, a black girl, black and young from *Saint Domingue* or *Hayti* as it is now called, in the Carib Indies, and she it was who occupied the Chamber of Mirrors, and this was fitting for in my mind she was the most beautiful of the four having short curly hair, large eyes and large mouth, and firm young limbs with rounded breasts and pert bum, and what made me mad for her was the way her torso curved into the small of her back like a young tree. She was very black though claimed an Italian, a Genoese sailor, for a Grandpapa. Alas it was my misfortune to dote on her and she was merry and showed a liking for me too, but would not cheapen herself she said by going down *gratis*, or with someone she *knew*. Old men preferred her and I used to wonder what went through her mind as she lay on her back and looked at the reflections in the ceiling, reflections I assumed of fat old men with dimpled arses, or thin and scrawny ones, varicose and pale, and one day I had the temerity to ask her. 'God Bless You, Zeppo,' she cried, ''tis I have them upon *their* backs, very few old ones can have me any other way. I straddle 'em and ride 'em thus for that's how they prefer it.'

Item, Lady Secret Rose, the Chinese, born not in China at all but in Barcelona; indeed there was no touch of China in her at all, her Father being a Malay who had levanted from a Dutch merchant-man some twenty years before – but she had a slant-eyed look and a yellowish tinge to her skin enough to pass to the ignorant for an Oriental. She was most popular with the youngest officers but not with me who found her shrewish and tart in her off-duty hours. Once I asked her if she could account for her popularity – she said if I could find ten napoleons of my own and not the House's I might find out, then Dolores butted in with this remark: 'Why, Zeppo, did you not know what they say about

Chinese girls?' 'Nay,' said I, 'except that they have small feet and eat birds' nests.' 'Well,' said Dolores, moving beyond the reach of Lady Secret Rose who was working with her needle, 'Well, they say their bodies are formed quite differently, in, well you know, *those* parts, which are said to lie *sideways*, instead of up and down, sideways like your mouth . . .' at this Lady Secret Rose leaped to her feet with a scream and chased her mocker round the table, which nevertheless caused her to raise her voice to finish her taunt, which went thus: '. . . so all these young lads pay out good money to find if it's true.' 'And is it?' I called, whereat Lady Secret Rose turned on me and for a time I was hard put to it to protect my eyes from her nails which she grew three inches long and painted, this being a Chinese trick too. She could not read Spanish, which was her native tongue, let alone the Characters on the paintings in her room and now I realised there had been sarcasm in Madame's assertion that she would.

Item, Ishtar, who said she was Egyptian and maybe she was, having found her way back with the rump of Boney's army left by him to stew by the Pyramids ten years or more ago, for certainly she was the oldest of them all, and the smallest too being an inch or so shorter than I, and always put me in mind of a sparrow. She soon built up a small but very faithful group of customers who came to her as much for the *haschisch* (of which she had brought a very large store) as for the carnal delights she offered. She was something of a blue-stocking, given to books which she could read in French and later in English for she made me teach her the tongue, and often would talk the small hours away while the heady smoke bubbled through the rose-water, and her customer became glaze-eyed and pallid with it.

Such were my Aunt's nieces – Brigid, Dolores, Lady Secret Rose, and Ishtar. Madame named them for me the day they arrived, all dressed most soberly in black and handed down from their carriage in the Square below us by a Captain of Dragoons whose troop had escorted them from Madrid, and they seemed almost what Madame put out about us for the Commonalty to believe, *viz.* – she was a widow with four nieces left her by her deceased brother, and they were her wards she hoped to marry off to Colonels at least. When I pointed out the absurdity of this tale – as how could one woman be brought to bed severally of a Dane, a Black, an Arab and a Chinese, she said, 'My brother was also a Colonel and campaigned in every corner of the World in the Service of his Emperor, and his wife went along too, both being took off by the Yellow Fever in the Indies. Thus my brother – as for my sister-in-law, she was no better than she should be, and it would be censorious and unchristian to speak ill now of the dead.'

All this she said to me in play, but once I heard her say it to a Jesuitical Priest who came with three Alguazils on a complaint that she kept an unruly house that was a scandal to the town, and she said it then so straight they believed her, which was in July when the French Garrison was much reduced and the inhabitants more ready to voice what they felt, but to write of this now is to presume on what is yet to come.

3

For the first months all went very well for us indeed and I came to understand why Salamanca should be a good place for the Trade. To the North and West of us Marshal Soult campaigned against the Galicians and the Portuguese, to the South and East of us Marshals Jourdain and Victor took on mad old Cuesta in Estremadura, and there was, in consequence, a steady coming and going of reinforcements and reserves, of sick and wounded, of subalterns and Generals from both campaigns, and soon it was known all over Old Castille and the Kingdom of León that Madame's House in the Great Square was just the thing to rally a man before a fight or after one.

We were soon in a routine which I found pleasant enough: at ten in the morning I would rise, and with Marinetta clean out and air the Publick Rooms, then she and I went, with our Grenadier, to Market. After a light lunch, back to bed from which the chatter of the nieces – should I say my *cousins*? – drew me in the early evening. This was the time I liked best, when we would all be together in and out of the kitchen where Marinetta dressed up succulent and exotic dishes for dinner, or the Publick Rooms where the girls worked with their needles and Madame went over the accounts and lists of officers she knew to be in Town. The time I liked least followed, if not enough were engaged for the evening, for at eight o'clock she would then send me out with invitations discreetly worded; the Grenadier came with me so I was not molested, but any of my old acquaintance I chanced to pass either cursed me or cut me, which I could not abide. But as the reputation of the House grew these evening excursions became less necessary.

Each night was a feast followed by gaming and all I had to do was play the butler and keep sober – which I did quite easily after Madame threatened I should be put out of doors next time I was drunk. Sometimes, but very rarely, not above three or four times, the Clients themselves gave trouble, either by being drunk, or quarrelling at cards, or offering violence to the Girls, which was a sort of pleasure Madame would not permit, though the other way about was current and approved, especially with Brigid who kept instruments of correction for the purpose. Madame kept a case of pistols about her and one of these snapped in a Brute's face usually calmed him; and he was never allowed back. This last was what kept our lives so peaceable I am sure; this and the fact that what was offered was so genteel, so refined after the rigours and privations of campaign, that only those who valued the contrast came. My day finished towards dawn when I handed out hats and coats and took, as discreetly as may be, gold napoleons at the door, sometimes as many as fifty in an evening, and rarely less than thirty.

I recall especially one jolly time in April when we entertained two Captains of Infantry and an *Aide-de-Camp* who had fought in the campaign just concluded against Cuesta at Medellín, where the old fool lost ten thousand men and was ridden over by his own cavalry which did him no good at all but did not kill him. I confess I laughed and laughed when these officers recounted how it went, and almost wished I had been there to see it, so much I hated that man for the danger and misery he had brought me at Cabezón and Medina de Rioseco, and the death of my friend Rafael.

Not all the news that night was so good, and what was bad, bad that is for our guests, was not of battles lost but of men murdered by the *Guerrilleros* up and down the country, and especially between Salamanca and Oporto in Portugal, which Soult took and sacked the day after Cuesta was thrashed at Medellín. And having got into Oporto he could scarce get a message out without he sent a company of Dragoons or more to carry it, for the *Guerrilleros* cut off the heads of couriers they could catch and this in redress for murders and looting done by the French. And one name mentioned above all others was that of the *Garrochista* and bullfighter Don Julián Sánchez – he who had carried off a convoy at Carnival-Tide, he who had worked the bulls before our eyes at my Father's vineyard.

It seemed that all now feared to go beyond the City with less than a company for Julián had at least an hundred men and all well-mounted, and if the numbers were on his side at all then he would attack if you stayed and catch you if you ran; he took no prisoners, they said (but this was not true, he took many) but killed all who came to his hands.

'But what can one do then?' asked a Swiss Lieutenant, a *Voltigeur*, and only just arrived in town. 'I am to go tomorrow four kilometres or more on the road to Ledesma to bring in some sheep and I'll not have more than twenty men with me. My God,' he continued and slapped his forehead, 'I see it now – the Colonel has picked me for this chore because he foresaw the others would refuse it.'

At this some looked serious, and others laughed, and each put forward the expedients he might employ – as ask for an hundred

men, or discover what other parties might be out on forage and if
they could go together, or if he could somehow devise things so
that the *Guerrilleros* would swoop on another group, not his – and
this put me, who was serving them wine, in mind of a possible
wrinkle they could exploit, and up I spoke, for I liked to talk with
these officers, especially the ones nearer my age, and many were,
man to man.

'Why,' said I, 'if I were coming across the plain and saw
Sánchez's men coming towards me, I'd make for the nearest village
and fire it before he reached me . . .'

'What possible good would come of that, young man?' asked
the *Aide-de-Camp* who was the senior present that night.

'I know this Julián Sánchez,' I said, 'and for all the cruelties and
barbarities that are now laid at his door I know him for a good
man, and even a gentle one. If he entered a burning village he'd
stop and put it out and succour those living there, and while he
did you could all get off.'

I was much gratified by their reception of this stratagem which
they all hailed as a master ploy of military art – 'A Joseph to catch
a Julián,' as one of them said, and when he left the Swiss
Lieutenant, whose name was Coulaincourt, and had soft brown
eyes and a soft brown moustache he often stroked, gave me a
napoleon, 'for yourself, for yourself,' he said, but I paid it up to
Madame with the rest for that was a rule of the House, that gra-
tuities went into the common purse, only presents in kind could
be kept by the receiver.

Such were the early days at La Granace's House in the Grand
Square, and I think of them now as happy ones, but they did not
remain secure and untroubled for long, for shortly a new matter
entered in, one to upset the even tenor of my days and bring me
dreadful worry and frightful anxieties, as I shall now recount.

PART THREE

CHAPTER VI

I am Forced into a Career Fraught with Dreadful Dangers, yet Contrive to Make Shift.

I

One bright morning at the end of April I received a call I had not looked for – at the time I was sweeping the stairs near the top of the house (my first chore of the morning done before any were up), and heard the bell peal far below, and then peal again, so I cursed it a little and pondered whether or not to leave it, but again came the clamour so I left my dust-pan and brush, took off my apron, and went all downstairs to see who was there. Following Madame's exact instructions I slid back the Judas before unfastening anything and found myself face to face with – Rubén García, whom I had not seen since the night of Carnival.

'Ah – Rubén, 'tis you,' I said.

'Ay, it is. Come man, will you not let me in?'

'No,' said I, 'for where would be the point? All here are asleep but me, and save for the Cook are like to be for several hours yet.'

'But, Pepe, 'tis you I am calling on.'

'I?'

'You. I have important matters to talk over with you. Now come on and let me in, for I feel a fool gossiping here on the step and what I have to say should not be heard by others.'

'Well, well. I suppose Madame will not mind, since she knows you too.'

'Ay, she knows me well enough.'

And so, but feeling bemused and a little nervous too, I pulled back the bolts and undid the chains, and let him in.

'You'd best go on into the Publick Room,' I said as I rebolted and made all secure again, and followed him into the room where Madame had first welcomed me. It was in darkness until I had pulled back the drapes and pushed back the shutters and let in the soft sunlight, warm air and the noise and bustle of the Great Square below. It was not yet cleaned out – in consequence there was a litter of bottles and such, and plates with half ate fruits and scraps of fowl – for Marinetta had dressed up twelve brace of duck the night before, and I forget what else.

'Well, what can this matter be, then, Rubén?' I asked.

'First let us sit down,' he replied, 'for the telling will take some time. I say,' he went on 'can you not find something to refresh us, pick us up, you know?'

I fetched some lemon water from a cabinet and two glasses, and then sat opposite him in one of Madame's fine white and gilt chairs. He was on the ottoman and now I could really see him I confess he looked a swell, and me in just my shirt and breeches. He had a fine new coat, dark green and cut in the English style, hessian boots, he carried a fine high hat, and wore a fine gold signet seal dangling from his vest.

'You look very well,' I offered.

'You mean my clothes? Aren't they smart? I have been told this green sets off my hair most choicely. Well, Pepe, I think I can put you in the way of such good things, if you've a mind to them.'

This was so much the style he used when in with the murderer Pepe Clemente and the Witches that I became more wary yet than I had been before. 'I'm sure I lack nothing here,' I said, 'I, too have three fine . . .'

'Come, come, Pepe – she works you hard, you've not been seen out these four weeks, except to market with that old harridan, and a Grenadier as escort.'

This was true, but more out of fear I had of the people than for any restraint that was laid upon me.

'And I tell you what, Pepe, if you'll do some small deeds for me I'll see you get a duro a day, nay I'll make it two gold dollars a week.'

This thought did please me for although I did not want for anything, I lacked one thing in my situation, and that was ready cash. Once I asked Madame for some and she said no – that I had only to ask for whatever I needed and she would see I got it. Another time I tried to keep back some change from marketing, but she kept her accounts so carefully 'twas detected, and I rebuked, though I swore it was but a slip on my part.

'I can see I have you interested,' and he smiled his twisted grin, 'so here's the matter. You are well situated here, are you not? to spy for the Patriots and the British.'

'To spy . . . ?' but my tongue failed me as cold fear gripped me, and then bewilderment too. 'But Rubén, I thought, I thought . . .'

'What, good Pepe, what did you think?'

'That you were in the service of the French.'

He frowned now and the corner of the scar of his forehead puckered. 'Pepe, I'm in no-one's service but my own. However, 'tis the French who pay me, and the French who will pay you.'

'To spy on 'em?'

'I did not say so. I said you are well placed here to do so – with officers coming here every night and often from every corner of Spain, much wine drunk,' he looked around at the litter, 'they gossip and game and whore and you stand amongst them like a flunkey and with your gift of tongues understand them all; I have it right, I think?'

I nodded dumbly for still my heart was beating too painfully to do aught else.

'Well then, here's what you do. You go to Rector Curtis . . .'

'Mr Curtis?'

'Ay, that old Irish fool, the friend of your Father, and he'll receive you for that old acquaintance where I fear the rest of the

town will not, and you spin him a yarn of how you'd like to help
the cause of Liberty, or the Old Monarchy, or Religion, or what
you will, but do it skilfully for he must not know you've come to
him knowing he is a spy . . .'

'Mr Curtis a spy?'

'Ay, 'tis what I said – he's an agent for the British, what they call
a *Correspondent*, and working between 'em and this Julián Sánchez
who is so much trouble to us just now . . .'

'Then why not . . . ?' and I shuddered thinking of the gibbets
outside the University and in the Market which were new furbished every week with spies, or cut-throats, and no rank
respected either, ten days before a Cathedral Canon had been
strung up, a most worthy old man and of good family.

'Why let him go on? Because if we wrung his neck there'd
soon be another, and trouble to us finding out who, so it's better
to leave him and use him. And that, dear Pepe,' and he leant forward and put a hand on my knee, 'is why I'm here. As I said you
will convince him of your desire to help the British, and bit by bit
let him understand how well placed you are to do so. And then to
convince him you'll let him have titbits and tattle that I shall contrive to send you and you'll soon see how well all goes. Well
then, Pepe, that's it. I think you should start right away – you can
call on the Reverend Gentleman this very forenoon if you wish –
there's no reason for delay.'

'But how will this help the French?' I asked.

'You are not so silly I think as not to see how. Why, some of
what you tell him will be misleading, that is how. But also I shall
expect you to pick up hints and news from him – especially concerning Julián Sánchez and his bandits, who must be put down.
See Pepe, there's a price on the brigand's head – help in his capture and you'll get a share.'

I did not like it, I did not like it at all. Till then I had been
happy and all around me was conformable and safe for such troublous times. I should like the money, that's true, but not at the cost
of meddling in such dangerous games which I could see would

most likely bring me to the end of someone's rope, it would not matter whose. So I stood up and paced about a bit, and then said as much to Rubén.

He stood up too and his pale blue eyes were like ice – he put his hand to an inside pocket and pulled out a paper bound with red ribbon.

'This, Pepe, is a warrant to bring one Joseph Bosham, a known English Man before the *Juge d'Instruction* in the Town Hall, as soon as may be, that he should answer if he can to charges of being in the pay of the British Government and a known and notorious spy.'

I sat down again – 'twas either that or bring back up the lemon water.

'Well, if you do as I say, today, this afternoon, I'll file it – otherwise a Beadle will be around to serve it this evening.'

I wiped the cold sweat from my brow.

'All right, Rubén, all right. I'll do it. But I'll call on Mr Curtis at six for then I know he takes a dish of tea and welcomes visitors.'

'Very well, very well.'

'And Rubén. I shall be paid too?'

'Of course, dear Pepe, of course – and here, let me give you a duro now as earnest of my good faith.'

It will be readily understood how I fretted and worried the time away till six, and indeed so upset was I that 'twas remarked on by the company when they came down to break their fasts at about four of the afternoon as was their custom.

The girls offered me banter on my silence and pallor, and Lady Secret Rose affected to believe the cause was that I was in love, which provoked much merriment at my expense as they vied with each other to get me to say which of them it was had caught my heart; only Dolores was kindly, looking at me from her big black eyes that seemed a little sad, for she already knew how I loved only her of them and while she never offered herself to me, for it was not in her to do it for love, at the same time she was sorry to see me suffer.

Madame too understood me well enough to know 'twas not a heart sickness I suffered from and when Marinetta had cleared away the coffee cups and fruit she bad me come to her room where, to cut it short, she quizzed me narrowly, but I could not tell her what ailed me, at which she concluded thus: 'Zeppo, there's not much in this world that can't be set to rights with money and you know I shall do aught in that way that's needed – and if for some reason you cannot ask then I beg you bring to mind the ring I gave you against a time when things seem bad. You have it still?' I agreed that I had, though in fact it was hidden away privately in my Father's house in Los Arapiles where I had not been for three months nor knew if I would be welcomed if I went there. ''Tis worth all of a thousand napoleons, being a gift from an Indian Prince, and that's a sum will buy you time, at least.'

Well, it was kind of her to say all this, but not much to the purpose. Rubén would sell me the Warrant for it, I had no doubt, but he would be back the next day with another.

And so the time went by and at half-past five I got my stick and coat and hat, made my excuses to Marinetta that I might be in later than usual to help her prepare the Dinner, and asked her to lock the door behind me, which she did.

2

It was a beauteous calm evening, warm and balmy after the hot afternoon, the first really warm we had had that Spring, and the first Martlets and Swallows were swooping down the long honey-coloured alleys as I made my way between convents and colleges to the Irish College, that was once the *Colegio Mayor de Arzobispo* before the reforms. The Porter recognised me from the time when I was studying and was used to call once a month, and led me through the huge handsome hall and up the narrow stairs to Mr Curtis's door where he bade me wait hat in hand to see if I would be received. The place was wondrous quiet after the bustle and toing and froing and sporting and singing of the Irish Seminarists who had now all gone – many with Sir John Moore, on Mr Curtis's advice and instruction, and others later to Lisbon, where all listed, and mostly in the Portuguese regiments since they could not serve as officers in the English on account of religion and lack of funds to buy a commission – all this by the way though perhaps I thought on it at the time to pass an awkward minute or two waiting to see how I would be received.

At last the Porter reappeared and in I went, though feeling I was about to be met with punishment and recrimination rather than by an old friend of my Father's who had so often shown me kindness and offered me help.

The room was not large, and cluttered up with papers, books, ornaments, and I know not what except that by the high sash window stood a large brass telescope on its tripod and an astrolabe beside it and to one side a large clavier, much larger than my Father's, and properly speaking a *fortepiano*. It was made by *Stoddart* of London. Near this stood Mr Curtis, his white hair puffed out against the light of the window like a nimbus, and holding in his large fine hand a cup and saucer which he presently set down to receive me and introduce me to his other guest already there. This, like Mr Curtis, was dressed clerically in black frock-coat, white bands, black breeches and stockings, but was a very different figure altogether, being smallish with a very pale face and yellowish hair that was already balding though its owner was not much above my age. There was withal an impish quality in this stranger's eyes (which were blue and slanted outwards somewhat) that I found instantly attractive, or rather as soon as I had studied him a little, for immediately my first reaction was one of consternation – I had not expected a third person present. Mr Curtis named him as Father John Reaney, a priest from Dublin and Liverpool, and I shook his hand which was freckled and slight.

Mr Curtis now served us tea in dainty cups painted with strange blue pictures on a white ground with lattice bridge and a drooping tree, but not done with any naturalness though the effect pretty. There was now an awkwardness in the air that I tried to dispel by remarking on these cups. 'It is a design of Tom Turner's,' said Mr Curtis, 'in the Chinese style, and has already proved most popular in Hibernia, especially with the Ladies of Dublin, I understand. Have you come across it before, Father John?'

'Indeed I have, and there are many imitations too, commonly and cheaply bought and used by my Irish parishioners in Liverpool; it makes me quite homesick to see and handle them.'

Father Reaney had a marked accent which was Irish but flattened and nasal.

I asked him how long he had been in Salamanca and there was a hesitation and I fancied a wrinkling in Mr Curtis's brow and perhaps a shake of his head in warning. At all events Father John answered thus: 'Not long here at all, not at all. A few weeks only. But I hope to stay and continue my researches under Mr Curtis into *Astroscopy* in spite of these troublous times, for that is why I am here.'

We chatted of this and that and when he asked if I liked music and I said yes he told how he had brought sonatas for Mr Curtis by the Dublin composer John Field and what he called *nocturnes*, which were a novelty; but the silences grew more prolonged and I would not state my business before this stranger nor would I go without I had done what I came for, for I feared what Rubén would do if I failed. Nor was Mr Curtis helpful – he spoke little and I could not but sense the strongest disapproval in his manner towards me.

At last growing despair overcame my timorosity and I spoke up like a man.

'Before I go, Sir,' I said to him directly, 'I should like to speak to you alone on a matter of some peculiar urgency to me.'

At which Father John Reaney leapt to his feet, set down his cup, and with not much ceremony, but profuse apology, took himself off.

'Well Joseph, what can it be you want of me?' asked Mr Curtis gruffly when his co-cleric had gone. 'I hope it is not money you are after, for I have none to spare and no inclination to lend it to a profligate. I am sorry to speak so sudden and bluntly and would not have done so had you not contrived for me to see you alone. But you have, and I think I should speak freely. Your present way of life, the company you keep is a source of great pain, even I should say misery, to your Father, and to a lesser degree to me and to all your ancient acquaintance. I wish to have little to do with you unless you have come to enlist my help in returning to a life of usefulness, rectitude, and moderation.'

This was an opportunity I could not afford to let go by, but before I took advantage of it I must allow Mr Curtis to take snuff and wait till the consequent sneezing was done. At last I leaned forward and said as earnestly as may be: 'But that, good Sir, is truly why I am here.'

'You must pardon my incredulity, but your history over the last three years has done little to presage an early or easy reform. But Joseph, if that is your desire, your very first step must be to leave your present abode. Your Father would not perhaps welcome you immediately, not without the office of a benevolent intercessor – but that duty I can perform and gladly, and meantime we have many, very many places you can stay here,' and his gesture indicated the empty college about us.

This offer, kindly meant, spelled ruin to Rubén's scheme and therefore to me. I took time to collect my wits and then began again.

'Sir, I cannot leave my present place . . . no, I beg you, hear me out, I beg you, Sir, at least give me a hearing. You spoke of usefulness, rectitude and moderation. That my life in that place is not without the last two is something I shall not persuade you easily, but so it is. What others may do there is not the case – for myself I do not whore, I drink little, and eat carefully. I work hard for the Lady who runs the establishment who is, as I'm sure you are aware, a connexion of my Father's and to whom I owe much. But yes sir, you are right to say my present way of life lacks usefulness, and that is why I am here – to seek your advice, for I have the means to make it useful.'

Here I paused to see how well I was marked, and found Mr
Curtis still eyeing me most balefully, indeed I began to fear that
old man though he was, and big as he was, very much larger than
I, he might yet take a stick to me and drive me out. I hurried on.

'You seem to know something of the place, Sir, and so you will
know it is much frequented by officers of the French Army from
the least to the greatest. Only a week gone we had General
Dorsenne's *Aide-de-Camp* amongst us, and have had several others
of his staff. Now, Sir, in those surroundings they talk . . .' and I
went on to say how I frequently learned all sorts of news at table,
at gaming, and so on, as of movements of troops and even of
strategies scarcely framed in their creators' minds before babbled
out over the third or fourth bumper. I concluded this way:
'. . . Sir, I believe I could be useful, for surely all these things,
directed to the proper place, could serve the cause of the Allies in
their struggle to throw over Tyranny. All I lack is the means of so
directing what I hear.'

I paused for a slight shift in the old man's attitude was evident:
it seemed to me he listened more attentively, his alert old head
slightly cocked to one side, his mottled hand slowly rubbing his
large and aquiline nose.

'Whether or not I believe your intentions,' he now said,
'whether or not I now trust your goodwill, I am not yet sure. But,
Joseph, I must in any case ask – why single me out? Why should
you think I know where to direct you with these informations?'

'Sir, I know that when Sir John Moore was here you billeted
him, you instructed your seminarists to join his army, you per-
suaded an Abbess to mortgage six thousand gold dollars worth of
convent plate against a Bank of England draft to pay contractors
(this I had learned of my Father in January). It is not foolishness
then on my part to seek you out in this matter, though it seems I
must resign myself to the possibility it was error.'

The long and the short of it was this – he would not admit that
he collected, sifted, valued the news of the Province and
despatched it to Wellesley campaigning then up the Tagus to the

South, but nor did he outright deny it; and we left it in the end that when I had news that might be useful I should send them discreetly as may be, by a seller of flowers who would call at Madame's house on such days as I set an empty flower vase in the window, and that I should hand to her what I had.

At last I let myself out and went downstairs with a lighter heart than when I came, and before I reached the lower floor I could hear the strains of Mr Curtis's *fortepiano*, no doubt playing a *nocturne*, and I thought of returning to ask him whose the music was he had played at my Father's the day Fernando brought us news of Mondego Bay and Vimeiro, but I thought it best to go on.

Had I not done so I should have missed a surprising sight in the Porter's Lodge – for there I ran into, so she could not avoid it, none other than Violeta Martín, Don Jorge's recently widowed daughter, in black weeds and her face almost hidden with veils, but I knew her by her trim figure and tuneful voice, for I was near enough behind her to hear her asking the Porter directions for the rooms of Father John Reaney. When she turned and saw me she would not speak to me, ignored my proffered hand, and swept away with an air of cold disdain.

This, though I did not know it then (for what ground had I for suspecting Reaney was not what he seemed?) was the first seed that grew to strange and wonderful adventures I would share with Violeta in which I would do her and another Lady (a Princess and a Goddess) much service and many good turns, but all this far in the future yet. But still I marvel that such, for me, momentous events as would shape my later years entirely had their beginnings here in the lodge of the Irish College when Violeta Martín asked directions to the rooms of 'Father' John Reaney.

However, I had not then nor now the gift of prophecy and my only thought as her black taffetas rustled away over the stone flags was – well, perhaps she'll treat me less haughtily when she knows I am working for Mr Curtis in the interest of the British and the Spanish Cortes in Seville which I knew her family favoured; and things turned out thus sooner than I expected, for the first day I put up the empty flower vase who should be the flower-seller come for my news but Violeta herself, and then and subsequently she favoured me with a shy smile instead of cold reproof, and murmured thanks in place of scorn.

3

All went well enough until the twenty-ninth of June (1809) – the Feast of Saints Peter and Paul and the day for one of our grand *romerías* or pilgrimages or picnics out into the country, like that of Saints Philip and James on which Rafael had betrothed with Isabella and I ensnared with Angelica, so long ago it now seemed, but described above in my First Volume.

This of Saint Peter was the same sort of High Day: all the best in the town in carriages, sumptuously provided for with cold meats, salads, wines, and sweetmeats, and all dressed up in our Summer best went along; and Madame today made an exception of her usual rule to keep her four *nieces* mewed up from publick gaze, and hired us a fine *britzka* in which she and her four chiefest assets lolled at their ease beneath their parasols. For me she procured a fine chestnut hack to be their outrider – this and the mules pulling the *britzka* she had of a Captain of *Artillerie à Cheval* whom she favoured at the time, and he came too on his own mount. (Often she took a lover thus and out of affection or carnal desire, not for profit. At these times I made up a pallet on the floor of the Publick Room.) As for the hack, I found him mettlesome, for to say truth I am not too at ease on a horse, but was glad of him by the end of the day.

We made a splendid equipage, but the girls looked like any man's dream of carnal delight, for all were dressed in white and in the new *classick* style of the time, *viz.* – shifts of finest muslin gathered under the breasts to fall straight in pleats to the feet, leaving arms and much of the breasts bare, and what they covered they not so much covered as lightly veiled – never had I seen such a delectable group as these my four charges I shared with Madame, as I rode behind and watched the play of sunlight fall across their laughing faces through the lacy parasols and heard the chatter and banter they indulged in, and most of all my eyes lingered over the blackish, purple hues of Dolores' flesh which sometimes glowed ebony, sometimes dark gold where the sun fell, and shone like the skin of a ripe aubergine where the shadows were deep.

No doubt we were the best outfit there, for already the Wars had brought down the prosperity of the Town's richer families and especially only those whose support for the Occupants was known and assured had mules or horses – since all such were now drafted into the armies. The rest had to make shift with donkeys and some resorted even to oxen hired for the day from peasants who were allowed to keep such beasts as were needful for ploughing and bringing in harvest; but this was taken in good part and there was much jollity and laughter amongst those who found such low animals unversed in drawing chabriolets and landaus. Amongst those with mules I marked Banker Zúñiga with Doña Elvira, amongst those reduced to humbler circumstances the Martíns. Neither group acknowledged my salutations, nor did the Martíns respond to those offered by the Zúñigas; however, for reasons given above Violeta gave me her shy smile, though not dressed in the humble garb she affected in her guise as a flower-seller.

Finally in this rout there were the French – some three or four carriages of French officers and as escort half a troop of Dragoons, and these not well mounted, just twenty men, and this was thought to be enough for a very good reason, as I shall now expound.

Three weeks before I had received, by publick messenger, a request from Mr Curtis that I should call again for tea, and since he had couched his invitation in politest language I felt able, nay happy to attend him. The occasion too was pleasant – he declared himself pleased with some of the news I had given him and for what had not turned out so well, indeed in one case had occasioned Don Julián some loss, he did not hold me accountable. The long and the short of it was he hoped to continue the association, some of his earlier opinions he now held in doubt, and he had been pleased to say so in a letter to my Father, who, he intimated, was now recovered somewhat of his illness of the Winter, though slower in his mind than he had been. He felt I should make a visit thither soon and I promised I would.

In the midst of all this Mr Curtis was called to his door by Father Reaney, the supposed student of Astroscopy, and there followed a quite long consultation on this subject between them, during which I was left to my own devices. The Devil finds work for idle hands, and in this case eyes, for what should I see broadly displayed on top of a pile of correspondence on the scholar's desk but a most unscholarly epistle couched in simple rough terms but signed clearly and with a flourish *Julián Sánchez García, Captain commissioned in the Army of the King of all the Spains in His Absence by His Majesty's Supreme Junta, Seville*, and the content of the missive was this – that Don Julián proposed to attack with his *partida*, now numbering near two hundred men, the fortified church at *Fuente de San Esteban*, half way on the road to Ciudad Rodrigo, and this to be on the twenty-ninth of June, St Peter's Day. For which enterprise he begged Mr Curtis's assistance in the form of twenty dollars gold, English Sovereigns or Guineas would do, since he owed the villagers in that area so much for fodder supplied in the Winter and he wished to be assured of their support before embarking on such a dangerous enterprise.

All this I scanned and conned while Mr Curtis and Father Reaney gossipped of the stars, and the upshot of it was Rubén paid me three extra dollars for these news which pleased him mightily, and on that very day, the twenty-ninth, the day of the *romería*, all the French troops that could be spared in the area (not many for their armies were much stretched at the time, of which more anon) were concentrated in ambuscade in the vicinity of Fuente de San Esteban and all thought Don Julián would be caught. And since San Esteban was a clear ten leagues from the

Fountain of Saint Teresa, high in the hills on the Alba road and the object of our pilgrimage, none expected sight or sound of *Guerrilleros* or soldiers, save the few escort we had, and a day of festive peace was looked for.

The spot we had chosen was higher than the Town and cooler; it was always refreshed by St Teresa's Spring, oaks provided shade above a floor carpeted with aromatics as wild lavender, thyme, and thorny sage. Once arrived the Lieutenant of the Dragoons posted four *vedettes* out in the thickets to North, South, East and West and with these sentinels about us we settled down to pass the time as delightfully as we might.

Bright poppies and blue cornflowers nodded by the roadside; bee-eaters and blue rollers gladdened the eye amongst the branches. To the North and the topmost spires and domes of the City flashed through the heat haze and to the West those flat-topped eminences, Los Arapiles, that sheltered my Father's hamlet hidden on the other side, brooded like whales above the corn, still bluey-green, and oaks. Sometimes I thought on my childhood days there and on my Father and Tía Teresa whom I vowed to myself to visit soon and make amends for my absence and allay their fears of a life of dissipation; and sometimes I lay close to Dolores and she let me stroke her arm, warm, smooth and soft in the heat, which love play brought on tremors of desire almost too sweet to be borne.

Thus pleasantly the afternoon passed, and when we had dined the Swiss Lieutenant of Voltigeurs whom I had befriended earlier came and sat near us and regaled us with tales of *Guerrillero* hunting. Now the Sergeant of the Dragoons, a loud-mouthed, uncouth fellow, a Pole, who, no matter what language he attempted, we could hardly comprehend, tried to cap Coulaincourt's tales in the way men do when vying with each other. It seemed he had been stationed in the block-house at this same Fuente de San Esteban, where Don Julián we supposed was even then being reduced to nothing, but he had been there in the Winter.

'One cold morning, I on tower of Church,' he said, 'on watch. It all very cloudy – no, that wrong, it were, how you say, *foggy*. Dank you, foggy is the word. But when the sun he come up, the foggy lift a little, just little and what do I see but one man rides a mule out of the village under the foggy but the foggy has gone a little and his head and the ears of his mule are above the foggy, but the rest cannot see. It is a laughing sight thus – the man and the ears of his mule. So I say to me – here is a spy who goes on his way to Julián and we will catch him now, for we are good mounted and he only a mule. So I have my men together very quick, and soon we are off and after him, and with the foggy very lifted now, he give us good sport, like hunting the pig in the forests of my country.'

This Sergeant went on with his tale of how they hunted the spy, for so he was, letters beneath his saddle confirmed it, and he gave them a good run, before turning at bay – 'Just like the pig with the great teeth, yes?' between two oaks, and actually took off two of his men before they overpowered him.

'What happened then?' cried sweet Dolores, still warm against my arm.

'Ah, we were angry against him, very angry,' said the Polish Sergeant, 'so we pulled down his pantaloons and severed off his balls, and then made him run about thus which made us laugh until he fainted. Then we cut off his head.'

'Mother of God,' cried the gentle Brigid at this – she was at the time fondling idly with a small dark Bavarian who found her blond hair and tall figure much to his liking, 'that is quite the most horrid story I ever heard.'

'You are soft,' said Lady Secret Rose, who, by and by, in daylight, without benefit of paint looked scarce Chinese at all, 'any who help the *Guerrilleros* deserve much worse – I should have lingered out his death much longer than that, I promise you.'

'Whatever he deserved should not have been done on him so sudden,' said little Ishtar, raising her eyes from her book which was by a Philosopher called Montesquieu. 'Punishment meted out

without rational purpose is as contrary to the welfare of the community as the crime it punishes.'

'But in this there was purpose – to provide example to others,'
protested the daughter of a Catalan whore and a Malay levanter,
and they would have quarrelled had not Madame lifted her head
from the lap of the Artillery Captain and shushed them.

Well, this foul tale was not so much to my liking either –
for there but for the Grace of God go I, I thought, thinking
of this poor spy or courier – and to change the subject I spoke of
the boar-hunting in our country and especially in the forest of the
South of Los Arapiles, which fateful hills I showed them, at which
my friend Coulaincourt, the Swiss, exclaimed that he had never
hunted the boar, and so I engaged to arrange such sport for him
when Winter came again if he was still amongst us.

Earthly bliss is never sure and at about four after noon just
when preparations for our return were being put forward, the first
hint of danger touched us like a cold finger in the night – a small
boy, with sharp eyes, in a party near us, swore he had seen a
horseman walking briskly or trotting between the trees a half-mile
off, a horseman he said who wore a yellow coat and carried a
lance and seemed to be scouting about us not coming nearer or
going off. A sort of chill of doubt spread amongst us which caused
the more timorsome of us to urge a speedy departure and the
more temeritous to pooh-pooh and ask why one horseman should
frighten us so.

Then a flock of pigeons rose from a dell a quarter mile off, but
near the road we must take, rising from the thickets with wings
winking in the sun before circling up and away and clapping in a
covey straight above us, and Madame's *Capitaine d'Artillerie* now
stood up and put his glass to his eye. He remained thus while a
man might count to fifty and while he did we were all sensible
that his cheeks had lost colour. At last he pushed in his glass with
a click and pronounced that there were at least four more
mounted yellow coats concealed in the thickets below, so many
seen implied many more hidden, and he doubted not we were

faced with an ambuscade of Julián Sánchez's *Lanceros*. A whiff of grape would flush 'em out, he added, and I forbore from pointing out he had left his eight pounder in the Artillery Park outside Salamanca.

A hasty council of war was now convened out of which came the following plan – we should put together our moveables and trappings as quick as may be, but with as little outward show as possible for 'twas thought the *Guerrilleros* would not attack us till on our way back – else why had they not attacked us before since they could whenever they might? and this reasoning led on to the second part of the plan which was that we should try to get off by whipping up the animals and stampeding them off not to Salamanca but to Alba which was nearer and the road descended more steeply, and where a garrison of two hundred Bavarians held the old castle and had a battery of four pounders too. Coulaincourt suggested firing the first village we passed through on the way – 'A Joseph to keep off a Julián', he called it – but there was none in this case.

Now dissension broke out amongst the Salamantines for first those with donkeys and oxen said they would never get off and asked to be taken up by those with proper beasts in their shafts, who refused them saying they were well-freighted already, at which the first shrugged and said after all they had nothing to fear from Don Julián, they were not *Afrancesados*, and this set altercation going more furious than before for now the split in our Society became clear and bitter as one party accused the other of siding with murderers and vagabonds and were answered by being named treacherous lick-arses of an intrusive upstart.

In the midst of all this the Lieutenant of Dragoons called in his *vedettes* – two only, and they posted the nearest, answered the bugle; five were sent after the missing two, discovered one with his throat cut and his horse gone, were suddenly fired on from close quarters, and only four came back, lickerty-split and threw all into panic. Horses reared, mules kicked, oxen bellowed, dust flew, birds rose into the air, women screamed, and all was utter confusion, but in all Madame's Capitaine kept a sort of *sang-froid* for he managed to separate out four or five of the best carriages, including our *britzka* and the Zúñiga English-made coach, and sent them off towards Alba with the dragoons and other mounted men and boys to keep at their flanks and sides; and so we got off leaving the rest milling and churning like fowl in a yard where a fox has got in, and it must be thanks to him and the fact that the *Lanceros* were a quarter mile back waiting for us to go the other way that we escaped with scant further hurt, for their pursuit was delayed by those we left behind.

Nevertheless the fleetest of them caught our rear-guard just as we approached the narrow bridge and I saw beside me two Dragoons, and one was the Sergeant, Pole or Lithuanian, who had told us of hunting a spy near San Esteban, and they were caught by the yellow jackets – brown men with huge moustaches – and speared on their lances, the Sergeant with such force that the point came through his chest, pennant and all, piercing his heart and lungs so blood blossomed from his mouth and chest like a bunch of crimson poppies, before my horse which I had contrived to stay attached to, but only just, swerved on to the bridge and carried me to safety beneath the guns of Alba.

It is not much to say that the outcome of all this was that Wellesley and the British got out of a scrape which might have been the end of them, and later in October, the Spanish armies inflicted on the French the defeat of Tamames, which led to the temporary liberation of our town.

We were kept two days at Alba (scene so many years ago of my one unhappy attempt at the Art of Toreo) waiting for an hundred men to be free to escort us back to Salamanca, for so many were now thought necessary for safety anywhere outside garrisoned villages and towns, so vigorously and with such skill did Don Julián pursue his horrid trade of murder and kidnap, and during these two days I had time and cause to speculate on what had happened. And this is the conclusion I came to: the letter I had seen at Mr Curtis's was spurious, it had been the cunning old man's design that I should see it; because I had seen it and reported it, troops had been drawn off from Salamanca and Don Julián had been able to move in close to the City for his operations, nay right into the City itself – the raid on our *romería* being only one of several incidents over twenty-four hours, the others being the carrying off of various cattle both draught and provisionary and the removal of gold plate from the smaller cathedral; and through this I realised that my situation, which had never been comfortable, was downright dangerous. In fine: Mr Curtis knew I brought him news mainly false, but was useful perhaps for giving false news in return; Rubén knew the news I took was false, and would now believe that what I brought him was false; both knew me as a spy not to be trusted and therefore one who could at best be put aside, at worst exposed and made an example of. I had heard of such out in the forest crucified with their privates cut off and stuffed in their mouths, and in Town the strappado and the rack were followed by the garotte and the gibbet – the only way out I could see was to fend for myself and, instead of waiting for each side to give me *false* news for the other, seek out *good* and *true* news for both and thus earn their trust and a reputation with both for honesty. *Reputation* I divined could be earned not only in the cannon's mouth but also in the lap of a whore, or at any rate by listening to the drunken mumblings of those so fortunately placed.

Opportunity soon rose to put this new plan in train, for in the next week or so there was much bustling in the Town of troops and baggage trains and guns and so forth and setting up of hospitals, for there were those who were wounded and more too who suffered from famishment and footsoreness as they had come on long marches and those ill provisioned for; and few would tell of what had happened and of course no official news at all, for the French were less willing to admit of discomfort or defeat even than the Spanish. But in Madame's Publick Room it was different and these new clients we had, often with hurts, and all burnt by the sun and their clothes in tatters, and thin almost to starvation, would, with a bottle or two, let out with many angry curses, what had befallen them – and this was it: they were of Marshal Soult's army that had stormed and sacked Oporto in Portugal at the end of March, but they had only six weeks to enjoy the fruits of this victory (save what they brought away – enough for most to spend several nights at Madame's) – for the English had come at them from Lisbon and by devious means – as crossing the Duero (or *Douro*, to Portuguese that river) where none thought it possible – had twisted them out of their citadel 'as easily,' said one of them, 'as a fish-wife winkles the flesh out of a whelk on a pin.' Followed a dreadful retreat, not East to Salamanca for the British and Portuguese had got between them, but North into Galicia and only then East, and hounded and ravaged by *Guerrilleros* all the way until they reached the open country of the *campo* and could at last get back into a sort of marching order for the last sixty or so leagues back South to our Town – and in this last heat and thirst took off as many as the *Guerrilleros* had taken before.

Then for a time it was rumoured the British might come our way and there would be a campaign on our doorstep, which put us in something of a fright, but this proved error for Wellesley – for it was he again, the Victor of Vimeiro, whom Fernando had seen on the sands of Mondego Bay, who was the 'fish-wife with the whelk pin' – Wellesley went South to join Cuesta near Plasencia, and we all breathed again. Well, all the news of the French I passed on to Mr Curtis and I doubt not he knew them well already, but at least he'd thus know I was in earnest and giving him what was true, so perhaps he would not have me kidnapped and handed over to Julián's savages as happened I knew to some.

On the twenty-fifth of July I did better yet for on that evening we had fifteen officers in, most from Soult's field army that had been regrouping and re-equipping in camps outside the town for three weeks, and fifteen was more than Madame liked at once for it was too much for the girls, and sport and drunkenness grew wild in such large company and breakages were added to her expense, but her *Capitaine d'Artillerie* pleaded with her and on this account: in two days' time all would be off, every man that could be found or spared, that was fit enough to march and fight, none would be back for they were to sweep the British into the sea and then march on to Andalucie and Seville, to a land of gypsy girls with swirling dresses and long black hair, and orange groves and vines, the very garden of Spain; those of us, the Captain added, who are not killed on the way – and so she let them in, considering there would be less custom in the coming months and she should make hay while the sun shone. This I straight reported to Mr Curtis through Violeta in her guise of flower-seller and whispered to her as I handed her my packet that he should note it well for I was sure what I said was true.

The upshot was that Wellesley – by then recovering from his victory at Talavera, recovering for it cost as dear as it won – knew well in time of this threat to his flank from the North and withdrew into Portugal to leave the Spanish Armies, which had left him wretchedly in the lurch in the matter of promised supplies, to fend for themselves. Cuesta was beaten once or twice more, I believe, had an apoplexy and died, and the rest were bundled out of Andalucie and bottled up in Cadiz, so what the Captain said was true, though whether he lived to enjoy the gypsy girls and the oranges we never discovered. But what I say is this: had I not given the news of Soult's decision to go South in good time the British might have been caught on the fever-ridden banks of the Guadiana and all lost, and with them the hopes of Europe for a future free from Tyranny.

By the by, after the Battle of Talavera, Wellesley was made Viscount Wellington and from then on was known as The Peer.

Chapter VII

Of Devious Schemes Resorted to, Necessary for Survival in Difficult Times.

I

'Tell me, dear Zeppo,' Madame asked one morning, or rather early afternoon, in October, 'what of this Duque de Parque they talk of and this rabble he has brought together in the South?'

'Tell you, Madame? How should I know aught of such things?'

'Come, come, boy,' and she leant forward from her many pillows to tweak my cheek, and as she did so her full breasts swung forward with her night-gown. Then she lay back again, took up her coffee cup and a cinnamon sippet, but before she nibbled went on: 'I know well enough you get news of the British and Spanish before most of us, and what you pass on to Rubén and what you keep for yourself is no concern of mine. But . . .' and here she did have a nibble at the biscuit, '. . . now, just now, I feel . . . *exposed*, a little *threatened*.'

She looked straight at me, and though her full red mouth, just newly painted, smiled, her eyes, round which I marked a fine lace-work of lines and wrinkles, looked solemn, and then even as they flinched away, a little wary.

'Why should that be, Madame?' I was sitting on the edge of the bed, which was high enough for only the tips of my toes to touch the thickly carpeted floor, and sipping my chocolate, for I did not yet have a taste for coffee early in the day – I found its action on my bowels too quick – having bedded with her since her *Capitaine d'Artillerie à Cheval* had set off for Seville. This not for any carnal satisfaction, but for company's sake for, as she said, she could never sleep without there was someone to put her arm round.

'Why? Because this Duque de Parque is marching hither, it's said, with an army of ten thousand, and the French will be kicked out, that's why.'

'Madame, it's not possible.'

'Why not?'

'That Army of his is a rabble – I know, I was part of it once. 'Tis what is left of mad old Cuesta's host, he that lost more battles in a week than . . . than Dolly has lovers. That mob could never win a battle.'

'How many French would be needed to beat this Duke of the Park?' she giggled a little at this then fell serious, nibbling her biscuit while waiting my answer.

I thought, and wishing to allay her fears, pitched the number low. 'Three thousand,' I said.

'That is childish invention. Be serious.'

'Madame, I'm no soldier. There are plenty who are whom you may ask.'

'Well, I'll tell you, Zeppo, since I've enquired already of a Lieutenant of Sapeurs, whom I'd fancy were he not willing to pay Brigid more than we can afford to lose, for he is a gentle, oldish man and would comfort me well, I'm sure, and clean too, so Brigid says . . .' (this all said to rebuke me and raise in me the monster of envy, which, by the by, is one vice that scarcely ever bothers me) '. . . this lieutenant says that odds of five to three if the soldiers are good on the French side, but only five to four if they are not; this if the Spanish are well led, which by all accounts is the case with this Parque. Zeppo, how many good troops could gather together on Salamanca in the next six days?'

I had no exact idea of this at all but a shiver ran down my back so I pulled my gown closer round me; for I was sure there could not be more than four thousand within sixty miles, and if there were they would be *Sapeurs*, wounded, garrison troops, Belgians, Neapolitans, and God knows what all, for we had not seen a proper young fighting soldier in a month or more, a matter Madame's nieces were inclined to grumble at. Even the Bavarians from Alba were gone.

'Marshal Ney. They say he has a fine army in Galicia. Will he not come down on this Parque to save us?' I suggested.

'No, Zeppo, he will not. For that is another matter I heard gossip of last night when you were already dozing. He will not come for two reasons – first General Marchand who governs here in Dorsenne's place is one of Soult's men, whom this Ney hates; and secondly because the town of Astorga yet holds out against him and he durst not leave it unreduced in his rear. And Victor and the King are following Soult into Andalucie for the plunder.'

I marvelled aloud at her comprehension of matters usually thought beyond women's capability, or at best unsuited to it. She raised an eyebrow at me. 'Zeppo, pour me some more coffee. For eight years I have run the sort of enterprise you see me now engaged in – in Milan, Vienna, Naples, and for a short time in Lisbon, and I should not have survived had I not mastered the elements of military strategy; for the secret of a good profit is to be near the fighting men who will spend lavishly and gratefully on any house of drabs that has some quality about it, which they will not do in a dull garrison town where all is settled and they have their mistresses or wives, and if they want a tart as well, well that's all they want and a dollar for half an hour is all they'll spend. That's how Naples had become, and that's how Madrid is now. So we keep near the fighting, but not too near. And now I fancy it is too near. I tell you what, Zeppo – I think this Marchand will be beat, and beat soundly, and this Parque will have the French out of Salamanca before the end of the month. Earlier perhaps.'

By now I was well frightened and, as I recollect, pacing the carpet and wringing my hands. 'What shall we do then, Madame? We must be off, I think,' I cried, and so forth, for I fancied I could feel the cold collar of the garotte about my neck.

'Well, yes and no, Zeppo. I think *we* should be off, that is the girls with me and Marinetta, but you shall stay.'

'Oh Madame, they'll hang me as soon as . . .'

'Now quieten down. I insist. Zeppo, I'll turn you out of doors this instant if you do not cease your blubbering. There. There, there. Now that is better, is it not? This then is the matter. I cannot think we shall be gone for long. The way things stand – the Spanish Armies in the South faced with the King and three Marshals cannot last a month or more. Astorga will fall. We shall be back before Christmas – earlier, I make no doubt. And meanwhile I want you here to keep an eye . . . Zeppo, will you listen? I am not going to have this house pillaged in my absence, I will not be put to the expense of redecorating . . . Zeppo, please listen. They will not hang you. They will hail you as a hero; they will place garlands round your neck, not nooses, above all they will respect your wishes when you tell them to leave this house locked and barred and untouched . . . How will they do this? Why will they do this? Come back to bed and I will tell you.'

2

Followed a conversation, schemes and stratagems being the greater part, which soothed me in some measure, for I saw if all worked out as we put it together, well, I might get off with some advantage to us both – but it seemed a terrible, perilous plan even when we had refined it and looked at it from all sides at once. It did not need much to go wrong for me to end up hanged or worse and I said so repeatedly, but she tushed me and shushed me and soon I gave in, and all this time lying close to her in her giant bed, her heavy brown and reddened hair about the pillow, the weight of white buttocks and thighs in the down beside me, and the smells of her body, a little sour beneath the scents she used, wafted in my nostrils every time she moved. And when at last she said, 'Will it do, Zeppo? Can you carry it off?' I sighed and sighed again, and at last flung myself back in the pillows, and nearly tear-ful said, 'Madame, if that's how it must be, then that's how I'll do it, but my heart misgives me yet,' at which she gathered me up to her and offered me intimacies that comforted, though none, of course, sinful.

When we arose we set in train two days of toing and froing, all covert and clandestine, so none knew all that went ahead except us, though Rubén knew most of it, and perforce I had to slip away to Antonio's and find gap-toothed Suero and his gypsies and offer them more of Madame's gold than I had seen (I mean for my own use) in a month to run messages for us to Marchand, these pur-porting to come from traitors amongst Julián Sánchez's *Guerrilla*, and Frenchifiers on the Duque de Parque's staff, and so forth. And also I had to send messages to Mr Curtis, Violeta, and so to the Martíns and other loyalists in the Town, so it should be known to them that what was to come about, which was inevitable anyway so it is not on my conscience – namely, the defeat of the French as prophesied by Madame – was brought about in some measure by me, and also through the good offices of Madame her-self, though this part of it only hinted at, not said so broadly. And all had to be managed in such a way that the French believed and would continue to think we were helping them – thus Rubén took me to the General himself and I boldly warned him that Suero and the Gypsies were not to be trusted and need not be believed. But this too late for Marchand wanted to believe what Suero told him, that if he moved fast he could catch the Spanish before they came all together and destroy them piecemeal; but not so late that it would not be said after that I had told truth and Suero was a deceiver. Thus and thus both sides came to think us honest.

Three days after our first talk on all this Marchand took his Army off – just five thousand and all paymasters, barber-surgeons, pioneers, wounded not yet recovered, young conscripts, and not half of them French – and left scarcely an hundred in the Town with an hundred Dragoons. Next morning Madame was off, with her nieces, Marinetta, and the Dragoons as well which had been promised her as escort to Madrid and kept back for that purpose, though they carried despatches too.

Before she went she embraced me very fondly, we were alone in her chamber, then held me by the shoulders and looked at me from golden eyes that wept a little, and said: 'Zeppo, take care; and if aught goes wrong, very wrong, you know you have the ring I gave you.'

'It is yet hidden away at my Father's house,' I cried.

She frowned at this — 'Please get it, Giuseppe, and once you have it please keep it always about you,' she thought for a moment then continued, 'meanwhile, and because even the distance to Los Arapiles may not be easily crossed by a man alone in the next few days, here is another resource,' and she let go my shoulders and her taffetas rustled as she moved round the great bed where, on the other side, she discovered a panel in the wall that opened and inside it a porcelain coffer, not above the size of a small book. 'It has always been my habit,' she said, 'to keep some insurance about me, but I will leave this here for you now, in case you should not be able to fetch the ring I gave you before. But mind. The first ring is yours — these are a loan, and you must use them to buy off any attempt the Jesuits and such may make against this house while I am away.'

By now I was at her side and I could see the coffer held three more rings — the brilliants not as big as the one she had given me but together worth as much or more. She replaced the lid, which was painted prettily with cupids and roses, and pushed the panel to.

Then she embraced me again and I led her down to the Square where a seven foot Dragoon in green with red facings handed her into her coach where her nieces and Marinetta already attended her. The coachman whipped up the mules, and in a clatter of iron wheels on granite paving they were gone, the last I saw of her for eight long weeks.

I made fast the house, which had had extra locks and fastenings

and bars with padlocks added, and took myself off to an attic
lodging I had prepared, where I waited the outcome of our
devices for a further full three days, during which I went not
abroad, hardly slept or ate, and almost starved myself to death
with worry and anxiety, but all fell out much as we had planned.

On the nineteenth of October at dawn all the church bells
rang, and looking down from my attic window, set in the leads
above the Town, I could see the Squares and streets filling as all
tumbled out to the news that at Tamames, a village some ten
leagues or more to the South and West, Marchand had been
routed, with loss of nearly two thousand dead, that Parque was
victorious, that our Town and Province were free of the French –
and going down I heard, bit by bit, as more news came in, what
I knew already, that the French had attacked a position held by
only six thousand, not knowing that this number twice over lay on
either flank, concealed by forest and hills. The Spanish centre
held, the trap was sprung, the French broke, and what with Don
Julián's *Lanceros* and a hostile country very few, if any, got off, and
those that did fled to Zamora and Toro to the North and sheltered
there behind the River Duero, where outposts of Ney's army
were already posted.

3

In the week or so that followed I renewed my acquaintance and
even friendship with many who had scorned me in the past for my
Aunt and I had laid our schemes so well that all accepted
Marchand had gone where and when he had through information
I had put before him. At the Martín house I was welcomed again,
though Fernando was no longer there, being now one of Don
Julián's *Lanceros* and out campaigning along the Duero and East as
well against the return of French Armies. There – at Don Jorge's,
I mean – I dined and supped on three or four occasions, and
what surprised me was that at their table I always found Father

John Reaney, the student astronomer, and not only was he always there, but, it seemed, on terms of filial closeness with Don Jorge and Doña Regina, and closer still with Violeta whose hand he sometimes took, and once I saw him kiss it in a fashion quite unbecoming in a Priest; she blushed, but whether for shame or pleasure, I could not discover.

Early during this time I was much gratified to be called to the Chamber in the Town Hall where once I was quizzed by Dorsenne, and there was received by the Captain General el Duque de Parque, whom I found to be a most obliging and condescending personage, to the extent he shook my hand and thanked me for the part I had played in his recent success, and offered me a glass of wine which I was pleased to accept. During the brief exchange that followed I was able to satisfy him that I was a connexion of his acquaintance the Marquis of Monterrubio de la Sierra on the distaff side, and this seemed to content him.

This, one would think, would set the seal of almost royal approval on my habilation as a friend of Loyal Spain and the British, but Mr Curtis alone remained crusty and curmudgeonly yet, for when I offered to call on him his porter told me he was not in, and later he sent me the following note.

Joseph
The pleasure I might have had at hearing reports that you are a patriot is vitiated by doubts as to their veracity. That's as may be, and I must beg mercy of Him Who condemned the Pharisees and taught us of Joy in Heaven at one Sinner Repented if my judgement in this is wrong. However, my purpose in writing is not to repeat my earlier censures, nor put before you later grounds I have had for doubting your good faith (*Did he refer here to* his *bad faith in laying a trap for me with his false letter from Don Julián?*), but to urge you to visit your Father, who is not well and would like to see you.
              Yr servant, and yr Father's friend, as ever,
                      Patrick Curtis.

I intended to go as soon as may be, and indeed before three weeks were out did so, as I shall relate, but in the meantime was much occupied with all that went forward in town as of Masks and Balls, of *Tertulias* and Plays – for every day brought better news and all were jolly with them, for none now expected the return of the French; though I was not so sure, not out of my own judgement but because of Madame's certainty she would be back.

The good news they had were that in the South Soult could not move for fear of the British on his flank, in the North Junot and Ney were hemmed by the Galicians on one side and by our own Parque's army that increased in numbers daily and was spread along the Duero waiting for a favourable opportunity to cross it, and that a huge host led by one Areizaga was even now marching on Madrid to chase out Joseph for the last time, which he was bound to do having an advantage of two to one.

And the bad news reached us on the Twenty-Third of November that this same Areizaga had lost thirty-six thousand out of fifty-two thousand men at a battle near a town called Ocaña twenty leagues South of Madrid – and that was a sudden end to all our merriment. By evening of the same day units of Parque's army were coming through town from the North, having abandoned the Duero line, and I knew it was time to shift my course to the starboard tack as sailors say, or face right about as a soldier might have it.

First I enquired where I could – in the Town Hall, at Jorge Martín's, even of soldiers passing in the street – what they thought *el Duque*'s plans were, and all agreed he was concentrating as quick as may be on Alba, which, with its strong citadel and the bend in the river then in flood, he hoped to hold more securely than he could the Duero or Salamanca itself, and wait there new orders from the Junta in Seville. Then I sought out Suero in the back room of La Covachuela.

'Carry news for me to the *Gabiné*, O Calo,' I demanded of him.

'What news, *O Busné*?' he asked, 'and which of the *Gabiné*?'

'Why, the *Gabiné* at Zamora – and the news is that if they

would catch the *Senjen* soldiers they must march on Alba as quick as may be.'

He gave me his gap-toothed grin and said: 'I doubt not they know that already.'

'No doubt, but *Calo*, I would have them know that it is something I wish them to know, so they may know I wish them well.'

'O little *Busné*, almost I think you could make the *hokkano baro* (by which he meant the Gypsy Swindle) like one of us, you are so sharp – but how will I get through the *Senjen* lines to deliver your message?'

'With gold?' I suggested.

'Ay, with *sonacai*, little *Busné manclay*.'

I gave him what he asked from Madame's store and he promised he would deliver my news to the first French General he could find, and would be sure to see it bore my name in cipher Rubén had given me before he left.

There remained one last thing to do – and that was visit my Father at Los Arapiles, as suggested by Mr Curtis, before the wars returned more nearly to make the trip difficult or dangerous, and partly I had it in mind to pick up Madame's ring for I felt sure on her return she would demand of me whether I had it or not and the three small rings she had left with me she would require back; and in the meantime there would be some days ahead both before and after the coming battle when I might need all I could lay my hands on if ever what side I was on, or had been on, was doubted.

CHAPTER VIII

A Visit to Los Arapiles Discovers an Old Man Wandering in his Wits.

I

Throughout the last fortnight of November the rains fell almost without ceasing and when I set forth on the Twenty-Sixth, having postponed my departure in hope of more clement weather for as long as I dared considering the possibility of a battle in the neighbourhood, the ways were deep and miry with the water lying in the ditches and potholes like a thick red soup and the sky low, sometimes so low that mist drifted across the Arapiles as I neared them on my mule, and always the rain. The village seemed deserted as I clopped through it, I saw no-one nor any living thing at all, not even a dog or hen, and no smoke from the roof vents and no peeping at the sacking that covered the windows, so that by the time I reached my Father's door I wondered if all had fled, knowing of imminent fighting in the neighbourhood; but as I waited after giving the door a good knock I could hear the movements of Tía Teresa within as she came to unbolt the door, and above the steady drumming of the rain fancied I could detect the tinkling of my Father's clavier.

Almost I did not recognise the good old lady when at last she opened up: her face in less than a year had fallen in and taken on an ashen pallor as of dirt or ground-in plaster, yet my Father was ever insistent she should wash; her body, still large-framed, seemed sunken so her old gown hung loose about her, her eyes and nose watered constantly and her hand shook.

'Is it you, José? Well, well, is it really you? Ah well, you'll want to see your Father, and mayhap he'll let you, I don't know I'm sure, but you'd best come in.'

Chilled by this doubting welcome I entered, nor did she offer to embrace me as I expected. As I removed my hat water tipped from where it had gathered in the brim, and I looked for a scolding from one who had once been so nice about her floors, yet got none, instead this: 'José, did you walk here? No, by your boots you did not. Then you'd best get out again and take your mule or whatever in to the lean-to, then bolt it and come back in by the garden, quick now or it will be gone before you know it.'

Well, I did as she said, but much disturbed to think things had come to this, that I could not leave a mule tethered to the hitching ring by my Father's door, without it might be lifted; the stall was empty too, and the garden desolate with nought but six cabbage stalks and only two of the fruit trees left, stumps where the others had been, and the raindrops plashing in the red mud where in the past, even at that time of year, I should have expected greens and the like in some profusion, and the stone lid on the well was cracked.

The kitchen was cold though Tía Teresa now occupied herself with a bellows on the charcoal trench she used for cooking, but there was no life in it, just white ash that swirled around her. 'I've told him you're here,' she called above the noise she made.

'I'll go up then,' I said, not wanting to linger in such cheerless gloom.

'Not yet. He said to wait. It was a surprise to him, your coming, and he wants to think on't for a space.'

I sat down, and soon Tía Teresa gave over pumping useless air at the dead embers and sat down too, but at the far end of the table.

'It's been out these two days,' she said. 'He won't have it going unless there's cause, and that's twice a week when I make the soup,' and she pulled her shawl about her with shaking fingers.

'Most part of the day I stop in bed,' she went on, and gestured to the alcove where I had slept throughout my childhood – 'it's warmer there. But I thought I should try to start it up for you. Though the Lord knows why.'

We sat in silence and I listened to the rain and for the sound of my Father's clavier, but nothing now. Slowly I itemised the changes since last I was there, and what they came to was that the place was bare, bare and dirty – no country hams or sausages drying from the ceiling, just one bone with all but the very last scraps of meat gone from it; no herbs. Where on the dresser there was wont to be a pair at least of good white loaves there was only a large crust, and that grey. The pots no longer shone, there was grease on the table at my elbow. I wondered what ailed Teresa that she should let all get to such a pass, and supposed it must be illness, old age, or both.

Then, as I thought this, I heard my Father's step on the boards above our heads, but instead of the call to come up that I expected, the creak of the stool by his instrument and then at last his music.

It was a sonata of Scarlatti's I knew well for he was used to play it often, it's known, I think, as *il Corteo Funebre*, for it repeats again and again a noble solemn tune with an almost funeral rhythm, though not so slow as all that, so perhaps it is not well-named after all, but the tune goes thus: *Ya* ta ta *ta* ta *ta* ta *ta* and then the other hand picks it up so it is never completed, the first note coming *Ya* as it were on the last note *ta* – that is the last note thus becomes the first note. What happened now was that my Father attempted it six times and each time failed to bring in the left hand at the right moment, so all was left hanging aimless in the air for a beat or so, till at last it came so late as to sound empty and without meaning, at which he would go on for half the phrase and then stop and go right back to the beginning, but always that empty break came again, and this done, as I say, six or seven times. Then the lid closed, but not smashed shut, that was not my Father's way, just closed, and silence but for the rain.

At last the stool scraped back, we heard his step, then he called.

'Joseph, are you really there?'

'Yes, Father.'

Silence again; then, 'Well – you had better come up, come up. Ay. Come up then.'

And so I did.

2

He was standing by the window facing away from me yet I could see, even from his back clad as ever in black broad cloth, that he too had become woefully thin. I waited for him to turn and my eyes wandered over his study, at the book-shelves where *Lazarillo de Tormes* still sat high on the top shelf, at the large table and six good chairs, at the *pot-pourri* and at all the other objects so familiar from my childhood, and after what I had seen below stairs was happy that after all not much had changed here. Save him whom I had come to see – for he turned now and looked straight at me and I saw his eyes deep sunk in dark sockets, a face lined and grey, with beard more thin and now white not grey save where it was stained, and quite unkempt so no two hairs were of the same length. He waved me to a chair with a hand thin and claw-like, nor did he offer to embrace me either, so I sat with feelings mixed between hurt and bitter and angry, but not strong, yet, for I was puzzled too. As I say, I sat and waited.

'Well, Joseph, you have come. What for, pray? We have little or nothing here for you.'

'I came, Sir, at the request of Mr Curtis.'

'What will you gain from him by coming?'

'I pray you do not be so sharp with me. I came because he said you were not well, and he thought I should see you.'

'Why, this is bad news. He must think I'm dying. Well, I may be, 'tis true I may be. So he sent the Prodigal back to me, eh? Nay, he's a sentimental man, a sentimental man to think you will reform at my deathbed.'

'Sir, you do neither of us justice – he told me to come out of his concern for you, thinking a visit from me might cheer you, and for that reason too I fell in with his wishes.'

'He may be sentimental, but he's not a fool. He cannot imagine a visit from you will cheer me.'

And he turned back to the window and seemed to watch the rain run down the panes.

I listened to my heart-beat, and felt the sweat in my palms – how I should have loved to take myself off then, give way to the anger he had knowingly provoked, and be off. But that is no doubt what he wanted.

'Still here, Joseph?' His voice was even lower than before. 'Why stay?'

'For your blessing, Sir, if you are like to die.'

'Oh ay. An old man's blessing, but that won't buy you a new suit of clothes.'

'Why are you so hard on me, Sir? I have only come to talk to you, cheer you on this dull day, bring you the news if you wish to hear them . . .'

'You could have come these nine months, Joseph, to bring me news.'

'I did not know you had been so poorly.'

'No? But I've known what you've been doing, and you know I know. And I know with whom you have been lodged. Is not that it, my boy?'

'Tongues wag, Sir. And they get things wrong. None but I know what I was doing.'

He had no answer to this, but at length sat himself down also, but with a grunt or two as if his old bones ached, which was painful to see for even up to a year before, at Christmas when we had made that perilous journey to Torrecilla and fallen in so extraordinarily with no less a person than the Emperor of the French, he had been agile enough, despite his earlier apoplexy. And there we both sat in silence for upwards of half an hour and the light deepened about us, for early evening was coming on, and neither of us spoke. But I thought, as I was bound to, of the past, of the lessons he had given me there in tongues and botany, and *Robinson Crusoe*, this being the period when my education followed that of *Émile*, and I know not what all, though most I had forgotten, and I wished he would find it in him to offer me some kind word, but he said nothing, though once or twice he drew in breath wheezily as if to speak, but then let it out again, and sometimes he cracked his knuckles, and sometimes he stroked his beard.

And then just as I was ready to burst into sobs, so heavy was my heart in me with a mixture of frustration and despair at his hardness, he lifted his head and, 'What Joseph, still here?' he said, 'well then, call to Teresa for a light, and I'll talk to you if that's what you've a mind to.'

With alacrity I did as he asked, and when a tallow taper was set between us, for that was all there seemed to be in the house, we sat down as before, and I listened to what he had to say, which was, as near as I remember, much on these lines.

'I congratulate you, Joseph, that on being grown to manhood, you have turned out so well fitted to the times we live in, and for that I did not intend it nor understood these times, it must be seen as some act of blind providence that it should be so. For I see you are grown a *rational* man and the times are *rational*, and so you are fitted to them, and no doubt you will continue to do well. You look askance. Why? Because I seem to speak sarcastically of Reason, when all my life I have tried to regulate myself and my affairs according to what paths of conduct she seemed to indicate? No, no. I do not speak ill of Her. Only of myself, who failed where you have succeeded so well.

'I always congratulated myself,' he went on, 'that I was born at that time when the blindness and the cant and the superstition of many centuries were being rolled away like the mists of a foul night before the bright rays of the newly risen sun of Reason. It was the Mathematicks, so pure, that started this Golden Dawn, the Mathematicks that put the Planets in their orbits, that learnt to

measure a curve, that could describe and predict the path of a
Heavenly Body to the end of Time. Sublime Isaac did this,
Sublime Isaac. He resolved the operations of the Moon to two
motions – a forward motion of a certain velocity, and a second
motion as of the Moon falling to Earth by gravity, which is to say
she follows the Law that every particle of Matter, whether in the
Heavens or elsewhere, behaves as if it attracts every other particle
with a force proportional to the product of the masses and
inversely proportional to the Square of the Distance. You know
Joseph with laws like this one day Man will put himself on the
Moon, ay, and get further.'

Here he looked at me at last, his eyes glinting and wild in that
poor light, the shadows of the new hollows in his face as deep as
pits, and I thought to myself, here is a man who is mad, but I sat
fast and heard him out.

'Well, Joseph, what sort of man shall be put on the Moon, eh?
What sort of man? It cannot be he will be one of the old sort,
blind, and stupid, dull and unsensible of where his interest lies. It
would not do to have an unreconstituted *Human* there; why, he
would try to eat it presuming it was cheese, or look for the Man-
in-the-Moon there before him with his Lantern, his Dog, and his
Bush. Nor would a Lover nor a Poet do, for odes and raptures are
not worth the air that breathes them, and air will be short on the
Moon, but Moon Dust, Joseph, the ashes of the Moon, those
would be something; for who, Joseph, would not like to let the
ashes of the Moon slip between his fingers?

'No, Reason requires it shall be a reasonable man who first
takes that step beyond our sublunary state and Reason shows us
the way to make men reasonable: for if the Planets obey the Laws
of Reason, why should not man do so too? and he will Joseph, he
will. Already, in you, he sometimes does.'

Here he paused and thought again, and as he did he drew an
ellipse with his finger round the candle-flame, and then was off
again.

'Joseph, there is to be a Mathematicks of the Mind, a Differential

Calculus of the Soul, a Science of Society. These things are possible – I have always thought so and other better men than I. *Locke*
affirmed morality is – must be – as capable of exact demonstration
as Mathematicks. And *Leibniz*. Leibniz, the man the Emperor
with his Metre Rule so praised, what did Leibniz say? "If contro-
versies arise there should be no more need of disputation between
two philosophers than between two accountants. For it would suffice for them to take their pencils in their hands, to sit down to
their slates, and say to each other (with a friend to witness), '*Let us
Calculate*.'" This last he produced in a mincing voice like a child
repeating its lesson by rote, and this bewildered me for often had
I heard him recite it before, but with joyful seriousness, as it were
a message of hope.

'And here's another, Joseph, here's a good one to point the way,'
and he stood up and found a small octavo volume on the shelf
near where he sat and held it up to the flame in one hand and
peered through a hand glass held in the other. '"To find a *univer-
sal canon* to compute the *morality* of any actions, with all their
circumstances, when we *judge* of the actions done by our selves, or
by others, we must observe the following *propositions* or *axioms*."'
This again he read in a whining sarcastical voice as above. '"One:
The *Moral Importance* of any *Agent*, or the *Quantity* of *Public Good*
produc'd by him, is in a *compound Ratio* of his *Benevolence* and
Ability: or $M = B \times A$. Two: In like manner, the *Moment* of *Private
Good* or *Interest* produced by any person to himself is in a *compound
Ratio* of his *Self-Love* and *Ability*, or: $I = S \times A$." From this you see,
Joseph, we may calculate the *benevolence* or *Moral Importance* of
any *Agent* to the ineffable benefit of Mankind.

'But this is childish footling stuff to the constructs that are to
follow. Isaac made a Mechanism of the Heavens – if the Cosmos
itself is clockwork then so must be our smaller minds that thus
contrive to comprehend it – that is Rational, is it not? Perhaps a
complex clockwork, but clockwork none the less.

'How does it go on? "Mind is the product of sensations". That
is a good one. "Man is made up of vibrating particles or

Vibratiuncles" which respond to sensations; and, since it is inconceivable that there should be a gap in the chains of Cause and Effect that make up the Cosmic Process, Mind must be the product of sensations, must be the effect of stimuli producing sensations combined inexorably by various laws of Association. Our impulses are formed by appetites and desires because their satisfaction gives us pleasure and their frustration gives us pain. And so, Joseph, we can now boldly state the moral equivalent of the Law of Gravity. It is nothing other than the Law of Self-Interest. You see what I mean, Joseph, when I congratulate you on your Rationality and Moral Soundness?'

I felt here a strength of feeling against me beyond what I had hitherto been sensible of and was quick to riposte with this: 'Sir, you oft-times taught me that a Man of Sense was a man passionate to do good because of the happiness it gave him, a happiness that might move him to tears, as I have seen in your own eyes, and indeed I have learnt to weep at beauty and goodness myself, from your example. And this sense of goodness you said was natural . . .'

'But corrupted out of most of mankind by false society and civilisations founded on greed and superstition; Oh ay, Joseph, I remember it,' and again that voice like a violin badly bowed: '"I had rather search for Nature's Law in a Naked Indian than in some spruce Athenian; in a rude American, rather than in a gallant Roman; I would fetch the Law of Nature from the Scythian, from a Barbarian – there shall you see it without glosses or superstructures, without carving or gilding,"' and then his ordinary voice, but lost and quiet: 'Joseph, I have seen two soldiers hold a baby each by one foot while a third cleaved it with his sabre. Sucking pigs are thus cut up for Epiphany. And when I saw this here in this village, and the child was María Victoria's, you remember her? it seemed to me then that here was an action that lacked carving or gilding, that lacked the superstructure the Law gives to the Hangman when he performs the same favour for him or her judged by Society to merit such treatment. Is there not a paradox here? Some Contradiction? I wish I could fathom it out, but I think my brain is tired and addled and does not see so clear as it did.'

And now I was moved to the happiness I should feel if I could see him but a touch restored to do good, and so I tried to cheer him thus: 'But Sir,' quoth I, 'the soldiers who performed this dreadful act were not the product of their Human Nature, but were made brutes by the society that framed them . . .'

'Oh yes, Joseph, oh yes. I had quite forgot,' and he pulled himself up and went on with, I thought, more cheerfulness, 'how good of you to remind me. It is of course self-evident that man is the product of what is around him – how could a *conglomerate of vibratiuncles* be other? and therefore of the institutions under which he lives – all we have to do is reshape these institutions in accord with the invariable and determinable laws of nature, for we must never forget or doubt that Reality is subject to Reason, and the System delivers the Good. What are the natural laws of which I speak? Why Gravity, I mean Self-Interest, embodied in the principle of pleasure and pain, from which we extract the sublime algebra that equates the good of the many with the good of one. Much has already been done. I have seen in my time many improvements, many projects that have brought much amelioration,' and he rattled them away like a child repeating his lesson by rote, 'navigation, cattle-breeding, cotton-spinning, and sanitation. The metre rule. The Metre Rules, that's right, is it not? From all this we shall have, almost we have already, Social Sciences. We shall have Enlightened Ministries to enforce, I mean encourage, the findings of these Social Sciences. Sciences which will give man a true theory of his own nature and thus enable him to control his own destiny. Or give some men the power to control the destinies of most. Well, whatever the beginning, the end will clearly be glorious and paradisiacal. Oh yes. These views, I assure you, are fairly suggested by a true theory of human nature. But Joseph,' here his voice lost its manic note and fell away again, 'I am forced to admit all this is in the future, a future sure to come for all Reality is subject to Reason and the System will deliver the Good, but in the meantime Reason sleeps and all about us are the phantasms that haunt her dreams, as barbarity, brutality, greed, theft, murder, rapine, revenge, sickness, hunger just as there always have been, just as always. And there is manipulation of men's souls, and men believing mumbo-jumbo like the Afric Heathen, not out of Faith or Goodness, but because that way self-interest lies, and tomorrow it will be the mumbo-jumbo of the Sciences of Man, no different from any other mumbo-jumbo, and men lie doggo, and rut, and drink, and seek to go like pigs, like pigs in their own filth, because it is easier to live thus, than otherwise. And this common desire to be enslaved by contentment, to live like pigs in their own filth, will always be the weapon, infallible weapon, of the ambitious, the greedy, the cruel, the power-hungry whether the intermediate tool is Christianity or Social Sciences and, but, oh Joseph, I'm tired. Joseph, I'm very tired . . . Joseph.'

He nodded a moment and I thought he was done, but then he pulled himself up again, and spoke at last with more coherence than he had yet achieved.

'Joseph, you asked my blessing. I give you this instead. I would see a world where each man seeks the Truth and is left by all other men to do so in what way he likes and interfere with none and be interfered with by none, and where Science and Knowledge are helps to him in this search and also help by removing as much as may be from his shoulders of meaningless toil and pain. But what I do see is a world of interference, of control, of dullness, of brutality. A world where force, strength and guile and cheating are the only real virtues, these and wilful blindness, and where Science and knowledge are not paths to Truth, but to power. In this world, Joseph, I would have you strong and courageous, ready to be alone at all times, and at all times ready to listen to the dull and confused promptings of your soul, yet doubting at all times that there is such a thing as a soul; seeking with all your might to disentangle what is good, and kind, and true from what others say are good, and kind, and true, knowing that they do only to serve their own ends whether those ends be the manipulating of others or the pig-like satisfaction of doing nothing; above all, I would have you doubt your own deepest insights into the True, the Kind, and the Good, for self-interest is the worm that corrupts the very purest of thoughts and actions.'

He paused again and mused a little, and then went on – his voice slower than before, but firmer.

'Joseph, some weeks ago I had a sort of vision or dream of what I take to be the best we can hope for and I offer it you now as a type to keep in your heart and ponder on. The man I see is no Hero, or Slayer of men, nor builder of Palaces or Prisons. Nor is he wise as other men are wise with measurement and deviousness. Nor is he a scientist or a law-giver or any other sort of man who puts a circumscription round life and says – "because this is how I have calculated then this is right and all else is wrong." Nor is he like a Christ bleeding on a Cross so women may weep over him. He is none of these.'

I waited, then had to prompt him with a muttered, 'Pray go on, Sir.'

He heaved a deep sigh, and continued thus: 'Here is the Man I saw in my dream. He is old, but strong. He is simply clad in a worsted gown as it might be like a Friar's habit, but this only because it is serviceable and no more, and has no vanity about it, and no-one has suffered to make it. He is certainly not religious – and this is clear from his face, which is burnt brown and though kind has a thoughtfulness in it that shows he has studied the world much, and himself especially, and though he has not found all to his liking, is ready, as I am not, to live with it for a while yet. And he has studied all his life how best to be useful, how best to be kind, and has put away the vanity of religion that provokes the veneration of others or seeks a spurious happiness beyond the grave. In the same way he knows that he cannot teach without passing on corruption of manners, or fastening on mental chains; he cannot till the soil without pandering to greed, his own or others'; he cannot sing, or play music or perform in any craft or art, without he becomes enslaved by the plaudits of those less skilled; and so on, Joseph, the catalogue is endless and I am tired.'

'Then what does this man do, that can be useful only with no tinct of corruption in it at all?'

'Well, Joseph, this is it. He carried a large earthen pot, with a stopper and a cup, and this he fills each day at some choice spring, and he offers water to any who ask him, and he takes from them only what he needs, and if he cannot get thereby a *cuarto* a day for some bread and salads, then that day he does without.

'There we have it, Joseph: what I should have tried to be, what you will never be. But there is one other Law you can follow with a clear conscience, and that is: survive. One day things may be better, until then, survive. Don't wait to be hunted to hide, survive. There is no such thing as enlightened self-interest, but self-interest will keep you alive, survive. I think you will be good at this. I know already you are good at it. Not good – accomplished. Survive.

'Well. Now I shall go to bed. I shall not see you again. I do not want to see you again. That ring of Annabella Grannacci's is where you left it; it is what you came for. Take it and with it, well, my hope that you may survive,' and here, quite suddenly, he blew out the flame but left the wick smouldering and in the sudden darkness I felt him stumble past me towards his bedroom. The strings of his clavier chimed as he bumped into it, and then I felt his hand on my shoulder as he went, but whether this was accident or design, I do not know.

3

I waited twenty minutes more, hearing him move in the darkness of his room, and then the ropes of his cot creaked and at last I think he slept. I found the taper by the glow of its wick and blew it in again. By its light I took down *Lazarillo* from the top shelf and behind it discovered Madame's ring, where I had left it. I put back the book.

By the same light I found my way downstairs again to the kitchen. Teresa was still up and had got a fire going and on it a pot of thin soup. As she watched me eat she said: 'Has he gone to bed then?'

I nodded.

'He sleeps up there again now. I don't know why. Did he talk a lot?'

'Ay.'

'I heard him but not clear enough to mark the words. Did he go on about a water-seller?'

'Ay.'

'He talks a lot to me too during the day, but not much sense in what he says. You are clever enough to know, Joseph, is there much sense in what he says?'

'Not much.'

'No. I thought not. He'll not last much longer, and then what will become of me?'

Soon she gave me a blanket and herself retired into the alcove behind the curtain, but I could hear her snuffling about, and could not sleep myself either so I asked her: 'When did the French come here?'

'Last Spring. April.'

'Why?'

'We thought for fodder and animals, and that was part of it.'

'What else?'

I heard her sigh. 'A month before some ruffians broke into Manuel García's bakery and beat him and stole his flour and his money.'

'Rubén's Father.'

'Aye. They did it on account Rubén serves the French in the Town Hall. When the French came they broke into every house save two – García's and this one.'

'That's strange,' said I, 'for the most part they are terrible strong against Priests.'

'Ay. Well there was talk about it after. Some said there was a

Lady in Town, an Italian, that keeps a bawdy-house, and she kept them off for she favoured your Father. But I can't believe that. Your Father never had to do with that sort. No. But others said 'twas on account of you, that you, like Rubén, are a Frenchifier.' Again she heaved her dreadful heavy sigh. 'I was glad we were spared, at first. José, they did terrible things here. But since then those that are left have naught to do with us at all, and it's become horrid lonely. It's a shame, José, a terrible shame. I know your Father is a foreigner and a scholar but he cared well for the simple people here and would do so now an they would let him, but they won't, and he mopes.'

That was all she would say, though I fancy she cried a bit. Later she snored.

I tried to doze the night out, but the fire went out and there was no more wood to put on it and I was cold and wet. At dawn I found my mule gone from the lean-to, in spite of the bolt. I was not much troubled, apart from the inconvenience, since I had lifted it from an alley near the market for the occasion. The rain being stopped, though the sky still overcast, I made my way back to town on foot.

The next day Generals Kellerman and Marchand won a battle at Alba. Parque got off lightly, however, and, with Don Julián's *Lanceros*, occupied the fortress town of Ciudad Rodrigo. This was still close, only fifty miles away, but they were well locked up there, so by Christmas, as she promised, Madame was back and the girls with her. She was pleased I had managed our affairs well in her absence, and gave me Dolores for a night, together with new clothes and much else.

Followed a period of some security when little changed in the Town for two years, though battles enough in the rest of the country: the British came near, then melted away to the Lines of Torres Vedras leaving Ciudad Rodrigo to be captured by the French, though Don Julián got off and went back to marauding and murdering in the mountains. The following Summer (1811) they were as near again as Fuentes de Oñoro sixty miles off, but that Winter were back again in Portugal. Throughout this time I maintained my credit with both Rubén and Mr Curtis by keeping what I thought to be spurious and invented in the informations they gave me to myself, and passing on what I knew to be true or at least likely, and so fulfilled my Father's kind instruction and survived. He too was more diligent in his own interest than expected and also kept alive, even I believe with some slight improvement in his circumstances, the consequence of the charity of Mr Curtis and others, until the Autumn of 1811, when it was reported to me he died of an ague.

At about that time, or a little before, Coulaincourt returned, the Swiss Lieutenant, and I kept my promise of a wild boar hunt, which almost fell out ill for both of us for again we believed news I'd had of Mr Curtis that all Don Julián's *Guerrilla* had gone into Portugal. However, we got off unhurt by employing the stratagem I had earlier devised, that is we fired some empty cottages in our path and the *Guerrilleros* stopped to put out the blaze. The next to happen was the Irish College closed and used for French billets, Mr Curtis and Father John Reaney locked up in a house in Town and lucky not to be shot or hanged for the spies they were, but not before I was given a message to take to the Peer, then in Freneda in Portugal, which I undertook for with their arrest I felt my own time in Salamanca had a term to it.

This adventure near cost me my life, but turned out well enough in the end, so I was able to return the following June (1812), by when I was Brevet Ensign and Aide to Captain Branwater of the Eighty-Eighth – the Connaught Rangers.

Madame and her Nieces withdrew ahead of us to Madrid, and thence I believe to Valencia.

On the twenty-second of July (1812) I served with the Connaughts at the field of Los Arapiles, or Salamanca as it is sometimes known, where I received a trifling hurt, later was in the terrible retreat from Burgos, through Salamanca to Ciudad Rodrigo, and then the marvellous swift advance the following

Summer to the Pyrenees themselves the North faces of which, and especially the Pic du Midi d'Ossau, like a giant broken tooth, I can see from my window as I write.

With the History of the Late Wars in front of me I must recognise that what happened to me in those Glorious and Fateful Years must seem dull and tedious compared with the Heroic Exploits of those who served less humbly than I, and so I lay my pen aside here, thankful at last to God and my Benefactor that I have here in Pau a secure place to end my days in, in the house of Captain Branwater, with the upbringing and education of the Darling Boy these wars left in my care as my chiefest duty and greatest delight.

VOLUME THREE

Apsley House
London

10th February 1824

The Duke has received Mr Bosham's letter of the thirteenth of January. He regrets that he can make neither head nor tail of it. The Duke agrees that he is indeed fond of children, his own and other people's, so be it they are well-favoured and well-mannered. He does not feel this trait – one he shares with most – entitles Mr Bosham to entertain hopes of preferment or pension from the Duke. As far as the Duke is aware there exist no grounds at all for him to feel obliged to Mr Bosham, though if Mr Bosham would be so good as not to write again, a sort of obligation would occur, though not one to be honoured with money or position. If, however, Mr Bosham cannot refrain from putting pen to paper, the Duke begs him to place before the Duke whatever it is he is trying to say, in clear and unreserved language.

Wellington

PART ONE

Chapter I

A Short Chapter, Introductory to the Third Volume, offering Examples of a Softness that Honours a Noble Nature.

I

That the kind and gentle side of Your Grace's nature is drawn forth in publick by the company of Children, that the steely visage appropriate for War and the mask of the Great Man of Affairs relax where innocence and playfulness are abroad, are known and attested by all who have seen Your Grace in surroundings and circumstances other than the most ceremonious and solemn, other than where shot and shell were flying, and, God Willing, women and children all well to the Rear. It has twice been my great privilege and pleasure to witness Your Grace in the company of children and both times I confess I was touched by what I saw.

The first occasion was in November of 1811, in the Portuguese hamlet of Freneda, not above a league or so from the Spanish border where, having just delivered dispatches to the *Guerrillero* Chieftain Don Julián Sánchez, who had rewarded me for a service arduous but not above the call of duty with a silver duro, I took my ease in the warmth of the sun and drank your health and his in the rough red wine of the country.

A small market was in progress – a few stalls put together from boards and trestles, and the peasants selling vegetables as cabbages, carrots and onions, with cheeses and sardines in oil as well. Amongst them one fellow stood out, a pedlar who had made his way from Oporto or Lisbon with a donkey load of things from Albion itself for homesick soldiers to buy and remind them of distant hearths, as Real Old Harrogate Toffee, Mr Dobson's Butter-Scotch, and Liquorice from Pontefract. There were too articles of a more useful sort – clasp-knives of Sheffield Steel, flint wheels with strips of lint for lighting pipes, pencils in brass cases, spirit stoves on which a small kettle could be boiled, and tinned tea-pots from the manufactories of Birmingham – such things as might make a common soldier's life abroad and on campaign a little easier; but at this hour of which I speak, being in the afternoon and most of the army thereabouts at their cooking-pots, this fellow was doing little trade.

I am sure Your Grace has no recollection of what happened now, for out of the great events of those six tumultuous years what I am about to record must be considered the most trivial and trifling occurrence – yet to me the scene and your presence on it is as lively in my mind as the sight of Your Grace upon more than one Glorious and Sanguinary field; and I must crave your indulgence in thus putting you in mind of it again.

2

Your Grace came forth from a neighbouring house, no bigger than the rest and no less humble, yet it was the General Head-Quarters of your Staff; you paused on the threshold, looked up and down, and then, quite unattended, strolled into the street and between the stalls, for all the world like a country squire amongst his tenantry. You were dressed, as I recall, in a grey frock-coat and grey trousers with a cape which shortly you removed and carried over your arm, for the sun was warmer perhaps than you had expected. On your head a small cocked hat – no plumes, no lace, no bullion, no sword, no pistol, not even a cane, and thus you took a little recreation from the Cares of Nations that beset you. Presently a small girl came up to you, a Portuguese, and taking you firmly by the hand with such familiarity as spoke of earlier meetings, indeed an established acquaintance, led you to the stall where the pedlar from Lisbon displayed his English wares. The girl was not above seven years, perhaps less, thin, dark, and a little pert – dressed cleanly in a white smock that set off her brown skin and with her dark hair in braids tied with a red ribbon.

Now this Miss questioned you earnestly, and all the time you kept her hand close in yours, and I suppose she wished you to explain the strange objects before her and especially the toffees and so forth, which though unfamiliar to her yet suggested by their smell and appearance pleasures fit for a childish palate. Anon, with easy formality, you addressed yourself to the pedlar who straight put up a pennyworth of wrapped butter-scotch in a screw of paper, which, the transaction completed, you offered to your companion. But now a shyness overcame her, perhaps she would not like these foreign dainties, and so to persuade her of their excellence you must draw one out of the screw, unwrap it, and after tantalising her with it for a moment pop it in . . . not her but your mouth. Miss frowned now, perhaps a tear glistened; to forestall it a second piece was quickly exposed and this posted where it most properly belonged. A space while one might count to twenty then smiles and glee on both sides, and two satisfied parties continued their perambulation, still hand in hand, of the tiny square.

3

The second time I was able to observe Your Grace in the company of children was during an all together more ceremonious and formal affair, it being in the Town of Pau, in Béarn, on the occasion of Your Grace's triumphal visit to that place on the fourteenth of May 1814. You were, I believe, on the way from Toulouse where you had lately won your all but last and all but greatest victory against the Tyrant's Armies, posting to Madrid on business of state, the peaceful future of ravaged nations being then your close concern. The town was at pains to make it clear that whatever its record in the past of support for the Tyranny lately ended, it now sought only to acclaim its Liberator and the Restorer of its ancient Kings. The Mayor and Corporation turned out to welcome you beneath a Triumphal Arch inscribed thus: *A Lord Wellington. Il nous a rendu les descendants de notre Henri* – this being a reference to the Bourbons as the linear successors of Henry the Fourth of Béarn and Navarre, he who found Paris worth a Mass, whose first capital was Pau. There were speeches and banquets, music and toasts and endless compliments for every Notable in Béarn, and I'm sure Your Grace's patience must have been stretched for all was done, to be sure, for the gratification of the makers of the speeches rather than out of sincere feeling for him to whom they were addressed, and this is usual, I suppose, at such functions.

But at the end of it all there came one simple ceremony which it seemed pleased Your Grace more thoroughly than all the rest, and here I must take my place on the stage of history and claim a portion of the credit.

At Pau, there was, and still is, an Academy for Young Ladies run by a Madame Hugues which at that time boarded and bred up young girls aged seven to nine and to which scarce a week before I had been appointed Teacher of Foreign Tongues, this on the rec-ommendation of my friend Captain Branwater who was of the garrison there, he having released me from my duties as his Ensign and Interpreter; and acting on my suggestion it was decided to employ six of the most becoming of these girls to come forward at the end of the banquet and present to Your Grace wreaths of laurel, which they most prettily performed.

No doubt the Mayor and other dignitaries had planned that this pleasing ceremony should be no more than the matter of a brief moment but Your Grace, refreshed by evidences of innocence and sincerity (for there's no blinking the fact – two months before there was not one there who had not had the tricolour for his sash of office), drew out the moment so it lasted a full half hour. As I recall it you embraced the chief of these young ladies very warmly, then let her take you by the hand and introduce you to each of her friends and to each you made your bow. Then, while His Worship and all His Worshipful Company hemmed and coughed and shifted from one foot to the other, you went down on your knees before these tiny nymphs and each in turn had to place her wreath on your brow, and then receive your compliments on her handiwork. Finally you bestowed a kiss on the one whose laurels clasped your temples most neatly, and kept her by your side during the following progress through the streets.

Your Grace, I do not dwell on these instances of the fineness of your feelings for children and the joy you take in their company out of any desire to draw profit from these virtues, save the profit of an example all should follow; yet my knowledge of these generous and unconsidered acts and the large heart they spring from leads me to feel sure Your Grace would condemn a failure in duty to Your Grace and to my Charge, a young boy nine years old bred up strong and bright by me and at the time of Your Grace's visit to Pau just eleven months old, and so I humbly draw Your Grace's attention to the existence of this Charge.

My post at Madame Hugues's Academy sustained me for scarce two years; with the return of settled times her establishment increased; girls of more mature years were enrolled; a most unfortunate misunderstanding concerning my relations with one of these, exaggerated by the malice and envy of those who coveted my position, secured my unjust and untimely dismissal. For some months I was hard put to get by, and only the trust of the Boy prevented me from cutting short an existence grown burdensome; at this time I wrote Your Grace, Your Grace replied, I had hope of relief from my miseries, but before I could advise you more fully of my circumstances, as you requested, the need was removed. Captain Branwater returned with his dear wife to Pau whose climate he believed would recommend itself to her sickly constitution – indeed it is mild though wet – and finding me in most dolorous circumstances was moved, out of memory of past trials and hardships shared, to give me a place in his household, which I held until only the other day. Alas, it is ever my misfortune to be misunderstood, accused where honour forbids the truth should be published abroad, and the matter of a Purse of gold *louis* remains between me and my benefactor.

Your Grace: Truth, the Boy's future, the desire he will no doubt one day have of rewarding those who have been at such pains to bring him up properly, all demand that the circumstances of his Engendering and of his Birth should be brought to Your Grace's attention. This the following pages set out to do, and as fully as may be, so none may find it possible to question them. If Your Grace will only peruse them then I find the Faith I have in the Special Compassion I know Your Grace has for the young – as exemplified above – prompts me to be sure that the very dire need suffered at this time by the Darling Boy will be swiftly alleviated, and the care I have been put to on his behalf in the past, and will cheerfully shoulder in the future, will not go unrewarded.

CHAPTER II

Salamanca, so recently the Scene of a Glorious Triumph, is Abandoned again to the Mercies of a Rapacious Foe; on the Retreat I fall in with Mistress Flora Tweedy, an Heroine too late introduced if what I write were Fiction merely, but an Heroine nonetheless, in Fact.

I

We were sitting down to dine, just about two o'clock in the afternoon, that is Don Jorge, Doña Regina, Doña Violeta, and I, in the Martín apartment when we heard a clattering on the stairs and in came *Capitaõ John Reaney* of the *Eighth Portuguese Caçadores* with the rain already blotching his brown uniform, and the shoulders of his cloak black with it, and the green plume in his shako ruffled.

'The jig's up,' he said without ceremony . . .

But stay. I perceive I have plunged too inconsiderately into my tale again, without proper consideration, that is, for any reader who has followed me faithfully thus far – and this out of a desire to push swiftly on to what is the sweet kernel too long delayed of these memoirs, namely how Mistress Flora Tweedy, whom I have yet to introduce, daughter of Major Tweedy (deceased) of the Eighty-Eighth, came to be with child and was delivered at the Battle of Vitoria, and was not heard of again, leaving me with her infant, a fine boy, to bring up as my own. With my tale hurrying on to these scenes both elevating and affecting I see I have left much unexplained – how in the Summer of 1812, before the battle, 'Father' John Reaney threw off his spurious canonicals, stood revealed for what he always was, an officer serving with the

Portuguese, and a layman free to marry; how he married Violeta Martín, she who five years before kept the door for me and Angelica, and was sister to my dear dead friend Rafael; how through the many true and useful informations I had laid before Mr Curtis concerning the French, and with Violeta in her guise as flower-seller as go-between, I had regained a reputation for loyalty and even bravery with the Martíns and other Salamantines and was now welcomed amongst them as in days of yore; how . . . but after all, these are not to the point: I shall not dwell on all this, nor on how I came to be in the British Army, served at the Battle of Salamanca and was wounded there, but will push on to show how Doña Violeta and I came up with this Mistress Tweedy aforesaid on the Retreat to Ciudad Rodrigo, were separated from our friends, suffered many privations, and eventually came up with the armies again at Vitoria, as above, where both ladies were brought to bed.

So back to the Martín apartment in November 1812, and in comes Captain Reaney, as described, and 'The jig's up,' he cried, 'the Crahppos are feeling round our right and the Peer is pulling out. It's back to Ciudad for you, my Darling, so get your things together as we planned, it's time to be off.' He turned to me. 'Joey, you know what to do. Get her down to the Baggage Train as quick as may be, keep her close for me . . .'

'I'm staying here, Johnny,' cried Violeta.

'That you are not. Now all has been decided these ten days – Joey, go get her bags, which are packed and ready, I know.'

'Johnny, if you and Papa and Mama are staying here, then so am I.'

Violeta's temper was now up; small and large-eyed like a doe though she was, she had a temper would stop a drunken trooper if need be, and I doubt Johnny would have had his way had not her Mother now intervened, Doña Regina, she who had filled me with awe and even terror when I first lodged there as a student so many years before.

'Violeta, you'll do as your husband requires of you,' she said in tones as icy as Greenland's Mountains, 'go get your things.' 'But,

Mama –' and here Doña Regina raised one brow and set her lips in a line – a pause, a silence – then Violeta broke and wrung her hands, 'But I'm sure I'll never see you again, never again,' she sobbed, but did her husband's and her Mother's bidding.

I was an half hour loading up one ass and saddling another in the courtyard below and when I returned I discovered Capitaõ Reaney of the Eighth *Caçadores* had gone and the Father John Reaney I had known before was back in his place, which made the embrace his lawful wife Doña Violeta now shared with him look like something out of a French Novel – thus to see a Priest in black with white bands and shovel hat on the table beside him, so fondly kissing and cooing. But soon he left off and turned to me, and thus continued: 'Now, Joey, mind how you go – the Army's moving off in three columns and I'd have you take the centre one for the marching right is where the Spanish are and I make no doubt they'll cock things up, and the marching left is where the French will be closest, so you'll be safest in the middle. Your best plan is cross the river by the Bridge but then head down the far bank till you come up with them, but if you don't within a league then cut back to the main road but once on the main road keep to it, don't cross it. You're bound to come up with them . . .'

But now Violeta claimed his attentions again and perforce he had to comfort her with, 'Now don't fret at all, my Love, not at all. I shall be as safe as you, I make no doubt, snug with Mr Curtis in his lodgings and a Winter of Astroscopy in front of us. And I shall be able to keep an eye on your parents here, so all will go well, you'll see how it shall. Why, Dove, now look at me cheerly, I make no doubt I shall get me a position at Greenwich when all this is over, so much of the stars I shall have studied and nothing else to do at all,' and so a little more in this vein, but not much, and then we were off, with hardly another look at those rooms that had been so dear and so familiar to me for so long and which, had I but known, would present so different and horrid an appearance when we returned.

'Well, well,' I said to Violeta as we jogged and slithered over the cobbles down towards the bridge, 'who would have thought there would be such a dismal end to so glorious a campaign,' but then I remarked that she was crying a little, that with this and the rain which was now fairly tipping out of the black sky above, and the sullen faces, unbelieving, of the townspeople that were to be left to the French again about us so almost I wished I was not in my red jacket of a British Ensign at all, with all this I saw she was not marking me, so I resolved to keep my mind on getting clear of the Town as quick as may be, and kept my thoughts to myself.

Yet they ran on as they were bound to with such an *exemplum* of the frailty of human hopes, nay of human achievements to dwell on. Not six months before I had seen the Peer himself, mobbed by this populace that now looked so dourly on us, garlanded with flowers, deafened with acclamation and adulation, on his horse in the Great Square, and trying even then to write off an order on his *sabretache*, for the French still occupied the convents by the river (whose ruins Violeta and I were passing) and had to be got out somehow. And what of the greater triumph yet, a month later, the greatest Battle of All, fought round and in the village of my childhood, and on the Arapiles themselves, the Battle that had seen such utter routing of the Eagles, well, where had the fruits of all that gone? And what of Fernando's leg, had that too gone for nothing? Had all the lads who died there died in vain? These questions I asked myself as we crossed the Roman Bridge and headed down the river bank as Reaney had instructed.

'Pepe,' Violeta presently called, and I turned and looked back up at her, riding on the ass behind, for I was leading the one with her bags and such, 'Pepe, should we not head South soon, head for the Ciudad Rodrigo road?'

'Leave it a league, Captain Reaney said,' I replied, 'we've hardly gone a mile yet,' and indeed beneath the black sky and in spite of the rain which was now so fierce I had to shout above the noise, and both of us already quite soaked to the skin, we could still discern the Towers and Domes of the Cathedrals above and beyond the river that swirled and eddied brown and silver beneath the lashing from the sky.

'But I think with this rain we had better be on the road – Look, between the poplars, look . . .'

And where she pointed I could see long lines of brown and red beneath the trees, and above the roar of the rain hear the squeal of carts. Ahead of us there was nothing, nobody, and the force of the storm and the fear of the French now combined to make me wish to join my fellows, for it was so dark already, although not yet four o'clock, that I feared we'd miss our way, take a tumble into a ditch or the river itself, and no-one by to help us, so at Violeta's continued insistence, I pulled on the rope bridle and soon we were up in the poplars and on the Ciudad road and amongst a regiment of Portuguese.

And thus it was, in despite of Reaney's advice, we fetched up on the left of the army, an accident that led finally to separation from our fellows and the strangest time of my life – but before that other things befell us, that in fairness to this Boy whose life and welfare have been my sole concern these ten years, I must record.

These Portuguese were marching in good order though already their brown great coats were sodden, their faces dour, their moustaches lank and drooping beneath their shiny black shakoes, and hardly a word from any, just the tramp, tramp of good British boots on the stones, save where the road dipped and the ditches already flowed over it. The road was wide enough for us to go with them for a time and so we did, and we could see ahead, when the gloom and rain allowed it, the black coats of a brigade of Brunswickers. I doubt not though that we should have been with these Portuguese till nightfall and bivouac for we could not make better speed than they, except that, as always, there were halts and delays and with these we got on ahead of them, and then ahead of the Brunswickers, and this brought us up at last with a British Line regiment, the Seventy-Fourth. This cheered me for I knew we would soon be in with the Eighty-Eighth, the

Connaughts, since all were part of Thomas Picton's Division, commanded by Edward Pakenham since the former's hurt at Ciudad Rodrigo, and thus fetch up with Flora Tweedy who would be good company for Violeta – and perhaps Captain Branwater too, and many other old friends. But night came too quickly, two hours too early with the rain and cloud, so you could not see your hand in front of you by five o'clock, and I suppose we were not more than five or six miles from the City and who knew where the French were, though we knew it rained on them as it rained on us, and in this extremity we had to settle and wait for the dawn without coming up with the Connaughts, nor with the Baggage, and this was great hardship for Violeta, and indeed all around us.

We got in under an oak, Violeta and I, and some of the men around us, with blankets and coats, and somehow managed to be warm, though certainly not dry, and there was no question of fires, and no provisions either so we were forced to beg some rain-soaked biscuit of a Corporal near us, and this was all the food we had that day. We now contrived to get some rest, though with difficulty since if the rain abated at all our ears were assailed with the oaths and grumblings of the men about us. In all this Violeta, now seemingly recovered from the grief of parting, showed her usual courage and good sense and even good spirits, so she gave back the chat of one man and made all laugh, and scolded another who wished to remove his boots for the sake of his feet, but she told him it would be the ruin of him if he did since they would never go on again, and all this in her broken English picked up from Johnny Reaney.

2

The officers had their men standing to arms and in marching order well before dawn and waiting for provisions still, but none forthcoming, and so starving as well as wet and cold, we were on the march again as soon as it was light enough to see the back of the man in front, Violeta, I and the donkeys as before and the rain still.

Soon another trouble – the French; but the first sight of them not much, just a troop of Dragoons scouting through the thickets to our left and just out of musket shot, though a good rifleman might have given them a start. Still there they were, and shadowing us for an hour or two, and so the men were constrained to march in fighting order, in open column of companies ready to deploy against attack, which meant many men off the road and up to their knees sometimes in mud and water, and all grumbled as to where our horse were that should have driven these off.

At about ten o'clock we were brought up against the regiment in front and as we drew nearer I was sure they were our old friends the Connaughts and B company in the rear, for in spite of the noise of marching and of rain, of squealing carts and hooves, and even occasional gunfire in the distance, we could hear the steady chanting of the song our old friends Nolan and Coffey had taught them, not an Irish one at all, but cockney I believe, and for all that adopted by these particular Hibernian ruffians as their marching song.

> I don't want the Sergeant's shilling
> I don't want to be shot down –
> I'm really much more willing
> To make myself a killing
> Living off the pickings of the Ladies of the Town . . .

Just then a flurry of rain riding on a rising wind almost swept away the next lines, but I knew them too well for them to be put out of my head, having marched with them from Ciudad Rodrigo to Salamanca; I'd heard them as we marched across the fields towards the gunfire and Los Arapiles, and I'd heard them echoing between the tall palaces and churches of Madrid itself –

I don't want a bayonet up my bumhole
I don't want my cobblers minced with ball
For if I have to lose 'em
Then let it be with Susan
Or Meg, or Peg, or any whore at all . . .

and so breaking into a run, we clip-clopped across the gap, and came to no harm, there being no French in sight at that moment, and sure enough there was Coffey, tall, beef-faced Hero that he was, with his hair bleached to straw and now lank beneath his shako, marching in the next file to last, and Nolan, a trimmer, smaller figure in the file before him.

Immediately they knew us and as we fell in beside them, 'Mother of God,' Coffey called, 'Look who's here, but if it isn't that little divil Joey Bozzam, himself, and see if he hasn't a couple of hinnies with him, trust the auld sod.'

'No, is it really you, Joey?' called Nolan, 'now trust little Joey to have picked up news there was some sort of festivity toward, he has a nose for the booze, like Mother Riley herself.'

'What festivity is this then?' I asked, wiping the rain from my face.

'Why, 'tis well known Atty has laid in several hundreds of t'ousands of booze at Roger's Town for us, else there'd be no reason otherwise for us not to stay at Sally Mankers, no reason at all. And it's a good reason you've brought your doxy along, there being a shortage of the commodity at Roger's Town unless it's better nor when we were last there.'

'Well, that's as may be, boys,' I said, 'but this is Captain Reaney's new wife, and you'll treat her with proper respect I dare say.'

'Mistress Reaney, how do y'do? Much obleeged to make your acquaintance, I'm sure. But Joey, y'niver let this Lady marry that auld fornicator did you? Why, Father John Reaney's been up and inside more petticoats than Kevin Nolan here has had hot baps for breakfast. But then, Madam, I'm sure I mean no offence and Reaney's a reformed man now, and will only put on a priestly gown for the very best of purposes in the future, I'm sure, for with a bride like you he'll not have eyes for any others.'

With which piece of gallantry Coffey bit off a chew, planted it in his cheek and took up his song where he left it:

> *On Monday I touched her on the ankle*
> *On Tuesday I touched her on the knee . . .*

'Is the baggage far in front, Kevin?' I now asked his friend, for further sense from Patrick Coffey seemed a lost cause.

'Ay, 'tis,' he called, 'not above a quarter mile, I hope.'

'And is Mistress Tweedy still with you?'

'Ay, Joey, she'll be there, I'm sure on't.'

'For I think Captain Reaney would approve it if I gave Mistress Reaney here into her care, if I can find her.'

'Ay, Joey, she'll be in good hands with Mistress Tweedy, and I'm sure you'll find her up in front, and if you do be sure to tell her we missed her sorely last night in the rain with her tay and champ . . .' and here he too went back to join the others in their song:

> *On Wednesday such caresses*
> *As I got inside her dresses*
> *On Thursday she was moving sweetly . . .*

'Why,' asked Violeta, her voice sharp, 'did those men say those things about Reaney? How should they know him so well when he's an officer and a gentleman and they just ordinary folk?'

Well – Reaney's history was this: first he was a seminarist at the Irish College but on Mr Curtis's advice listed with the Connaughts in 1808 when they came through with Moore, and that's when Coffey first knew him. At that time Reaney yet kept his cassock with him, and professed one day he'd be priested, which Coffey and Nolan would not credit, but decided the Cloth was kept to aid him in seductions and intrigues, and such was still his reputation. In 1809 he transferred with many others of his co-religionists with some education to be a Lieutenant and later a Captain with the Portuguese army then being trained up by the British, but latterly put on his cassock again to spy for the Allies in Salamanca. Most of this history Violeta knew of course – just that of his being with the Connaughts a few months in 1808 and 1809 being unknown to her.

'And sure he's a real gentleman,' cried Coffey, after planting his chew beneath my donkey's hooves, 'sure Reaney's as proper a gentleman as you'll find in Dublin not a Prod, for his Aunt keeps a shop in Eccles Street and was she paid for his schooling.'

'And who,' Violeta asked, 'is "Atty" that keeps all this drink waiting for them in Ciudad Rodrigo?'

'Why Atty,' said Nolan, 'why Atty is Atty, Nosey, the Peer, the auld sod that beats the French.'

But even as he spoke a bugle sounded up clear and close to us and a Lieutenant came running down the column which in response to the call was already fanning out in line across the road – 'Come on, my lads, now look as lively as you may, now then, now then, dress up properly from the right – what are those two God-damned donkeys doing there? And you, Sir, where's your piece? Well, I'll see you later, now get those animals and the Lady there behind the line and ten yards back. Right, lads – hold it like that, wait for the bugle. Now.' And as it came again the pattern shifted with kaleidoscopic geometry and two hundred men moved into square, with, miraculously, Violeta, I, the officers, and two donkeys inside it and all this done in three minutes, and in pouring rain and on empty stomachs.

The cause of it all was now seen – a cloud of slate blue uniforms on black horses was on a low ridge about three hundred yards off and gathering into line even as we watched them, quite distinct despite the rain.

'Well, who are they then?' I heard a voice say, and a Captain who had his glass to his eye answered: 'Hussars. Troisième. I know for they have black slings, all the others have white – they were at Los Arapiles, I mind them well. Oh come on, Summers, you remember, they came on at us quite hard then, just as we were going in.'

'Oh ay, I remember. And that fool d'Urban was almost too late flanking them.'

'That's it. And that same fool d'Urban should be here now. How the blazes did they get so close without our cavalry saw them?'

'Where are the God-damned cavalry?'

'Well, it's a question we shall want to know the answer to, you may be sure. Now look lively, for here they come. Bugle.'

As he spoke the front line dipped over the ridge and came down towards us, then another, and then another. Our bugle sounded and the men presented their pieces, with bayonets fixed.

'What would you say – three hundred?'

'Not more.'

'They'll be no trouble.'

In a moment they came into view again out of the dip, trampling down the low, sodden thickets of lavender and sage, the boughs of the oaks brushing their black, red-trimmed shakoes, the drawn sabres of their officers gleaming dully, but at an hundred and fifty yards they drew rein and we could see them clearly now, a line of horse three deep facing us and could hear the swing and click of harness, the snorting and pacing, and a French oath as a horse's head went down to tear at the shrubbery and was yanked back up.

'Hold steady now. I'll flog any bugger that lets off his piece before the word of command, and that won't come till they're a hundred paces nearer.'

But the Hussars knew better than to come on in any nearer to us, and a moment later, also to a bugle, turned on the left rein and began to trot along our flank and then on to that of the square along from us.

Meanwhile a horseman came down on our right, on the opposite side from the French.

'Mister Lynton?' he called.

'Here Derby, you old renegade,' our Captain answered.

'General Pakenham requires you, if you would be so good, to have your men proceed in square as well as you can keeping your distance from the Fifth ahead of you, keeping it all even if you take my meaning.'

'Listen Derby, you reprobate, you know my men will keep station with the Fifth, but you just be sure the Seventy-Fourth keep their distance behind us.'

'Quite so, Lynton, quite so.'

'And Derby – where in hell are our horse?'

'Not too sure about that, Lynton. That's why the General requires you should move in square. Seems the horse took the wrong road, damn it.'

And he touched his crop to his hat, which was a high one and belonged to no regiment on earth, and trotted on down to the Seventy-Fourth.

'Right, men. You heard the order. Now let's see how well we can keep station – dress to the right. Wait for it . . .'

A rumble of abuse now broke out all round: 'March in square! This isn't a fucking parade ground. We'll be trooping the fucking colours yet. Sarge, my fucking boot's coming off. Much more of this and my fucking arsehole will be fucking square,' and so on so I feared for Violeta's ears and would have begged her to close them if I had felt I could without bringing scorn on us.

'You there, you'd better explain now what you're at.'

'Oh come on, Summers, you know him.'

'Do I, Lynton?'

'Yes, damn it. He's little Joey Bozzam. The nutter poor old Branwater paid out good money for to some gypsies who were going to cut him up for being a French spy. Last Autumn, it was. A bit before we took Roger's Town.'

'Oh aye, I recall it. Branwater did it because he thought he was some sort of Englishman, or English boy, on account of him speaking the tongue and being small.'

'That's it. Well, Bozzam. Branwater's on the Staff now. General

Pakenham's that is. Now who is the Lady and where did you get those mokes?'

I explained our situation, Violeta's and so on, as above, and this Captain Lynton, who had only been a Lieutenant last time I saw him, said he'd see us moved up to the baggage as soon as opportunity arose, but while 'the damned Hussars' were about we'd best stay where we were, which I was happy to agree with.

But the incidents of the morning were not over yet. We marched on for a space, but very slowly, the difficulty being keeping formation over rough ground, and the men began to grumble more and more, especially when the Hussars trotted near, which they did every quarter hour or so and all had to be halted, the square dressed, faced out, and prepared to fight again. And the rain never let up at all. As I say, this for an hour or so, then suddenly a commotion broke out over to our left as of shouts, a horse neighing, and three shots, then over a rise some two hundred paces off came five red coats, one clutching his shoulders which seemed half shot away, and his face ashen at the blood that poured through his fingers. He was helped by two of his muckers and behind them trotted ten French Hussars, three with their fusees out and the rest with their sabres drawn, and just before these runaway red coats could get where our muskets could cover them the Hussars overtook them, rode two to the ground and sliced the arm off another, so the remaining threw down their pieces and waved their hands in the air signifying surrender. All this took place to a barrage of abuse and cat-calling from our men who offered to break ranks and go to these men's rescue, but our officers threatened to shoot them if they did, and some let off their pieces and had their names taken, no doubt to be flogged later for not holding their fire, and all in all our officers were right for there was nothing to be done.

The man who had had his arm off, almost off for it hung by a strip of sinew and rocked to and fro quite independently like that of a broken doll, now screamed and screamed at what had been done to him, and it was a sad sight and sound which caused many of our men to shout and call on the French 'to finish the poor

bugger off', and whether it was because they heard us or thought
it out for themselves I know not, but one of the French who had
been standing and looking at the man as if he were a problem he
knew no answer to, pulled out his pistol and blew the poor
maimed man's brains out, which was a mercy, I suppose.

Some ten minutes later when we had marched on, we saw
some cattle out in the woods, the big, black cattle bred up for the
bullfights, two cows and two calves, and it seemed likely to us the
men we had seen taken had broken ranks to get after these cattle,
at which our Captain made an example of them, saying the same
would happen to any of us who offered to do likewise. Yet by the
end of the day many did, will they or will they not, out of exhaustion and hunger and cold, for no food came until dusk, and the
rain never stopped, and our horse never showed, so we were
marching in fighting order the whole day, and there was no
chance of getting Violeta up to the baggage safely.

3

Darkness fell early again and imperceptibly, with the clouds continuing low and the rain not ceasing, and at about four o'clock the
whole column came to a halt, our four companies of Connaughts
happening to be in a sort of declivity or dell and the ground
exceedingly wet. For half an hour we stood to arms thus, then
word came down the column that no further progress was
expected that day and so arms were piled, pickets put out, and we
made shift to bivouac as we were, which was not really possible as
the men were quick to point out. However, the next thing was a
sack of dried beef and a half-firkin of rum brought down on an ass
for us and this caused a little cheer, but only a little, though some
of the men became very drunk very quickly on a third of a pint of
rum each put away as quick as you might drink so much water,
and they not having ate for twenty-four hours. At this Coffey and
Nolan went up to Captain Lynton, saluted smartly as if to signify

here were two soldiers who could be trusted out of the rest, not having fallen into any ill-discipline of any sort, and Coffey spoke up thus.

'Captain Lynton, Sir, and humbly beggin' Your Worship's pardon, but may we have a word with you?'

Permission granted, he continued: 'It's about this young Lady here Sir, an officer's wife and with nought but a bog to lie in, and a rabble of drunken Irishmen about her. We're thinking, Kev and me, that this is no sort of a place for one so gently raised.'

'Indeed it is not, Coffey, but I am at a loss to know how you hope to improve her lot. As you see, Lieutenant Summers and I have done what we can for her and I fear that will have to suffice for tonight.'

This was true, a sort of tent having been set up for her made of a tarpaulin and a great coat with a musket for pole – but really it did very little for her and clearly she was now feeling the wet and cold very sorely, having the shivers almost all the time and refusing rum for the smell of it made her sick, and not able to chew on the beef. Yet she contrived to keep cheerful, though with much effort.

'Well, Sir, me and Kev have given the matter some thought and believe we could, without any risk at all, conduct her through the lines to the Baggage Park, where she can be placed in a covered waggon, and where Mistress Tweedy I'm sure will have some hot tay going for that woman could keep tinder dry in Noah's flood. Begging your pardon, Sir, but this seems to us the best idea, she being, if you'll forgive me, Sir, already half-dead with the cold and all.'

At this Nolan stooped, looked at Violeta, straightened, and added: 'Sir, she'll not last till morning here,' and he shook his head, 'no Sir, and I know the signs.'

'He knows the signs,' agreed Coffey.

Now this Captain Lynton was a young boy and had joined the regiment with a bought commission just eighteen months before, and while he had shaken down well enough to be confident in

any situation where his course was clear, was ready to be swayed
by the first advice proffered when it was not, and after hemming
for a moment or two he finally agreed. Immediately I saddled up
the asses again while on Nolan's suggestion the Captain scribbled
out a pass and an explanation.

With Violeta mounted again and me leading off – 'Hang on,'
called Captain Lynton, 'There's no need for three of you to go, no
call for you to be off too, Bozzam.'

'Begging your pardon, Your Worship,' I replied, for I had feared
some such interjection and was prepared, 'but Captain Reaney
was most earnest and particular that I should not leave Mistress
Reaney here until I had seen her safe into the hands of her married sister in Ciudad Rodrigo. And these cattle too, Sir, they
belong to the Lady's Father and he has my receipt for them and I'll
not let them out of my sight except against payment of what they
are worth.'

And here Violeta, bless her heart, through her chattering and
shivering and all, added her plea. 'Captain Lynton, this is as he
says, and he is a very good man who my husband says should stay
with me,' and so all four of us set off down the lines for Lynton
had made out his order for Nolan and Coffey, and did not want to
alter it.

The way to the rear was tedious, what with the dark, the rain,
the bogs, and one stream above knee deep and running fast, and
several challenges from pickets including one fool who let off his
piece at us and brought down a branch which tipped a quart of
water down Coffey's neck, but we made it and within an hour
were snug and nearly dry beneath the largest waggon in the
Baggage Park.

There was a bale of straw strewed out beneath us, and blankets
and great coats too; a pair of spirit stoves hissed and spluttered, and
gave out a good light as well – on one of them a kettle for tea
laced with rum was coming to the boil and on the other a large
pan of Champ, pea and potato stew. The Goddess (or Princess at
least for as she was wont to say all Irish girls are the daughters of

Kings), who presided over this scene of homely warmth, was Mistress Flora Tweedy, of whose history more anon, and she dressed as always in her soldier's red coat, her green and red plaid skirt, with her long nut-brown hair looped about her ears. She and Violeta, who was soon very much recovered, chattered away nineteen to the dozen as if they'd been acquainted for years, though for all I know they'd only encountered once before and that tending the wounded on the field of Arapiles five months before. And crouched down there with us with the light from the stoves glowing redly on their faces, now beaming smugly with the food and the rum inside them, and cradling their hot mugs in their hands, Coffey and Nolan, pleased as ever to have found the snuggest niche in the Army.

Presently though, a limping step came splashing near and then another face familiar from the Summer before suddenly swung into view, upside down, as its owner bent down to peer at us all below the floor of the waggon.

'Gracious me,' this face said, it being red and with very thick curly hair, yellow, that now hung down almost to the mud, 'it can't be. Well, I'm deuced sure it is. Coffey, Nolan, and by all that's wonderful, little Joey Bozzam. How extraordinary,' and he reversed his posture, crouched on his haunches, and, his face the right way up, went on: 'I just can't believe it. Well, aren't you going to shake a chap's hand and give me a spot of that rum to celebrate with?'

'Shit,' said Nolan, and made no bones of it at all, 'it's fucking Corporal Prigg. Now see here, Prigg, we're full up. Look, there's five of us under this waggon . . . Oh, come on, hey Flora love, Mistress Tweedy, tell him to bugger off.'

But Flora Tweedy just looked up and said, 'Eh, Corporal Prigg, is it?' and turned back to Violeta to continue her chatter on the subject of what was best to give a man with the fluid on his chest – a poultice of mustard, or hot inhalations from an infusion of balm, so this Corporal Prigg pushed his way in under with us, without ceremony shoving others' legs and elbows out of his way

until he was snugger than any and the rain was coming in on my
back again, for he was a big man this Prigg, above six foot, with
large red hands and the biggest feet I ever did see, and clumsy with
them as well, as will be seen.

This Prigg was a square peg in a round hole in the Army, and
was often the butt and Aunt Sally of all those near him, which was
why he sought out those whom he saw to be different from what
he called 'The Common Herd' and insisted that he and they
should 'stick together'. The fact is he believed himself a gentleman
of a sort, having been sent by his father, who was a prosperous
artisan in the Midlands supplying the new manufactories with
machinery, to an Academy near Nuneaton that boasted it could
make silk purses out of sows' ears by teaching lads to ape their betters. He had singled me out the day I arrived in Mr Branwater's
service; Coffey and Nolan he favoured also for though apparently
ordinary soldiers they were genuinely distinguished by their per-
spicacity, their talk, and their willingness for any jape out of the
ordinary.

Notwithstanding his attempts at ingratiation Coffey and Nolan
could scarce tolerate this Prigg and were almost always blunt with
him to the point of downright insult; and especially so on this
night when they no doubt saw the Midlander as a threat to their
supplies, and there being no mule with a hide so thick it won't feel
a goad – as Fernando might have said – the Corporal at last took
offence and grew sulky and testy and was like to spoil the amical-
ity of the company. Mistress Tweedy took note of this, and she
being imbued with a spirit of complete and impartial generosity
sought to pacify him which she did with inoffensive tact by bringing forth a third spirit stove, which, she said, was in need of repair,
and, 'Corporal Prigg, I would be much obliged if you would put
it in good order for me,' she said.

Nothing could have been better calculated to restore the
Corporal's composure. For it was his conceit that he understood
what he called the 'World of Engines' and could make them work
when they went wrong. Indeed he claimed the Recruiting

Sergeant who had inveigled him into the army had promised him he never would have to fight, or drill, or march, but simply apply his talents to 'fixing things' whether they be the officers' glasses or mapping instruments, or the men's flintlocks, and there would always be plenty of such employment for him. For this, and because the day before he had quarrelled with his father over the design for a steam engine, he had listed. Now he examined the stove, turning it to and fro in one hand, while with the other he twisted at a lock of his coarse hair, and his face took on a maniacal grin or rather rictus, and 'Mmmm,' he went, and 'Hah,' and 'Hum,' until at last he cried, so loud we all jumped, 'I have it,' and without taking his eyes off the stove, relinquished the lock he was twisting and thrust out his left hand into the company, knocking over Kevin Nolan's tea mug as he did so and: 'SCREW-DRIVER!' he bellowed.

This reduced us to silence so we could hear the steady drumming of the rain, then Kevin said, very coldly, 'Corporal, it is a matter about which I feel peculiarly distressed, that I do not happen to have a screwdriver about me, for sure if I did, I should know what I should recommend you to do with it.'

This sally had an unfortunate effect on me for it produced one of the fits I was then subject to of an uncontrollable attack of sniggering, giggling, and tittering which once started was like to continue for upwards of half an hour. Four of those under the waggon pretended there was nothing untoward in my behaviour having experienced it before, but poor Violeta began to be alarmed.

Flora reassured her: 'Pay no attention, Mistress Reaney, he is sometimes taken this way and it is best to leave him until it passes. It is perhaps an outcome of the injuries the poor man suffered, which would turn many a man's wits more completely than they have our Joey's.' Violeta asked what these injuries were, but Mistress Tweedy would not tell her, out of consideration of my feelings I suppose, though I am not troubled by my want, indeed at that time recollection of it was as likely to produce the *garrulactic paroxysm* as any other cause.

Mistress Tweedy was only partly right to ascribe my occasional affliction to injuries earlier sustained; it needed a risible event or recollection to set if off – the trouble was that once started, further comicalities would just keep on coming into my mind until exhaustion silenced me, and on this night, the second of the retreat to Ciudad Rodrigo, the memory that kept me laughing and tittering until the hiccoughs intervened was this . . .

It was a grievance for Prigg, on top of having listed in a Regiment of the Line and being expected to take his place there alongside his fellows as if he was a felon or an ale-house toss-pot or good-for-nothing Irish layabout, and stand up to shot and shell and ball, taking his chance with the rest, it was an added grievance that he was to do all this with the old Tower Musket or Brown Bess as his piece and not the new Baker Rifle – Brown Bess, he said was too weighty, he could not be sure of hitting a barn-door above fifty yards off with it, it was too long, and I know not what, but above everything lacked the rifling of the Baker weapon that imparted a spin to its ball which, for reasons I have never properly understood, though Prigg claimed to, made it travel further and truer to aim than a common musket ball.

It was Prigg's ambition to get his hands on a Baker Rifle, but this was a deuced hard thing to do, for Riflemen were trained most rigorously to take the greatest care of their weapons, which they groomed and coddled so it was said they'd sooner let an ordinary soldier handle their privates than their pieces. But one day, a week after the Battle, when we were pursuing Johnny Trousers towards Valladolid, but not too fiercely, leaving this to the Light Division ahead of us, and it being evening and bivouac-time, we heard a halloo from a dusty ravine nearby. On searching it we discovered a Green Jacket who had earlier gone scouting down there after water and had fallen, twisting his ankle so he could not walk on it; and while some carried him up (he was small, dark, Irish, and called Mike), Prigg retrieved his rifle. It was Mike's misfortune, and Prigg's, that Mike had an impediment of the tongue.

There we were then in the warm evening gloaming, with the heat of the day gone off, the swifts and the little owls of those parts flitting and swooping about the copse of pine trees we were in, and Mike comfortable on one side of the fire and Prigg on the other with Mike's rifle across his knee. A pair of partridges and a hare grilled nicely on the coals between them.

'This,' said Prigg, and he began to twist his hair, holding his head on one side with his rictus slipping on and off his face, 'is a truly very fine piece of kit, a lovely engine. First see how light it is,' and he hefted it up and about.

'B-b-b-b-b . . . ,' went Mike.

'By and large,' said Prigg, 'and on this occasion I know what I'm saying, I should guess this weapon is . . .'

'I-I-I-I . . . w-w-wish you w-w-w-wouldn't . . .'

'A-a-a-as I say,' said Prigg, who stammered too when excited or crossed, 'I do know a thing or two about this sort of thing,' and he now reversed the rifle so he could peer up the muzzle, 'you see here, Patrick, you see here, Kevin, the *rifling*, now that is its secret, that is the essence of it.'

Mike had now gone deadly pale, so I thought he was poorly and went to loosen his shirt.

'However, the firing mechanism,' said Prigg and reversed the weapon so the muzzle was over his foot, 'is a very neat piece of work. Notice this leaf spring, what a much finer piece of engineering we have here than on that old tube, for that is all it is. I'd sooner have,' he went on, snapping up the pan, 'a good old blunderbuss, at least . . .' at which the rifle went off and he lost three of his toes.

Which was why he limped and had served since with the Baggage, not being fit to step out with the rest any more.

Just as I had my paroxysm at the memory of this under control Corporal Prigg pronounced the stove not only mended but improved. He had, he said, looked at it all very closely and decided that its performance could be bettered by the addition of holes or vents near the wicks, which, with Nolan's bayonet which he borrowed for the purpose, he had now made. We were all invited then to watch him light this stove and compare its flame for brilliance and heat with those of the other two. Patrick Coffey was asked to hold it while Prigg got his flint wheel and lint going, which he blew into a flame and applied to the wick – there was a dull 'wump', like a paper bag popped, Coffey's red face with small blue eyes was brightly lit in a white glare and then he heaved the flaming engine out into the park where it continued to burn for several minutes in spite of the rain.

The space beneath our waggon filled with the stench of singed hair (Coffey's) and a stream of abuse (Coffey's) and then Prigg's excuse, said often and tetchily – 'I'm sorry, but it seemed like a good idea at the time,' and all this would have ended in a fight had not Mistress Tweedy now intervened and promised to kick both out if they did not quieten down, and such was the respect she was held in by all in the Division, they heeded her though continuing to bicker and grumble until all fell asleep.

And so I remember them now, on the second night of the retreat, three soldiers huddled together beneath their blankets and great coats, snoring and snorting in a stupor brought on by exhaustion and drink, and beyond them Mistress Tweedy still awake and sitting up, with Violeta's head in her lap which she stroked, and she hummed and crooned a nursery song, and all this seen by the light of one of the stoves left burning for the sake of a little warmth and comfort.

CHAPTER III

*A Night Disturbed with Dreams and Illusions, yet Important
Matters of Fact occur as well.*

I

It is a serious matter, and not to be undertaken lightly, not one to
be excused except for the most noble and generous reasons, which
I believe I have, to set down and perpetuate in writing a scandal
against a Lady's name, and more so when the first grounds of the
scandal were no more than the tattling and gossip of the Baggage
boys of the British Army – the scum, to be sure, of the scum of
the earth. And so I shall proceed now as circumspectly as possible,
reporting only what I heard and saw and drawing no conclusion
myself nor endeavouring to suggest one – at the end the reader
must judge and out of his own judgement not mine: let justice be
done for the Darling Boy who has ever been my care these last ten
years.

For all the rum taken, the exhaustion, and even the animal
warmth of those about me beneath that waggon, I slept only fitfully and while asleep was much plagued with nightmares as I
slipped off occasionally into something like sleep. At first my
mind dwelled on that occasion, after Madame's return from
Madrid with her nieces, when she rewarded me for my con-
stancy in her interest and the care I had taken of her property, by
inviting me to enjoy the company of one of her girls for a night,
my choice falling on Dolores – whose body to me was a garden

of delights and whose gentleness in her regard for me promised
kindness as well. For a time these memories remained entirely
pleasant, of her slowly and laughingly loosening her ribbons and
buttons – she was wearing a red velvet dress and several petticoats
and slips in colours of flame, bright yellow and orange – and
each article removed revealing more of her dusky satin skin which
seemed to glow in the lamplight, reflected again by the mirrors so
it splashed on her unexpected pools of softer light from unsus-
pected angles, moreover heady fragrances and odours which made
my head spin arose from her body and her clothes at each stage of
her unapparelling, until at last she stepped out of the final garment
and laughing turned herself slowly around in front of me, peeping from behind her elbow, as she loosened the ribbon that held
together her coils of wiry black hair. She was slender but not
scrawny, short but not dwarfish, her breasts were round and heavy
for her size and the nipples black with large black aureoles, blacker
than any of the rest of her; her belly was a delicious curve, a
parabola to the delights below, and her back an arch that exactly
echoed her belly in front until it swelled into her bum, two
smooth and unblemished mounds between which lay a shadow
more ebony than night.

She took me by the hand and led me to the edge of the huge
round bed and slowly uncased my frame, making a sort of pleasing game of not knowing how men's clothes were fastened, until
I was in my shirt only, and then kneeling in front of me she fondled me gently, cradling those parts I had entire then, saving only
what my Father's desire for hygiene had had removed, and no
doubt she did this out of habit being, on most nights, concerned
to give pleasure to older men befuddled with drink and jaded in
appetite, but all this was too much for me. Those pleasing heats
which Nature has ordained accompany the last moments of the act
of love now flooded out from the seat of such delights, infusing
my whole person with their glow, and I had to clasp the girl, my
arms round her shoulders and my face in the warmth of her fragrant neck as my spasm came and I spent myself on to her breasts,

where my joyce lay like orient pearls before slipping down to a nipple . . .

And at this pleasant point in my recollections I suffered the first interruption of the night, which was a soft light directed from a lamp over the straw we were all bedded in, turned this way and that, the face of him who wielded it quite invisible behind it, but his voice, though low, clear and his words distinguishable.

'Mistress Tweedy?' he called, 'Mistress Tweedy, are you here?'

At which the object of his search awoke and lifted her head from the angle of axle and wheel where she had rested it, and thus brought her face into the light. Though disturbed thus, her customary expression of calm did not alter, as she pushed back a tress of her chestnut hair that had been matted by rain and mud over her cheek, some strands of it lodged between her lips.

'Who is it?' she whispered, then, 'is it you, George?'

'Ay, Ma'am, it is . . .'

'What o'clock is it?'

'Just gone ten, Ma'am, and his Lordship is about to retire. His tent is close and he requires me to say he'd be much obliged . . .'

'Of course, George, of course. I'll be there directly.'

As kindly as she could she now made up a cushion from the blanket that she had had about her shoulder and lifting Violeta's head from her lap moved it to this new pillow, all as gently as may be, yet Violeta moaned in her sleep and suddenly fastened her hand on Flora's wrist as if to restrain her, which Flora could only unloose with difficulty, at which Violeta moaned again.

Thus free, Flora moved on her knees, her long hair about her shoulders and hanging in front of her, the tails of her soldier's red coat trailing below her waist, and her green and red plaid skirt snagging in the straw, and thus she moved towards the lamp. A hand appeared to help her up.

'George,' she whispered, as she took it, 'I'm in a horrid state, you know. I'm afraid his Lordship will have to take me as he finds me.'

The voice now had a laugh in it as it replied, 'Faith, ma'am, the whole army's up to its eyes in filth and I make no doubt his Lordship is in much the same case as you are, or worse.'

And then she was gone, and I did not see or hear her again until an hour before dawn.

2

I now composed myself, if not to sleep then at least, I hoped, to a return to those fond memories of Dolores I had been engaged with, but before I could this Corporal Prigg who was by me suddenly kicked out with his booted foot and caught me on the knee, then shouted, and notwithstanding the pain he'd caused me, I marked the words which were something on these lines: 'You must work three or four strokes by hand prior to throwing the eccentric rod in gear; and crown gear fits best with spur and so good father . . .' the rest being lost in mumbles. The consequence of these disturbances and discomforts was nightmare now overtook memory in the way it can when one knows one is dreaming and wishes to wake up, and cannot, and must let the dream take its course.

For what I dreamed was that Dolores was trying to bring me on again, I having already spent myself, and in this endeavour she employed a variety of tricks as kissing me and muzzing, as riding astride me and trying to coax me up thus while her breasts danced above me, and even she reversed her posture and went down on me with her mouth and tongue and teeth that daintily nibbled at me, the whiles presenting the moist velvet of her purple nether lips to my tongue, and this availed us somewhat, so that first she spent herself thus, or seemed to, and was the only woman ever did with me, so at last I began to rise again with the joy of this, but feeling me she came up thinking we should do it properly at last and as soon as she did all was lost, and for this reason, or so my dream said, that now I could see our reflections multiplied a million times where'er I looked and what distressed me so, in my dream, was not her form thus reproduced for ever, but my own face which for some reason filled me with horror, and which I could not take my eyes off.

Yet, in this dream, there was no reason my face should so transmogrify me into a child shivering with fear, for it looked at me as it always did, the eyes perhaps a little wilder and brighter than usual, the skin paler and beaded with sweat brought out by Dolores' ministrations, yet terrify me it did, and the more so for that the way the mirrors were angled I could not escape it but found it wherever I looked, either front on or seen in profile, with the sides reversed so what was my left in an ordinary single mirror appeared my right, and this added to my horror, for out of this I felt a strange illusion that when I moved I moved not to make the reflections move but rather the other way about – they moved to make me move, and for a time I was trapped in this compulsion, held slave to these grimacing, wretched, twitching reflections all about me, and a voice came echoing in my ear, and then split like the reflections into an hundred voices repeating over and over, so the chant merged and overlayed itself: 'There is no mirror like an old friend, no friend like an old mirror,' again, and again, and again.

'Twas Violeta woke me briefly out of this for now she too began to moan and cry and fidget and at last broke out in Spanish: 'Ah Juanito, Juanito, ay-eee, ay-eeee,' which is to say: 'Johnny, Johnny, alas, alas,' and then went on: 'Oh Johnny they will shoot you, I know they will, they will shoot you, oh Johnny let me come back,' and after some more in this vein which brought me up wide awake, her voice fell back into moans and groans and sobs and so bit by bit into silence and sleep.

I tried to get back to Dolores, promising myself to imagine away the mirrors, and for a time succeeded, but the interruption to her caresses and their natural fulfilment was now an even worse one for my fancy bred up a different horror, namely a repeated reverberation as of gunfire or explosions which came, it seemed, at intervals of about ten seconds, that's in dream time, though perhaps they matched the beat of the blood in my ear, and only Violeta's calling out about shooting made me hear them as sounds of war.

For now Rubén not Dolores was with me, taking me by the hand through a landscape of ruins, of large buildings whose roofs had fallen in, where walls were down, through court-yards where timber still smouldered as though all the ruin was very recent, and in my dream I thought these must be the Convents and Colleges General Marchant caused to be blown up, twenty of them, on his recapture of the Town, though they did not look like Salamanca buildings at all, at least not particularly so, they might have been anywhere, and as we passed through this landscape Rubén showed me the following sights: Partisans slumped and broken, bleeding from holes in the chest or their brain pans shot away, and 'Bury them and say nothing,' said Rubén; French soldiers with huge moustaches and frizzed out beards, their white pantaloons besmirched with blood or worse, forcing a covey of Carmelites in an arcaded cloister, and 'Bitter Presence,' said Rubén; eight priests garrotted in the Cathedral Square, their heads twisted this way and that, yet three of them still with spectacles on, and 'Nobody knows why,' said Rubén; a family starving, the Father with his head bald, his cheeks quite chap-fallen, and supplicating with stalk-like arms for bread or alms, and his woman about him cowled and moaning over a child who looked as if she slept but was no doubt dead, and Rubén and I, well wrapped up against the cold, he in a big bicorne hat and I in a high beaver, went by, and 'They are not our sort of person, are they?' said Rubén, and all the time the muffled percussion or explosion distantly repeated.

At last we came out of the town and the landscape was bleak and cold and grey and empty, with no trees or buildings, but a sort of swamp, so the mud, which was thick, came almost to the knees and walking was slow and difficult. An icy rain, almost a sleet, was driving across this mire, and fierce enough to beat on the eyeballs and make them ache. Then briefly this cleared and we were

approaching a low knoll, Rubén and I, on which two figures
stood, each with feet braced well apart, each wielding a stout
cudgel, and as we watched they slowly and in turn, to the time of
the distant thuds as it might be cannon fired for a ceremony, beat
each other about the head and shoulders. Both were bleeding
and had smashed teeth, yet neither moved, nor offered to run, and
neither cried out though both grunted and gasped as in turn the
cudgels were swung back behind their heads and then round and
down with a dull bump on cracked bones and split skin. It seemed
they had gone on in this way for ever and would go on thus for
ever, and as we drew near and circled them I saw that one was I,
and then a step further that t'other was Rubén, and turn and
turn about I felt the thud of cudgel on my shoulder, the stinging
jar in my hands as mine struck home, and . . .

'Joey, Joey, shush now. Calm yourself, poor boy, be calm; Joey,
you'll wake the others,' and I came to to find Flora back again,
stooped over me so her hair fell on my cheek, and pulling my
shoulder to wake me out of the dream.

3

I clung to her and she put her arm about me and soothed and
comforted me, then gently unhanded me with: 'There, Joey, you'll
be all right now I think. Leave me get the kettle on for tea.'

I looked about me and found the night beyond still black, the
rain still falling.

'What time is it?' I asked. 'Is it time to get up?'

'An hour off dawn, though I doubt we'll see it, for there's no
sign this weather will lift. You lie still and warm a little longer, till
the tea's ready. Sleep if you want, for I'm sure the dreams you was
in gave you no rest.'

I was frightened to shut my eyes again; the sight of her busy
with stove and pots and mugs, managing on her knees in that
cramped place, was more soothing than sleep could be.

In just over an hour it was light and we and all about us ready to move. Kevin Nolan and Patrick Coffey made their adieus and especially thanked Mistress Tweedy for her hospitality, and, 'Won't you stay, boys?' she cried from the seat of her waggon, where she already held the reins of her team of four, and Violeta sat up there beside her, 'I'm sure I can find you plenty here to occupy you.'

'No thank you kindly, Ma'am,' said Coffey, touching the peak of his shako which had suffered a dent in the night, perhaps kicked in by Prigg, 'but our pass is already expired and Kevin and I know better than to try our luck too hard. Yet we'll take the liberty to be back as soon as opportunity offers.'

'I'm sure you will,' said Mistress Tweedy, and laughed, then she shook up the reins, and 'Giddy up,' she called, so at the front Prigg and I heaved at the bridle of the lead mule and all went forward with Violeta's two asses tethered behind and the rest of the Baggage Train behind us and a battery of guns in front.

'I don't know why a lady like Mistress Tweedy should concern herself with the likes of Coffey and Nolan,' Prigg said presently, his voice raised above the slithering and miry trampling of the mules, the rumbling of the waggon and the screech of its wheels, but not so loud that she could hear, at least I suppose he intended she should not, 'they are a very common sort of fellow, don't you think?'

I didn't know what to say to this for I liked them both very well, was much in their debt, perhaps for my life. Prigg went on: 'She's of good family, you know. Father an officer. By and large I would not expect her to mix with the rougher sort.'

I knew her history as well as he did – that she was born in Gibraltar, her Father a Major in the garrison there and old and fallen into habits of dissipation, being a widower; that with these present wars he was called forth on active service, the first he'd seen since the American Rebellion, and that she had gone with him, fearing his age and health would not easily withstand the rigours of campaigning unsupported; that he had took fever on the banks of the stinking Guadiana, following Talavera, and that she was then nursing the numerous sick and wounded following that most sanguinary conflict; that, with his decease, she having no home, nor fortune, nor relations in England or Ireland she could turn to (her Mother, long dead, was Irish and Catholic, he Anglo-Irish, it being a love-match) had stayed with the Division, with the Ladies of the Division in the Baggage Train, and was known by all, not as an Angel or any such cant, but simply as Mistress Tweedy, the daughter of the Major that died.

But Prigg was not to be shook off the hobby-horse he had chosen to ride: 'Of course, she's a jolly fine girl, quite one of the very best, but I find it odd she'll keep company with that sort for some of the time, when she's been known to mix with quite a different set,' and here he leered down at me, with his inane grin, and pushed his big red hand through his coarse mop of straw hair. 'Did you mark she left us in the night? Was called away? Eh? It happens most nights now and has since the weather broke at Burgos and things took a turn for the worse there. They do say a certain other lady disliked the lack of amenities in that place and went back to Lisbon; but let them say what they will, I say Mistress Tweedy is a fine girl, and I'm sure you'll not say a word against her, Joey, not a word, and nor shall I either.'

Such was the gossip of the camp about this lady, and I should not repeat it for worlds, but that it might be in the interest of Another (who is all my care) to do so, as above; and is this connexion I must conclude with one more jot, before continuing the narration of my own life. It has never been my purpose to meddle in others' affairs, as I might be accused of doing here, just as I was the other day in the matter of Mistress Branwater's housekeeping purse I mistook for another – all happily now resolved.

In the first hour we went a scant two miles, so looking back down a long incline we could see where we had bivouacked, and the long column going back and beyond, threaded through the oak trees like a strand of brown and red pulled through some stuff of grey and green; but in front we discovered at the crest of this hill a group of men on horseback standing just off the road and a little above us, perhaps fifteen all told, and before we got there 'twas clear 'twas Divisional Staff, with General Pakenham in the midst and his Aides about him, scanning the terrain through their glasses, and couriers going off and coming back splashing us with mud as they went. So much was no surprise, but as we neared them we discovered in their midst one other figure – Familiar now to the World and, 'Jesus,' muttered Corporal Prigg, 'it's Atty himself,' and fool that he was he took off his shako, polished the badge on his sleeve, and tried to make his great mop of hair sit flat enough to set it back on straight, and as we came up with them he twisted his head to the right, brought up his hand in salute, and not looking where he was going stumbled and almost fell in a ditch.

Needless to say no notice was took of these antics; for all were quiet and deeply preoccupied with their business, but it chanced now that the artillery in front of us came to a halt by reason of some obstruction the other side of the hill and so we halted too and a local silence fell over us. Only the horses of the Staff snorted and shook at their harness, no doubt impatient like all of us with this third day of rain which glistened on oil-skin cocked hats, ran down in rivers over heavy cloaks, and carved runnels through the mud on splattered boots. So near were they we could clearly hear his Lordship's voice as he flung up an arm and pointed over the plain below us. 'Damn me Ned, but it won't do, you know. Be so good as to lend me a man to get down there to Paget, and let him know his proper place . . .' and then the voice broke off as the cold eyes beneath their high-arched brows turned and scanned us, the pale face, tired and drawn as it was, momentarily softened and two fingers came up to touch the front of his hat. 'Your servant, Ma'am,' he called, and looking back behind me over our animals, I saw Mistress Tweedy drop her eyes a second in the shadow of a bow and I thought her lips softened too in a smile.

'Did you mark that?' whispered Prigg to me, 'Did you mark it?'

And the cold voice went on, 'Get down to Paget, for confound me, I think the man's out of his mind today . . .' and at this moment the gun in front of us, a nine pounder with its caisson, moved off again and we after it, the noise taking all else his Lordship had to say from our ears, at any rate.

CHAPTER IV

In which I carry Two Ladies through Terrible Vicissitudes and Perils to a Happy Outcome.

I

The retreat thus recommenced in orderly fashion began to fall apart towards noon and by three o'clock most of what we saw of the army was an undisciplined mob, save only the Portuguese who kept their formations, and perhaps saved many lives by doing so, since they were thus able to drive off marauding French cavalry who ever hung about our flanks picking off stragglers, few of whom they put themselves to the trouble of taking prisoner but were content to ride down or sabre. The principle cause of this *débâcle* was the continuing failure of the British horse to provide a proper screen or cover for the marching men who soon tired of yet again attempting to proceed over difficult terrain in squares, for we were now in the wide basin of the Huebra River much criss-crossed with ditches and rivulets swollen with rains, but there were many contributory reasons too – as the weather took a turn for the worse, if one may believe it, by becoming colder – the rain congealed to driving sleet, and often snow, especially for us in the most southerly column who were by noon struggling through the foothills of the Sierra de Francia, and perhaps several hundred feet higher than those on the main road to Roger's Town; as also by the continuing failure of supplies except for biscuit and dried beef, which left many a man maddened with hunger; and as the fact that every step took us nearer to Ciudad Rodrigo and safety, and this the men knew having been over the ground before, many more than once, and for many a mad dash over the last twenty miles or so was preferred to another night and another day in the open with the weather ever colder and the French ever bolder, and the provision of drink and victuals unsure.

For all this I think we, that is Mistress Tweedy, Mistress Reaney, and I would have pulled through safe and sound to a warm Winter's lodging with Violeta's sister, but for an untoward circumstance which befell us and carried us off into a very different and very strange billet as I shall soon relate, but first another chance meeting occurred which I would fain not leave out since it is an example of the many kindnesses I have received from my benefactor and patron Captain Branwater.

I had already been advised, above, that my Captain was now on Divisional Staff – he had not been with General Pakenham and the Peer as we passed, but shortly I was much gratified to see his familiar figure trotting up the road towards us, accompanied by another officer whom I didn't know.

Now in the midst of all the business that was toward I had no desire to attract his attention away from the line of his doubtless arduous duties, for no better reason than to claim from him the courtesy of the time of day, so by slowing my gait a little I contrived to allow the lead mule to come up between me and the far side of the road up which he was hacking, but Captain Branwater was ever a keen-eyed young man – his eyesight is still better then mine, witness this trouble with the purse – and he espied me and pulled up his horse in front of us, and his companion likewise. Corporal Prigg, nearest them, and faced with two officers, contrived to halt the team and salute with all the obsequiousness he could muster, but of course it was not at him that they directed their gaze.

'By all that's wonderful, I declare that's Joseph Bosham. Mistress Tweedy, how d'ye do? How is it possible you have little Joey

Bosham with you? Come out from behind there, you rogue, and let me look at you.'

He was always wont to address me in these sort of terms, out of play.

'Well, Mr Branwater, that is something you shall have to ask of the gentleman yourself.'

'Ma'am, I shall. Now Joseph, where have you been these . . . four, no, nearly five months, and how do you come to be here now?'

'Your Honour,' I said, for I was not so unmannerly as to offer him a reply in the familiar mode we employed with each other in the presence of a strange officer who would not know my breeding or my background, and would see only a figure dirty and scruffy and undistinguishable from all the other red coats save by the smallness of his stature, 'Your Honour, the whole story would be too long to relate now . . .'

'But I'll wager it's a good one.'

'The kernel is I'm made responsible for Mistress Reaney here,' and I indicated the Lady, 'whose husband is Captain Reaney I know you are acquainted with, who remains in Salamanca to gain intelligence of the French. On his orders I am conducting her to her sister in Ciudad Rodrigo.'

'Your servant, Madam,' cried the Captain, and doffed his hat to Mistress Reaney, 'You vouch for this vagabond then, do you?'

She spoke up clearly: 'Of course, Sir; what he says is true.'

'Very well then – I could wish you in better hands, but he's brought you this far, and I daresay he'll bring you home safe if his skin depends on it.'

This said again in pleasantry, as above.

But now his companion intervened – a tall pale man, with dreadful spots on his forehead and cheeks, and something of a sneering mouth.

'I say, Branwater,' quoth he, 'is not this the fellow you told me of, you picked up in these parts of some gypsies and you took on as orderly? Odd history you said he had.'

'Aye, this is the one.'

'And he disappeared after the big Battle when Alec said an inquiry into his conduct there was in order?'

'Alec' was Alexander Wallace, our Colonel.

'Well, come on, Rigby, his situation in the army was not entirely regular . . .'

'Regular or not, he was either in it or not in it, and he was in it then and appears to be in it now. Desertion is a hanging matter, you know, Branwater. You ought to look into it, y'know.'

'Perhaps you're right, Rigby. Joseph, you hear that? It seems you have some explaining to do. Well, if I know you, you'll manage that all right, but I do think you ought to clear yourself and get back on a regular footing with us. Look me up as soon as you've seen this Lady safely lodged, and we'll sort it out – you'll find me where the Staff is, in the town itself I dare say, but enquiry will discover me. Now do as I say this time.' He saluted the Ladies again and as he stirred his mount into a trot I was warmed by his final remark: 'Say what you will, Rigby, I found him a deuced useful chap to have about . . .'

Of course Prigg was all agog about this talk of desertion but I pointed out to him I had never taken the King's Shilling, or been sworn into the Army by a Justice, as he had, and so was not so bound as he, and this shushed him up.

Towards noon we heard cannon way off to our right, perhaps some six miles off, that is North and West, but no sight of the French about us at that time – I believe it was the Light Division beat off the Crahppos at San Múñoz, not above a league from Fuente de San Estebán, of painful memory to me. At least that Rigby had been right in one thing – it was indeed in these parts I'd first fetched up with Branwater and the Connaughts.

Just after this cannonading we saw the first signs of disorder, namely a company or more of the Forty-Fifth quite out of any sort of formation went streaming by through the woods on our left, and some had thrown away their packs and some even their pieces, notwithstanding a Lieutenant and a Sergeant amongst them shouted and pleaded with them to stand and form up again – indeed we saw the Lieutenant draw his pistol and snap it in the face of a big, burly Scot, but the officer was a young lad and had not the heart to do it and so was brushed aside.

'I don't like the look of this one jot,' said Prigg. 'I mean I don't fancy our chances at all if the whole lot give way behind us,' and from then on he kept looking anxiously back and appeared far more agitated as time went on and more men went past us in much the same fashion.

About this time, the way being a little drier than before on account the track was stony and well drained, Mistress Reaney climbed down from her perch by Mistress Tweedy, with the excuse she wished to stretch her legs, and walked by me, and in our talk that followed I see now I should have been more careful about the way I spoke, but at that time had no idea what was in her head.

'Pepe,' she said, in Spanish, 'will the French be back in Salamanca now?'

'Certain to be,' I replied, 'not many yet perhaps, since they'll have most out after us, but some will be back in the town.'

'Oh, Pepe,' she went on, 'I'm so frightened for Johnny and Mama and Papa. The French will surely know where their sympathies lie, and if they don't there'll be those willing to tell them . . . I can't think they'll live out this Winter unscathed.'

Well, there was nought to say to this, for what she said was true. Indeed, I believe they were lucky to have got off so light the year before, when all, and Mr Curtis too, had been under house arrest and the Irish College closed – this under an order made out by Rubén García himself who by then held rank in the civil police of the Town. And this was the reason Mr Curtis took a house in the town and remained in it, for the French left the College looted and uninhabitable. The least our friends could now expect, in my estimation, was the same treatment as before – that is if Rubén was back amongst them again, and I made no doubt he would be.

'I would I were with them,' she sighed. 'I would I had never left them. Oh, Pepe, you know I have already lost my only brother, and one husband, I wish I were there.'

'This is foolishness,' I asserted. 'They stay to serve a good cause, that cannot be furthered by your presence. They'll be happier to know that you at least are safe.'

'Yes, dear Pepe, I know all that and it was said to me so often I believed it. But, Pepe, if they die, I should wish to die too, and I shall. And truly I should rather die with them, especially with Johnny, than die alone and after them.'

At this she burst into tears and so almost did I, I was so affected by what she said. When she was a little recovered, she said: 'Pepe, if I decide to go back, will you help me? Will you come with me?'

Of course I said no, nothing would tempt me to such a breach of my friend's instructions, such a betrayal of the trust he'd put in me, and I begged her to put such stuff out of her mind and not to think of it again, and presently she went back to her seat by Mistress Tweedy, leaving me to muse on the foolhardiness of women, especially when blinded by tender affections, for who else, I thought, would consider such a jaunt as to leave the column, in disarray though it was, and risk almost certain death, and not an easy one, either from the weather, or at the hands of a company of French Dragoons. Who else, I mused, but some one who had worse to fear at Ciudad Rodrigo, which was certainly not the case with her.

A little after, we passed the village of Tamames, leaving it on our left, and could now see to the right the horrid wall of granite and snow of the Sierra mentioned above, and the principle peak, the *Peña de Francia*, not always clear at all but awesomely glimpsed through driving clouds. The sleet was thicker and began to sting, as in my dream of the night before, or it settled in globs of ice across our shoulders and even on the backs of our beasts. More and more men broke from behind us and marched, or trotted, or even ran past us on either side in tens, fifties, and even hundreds, and all of course making better speed then us who could scarce manage more than two miles an hour, so Prigg and I began to consider the expedient of cutting the traces and using the mules to keep up with them, with the ladies too of course, but doubted that Mistress Tweedy would hear of abandoning her waggon thus. We were reassured a little later when we saw the Twenty-First of the Portuguese in dark blue standing steady with companies of the Twelfth *Caçadores* in brown and black deployed in skirmishing order in front of them, and as we came up with them some officers took the battery of nine pounders in front of us out of the column and posted them on a bluff on our right where they covered the track, and by these means brought many of the men to their senses, and before long we had almost two complete companies of the Sixtieth marching in fair order, and under discipline, on one side of us, and a mixed bunch of Irish, Germans and Brunswickers on the other, and these keeping station with us and going at our speed, all of which cheered us.

For an hour or two then we felt more secure and even believed we would get off unscathed, save by cold and exhaustion, which would soon be things forgot once we were in Winter quarters and snug, but at three or thereabouts, as the early dusk began to gather and we were looking for the order to park and brew up ready for the night, all fell apart again, and this was for two reasons, though I suppose either would have been enough on its own. First, all came to an halt, and from where we were, we could just make out, less than a quarter of a mile ahead and below us for the road was descending again, a small village, and the wind blowing from that direction, a confused medley of sounds came clear, including some shots, which troubled us, and then flames, as if a house was on fire.

A voice from the file nearest us of the reformed ranks said: 'Faith, I know what's going on down there,' and, 'Jasus, but so do I,' his neighbour replied, and looking at them I saw these two who had spoken had a wild and disturbed look in their eyes, and they ran their tongues over their lips and shifted uneasily, and soon I realised the whole company, perhaps sixty or eighty men, were in a like condition. A voice called out here, and another there, there was some laughter, and then a Corporal shouted: 'Well, lads, what are we waiting for – we know those Mother-Fuckers down there have come on the booze, and sure it's a shame it would be if all was gone, as it will be if we don't shift for our selves.' An officer answered: 'Come now, O'Leary – it'll be a flogging matter after, may be hanging, if you break ranks now . . .' 'Go fuck yourself, Lieutenant Sir, meaning no personal disrespect you understand, but you and the Provost Marshal can beat the shit out of me after, just now I want a drink,' and this Corporal O'Leary, a large man, now strode firmly forward, his arms linked with his mates' beside him, and first six, then ten, then sixty surged forward with him, and in a moment all were running down the hill ahead of us.

On the other side of us the two companies of the Sixtieth, being I suppose with their own officers entirely, held firm a little longer, but only a little, for a further temptation was now added to the first, namely a large herd of swine, perhaps fifty, the brown coarse-haired breed still with a lot of the wild pig of those parts in them, came into view, trotting and snuffling and rooting and snorting through the oaks and down towards the village, and the thing was this – each day the villagers of those parts, at this season, drove their pigs out into the forest to roam free and fatten them- selves on the abundant acorns that lay about, and this they could do confident that all would return of their own accord each night, for pigs are not stupid and value a warm billet when night comes on. Confident of their return, that is, without two companies of famished Irishmen between them and their styes.

It's not an easy matter to kill a pig cleanly, if you're not brought up to it, and while some of these Irish were, there were others who were not, and soon the air was filled with a screaming and a caterwauling almost more hideous than that of a convent of nuns with a company of French Grenadiers amongst them, and the sights to be seen as hideous too as of a pig breaking loose with its throat half cut and blood spilling as it went and a man reeking with gore in hot pursuit; of another porker with one leg off twisting and turning in terrible frenzy; nor was there any restraint on the part of the men, for though there was enough meat there to feed ten times the number, within an half hour of massacre all were killed or maimed so bad as to be as good as dead, and fires began to be lit in spite of the wet and cold, for the men now came amongst us, and looting amongst the sacks of flour and biscuit we carried went off with anything that was dry enough to burn.

With the halt in the march the numbers involved steadily increased as more from behind piled in, fighting broke out between those who had pork and those who had not, so many a nose was bloodied and one man at least took a bayonet between his ribs so he coughed out the almost raw gobbet of meat in his mouth and his life blood followed it; and now the men carousing the village caught wind of this supply of meat, and the men with meat went off in search of wine to wash it down, so soon all around us was a scene of utter riot with men staggering to and fro and jostling, shoving, fighting, screaming, and singing as all gave way to appetite with no restraint or order whatsoever, and the sleet still drove in on us, the darkness gathered, so soon all that was clearly visible was what was garishly lit by the fires, both those in the village and those in the forest, and a waggon, only two behind us, that had been pulled out of the column was tipped on its side and fired and was now a beacon that could have been seen five mile off, had the weather allowed it.

What of us in all this? Well, for a time Mistress Tweedy's waggon remained an island of order in all this chaos, at first out of the respect all in the division had for her, later because five officers found their way to us and this was as well, for soon no respect of an unforced nature would have kept the men from attempting some mischief on us, and especially the women, for not only wine had been turned up in the village but brandy too, and many were crazed with it. However, these officers sat with us with their pistols on their knees and their swords drawn and threatened all who came near us and indeed shot one dead who would not stop – and when I say sat with us I mean we were all now crowded on the bench where the ladies had sat, or in the small space behind the tail-gate, all save Prigg who had spied a wineskin let slip by a carousing gunner who went by clutching three in his arms, and, Prigg I mean, was now sitting against the wheel and drinking himself insensible.

The officers were of the Sixtieth and had the rollcall of their companies out, and were trying to pick out from the heaving, rolling, staggering rout about us those who could be labelled the ring-leaders or instigators of this mutiny, though most of the names they singled they seemed to do so as a means of settling old grudges rather than in any spirit of true justice – as: 'There's Williams, he gave me cheek once at Aldealengua, I mind the occasion well, prick his name for me; see O'Leary down there, cradling a pig's head in his arm – now he has always been more nuisance than he's worth to the regiment, we'll have him strung up, so prick me his name,' and so on. This shortly prompted Prigg from beneath us to speak up bibulously – 'All shall be flogged and hanged as pissing-well serves them right, flogged and hanged – this one for he has carved for himself; and that one for he has offended most perversely with a bottle; and, and, and . . . ,' here he contrived to stand up, 'I tell you what, Lieutenant,' and here he tried to come to attention and salute, 'I tell you what. Prick me out the name of Bosham there, for he's a desherter, he desherts, and desherts whenever he can he does, prick his name out for a desherter,' and then his knees gave from under him and he disappeared from view.

The influence of so much meat and drink gorged on empty stomachs soon had its natural and inevitable effect; within two hours of first halting before that village, the noise and shouting, the coming and going, began to dissipate, the cold and sleet took their toll too, and soon the men were crawling in closer and wrapping up, those who were capable of it, and trying to get into places where warmth and shelter promised some hope of survival; the fires burnt low too and soon all were out, and a most complete and utter darkness fell over everything with only the cries and groans of those still out in it to be heard above the moaning of the wind in the waggons and the trees. When all was quiet enough the officers suggested that we should make our way down to the village, where they said we, meaning particularly the women, should find a shelter more proof against the tempest than the waggon, and after some consultation it was agreed we should follow them, each holding the coat tails of the one in front, and it happened that at the end of this line – which would surely have been a comic sight if one had eyes that could see in the dark – came Violeta and then myself, at the very rear. I suppose we made fair progress for ten minutes or so, though often stumbling, then Violeta stood fast and still in front of me, while I might, had I been minded to, have counted an hundred; at first I thought all had stopped for some obstacle or sign of danger, but then it dawned on me she had let go the man in front of her, and since she did not halloo or even complain, I realised she had done so deliberately.

Just as I had this worked out in my mind, I felt her turn towards me, coming up close, and then her hand on my face.

'Is it still you, Pepe?' she said.

'Of course, but Mistress Violeta, what . . . ?'

'Shush, Pepe. Now don't, I beg you, shout or argue. Can you find your way back to the waggon?'

'I think so, but . . .'

'Then that would be best.'

And indeed with the others lost in the murk in front of us, there was no better course to follow.

Back at the waggon, and it took some time for twice we came off the road and fell into the ditch, and once I walked straight into an oak tree so the blow brought an explosion of lights in my head and I thought I had been attacked, we contrived to feel and fumble our way into the space between the sacks of biscuit and the driver's bench in front, which space was just wide enough for us to lie together, and so sheltered was it and covered in that we were snug enough, perhaps even more snug than those in the village, and indeed contrived to sleep a little, or at least I did, with Violeta's soft cheek on my shoulder and her forehead near my mouth and in this innocent embrace we passed the rest of the night; but all the time I was awake the thought went on nagging me that she had let us get free of the rest on purpose, though I said nothing of this then, being content, now we were so snug, to see how things would turn out in the morning.

At the very first glow of light, when her face was a greyness in the black about me, she woke and made her intention clear. 'Pepe,' she said, 'find our donkeys and take me back to Tamames. Now listen. I have a cousin will board us there for a day or two until the countryside is settled. Then you will take me back to Salamanca – for now I'm sure my place is truly there and it was a great mistake to come away.'

There was no remonstrating with her, and when she said she would go on her own without me if I refused, I saw clearly which way my duty lay.

One of our asses was gone – whether stolen or strayed there was no way of telling – but the smaller, which Violeta had named Paqui, would serve for her; I, as before, was content to walk. With the growing light we could see that all about us was utter desolation – the snow had begun to settle in the night for the wind had dropped, and was still falling in large flakes from a purple sky; it fell and lay an half inch on huddled bodies – some alive, many comatose or dead, on charred timbers, on half dismembered carcases of swine, on broken bottles and spilled wine-skins, and here and there a figure stirred or moaned, and one or two were already up and looking about them wide-eyed and aghast like spirits newly discovering themselves in Hell or Limbo.

'Well,' said Violeta, firmly, 'I cannot think there is much in the way of comfort or safety for us here – let us be off. 'Tis not more than a league or so, and I've no doubt we'll be there before the French are stirring.'

I handed her down from the waggon and then helped her on to Paqui's back and as I did so Prigg, beneath our feet, stirred out of his drunken stupor, opened one eye and said, 'Bosham, you're a desherter I know you are, and you misherable little wanker you, I declare you're desherting again.'

2

We made up into the woods, hoping thus to keep clear of the Army and the congestion on the road, where also we might be challenged, and walked parallel to it, but had gone a scant half mile before we discovered Violeta's wish that the French would not yet be stirring was far too sanguine; for over to our right, beyond a low ridge, we suddenly heard the trotting of horses and a jingle of harness. No expedient more efficacious suggested itself than to leap into the low boughs of the nearest oak, and then lean down to give Violeta a hand and haul her up into the evergreen leaves with me; Paqui now moved off a space, looked about her and fell to browsing off some stunted lavender nearby. All of this we accomplished yarely and just in time for now a troop of *Chasseurs à Cheval* in green and red, with their long fusees, pistols and swords, came trotting by, as quiet as may be, and just there deployed for a sudden swoop on the column below. In a moment or two all were in line, a bugle blew, with one concerted rasp fifty sabres left their scabbards, then all trotted, then cantered away from us through the trees and in a moment shots, shouts, screams broke out below us, and my blood ran cold to think of the easy slaughter they would carry on amongst that rout of half dead drunks.

'What shall we do?' cried Violeta, pressing herself against me, not only out of fear but also because the bough we were on was narrow.

'I think we should get down and go as quickly as we can further into the woods – for these horses will return hither, for it is their infallible custom to regroup after an assault at the point from which it was launched. Moreover these boughs are none too thickly leaved – we saw them clearly enough and if they look up they will see us.'

By the time I had finished saying this I was on the ground again and helping her down. Seeing us on the floor our faithful Paqui trotted up and with me running beside her we made off in the direction from which the French had come, that is over the rise which had shielded them from our view and from that of the allied column. Now we were faced with a sudden change in the terrain we had not bargained for, for on the other side the rise the forest gave out into what in Summer would have been a wide meadow with boulders and low scrub on the far side, above which the ground rose steeply into scree and rocks, with clumps of pine and fir and broom – a wilderness marking the beginning of the *sierra*. This meadow between was now a smooth open field of snow, unblemished save for the tracks of the French, and was a quarter of a mile wide. The noise below continuing unabated I calculated we had time to cross this plain and find cover in the boulders and bushes beyond before the French returned. Half way across and looking back I realised that our tracks might betray us, but now there was nothing to be done, so I urged Paqui on, and we did indeed reach this new cover safely, where we stopped to regain our breath.

Scarcely had we done so, and were about to climb further up the slopes away from the meadow and into deeper cover, than a most extraordinary sight captured our attention and held us where we were: down to our left and several hundreds of yards off, but walking up the very centre of the meadow, or rather plain of snow, came the figure of a woman – and unmistakeable from the faded red coat she wore and long green skirt that trailed in the snow beneath it, and as we watched she paused, raised her hand to her mouth and 'Halloo,' we heard, faint but clear across the icy wastes, 'Halloo, Mistress Reaney, Joey, Halloo,' and then she came on up the meadow striding firmly and briskly, as though on a country walk, as approved by Mr Wordsworth.

'Why, 'tis Flora Tweedy,' cried Violeta, 'we must warn her of the French,' and up she stood and was about to wave and halloo in reply when I pulled her down and just in time, for now over to our right a second troop of *Chasseurs à Cheval* had appeared at the other end of the meadow and was trotting slowly down towards Mistress Tweedy.

There was naught to do but wait for an end which we could only pray would be speedy and with as little pain as may be.

Mistress Tweedy saw the horse much at the same time we did, and for a moment checked in her stride as if calculating her chances of getting back through the forest to the road, but then went straight on towards them, and they straight towards her. Distantly the sounds of skirmishing came from below; more nearly the steady trot and jangle of the *Chasseurs* whose hooves churned up the snow in clouds of purest white; the pines and rocks above us were still and dark; and we waited for the horrid connexion of steel with bone, the blossoming of blood upon the snow.

At fifty yards from the leading file Mistress Tweedy stopped, and swinging her head from side to side shifted her long tresses off her shoulders, then she placed her arms akimbo, facing at the French directly, with her head held up.

They came on at her in threes, and two of the files passed on our side of her, the third on the other, and none of them checked or offered her any violence at all; they parted and went each side of her as if she was inanimate rock. And when they were passed she stooped a little and shook the snow off her skirts where it had settled in their passing, and came on up the meadow, as if nothing had happened at all.

The French having turned and like the ones before gone into the woods towards the road, Violeta now stood and waved and hallooed – I could no longer restrain her – Flora paused, cast about for us, saw us, waved, and altering her course came on up to us.

For all she had appeared so cool below it was clear from her pallor, and the way her voice quavered, that she was very much shaken.

'Holy Mary,' she exclaimed, 'that was terrible, that was terrible,' and Violeta ran the last ten yards to embrace her and lead her up to the boulder behind which we had been crouched.

For a time the Irish Girl could only shake and exclaim, 'I was never so frightened in my life; in my life I was never so frightened.'

I asked her: 'Why did you not run?'

'That would surely have provoked a drawn sabre and a swift chase, a chance for a Trooper to show off his skill at a gallop. My best chance was to do as I did,' and there was no denying she was right.

Poor Violeta was also much overcome for she divined that Flora had left the baggage train and come out into the wilderness solely to fetch us back, and she was much moved at the thought that her new-made friend, for thus she already considered her, had almost lost her life on her account.

'No, no, not on your account, dear Mistress Reaney,' cried Flora, 'but on that of this rogue, this imbecile, this *dwarf*, who not only did not impede you, but abetted and was accessory to your madcap scheme,' meaning me.

'But it was my idea, he only did my bidding.'

'I doubt that boy has ever acted solely in another's interest in his life – make no mistake, he saw advantage in it, and we'll plumb out just what in our own good time; but meanwhile I insist you are not to blame – no-one expects a girl not long married and then separated from a husband much doted on and in most uncertain circumstances to act like a Lady of Sense.'

Like Captain Branwater, Mistress Tweedy often affected a brusque and playful manner with me, so I took little offence, only at the word *dwarf* – I am *small*, not dwarfish – and now asked her how she had come so surely on us.

'Why, Corporal Prigg directed me to be sure – he overheard Mistress Reaney's plan to go to Tamames, and thence to Salamanca, and marked how you left the road. "Desertion," he called it, Joey, and may be, drunk though he still was, he had hold of a grain of truth in the chaff and straw that man calls his brain. Faith, what's that?'

For now we heard shots below us, and looking down saw the first troop, the one that set Violeta and me into our tree, come out of the forest and into the plain and in some disorder, firing with their fusees and pistols, and one, then two of their number dropped into the snow, and then a horse with a high whinny like a scream took off despite its rider's efforts to hold him, but his front legs buckled beneath him after twenty yards and he collapsed in a shower of snow, threw his rider for him, gave a brief kick or two, and expired.

The reason for all this came clear – brown and black uniforms, men brown of face with black moustaches, were moving from tree to tree and driving the horse before them with the accuracy and range of their rifle fire – *Caçadores*, and no doubt the skirmishers we had seen the day before. The French now milled about directly below us, and even then in some danger from the rifles, even at a quarter of a mile, for we heard the balls whining about their heads, and not far off us either. The Portuguese would not now venture out of cover on to the plain, nor would the *Chasseurs* go nearer the wood, so a deadlock prevailed.

While all this went on Flora and Violeta held a council together, for Violeta no longer proposed to go to Tamames and the way to Roger's Town was now surely blocked with French.

'There is only one way out,' Flora declared at last, 'and this is it. I recall a day last Spring, when we were putting ourselves together again after the terrible assault on Badajoz, some officers of the Division, and some ladies too, of whom I was one, went hunting and picnicking up the hills and valleys to the East of Ciudad, all this for recreation, and to follow the Agueda to its source was one of our aims. The country we passed through was one of the most lovely I have ever seen, being rich in game, filled with flowers, and shielded to the North by a rampart of mountains. Now those mountains must have been the ones we are now on the North side of. What we must do is cross them – presently we shall find brooks and rivulets; these we shall follow and they will surely be tributaries of the Agueda, if not the Agueda itself, and thus we shall come to Ciudad from the East and South and avoid the French.'

I urged the dangers and privations that would face us in the mountains, especially with the wintery weather, but when put to it to suggest a better plan could come up with nothing.

'Surely we shall find some shepherd's hut or charcoal burner's camp,' Violeta asserted. 'Not even in this wilderness shall we be quite without aid.'

'And we have almost the whole day ahead of us – in that time we should cross the watershed and be safely on our way down the other side,' Flora added, and briskly gathering her skirts about her, set her face to the slopes above us and stepped out like a man. Violeta followed and I took up the rear, leading Paqui, for the way was now too steep and rough for Violeta to mount her, and always I cast a nervous eye behind me lest the French should mark our ascent – but they were some way off now and preoccupied still with the little fellows in brown ahead of them.

The first two or three hours of our walk were not unpleasant, the slopes after the first ridge we crossed being gentler, and well covered with pines which sheltered us from the wind coming up now, and from the driving flurries of snow that occasionally came with it, only hunger troubled us and this no worse than the feelings of healthy appetite that accompany such exercise. My spirits were also lifted when at the second pause we had for a brief rest Flora turned to me and said: 'Joey, I'm sorry I spoke so harshly back there, you know it is not my way. I can only plead the fright I was still in which put me out of temper; give us a kiss and let us be friends,' so my cheek touched hers, soft like petals, and with a heart much lighter, indeed I almost felt like singing, I followed them on up through the woods.

We saw no living things at all, except some crows that rose cackling out of the tree tops ahead of us and then settled back into their perches like sheets of fire-blackened paper that had floated up into the hot air above a holocaust; there were signs of game though, as footprints of deer or some other cloven-footed animal as it might be goats or pigs, I lacked the lore to distinguish them, and occasional droppings, and in one place where we descended to cross a valley, for the way was up hill and down, not always up, though we kept the high mountains ahead of us, in one place I say we descended into a grove of beeches where holly bushes flourished beneath and here were clear signs some beast had been browsing – as leaves and twigs new cropped on the floor amongst the mast, and Paqui at least was able to satisfy her hunger on these, though they were no use to us.

In this fashion we covered perhaps ten miles before noon or a little after and were now faced with a long escarpment of rock and scree a thousand feet above us. It was an awesome sight, enough to daunt the stoutest heart, for the clouds and mists were driven constantly between us and it, and curtains of swirling snow like the ghosts of all the generations of man hurrying in huge crowds to the gates of Hell; though where we were we were now free of it, except occasional gusts.

'We cannot cross that without food,' I said.

'I'm sure I cannot cross it at all,' Violeta whispered; the way had been arduous for her, she being delicately nurtured and unused to campaigning and hardship as we were. Indeed for the last hour she had limped with her arm round Flora's shoulder, the heel of her left foot having blistered notwithstanding she had ridden on Paqui whenever the way would allow it – but this was not often as we got higher.

'Well, we must find food, I'm sure,' said Flora, 'but how?' and she sat on a lichen-covered boulder and cupped her chin in her hand with her elbow on her knee and sat thus for a minute or so.

Paqui wandered to a patch of heath which she began to crunch.

'That moke,' said I, 'I doubt if it will be much use to us up there,' and I nodded towards the ramparts of granite above us.

'You will not kill Paqui,' cried Violeta, with fire as well as tears in her voice. 'If you did, I would starve rather than eat any of her.'

Flora, without lifting her head from her hand, said, 'I don't think he could. I don't think you could kill Paqui without a gun or even a knife, could you, Joey?' Then she stood up and straightened her woollen skirt. 'Well, we'll make shift somehow. Joey, have you got your flint and wheel?'

I said I had, the English one I had bought off a pedlar in a Portuguese village a year before.

'Good then. I would have you get a fire going as quick as may be, and as large as you like. It will keep us warm; its smoke will serve as a guide for me so I may find my way back to you, and God Willing it will cook for us whatever I may happen to find,' and without more ado, she set off down the hill into a valley that was to our left, and was soon lost from sight in the trees.

Violeta and I gathered up tinder and wood and this was not difficult for there were many fallen branches about; which though wet on the outside, when I set out to break them down to convenient lengths, were found to be dry and friable inside. My trusty flint did its work without too much difficulty and within half an hour, much of it spent trying to coax a flame out of leaves and pine needles by blowing on the spark I'd made, we had a good blaze going and a plume of smoke blowing across the valley into which Flora had gone. We worked hard to keep it going, and built up a good store of logs for the evening and night as well, but soon Violeta complained that she would have to rest, as hunger and the pain of her heel were making her faint, and she stood by with Paqui, whose muzzle and ears she fondled, and who responded to her caresses by nuzzling back.

'Mistress Tweedy was right, I'll be bound, that you would not kill Paquita,' she said.

'If need be I would.'

'I do not think so. Well – do not say so.'

'If need be,' I insisted. 'If Mistress Tweedy returns empty handed, we'll be dead by dawn without food, despite the fire,' I said, this with some sureness for now too I was very weak, and the pangs were truly painful like cramps.

'It would be an evil act,' she said, and fondled the silly animal's nose all the more and flung an arm round its neck and held it close.

Well, evil or not, the more I thought on it, the more I thought perhaps she was right, for how would I do it? I imagined to myself searching out a heavy stone – it would have to be the heaviest I could lift and with a sharp edge. And then what if the first blow failed to lay her out, what if she was injured and made off and I had to follow? I imagined her frenzied and lashing out with her hooves, with her head bleeding and no doubt bellowing as only a donkey can. I thought of how a head wound can bleed. I remembered the pigs of the night before, and the Frenchman's horse shot down in the morning, and in it all an old phrase of my Father's came back to my mind, which once I had found too horrible to contemplate, but now I discovered sense in it: 'It is commonly held that few evils surpass the bestiality of the lonely shepherd who rogers one of his ewes, but I ask you, may not the shepherd later cut her throat for market? If the ewe is sensible of either act, which do you think she most resents?' Such was the effect of hunger and privation on my mind I now rephrased this: 'Granted the shepherd has no moral scruples about either act, which do you think *he* more enjoys?' And this caused me to giggle to myself so Violeta wanted to know what made me laugh, and of course it was out of the question I should tell her.

'That's most unmannerly of you,' she declared, 'not to share with me a thought that could brighten our dismal lot, and especially for me, who have brought all this upon you both,' and her voice trembled a little and I feared she would weep, but no; Violeta, for all she was little, ever displayed a steely fibre in her soul, and she soon returned to quizzing me about what made me laugh.

'Men are of a coarser nature than your sex,' I said, 'and thoughts sometimes come to them which would be beyond the comprehension of a woman.'

'Bosh,' she cried, 'I have been married twice and know most of what goes on in men's minds. The life I carry here,' and she patted her belly, 'was not conceived without some knowledge of how to go about it, you know.'

Well, such is the perverseness of our natures I was put more out of countenance by this speech – both on account of its plain speaking manner, and of its matter – than perhaps she would have been on discovering I should rather pleasure myself with Paqui than kill her, and I must have blushed and perhaps hemmed at it somewhat, for now she went on: 'Oh, men are so silly – they revel in tavern talk, but cannot face the plain and simple facts of how Nature has arranged our coming hither.'

'Nay, that's not the reason,' I cried, and looking out for some way to recovering my composure, catechised her thus: 'I am surprised on you, Violeta, that you wished to die with Johnny, if such befalls him, when you carry his unborn infant.'

Now it was her turn to be confused and it seems her bragged-of knowledge of things natural was not so complete as she would have had me think, for turning away she said: 'Oh that was yesterday and this morning. I did not know I was in this condition until Mistress Tweedy advised me some hours ago that this was the likely reason for . . . for things ladies know of and need not concern you.'

I don't know how this talk would have gone on, but now it was interrupted by a distant 'Halloo' which we recognised as Flora's, and we hallooed back till anon the red coat could be seen between the trees below us, and shortly we could discern that she was holding up her skirt as if she carried something in her lap and she was careful not to spill.

'It's simple enough fare,' she called cheerily, 'but it will serve, you'll see we'll not starve tonight,' and what she had was a pound and more of chestnuts, as many blackberries and a handful of filberts and hazels.

We set the chestnuts in the fire, and feasted off the others for removes while they cooked, and all in all did very well, and the warmth and fun of this primitive way of dressing our dinners put us in good humour, so we joked and grew merry, in some part at Paqui's expense, as calling out to her that broiled chestnuts would do very well, but broiled donkey cutlets would do better and she had better look to her behaviour, which pleasantries she took in good part, snorting and flapping her ears.

When we were done dusk was gathering and the snow coming on heavier, so we decided to bivouac where we were, hoping to cross the escarpment on the morrow, when we expected to be refreshed. So we pulled down more branches, shifted some boulders about and thus procured ourselves a sort of shelter as close to the fire as we could get, and when all was ready and the dark coming on faster, we crawled into this and lay up as close to each other as we could, with Violeta in the middle, our feet to the fire, and Paqui tethered behind our heads.

But the night was not to be passed as snugly as we hoped: first on account of the cold, for despite our preparations this was far more bitter than we had expected – the fire burnt low in an hour and the choice was presented, should we keep it in at the expense of frequently disturbing the warmth we built up between us, or let it out? After another council on the matter it was decided to keep it in as long as may be on account that once it was out it would be impossible to relight it in the dark and the wind and the falling snow. It was as well we decided thus for soon we were beset with another danger, at least we took it as danger then, and the fire was a comfort in this latest extremity.

The first presentiment we had of new trials was from Paqui who gave warning first by moving to and fro, and snorting, pulling at her tether, and finally bellowing, all this in what was now pitch darkness so we could not see what ailed her at all; but then over the wind came another sound, a long drawn out howl, answered by another, and then yapping, and we clutched ourselves in fright at this and Paqui redoubled her bellowing, for it was clear to us all that wolves had come on us, and were even now skirmishing around us, and I think at that moment we should have preferred to hear the *qui-va-là* of a French patrol or picket.

Soon we could see their shapes moving about just on the edge of the firelight – it was difficult then to be sure how many they were, later it seemed only three, but in the dark it seemed more, and they loped to and fro, grey shapes, padding with loose-limbed motion, muzzles hung low towards the ground except when at some special noise from us or Paqui they pointed towards us almost as if they had been gun dogs. In all this we were very frightened indeed, and Paqui more than us – she pulled about at her tether, rolled her eyes, sweated, lashed out with back hooves or reared on them, beating the air with her front ones, and bellowing almost all the time, so sleep would have been impossible on her account alone. We made up the fire, hoping that would scare off our visitors, and when it did not I tried tossing burning brands at them, but they only moved off a little, circled where the brands fell, and came back as close as they had been before. After a time they grew less active, sat in front of us, first upright, and their eyes lit up red at us, which was most frightening for they did not look like eyes at all, but as if they were spy-holes into heads filled with glowing coals; then one by one they stretched out on the ground full length, and closed their eyes and seemed to sleep.

That is what Flora thought, for now she whispered, or spoke low as she could and yet be heard above the noise and the wind, and Paqui still snorting and plunging about: 'I declare they have dined betimes, and come on us only for the warmth of the fire and the pleasure of our company.'

This, if it could be believed, was comfort, and perhaps there was truth enough in it for as the fire burnt lower the wolves edged closer, but to the dying embers, not to us: and that posed a problem, for I would not build it up again since to do so brought me nearer than I liked to the brutes; however, Flora, more convinced than I of what she had said, continued to put on branches as necessary until all we had gathered were gone; and when she did the first time the two near her leaped up so I thought they would be at her throat, but no, they shied away as if as frightened of her as I was of them, and only came back to their previous station when she was lying down with us again; but the next time she got up they did not move, though their eyes glowed.

'You know they wag their tails now when I approach,' Flora said later, but this I could not see and did not credit.

At last exhaustion overcame all else, all the branches were consumed, and fitfully we slept; I'm sure I should have dozed then had there been lions and tigers about as well as wolves.

Dawn found us all wretched, haggard, our bodies racked with cramps, our extremities numb, and my first thoughts were of complete despair – I did not see how we could live out another day and night in the wilderness, and that and more would be needed to get us to a village beyond the mountains where we could feel sure there were no French. However, the sun, which we had not seen for almost a week, shone briefly in a dawn made late by the height of the escarpment we had to cross; we watched his golden progress down the rocks and screes, and over the forests towards us, until he filled our glade with a glow that held little real warmth, yet it cheered us as we rose and shook the snow from our cloaks and from the boughs that had covered us. The fire was cold, and the wolves had gone.

Presently Flora repaired to the valley below again for more chestnuts, Violeta and I rekindled the fire as before, and all this activity set the blood flowing so that its tingling warmth was almost a pain, but our spirits continued to rise, and after we had broken our fast on the same fare we dined on, and none the worse for that, we saddled up Paqui, and set our faces firmly to the mountains ahead of us.

The slopes were soon almost precipitous, but still in trees, so we contrived to keep going by tacking to and fro and clinging to the trunks when we slipped or slithered. There was no question of Violeta riding Paqui, indeed at times I was for leaving the animal, which was in distress and had to be pushed and dragged, but neither Flora nor Violeta would hear of it. There was little or no more sun, the sky becoming overcast, but no wind. At about noon we came out of the trees and on to a sort of meadow but a foot or so deep in snow and sloping steeply up to the escarpment, which now presented to us a long barrier of battlemented cliffs rising from the meadow; these were like buttresses or turrets set in the walls of a fortification, and much split with cracks and chimneys that were filled with ice, that is they were broken and not uniform, yet they presented a most formidable and daunting obstacle and I could see no gap in them at all; to climb them was not possible.

'Well,' said Flora, 'we shall scout along the edge of this forest and shortly we shall surely find a way through – nothing in nature goes on for ever without a break,' and this we did, but first refreshing ourselves on the last of the cobs she had gathered earlier.

For a time our progress was easier – we were no longer climbing and we could look down from our great height across the hills and forests we had crossed to the Great Plain beyond, but could discern no towns or villages beneath the blanket of white that covered all. Indeed it seemed we were the only humans left upon the planet.

A raucous call above us, and then a mewing cackle as of crows, but higher-pitched drew our eyes upwards and in those silent icy spaces we saw a flock or colony of birds, black like rooks, in front of the nearest cliff to us, but several hundred feet above: they were not rooks at all; I think they were *choughs*, for they soared on spread wings and when they came down a bit were seen to have yellow beaks. And higher, but distinguishable because of their great size, three vultures sailed in slow circles on motionless wings, white with black tips, and I wondered if they had seen us, and divined an end for us in that frozen waste that would keep them fed for days, but though I shuddered at this thought I said nothing, for neither Flora nor Violeta had seen them.

What I now recall most impressed me of this stage of our ambulation was the silence – for when we were still, and the choughs had ceased their racket, there was nothing to be heard at all, not a single noise of any sort, and this was frightening once we were sensible of it, for it gave the scene a desolate feeling that lacked reality; and when we moved we fancied the sounds we made, as of gasping and footfalls, would reverberate across the snowy wastes and echo between the buttresses of the ramparts above us for ever. At other times I heard the rush of blood in my head, a noise they say is always with us, but never marked unless there be no other sound at all, and requiring a sort of effort to distinguish, but the effort made, could not be shook off, so I almost prayed it would cease, though knowing hearing and all other senses would be quite put down for ever if it did.

It was thus a relief at first when the wind got up again from the West, that is in our faces, and banks of cloud, lower than what was above us before, rolled towards us like clouds of cavalry at the charge, with ragged pennons that soon raced between us and those gaunt pillars of rock that ever stood between us and our goal; but the first flurries of driving snow that soon followed were no sort of relief at all, for the flakes caught in our hair and froze there, they stung on the eyes and blistered the lips. Worse was to come, for as we struggled on into this rack we became sensible that the meadow, if such it was beneath the snow, it could well have been scree and rock, was narrowing, the incline we walked across was steeper and the firs below us thinner and more stunted. Then we rounded a bluff and found ourselves facing across a valley, a ravine and, as we moved further into it, a chasm, about whose walls the wind howled and the snow whirled in eddies like the souls of those tormented by the winds of their carnal desires and passions. Yet even then we were not fully sensible of the plight we were in, with the distraction of the storm, till Paqui suddenly lost her footing, her hind legs slipping away from her on the scree beneath the snow; for a moment she flailed and kicked and bellowed, and I hung on to her bridle and heaved at it – though why, God knows, she could have taken me with her – and thus she got her footing back though clouds of snow and débris, gravel and boulders, continued to thunder down the slopes below us and into the bottomless ravine: for the fact of the matter was we were no longer sidling across an incline but were on a steep so close to the precipitous that a false step could take us down and down, as surely as if there was naught but space below us.

To turn Paqui round without repeating her slide – for she would not back to safer ground – was scarcely possible, and often she nearly went and me with her, but somehow we did it with Flora pushing at her rump and Violeta chucking and cooing to bring her head round and soothe her the whiles; and as we worked at it the very footing we were on seemed to shift and new boulders bounced away down the awful slope. How we did it and why we did it are mysteries to me, but I declare that in all the battles, skirmishes, sieges and assaults I have seen and been in, I was never so frightened as then. And it was the snow swirling *beneath* us that made it most horrid to the brain which turned giddy at the sight, a sensation made yet more horrid when a gust more fierce than all the rest plucked off my shako and sent it spinning away from us on the blast.

There was nothing for it but to go back and try our luck in the other direction beyond where we had first come out of the forest.

No doubt we made good speed with the wind and the snow now in our backs, and the footing, on account of the incline reducing, with each step improving, and there was still an hour or two, perhaps three, of daylight to be counted on when we passed our point of exit from the forest as near as we could judge it for our earlier tracks were already obscured; but though the slopes continued to be easier there was still no break we could see in the ramparts above us, and despair began to swell like a cancer in my soul, as the cold and weariness bit deeper, and no hope of relief seemed rational at all. Twice the words rose to my lips to beg Flora we should stop and rest, but I swallowed them back, knowing it was not rest I longed for but *requiem*, to lie in the snow with my coat about my head till sleep blackened out my brain for the last time; and once I stumbled and would have lain there but Paqui would not stop and my fingers would not loosen on the bridle, so either I should be dragged or else get up, and somehow I still had the will for the latter.

Yet the thing was this – this extremity I was now in, which seemed so physical, was not so at all but of the hopeless soul, for when, just after my tumble, a sliver of hope came to us I found that after all I had the strength to go on, and Violeta and Flora too, for I make no doubt they were in as sad a frame of mind as I.

Flora stopped and flung up her arm and coming behind her shoulder with her hair streaming away ahead of us, I followed where she pointed and saw three shapes, low and grey, trotting zig-zag across the snowy waste up and towards a huge pillar of rock that looked no more penetrable, scaleable, or negotiable than any others, yet as we watched, the wolves – no doubt they were those of the night before – reached its base, scouted along it, and then were gone.

We followed them – at worst these beasts knew of a shelter, at best a gap our eyes lacked the skill to see.

3

They were so close in front of us that it was easy to follow in their tracks, indeed not only had they marked the way for us, they had made it easier too, for they ran in single file and thus left a path of trodden snow just wide enough to walk in; and when we came to the foot of the cliff and then to the point where they had disappeared we found that what had looked like one buttress with a cleft from top to bottom, was two, and the cleft, the division between them, wider than it had looked from below, being all of thirty feet wide, and what was best of all this gap now widened in a funnel-shaped slope right up to a ridge above us that should be the top of the escarpment, and it looked climbable. Indeed the wolf tracks zigged and zagged right up it and even as we looked, straining our eyes through the whirling snow, a grey shape appeared on the crest, muzzle flung up to the sky, and again we heard the dismal howl as of banshees that we had heard the night before. In a moment its two companions joined the first and all three continued their ghoulish strains as if calling us on – but whether to safety or to our doom was yet uncertain, then they were gone.

This was now the hardest climb of all, the last few feet up as steep a slope as the one we had nearly plunged down, but the wolf path sufficed to get us up and over.

There was little in the view that now presented itself to our eyes to give us cheer, save for one thing only, and that was this: there was no higher ground ahead of us, though peaks and crags stretched away on either side. The rest was a flat of white across which the wind drove clouds of snow whipped up from the ground and mingled it with that which still fell; this plain stretched down and away ahead of us for perhaps a mile, and what lay beyond was undistinguishable on account of the tempest and the gathering dark. It was a dismal prospect – in many ways the worst that had faced us yet, for there was no sign of shelter, no hope of food, and all three, I should say four, of us approached the limits of our endurance, for the cold had taken all feeling from our feet and hands; Violeta especially was in dire straits for she moaned with every step, as if it pained her to move, and we had to walk three abreast supporting her between us, for if we did not she sank to her knees and seemed unable to rise again.

Our only continuing hope was the wolf path, which was filling in with the driving snow, and so we followed it as quick as we could, only hoping it would not lead us to destruction over a precipice, or into an interminable waste of ice and snow where we must surely perish.

After a mile or so thus, crags and rocks began to come closer to our left and towards these our path directed itself – as it did the slope became steeper again and I, at any rate, feared we should arrive again in a situation like that where Paqui had slipped, but before it came to this extremity, and with the darkness now almost complete, we found ourselves skirting along the edge of a broken rock face, feeling at places with our hands, and the track at our feet as likely a figment of our fancies as a reality, when a low whimpering and whining could be heard near, indeed very near, for the gale was still strong about us.

'It's the wolves,' Flora croaked, 'they are close about us some-where.'

She spoke as if this was a comfort – I prayed I should be uncon-scious from the cold and hunger before they attacked, and Paqui had much the same idea for now she bucked and whinnied, then bellowed and reared up, and to save my head from being dashed in by her hooves I had to leave her go, and almost as I did it seemed Flora and Violeta fell away from me into a darkness darker than the dark about us.

I stayed where I was, quite rooted to the ground, for I thought they had gone over a rock face into a nothingness so deep I could not even hear what surely must have been their dying screams; however, after the lapse of some seconds it was not screams I heard nor the distant thud of bodies on rocks or snow below but first a sharp yap, three times repeated and so close I almost jumped out of my skin, then Flora crooning and shushing, and finally her croak again, and that too very close: 'Joey, where are you? Joey, can you hear me?'

'Yes. I can hear you, but I cannot see you,' and I moved a step or two towards these sounds.

'We can see you now, against the sky, but not clear.'

'Where are you?'

'Here, in a cave. Come towards my voice, Joey. It's all right.'

'But the wolves . . .'

'You must trust them, there is no choice. And doubtless if you offer them no harm they will trust you.'

Sure she was right, there was no choice, and I edged towards her in the darkness, feeling along a rocky wall with my hand. The sky shut out above my head, the moan of the wind was less, its force no more than a breeze, then nothing. The air was still, dry, and with a dusty tang to it as you might get in a barn in July when it has been empty and dry longest. My feet brushed into something hard and brittle like very dry branches and whatever it was crackled and rustled so the odour came up more pronounced, then I felt Flora's hand on my arm, then on my face. Although I had looked to find her she startled me thus in the dark, I had not thought her so close.

'Joey?' she said, and there was fright too in her voice for a second.

'Ay.'

'Good. Lie down then here beside us.'

'Where are the wolves?'

'Close. They will help to keep us warm.'

At this I sobbed for helpless fear, but exhaustion and cold had so sapped me I could do no more, and I subsided into her arms, or Violeta's, I know not whose, and their warmth and the darkness, the dusty odour and the doggy one of the wolves were my last recollections as I sank into a slumber, or a state even nearer death.

Some time in the darkness I was woken by a moist warm nuzzling in my ear and at my throat, then round my lips. So far gone was I that I lay still and waited for the decisive snap upon my wind-pipe or the giant vein in my neck – not with fear, nor resignation, but a sort of sick longing – but it never came. The brute licked my eye-lids, snuffed round, found my hand, licked that too, then padded away. Some time later, perhaps only minutes, perhaps hours, I came more properly awake to the mournful ditty of their howling again, close, but outside the cave, and presently Paqui's bellowing was added as a burthen in the bass. The wind had dropped and the entrance to the cave, higher than I had thought, ten feet high and as many wide, was a hole in the darkness, a hole of unearthly silvery light – the sky had cleared and the moon shone. Soon the howling stopped and the bellowing too – I waited to hear our donkey's death cry, but it never came.

Later the moon, just past full and setting, shone directly upon

us. Because it awoke me and I wished to sleep more I murmured
a prayer that came into my head, whence I know not, but it went
like this:

> Lay thy bow of pearl apart
> And thy crystal shining quiver
> Give unto the flying hart
> Space to breathe how short soever
> Thou that makst a day of night
> Goddess excellently bright

and turned my face into the cave, at which I swooned at what I
saw there, swooned on a choking blubbery cry, for there before
me was Death Himself, despite my prayer, come now I knew to
take us off – gaunt with hollow eye sockets and teeth that glowed
white against the yellow of bone and dried up sinew, and on his
brow a gold diadem clear in the light of the Moon, so I knew this
really was old Dis Himself and no illusion or phantasm.

Yet when I woke the third time it was not in the horrid Halls
of Hades but still, so far as I could tell, in that hollow cavern as
dread to me now as that other place, and I durst not open my eyes
for fear of what I would see this time, but my ears were unstopped
and through them I heard the voices of Violeta and Flora, in
earnest interlocution.

'But who can he be?' was the first I clearly distinguished from
Violeta.

'A King, no doubt,' from Flora, 'a King of long, long ago.'

'A Moor?' there was fright now in Violeta's voice.

'Nay, longer ago than that perhaps. A Pagan King from even
the time before Our Lord.'

'Ay, there were savages in our land then, I've heard tell – they
who cut off the head of St James.'

Quiet and awed though their voices were, they spoke with
equanimity and I surmised now the horrid figure of Death I had
seen was not Death but the dead, and I opened my eyes.

That sort of light the harbinger of Dawn now filled the cavern and there again was that King I'd seen before, but now spied over Flora's shoulder, for she sat between Him and me: he did indeed look a sad thing now, far smaller he seemed than before, but propped up on a rock, or throne, a bag of bones held together by strands of leathery skin and naught majestickal about him at all, save his diadem of gold incorruptible, which proved to be beaten leaf thin and fashioned like leaves, oak-leaves.

I stirred and Flora heard me.

'Joey – are you awake?' She reached behind her and took my hand. 'Don't be afeared at what you'll see.'

Well that cave, or rather caves for there were two more chambers, was certainly a curious place, and would have been of great interest to any antiquarian, I'm sure; we explored it throughly and found much more than this King on the threshold of his palace, almost as if he was a porter, not a king, as *item*, with him two supine corpses one of which was what I had took to be a bundle of dried sticks when I stumbled in; *item*, in the second chamber three more but with what we thought had once been baskets, now crumbling away into dust; *item*, in the third, and this was the most strange of all, partly on account it was dark and we beheld it only briefly by a flame kindled in a handful of straw from one of those baskets, many more corpses, perhaps a dozen, laid out in a semi-circle or half moon about another monarch, but this time a Queen, who like her Consort was also on a throne, but in far more state than he – *viz.* a necklace of shells and tusks, a robe of skins, and what else I could not now say, so brief a glimpse of her did we have, but my recollection is touched with a deeper awe than I had felt before, as of a mystery and knowledge in that chamber beyond what I had ever felt, or sensed, or known, and almost regretted our intrusion, as something unmannerly.

We did not linger beyond this brief exploration, for the first view from the cavern's mouth that morning promised our trials and suffering were almost done, and we were anxious to be off. The sun shone, the crags behind us sparkled, but best of all was this: that beyond the snow-field immediately in front of us, a clear vista of mountain chain after mountain chain stretched in front of us for may be fifty miles or more to violet distances beyond the reach of sight, and none but what we stood on were capped with snow, but instead all dark green and verdancy and forest promising warmth, shelter, food, and surely habitations in what looked to be paradisiacal valleys, and no doubt the streams and rivulets would lead us to the Agueda and so to Ciudad Rodrigo. And not the least of all the occasions we had for uplifted hearts was the presence of Paqui still alive and well amongst us − for it seemed she had passed the night between two boulders and there either defended herself successfully with her hooves against the wolves, or perhaps, out of respect for us whom they seemed to look on as friends or masters, they had not troubled her.

As Violeta said, repeating a Spanish proverb, 'No-one ever yet saw a donkey dead.'

Our descent was truly a descent into paradise. First the snow gave way to grasses and a hundred channels tinkled and sparkled through the greens from the edge of the melting snow, and soon these met into streams and the streams into a rivulet which we followed into what was first little more than a dell, but soon became a valley, and these brief pastures were strewn with tiny purple flowers, like spears where they were in shadow and like chalices in the sun, and they were crocuses I suppose, but I had seen none before in Winter, only in Spring. And this was an indication of the country we were now coming into, for truly it seemed it never knew a Winter but only a Spring and Summer, for there were ever flowers about the waterside as violets, pinks, scabious, and buttercups and yet the trees were all in fruit as rowan with bright scarlet berries, and juniper with purple ones and spiny leaves, then hazel and blackberry off which we feasted and at last a shrub I had never seen before, and there were groves of them − dark-leaved like laurel, with white flowers that hung in clusters like pearls, and on the same boughs small fruits just like wild strawberries in shape and hue but when bit into had a yellow flesh, sweet and fragrant.

Yet for all this, all was not well with us – the way was not always easy, there were no proper paths and often the valley narrowed into steep sided gorges which left us with awkward choices – whether to remain above the rivulet and take the chance of the descent becoming at last too precipitous to manage, or whether to follow it in its bed where perforce we might have to wade in it or negotiate cataracts and water-falls. Often we had to wend our way back a half-mile or so and try another way through and the worst of these times Paqui could not be ridden and Violeta could not walk, her feet so pained her; and later, after we had eaten, she fell into a violent vomiting fit, and then complained of heats and cramps, so we were sure she had an ague at the least and perhaps a fever yet more virulent, as the tertian. And soon, in her delirium, she began to call on Johnny again, and then on her unborn child whom she feared to lose, and at last on Our Holy Mother and Her Son and all the Saints, and the least consequence of this was that what later became familiar to us as a paradise indeed, was now scarce appreciated at all or even cursed, for there was still no sign of what we most looked for, namely a habitation, be it only a shepherd's croft.

Perhaps after all it was Violeta's fevered praying that saved us, for at a point where the valley at last widened and the ground was almost level and like a park or garden we came first upon a path, then a place where a tributary stream had been coaxed through a channel of dressed stone away from its natural course, but followed the path, and thus at last to a low wall with a gate.

In short, we had come across a tiny House of ten of the reformed Cistercian or Trappist Order whose Superior, when I knocked him up, found us a disused hermitage on the hillside out-side his confines and there let us lodge for as long as we needed.

For all that our stay was occasioned by Violeta's prolonged ill-ness and slow recovery, I look back on the next six months as the happiest of my life, as a period of rest and repose untroubled by any cares but memories.

PART TWO

CHAPTER V

Of the Enchanted Time spent in the Batuecas, a Space for
Recollection, to set certain Records Straight.

I

> *Any Lancer of Don Julián*
> *I must love and cherish*
> *But the one who loves me back*
> *I must have or perish*

Sang Violeta as she plied her needle on a warm day in January (for all days were warm in that place), seated just outside our tiny cottage, the Hermitage, with Flora beside her and she sewing too. Below us the slopes of juniper and *madroño*, arbutus or Strawberry tree, as one of the monks had named this fruiting laurel for me, fell away quite steeply to the river below which stormed along today through its ravine, for though warm it did rain in that paradise, and had for a week, and the river was rushing and boiling round boulders above its usual bed. To our left we could see the wall that marched like a miniature of that in China I have seen engravings of, over the hills and down again, marking off the monks' domain, and beyond it fold on fold of pine-clad crags though with cork and olive on the lower slopes. To our right the valley wound up into the mountains we had crossed and the sun glanced off the snow so that it shone like burnished white gold and I could almost fancy I could see the Cave where the Oak

King kept his everlasting vigil with his Queen behind him in her tomb or Birthplace of Time.

> *Don Julián, your Lancers*
> *Look like clouds at sunrise*
> *Their blood red scarves are streamers*
> *That dazzle female eyes*

Violeta continued, her tune a gay and tripping *jota*, adapted all over the Peninsula for the exploits of our Hero, now known to all as *el Charro*, a word signifying all that typifies our Province; and Flora shyly joined her, for it was their conceit that Violeta should teach her Castillian. Now Violeta broke off, needle poised in the air, to admonish her companion.

'Mistress Flora, I beseech you, you must say *encarnADas*, not *enCARNadas*.'

'Faw, 'tis too silly,' replied Flora, 'when our great Poet has in-*carn*adine. *EncarnADas*, indeed.'

'And I pray you – just a touch of a *th* on the *d*, if you wish to be thought correct.'

'Well, well, let me see – *encarNATHas*.'

'Much better, Mistress Flora, though a trifle forced.'

'You must say *fawced*, not *for-r-r-rced*, unless you wish to be mistook for a Scot.'

And so they bantered on while I sat by, somewhat behind them, and ground some corn on a stone between my knees, a daily chore since the monastery afforded us barley but no flour, and Flora every forenoon baked or rather broiled us barley cakes on a skillet in place of bread from what I ground the day before.

And what they were now doing was this: they had privately removed their undergarments from beneath their skirts, as shifts and petticoats, undone the seams, and were letting in panels of stuff taken from a petticoat sacrificed for the purpose, thus to enlarge them for comfort's sake, for some two days previous when Violeta had projected this or some similar measure, Flora had put down the spoon with which she had been stirring a pot, and had spoken up thus: 'Ay, Mistress, an we can find two needles amongst us, I shall join you at it.'

'Nay, that's not necessary, you do too much for us already, with all the cooking,' for Violeta was convalescent, being still much weakened by our earlier privations, the fever that had afflicted her, and still lame in one heel, the result we thought of frost-bite as well as blistering – 'I may not be altogether recovered but I am surely able to do my own needle work.'

''Tis not for you I should be doing it,' there was a dry tone to Flora's voice and she looked her friend steadily in the eye.

There was a silence so I could hear the fire crackle, and the rushing of the stream below, till at last Violeta, who had dropped her gaze and on whose cheeks a blush had come, looked up again with a question in her eyes: 'Oh, Madam, do I understand you?' she cried.

'I think so. I shall lay up much the same time as you, I dare say.'

At this Violeta lifted herself out of the chair and hobbled across the stone-flagged floor and was received into a warm and tearful embrace, at which I surmised a period of female gossip I had best not hear was in the air, and took myself off for a space to walk in the woods, the rain having eased, and there picked a bunch of violets and primroses for I guessed the mood would be a celebratory one rather than otherwise when I returned.

Thus, as I say, both of them plying their needles, singing, and each with the other perfecting their skills in foreign tongues, and me grinding the daily ration of corn and hoping they would sing more than chatter, for the rhythm helped the tedium of my task.

> *A Lancer of Don Julián*
> *Has impaled me on his lance*
> *I'm sure he'll take me on his crupper*
> *All the way to France*

at which both began to smirk, then each saw the other's face and laughed outright.

'Holy Mary,' cried Flora, 'aren't we a fine pair to be talking of being placed on lances?' and they giggled all the more so I thought they might, in their conditions, do themselves injury.

At last Flora controlled herself and, 'Did you ever see *Don Julián, el Charro*?' she asked. 'He's a fine man.'

'Indeed I did,' said Violeta, 'but before he was a *Guerrillero* Chieftain – I mind well I met him once, out in the fields when my sisters and brother and Pepe here went out for a picnic. What a day that was, eh Pepe, I'm sure you mind it,' and she went on to describe it all, and I helped her out, so we put together the scene between us, just as I have described it in my Volume the First, but with some tears and sighs from Violeta for poor Rafael, and for her sisters Jara and Margarita – Jara had died of the consumption in the bad winter of 1809 and Margarita had married and removed with her husband, a Lawyer, to Cádiz where he now served as secretary to the Cortes, then met and drawing up its new-fangled constitution.

'How like the man that is,' cried Flora when we had done, meaning Don Julián in his exploits as *Garrochista*, 'but you talk of one Paco who plays the *charro* music on fife and drum – and is he an old round man with half his ear gone?'

'Why, yes,' I cried, 'that's him, and he says a wolf took it.'

'Wild cat, I think.'

'May be, it's all one – of course it must be the same man, but where, Mistress Tweedy, did you meet old Paco, for surely he left my Father's land these two years gone or more?'

'Ay, he did, and on account of the French who pillaged it, though he and his wife escaped with their lives. Following that he met up with the *Lanceros* and they took the two good old folk to Lumbrales, then their main Head Quarters, where they served *el Charro* well, he as ostler and smith, and she dressing their food for them according to the *charro* styles they favoured. But it was his music I remember him for, and most especially at the great fiesta there, twelve month last October, on the day of the Feast of Our Lady of the Pillar.'

> *La Virgen del Pilar dice*
> *Que no quiere ser Francesa*
> *Que quiere ser Capitana*
> *de la Tropa Aragonesa*

sang Violeta, supplying another *jota*, even more famous than the earlier ones, being in celebration of the heroic defence of Saragossa – *Our Lady of the Pillar, To be French did not aspire; To be Captain of our Army, Was her chief desire* – 'but what great fiesta was this, Mistress Tweedy; held in times of war it cannot have been like the old ones?'

'Well, I cannot speak of what I have not known, but if your feasts in time of peace bettered this one, then I hope I may be spared to return to see them once old Johnny Crahppo is driven off at last.'

'But of course you shall,' cried Violeta, 'and be guest of Mr Reaney and me; oh, dearest Mistress Flora, let us engage now you'll come. You will make me the happiest creature in the world if you do.'

'I declare I am most obliged to you. It will be a great honour to take up this invitation . . .'

'Pooh, now I believe you are mocking me for my too great civility – but I mean it most sincerely.'

'And I accept most sincerely too – but do you wish to hear of this Fiesta of the Country I attended?'

'I want nothing more, and I shall be quite mum, and you too, Pepe.'

So Mistress Tweedy bit off her thread, sorted out another, and when she was ready proceded with the account of how, Ciudad Rodrigo having fallen to the French, Don Julián marauded thereabout for many months, and one day, being the Eve of the Feast aforesaid, and lacking meat to eat on the Day, planned a daring raid on the Cattle the French grazed on the *glacis* outside the Town, right beneath their guns, and he was able to do this having heard from spies that General Reynand too planned a feast – it was the garrison's custom to curry favour with the population by occasional observances of local custom – and would go out that morning to choose the oxen he would have roasted whole in the City Square. Thus Don Julián was able to fall on the herd know-ing the gunners would not shoot for fear of hurting their General, and so carried off not only the cattle but the General too, much to the latter's *chagrin*. The French cavalry now made *sortie* in force but were well beaten back with heavy losses and all in all the *Lanceros* had much to celebrate in Lumbrales the next day.

'And you see,' said Mistress Flora, 'I was there at that time with three companies of the Connaughts and twice that number of Portuguese with guns too, sent by the Peer to hold Lumbrales for the *Guerrilla* should the French decide to take it, though they never did. Well, we had a fine old time I can tell you. In the forenoon there was a tryout at bull-fighting, but the cattle were the wrong sort, not bred for it; nevertheless Don Julián put on a fine display of his old profession much applauded by all, and then old Paco, dressed in his *Charro* suit of black velvet with tassled sombrero came out with flute and drum, and four or five others with him, and struck up your gay *Charro* music, and soon all was spinning and clapping and stamping so the dust flew in the air to our waists . . .'

'Did you take part, then?'

'Why, of course, for though a Princess, being like all Irish girls the descendant of Kings, it is also true that the Irish girl comes dancing from her mother's womb . . .'

'But that is a Spanish saying, a *Charro* proverb!'

'And an Irish one too. And after, some Paddy or Mike found a fiddle and borrowed a flute and we gave them a *ceilidh* for your fiesta, and then the Portuguese found guitars, and improvised drums with dried peas rattling in them and took their turn, danc-ing in a circle first this way then that and twisting their feet most

neatly and nimbly; and all the warm afternoon the smoke of wood
fires and smell of broiling meat drifted through us till it was almost
dusk, and the air nippy, and the wine went round in skins. There
were gypsies too with their wild music, but not at that time much
liked, for none could dance their oriental measures, and soon it
was back to honest Irish and plain *Charro*. Patrick Coffey and
Kevin Nolan were there, you mind them, Mistress Violeta? and at
first Coffey would not dance and swung his fist at those who
called him to, but at last I took his hand and led him out, and faith
he was wilder and more apt for it than all the rest once he was
going. Oh, it was a grand day, a grand evening, and we feasted
until dawn, I dare say – and I mind now Don Julián, *el Charro*, sitting at table above us, beneath flaming torches, leaning back in his
chair, and smiling through those great black whiskers, and smoking a *cigarillo* and all the time trying to make his honoured guest
General Reynand crack his face beside him, and I doubt he ever
did, the only glum one there, I'm sure.'

'Well, he's scarce to be blamed for that, Mistress Flora, I'm
sure,' laughed Violeta, then turned to me, 'Pepe, was it not about
then you fetched up with the Connaughts and put on your scarlet coat? It must have been much at that time, I think.'

'Ay, it was. Well, a month later.'

'Since we're telling tales to ease the dullness of our chores, let's
hear how that fell out, for I never did hear it before now, I'm sure.'

At which I stood up – 'The corn is ground,' I said. 'If you want
to hear of it Mistress Tweedy'll tell you, for she knows it as well as
I do,' and I took myself off into the woods and down to the river,
for it's not a tale I care to listen to and I hoped thereby to avoid it,
but I could not for now it was in my mind, and no matter where
I went in that paradise where shy irises already peeped purple in
clumps beneath the boulders and clouds of snowdrops nodded by
the river beneath a copse of alders; or higher up above the scree
amongst the juniper whose spines prickled when I grasped them
to stop a slip or fall; or pushing through the gum cistus, not yet,
even there, in bloom: no matter where I went the tale unfolded in

my mind more completely and with more logic than Flora's telling, for I'm sure she did not know the half of it.

2

At about the time of the feast Mistress Tweedy had been speaking of, General Marchand at last closed the Irish College in Salamanca and took Mr Curtis off and 'Father' John Reaney (who remained undiscovered for what he truly was, except to Violeta Martín whom he courted discreetly, and her family) to a house near the Great Square where they were put under most secure house arrest; and with this done the chief amongst Mr Curtis's couriers to the *Guerrilleros* and the English were severally caught, tortured and garrotted, as they came to his rooms at the college and found not him but Rubén García sitting in his place, and tinkling out a French Air on the Stoddart Grand.

And that it was Rubén himself that did this I knew, for he himself sent for me thence and thither I attended him, on All Hallows' Eve, that season having coming round again when girls stand on their balconies and seek their husbands-to-be in the crowd below, though few out that year for fear only French would pass in the streets.

Though I expected him it was a shock to see Rubén's flaming hair above the raised lid of the *fortepiano* instead of Mr Curtis's white nimbus, to see his blue eyes with the livid scar above, a shock, for it was a blasphemy he should haunt the rooms and handle the objects of that good old man and wait like an hermit crab in an oyster shell for the unsuspecting to swim into his reach.

'Well, Pepe, I'm glad you came. Won't you sit down? These rooms must be very familiar to you I think. I find our host has some excellent Indian Tea here, almost an offence in itself these days, would you not say?' He referred to the Berlin Decrees which contrived without success to occlude goods originated in Britain or her Colonies from anywhere in Europe.

There was nothing for it but to accept and presently I was making the tea myself, for Rubén had not the skill. He pronounced the infusion excellent and promised himself to use up the caddy before he left, now he knew the trick of it, then set down his cup.

'Well, Pepe, let's to business. It's a simple matter I require of you. You must go to Freneda, which is in Portugal and the Head Quarters of *Milord Velintón*, and discover there for us what his intentions are in Spring.'

I suppose my feelings showed; it could hardly be otherwise. I recall I could no longer hold my cup and saucer.

'Nay, I'm sure you'll be welcomed there, for they will have felt a lack of news from Salamanca,' here he gestured about the room, 'and we shall give you good ones to carry – how Mr Curtis is taken and this cell closed, how the best brigades of the Guard are being moved back to France and there's talk of a campaign against Russia, and so forth – all they shall have known already or will soon discover anyhow, and thus they shall believe you to be honest. No danger will attend you at all. And of course while you are on your way but yet in French-held territory you will have a passport signed by Marshal Marmont himself if you like – though I dare say my name and a couple of Generals will suffice.'

By now I was enough recovered to protest I would not go.

'But you will, Pepe, you will. For if you are still here, let me see, Wednesday the day after tomorrow, I shall have you arrested and later garrotted in the Market Square, right on the spot where my friend Pepe Clemente died. Do you remember him? Give time for the formalities to be observed, as putting you to the question and such for a good confession will be required – preferably one inculpating the Martín family and Violeta Martín especially who has been seen about these rooms – and I think we can promise to send you off Sunday about noon. Unfortunately *el Suero*, the gypsy who spun the screw for the other Pepe, is not in town, but . . . you'll do it?'

I nodded. Two considerations had brought about this change: I doubted not that I should fail under torture and thus by avoiding the occasion and going on this errand I should save Violeta's life; second it had occurred to me that once in Freneda I should not need to return.

'Perhaps you think that once in Freneda you need not return?' Rubén asked. 'Well, I think you will.' Here this Devil incarnate went over to the big bureau and unlocked a drawer. 'I found this amongst Rector Curtis's papers,' and here he drew out a piece of legal vellum bound with red ribbon which he now loosened. The parchment creaked as he unfolded it. 'This,' he continued, 'is your Father's Will. Such a loss for you; I see you are already in mourning. I imagine Rector Curtis has not communicated its contents to you directly for you would not believe him without the proof, and that I have here. This document declares you to be illegitimate . . . wait, you are Joseph Bosham? of course, and therefore not able, under the clauses of the entail, to inherit your Father's interest in several pieces of land hereabout which now revert to the Estates of your connexion, less a connexion than you thought, the Marquis of Monterrubio de la Sierra. It is true, José, see. Here and here. I admire his discretion in not naming your Mother – he simply says you were not born in wedlock. Oh yes. You do inherit his books and moveables. How charming.

'Now if you return before the first of December with the information we require I shall burn this in front of you. If you do not, I shall lodge it with the appropriate officer in the Legal Department at the Town Hall.'

Again I required some moments before I could compose myself enough to reply, but when I did it was on these lines: 'Burning that document will scarcely save me my inheritance, for surely Mr Curtis has read it, and doubtless there is a copy somewhere . . .'

'Indeed, Pepe, you are right – he has not only read it but was a witness to it, his signature is here. As to a copy – well there may be, there may not be, but only one person there is who will know of it and that is Mr Curtis.'

'So?'

Rubén stood up, moved to the window where he fiddled for a moment with the telescope that still stood there, pointing to the stars.

'The Rector is a valuable prisoner – we had thought to exchange him for a General or two – only the other day General Reynaud was carried off by that murderer Sánchez from beneath the guns of Ciudad Rodrigo. However . . . the news we require is also worth a General or two and if you bring them back I shall put the Rector in your hands to do with as you like.'

'What could I do with him?'

'Well, you do not take my meaning – give us our news, and, by-the-by, it must be a document, which you will have to come by somehow, for we are not so green as to take your unsupported word, bring us the news thus supported and you shall only have to give me the nod for Rector Curtis to be shot while escaping, and thus your inheritance will be secure.'

I knew then, at that moment, I should never be able so to betray my Father's old friend, though he and my Father it seemed had betrayed me and I felt most sorely about it, more sore and bitter than I can now say; and then I thought on it some more, and such is our readiness to believe what we want it seemed to me that if on my return Rubén would let me see Mr Curtis I might persuade him to keep mum about my Father's Will, which clearly had been framed in his recent madness and would never therefore be proved, and this in return for not asking Rubén to kill him. In short, the Will would be suppressed, and Mr Curtis's life saved.

'Ay, of course,' said Ruben when I asked if I might be allowed to see Mr Curtis on my return, 'and you may knock him on the head and save us the trouble, if that would suit you.'

There only remained for him to tell me what news he required: 'Well that's not difficult – 'tis simply this: the whereabouts of Milord Velintón's siege train. Is it still in the South and destined for Badajoz again or has it been brought North for Ciudad Rodrigo?

I repeat, José, I want something in writing, anything, a field order, a requisition, anything, so be it is in English, and says clearly or hints so there can be no doubt the whereabouts of the siege train.'

Having mused thus far I found myself on a lichen-covered boulder in the midst of the River Batueca, for that was the name of our stream, the Superior of the Monks had said, and wondered how far in her account to Violeta Mistress Tweedy had gone – further, I supposed, for none of this so far did she know. Yet most of what followed was clear to her and my stomach sank and my blood ran cold to think that will I or will I not I should soon have to return to the Hermitage to face Mistress Reaney's scorn – I doubted she would speak with me again or have me near her and as these thoughts and feelings ran through my mind I peered into the pool below which was deep, and the water boiling into it one end and tumbling out the other so its roar bewitched me, and truly I felt it would be best to cast myself in.

I reached Freneda safely, a tiny village less than a day's journey from Ciudad Rodrigo, and found Don Julián there on a visit to the Peer with news of his own, news which I actually heard him deliver, and this was my own first sight of Britain and Europe's Hero, who welcomed the *Guerrillero* Chief with an embrace and then quizzed him on the details of his exploit in capturing General Reynand and his cattle, which, when he heard, set him laughing – a terrifying cachinnation, very loud and long, like the whoop of the whooping cough, repeated again and again. Afterwards Don Julián thrust me forward and said I had news of Mr Curtis, at which His Lordship grew solemn and fixed me with his eyes beneath high-raised brows and proceeded to categorise me most carefully on all the circumstances that attended Mr Curtis's arrest, which I answered as well as I could though confusedly, out of consciousness of the ambiguity of my position and awe at the presence I found myself in. At last the Peer concluded that if I returned to Salamanca safely I was to be sure to get news to the good old man that Lord Wellington fully expected to lodge with him that Summer and meanwhile he wished him to keep his spirits up.

In all but this detail that brief interview has almost passed from my mind, which is strange when I find it so easy to recall the night spent in Torrecilla de la Abadesa with Buenoparte three years before – and I must confess I have always felt myself more at ease with a known and obvious rogue than with a man with whom I can find no material fault. This strange man who was so brusque yet informal, who laughed so demonically yet kept a solemnness behind his eyes, this General who has said 'Nothing except a battle lost can be half so melancholy as a battle won', which is a strange thought for a General to have, left me as ill-at-ease as I have ever been, and I was glad to be out of his presence, though I noticed, when we were, that Don Julián, that proud *Garrochista* and veteran of five campaigns, came away like a small boy unexpectedly rewarded by a loving but remote parent – his cheeks glowed, he smacked his boots with his crop, his eyes shone and he muttered oaths in his whiskers, now grown prodigious, all of which, in its rough way, seemed to express the very seventh heaven of delight.

Well, Don Julián rewarded me with a silver duro – it should have been thirty – to drink his health and the Peer's and I was left to my own devices, for none suspected aught ill of me, and I was free to wander as I might about the tiny village, and in the three days I was there caught sight of the Peer twice more, and once all unattended walking about the square with his hand in that of a Portuguese child for whom he bought a penny-screw of butterscotch of a pedlar who had brought English wares from Lisbon. It was as well Rubén had sent me and not a bravo for such a one could have hit the mark and got off too, so openly did his Lordship go about the place.

I found the news I wanted easily enough and a paper to support it, being a receipt for five barrels of salt beef 'for the men with the Siege Train at Almeida', which was a small fortress some ten miles to the North of Freneda, so clearly the Peer's design was on

Ciudad Rodrigo, not Badajoz, and this receipt I got my hands on in the Commissariat offices in Freneda by pretending to the clerk there that I was a farmer owed for some wine and sending him off to look at his ledgers, and now there was nothing to do but return to Salamanca, but I was more and more loth to do so, and only finally moved when the day after I had my paper I was suddenly accosted thus in the street by a lady dressed in furs, for the weather had turned chilly, and whom I at first did not recognise: 'Jesus and Mary, it can't be! But it is – Pepe Bozzam,' but at her voice I knew her well enough.

I did the worst thing I could – I ran, and left Marisa Von Schmidt standing there in a doorway, her hand held out and her mouth open in surprise, Marisa Zúñiga as was, the prying shrew who played the guitar in the Italian style and was always ready to proclaim me a liar to any who would listen, she who had married a Hamburger in the King's German Legion. Well, having run from her in fright there was nothing to be done but be off in earnest, though I was reluctant, for she would surely raise some sort of hue and cry to have me examined at least and I had no desire to end my days on the end of a British rope.

I almost got off – first across the Agueda North of Ciudad Rodrigo, and thence to Lumbrales; all done easily enough for I had a pass from Don Julián, who believed of course that I was returning to Salamanca in the British interest, and thence to Fuente de San Esteban where I knew there was a strong French force garrisoned in the Church, and indeed I was in sight of this church when I was taken.

I was on a mule, the first snow of the year had fallen, and was kicking up behind me, but those on my tracks, relentless as bloodhounds, were better moun . . .

No. This will not do. Without doubt my gift for narrative, especially descriptive of action, is here taking charge – neither did it happen thus, nor did I remember it thus on my boulder with the torrent of the Batueca tumbling about me, nor must I describe it thus now, seated here at the deal table in the attic Captain Branwater has disposed for me as a private place where I may pen these memories – there was no stirring chase through the oak trees and across the snow, no last stand in which I brought down one or two of my pursuers before being taken, no rescue at the moment of direst extremity – well something of this last, but not much.

To the point then. I left Lumbrales with a heavy sick heart and purposely loitered every step of the way over the furzy hills and down into the oak-clad plain, and cast my eyes ever backwards longing for pursuit, and forward with a failing spirit. Why? It would be easy to say that I had come to Freneda to save my neck (and Violeta's) from the garrotte, which is a motive that may be despised but which the generous of soul will excuse – indeed my Father's behest (worth more than his *bequest*) was 'survive', and so I displayed filial piety in going thither. But in my return I had only one end – to secure my inheritance; and thereby encompass the life of a brave and blameless old man. For all my faults I had never until then acted solely out of greed, which is what it was, howsoever I whipped up the flames of my righteous indignation, fed with bitterness, at what I was like to lose.

Easy to say and write. Yet that is not the whole story – the motives of the considering man are never simple; I delayed my return for another reason too and that was fear of a sort, in a way an honourable fear. I have heard tell of moral cowardice – the sin of him who out of fear of the censure of others is unable to do what he knows to be right. Is then cowardice of a sort which leads *to* instead of *from* what is good, which keeps one *from* an evil action, to be called *immoral* cowardice? (I do not refer to fear of punishment, there was no danger of punishment in returning to Salamanca, only the prospect of considerable reward.) If *yes*, then immoral cowardice slowed the gait of my mule, for what I feared was not that I *should* give the nod to Rubén for Mr Curtis's demise, but that I should not be able to, and as for substantially facing the man and appealing to him to suppress my Father's Will, well, I was now close enough to the event to be sure that that was quite beyond my powers, moral or otherwise, to sustain.

And so it was a relief when, with my mule still an hour's ambling gait short of Fuente de San Esteban, I discerned behind me the brisk trotting of a troop of horses, doubtless pricking down through the oaks on the trail I had left in the powdery snow. I drew rein to wait for them, and looked about me at the grey sky, the sombre trees, the powdery snow lying on the dried brown twigs of lavender and sage, all that was left of the Summer gone, which rattled when a sparrow fluttered in them or when the icy breeze shook them, and all that I wished for then was a flask of *aguardiente*, for to pretend I was not terrified would be absurd – I was near dead already with terror alone, and my teeth so chattered with it that I could not speak when at last they came up with me and circled slowly about me just out of pistol shot in case I should resist them.

There were ten of them, in jackets once yellow, now frayed and faded, with bearskin busbees decked with blood-red scarves to show they were now under the British General, and fur pelisses. They carried lances with tatters of yellow pennons, and carbines and holstered pistols; and for a time, as I say, they scouted about me, keeping the shrubs and trees which crackled beneath their hooves or shed their snow in crystal showers when their busbees brushed them as often as may be, between me and them, and thus they drew nearer until at thirty paces I knew the stocky, dark-browed leader to be none other than Fernando.

'Well, José,' he called, in his gruff and still familiar voice, 'Will you come with us?'

But I could not at once reply, for my teeth were chattering, as above; so at last he came boldly up and took my bridle.

'*El Padrón*,' by which he meant Don Julián, 'wants you back at Lumbrales. If what they say there of you is true, I should do you the kindness of putting a ball in your head now, for there will be worse than that to come.'

At which I must have near fainted, for he swiftly added, 'Never fear, José, I could not do it. Besides he is most strict now that there should be a proper hearing and examination of evidence in these cases, for that is the British way and we are in their Army now.' So saying he led off my mule and so we went, back up through the woods and into the hills, and his troopers about us, all in good order.

After a time I was able to ask him, 'What, good Fernando, am I accused of?'

'Of spying, José, of spying in the French interest. 'Tis laid against you by Marisa Zúñiga, now Von Schmidt, who gives herself airs for her husband is to be a *Junker* or German Lord when his Father dies. But proof is lacking, so I doubt not you'll get off, for we'll not find anything on you, I'm sure.'

He apprehended the meaning of my continuing silence.

'You have it on you, then?'

I answered in English: 'I could dispose of it if you gave me opportunity.'

We jogged on. I tried again, still in English.

'They will kill me, will they not, otherwise?'

Still no answer.

'You will not like to see an old friend go thus.'

At last he spoke, but in Spanish and in one of his blessed proverbs: '*Por la calle de luego, se va a la casa de ahora.*' – By the street of then the house of now is reached.

I tried once more but was rebuked: 'Speak Castillian, José. I would not have my men think we spoke in secret from them,' and so I was silent and fell into blank despair.

However, the ties of ancient friendship proved as strong as I hoped after all, and this is how Fernando contrived to get me off: after an hour's more jogging and dusk coming on he spoke again, and again in English – 'There would be no profit in letting you ride off with no where to go or hide. My men would soon hunt you down and skewer you like a pig. But just outside Lumbrales is a gypsy camp – you know the tongue, perhaps you know some of the tribe. It will be dark as we come to it – when I give the word make a break for it; it is in a declivity where there used to be charcoal burners . . .'

I said I knew the place, having passed it that morning on my way out.

'There are thickets,' Fernando went on, 'which we shall search, while you go on to the gypsies.'

And so it fell out. After no worse fright than a couple of pistol balls near my head from the more alert of his men I reached the camp, where I hid between a pile of logs and an old turfed hut, and listened to Fernando's men thrashing about in the thicket while the gypsies hurled abuse at them for disturbing their evening. At last the *Lanceros* went off and I was just about to make myself known to the gypsies by standing up and calling to them when I was seized from behind – my presence having been detected from the start – and they bundled me into the hut where to my surprise (but it was no distress to me – for reasons I have not fully entered into I was past caring) they fastened on my neck a chain that was stapled into a large stone I could scarce lift let alone walk with. There, for the time, they left me, though I was aware of much talk, as of a *council*, going on outside, and later Suero for he was amongst them, came and asked me who knew I was there, and I told him some of my case.

I was there a fortnight, always chained like a dog but in some comfort else – warm, with wine and good food, even meat, and twice a day they came and offered me abuse and then reverence in turns, though exactly how I could not tell, for I do not have their tongue off perfectly by any means.

Amongst them, as above, Suero with his wicked grin, and nimble fingers apt for the guitar, and Pedro, bald-headed with broken hand, and Luis with long hair and a woman's voice, and I asked Suero the second day I was there, why they kept me chained and treated me thus, and this is what he told me.

They looked on me, he said, on my arrival, a vagrant hunted by the authorities, and not one of their own kind, as a gift sent from Heaven, for it meant that that year they should be able to perform a custom long fallen into desuetude, but which if revived would bring them great good fortune. In short, I was kept to be emasculated and then strangled to death on St Lucie's Day, ten days off. It seemed Fernando had put me in a scrape as bad as the one he had had me out of.

I asked Suero if he would be executioner.

'No, *Busné*, it will be our *Manclay*, our Count, he who comes with hawk and hounds, he will strangle you in the end.'

'In the end, *Calo*?'

'Much is to be done first.'

'Why, O *Calo*?'

'Why, *Busné*? Why, in honour of our *Beluñi*, our *Ostelinda*.'

'I do not know those words, *Calo*.'

'They signify *Queen* and *Goddess*.'

'And what is this Goddess's name?'

Here he gave me a queer look – he was sitting on his haunches at my feet, and hitherto had made signs in the dust between his knees with a twig, but now he looked up at me, and the whites of his eyes glowed in the gloom of the hut.

'She is the same Goddess as yours,' he said, '*Maria Majari* – the Virgin.'

Another time I asked him if he would not for old times' sake conspire with me to get me off; and he flashed his gap-toothed grin at me and said, 'What old times were those, O *Busné*? Have you *sonacai* about you now? Can you tell me where is buried treasure?' I told him he should seek out Fernando in Lumbrales and tell him of my plight, but had little hope he would, and no certainty of the outcome, for where could I go if Fernando got me off again except to a different scaffold? Better to die for a Gypsy Goddess, I thought, than for a Spanish judge or an English Provost Marshal.

On the Eve of Saint Lucie's Day they came to my hut and dressed me up in fine clothes – well, fine to the Romany people, as breeches of black velvet though much worn, vest sewn with beads of glass and tarnished silver, and they fastened ribbons on

my shoulders and pom-poms on my shoes, and took me out into
the middle of their camp where all came to me and called me
Eraño, by which I understood them to mean Lord and Master.
Then they sat me on cushions in front of the biggest of their fires
and one of their ladies came and sat beside me, also decked out in
tinsel frippery, and they paid us homage, as if she were Queen
and I her Consort. There followed a Feast, with Gypsy Dancing,
and . . .

3

No. This will not do either. This is all phantasy, or most of it. If
there was ceremony, it was squalid; if there was dancing and music,
I was too terrified to mark it. The truth of it is this – one cold
December morning, with a sky like lead and crows in the trees,
when the black twigs of the oaks glistened with the rain of the
night before, all that dirty tribe, there were not above fifteen of
them, all blue with cold and shivering as much as I, took me out,
stripped off all I had on, and bound me to one of the trees that had
been lopped back to three stubby branches by the charcoal burners the season before, but high up with my head in the crutch of
it so I could see the road above us, less than a furlong off, and my
arms pulled back over two of the limbs, my knees bent and my
ankles pulled round the trunk with a cord to fasten them. Having
trussed me up thus – and they even lacked rope for it, and used
strands of a ground ivy called *periwinkle* – they went back to their
fires and pots, and it began to rain, a cold sleety sort of rain, so that
with the cold of it, the tightness of the thongs about my wrists and
ankles, the cruel way my arms were twisted and the pressure of the
rough bark on my naked shoulders and buttocks, I almost prayed
they would have their meal done quickly and get on with what
they had to do.

But they took their time and then Suero did indeed strum a
little and three or four of their drabs attempted to turn, but the

floor was wet and mud splashed up their legs so they soon gave in and went back to their stew.

Three bedraggled urchins, hair lank, wet and greasy, unshod with their feet in puddles, dressed in sodden rags, came and stood before me, thumbs in mouths, not above seven or eight years of age and all girls. They stared at me with blank gaze so I grew ashamed of my nakedness in spite of all.

At last their elders pushed away their platters and in two and threes gathered round my tree, but still about ten yards off, and all stared up at me from blank, black eyes, with the rain still streaming down their faces, and they seemed to be waiting for something, and at first I could not tell what, but then by craning my head round and twisting my neck I could spy their Count with his lurcher, and he was sharpening a knife, or rather sword-bayonet no doubt filched from some dead Rifleman. He was most earnest about it as if he wished it razor keen; and over the rasp of his stone the women began to croon a low sort of wailing dirge which I recognised, having heard it before from the gypsies about Salamanca. A sort of lament for their wandering exile, Englished it goes like this:

> The region of Chal was our dear native soil
> Where in fulness of pleasure we lived without toil
> Till dispersed through all lands 'twas our fortune to be
> – Our steeds, Agueda, must now drink of thee . . .
> Our horses should drink of no river but one
> It sparkles through Chal 'neath the smile of the Sun
> But they taste of all streams save that only – and see
> Our steeds, Agueda, must now drink of thee.

Now the Count was done and he came through their midst with his bayonet, and his woman following holding a brass basin with the lip cut away in one part, a barber's basin used for shaving or bleeding, and all fell silent so I could hear naught but the steady fall of the rain, naught save another song, undistinguishable before

because of distance and the gypsy lament, but now quite clear and
growing stronger every second . . .

> *I don't want the Sergeant's shilling*
> *I don't want to be shot down*

. . . and daring for a second to take my eyes off the Count's knife
I raised my head, shook the rain from my eyes and saw coming
down the road above the gypsy camp a company of red coats with
an officer on a fine bay mare in front leading a mule loaded with a
wicker and moleskin trunk, and a couple of waggons at the rear.

> *I'm really much more willing*
> *To make myself a killing*
> *Living off the pickings of the Ladies of the Town . . .*

One or two of the gypsies too now looked back over their
shoulders, but the Count came on, eager to carry out whatever it
was he was thinking on, and as he did I tried to shout out, but my
throat was tight and hoarse and only a croak came . . .

> *I don't want a bayonet up my bum hole*
> *I don't want my cobblers minced with ball*

And as His Lordship came with *his* bayonet for *mine* I at last got
some rain on my tongue and round my mouth, so my throat
cleared . . .

> *For if I have to lose 'em*
> *Then let it be with Susan*
> *Or Meg, or Peg, or any whore at all . . .*

. . . and at last they broke off for I hollered, and hollered, and had
the wit to holler in English, and I hollered all the more as the knife
made the first cut.

The first and last, for Patrick Coffey, until that moment Corporal Coffey, threw up his musket and with a snap at two hundred paces took off the Count's bonnet, and gave him the fright of his life, and as he did Captain Branwater drew his sword and spurred his little mare down the bank, hallooing wildly as if on a view, came through the thickets, and into the shabby tribe who fled in all directions before him, to cut me free, before I could receive any further hurt.

Coffey lost his Corporal's stripe for firing without command but said: 'Faith, I could do no other, for I heard the poor cratur had our tongue like a Limerick bhoy and I was sure he was none of your heathen Diegos at all'; and I lost that that has left me free from one temptation at least, though not all have believed me since, and I suppose I may call the loss a blessing.

'Halloo,' called Flora Tweedy, and the brown cliff streaked with lemon-yellow lichen above my head reverberated her cry, 'Halloo, Joseph. Joey, where are you?'

After a pause I raised my chin from where it had been cupped in my palm, and 'Halloo,' I answered, 'Mistress Tweedy, this way,' so that presently I descried her red coat and her long chestnut hair coming through the alders and the rowans below. At last she stood on the bank, a few paces from my boulder.

'Are you coming back yet?' she cried, voice still raised above the plashing and laughing of the water.

'What did you tell Mistress Reaney of me?'

She tossed her hair back over her shoulders.

'The truth, I suppose. That we found you on our way from Lumbrales to Roger's Town; that you had missed your way, were half-starved, and poorly.'

'What did you say I was doing there?'

'That you were returning to Sally Mankers with false news for the French, that by the time you were recovered the occasion for these news was gone; and so you stayed with us and listed as Captain Branwater's orderly.'

I shrugged and stood up.

'There's no harm in that, is there? Mistress Reaney can see none, I assure you.'

Taking her hand I jumped back on to the bank beside her.

'Come on, Joey, don't be such a silly. You cannot believe I would tell her aught to your discredit without there was a reason – even if I knew the whole story, which I don't.'

Together we made our way up to the Hermitage and as we went the odd story of my rescue was still in both our minds, so she knew what I meant when I said: 'How was it you came by so pat to save me?'

'Your friend Fernando came to us and said you were there and like to suffer; so Captain Branwater took the company on a detour that way – he did so for Fernando said you were English, and that's why the Captain paid the Chief Gypsy three gold guineas for you – and another for his spoiled bonnet and the fright he'd had.'

This was news to me, that Suero and Fernando had been the means of my escape, which I had until then put down to Fortune. Mistress Tweedy continued: 'The Captain thought you were English and near ten years younger than you are. It was quite a joke in the battalion when it was found he had a Spanish Rogue for his money, instead of an English drummer boy.'

At which I fell silent again, hurt to be called *Rogue* (though God knows I had worse on my conscience at that time than I have yet had courage to set down) until she squeezed my hand and began to tell me how a cat had arrived while I was gone, had taken some milk and some scraps and seemed likely to stay: ''Tis one of the tabby kind and has a torn ear, so must get in fights.'

'How are we to call it?'

'*Him*. Why we discussed that, and it was Mistress Violeta's conceit, bearing in mind he is a fighter, to call him *Wellington*.'

She coloured a little at this, and I forebore from remarking that Fighting Toms were usually Lovers as well as Fighters.

Chapter VI

The Same, Continued

I

One evening in the last week of February of our sojourn in that paradisial valley came a thunderstorm, a rare thing at that time of year but following a spell of almost Summer-like warmth that had brought forth yet more flowers, more than one would have thought possible, including daffodils, yellow star of Bethlehem, a purple lily whose name I did not know, and white ramsons whose leaves we chopped up for garlic flavouring for our stews. The storm coming late and at first distant, we had supped and were already snug in our cottage, the Hermitage, and gossiping away the last hour or so before bed, when the first rumbles tumbled about the peaks behind us.

The Hermitage was just one room, being not really a proper dwelling place at all but a cell and chapel used by any monk from the Trappists below inspired to even greater mortification, yet more single-minded devotion than their strict rule already enjoined, and at the time we arrived was not in use. It had but one door, one window, an unfurnished stone altar, and a small alcove near the door. With the Superior's permission we had made a fire near the middle, under the window, which was of course unglazed, and by this evacuated some, not all the fumes – however, there were not many of these, for the Monks had a store of charcoal which they invited us to be free of, as also goat-milk, cheese, fruits and vegetables, eggs and so on, nor would they take payment (not that we had above two silver duros to offer between the three of us) but imposed one condition only, namely that the two women should never venture within their wall, and so 'twas always I who went for provisions, and asked for any news.

In fact there were no news, beyond what the Superior told us when we arrived, namely what he had had of a shepherd who had lost his way six months before, that the French and the British had together invaded Spain, which prompted him to advise us that we were right to rest up at the Hermitage since to go about the country might be dangerous with foreign soldiery abroad. So self-sufficient were they, so cut off at the end of a long valley, with the nearest village two leagues away and living as simply as themselves, they had remained blissfully unaware of all the cataclysms of our century.

We had made our primitive lodging as snug and comfortable as may be – the Ladies had a bed of rugs thrown over broom branches by the altar, while I couched similarly in the alcove by the door; we had pillows and cushions stuffed with straw, and three stools also borrowed from the monastery, a plate each, a knife each, three cups hollowed from wood, two pans to cook withal, and that was the sum of our moveables, and they were sufficient. As I say, we were snug there, for the weather was never really cold, no frost all Winter long, and there was naught to bother or disturb us save memories of the past and presentiments of the future.

On the evening of the storm, as I recall it, Violeta was quizzing Flora about what was to come of her: not out of idle curiosity, nor in order to censure, but out of concern for her friend, whose predicament she took to be lamentable and desperate. Not so Mistress Tweedy, who sat on one side of the fire, quite quiet and tranquil, with Wellington upon her lap whose throat she sometimes tickled. 'Nay, Mistress Reaney, don't take on so. Things will work out for me, for us,' and she gave her belly an affectionate pat, already swelling a little beneath her green and red plaid skirt, 'I assure you. I am not ruined you know, at least very little more than I was. For what is ruin, but loss of reputation, and how can I who tramped about these hills and valleys, mountains and plains, in the unchaperoned company of a thousand men, for three years, how can I be said to have reputation?'

'Oh my friend, you have reputation for naught but goodness and kindness, I am sure . . . what is it?'

'Thunder. Did you not mark it?'

For a moment we were all mum, then it came again and the cat too pricked up an ear.

'Ay. 'Tis thunder. But Mistress Flora, how will you make out? How will you get by?'

'Well, well, as to that I shall have to see. But I make no doubt if I chuse to make my condition known where perhaps it should be known, I shall do very well indeed. Yet for that reason I may prefer to keep close; I should not like to be thought a fortune-hunter.'

At this perhaps a little colour rose in her neck though she remained composed and continued to soothe the cat who was now sensible of the distant storm.

'Oh, how glad I am,' and here Violeta clapped her hands, 'you must mean your Lover is free and will marry you, being a man of honour, when he is advised of the consequence of his wicked-ness . . .'

'Nay, you mistake me,' and here Flora sounded a little severe, 'but first – I do not count what happened wickedness, and not because I hold 'twas as much my deed as his. No, I am afraid he is not free; he is already married, but I am sure will, nevertheless, make very good provision for me an he knows he has occasion – he has done so for others I believe.'

There was a louder roll of thunder and Wellington the Cat now dropped to the floor where he paused to lick ferociously at his shoulder as if bothered by some flea or tick, then, the thunder apparently forgotten, he stretched out in front of the fire, but head still up and eyes alert. He was, by the by, not a full Tabby, having white bib and belly, and flanks more mottled black and tawney than striped.

'You make him sound a libertine,' it was I who spoke this time, and instantly regretted my intrusion into what, had our circumstances been more congruent to those pertaining in polite society, would have been that after supper hour when Ladies are wont to gossip alone, for there was now no mistaking the severity of Mistress Tweedy's reply.

'The Gentleman in question is assigned to duties whose gravity may be equalled by others' but is not I believe surpassed. He discharges them with meticulous nicety. I do not think he should be denied what solace he can find in the midst of such trials, nor should he be censured for doing so.'

'No, I am sure he should not,' I mumbled confusedly, and the thunder drowned my mumblings. This time the storm was close enough for the lightning to be discernible, despite the sacking draped over our window, and presently we heard the splashing of heavy rain-drops, not yet abundant in numbers but promising worse to come.

Violeta put aside her sewing. 'It puts me in mind of that great storm before the battle,' she said.

'Ay, that was a storm indeed,' said Flora, her composure quite recovered, though in truth it had not been much ruffled.

'Reaney was hurt there. Oh, how I wish I knew he was safe now. How I wish it!'

'You too were wounded, Joey, I think.'

'Scarcely. A spent ball hit my brow in the first attack – when I recovered consciousness, it was all over. All I then had were two black eyes, and an headache; and a stupid loss of memory which deprived me of all sense of where I was, or where I should be for a day or . . .'

I realised both were smiling, so I stopped, far more out of countenance than Flora had been.

'Here it comes. Lord, how heavy the rain is, and how bright the lightning. Almost it frightens me. And the cat too – I declare he is trying to get beneath your skirts, Mistress Flora. Welly, Welly, Welly come out. My, you should be ashamed, you reflect none of your namesake's virtues, I'm sure, come forth, you naughty creature . . .'

But as to his vices, that's another matter, I thought to myself, reflecting on the caterwauling of the night before, as well as his present situation which now seemed to alternate from being between the legs of one woman and in the arms of another, but I kept silent this time for I felt that thought expressed would have raised Mistress Tweedy's ire in good earnest, and I should have spent the night beyond doors with the cat, I make no doubt.

Almost I wished l had, for as it was, what with the thunder and the talk before it, I could not get out of my mind the events of that day, the Twenty-Second of July gone before, which, for all I have seen many terrible things and suffered much, I still count, and pray God I may always do, the very worst in my whole life.

A fortnight before that, early in the month, when our army faced Marmont's across the Duero, some ten leagues North of Salamanca, Captain Branwater had imparted news to me of truly dreadful substance – namely that following a standing order recently made all regiments were expected to muster every man possible in the battle line, this on account of the evenness with which the two hosts were matched, and that Colonel Wallace had noted that he, Branwater, was now the only officer in the Brigade who retained a personal servant.

'I'm sorry, Joey,' he had said, tapping his boot with his crop, his habit when put out, 'but Alec said it just won't do and you'll have to take your place in the line with the rest until we've given this Marmont a drubbing or two, and seen him off, which all expect in the next few days.'

I urged all the circumstances extraordinary to me which I believed should except me from this order, *viz*. – that I was a gentleman; that I had only listed to help Captain Branwater with my

knowledge of the language and the country and this out of gratitude to him for saving my life; that I was quite unskilled in
military arts: but none availed, least of all the latter – 'For as you
know, Joey, in most regiments every third man is a Portuguese
trained up to fight like a Briton, and most as little in the way of it
a year since as you are now, and some even listed only a month.
Besides, you have told me, and I have told others, how well you
did at Cabezón and Medina four years ago, so I'm sure you'll do
very well.'

I reminded him that I had fought then as an officer, at which
his brow darkened: 'Come, come, Joey,' he said, 'you must know
talk of that is nonsense,' and I said no more for I did not wish to
anger him.

So for a fortnight I carried my musket and my pack and my
sixty rounds of ball and cartridge, bayonet, blanket and kettle, and
all the rest, humping the lot from Toro to Salamanca on the last
three days in a most blazing and enervating heat, and expecting
every day the worst to happen, *viz.* – a general engagement, for
almost every day on that march we could see the French, often
they marched parallel and within two furlongs, so it came to cannonading, but never – where we were, at any rate – to musketry
or worse. When cannonaded our officers usually ordered us to lie
down so shot and shell passed over – a most judicious practice and
one which, had Rafael resorted to it at Cabezón, might have
brought him off unhurt and Violeta unbereaved of her only
brother; but that by the way.

As I say, we sat on the Duero for ten days and then marched to
and fro with no hurt save that inflicted by the sun and drought,
for three more. At the time the purpose was a mystery – with the
History of the Late Wars before me I now discover that the
armies being so evenly matched neither General was prepared to
risk a battle without some advantage, as of the ground, on his
side. Meanwhile we were always falling back towards Salamanca
for Marmont was always trying to get round us and on to our
communications with Ciudad Rodrigo, which following the

siege of the previous January was now the allied magazine. Thus on the Twenty-First we came again to the heights, no more than steep Downs, North of Salamanca, known as San Cristóbal, and we, that is the Third Division, under General Sir Edward Pakenham, were placed on the extreme right of our Army's position on a knoll overlooking the ford across the Tormes at Cabrerizos, barely a half-league North of Santa Marta where Rubén, Fernando, and I had hunted crayfish eleven years before and had had our first sight of an army, which occasioned Fernando the loss of a sock.

The next day he would lose the leg to put in it, for he was with the army, but I did not know it at the time.

We came to this knoll in the middle of the day of the Twenty-First and rested up there with our cooking pots over our fires, and I was glad to see to the South and East, in the woods and hills that lay towards Alba, little sign at all of the French: it was said they had gone off a league or so towards the fords at Huerta and Babilafuente, and so I reckoned another day as a soldier of the line had passed with no worse hurt than sore feet and an aching back. All around us was the dying bustle of a division preparing to bivouac, as of tents being raised, arms piled, the canon trundled into an improvised artillery park, the snorting and champing of horse as their riders groomed and foddered them, the coming and going of officers as pickets and *vedettes* were appointed, and I began to feel so long as things continued thus I might yet get to tolerate the life, for a short spell anyway.

This feeling was buttressed by news we presently had of Kevin Nolan who ever made it his business to seek out what was going on and to that purpose had slipped away to hang about the Divisional Staff to see what he could pick up. He returned looking glum, and this was what he said: 'Well boys, I make no doubt there'll be no great battle this Summer, for I've just heard there's more French coming up, and they're at a place called Pollos now. Sure Joey here will tell us how far off is that.'

'You're a great idjit,' cried Patrick Coffey, 'Pollos is the village on the Douro we were at four days since.'

'Why so it is, Patrick,' said Kevin, always equable, 'and moreover the King's Army is coming from Madrid as well, so before the week's out we'll be back in Roger's Town and on the line of the Agueda, or even in Portugal.'

I had already marked most of the Army called the River Duero by its Portuguese name *Douro*, since it was in Portugal they first came on it.

'So there'll be no fight?' I asked, for I wanted to be sure.

'Not unless this Marmont blunders in the next two days, and he's shown no sign of it yet.'

'Well that's a mighty shame,' said Patrick, lighting up his clay and spitting, 'for our numbers are even and we could lick them in straight fight. I some times wonder if Old Nosey's nerve has gone.'

'It's always been said his first care is for the lives of his men, as is the way of all good commanders,' I now propounded, 'he's surely right not to risk all on an even throw.'

'Aye, but that's my point – our numbers being even the chances are not, for man for man we can always lick old Johnny Trousers.'

So the dispute went on, but my heart was much lightened by what I'd heard and I was hard put to conceal this, for it was ever their phantasy to believe there was no greater joy for a soldier than facing shot, shell, ball, sabre, bayonet, which, with only as much consideration as was shown in their Marching Song, must be seen to be foolish nonsense.

At about this time a truly marvellous and portentous sight appeared in the West which silenced these gossips: the domes and spires, the Cathedrals and convents and colleges of Salamanca were now lit by an extraordinary magical effect, as of the sun shining round and beneath huge palaces of purple cloud, piled higher and higher to the very zenith of the sky where they were capped with an anvil-shaped plume of purest white, and already lightning flickered in these clouds and thunder rumbled.

An hour or so later, as an early darkness was coming on and that huge cloud was now almost above us and the sun quite obscured, we discovered that the army was not fixed after all, and leaving our game of football, a favourite pass-time with Coffey and Nolan, we stood on our knoll and watched it passing division by division, column by column beneath us, forty thousand strong, and some into the ford below, others down to Santa Marta, and some up the road into the Town there to cross dryshod by the Roman Bridge, but we remained fast where we were for the night. Kevin said this was a sign all the French were across the river to the East, and our place in the line by this latest manoeuvre quite reversed – whereas before we had been the right flank of our army, we would soon be its left, and all this without moving a step. Well, I daresay he was right, and I hoped when we should next be called upon to alter our position we should be able to do it with as little effort, though I doubted we should be so fortunate.

At about six or seven o'clock the storm broke on us and put all thought of strategies and tactics from our minds, I think few of us cared much where the French were, for it was the mightiest storm I have ever witnessed. Lightning and thunderbolts rained down first over the City, silhouetting its monuments against the inky blackness of the sky, then came on all around us, with a roar of thunder more grand than any cannonading, and cloudburst after cloudburst, so soon all was soaked and the red earth of our hillock was washed away in gushing runnels right down to the bare rock in places, and this in only moments. By the lightning we could see the poor fellows of the Light Division, the last to cross the river that night, caught up to their waists in the flood, their rifles above their heads, and truly we saw one poor soul struck and no doubt killed by the bolt or drowned straight after; and between the peals of thunder, though in truth there was very little respite, we marked the terrified neighing of horses, some of which broke loose and could be seen in the flashes which came so close as to seem prolonged, careering down the further bank between the poplars and aspens, manes and tails tossing, white eyes rolling.

In all this, feelings of sublime grandeur alternated with those of fear and both at last gave way to those of that hilarity that only rankest buffoonery can provoke, and this because our Corporal now came amongst us, the egregious Prigg, not yet retired to the Baggage with his self-inflicted wound, and on this occasion with an absurd design he said would make the four tents of our section proof against the storm. What he wanted us to do was hoist two of them above the other two, to provide a double layer, and thus he said keep all our gear and ourselves the drier, notwithstanding that each remaining tent would now have to shelter twice as many men as before. We humoured him for a time, but when the weight of the first dismantled tent, already sodden, was thrown on its neighbour and it collapsed, and him inside it so the fabric heaved and billowed about like a great black monster in the almost dark, we went away and ensconced ourselves as comfortably as we could in the two left us. When Prigg had extricated himself, he came and begged to be let in, which Coffey refused, saying we were now too crowded, and this Coffey partly did to avenge himself for the loss of a football game Prigg had caused a month before, but he gave in in the end when Prigg whiningly threatened to fetch a Sergeant to make us obey. Once in he excused himself again and again with his old refrain of: 'I'm sorry, but it seemed like a good idea at the time; I'm sorry, but it seemed like a good idea at the time.'

As I say the risibility of all this countered the terror and some of the discomfort caused by the storm, which passed by midnight, leaving a rain-washed sky filled with stars beneath which all presently slept.

2

We stood to an hour before sunrise, on what was to be the worst day of my life, and no hint then of the horrors to come. Below us the grey plain and hills turned to tawny stubble, yellow corn, and the dark green of oaks still with a soft bloom on them like that on a grape – this the rain of the night, shortly exhaled by the sun to lie in lilac-tinted mist above the river and in the folds between the hills. A stork rowed through the air above it and between the poplars below us, its great white and black wings like the sweeps of a river barge, and up above us a lark spilled its song until, no bigger than a Mote in the Empyrean, its winking wings caught the first beams of *Sol*.

And all across the plain to the East and up into the hills towards Alba our great host stirred itself, bivouac fires were lit and an hundred columns of thread-like blue smoke rose into the sky as kettles were boiled up; horses neighed, and here and there Staff bustled about, a squadron of Dragoons rode out to see what the French were up to, a bugle blew and was answered by another.

After stand-to and our Sergeant telling us there'd be no move for us for a time Coffey said: 'Kev, you be off now down to the Baggage Park and see if you can wheedle a screw of tay out of Mistress Tweedy, and Joey, you take this kettle down to the river, for we'll have a brew-up to chase out the damps and cramps of the night.'

'Those are very fine suggestions,' said Prigg, and repeated them as if they were his own.

Down by the river as I stooped to fill the kettle I came upon a strange sight, a man crouched amongst the reeds, and so still the moorhens scooted and chirped by him as if he were not there – indeed I had not seen him myself at first, so when I had recovered from the start his presence gave me I wondered if he was not a spy sent to discover our Army's dispositions, a suspicion strengthened by the fact he was busily sketching with pencil on a pad of white paper.

'Well Sir,' he said, 'what are you staring at?'

'Nothing, I'm sure,' I replied, 'I'm just here to fill my kettle.'

'Then get on with it.' His tone was petulant, even irascible, and now I looked more closely I saw he was a Gentleman and one of rank. He had a large nose like the upside-down bow of a ship, thin lips, and masterful chin. On the bank beside him was the gear of an artist – colour-box and so forth – and a Dragoon's sabre and a Dragoon's white-plumed helmet.

As I straightened with my kettle full, a Lieutenant also attired in the accoutrements of a Dragoon came by and saluted smartly: 'General Marchant, there's an order just come from the Commander,' and 'Right, Naseby, I shall be along presently,' said my artist, and began to pack up his stuff.

This General Marchant did well enough before dusk, but was shot in the groin and the spine which killed him, none of which I knew then, but reflected only to myself that it was an oddly led army I was in where Generals spent the morning at their sketching.

Back on the hill the morning wore on pleasantly enough, though by eleven or before the day was hot, yet the air remained extraordinarily clear, the result no doubt of the storm before, so we could see great distances clearly, perceiving details normally lost, and this persisted till late afternoon when there was smoke and dust enough to obscure all but the closest view. All in all it was more peaceful a start to the day than was usual when we would have been marching along in the heat and the French with us, and artillery fire to interrupt our progress, as above. Of course it was not entirely peaceful. Towards nine o'clock we heard the distant crackle of musketry and the deeper thump of cannon quite fierce and prolonged, and this I supposed to be about a league up the Alba road, but due to the rising ground hidden from us. About then our officers came among us and set us to throwing up an earth work with palisades, but whether this served any military object other than to keep us from being idle, most of us doubted. At ten the Baggage Train began to move out of its Park below us with an escort of Dragoons, heading into the City to cross by the bridge, and this cast more gloom on my fire-eating companions for they took it as a sure sign we would soon be following it down the road to Roger's Town: in short everything indicated the prognostications of the night before were justified and an orderly retreat, each division covering another's movements in turn, back to the security of a fortress town would shortly be under way.

When our orders to move came there seemed no reason to doubt this was still the case; Kevin discovered we were to march South by West across the plain behind the main force of our Army (which pleased me you may be sure) to assemble again near a hamlet called Aldea Tejada.

'Do you know this place then, Joey?' asked Patrick.

'Certainly I do,' I answered. 'It's a league South of the City and I know it very well, it being a scant two miles from a village called Los Arapiles where I passed most of my childhood.'

'So how far have we to march then?'

I calculated a moment: 'Five miles or two leagues at most.'

'Well boys, that's not far; and a lot less than yesterday,' and so saying he hoisted his pack on his back and fastened his straps beneath his arms, and just as I was doing likewise we heard another roll of gunfire, more persistent and deeper than before, as though several batteries were now in action, and coming from a point more Southerly than before; and now there was some smoke too, billowing then spreading like a white stain in the still blueness about five miles off.

'Why, Joey, what is it? He's gone quite pale.'

''Tis nothing . . . well, this: can you make out a height, flat-topped above the plain beneath that smoke?'

'Ay, and another beyond it. They must overlook most of the country there about,' said Kevin. 'It looks to me as if they are disputed, which one would expect.'

'Ay, they dominate all the plain about there,' I said. 'They are the Arapiles from which my village takes its name.'

'And the village lies near them?'

'A mile to the West, in a dip.'

'Perhaps you fear for the people there. I should not though, for surely all will have left it by now.'

'Most left two autumns since. 'Twas twice ravaged by the French.'

We crossed the river by the Santa Marta ford at noon but now there was no Angelus, the bell no doubt having been long since melted down for ordnance or shot, by one Army or another. Yet it was strange indeed to march along that road with Kevin beside me and Patrick in front, in the midst of three thousand men, and that less then a tenth of the whole host, where eleven years before the French had marched and Rubén, Fernando, and I had watched with thumbs in mouths and then swaggered beneath the poplars beside them; but soon recollections of that day fell behind with the ford itself, for now instead of taking the road to the town we set off up hill and down dale away from the river, so soon all there was in front of us was the rolling plain beneath the baking sun, the stubble where the corn was cut, but most of it still stand-ing which occasionally we trampled on which seemed a shame and a waste, but also much fallow, just brown parched grass, for latterly there had been few to plough and sow and little inclination since all that grew was took by the French.

Over on our left the gunfire continued towards the Arapiles and smoke hung over them; but at least it did not seem to come nearer, nor grow in intensity, indeed all seemed much as it had on other days. In short we swung on merrily enough for all the dust and heat, and when the band did not play Patrick led the men about him in his favourite song, which I knew well enough by now to join in:

> *On Monday I touched her on the ankle*
> *On Tuesday I touched her on the knee*

. . . a pair of kites circled and soared above us and a hoopoe flapped out of a copse of oaks left standing in a dip. And some time about then, though of course none of us knew it, some where about then as we were marching between Santa Marta and

Aldea, it must have been (if I am to believe the History in front of me) that Lord Wellington was dining off a cold chicken in the garden of a farm house a mile or so off between us and the Lesser Arapil when a Staff Officer rode up and 'My Lord, the French are extending to their Left,' he said. 'The Devil they are,' the Peer replied, and threw the drumstick to the ground, wiped his fingers, mounted and rode up on to that height where once I had brooded over Rubén's streaming scalp and later entertained poor María Victoria – she in her white shift with poppies in her hair.

> On Wednesday such caresses
> As I got inside her dresses
> On Thursday she was moving sweetly . . .

. . . and after watching the progress of the French to the West, beyond the village, their front division spread out in a most unmilitary fashion, his Lordship put up his glass, and, 'By God, that will do,' he said.

Meanwhile we plodded on, the gunfire so monotonous I almost forgot it, the sweat now pouring down our faces and soaking into our jackets still damp from the night before, hoarse and tired after three hours marching, but still singing, until at just about three o'clock we came up with Divisional Staff, we being the last company in the division then, came up with them and grounded arms, for all about us were already getting out their pots and kindling fires . . .

> On Friday I had my fingers in it
> On Saturday she gave my balls a wrench

. . . six horsemen coming across the plain from the Lesser Arapil, but two well in front, one of them in a blue frock-coat and small cocked hat, dressed like a country gentleman out hacking (and 'By Christ,' said Patrick, 'if it isn't old Atty himself'), reined in in front of our General, not more than twenty paces from us and pale and breathless as he was, leant forward and tapped our General on the shoulder with his crop. 'Ned,' he said, 'move on with the Third Division, take the heights in your front, and drive everything before you.'

> *And on Sunday after supper*
> *I had the fucker up her*

. . . 'I will, my Lord,' the fool replied, 'if you will give me your hand,' which his Lordship duly obliged with.

> *And now she's got me up before the bench*

It's no simple and straightforward matter to get three and a half thousand men out of marching and into fighting order, all arranged by brigades, regiments, and companies, properly stationed, dressed and distanced, and it was close on an hour before we were ready to move, and hotter and thirstier than ever when we were, and short in the temper too. All the while I was growing more frightened, for it seemed the only height the Peer could mean was that of the Greater Arapil which stood three miles to the left of our front, steep and ramparted with cliffs and impossible to take I should have thought if properly held – indeed later many Portuguese lost their lives attempting it – but before we moved off it became clear that the height intended was a Down a league West of the Arapil, along which the French Left was stationed and about two miles due South of us.

At last we were ready, the infantry drawn up in two brigades in open column of companies, that is to say each company of up to an hundred men arranged in two files marching fifty abreast, with a space equivalent of fifty men between each company, and a similar space between the two brigades. We, that is our company of the Eighty-Eighth, were tolerably near what appeared to be the rear of the left hand column, that is there were ten or a dozen companies ahead of us of the Forty-Fifth, and Seventy-Fourth; I was positioned eight men in from the right in the rear file; on our left there were a regiment of Portuguese *Caçadores* in open skirmishing order with three companies of British Rifles in green jackets and blue trousers with them; far over to the right near a thousand horse, and in our midst eight guns – thus being towards the rear and in the midst of this vast concourse of men and *matériel* I took some comfort: it looked to me that the worst of what had to be done would be achieved before I got there. Only ignorance of military formations can excuse this, coupled with my natural tendency to see the best side of things – my cheeriness should have been belied by the comportment of Coffey and Nolan: both were pale, Patrick in front displayed a sort of irritable impatience, Kevin beside me was thoughtful, it seemed, then I marked the tiny beads of a rosary almost concealed in his fist half-inching one by one between thumb and forefinger; yet still I did not or would not believe the worst.

We fixed bayonets. The Colours in our midst were unfurled, the Colour Party being in the company ahead of us, and fluttered bravely across our line of march for a breeze from the West had come up. The band began to play and the Lieutenant in front of our company, Lynton was his name, turned to us and said, 'Now, boys, let's sing with the band if sing we must, for none here wishes to die with a bawdy song on his lips, I'm sure,' then he drew his sword, the Sergeant blew his silver whistle, 'By the right, Company, March,' and we were off. It was four o'clock or a little after.

There is a sort of lightheadedness at such times, a giddiness, a downright irrational irresponsibility, and not just from the rum – blue skies, bands playing, flags blowing, the ground shaking to the tread of feet, horses neighing, cannon wheels rumbling: almost it's enough to make one forget the steady roar like surf beneath all, the roar of the battle we were marching into. Patrick turned and gave a cheery wink over his shoulder to me, Kevin kissed the cross of his beads and put them up, and I felt a fine man indeed as I changed my step to get in with theirs, a fine man amongst fine men.

We marched thus for twenty minutes before the uneven terrain of low falls and downs we were going through began to drop gradually away into a more even plain – a change that gave us a clear view of what was toward. The first thing was over to our left above the green of the Rifles and the brown of the Portuguese, but close enough, a most magnificent and stirring sight – namely two brigades of cavalry – the heavy Dragoons in front and the light behind, the heavy in brass helmets and red jackets, the light in tall brown fur caps with blue dolmans and crimson and gold sashes, close on two thousand of them, and just as we drew level they began to walk forward and the westering sun flashed from their giant sabres as they drew them and the ground trembled beneath their hooves.

Beyond them the view unfolded and now I glimpsed the belfry of my Father's church, but the bell taken, in a dip, with three more divisions like ours ranged on the downs above it, and beyond that the Lesser Arapil, its slopes thronged with scarlet, and it seemed to me that it was in front and beyond the village, that is to the South and East of us that most of the fighting was taking place – here was cannonading and French light troops in open order skirmishing about the outer sheepfolds and smaller cottages, while beyond them stood their main body, deep ranks of blue and white and a long line of cannon that flashed and banged, flashed and banged, pumping round puffs of white smoke into the clear air above them. All this a mile and more, perhaps two, off to our left, and glimpsed over and in front of the ranks of our cavalry, and none of the shot coming our way, so still it seemed a sight of colour and even beauty, a great thing to be part of.

About now our direction of march changed obliquely to the right and West, so all this fell away behind our left shoulders and now to our left front we could clearly see the height or Down we were making for, still a thousand yards off, and as we dropped lower into the basin in front it correspondingly seemed to rise higher, though never much, for it is very low in truth, unless it supports, as it did then, a long line of blue and white – which had the effect of making it seem as dangerous to attempt as an Alp or Pyrenee. Our approach had been marked. Some cannon were now deployed and in a moment or two the first shot and shell fell on our foremost ranks. This did not bother us particularly, being at present towards the rear as we were, though soon we found in our path the maimed bodies of the fallen and these did nothing for my spirits at all – although not yet under direct fire it was about then I discovered what should have been clear an hour before, that I was caught up in a Battle, which is to say a *machine*, a *mechanism* that keeps even the most watery of joints, stumbling and shaking, on the move, one-two, one-two, to the beat of drum and the wail of bagpipe, pushing me on into something I knew I wished no part of at all. I was in a place I hated to be in, already suffering sights and sounds that terrified me, about to do things beyond my nature or ability to do. I think then I looked wildly about me for Kevin glanced at me and 'Steady, Joey,' he cried, for the noise was already far too loud for ordinary speech, 'Steady – not long now,' and his last word was drowned by a bigger explosion than all before, behind my right ear and I thought we were blown to bits, but glancing back discovered our cannon on the crest of the slope we had just crossed, banging away above our heads and all together at the French across the plain.

About now shouts and musketry on the right drew our atten-tion and above the heads of our other brigade we could see the sudden onslaught of French Troopers, the flash of sabres, the rear-ing of horses and their screams, the cries of men hacked in the shoulder and head; and then musketry to our left and a cloud of French light soldiers had come down the slope in front of us and were engaging our Rifles and the Portuguese. It seemed to me at this point that the ardour with which we were resisted on both flanks would have perfectly justified a halt and a retreat – even the most elementary of military manuals I am sure say that to be flanked on both sides at once argues that a position is untenable, but no, we went steadily on, obliquely up the slope towards the crest, and as we did the French Riflemen, *Tirailleurs* and *Voltigeurs*, fell back, and cheers further off on our right, discernible above the din, and the sight of our Dragoons engaging the French horse, showed the respite I longed for was not to be. Yet still I comforted myself on my position, in the centre of the column with forty files to my left, a company to my right, and two thousand men in front.

At this moment the bugle blew, Lieutenant Lynton in front of us flung out his left arm, the Sergeant on his right blew his whistle and did likewise and the true dreadfulness of our formation came home to me. What happened was this: the end files on my left halted and marked time, the files on my right quickened and lengthened their strides and the whole brigade by companies thus formed line, the right hand files of each company sweeping round to lock into place beside the stationary left hand files of the company in front of them. I believe what we did is known as 'bringing our right shoulders up'.

The effect of this madness was that we were now a thin red line, only two deep, and Patrick Coffey alone stood between me and the whole French Army. Behind us the other brigade had performed the same nonsense, so they too were now a line two deep, following an hundred paces in our rear. The crest was only fifty yards above us and now suddenly filled with phalanxes of blue with muskets levelled at us; I heard the Lieutenant carrying our nearest Colour, now ten yards from me, shout, 'That fellow is aiming at me,' and the boy next to him answered, 'I hope so for I thought he had me covered,' and then a thousand muskets flashed in front of us, Major Murphy riding before the Colours fell, his stirrup caught, and his horse bolted, dragging him rolled and tumbled in the dust and grit down the corridor between the armies, Kevin was gone, but no, simply he had moved forward into the place vacated by Patrick's neighbour the top part of whose skull was shot away, my left hand neighbour pushed me into Kevin's place and I remembered the rule – fill in towards the Colours; a wild voice screamed from another horse nearby and I saw it was Pakenham himself, our under-age General – and 'Let them loose,' he was bellowing, 'Let them loose,' and our older

Colonel called more coolly, 'Right lads, push on to the muzzle,' and what was left of our line fired an answering volley and charged across the gap, all hollering and screaming like madmen, before the French could reload.

From where I was lying I saw Patrick Coffey himself reach up and wrest from the dying hand of a Frenchman his silver and gilded Eagle the 'Jingling Johnny' he later called it on account of the silver bells on it, then I put my head under my arm and kept as still as I could, for the second brigade was coming on after the first and like to trample over me.

When they had gone too I tried to take stock of my situation – I was dazed, deafened, blinded by smoke and dust; though not hurt I expected to be maimed or shattered at any moment; it seemed quite clear to me that the advantage of the slope above me was with the French, that numbers were too (though in this the History tells me I was quite wrong, that owing to a blunder on the French Commander's part and the quickness of ours in exploiting it, we had at that point of the field an advantage of two to one), that in only a matter of moments all would be hurled back, or all that still survived, and the ground I was on would be overrun with bayoneting, sabring French; in short, it was time to get myself off while these gallant lads above me held back the tide. Where to go? Dazed I was, and out of my mind with terror – where to go but home, and that's where I made for though the nearest hovels were still five furlongs off.

However, I was dogged in my desire to get there, and would not willingly allow myself to be put off it, having thus got the idea fixed in my mind, and this despite the fact that obstacles of the most weighty sort were put in my way – as a cavalry charge of some two thousand horse, for I had scarcely got clear on my way when more bugles blew up on the hill down which and round which we had come, bugles high and shrill, answering each other in rising crescendo, and then over the top they came, the two divisions of cavalry we had seen earlier on our left, now at a steady trot which even as I halted, right in their track, became a canter.

There was a shallow ditch running through the sharp corn stalks at my feet, dug in times of peace to mark the boundary between two parcels of land, and into this I buried myself; but not before I had seen an extraordinary sight and that was a covey of larks or fieldfares spin out of the stubble in front of the horse and wheel away above my head, and as I did I thought, 'They'll have my empty skull to nest in, in the Spring.'

Yet the horse followed the birds over me, file after file after file, then a pause, and then yet more, and I took no hurt at all, save a shaking from the ground that quaked beneath them, though by reason of keeping my face in the dirt missed what our Commander categorised thus: 'I never in my life saw anything more magnificent,' but then he was not so close to it as I, nor perhaps did he see the punishment they did, and for all who may read this and have read thus far with excitement at these great events mingled perhaps with amusement at my expense, I beg them now to pause a moment and consider this: a heavy cavalry-sword has a blade above a yard long and weighs several pounds; wielded by a strong arm backed, if it's done properly, by much of the power of his galloping charger, it inflicts a wound more terrible than any caused by shot or plosive shell; a wound that is rarely immediately mortal, but cannot be recovered from if the blade had gone home truly, for it will have butchered its way through collar-bone and ribs, lungs and liver, and left one side of a man hanging loose from the other. I judge it to be more than should be asked of any man to put up with handling of this sort.

Once the cavalry had gone by, led by the General I had seen sketching at dawn on the banks of the Tormes, who was shot dead in spine and groin some minutes later, though after sabring a few himself, I make no doubt, the rest of my way to the village was tolerably clear, and I picked myself up and ran as fast as my already foolishly weakened legs would carry me, but so passed across the slope down which our Fifth Division had marched on its way to engage the French, and they having been cannonaded had left some litter behind them as dead, maimed and dying, and a spent shot on which I stubbed my toe – the impetus of my charge and the slope falling away, I fell heavily and awkwardly, both knocking the wind out of my lungs and stunning the side of my head on a low boulder so that for the second before I fainted away, I felt sure that after all I had been hit.

I was not unconscious for long – when I came to the roar of battle seemed no further nor nearer. I opened my eyes after a space during which I became almost sure that I was not badly hurt, but found some difficulty in bringing them into focus – a symptom I believe of concussion; what I eventually made out a yard or so from my face was a clump of pink and white everlastings, but already faded and dried by the Summer heat so much they resembled in their life-like but dead repose the *immortelles* sold here in Pau market in Winter when the season for fresh flowers is gone, and in their desiccated beauty found a sort of peace or comfort and, feeling a gratitude that they were there, fell to a study of them for several minutes. But nothing lasts for ever – they had survived, dead though they were, the drought, the storm, the reapers, and a division of foot that must have passed by within yards, but now as I watched first the air above them seemed to bend then shimmer, then before my eyes the outer petals shook, turned grey, black, shrivelled until at last the dead but miniature suns they were burst into stars of live brief flame.

I lifted my head some inches and thereby altered my whole perception of the landscape – the dried grasses, tansies, cudweed and everlastings all about was on fire – a low fire, whose flames were often invisible in the sunlight, but which blackened then consumed all before it as it moved unevenly in fits and starts, pursued by the breeze like dust before a broom. Ants and spiders scuttled in its van, a tiny pale blue moth fluttered above before its wings too shrivelled in the heat and it dropped in.

This small fire and there were several like it, was caused by the cartridge papers that now littered the field and blew about it – clearly it prevented me lying where I was longer and I set off again for the village. I suppose I was lucky to be able to; a soldier I passed who lacked a foot was now much bothered by one of these fires which he endeavoured to extinguish with his bonnet.

I passed into the village on the North-West side, away from the track and quite near the church, and thus came to my Father's cottage without a challenge though I passed near where the wounded Fusiliers and Guards were brought who had defended it, and a handful of French prisoners too. The bombardment of the village had ceased, the French guns opposite now being occupied with the divisions that generally assaulted their front.

My Father's chimbley, the unique feature of the house, had fallen and partly dropped through the roof – the result I thought of shot, but this, as will be seen, was wrong. I paused at the latch gate in the wall. The garden had grown rank then dried into deadness; there were almonds ripe on the one tree and the brown nuts dropped through their withering cases into the wilderness below; one hive was still upright and the busy bees maintained yet the commonwealth my parent had been so pleased to study, and a line of self-seeded tomatoes ripening green and red stood witness to his last attempt at agriculture; the chicken hutch shattered and empty, the stone cover on the well split. The door to the kitchen swung broken from one hinge and the lintel was blackened, and that of the lower floor window too, by the fire set there by retreating French the Autumn before. I pushed in and for one second the darkness, the coolness and the almost silence (for the noise of the battle though still tremendous seemed now remote) near broke my heart with familiarity so almost I thought to hear Tía Teresa admonish me to wipe my feet.

But then my eyes grew accustomed, for it was dark only by contrast, and I apprehended the continuing ruin of my home, and worse than ruin: my gaze crossed the litter of fallen plaster, broken crocks, charred moveables to a larger pile of what at first I thought was refuse lying by the stairs and covering the first three steps.

This is the truth of the matter, near enough. News had been brought me the previous autumn of their two deaths – Tía Teresa's and my Father's, and, for two reasons, after hearing them, I had stayed away until now, the day of the Battle. The first was his Will, but that perhaps by way of excuse; the second was out of guilt at the manner of his death, which, to be brief, was the result of my friend Coulaincourt employing a 'Joseph to keep off a Julián'.

Tía Teresa died in the fire, I was told, my Father five days later, but of what, unless shock and old age, was not made clear: María Victoria's Mother brought me these news, and that all who had been in the village and survived this last assault had now left. She omitted to say that they had neglected to bury the dead before leaving.

The heap of refuse at the foot of the stairs was what was mortal of Tía Teresa. The tatters of her black skirts still clung about her bones, and her shawl was wrapped about her head. Beneath it, still attached to her skull her white hair peeped and even stirred in the air I caused to move about her as I stooped. She had not been burnt at all, but perhaps suffocated in the fumes. I mounted the stairs – one rotten gave beneath me – filled with dread at what I now felt sure I must find.

The first room was where the chimbley had fallen, bringing in the roof and smashing his clavier to the floor: wind-blown leaves, dust, bird-droppings, and a pool of water from the storm of the night before betokened that it was not shot of the raging battle had brought it down. Many of his books were scattered about the floor – Newton, Descartes, Priestley and Bentham, and the pages that stirred showed signs of mildew; but his brass microscope still gleamed on the table. As I lingered, not wishing to go further, I was suddenly jarred with fright by the swoop and tweet of a swallow, all two-pronged barred tail and red blush of breast, visiting its young, surely by now its second brood, in their mud pellet home in a ceiling corner above the shelves; then it was gone back through the roof to skim and flit above the blood, terror, and heat in the valley beyond.

I pushed into the inner room, a dried lath cracked beneath my feet, and I discovered what I had feared – the old man sat up in his cot against a pillow, the sockets of his eyes eyeless, the skin

on his brow yellowed and cracked to show the bone, yet some
of his straggly beard still there. The tatters of his night-shirt still
cased his ribs and did service as a shroud. What was most odd
was the ruins of his learning strewn about him – his books
open, many with the pages, ripped, as if in frenzy he had tried
to spoil them.

I drew nearer and discovered the Will he'd left with Mr Curtis
was not his Last Testament – for in his hand, on the coverlet
above his knee, he held a framed slate he'd used to school me and
then the children of the village. On it three words inscribed:

– NADA . . . NIENTE . . . NOTHING

3

How long I remained there I cannot be sure – perhaps an hour,
for in that time a sort of leaden gloaming gathered in the room
and the noise of gunfire first grew to a terrible crescendo as the
French mounted a counter-attack between the village and the
Lesser Arapil and then receded as it was beaten off so that I heard,
when it came, the chink and scrape of stone, and a muttered oath
in the garden below. A Winter storm had blown the casement in;
its broken frame and shards littered the floor and splintered
beneath my feet. I looked out, and below me, but not far, indeed
quite close for it was after all but a cottage and a tall man like Mr
Curtis could not stand upright in the kitchen, below me in the
tiny wilderness of the ruined garden a soldier, one side of his face
blackened and his coat beneath in shreds, one arm coated in
drying blood, was trying to shift the broken cover off the well. He
must have heard me, for now he looked up.

'I say,' he called, his voice cracked, 'do you know if this is dry
or not?'

'I . . . I don't know. It never dried before.'

'Then give us a hand with it, there's a good chap.'

I came down and shifted the lid for him – he was a brown-haired youth, an Ensign of Fusiliers – and we dropped a pebble in, listening for its echoing splash, and marked the silver rings expanding in the blackness below. I found Teresa's bucket and rope, where they'd always been, just inside the door, the bucket a wooden one made ten years before by Fernando's uncle who had the cooper's art, and we found it still held water as on the day he proved it.

The Fusilier plunged his face in it then made me tip it over his head so the water cut runnels of silver through and across the powder burns on his cheek, at which he winced and shook himself.

'Dear God, that's better.'

I let the bucket down again, heard Teresa's voice warn me not to let it bang against the sides, felt the weight come as the water flooded in, and pulled.

'Well, thanks,' said the Ensign, as I offered it to him – he was now lying with his back to the almond tree – 'but there's others outside need it now more than I . . . be a good chap and take it to them – this arm of mine is deuced painful . . .' He paled and groaned as he tried to move it. 'And I think it beyond me to carry a bucket.'

'Do you need a surgeon?' I asked.

'If you find one unoccupied, then perhaps yes I do. But my arm's not bleeding now, I think, so I'll live for a bit longer with it. It hurts like the blazes but I have an affection for it, and though doubtless it will have to come off, you need not hurry with the saw-bones.' Here he closed his eyes and I thought had fainted, but anon he opened them again. 'Run along, there's a good chap,' he murmured.

In the little square by the Church I found more wounded and went about them with my bucket, refilling it several times before an officer amongst them declared them satisfied and suggested I should go beyond the village, where he made no doubt I should find many more who would be grateful for a drink. I was somewhat loth to do this, for the battle still raged beyond, though certainly further off; however, I still had on my red coat, and he his Lieutenant's epaulette, so I deemed it an order, and set off.

I need not have worried, indeed my new occupation seemed likely to keep me out of harm for many hours, for although the nearest fighting was still less than half a mile off, and that very fierce indeed where the French centre still held – though even on my first trip they began to fall back up the slopes towards the Greater Arapil and beyond – there were between many hundreds of wounded and dying, perhaps thousands, for this area East and South of the village was the cockpit most bitterly contested in the field, the one place where for a time the result of the battle had been in doubt, and this struggle had left a litter of smashed and maimed beneath a pall of dust and smoke. Amongst them more of the tiny fires I had witnessed before flared up sizzling and crackling through the trampled thistles and stubble, dried flowers and brown grass.

I continued here for several hours. The noise of battle drew off steadily, dusk gathered, the dust settled and the smoke dispersed; the hideous screams of the newly hurt became less frequent, less piercingly close, and moans and sobs were what guided me once the darkness fell. For a time I made distinction between the colours of the uniforms about me, pedantically favouring the brown over the blue and the red over the brown, but soon found myself in places where the blue predominated and the oaths and prayers were in French, Polish, Italian and tongues other than the Portuguese, German or English. Moreover, in one of the rare moments I allowed my mind to dwell on the parcel of bones in my Father's cot, I seemed to hear his voice rebuke me for such niceness.

With the final moments of the day I recall I paused on a low knoll, a spur of the Lesser Arapil, from which I had an extensive view of the plain, and there let my aching back straighten and my stiff arms rest limbs surely an inch longer from those buckets (I had taken a second from a smashed up cannon) yet not a thing to complain of when so many about were shortened by far more.

There I saw, beneath a bank of low black cloud, the last nail-paring of crimson sun whittled away by the turning earth and knew the hill a league off that masked it was that where our Division had begun its attack. I wondered how Patrick and Kevin fared, if they were hurt, if I should look for them, but the suffering nearest claims one's first duty. In the other direction, on the slopes that led up to the oak forest and the road to Alba, a line of muskets flamed orange, and then again, and a group of horse wheeled to a distant bugle. Behind the Greater Arapil and out of my view, cannon still thudded.

There was nothing majestickal or sublime in the scene, nothing at all. Distantly I could hear the bells of Salamanca peal, those that were left, but their message had nothing to do that I could comprehend with what lay about me. Nearer at hand a line of dim lamps signified the approach of waggons called back from the Baggage Train, and, in a converging line, some carts and carriages from the Town itself also came for the wounded. Though I did not know it then, Flora Tweedy was with the former, Violeta Reaney with the latter, and both laboured till dawn; for a time they met and became briefly acquainted – but so wide was the expanse, so great the number of hurt, near on sixteen thousand I believe, I did not meet them.

But the night was not without its coincidence for me – amongst the voices that called for help, for a surgeon, or for a hand to hold as they died, there were few, indeed I only heard the one, that called in Spanish, and this because the Spanish Division in the Army had been held back in reserve. The one I did hear was familiar enough, though wrenched by pain from its normal gruff friendliness, and was that of Fernando.

On account of his intimate knowledge of the ground he had been sent by Don Julián to Lord Wellington to act for the latter as guide, which service he had performed till struck in the knee by a ball which shattered it. I stayed with him for an hour until two drunken surgeons came up – these gave him a mug of rum to drink off, a piece of leather to bite on, and bade me hold him down while by the light of two *Argand* oil lamps they sawed through his hip and took off his leg. As they did I recollected my studies, long since abandoned, had tended to their occupation. A boy with them smeared the stump with tar from a can, and they went on to their next. They were not with us above five minutes.

The darkness came in on us like a tide as they moved off and after a time I supposed Fernando slept or was in a faint and so endeavoured to disengage my hand from his.

'Pepe,' he murmured, 'before you go, do me one further favour.'

I assured him I would do all I could for him. He asked me if the surgeons had taken away his leg. I had to tell him no, that it lay on the ground beside him. He then asked if I would find it and bear it off some distance, for he did not think he would bear the sight of it when dawn came.

I did as he asked, and that was the last I ever saw of him, for when in the morning I returned to where he had been he was gone, and I presume taken to an hospital.

I don't remember all that we talked of while we waited for the surgeons, but some of it was recalling happier times as *romerías* and especially that when he went with Rafael and his sisters to my Father's vineyard. Also he was very proud of how Lord Wellington had spoke to him when they dined earlier that day – he had recalled to the Peer the landing at Mondego Bay, which greatly interested his Lordship, that Fernando should have been there. No doubt he was as full of proverbs as ever. That we had ever been less than friends we forgot for yesterday's bad fruit is out of mind when market day comes round again, and tooth and friend – you must suffer the pain of one like the vice of the other.

The thunder rolled away round the peaks above us, the rain eased, and soon all I could hear was the leaves of the trees above the Hermitage disturbed by a breeze just sprung up which displaced and scattered the water on them so it fell like the last echoes of the storm. Wellington now stirred and presently came on to my pillow where he pushed his face against mine, his way of signifying he wished to

be out. I got up, opened the door; he paused on the threshold, sniffing the rain-washed air and savouring with his eyes the moonlight
just then flooding from behind the last of the cloud so, as I watched,
the valley which had been black before took on silver and purple
and the shapes of trees, boulders, and mountains became distinct.
Below us the river chattered, perhaps more briskly than before.

'Are you going or not?' I murmured; then off he trotted across
the grass in front of us, tail up till he reached the bushes at the edge,
then he leaped and was swallowed by the darkness of the wood.

'Joey, is that you?' I heard Flora whisper as I shut the door.

'Ay. I was letting out the cat.'

'Joey. You were moaning and crying earlier. Are you recovered
now?'

''Twas a dream, I suppose. But gone now, with the storm,' I
said, though I do not think I had properly slept at all.

'Joey, in the morning, I pray you fetch us some oranges from
the monks; I have a great longing for oranges.'

When the sun was well up I took Paqui down to the monastery,
or more properly I should say she took me, for I rode upon her
back, and all the way down discovered new beauties on the path
for all it was so familiar, for each new day of burgeoning Spring
brought out more flowers, or brighter greens as new ferns
uncurled and mosses spread, and clouds of sharp pink in the beech
buds above my head; and as I rounded the corner near the door of
the monastery I entered a bank of fragrance, for the mimosa buds
I'd marked in previous days had opened and the sprays of soft
yellow were like slow spreading jets shot from a living fountain,
and above this tree and all around it fluttered and played a host of
yellow butterflies whose motion alone betrayed them when they
came near the flowers, so like was each yellow to each.

I tethered Paqui to a ring set in the old mossy wall, pulled the
chain that linked with a bell somewhere inside, and sat down to
wait, for always it was some time before the Superior came to
answer. The river chattered round its lichened boulders, a yellow

wagtail perched, fluttered and cheeped, bobbed its tail, perched, fluttered and cheeped, bobbed its tail from rock to rock, jewelled dragonflies hovered and darted, hovered and darted, and from the top of an Arbutus nearby a white-throated ouzel delivered itself of its chuckling song.

Yet was my heart heavy – partly because the shadow of my night thoughts still floated in my brain like a carrion crow seen nearly but in the corner of the eye, partly out of that premature nostalgia that always visits our enjoyment of what is transient – not that that valley is transient, but that soon we should be off, for Violeta talked more of Mister Reaney and Flora spoke of the better weather coming and Armies on the move.

The door creaked behind me and the Superior stood in it – a tall, large man with close-cropped grey hair, short-cut beard, weather-beaten face deep-lined by toil and waking nights spent on his knees, and sad wise eyes beneath high brows that yet had a sort of doubting, quizzical twist to them. He shook my hand in both his, which were large and very strong, his daily greeting. He was the only one there I ever talked with, having I suppose dispensation from his Rule of Silence where acts of Charity towards the world outside were in train. He had barley for me, three grayling brought as a gift by a family of cork strippers who worked in the forest below, and for which his company had no use, it still being Lent and they eating no flesh at all in times of penance, and a dozen eggs of which they also had abundance at that time of year for the same reason. I asked for oranges whereat he smote his breast and '*Mea Culpa, mea culpa*,' he cried, but with a smile, 'how we have neglected you,' and putting his arm round my shoulder urged me into their trim but tiny orchard where six orange trees stood beneath a cypress, laden with bright fruit glowing like golden lamps in the dark green night of their glossy leaves.

Back up at the Hermitage I found the place deserted and so wandered out to find where my companions had gone. Guided by Violeta's voice, warbling as usual one of her gay high-pitched *jotas*,

I came upon them by a pool, but Actaeon-like stayed where I was in a shrubbery for they had been bathing, after first washing out their clothes which were spread on the lawn about them. Now Violeta was combing out Flora's hair and the bright sunshine played in ivory shades on her shoulders and arms and this is the song she sang, which made them both laugh, but drew from me a fit of weeping that lasted all the way back to our cottage, for I did not disturb them, and this weeping continued while I tried to dress our dinner, so much so that our cat returned and filched a fish from beneath my eyes, and when we came to dine I had to do without –

'*Ahé Marmón, onde vai Marmón?*' she softly crooned in dialect, by way of introduction, '*Ahé Marmón, onde vai?*' – 'Hey there, Marmont, Marmont, where are you going?' Then snapped her fingers like castanets about Flora's wet hair, and Flora clapped with her to the cheery rhythm.

Velintón en Arapiles
A Marmón y a sus parciales
Para almorzar les dispuso
Un gran pisto de tomá-á-á-á-tes

Y tanto les dió
Que les fastidió
Y a contarlo fueron
A Napoleón:

¡Y viva la Nación!
¡Y viva Velintón!

Wellington said to Marmont, Come and eat with me
I've dressed at Arapiles a dish for two or three!
The Frenchman brought his friends, but neither three nor two
Had stomach for my Lord's tomato stew:
Perforce they had to scarper, and tell Napoleon –
So long life to our Nation, and the same to Wellington!

PART THREE

Chapter VII

*Mistress Reaney Indisposed, Unseasonable Weather, and
Paqui gone lame, bring us late to Salamanca, where we learn
News – Some Distressing, Some Curious.*

I

The last week of April Flora Tweedy said would be time enough
to move, for she did not think we were above three days journey
from Roger's Town and the army would be there until the First of
May – on account of the green forage not being forward until
then, and armies unable to march without it, all winter fodder
having been consumed. But we suffered several delays before we
finally set off – the first of these just about the beginning of the
third week of April when Violeta Reaney suffered a flux of blood
so that she and Mistress Tweedy thought she was like to lose the
baby, she being then in her seventh month (as Mistress Tweedy
was also) and so they decided she should lie up until quite recovered. This notwithstanding, she was much distracted by fear the
Army would have gone on and who knows what battles and
sieges, marches and skirmishes that might take Captain Reaney
from Salamanca before we could get there. And another consideration was that he must think her dead, having had no news of us
save perhaps that we had disappeared on the retreat, and so would
not stay for her, even if the Army allowed him.

Mistress Tweedy contrived to reassure her: 'I pray you mark
me, Mistress Reaney,' she said when one day Violeta was in a fit of
the dumps which would not yield to pleasantries nor fine weather,

'we have had no rain for a month or more, none really since that thunderstorm; yon brook is as low now as I dare say it is in Summer . . .'

'To what end tends this?' Mistress Reaney sulkily interposed.

'Mark me, I say. If the whole Province is in drought, there'll be no fodder yet, and campaigning delayed.'

In this she was right – for after four years with the armies and a childhood in garrison with her Father, her understanding of these things bettered that of many a General; however, the very next day the drought broke, and though we might have moved then or the day after, it rained so hard and without a break, we were put off for another week or more.

So with all this it must have been about the Seventeenth of May (1813) we left our cottage, picking our way down the valley of the Batueca; I in front leading Paqui, Violeta riding her, and Flora walking beside. With a small bag filled with barley cakes, and another with the last of the season's oranges, and six cold omelettes and six small goat cheeses wrapped in fresh sweet chestnut leaves, we were provisioned for three days at least by when we made sure we would be in Ciudad Rodrigo.

For all my two companions, with the uncertainties that surrounded what kicked in their bellies and what the outcome would be, were relieved to be at last on their way, they were sad to leave the place, and I, I was downright miserable, for never before or since have I been so content as I was those six months, and if I could I would return there.

We rose before dawn on the day of our departure and brushed out the place leaving it as it had been when we first arrived, then I took down the moveables lent us by the monks and made our adieus and offered our thanks for all we had had of them; and not by way of payment but to signify our gratitude offered them a cloth bleached white and trimmed with lace, then daintily embroidered with flowers about a cross that Mistress Tweedy and Mistress Reaney had worked up that it might be part of the Monastery altar furniture, as a napkin for the Server at Mass.

The Superior was much pleased with this gift, exclaiming often at the art of it, and asked me to assure the Ladies that it would be put to as good and proper use as the Ladies hoped. I had been bound by most fearful oaths to keep mum about the provenance of this napkin, and I kept my word: its earlier incarnation, before metempsychosis, of which, as is the way with the Transmigration of Souls it had no recollection, was as Mistress Tweedy's petticoat. It would be a churlish and too nice consideration to disallow its function polishing the Sacred Vessels on the ground of its earlier profane life round a lady's belly and bum: are we not taught that that finer part of what now inhabits our mortal clay will in Eternity sing praises round Our Lady's Throne?

The consequence of this was the goat cheeses as above, and some early salads, which the Superior now thrust upon me before giving me his last blessing and farewell, so we were almost too much laden when we at last set forth. Wellington, the cat, followed us a little way from the Hermitage, occasionally running on ahead and waiting, ears and tail erect till we came up with him, but left off as we came to the Monastery wall, preferring to stay in his old country than go with new friends, as is the way with cats, at which Violeta was affected and shed a tear or two, but we assured her he would get by without us, would return to mousing for the monks – an occupation he doubtless only left on account of better pickings with us.

All regrets, at least on the part of the ladies, soon dissolved, and this not only for the prospect that lay ahead if all went well, but also for the day and the landscape – the former being warm and sunny, the latter beyond description beautiful. Pine clad crags, aromatic with the heat, shimmered above us, then gentler slopes of shady cork trees, their bark stripped to reveal the soft red hue of their trunks, and beneath them broom just bursting into gold and pearly sprays of blossom, and gum cistus or mountain rose unfolding papery flowers of white streaked in the centre with crimson. Swallows swooped about us and the cuckoo's plaint rang echoing between the cliff's, butterflies performed their awkward ballet above the blooms and bees fumbled noisily at the smaller flowers. We halted in shade beside a pool after two hours walk through this paradise, ate omelettes and oranges, and thus refreshed continued down the river bank where there was a path of sorts, confident we should soon be in Ciudad and meanwhile had naught to look forward to but the continuing beauties of the way.

In the early afternoon we passed through a tiny hamlet of cork strippers and charcoal burners where the people spoke an ancient sort of Spanish as it might be they lived in the pages of the *Quixote*, but were as friendly as we wanted and as helpful as they could be. Like the monks they knew little of wars or the French; an old man asserted he had been to Ciudad Rodrigo as a boy in the company of their Priest, long since deceased (they relied now on the Superior for wiving and shriving), but he could not give us particular directions having forgot them. However, all agreed that two leagues further on our stream debouched into a larger river and this flowed towards the West, so Mistress Tweedy made no doubt it was the Agueda and would lead us to Ciudad; after taking a cup of wine with them, we went on our way.

The valley widened, became less splendid, though still empty, and hotter too, so that we were much bothered by the flies – then about two hours before dusk Paqui cast a shoe, which was no surprise, a farrier had not been near her for six months or more; and straightway she went lame. Violeta would not ride her thus and got down to walk, but after a scant mile complained of cramps and dizziness so we had to stop by the path-side and wait for these to pass. Thus it was almost dark when we reached the river, which ran through a wide, forested plain. At this confluence of river and stream we decided to bed up for the night.

The next day the ways were harder, the sun hotter, Paqui continued to be lame, and Violeta was visited with dizziness and vomiting if she walked more than a mile – the consequence was we went scarce three leagues, and the days following no more. It was not till the Twenty-First of May we came on a village with a farrier and he took our last duro for his pains. Thus we were fatigued, hungry, and destitute when we arrived in Ciudad on the Twenty-Second, just two days after the Allied Army left, and such was now Violeta's condition we were constrained to lie up there at Mistress Reaney's sister's house for two days more, and it should have been longer but Violeta was ever eager to press on as soon as may be and this the more once we had discovered news of her husband.

These were as follows. In February Mr Curtis and Captain Reaney had come to Ciudad after imprisonment in Salamanca and then an exchange of prisoners. Reaney had come straight to his sister-in-law's house and there discovered his wife had never arrived which threw him into a fit of melancholic distraction so his life was despaired of. He had recovered, thanks to Mr Curtis's counselling as much as to his connexion's care, and in April had rejoined his regiment of Portuguese in the Fifth Division, in cantonments to the North of Freneda, and had gone with the Army two days before, as above, and Mr Curtis too.

All this excited Violeta greatly – and it was her fancy that she must get after her Johnny as quick as may be, for she did not trust him not to be wild and foolhardy in the fighting coming for as long as he thought himself a widower.

It was a strange thing, this about news – for we heard at Ciudad of how the Emperor and his Armies had suffered dreadfully in Russia in that Winter gone, we had news of London fashions, and of how England was now at war with her late Colonies now the United States of America and had burnt their Capital, of how the Cortes had framed a Constitution at Cadiz which pleased the Liberals but angered the Army and the Church – of all these things the sheets, both English and Spanish were full, but naught could we learn of any certainty concerning our friends and Mistress Reaney's family in Salamanca a scant twenty leagues to the North of us, where, did we but know it, terrible things had been done.

Violeta's sister begged her to remain longer, for daily news were expected and not least of another battle, and she said we should wait till all was certain, but Violeta chafed and fussed so

that we needs must be off, and Mistress Tweedy too felt no inclination to linger for though there were British wounded and sick
in the Town they were not like to stay, and the garrison was now
Spanish.

I too felt I should be off, for the Colonel left there with these
British, an elderly and gouty officer much addicted to Sherry
wine and bad temper, questioned me as to who I was, recollected
some garbled version of my history, and decided the only way for
me to avoid Court Martial at his hands for desertion was to get
North after the Army and join my own regiment where, he said,
my own officers might have the joy of hanging me.

Before we left though, we did see one thing of slight interest
and that was posters fixed to the wall of the Town Hall, one
announcing that officers and men of the Light Division would
perform (I suppose had performed) *The Rivals*, and another
announcing A *Mid-Summer Night's Dream* done by the
Connaughts – 'Ay,' said Flora Tweedy, 'that's your Captain
Branwater for you – his favourite reading is the Bard. But who
played Bottom the Weaver? Why, Patrick Coffey, I'll be bound.
Well, I'm sorry we missed *that*,' which left both Violeta and I as
bemused as ever at the antics these soldiers were up to when they
were not fighting.

We left the city on the Twenty-Fifth of May and set off across
the plain in much the same order as before, but well-provisioned
this time, and with money too, but still only Paqui to carry us for
the Army had taken off all but such oxen and cattle as were essential for the coming harvest, and indeed only a plea from Violeta's
brother-in-law to the *Corregidor* saved us our moke. Before we left
I bought an old slouch hat to replace my shako lost in the blizzard
on the Sierra de Francia, and was grateful for this for the Sun had
been bothersome thus far.

We reached Salamanca on the Twenty-Ninth of May but before
I recount our arrival there I must first dwell on a strange
encounter on the way whose meaning was hidden from me then
but which came plain a month later.

On the morning of the fourth day a party of gypsies came up with us, travelled beside us for a furlong or so and then went on. There were four of them, three men and one woman, which was unusual for their women, who are chaste, remain in their camps while the men go abroad thieving and swindling, and when they do travel travel all together – but now, as I say, three men and one woman and all mounted on ponies which were dressed up to seem spavined and blown but which Mistress Tweedy, who had a good eye for horse flesh, said were in better condition than they seemed, indeed she thought these Romanies to be well-mounted.

The leader of them was a large man, large for a gypsy, and yet darker than the others; he had gold earrings and silver embroidery on his waistcoat, a lurcher loped at the heels of his horse, and his large knife was silver-mounted – in short I recognised him for the *Count* of that encampment of gypsies I had lodged with for a space before joining the British Army, and he recognised me too for after looking me over a second and third time he smiled, his white teeth flashing in his dark face, and he touched the ivory pommell of his knife.

'Is it really you, little Lord?' he asked, 'and still in the red coat of the soldiers of the *Londoné*?'

I agreed that it was I.

'And on your way to *Helmantica*?'

This was their name for Salamanca.

'Are not the *Gabiné* there yet?'

'I think not, O *Manclay* of the *Rom*,' I replied, for only the evening before we had had it off a courier returning to Ciudad that the British were in and the French out with hardly a fight at all, which had cheered us greatly, you may be sure. 'The Armies of the *Londoné* have the place in their hands again.'

At this he frowned and the lady behind now spoke to him, querulously and questioning, but too quick for me to understand. She did not like his answers for she spurred on her pony and came level with me. Now I recognised her too, for till then I had marked only the dark face, wrinkled though not old, the gold coins winking on her wrist, the dirty flounced skirt that typify all her tribe, recognised her for Suero's wife or woman, and she had a grubby infant, wizened and brown and tied to her back with grubby bands, no doubt his son.

'You know me, *Busné* Lordling?'

'Ay, I know you, *Calli*.'

'You say the *Gabiné* are gone from *Helmantica*?'

'I hope so and am sure so.'

'And what of the *Senjen* that worked for them?'

'They will surely be gone too, for now there will be many in the town to call them traitors.'

At this she spoke briskly again to the Count, he answered her, and now pricked their ponies into a trot and were soon gone from us.

Violeta Reaney was much disgusted with me that I could speak their language, categorising them as thieves, murderers and cannibals.

A short time later we came on signs of a skirmish, but one a week old from the way the vultures, crows and foxes had already reduced the dead to bones, and the peasants plundered all the poor souls had carried or worn. Yet it cheered us to see that all were French, or so it seemed from the tatters left, and '*Ahé Marmón, onde vai, onde vai*,' Violeta Reaney sang.

2

On the evening of the Twenty-Ninth we first saw again those rose and honey-coloured spires, towers and domes soaring on their cliff above the poplars alongside the Tormes – how different a view from when last seen in that terrible cloud and rack and rain of the first day of the Retreat – all smiling now they seemed, yet we approached with mixed feelings, for we yet feared to discover ill news of Captain Reaney and the Martin family, and as we drew nearer we discovered the deceit the City's distant beauty masked – the whole Southern and Western quarter of the Town which we could now see clearly across the river was in ruins and dilapidation, the colleges and convents of the area reduced to rubble so what was once the flower of all universities anywhere was now destitute of over half its buildings. We crossed the Roman Bridge and all to our left was like a landscape from Hell so we could see clear up the slope to the Irish College itself, still standing, where before six or seven buildings as fine would have obscured the sight of it, and now, as I say, naught but broken walls and tumbled arches, with a sort of shimmering stillness around and above it broken only by the heaving into the air and untidy flight, the squawk and flap and peck of several giant crows and kites that still found carrion amongst it all. What dismal reflections on the Vanity of Human Learning were provoked by this sight, what horror at the Consequences of War! Yet the crown of all still stood – the cathedrals old and new and the *Clerecía*, and the old Schools with their tricksy carved gate where the students used to gather before disputations to point out the frog carved sitting on a skull which was deemed a lucky thing to do – these still stood, but so much was gone, so much gone, all the streets and alleys empty of students and religious where before there had been so much noise and bustle, gossip and news. How sad it was to see as we passed along the Street of Booksellers the shops broken in and empty now save for a few old volumes scattered on the floor and pavement, and the slogans painted in fine red lettering now fading but still recording academic triumphs of past years as how *Ramón López* became a *Licentiate*, a *José-Luís Guijarro* a *Professor*, a *Rafael Portillo Chief Beadle*, but all so many years ago, none freshly done! And what was the cause of all this ruin? – Why, military necessity, that least necessary of all imperatives for most transitory. General Dorsenne had fortified three convents by the bridge the year before and to make the taking of them difficult had ordered the levelling of all that stood around them. Yet when the time came they withstood the English siege a scant week and then were levelled too, and let it be said the French pulled down five and twenty colleges for the three the British blew.

It was a relief to come out of that quarter and up the *Rúa* and so into the Great Square, that most perfect of all in the world, to find some life and light and bustle still toward, and see too a handful of red coats, including a picket at the Town Hall where the Jack stirred in the evening breeze beside the white flag of the Spanish Bourbons; and now with lighter hearts and jaunty steps we pushed on to the Martin apartment where Violeta made sure we would be made welcome, where she looked to find Captain Reaney himself, or surely further news of him. But again despair and worse were ahead of us: first we found the stairs to her door littered with plaster and rubbish, the door itself boarded up and no sign of life at all – at sight of all this Mistress Reaney fainted and Mistress Tweedy, catching her and letting her to the floor as gently as may be cried out to me: 'Quick, Joey, quick as you can, run and find some help, for in her present state her life itself may be in danger at this shock, and even more perhaps when she finds the causes of it all, for I doubt not but some calamity had fallen on her people.'

Where to go was a problem, but then I remembered that the lodgings Mr Curtis had taken, and had proposed to return to when the British left the October before, indeed return to with Captain Reaney in his disguise as a Priest and Scholar, were close, scarce a hundred yards off in the Calle de Zamora, and thither I hied as fast as my legs would carry me. I found the good man there, but alone and his house in disorder as if he was just arrived and unpacking or just off and packing up, but there being no time then for proper greetings or explanations, I simply told him the reason of my sudden appearance, and he called to him his servant and his housekeeper and the four of us rushed back to the Martins.

On the way he found time and breath to say this: 'It's a hard case, Joseph, a hard case, and out of all the miseries these wars have visited on us, this is one of the worst – what Mistress Reaney must now bear, and we too in the telling of it.'

My heart failed but I asked him to tell me now what he meant before we got there.

'Poor hapless girl,' he cried, as he pushed his way down the alley, the tails of his black coat billowing behind him, his nimbus of white hair streaming about his head and from beneath the brim of his hat, 'poor hapless girl. For you must know, Joseph, her Father was accused before the French, and by none other than your acquaintance Rubén, an evil man, Joseph, a very evil man; and so Licentiate Martín was arrested and later shot . . .'

'And Captain Reaney?' I contrived to ask, but we were already at the foot of the stairs, and I had to wait for an answer while Mr Curtis directed his servants to take up Mistress Reaney, she still being in a faint, with Mistress Tweedy in attendance.

In the course of the evening, during which a doctor was sent for who bled Mistress Reaney and prescribed she should lie up a fortnight until her time came, for so close was she now to it, and Mistress Tweedy too, and during which Mr Curtis changed his plan which was to move back to the College, this being the reason his moveables were packed up, and resolved to stay in his lodgings, which, though nothing grand were commodious enough, and indeed it later transpired the Peer himself had stopped there only the night before, during this evening I say, bit by bit I pieced up the history of our friends and acquaintance during the six months of our stay in the Valley of Batueca.

First, under the returning French, a terrible proscription of all who had helped the British had gone on, this largely managed by Rubén García, and including the close arrest, in prison this time, of Mr Curtis and Captain Reaney, with Don Jorge Martín and many other of his friends and intimates – 'But not that Banker fellow,' said Mr Curtis, 'Not Lorenzo Zúñiga – he got off, and his family, but only the Devil knows what it cost him in gold coin, the Devil and Rubén García.' For many weeks Mr Curtis and Captain Reaney had despaired of their lives but then in February, by when a terrible famine raged in the City and the Poor were dying of it, they were exchanged for a French General and a

Spanish Frenchifier who was like to be crucified by Sánchez's *Lanceros* if he was not got off. And so in February Mr Curtis and Captain Reaney came to Violeta's sister's house and there learnt that Violeta had not been seen at all, nor I either, and by careful questioning in the Third Division, and of the officers of the Connaughts particularly, they presumed we had fallen in with the French and been slaughtered.

Then, as above, Reaney had fallen into a distraction, but recovered and had rejoined his regiment, which, Mr Curtis asserted, had never come back through Salamanca at all, but was off on a terrible swift and secret march North through the mountains of Portugal; so much he had gathered from the Commander's lips himself at table the night before, and that very morning the Peer had ridden off in great haste to join them, the division or so outside the City not being the main force at all but only the right wing of the Army, by which bluff he hoped to get round the French right and make them retreat towards France without a battle.

Mr Curtis had come back with this division, opened up his lodgings first for the Commander and his Staff, and now for us, and yet had had time to find out the fate of many of his acquaintance, which was that Don Jorge Martín and many others had been tried and shot, and that Doña Regina, Violeta's mother, being now without kin in the City had gone off to live in Avila where she still had a sister alive and whither Mr Curtis and the Doctor now proposed Violeta should go as soon as she, and her child too, if not miscarried, which they feared it would be, were able, and meanwhile letters should be sent to tell her mother of her safe survival and return.

I slept that night in Mr Curtis's attic and through the exhaustion brought on by our marches and the news of the previous day woke late to learn Mistress Violeta was still in a state of collapse, though conscious and her baby still snug within, so discovering there was nothing useful there for me to do I begged a dollar of her and set out to take a turn round the town.

This proved a melancholy business – first on account of the widespread destruction which was not only of the colleges and convents but also of much of the market area and the shops of artisans about it – these being the people who had most resisted the French and whose homes and places of business had been razed; then for the general appearance of the few people about which was mostly thin and ill, and there were *queues* at the bakers and meat-shops which had nothing to sell but plucked birds and black puddings, the former no doubt crows, the latter filled with sawdust. Thus the life and the gaiety of the Town was quite gone – it seemed beyond belief that here just four years since were balls and *tertulias*, theatres and concerts, the Summer *paseo* after the *corrida*, and streets filled with sellers of drinks and sippets and throngs of people to buy them. As I thought on all this and the dismal scene before me, a great melancholy came on me and I began to doubt I should remain there after all, as I had somewhat thought I might, for what was there now to keep me? All my old acquaintance dead, gone or estranged; my inheritance no inheritance at all, thanks to my Father's Will and what would no doubt turn out to be a too nice and pedantic performance of its rubrics by the appointed executor, Mr Curtis . . . these were my thoughts as I turned out of the Square and round to Antonio's Tavern in the cellarage beneath.

Here at least not much was different – Antonio himself still served, his melancholic face perhaps yet longer and even greyer than before, his apron strings a touch more strained by a corporation grown bigger despite the famine of the Winter, his eye still sharp and his fingers nimble so the *cuartos* and the *ochavos* still flew from his tray to his pocket and an egg was discovered in the ear of a serving girl sent with a jug for lemonade; yet even these old japes seemed dull after the first new exhibition of them, and their performer himself seemed jaded by them.

I missed too the twangling of guitars, the spirited clapping, and high wailing voice of *el Suero* and his friends, though there were yet gypsies there, by the window, and as I turned with my second glass I saw them properly for the party who had passed us on the road the day before.

The Count now left his low bench and stood before me, his company followed, with Suero's wife, so all were ranged in front of me, the Count in the middle with his hand on the gleaming hilt of his heavy Manchegan knife.

'It is the *Busné* Señorito again,' he murmured, 'he who was acquainted with Suero.'

'Ay, *Manclay*,' I answered, 'I counted him a friend.'

'A friend he was, *Busné*; but for his idea of selling you to the *Londoné* soldier I should have cut off your *janréles* for *María Ereria*; and I think She was angry with him for this for from that day his *sustíry* has turned out bad and ended here, a year later, on the gallows, and his friends with him – Antonio with the twisted fingers and Luis who walked like a woman, all garrotted in the Square. Señorito Pepito, do you know why I tell you all this?'

'No *Manclay*, I do not, but what you have said distresses me more than I can say,' and this was true, for indeed I had a liking for Suero with his gap-toothed grin, his nimble fingers, and his singing, and he had saved me in much the way the Count had said.

'Well, I will tell you. The *jal* was twisted on their throats on the order of another friend of yours, the truest *Bengué* of all (by which he meant *Devil*), Rubén, the *Judio*, he with the hair like flame.'

'He is no friend of mine, *Manclay*.'

'Do you look pale now, little Lord? Is that sweat upon your brow? I think he is your friend. You used to bring gold from him to Suero, and Suero brought you news of the armies which you took to him. Is that not so? At the time you lived in the house of the *Gabiné remacha* (he signified *French Bawd*, by this). I am right this *Bengué* was your friend.'

They were now closer to me and I could smell the garlic on their breaths; the dim light gleamed on the steel of the Count's knife, for he had drawn it a little in its scabbard. There was naught to do but scream, but as the cry rose to my lips there was a noise behind, one which turns the blood cold of all who hear it, the heavy click of flintlock cocked, and turning they saw Antonio at his counter with a heavy blunderbuss in his hands.

'I'll have no killing here, Gypsy,' he said.

The Count raised his hands palm outward and his voice took on the whine that typifies their tribe. 'I don't wish to kill him, Landlord; I only wish to discover if he knows where we may find this Rubén now.'

It did not take me long to convince them that I was innocent of any such knowledge, beyond guessing their *Quarry*, for that was what Rubén had become since double-dealing with three of their tribe, had gone off with the French and would be found in their camps, not in Town; and at length they left, though not before Suero's woman had cursed me and spat at my feet, no doubt fixing on me the *Nasulo* or Evil Eye, and this perhaps is the reason why my life thereafter has been one of continued ill-fortune, and this she did because she blamed Suero's ill luck on me.

After they had gone I thanked Antonio for his action in saving my life, and offered him a glass of wine which he took.

'I have my reputation to think of,' he said as he drew it, 'Your health, *Señor*. Your Honour cannot conceive how times have changed and the trouble there is now if a man dies here or is knifed. I do not read or write readily, why should I? I have no need of the art in buying and selling wine. But if a man dies here now I have to fill in affidavits, sign testimonies, get counter-signatures, and I don't know what for them at the Town Hall. In the old days it was send for the Priest and the man's relations if known, and tell the *Alguacil* what had happened, and that was all. Now it is paper, paper, for a month.'

'But now the French are gone . . . ?'

'Listen. Up there,' he pointed up towards the Square, 'there are thirty scribblers employed where five served before. All Spanish, educated folk like yourself. Now do you imagine they will readily give up such easy employment as pen-pushing, just for a change in our Rulers? I don't think so. There were three in

yesterday all cockahoop for the new Superintendent of Drains had
agreed they were needed. What have drains to do with clerking?
I tell you, *Señorito*, from now on whoever says they rule us, it will
always be the scribblers. They are in the woodwork, and tearing
a house down and rebuilding it does not get rid of the pests, it just
makes them more active.'

Thus Antonio; but he had one more trick. As I settled my
account I discovered a folded paper magicked on to his tray by
sleight of hand, my name on the front, a blob of wax on the
back.

Inside I read this:

23rd May

Zeppo:
    Go to my room, you will know where to look there.

                                                    A La G

I left the change on the tray, Antonio knocked it with his
knuckles, and the coins cascaded into the purse he held open at his
belt.

Back in the Great Square I found the door to Madame's house
barred, the bar padlocked, and the place empty. There was no way
in without the help of a locksmith, and a locksmith who could be
bribed at that; this would need money which I had not got, a
considerable outlay perhaps yet I doubted not there would be a
handsome return, yet how to get the chinks quickly was the problem, for quickly it would have to be: for if I was known to a
tavern-keeper and to a gypsy as a friend of Rubén, then to whom
else also? Only the promise hinted in Madame's letter now kept
me in Salamanca – every other consideration prompted a speedy
departure.

For this reason the news Mistress Tweedy had for me – that she
and Mistress Reaney planned to set out on their travels again the

very next day and North after the British, not East to Avila – was most welcome to me and when I offered to continue with them as groom and lacquey, she mocked me with a courtesy, bussed me on the cheek, and exclaimed: 'Why, Joey, that is just what we hoped you would say'; and on questioning her further I discovered that though Mr Curtis and the Doctor had argued that they should stay and letters should be sent to her mother and Captain Reaney, Mistress Reaney would not trust to the posts in such difficult times; she still had such fears that Johnny Reaney would be killed in the campaign then started out of a foolish desire not to live without his wife, that she felt she must follow or go with the letters and get to be near him as soon as may be; and there was no shifting her from this resolution – indeed they had had difficulty persuading her to lie up another day, especially when it was heard that the British Army outside town under Sir Rowland Hill, then on the Down of San Cristóbal, was already moving off.

So I had now only an afternoon in which to find money and a corruptible locksmith and was about to rack my brains for it when Mr Curtis's servant brought me a note, which directed me to attend him in his old rooms in the College as he had a private matter to discuss with me. Though I did not relish an interview with him, for he had been churlish and chiding with me the night before, I set off with a lighter heart, hoping that perhaps he had now come to a just and wise decision regarding my Father's Will, purposing even to suppress it. Needless to say this proved a false hope; Mr Curtis had ever been a man constant and fixed in his opinions, and now, with increasing age – he was over seventy – he was grown downright stubborn. However, I got what I needed, as I shall now relate.

The way to the Irish College was through some of the ruined places and was sad; a cloud of urchins gathered round me, thin and dirty, clothes ragged – signs of real calamity for normally the pride of the poorest Spaniard keeps his children neat, and fixing on my red coat they pulled at it and called after me: 'Eeenglish, *Inglés*,

Inglés, penneees pleeese, pennees pleeese, *para pan*, for bread,' and they pointed at their open mouths, so I was constrained to give them the few coppers I had left of Mistress Reaney's dollar.

The College had not been much knocked up being kept by the French for billets, but it was blank and deserted with no porter at the Lodge, and my footsteps echoed through the great hall: soon, however, I discerned a familiar noise, the melancholy jangling of the Rector's *fortepiano*. What he played this time, like what he had played for my Father and me the day Fernando brought us news of Mondego Bay, seemed to make most moving music out of the simplest material – a phrase of three descending chords, though there were hints in the rhythms and in a tune that seemed to try to appear but did not of that earlier piece that had made my Father dance. I paused on the threshold, hand raised to knock until the music rippled and trickled away to come to rest on two slightly peremptory chords which brought to mind Mr Curtis's phrase – 'a gesture of Farewell'.

He rose from behind the keyboard, waved me to sit down, but himself remained standing near his instrument, with his back to me, his hands clasped behind him so I could see them clench and unclench above his tails, his white hair fluffed out and lit by the afternoon sun, and thus we remained while I might have counted an hundred, and I had time to look about me. Nothing much had changed, or more properly most had been restored as it had been – the telescope, the books, the china blue-patterned in the Chinese style, and other instruments as a microscope I did not recall seeing there before but which was familiar.

At last he turned.

'Joseph – I have debated with myself all night to determine what to do with you,' he began.

This seemed an impertinent opening, but I kept mum.

'The City is yet in a state of some disorder – it is doubtful who exactly is in proper authority; yet soon, today even, a Civil Governor will be appointed with the approval of the Cortes in Cádiz. Now once this is done there will be many here who would, I am sure, and quite properly, lay information against you and ask for your arrest, an they knew of your presence in the Town.

'But then again you still wear the coat of a private soldier and the badge of a proud regiment, not of Spain, but of Britain, and albeit your record in that Regiment or what I know of it, does not excite respect and there is I believe some question you should come before a Court Martial on a charge of desertion, this perhaps privileges you as regards the Town. I am not sure.'

It seemed the old . . . I almost wrote *fool* but respect for my Father's friend cohibited my pen . . . man was determined to hale me before some Court or other, and I wondered aloud if I should not be off while I had the means – however, he asked me to hear him out.

'Now there is this foolhardiness of Mistress Reaney and Mistress Tweedy, together with the generous encomiums they place upon you, and the continuing uses they will have for you: to be blunt, Joseph, they wish to beg you off.'

He took a turn round the room.

'Well, there it is, Joseph,' he said at last, 'I have decided to let you go with them. I hope, I can do no more than hope, you will not betray their trust.'

Since he seemed done, I again moved as if to be off.

'Stay, Sir,' he commanded. 'We have yet some business.' He took another turn, 'Your Father left a Will . . .' and here he went to that same bureau Rubén had opened and he drew out the same piece of red-taped vellum; '. . . I witnessed it and am made executor, which duty I must now perform. I shall be blunt with you, Joseph, for as you know I am not disposed to mince up what I have to say with herbs or garlic to make it palatable – nor does your history warrant the respect I should owe . . . well, I shall be brief.'

'I think, Sir, I know the main part of the Will.'

'Speak up, Sir, you speak too soft.'

'I said, Sir, I know the main part of the Will.'

'I think not, for your Father told me that he would never divulge it to you.'

''Twas not from him I had it that I am a Bastard, but *from another*, who had as ready access to the contents of that paper as you.'

'As ready access to the contents?' And he paused as one who has heard a distant noise and waits for it to be repeated, as it might be thunder or gunfire, before determining its nature, then he struck his forehead: 'Your *Mother* told you? After all, *she* told you?'

Here he sat down at his table and hemmed a little and tapped the polished surface with the Will. I kept quite still, not venturing a word, partly because my outspokenness had temporarily exhausted what stomach I had for this encounter, partly because I sensed that I might dam the flow of disclosure that seemed imminent.

'Well Sir. Well. Your Father went to lengths, some lengths in the first place to keep it from you. He sent her money, all he could afford, and asked her to keep quiet, and she sent all back but vowed with what seemed unimpeachable sincerity she would never tell you, and he had to believe her – he was in no position to do otherwise. But Joseph, he said to me that for all the wickedness of your Mother's employment she was in her way an honest woman and could keep her word. She had not betrayed him before, and would not do so again, he said. And yet she did, and yet she did.'

I did not see why *Madame my Aunt*, for I now guessed this was the 'she' he meant, should be diminished in his sight and again I found a sort of courage: 'Sir,' I said, 'I assure you Madame la Granace did not betray my Father's trust. After his death and in her grief at it, she admitted a liaison many years ago. She did not suggest I was the outcome. That my birth was illegitimate I had of another source.'

Mr Curtis became very confused at this and continued to hem and cough awhile, pulled out his great kerchief and mopped his brow, stood up, and sat down again. When he spoke at last it was in a softer tone: 'Well, lad, well. Perhaps I have been hard on you.

I'm not sure. I must think on't. But if you knew this then perhaps what I count your worst crime may be if not condoned, then comprehended. It cannot but have been a shock to you, a shock that turned the affection and duty of a lifetime to a sort of hate perhaps . . .'

All this seemed idle to me, I could make no sense of it, but at last he pulled himself up and some of his usual brusqueness returned: 'Joseph, this is the matter, and I must deal with it now, and I'll think on the rest later when you are gone and I can be calm about it. There is a clause to this Will which leaves all the moveables, as furniture, books, instruments and so forth to you, for your Father reckoned he had the right to will those whereso-ever he wished and I assured him this would certainly be the case in Law. Now as executor I should have seen that you came to this inheritance promptly, but on the very day I received news of his death I was taken from here to that house where I have since lived when in Town and placed under close arrest there, and thus remained until the Town was first freed from the French a year ago. I assumed that by then you would have sold up those move-ables yourself; it was only this Autumn, or rather early Winter, after you had gone off again with Mistress Reaney in your care, that I was siezed by a whim to visit my old friend's house. Joseph. What I found there filled me with horror. Your Father's bones and those of his Housekeeper still uninterred, a full year after their demise. Horror, and I fear a hatred for you who had I presumed left them thus. Before the French arrested me again I was able to see to their decent burial and the removal of the few articles unspoilt by weather, time, and the ravages of War. These are what you now see on the sideboard, and if you will take them, or twenty guineas from me for I shall, for your Father's sake, buy them of you if you wish, I shall have done my last duty for him.'

With a melting heart and a tightness in my throat I stood and looked over that pathetic collection, all that survived of my Father's faith in wisdom and Rationality. Beside the microscope there were thirty or forty books, some with pages torn or singed, but all more or less entire, the only ones left thus from his whole Library, I must suppose. Alas, I thought, that the very forces engendered by the new sciences cased in these volumes and instruments had brought him to his miserable death and me to destitution, and the end of all decency everywhere; this I thought as I turned over his Priestley, his Locke and his Descartes, and one of his most recent purchases, *An Introduction to the Principles of Morals and Legislation.* I opened this where he had left a mark and read where he had marked the margin: 'The object of all Legislation must be the greatest happiness of the greatest number . . .' and for a moment the room swam before my eyes and nausea rose in my stomach so that I thought I should faint or vomit, for that line reaved me back three years and more to the table of the Emperor and his canting justification for Tyranny.

I put the book down and then my eye fell on another smaller volume.

'I should like to take this, Sir,' I said, holding it up.

'Of course,' he delved for a pair of spectacles and pulled them on. 'It's of no value – the twenty guineas are mainly for the microscope which is a good one. I pray you take up the purse and do not worry about this book. Sir, I am not a dealer in second-hand books, I assure you!'

He spoke thus because I had my hand in my pocket searching for change: for now I had a desire to be square with him – but I had given it all to the urchins.

There was nothing now to do but go. I pocketed the purse and the book – 'twas the *Lazarillo de Tormes* which I had always been curious to read since my Father damned it as wittily ironical but tending to vice. I wondered if he had changed his mind latterly: I recalled a cabbalistic remark he had later made imputing a sort of truth in fiction not communicable by other means.

With my hand on the door the Rector spoke up one last time.

'Joseph. Your Father was a good man and I would have you honour his memory. On my side I shall try to think better of you than I have. Would you shake hands, Sir?'

I did.

'There then. Now be sure you take good care of those girls.'

I walked down the stairs slowly and so heard after a moment or two the *fortepiano* again: this time the music opened with a plaintive, almost uncertain sounding phrase of three notes which were followed after some development with a longer, extended, almost singing sort of tune, but still sad, and these alternated and interwove until I reached the Hall. Only then did the music move into a brisker, jollier sort of mood, but by then I was too far away to make much of it.

3

I laid out one of my Father's gold guineas on a locksmith's talents and four more for his silence, and thereby made an outlay for a better return than any received from any other venturing with money in my life, though as shall be seen the profits did me little good, for I had them in my hand for less than a month.

Once in our old rooms, and the locksmith dismissed. I found I could no longer keep out of mind what Mr Curtis had let slip. In truth, that Madame was or claimed to be my Mother was not the surprise it might have been: I had already presumed as much might be the case eighteen months since when news of my Father's death was brought to us where now I found myself alone, for on that occasion her grief would have seemed madness if expended solely for an old and long forgotten brother-in-law, and she had lost her composure entirely when the manner of his death was revealed – how Coulaincourt and I, with four others out boar-hunting, had come on *Guerrilleros*, how we had fired the village to keep off the pursuit, and thus got off. Then it was anger not grief that overcame her for she took me by the shoulders and shook me and cried: 'Giuseppe, you had the ring, did you not have the ring about you?' and when I had admitted I had she had insisted that the *Guerrilleros* could have been bought off with it and would not listen when I protested that they would simply have taken it and then killed us. 'Give me back that ring, you wretch, you degenerate, you pimp,' she had cried, and such was the tempest of her rage, I had never seen the like before, I had fetched up the chain which supported it round my neck but before I could undo it she snatched it from me so the chain broke. Well, she had ranted on a space about what a good kind man he had been, and then: 'Oh, the injury I did him, the injury I did him,' she moaned in a sort of hysteria, 'and he so kind, so kind.'

She had not turned me out of doors, as I feared she might, but she did not speak to me for two days, and it was on the second of these Rubén called me to Mr Curtis's rooms and sent me off on that fateful mission which ended in the British Army, as above, and often I had wished to have the ring about me, especially when amongst the Gypsies, but I had lacked the courage to ask it of her before I left, indeed I left without any *adieus* at all.

These were the painful scenes in my mind as I picked my way about those desolate rooms, and all the time found myself increasingly loth to go to the panel in her old chamber, which I was sure was where I was directed, and so wandered upstairs and down visiting each room save hers in turn. At the top the four chambers of her nieces were, like the others, reduced to bare walls and the heaviest furniture, as if all that would fetch a penny or two or had cost as much had been fetched downstairs in a hurry: thus in Brigid's room the convent grill stayed bolted to the window but the saintly pictures were gone, and I wondered if they were back in Church or Monastery, and what aura of the scenes they had witnessed on Brigid's couch still hung about them; in Ishtar's nothing of her tent or silver, but the odour of *haschisch* lingered yet; in Lady Secret Rose's room not even an odour recalled the spurious oriental delights she had offered her clients, just the shards of one of her tall vases betokened the haste of their departure.

Lastly I ventured into Dolores' room. Here less was changed than in the others – the mirrors were too heavy and perhaps too well fastened to be quickly moved, and the big round bed like-wise. Yet with the drapes from the windows between the mirrors gone, and sunlight filtered through laticed shutters lying in bars across the floor and bed, it was perhaps the most changed after all; the noises of the Great Square as the few shops still in business reopened for the evening came faintly up and the mewling of swifts swooping for insects between the chimney pots.

I sat on the bed and the myriad reflections sat with me – in pro-file, three-quarter face, reversed; I stood and they stood too; I smiled to think I had had the illusion that when they moved 'twas I was forced to follow, and they smiled back. Distantly a clock struck five, and others echoed. I searched the glasses for one that would give me back my face direct, then recollected the only one that could was that above and I lay on the couch and dimly saw my body floating above in the gloom, for the ceiling was high. My face I saw was a little solemn but no fright, and I wondered deeply for a space at my foolishness that I who had seen so much horror and evil in the World once flinched away from my own reflection. No special wickedness was in those lips: they have deceived and flattered (I mused), cajoled, pleaded, whined, abused, and cursed like most others, but ordered no deaths; if the eyes are those of an unregenerate coward, they are also the eyes of a man still alive, who never murdered nor even maimed another; and if my stature is small (my body then barred by the sunlight), that is no fault of mine and at all events it is a body that has caused less distress than most; and so on and thus I categorised my physiognomy and physique until the half hour was struck.

I rose refreshed and stronger, ready to see what Madame had left me, to face disappointment if I had been forestalled, to stom-ach any further revelation which might be attached, for I felt sure there would be a letter, whatever else, and almost I hoped most for a letter.

The bed was gone from her chamber and all the moveables, and I remembered with a pleasant warmth how it was the most

comfortable I had ever known being *down* in the mattress and the
covers down-filled too, and how she valued it above all other
possessions. My feet echoed on the boards as I walked across to the
panel. It yielded softly to my touch, revealing in the recess that
same tiny porcelain coffer with cupids and roses as had been there
before. The fine china rang as I lifted the lid – inside it was my
chain, my ring, and a paper quite large and written all over.

The sun flowed into the stone, the sun entire, and lay there
winking back from the palm of my hand, then I slipped the
chain – she had had it mended – over my neck and the ring
beneath my shirt, and read, at last, as follows.

Well, Zeppo, if this is in your hands I am mightily pleased at
the thought, and whose else I cannot think – for none but
you knows of our little *cache*. Truly I have a hope you might
yet come back and find it, for having despaired of you, and
thought you gone for ever, what should I hear when we
returned five months ago but that you'd been seen in Town
in the Summer, and that in an English red coat, even that
you were at the great battle and came off whole. Well, now
we're off again and in haste, and I think this time the last, for
I fear the jig is up with the French, they are too much
extended.

'Tis eighteen months since Carlo Bozzam died and I was
in such temper with you, and Time heals all they say, but
what I say is that by closing one wound it opes another, for
while my anger with you is cooled, nay quite gone away,
and I see you was right that those brigands would have took
ring and life an they had the chance, I have wrung my
hands at the thought of what harm I might have brought
you an hundred times a week or more, and the pain caused
by my silliness increases daily – for always I ask myself: 'Is
little Zeppo alive? If not, had he had his ring perhaps he
would be?' And Zeppo, if 'tis you reads this, then you are
alive and can look with kindness on your Mother's folly, and

take back your ring to hold it again against a day you'll need it.

For yes, Giuseppe, I find I can write here what I ne'er could say, and call you my son, for that is what you are, and I'd hug you now, and kiss you, an you'd let me, my own darling boy; but Zeppo, this is not all you should know, and now, with Signor Carlo gone, I can tell you the rest.

Zeppo, you was not the son of that kind, wise, good man, and I did him the greatest injury in making him believe you was, though I believe he latterly doubted it himself; the truth on't is this – when my sister was big with her second, her first having miscarried, I, being flighty and forward, was bedded by a scholar Signor Carlo was giving lessons to out of charity – though to tell truth 'twas more I bedded him than t'other way about. As indeed was very much the case when a few weeks later, suspecting I was then with child, and fearing the consequences when it was known, I exercised all my art on Signor Carlo himself – and this I should say on his behalf – my sister was a cold woman though a good one and kind, very religious – and he had had none of those comforts all men wish for and a husband has a right to enjoy, for several months, so it was not hard to bed him once my mind was on it. When my time was come he spoke up for me, would not let me be put out of doors, thinking then you was his, and my sister being much weakened by her own lying-in, and wasting away, a virtue was made of my own case and I suckled her child at one breast and you at t'other.

A year later, Zeppo, I had an offer of a Bishop I could not refuse, and well, Signor Carlo's house was a quiet dull sort of place once he'd mastered his passion for me, which was quite soon the case, and he and my sister took you on when I said I was going will they or will they not, and promised to raise you as if one of theirs.

Zeppo, she was a better Mother for you than I should have been, I promise you that, and you'll agree I'm sure.

Well Zeppo, that will do for now, though there's much more to be said, much more I could write, but these above what matter. Marinetta calls me that the coach waits and we must be off.

Your Affec. Mother,
                    Anna Granacci

P.S. I've had a value put on the ring – it is worth five hundred guineas, the stone being good and from India.

CHAPTER VIII

*A Grand Competition for a Cup, Recalled; a Feast;
and a Review.*

I

Albeit the next morning was warm and sunny and the larks filled
the sky with spilled showers of song above the blue-green seas of
heaving corn, as we climbed the long slope up the San Cristóbal
Down and the domes and towers sank between the folds of the
hills and the twin Arapiles rose from the plain a league and a half
to our right, it might be supposed that my thoughts and recollections were of a melancholy, even tragickal nature, as of marching
up the same slopes with Rafael five years before with our ragged
crew of peasants and students, or of my Father/Uncle in his grave
beyond, or of lovely places never to be seen again, but no, for
when we were nearing the crest and passing across a long, wide
declivity or Dell, well-grassed, Violeta, riding on Paqui, flung
out her arm, and 'Whatever are those?' she cried, 'I never saw
their like before.'

What she thus adverted to were eight piles of stone, cairns
built up to five feet high, and placed in pairs, or rather it seemed
in one group of four with one pair on its own nearest us and
another on its own at the furthest end of the dell, but this was the
wrong way to look at them, as Flora and I tried to explain, for in
fact the two nearest us were paired with the two opposite them an
hundred yards off; the third pair that backed on the second really

went with those that faced them another hundred yards off, and what these were was *goalposts* and the space between *pitches*, so there were in all two pitches and four *goals*, and Coffey and Nolan had directed their erection the Summer previous.

'It was the third week of June when the army stood here for a week with Marmont in front and the Forts in the Town yet untaken,' said Flora, 'and all restless and uneasy expecting a battle which never came, so the officers proposed some exercise or sport to keep the men amused and Patrick Coffey suggested a tournament of Football.'

'What pray is *football*?' asked Violeta, 'Some exercise or practice connected with the arts of war?'

'Not exactly so,' said Flora, and at this began to laugh and I did too, and more and more so, so before long one of my fits was on me, for there had been much to laugh at in Coffey's *Grand World Competition at Football* and the recollections of it set me off.

For what had happened was this – Sir Edward Pakenham had directed our Colonel, who had passed it on to company Commanders, that a festival of *Cricket* would serve, but Coffey had said this was absurd, not many could play Cricket, in fact in all the Connaughts only three Black Jamaicans who had learned it of Plantation Owners, two Hampshire country men and Corporal Prigg whose Academy had fostered the game as *Gentlemanly* were all that had the art, whereas he said all could play football, and if not could learn, for it was a simple enough game, and the Hanoverians and Brunswickers, Portuguese and Spaniards could get up teams as well. He said all this loud, and Coffey had a loud voice, and the men about him all threw up their bonnets and said 'Aye, let us play Football, for Cricket is tedious and slow,' so Lieutenant Lynton told Captain Branwater whose servant I then was, and Captain Branwater told Colonel Wallace who told Sir Edward, and Sir Edward said ay, and back the word came, football it should be if Coffey would set it all up.

It was a grand thing to see how busy he was then: all morning he bustled about the division, bivouacked in neat rows along the reverse or Southern slope of the Down above the Dell, with Nolan behind him offering counsel, and I went along too with a pocket book and pencil borrowed of Captain Branwater to set down the teams and act as interpreter, and by two o'clock six teams were drawn up, *viz.* – one for Portugal from their Ninth, Twenty-First, and Twelfth *Caçadores*; one for Spain from the *Lanceros de Castilla* as Julián Sánchez's troops, now regularised as Light Cavalry, were known; one of the Duchy of Brunswick and another of Hanover from the King's German Legion; one for Scotland from the Seventy-Fourth; and one last that called itself *The Saints* for it was mainly Irish from the Connaughts, and Erin is the Isle of Saints, this last led by Coffey, with Nolan in goal, Prigg in the defence (he still had all his toes), and eight other of Coffey's acquaintance, which Coffey was sure would beat all the others easily.

'Now,' said Coffey, having called the other five leaders or Captains about him, and with me trying to keep pace with him in Spanish and French which a Bunswicker had off well enough to put into German, 'now, to keep the interest alive all afternoon we'll not play sudden death, by which I mean once beaten you play no more, but we shall divide into two groups: the Saints with those of Portugal and Brunswick, the Scotch with those of Hanover and Spain, and in each group each team will play the other two – thus all will get two games at least. Then the best team in our group will play the best team in theirs to decide the winners,' here he dropped his voice a little, 'and I make no doubt lads, that will mean we play the Scotch in the Final, for no foreigner ever yet had the art like the native born, but as I say it'll keep the interest up to start in groups.'

('It seems very complicated,' said Violeta, 'and I don't understand why you two cannot stop laughing as you tell me of it.'

'Bear with us,' I managed to splutter, 'you will understand all presently.')

The pitches were paced out, and the goals made of piled stones, as above, the General rode up to the crest and saw Marmont was keeping a good league off or more so said all but pickets could leave the line to watch, and just as the men stripped off their coats and shirts, for it was a hot sultry sort of day, and were ready to begin, who should come by on his fine chestnut colt, and all trim in his blue coat, but the Commander himself, and, 'What's going on here, Ned?' he called.

'A tournament of Football, my Lord; the men requested it to pass the time.'

'Excellent plan, Ned,' the Peer replied, 'see an extra ration of rum is given to the Regiment that wins. No, Ned, I'll go further – I have a silver stirrup cup in my tent which my man will bring over for the winners. Now mind you play fair, lads – good knocks but no broken limbs.' And the teams gave him a cheer which he acknowledged with his crop to his hat, and so hacked off down the line, remarking to his Aide that such sports were a good thing and should be encouraged in schools, though not the very best schools – a gentleman might ride or fence, but should not play with a ball.

'Jasus,' said Coffey, and his eyes went small and seemed to burn red, 'we'll have that cop, I swear by Our Lady we will.'

At three in the afternoon all the matches started and to begin with all went well: the men not playing sat on the grassy slopes in their companies, finishing off their meal, smoking their pipes, and cheering on the teams they favoured and jeering at the others. A Board had been erected at each pitch on which the teams names were chalked, the scores and so forth, and all beneath a big-lettered heading – '*World Competition at Football for a Cup*' which added tone to it all, as I heard Corporal Prigg say, he jumping up and down at the time so his mop of hair fell over his eyes and flicked out again – 'just loosening up,' he said, when asked what he was doing, 'always did so at College before a game, you know. You should do so too.'

'I only put him in for his size,' said Coffey to Nolan, who grumbled mightily when Prigg took the field along with him.

In the first game in Group A the Saints beat the Brunswickers by two goals to one and all on both sides seemed satisfied and the spectators too; then the Portuguese came out to play the Brunswickers and at sight of them Coffey turned a little pale – four of them were Blacks, from Brazil or some place in Africa it was said, and were very very big. They beat the Brunswickers by five goals to one and one Brunswicker was carried off with a dislocated shoulder.

As Coffey led his team out to play these Portuguese knowing he had to beat them, for a drawn game would leave the advantage with the *Vamoosers* as they were called, he was greeted with more boos than cheers, and the reason was this – the Regiment had now had time to see that the team was his, his friends from two companies only, and all felt it was not the best possible, and it would be a shame if we lost.

Meanwhile, on the other pitch the Highlanders of the Seventy-Fourth were coming out to play the Hanoverians, the Spanish having been beat by both ('Well,' said Violeta, 'there's no disgrace in that I'm sure – it seems a very childish way of going on, and no shame to be poor at it,' at which Flora and I laughed the more and when we explained why – that Violeta had displayed, albeit negatively, just that sort of partisanship which was soon to bring chaos on all, she grew a little moody and had to be told we teased her). Sulphurous clouds were building up in the East, the midges flew low, tempers high, and the guns down in the Town thudded steadily away against the convents stubbornly held by the French.

The last game in group A was hard fought and in the first *half* of twenty minutes one goal apiece was scored, Coffey for the Saints, and the biggest of the Blacks, known as Pele, for the Portuguese. This latter spoke English of a sort and was thought to be a runaway slave from British Guyana, and what was clear was he was more than a match for Prigg whose job it was to *mark* him, that is prevent him coming near enough the goal to kick the bladder at it; indeed whenever the ball came to him he always ran round Prigg by jinxing to the left and running to the right, or the other way about, so the crowd began to jeer and hoot all the more, and only Nolan's skill between the goalposts saved the Saints from a drubbing.

With three minutes to go (a tinker from Limerick kept the time with a fob watch filched from who knows where) Coffey scored again, and then ran all round the pitch waving and hallooing and jumping up and down and hugging each of his team in turn, even including Prigg, by these means hoping to waste the time out, but when the Tinker held up his watch and said it was done there was such a booing, even from the Connaughts, let alone the Portuguese, it was decided to play the last three minutes again.

Almost immediately Pele had the ball, came down the field, dropped his shoulder to send Prigg one way, and himself went the other, but Prigg was almost ready this time and though he could not get his feet to the ball was able to throw himself on it – when, finding it in his hands, he stood up and carrying it now beneath his arm like a stolen chicken, ran for the Portuguese goal and, 'Hey, what you tink you doin, man?' shouted Pele.

A dreadful argument now broke out with fists raised and worse, for while Coffey conceded Prigg should never have done this he wanted to start the game again as if nothing had happened, but Pele said no, a goal should be counted for the Portuguese. 'Look, man,' he said, 'that spherical leather I was just about to pro-pel past Nolan like a tunderbolt man, he had no chance at all, no chance,' and so on, and since they played with no Umpire there was no settling the dispute, until at last Captain Branwater was called on to decide it. He acted justly, all agreed, by saying Pele should kick the ball from a spot four yards from the goal with only Nolan in his way, which he duly did and scored.

Meanwhile on the other pitch the Germans beat the Scotch, whereat the Seventy-Fourth to a man came down from the slopes, beating on their kettles as they came and began to fight everyone in sight, not just the Germans, so only the storm breaking and a troop of Dragoons sent in to clear the Dell ended the riot.

The Final was never played – that night a red-hot shot fired the

Convent of San Vicente, next morning the French inside surrendered, Marmont moved off North, and we came down from San Cristóbal behind him. For several days all Nolan would say, if Prigg was near him, was 'What the fucking hell was that, Prigg? What the fucking hell *was* that?' and Prigg's answer was always, 'I'm sorry but it *seemed* like a good idea at the time; I'm *sorry* but it seemed like a good idea.'

Thus Flora and I recounted this history until we were descending the North slope of the Down and all sight of Salamanca, and the Arapiles, was gone, and all the time we laughed so in the end Violeta had to laugh too, and an old woman riding up to us on a donkey had to stop and scratch her head at the sight of us, and no doubt we were as comical a sight as any on the day of the *Grand World Competition for a Cup* – two young women like barrels, one perched on a tiny ass, and me shabby and ill-kempt in my old red coat, but leading the way like some Moorish Pasha with a Harem, and all laughing and laughing.

It seems to me now that Flora put us in the way of all this merriment to get us out of our own country without either of us falling into the dumps: for I suppose none of us ever expected to return, and I don't suppose any of us ever has, leastways – not me.

2

We continued thus on the road to Toro and made good progress the first two days, covering all of forty miles to arrive there at nightfall, having passed the first day at Fuentesauco; and this good progress was partly on account of the road being easy without too much hill, and on account the girls and Paqui seemed to have rested well at Mr Curtis's, but mainly because Violeta was now yet more passionate to be up with Johnny Reaney before there was a battle, and we knew we were only a day or so behind the army and this hardened her purpose and furbished up her strength. At the *posada* (which is to say a sort of inn where bedding may be had but little else – the traveller brings and cooks his own food) we heard that a great body of the army was camped only three miles off on the banks of the Duero – so Violeta was for pushing on but Flora said no, it was not certain Reaney's regiment was there, it was almost dark and we might lose our way, the morrow would do.

Another thing that helped us make such good marches was the chinks we had, for Violeta still had five dollars from her sister in Ciudad, I had the guineas, my inheritance, and so for supper that night we had a chicken; but not before I had been to some trouble to get it for this town Toro, which was only small, had seen more armies in the last two years than Pompey the Great saw in all his life and the people had become skilled at hiding their fowl from the French who took them, so they could sell them to the British who paid too much, as much as a crown for a bird – which is what was wanted of me, the Vendor thinking I was of that nation.

Well, I soon disclosed to the old woman to whom the Barber had directed me as being the most likely to have a fowl, how well I had off her tongue and called her liar and thief until she let me in at three pesetas which was half what she hoped from the German she had promised the fowl for the next day.

But news travels fast amongst beggars and fleas, as Fernando would have said had he been with us, and even before I was back at the *posada* Maritornes, the Galician serving-girl, was fetching down the big open skillet from the loft where it was hidden, her Mistress was pumping the bellows over the charcoal fire that burned in a pit in the middle of the publick room, and Angel, her husband, was sharpening his knife. This Angel was a big man with moustaches and a foot off, which betokened he was a soldier with good reason for a discharge, bulging cheeks, large brown eyes, and a floppy-brimmed hat which he never removed save to fan the coals; as I say, notwithstanding the usual rule of 'cook your own', he took the fowl from me, wrung her neck and passed it to

the two women who plucked it and drew it while he still sharp-
ened his blade. Then he lopped it up into pieces, twelve or
fourteen I dare say, for it weighed all of six pounds, and these he
dropped into the pan where a cup of good olive oil was already
smoking.

Now his wife returned from some cupboard or press or cellar
with dried hot peppers and garlic; the Barber appeared with four
onions, his contribution; the woman whose chicken it first was
arrived with a handful of parsley, her passport to the Feast; a Priest
chanced in, a jolly fellow in a soutane, and he had a chunk of
bacon; a thin, leggy man dressed in black, very old-fashioned, they
said he was the Doctor, produced four nearly ripe tomatoes; and
so on and so on, there must have been fifteen or twenty and the
pan now piled to its lip with apt ingredients, the last being three
pounds of rice, and all these Angel stirred and turned, stirred and
turned for ten minutes or so, flapping at the coals with his hat. An
excited buzz settled over the room as all drew up stools or spread
cloaks on the earthen floor; candles and lamps were hung from the
rafters or placed on the lintels. There were three men from the
fields (from the orangy-brown of their faces); two *Lanceros* (from
their yellow jackets); several girls and mothers; and small children
who pushed and scrambled and wriggled and twisted among us;
and three infants who squawled and chortled by turns. At last
Maritornes, who was broad-faced, flat-headed, and saddle-nosed,
with one eye squinting, and the other not much better, and little
bigger than a dwarf, but jolly and laughing and given to coarse
humour, so none was offended at her appearance, came in with a
pan of boiling water which she poured with much cursing from
her, and hissing and scalding clouds of steam, into her Master's
pan.

He now clapped a lid on, straightened up with his hands rubbing his back and – '*Pues Señores,*' he said, '*Echaremos un cigarrito,*'
let us make a cigarette – by which he signified his stew demanded
twenty more minutes.

He now discovered in an inner pocket his embroidered cigar

case (and the Priest, the Doctor, the Barber and others the more prosperous there all did likewise so it was comical to see them all at it together), and a book of fine paper milled in Valencia from which he tore a leaf and put on his lip. (The Barber, more gainly, kept his paper dangling between the middle and forefinger of his left hand while following Angel in the rest.) Next he rubbed down about a third of a cigar between his palms, jerked the baccy into the paper, rolled it up into a squib, doubled down the ends, stuck one in his mouth and lit the other. Satisfaction all round, save from the urchins who now watched eagerly who would be finished first so they could fight for the butt and the last puff with it.

All this while the pan simmered, emitting little gasps of vapour whose savour was *transcendental*, Flora and Violeta gossipped with the women the Barber was sent for his guitar, which presently he strummed, and by and by I found the Priest beside me. He offered me a whiff of his smoke which I accepted, then he smiled at me and spoke as follows – 'Sirrah, I do not know you, but you are a good omen, I am sure, a sign sent from Our Lady to cheer us. Like San José on the way to Bethlehem you come with an ass, but better than Pepe for you have not one Lady ready to give birth, but two; well, all this is nothing, but what really signifies is this,' he took the *cigarrito* from his mouth, studied it, wetted the already soggy paper between his lips, and drew on it again, 'do *you* know what really signifies?' he asked.

Perforce I shook my head.

He turned to face me, prodded my stomach with his podgy finger. 'You,' he continued, 'are the first travellers not soldiers, and you are not a soldier, that is plain for all your coat and the one the Lady wears, you were never a soldier, the first travellers I say in three long years to fetch up here with money for a fowl, in three long years. I declare,' he concluded, 'I declare you are a sign the Torment in Toro is over,' and with that he embraced me and ushered me to a stool near the fire from which I was able to see the arrival, held high above the heads of those by the door, the arrival of a *borracha*, an entire pig-skin with feet and neck still on, filled with wine and this not the last to arrive that night.

The wine of Toro and Zamora is heady and strong and promotes prejudice and argument – for this reason it is much drunk at the University of Salamanca – but that night, at least for as long as I was sensible, all were in amity and concord, though there was little peace. Once the food was eaten – and it was as paradisial as its promise – a space was cleared, the barber strummed and the girls fandangoed; Mistresses Tweedy and Reaney even took the floor and sailed and bobbed full-bellied like nothing so much as embarked traders on the flood, rich with merchandise, so all laughed for them and cheered them; three British soldiers from the lines in the plain below arrived, smoked their clays, had wine, and then did a comical dance, their arms about each other, kicking their boots in tiny quick steps in the dust, which they assured me in thick accents I could scarce understand were better done in *clogs*; Maritornes sat on every man's knee in turn, including mine, and was much fondled and kissed; and so most of the night was passed, and any dissent there was was limited to an assault by the Doctor on an empty pig-skin hanging in the window, which he said was King Pepe himself (meaning Joseph Buenoparte), and should be kicked from there to Burgos, to San Sebastián and so back to France; and at last there was three cheers for *el Señor Velintón*, for *los Ingleses*, for Spain and Santiago, and all concluded with *Ahé Marmón, onde vai . . . y viva La Nación, y viva Velintón* .

3

Dissension there may not have been that evening, but the next morning saw the first, and I suppose the last, that ever there was between Mistress Reaney and Mistress Tweedy, and it came about in this way. We set off just after cock-crow to cover the league between us and the general bivouac of the army, this in spite of a head that swam and a sickness from too much wine in my stomach – my

Companions seemed unaffected though perhaps dark round the eyes through lack of sleep, and, as above, touchy in disposition.

It was a lovely morning, much like that before the great battle a year before, and the country similar too being Downs and Plains and a great river winding through, though this, being the Duero or Douro, was even wider and greater than the Tormes which becomes its tributary some leagues to the West of Toro, and soon we heard the sounds of a great camp breaking up and an army preparing to move, as of bugle calls, waggons screeching, drums beating and so on. Then, coming over a rise, we saw on the plain below us two divisions of the army drawn up, their Colours uncased and drifting in the light airs, their right flanks on the road we were on, the baggage in the rear just below us, all as if a battle was about to commence, but to my great relief no sign of the French.

At this moment we were challenged by a *vedette* of the Third King's Own Dragoons, who emerged from under an oak-tree with his carbine levelled at us.

'La! but you did give me a fright,' called Flora Tweedy in response to his *Who Goes There*, 'I pray you put up that thing and come and tell us what is toward,' so this fellow (who was, by-the-by got up in the oddest helmet of gilt and horsehair which when Mistress Tweedy twitted him on it, he blushed and said it was a new design said to be done by the Prince Regent himself, and none of the fellows liked it,) trotted over to us and presently began to explain to the Ladies that what they saw was a Grand Review and March-Past in front of Lord Wellington himself; so we composed ourselves to enjoy the spectacle, and I do not think it is fancy on my part that prompts me to say Mistress Tweedy became a little pale, then blushed, and bit her lip until at last the Staff appeared over to our left and His Lordship dapper and neat as ever in his blue coat at the front, at which she gave a little gasp, and, 'I pray you sir, have you a glass I might borrow?' she asked.

The *vedette*, he was a Corporal and well-spoken, had one though it was only small, scarce more than a toy, but Mistress

Flora put it to her eye and, 'Aye, there he goes. There he goes,' she murmured.

'And behind him,' said the Trooper, who was too callow to perceive that she had eyes for none but the man in front, 'the Prince of Orange, a fine young man, then the larger, heavier man is Marshal Beresford who commands the Portuguese and gave the French a licking at Albuera, General Murray, Lord Aylmer . . .'

'Aye, aye,' said Mistress Tweedy, and marked him not, 'well, he looks fit. I must say he looks in very good health – what do you say, Joey?' and she handed me the glass.

He was sat up very straight, and very firm in the saddle in a sitting trot, his face tanned and lean, his eyes high-arched, his nose like the prow of a fighting ship. When he moved his hat to acknowledge the cheers that came by battalions I could see his hair was short but plentiful, and ever and anon he spoke in an aside to his Aide, and once laughed, that high laugh like a horse's neigh I heard in Freneda I make no doubt, though now too far off to hear it.

'Aye. He looks well,' I said.

'I pray you give me back the glass then,' said Mistress Tweedy.

'What divisions are those below?' Mistress Reaney now asked.

'The Sixth and Seventh,' said the Trooper. 'See, that is Lord Dalhousie his Lordship is greeting now, he commands the Seventh.'

'Then the Fifth is not here, pray where are they?'

'The Fifth, Ma'am, went off North today from Zamora in the column led by General Graham. Towards Medina de Rioseco, I believe.'

'And the Third?' asked Mistress Tweedy.

'They are to our right, a league off, and march with us I believe.'

And that was the cause of the dissension, for needless to say Mistress Tweedy was for staying with the main body of the Army and perhaps rejoining old friends in the Connaughts who could be trusted to take news of her return and her condition where they would do most good, while Mistress Reaney had Captain Reaney ever in mind and was for pushing on towards Medina, but now we noticed the Review was finished and all were quite still below. The Staff had reined in and stood fast, all the officers, the Commander included, uncovered, the men presented, and the massed bands began to play that slow and dirge-like tune – *God Save the King*. Then when this was done all covered again, the bands struck up *Rule Britannia* in more sprightly rhythm and all marched off in open columns of companies, wheeling about the plain so each could come past his Lordship and salute.

While all this went forward my two companions skirmished on till at last Mistress Tweedy said: 'Well, I declare there's no deciding between us, we must ask Joey to cast a vote; what do you say, Mistress Reaney, will you abide by what he says?'

Mistress Reaney put out her bottom lip and her brow furrowed, but at last she nodded, which we took to mean yes, she would do what I said.

I heard their arguments – Mistress Tweedy urging that in the baggage train below there would be women who knew from experience if not from training the arts of midwifery, and, more important, waggons to carry them – 'For I assure you we shall not be able to get up and walk as if nothing has happened,' to which Mistress Reaney stuck out for the fact that there was waggons with the Fifth as well, 'But a day's march ahead of us . . .' 'We caught these, we can catch them . . .' 'But Joey can go and find Captain Reaney, by this evening, and we can rest up with these . . .' and so on and on. I pondered a bit, said I would think on't, and got myself off to where I could whisper to the Trooper without they heard what I said.

And he told me that the French were at Valladolid to the Right and the East, so I voted to go North.

Mistress Tweedy said, 'Good then, let us go North,' at which Mistress Reaney burst into tears and said no, no, Mistress Tweedy was right and always knew the best, they'd go straight down to the Baggage, so soon both were arguing on the opposite sides to what they had held to before, but appealing to me again I remained steadfast, and presently we were on the move North, after General Graham and the Fifth Division, or, more properly, Captain Reaney and the Eighth *Caçadores*, or more properly still, away, as I thought, from the French.

CHAPTER IX

*We Reach the Basque Lands, but Mistake our Way, and after
Dangers Survived, Blunder in amongst the French, who yet
provide Us with a Commodity we despaired of – a Mid-Wife,
and she an old Friend at that.*

I

It is already a commonplace of military manuals, one dwelt on in
the History of the Late Wars now before me, and by Captain
Branwater when he's drinking port with his friends after a day
fox-hunting over the Béarn Champain (a sport he has become
recently much addicted to and has a pack of hounds bred in
England and sent out for the purpose), that Lord Wellington's
march in the next eighteen days was as swift and secret as any previously known and this especially in the latter week, when the
whole army disappeared into the uplands of the Ebro North of
Burgos to reappear over the mountains in five homologous
onslaughts, like so many thunderbolts, on King Joseph's Army in
the Valley of the Zadorra by Vitoria.

Since the French did not know where he was, nor in what
strength, since all said the paths and mountains he was in were
unmapped and crossed only by goat-tracks and it was unthinkable
he could negotiate them, it is little wonder we could not keep up
with him and were soon lost ourselves; and how it came about I
am still not quite sure to this day, but on the Eighteenth of June
we being in a hill village some three leagues North and West of
Vitoria heard gunfire, as of cannon and sharp musketry which
frightened me but cheered both my Companions for in three

days we had seen no soldiers at all, of any army, and notwith-standing my expressed fears they needs must do naught but march towards the gunfire and me with them. After an half hour or thereabout, and the noise of battle coming ever nearer, suddenly round a bend in the track (for it was a narrow and winding valley we were in) came the waggons and baggage, escorted by dragoons, of a whole division, and at a brisk trot as if they were pressed from behind, and the thing is they were not the Fifth nor the Third, I know not what number they were and did not stay to look, for they were French.

They were yet half a mile off and I managed to bundle Paqui and my two Charges, who were now very far gone in their condition and more like firkins in skirts than the young if buxom ladies I had known the previous November, off the road and into a copse of alders by the stream.

The events that now took place were the cause that directed us to my Ladies' final place of lying-in, but our situation helped as well – that is, that our copse was on the East side of the track, and the combat was developing on the heights to our left, that is to the West.

First, along these heights we saw a regiment or more of foot in open column of companies, moving in good order and deployed to turn and fight, with *tirailleurs* skirmishing in open order behind them, firing off their pieces at a foe still not visible to us. Next the Baggage Train clattered by, the dragoons stern with carbines unholstered, the lean French women whipping up their cattle and shouting abuse at them, then a battery of guns whose commander, observing a good clear grass slope also up on the left and a little in front of us, turned off, climbed the ridge, unlimbered, so soon they were banging away at targets to the North of us and still out of sight.

'I make no doubt,' I said to Flora, 'some red coats may soon appear, but I fear they may be the last we see,' and even as I spoke a round shot fired from the other side of the ridge at the French cannon passed over their heads and crashed on a rock just outside our copse, not fifty yards off, where it splintered with a great clanging noise and shard passed quite close over us. 'I conclude,' I went on, 'we had best move off away from all this, and take stock what to do when we are no longer fired on.'

'Or we could lie down where we are and let it all pass over our heads,' said Flora, though we were already pretty much crouched down, you may be sure.

But now another shot landed, nearer than the first, and this time a splinter fortuitously struck Paqui on the rump, which acted like the sharpest spur or goad, so that, frightened already by the considerable noise about us, she tore her bridle free from my hand and set off at a gallop across the stream that meandered through our copse and up through the broom, now in pod, that dotted the Eastern slope of our valley. I had two thoughts as I pursued her – one: I did not wish to lose her; two: I estimated she did well to withdraw the way she did.

I caught her two furlongs up the slopes since she paused at last in a declivity to graze awhile – where there's grass there's donkey – and soon, albeit breathless, red in the face, and not a little scared, for the skirmish was now developing briskly below us, Mistresses Tweedy and Reaney joined me there, and they were right to have come for even as they joined us two companies of French foot entered our copse and deployed there to cover the withdrawal of their regiment, and the firing fell into a steady roll. I put it to my Companions that beyond the ridge we were much less likely to be caught up in the fray, and so we crossed it. Casting a last look back I saw a line of brown and black, Portuguese *Caçadores*, just coming into view at the top of the valley, but judged it better to keep mum.

We were now in very wild and broken country – and for the first time off any track. Our first aim was to get clear of the fight and this took us a mile due East when we paused to get our breaths again and noted the gunfire going off from us and no human, fighting or otherwise in sight. We took counsel together and decided that since we had no idea how the fray was going, that we were likely to be shot, or run down, or captured by the French, as fall in with the British, our best plan was to continue for a time in the same Easterly direction until our situation was clearer. But the country thereabouts was exceedingly broken into ridges and ravines, into hills and downs that rose very steeply, though not very high, and were often wooded; we found few tracks and these sometimes came to nothing or after starting well for us took a bend to the South which was the direction the French were in: in short we were soon well lost in this Wilderness, and once even passed the same spot twice. We continued thus two days, until midday of the Twentieth, by when we were starved, cold, helpless, and despairing, for the first evening of our wandering the weather turned unseasonably bitter, and rain, very cold rain, fell in torrents all through the Nineteenth. All in all these were as bad a two days as we had had since crossing the Sierra de Francia seven months before, in dead of winter; and this weather Mistress Tweedy said, and said more than once, was 'a bit over the odds', it being a day off Mid-Summer's Day, but could not explain the expression when we asked her to, though she said it was one of her Father's and to do with Horse-Racing – which left Mistress Reaney and me none the wiser, though we conceded that if it pleased her to do so we would agree that the weather was indeed 'a bit over the odds.'

As above, this continued until about midday on the Twentieth – which was still a cold wet day, but improving, the rain coming down in squalls from the Bay of Biscay, not continuing in torrents – when we came down a hill-side and saw a good road, a *chaussée* running North and South across our path, and a small hamlet by it; we came on a bit and saw this valley open out below us on to a rolling plain with hills and woods in its midst and almost straight ahead, about a league off, a not inconsiderable town the twin spires of whose cathedral were just then caught in a shaft of bright sun that set them off well against the greeny-blackness of the forested range beyond.

This cheered us, for it was now a case of taking shelter and warm food from the Devil himself if need be, my two Ladies being in the very extremes of exhaustion and moreover complaining of belly cramps which could, for all we knew, be the first pains of parturition; however, our spirits thus raised were soon dashed, for a rise in our path, and the rounding of a shoulder on our right brought us a fuller view of the plain than we had yet had, and what we saw was a magnificent and dreadful sight.

'Holy Mary, Mother of God,' Mistress Tweedy was moved to exclaim.

In front of us meadows and orchards stretched for a mile or so to a river which meandered East to West down the plain before losing itself amongst hills of some steepness and consideration, about six miles off to our right; a mile or so beyond this river, not on it, the town seen before stood to our left – and between the town and the hills, on uneven but rising ground, sloping up and away from us and the river so all were presented to our view, there marched and counter-marched fifty thousand men or more – Regiments in Line, Brigades of Horse, Batteries of cannon, with flags and plumes blowing in the wind, the uneven sun glinting off bayonets, and oil-skins still wet, and distantly came the rumble of iron-shod wheels and the strains of martial music.

The British we had lost; but the French, three armies of them parading before King Joseph himself, we had found.

Mistress Violeta Reaney began to cry, at which Mistress Flora Tweedy flicked her long hair back over each shoulder, pressed her lips for a second as if she counted or prayed, then, 'Come, come, Violeta, we must not give way to the dumps you know. We have come a long way and been through much, and must not now let a few thousand Johnny Crahppos discompose us,' at which Mistress Reaney managed a smile with a sniff, like the sun then gleaming through the racing grey clouds, and said, 'Oh Flora, 'twas not out of fear I cried, but out of disappointment – my Mister Reaney will not be found here I'm sure,' but what she said was cut off with a gasp and her hand went to her side and she blenched. Flora cast a quick look at her and then said briskly, 'Come on, Joey, find us some shelter I pray you, we have come I believe to such a pass where we must ignore such inconveniences as *those*; at any rate we must be sure they incommode us as little as may be. There are none I can see this side of the river, and a village only half a mile off, you must get us that far if you can.'

Well, with my arm round Flora, who also used a stick I had cut her, and leading Paqui, who still bore Violeta, as she had for an hundred or two leagues and more I dare say, I got them down to this hamlet which was barely that, just four or five hovels, and found all deserted and ruined, as if not lived in for some years, a circumstance then frequent on account of the Wars – there was no hope there of comfort or of food, so, 'Press on,' said Flora, 'press on to the next and better luck, I hope.' We crossed the carriage-way a furlong above the bridge over the river which was held by a troop of green-jacketed dragoons; their officer raised his glass at us, but, 'Pay no attention,' said Flora, 'and he'll ignore us,' which he did, though two of us were in coats of a British Regiment of the Line, and now we saw ahead of us another village, more considerable than the first, for it had a bell-tower, and so a church, much like my Father's with a stork's nest on it.

This second village was also deserted, or almost, for one inhabitant remained and fortunately so, as I shall presently relate, but this evacuation had been more recent, indeed so recent as to be of that very morning, for we found the streets clean and well-appointed, the houses not dilapidated and the doors of all, of all but one, securely bolted and in some cases barred. Thanks be to Jesus and His Mother, or so said my quite forspent Companions, for the one householder who had neglected this precaution and left the door on the latch.

And thus it was we came, at about four of the afternoon, on the Twentieth of June 1813, to *Gamarra Mayor*, a village on the River Zadorra, one mile and a half North-East of the capital of the Biscayan Province of Alava, that is – VITORIA.

2

In Biscay the peasants hold the fertile and well-watered land they farm securely, and so are prosperous – thus much I remember from the proceedings of my Father's Economic Society (should I have said *Uncle's*?) and the interior we now found ourselves in bore witness this is indeed so. The cottage was two-storeyed, the ground floor being stabling at one end, as is usual everywhere in Iberia, the cattle gone but fowl still about, the manger still full with new mown hay in which wild flowers as tansies, poppies, and blue cornflowers could be seen, which pleased Paqui mightily, and at the other end a work-shop and tool-store filled with brightly kept implements of more variety and more modern design than I had seen in Castille or León – as, above the normal scythes and sickles, a mechanical gin for separating, but what from what I could not guess, and so forth. A set of open wooden stairs with banister quaintly carved led to the living quarters which were three rooms – kitchen with pantry and closets, living room with a cot for a child as well as table, chairs, spinning distaff hanging on the wall, and in the last room a fine large bed with quilted covers.

Flora stood in the midst, hands on belly and looked about.

'This will do,' she said. 'It will serve very well for our lying-in; do you not agree, Mistress Reaney?'

'Ay, it will do very well, though perhaps a shame there's only one bed.'

'Well, we must share it if put to it, otherwise take turn and turn about.'

They continued to explore, opening presses and cupboards. 'We must look after all well,' said Flora Tweedy, 'and leave all as we find it, with proper payment for consumables used.'

'But of course,' cried Mistress Reaney.

'Oh la, 'twas not at you I directed the remark. I meant it for Joey's ears.'

'You know,' I said, 'why this village is deserted.'

'Well, I suppose they expect a battle.'

'You have seen what a battle can do to a village.'

She bit her lip a moment, then shrugged. 'Let them have their battle if they want. There's that knocking in here to come out,' and she patted her belly again, 'that will not be put off by the Day of Judgement, let alone a battle, and to tell truth, Joey, I have not the strength to carry it a step further.'

'I have found bread,' said Violeta from the kitchen, 'which is brown, not white like our Castilian.'

'Then Joey will go below stairs and find us some eggs . . .'

'And what is this yellow grease?'

'That, Mistress Reaney, is butter, which is used in these parts for oil – it melts to an oil when heated.'

'It tastes quite excellent,' said Violeta, licking her finger. 'What vegetable is it made from?'

'No vegetable at all but from the cream of milk.'

'You astonish me Mistress Flora. What then do these Basques do for cheese?'

'Why milk is so plentiful they have enough cream for cheese as well as butter. 'Tis the same in Ireland – or so my Father said, for I was never there. However, the Navy brought salted butter to the garrison at Gibraltar. Joey, why are you standing there? First you must get eggs, and then I think you'll have to be off.'

'Off?'

'Aye, Joey. To fetch us a midwife – for I doubt you have the skill, and even if you claim it I should prefer you did not practise it on me.'

'I'll look for eggs,' I said.

Apprehensive already for the other errand she had suggested, I was now given straightway a sharper fright. As I descended into the stable I saw the door to the street was open – foolishly, like the absent tenants, I had forgotten to bolt it – and a large figure, black against the light, almost filled it, so large I thought it must be a Grenadier of the Imperial Guard at least. But whatever this monster was it was not a French soldier for at sight of me it backed off into the street as if more frightened of me, than I of it.

So with the first dizziness of my scare somewhat under control I got down and to the door and dared to look out rather than slam and bolt it.

A yard or two off was the biggest woman I did ever see, and the ugliest as well, save only perhaps the eccentric Tía María of Los Arapiles, she who chased Rubén, Fernando and me from her yard the day I almost had Rubén's head off; but this woman was bigger yet, and perhaps uglier. She was six foot tall with a head small in comparison with the rest but large all the same, wrapped in a greasy shawl, with pig eyes lost in a huge round, pasty face which had straw-coloured bristles to its several chins, then below this a black dress much patched which seemed to burst at the seams, and huge round shoulders as I have seen before only on the Smith who worked in the forge near Salamanca market. The rest of her was in proportion, indeed in just proportion for she was round, globular – diameters drawn at random through her mass would all have had a like length, whether up and down or across.

For a moment I wondered if my Good Star yet shone and here was a midwife sent from heaven to save me looking for one across a battlefield, but this, this lump, now made a strange croaking noise, tilted her head a little to one side as far as her massive neck would allow and with a podgy finger, like a sausage, pointed to her mouth. From this I surmised that with her physical deformity she was further afflicted with dumbness or simpleness or both – indeed further reflection suggested this must be so, or else why should she be there when all else had fled?

We watched each other thus – she croaking, I puzzled for I wished to understand her croaking, then a look of resignation or despair passed over that monstrous countenance, she backed off a pace or two, lifted her massive shoulders, turned and waddled and rolled her way up the street, and as she went she tried each door, as we had before her.

I went back indoors and this time fastened up, adding a beam I found on the floor to the bolts already there. And what with all the tremendous events of the next forty hours it is not to be wondered at that I entirely forgot the Fat Woman of Gamarra Mayor, until she next, and with wonderful contingency, came into my life again.

I chased the black and brown speckled hens with their rooster up on to the rafters and found four eggs in the straw about the place – they were large and brown, so I wondered if the Girls would be nice about them, preferring white as more wholesome, but this I need not have feared for they were hungry for any food and would have dined well off worse.

I had plenty else to fear though and with good reason for after we had dined off eggs *revueltos* with herbs in butter, as Violeta termed it, which made Flora laugh for she took it to mean *revolting*, and bread with fresh milk found cool in an earthenware jug, Mistress Tweedy returned to the subject of a midwife.

'But where shall I engage one?' I objected, 'it's not possible there's one to be had for miles.'

'Stuff,' she replied, 'there is a considerable town within a league, with midwives in plenty, I make no doubt. Ooof!' This last provoked by a spasm that now gripped her, but passed, leaving her face greyish, and a sheen of perspiration shone on her brow. 'Mistress Reaney, be so good as to lend me your arm, I think I should be better on the bed in the other room.'

At this Violeta sent me such a look of fear and despair over her shoulder as she helped her friend up and away, that my heart almost melted.

'But it's all behind French lines,' I cried.

'Joey,' came through the doorway, 'it may well be *Pandemonium* itself, and *Beelzebub's* cohorts drawn up between us and it, but you must go there and fetch a midwife. I promise you you must. For both of us.'

I damned them both aloud. Silence fell, and then the bed creaked.

'Joey?'

'What's the matter"

'Come here. I beg you.'

I went to the doorway. Flora Tweedy was now sitting back on the bed, her head high on the pillows, her chestnut hair plastered across her pallid brow, and in spite of her lump there was a frailty about her – she looked shrunken small in her man's red coat and green and red plaid skirt still wrapped about her. She gasped a little as if out of breath. Violeta sat beside her and held her hand.

'Joey. Come here. Now give me a kiss, a good buss, I pray you, and then be off.'

I hesitated, then went over to her, her arm came round my neck, and held me firmly as we kissed, lips to lips, held there firmly for a short eternity.

'You're a good lad, Joseph,' she said at last, 'and I don't say but what I've a corner of my heart reserved for you, after all these months.'

She pressed her cheek on my hand, which she still held, and then I took myself off.

I asked Violeta Reaney to come down into the stable so she could bolt the door behind me.

'How if I cannot get down to let you in?' she asked, as I harnessed up Paqui again.

'I'll get in,' I said, 'somehow. Hold still.' This last to Paqui who shook her head and ears as always when I tried to get the bridle on her. I hoisted up her heavy wooden saddle and strapped that on too.

'You're not so far on as Mistress Tweedy, at all events,' I said.

'Perhaps not. But not far behind either.'

'Right then,' I said. 'I'll be off.'

'Here, Pepe. Take this.'

It was a cornflower, a star-burst of blue, plucked from the hay stored in the rack above the manger. She reached up and threaded the stem through the hole in the brim of my slouch hat.

'You may kiss me now, José.'

I did. She was not so close as Mistress Tweedy, perhaps having
her Johnny Reaney in mind; she was always a sort of sister to me.
It was then a little after five o'clock in the afternoon.

There was only one way to go, and that down the street, which
was well-paved, almost like a town's, and so towards the river, and
as I went I thought I heard a baby's cry, so I waited a moment to
see if they would call me back, but it was fancy born out of anxiety or a desire to have the need for a midwife prevented, and we
jogged on. It was a change to be up on Paqui – the extra height
gave me for a moment a sort of confidence but I soon marked the
bridge, a narrow stone one, just wide enough for a cart, with
stone parapets and round stone blocks at each end. There was a
picket of ten hussars on the other side and the spurious confidence
given me by Paqui evaporated at sight of them, but it was well I
was on her: I doubt if I should have crossed if I had had only my
own legs to carry me.

I knew by the black slings that supported their sabretaches and
fusees they were of the Third Hussars, those that had charged our
Division's right at Los Arapiles and harried our retreat to Ciudad
Rodrigo, so, knowing them to be steady troops, I was not surprised that they held their ground in face of my approach. Their
sergeant told off two men to take me to their colonel, and he went
with them to their General, called Lamartinière, whose Divisional
Head Quarters was a large tent to the East of the Town, the main
body with the King being in the broken plain to the West. I
prefer not to recall too minutely what my feelings were while
these transactions were in train, the sensible will imagine them
well enough, suffice it to say I held myself together well enough to
answer the General's questions, which were on these lines, asked
in English through an interpreter.

'You are a British soldier?'

'No, Sir.'

'Why lie to me? You wear the coat of one.'

'Yes, Sir.'

'How did you come by it if you are not a British soldier?'

'I mean, Sir: Yes, I am a British soldier, Sir.'

And here I must remind myself I was on an errand of much urgency, this interrogation was a brutal and perhaps material interruption to it, if I was to do what I had set out to do I must get off quick, and I had learned from much experience – some of it recorded in these memoirs that to get off quick in this sort of situation is to give the answers wanted, whether true or false.

'A deserter?'

He wanted a deserter.

'Yes, Sir.'

'Why?'

This was more difficult, but inspiration of a sort came to me.

'I stole the donkey, Sir. Stealing is a hanging matter in our army.'

'Regiment?'

'Eighty-Eighth, Sir.'

'Division?'

'Third, Sir.'

Now there was a pause and all in the tent eyed me, for all I suppose foresaw the next.

'Where were they when you left them?'

'North, Sir. Three leagues North,' I answered briskly, for a brisk answer often disguises rank invention, and immediately all – General, Colonel, and Staff – broke into a positive bedlam of French oaths and curses, exclamations and rhetorical questions, with arms flung about, eyebrows raised, mouths pulled down and shoulders hunched, eyes wide, and the air full of flying spittle. At last the General flung up his arm and ordered silence, which fell like an executioner's axe.

'Was the General Head Quarters in the neighbourhood?'

'Yes,' I replied.

'Milor Velinton?'

'Yes,' for that again is what he wanted to hear.

Again the babble broke out, yet more animated even than before, and more extended: maps were brought out and unrolled,

orders were given, messages written, and at least three Aides
saluted with much jangling of gear and rushed away – whither, I
neither knew nor cared. For ten minutes this went on and I was
quite ignored but then a sort of lull spread out and the General
looked up and took notice of me again.

'We are much obliged to you,' he said. 'We have not known the
whereabouts of Milor Velinton for a month. What is your name?'

'Prigg,' I said. 'I was once a Corporal, but unjustly lost my
chevron.'

'Well,' perhaps you shall win it again. Take him and his donkey
to the baggage park, and presently we'll find occupation for both.'

So, feeling better, much much better, I was led off, and I quite
chuckled to myself as I remounted Paqui and a private soldier took
her bridle and led us off; and I was pleased to see the direction he
took was toward the twin spires of the Town, beyond which and
beyond the mountains behind them a fine sunset was now developing with high mackerel patterned clouds lit from below and just
tinged with rose and gold, promising better weather for the
morrow. Of course I had no inkling that the Peer was behind those
hills and not to the North at all, but that by the by, for what now
occupied my attention was this Baggage Park we then entered.

3

This, as all know who read the Dispatches and Reports of the
Battle, and the Histories and Memoirs published since, quite beg-
gared description.

Over a wide, flat plain, the flattest country thereabout, some two
thousand vehicles were drawn up in serried rows, and every type
represented from huge *fourgons* requiring a team of twenty mules to
pull them, through landaus, broughams, chariots, curricles, and
britzkas, to carts and waggons of the humblest sort; twenty thousand people – Ministers, Bishops, courtiers, clerks, commissaries,
contractors, their wives, their children, their lacqueys, their cooks,

their maids, their grooms occupied the avenues between the vehicles, so all had the appearance of a great Fair or *verbena* – such as that I've heard takes place in the meadows of Madrid at San Isidro or at Seville for the *Gran Feria* there, and there was a buzz of talk and coming and going, of music too, and laughter. Peasants and pedlars from all the country round who had fetched in provisions and hawked them about were now packing up and moving off while fires were lit and suppers prepared with what had been bought, and here and there the better sort were setting out tables, many furnished with the most glittering silver and crystal, and some even gold, in display more lavish than any I had ever seen, save on the altar of a Cathedral, so all in all it was a brave sight, a splendid sight, as grand as can be thought of.

And what was all this? Simply it was the accumulated loot of five years systematic robbery, carried on with the most brazen indifference to all the laws of God or Man – well, those at all events which relate to property – virtually the entire moveable wealth of a great nation. Generals who had ridden out of Bayonne with a horse and a spare suit now had here these huge waggons, barred and locked, and printed up neatly with legends as *Le Lieutenant-Général Villatte, le Général Darmagnac, le Maréchal Jourdan*, and so on and so on, but the largest and with armed guards, painted up in dark blue with yellow trimmings, were emblazoned thus: *Domaine Extérieur de S. M. L'Empereur*, and held the plate, the tapestries, the paintings and the statuary of the Royal Palaces of Spain, King Joseph's fee to his Tyrannical Brother.

Amongst all this my *poilu* leading me now pointed out six *fourgons* newly arrived from Bayonne, not Madrid, carrying five million francs – pay for the armies then camped around us.

As I say, he led me up and down these avenues for some time, perhaps twenty minutes, gossiping away in the manner of his kind with much gesture and exclamation as '*Oooh là, là, là*', and '*bien sûr*', '*mais c'est vrai, blague à part!*', for he had ascertained what his general had not, that I had his tongue off tolerably well, pointing out all these wonders, and we never seemed to be getting anywhere, or indeed heading in any particular direction and at last it came to me what was indeed the case, that he had fulfilled his duty by bringing me thus far and was now spinning out the time against when he would have to return to more arduous occupations.

'I suppose,' I said, 'in all this throng there must be a midwife or two.'

At which he looked up at me a little curiously – he was a lively man, small, some ten or fifteen years older than I – and said: '*Mais oui, bien sûr* . . . I doubt not that there are trades even more singular, every trade under the sun for it is a city on wheels, *une véritable ville qui roule.*'

I pressed the point – what else could I do? – at which he pulled one of those French faces, then presently made off, no doubt convinced that I was mad, like all *rosbifs*.

Dusk was spreading between the carriage, lamps and flambeaus were lit, bats whirled above like black papers in a wind against the luminiferous violets and turquoises of the sky, and I continued to perambulate the alleys of this monstrous caravan in several minds at once as to how to proceed – should I continue to ask for a midwife? Why not? In all that throng it was not impossible, nay perhaps even likely somewhere a wench would be in labour, and not so unreasonable a frantic husband or servant should be out on such an errand. Or should I press on out of this huge park and across the fields to the little town beyond – where at least one would expect in the *barrios* a shopkeeper here or a constable there to know where one might be found, that place being stable and stationary, not shifting its order and streets about each day. But what if I was challenged again? I could not but be sensible of my good fortune in moving about freely – could I be so sure that the next General I met would be looking for a *deserter*? Might I not now encounter one whose mind ran on *spies*? And all the time my mind went back to what was happening in Gamarra – were they coping? Had things advanced yet beyond their ability to cope? And an hundred phantasies filled my mind.

★

'GIUSEPPE! ZEPPO!'
    '*MAMMA MIA!*'
    Out of the light and darkness surged four figures – dark silks rustling, luminous petticoats flashing, hands (three pairs white and one black) reaching up, shaking, grasping, ruffling, tickling; four faces laughing, hair tossed, hair swinging – 'Zeppo, Zeppo, Zeppo, *Caro Mio*' – Brigid, Lady Secret Rose, Ishtar, and Dolores, pulling me down from Paqui's back, urging me, pushing me, arms round my neck, round my waist, almost carrying me across five yards of muddy grass to a grand open carriage, the largest open one I have ever seen, where sat amongst cushions, beneath lamps, with a small table set before her, with Marinetta on one side and a little man in black on the other, where sat, throned as it were, her auburn hair piled high round Spanish combs set with glittering stones, none other than – Madame, herself.
    'Giuseppe, *mi carissimo.*'
    '*Mamma mia.*'
    Four pairs of hands hoisted me from below, two arms, white and strong as ever lifted me and pressed me into the warm fragrance of her ample bosom, and so overcome was I, I now gave way to tears and sobs that lasted minutes before they were properly under control, indeed hartshorn and brandy were resorted to.
    The small gentleman in black, who appeared to be dining with her, offered to depart, but was urged to stay. 'Zeppo, he is the Minister of Finance, and looks after us,' Madame whispered to me.
    Such extasies cannot be continued long, and soon we were all sitting up in this carriage – the Minister, Madame, myself and Marinetta on one side, and the four Girls on the other, and what Marinetta apologised for as being only a snack, for this wandering life made provisioning difficult, but seemed an Epicure's Phantasy to me being jugged pigeons, a salmon galantine, and a cold saddle of mutton, all served with champagne, dressed up on the table between us, and Madame urging me on to more than my share for, she said, I looked peeky and seemed skinny, and surely needed feeding up.

'And how do you find us?' she asked, 'do you not think we manage this gypsy life well? Are we not better for fresh air and travel?'

I looked round from face to face and each smiled, pouted, nodded or dimpled at me – Brigid tall and pale, her blond hair pulled back and up above her head, Lady Secret Rose shrewish and cunning and not now at all Oriental looking, Ishtar very earnest with an octavo volume of some earnest stuff in English about a Pilgrimage on the table beside her, and Dolores, dusky and warm, fragrant and dark save for her eyes and teeth that glowed in the gloom against the velvet of her skin; and next to me Marinetta, plump, homely, but otherwise primped up in her best black gown and jet beads, good old Marinetta who kept house for them all as ever, who sorted out the inconveniences attendant on their trade, who made sure . . .

'Madame,' I cried, starting up so almost I upset the whole collation. 'Oh Madame, how fortunate I have come upon you thus, but I pray you excuse me, I must be off, but let me borrow Marinetta . . .' and so forth till she calmed me again and begged me to speak slow and with sense, and tell them what was the matter so they could understand it, and at last I did.

'*Deux jeunes filles. Les deux en travail*' and Madame shook her head and tutted, '*m'petit, tu exagères, il me semble que tu exagères . . .*' and she shook her fingers as if she had picked up an iron not knowing it hot, but I begged her not to mock me at which she embraced me again, and then all bustled about to get Marinetta up on to Paqui with the little bag she kept for such contingencies; the Minister called up a boy and presently I had a Grenadier with a lamp, and a pass, to go in front of us through the lines, so really it was hard to see how matters could have turned out better, that is, so long as we were still in time. Madame gave me one last embrace, and after making me promise to bring Marinetta back safely, we set off. We had gone a scant two hundred yards, less perhaps, when Marinetta leaned forward and tapped me on the shoulder.

'Look yonder. Do you remember him?' she asked.

I looked across the way and saw a fine, neat carriage, small but new, in glossy black and grey trim, closed and glazed, but lit within by a bright lamp hung from the ceiling. It had but one occupant and he sat up straight, dressed in a pale blue frock coat with his face white almost as if painted above a high collar, and the livid scar running from above his eye into the mop of flame-red hair – a chill came on me: after so much good fortune it seemed ill that Rubén should appear for in all my life things went bad when he did.

'What's he doing here?' I whispered.

'Like all of us, he's walking his chalks – I mean levanting. They say he has a chest of gold worth an hundred thousand francs beneath his seat. At all events he has sat there like that since we left Madrid, and speaks to no-one but his two servants who are bravoes and blood-thirsty villains by repute.'

As we came near the bridge we found the road that linked Gamarra Mayor with the town filled with marching men which frightened Marinetta – it was ever the fear of all in the Baggage Train that the Armies would march off and leave them all to the mercies of the Spanish, but our Grenadier had words with a Sergeant when the column halted briefly, who told us that news had come in that the British were in force to the North, with a Spanish army too, so the King had ordered a division across the river and into the hills above the village.[*] This frightened me for it meant the village would be occupied and disputed if it came to

---

[*] There is possible in all this the one historical, documented reference I have been able to find to Bosham's activities. In his account of the events of the 20th June 1813 Sir Charles Oman has the following: '*Late at night, apparently on a report from a deserter that there were British troops behind Longa* (the Spanish General operating in that area) *– indeed the man said that Wellington himself was on the Bilbao road – Reille took off the other brigade of Sarrut's division in the same direction, and sent it with Curto's regiments of light horse to join Menne.*' A footnote cites the report of the French General Gazan as a source for this story. See *A History of the Peninsular War*, Vol. VI, page 394, by Oman, Oxford 1922.   J.R.

a battle, and might be bombarded, but there was naught to be done then and I kept mum about this out of regard for Marinetta.

When all was across the river we followed on to the bridge and as we did saw four figures, cloaked close so even their faces were hid, coming towards us, and they brushed by us almost touching but on the side of Paqui away from me so I could not see them, yet I was aware Marinetta blessed herself thrice as they passed, and muttered a *Paternoster* and an *Ave Maria*, so I concluded she took them for gypsies and kept off from herself the Evil Eye – those versed in the arts of midwifery being especially prone to superstition.

CHAPTER X

A Meditation on Eggs, Yet Another Battle, concluding with Matters that will be of Interest to the Reader who has come with us so far.

I

There were soldiers in the village and on account of them Mistress Tweedy and Mistress Reaney had dowsed their glim, a lamp, and closed their shutter, so for a moment I thought they had gone, for they would not answer the door either. In the end I climbed on the Grenadier's shoulders and rapped on the shutter, calling their names, and presently Mistress Reaney came below and let us in, I paying off the Grenadier with a half-guinea by way of a *pourboire*.

What followed was all woman's business and I was pushed out of the way, indeed kept below stairs much of the time, though after half an hour Marinetta called to me and said there would be no birth before the morrow as far as she could tell – Mistress Tweedy being in a sort of labour but the spasms very distant from each other, and Mistress Reaney not yet started, but she sent me to fetch some water, no easy task in the dark but I found a well at the top of the street, then she said the girls were famished, would need their strength, and there being no more eggs she had me kill the smallest fowl, which is a task I never liked but carried out this time well enough. This she boiled up making a good broth for her patients, and she and I then supped off the legs, for by now it was close to midnight and we were peckish despite our supper with

Madame. I found a stone bottle filled with cider which settled my stomach and made me sleep till Dawn, which I did on hay on the floor near Paqui, and narrowly escaped a soaking when her lady-ship pissed at first light.

Thus wakened I put my head above stairs and learned from Marinetta that the situation was much as before, that since both Ladies were carrying their first the lying-in was likely to be pro-tracted, that Mistress Tweedy seemed in the way of having a hard time of it, Mistress Reaney had started, and she doubted not all would pull through well enough; then she sent me back up the street for more water.

This time I had the sense to remove my red coat and it was as well I did for the place was now garrisoned with Fusiliers of the One Hundredth and Eighteenth Regiment of the Line, and to my dismay they were barricading the North end of the streets with gabions, that is wicker baskets filled with earth, were breaking into and occupying all the cottages in that end of the Village, especially those flanking the barricades, and thus they made them into forts or blockhouses, knocking out firing slits in one place, filling up windows or doors in another. I reached the well unchallenged, indeed was not challenged at all for all were busy, and anyway I was no doubt took for an inhabitant of the place too stupid to get away, filled my bucket and turned to go back down to our house, when my eye met the worst sight of all so far, namely three cannon being brought across the bridge to complete our fortifi-cations, and one of these was placed in a second line of gabions just in front of the end of the bridge, blocking off our street and aimed so its fire would *enfilade* the whole length.

I stumbled back as quick as I could, slopping much of the water, but not particularly caring for I did not see what use it would now be, in fact I left it in the stabling, did not even bother to carry it up the steps which I ascended two or three at a time, or tried to, but I missed the top one and slipped thereby smashing my right knee most painfully. Marinetta came out the bedroom and enquired what was the matter and I put it to her straight – we should be off, there was a battle coming, we were in the middle of it, in a village that was to be bombarded.

I make no doubt the old lady was as scared as I for at these news she went as pale as the rag she was holding, but she put a better face on them than I. After a handful of Italian oaths or prayers, it was difficult to distinguish one from the other, she enjoined me to pray for a miracle like that which transported Our Lady's House from Nazareth to Loreto, for, she said, there was no other way the two Ladies in the next room could be moved for some hours to come.

When she was done I heard Flora Tweedy's voice calling and after a brief exchange between her and Marinetta I was bid go in.

As foreseen by Mistress Tweedy the day before, both now lay or rather sat up in the ample bed side by side. Mistress Tweedy was yet more pale and wan than before with shadows yet more marked about her eyes; Mistress Reaney on the other hand had now worked up a fine colour, indeed she was quite red in the face.

'Well, Joseph,' said Mistress Tweedy, 'What's this all about? We're going about our business too tardily for you, I see. But I assure you we're working at it as hard as may be, are we not, Mistress Violeta?'

'Ay, wonderous hard, Flora; 'tis more like labour than I thought.'

There was nothing for it but to tell them what I had seen, though I did not want to fright them more than need be, but I was briskly interrupted right at the beginning of my account.

'Joseph, we are not deaf nor fools. And Marinetta has eyes in her head and Spanish enough to stand at the window and tell us what is toward. So. You will be off now, I suppose – come here and give us another kiss for it is all I have to offer, which is a shame when you have done so well for us.'

Well, I heard a strange sort of rushing in my ears at this and felt a weakness in my legs not the result of my recent tumble, then a voice not my own yet coming from my mouth, for none else there spoke, as follows: 'I'll see if the hens have laid at all, for I'm sure you'll want breakfast, and there's naught else I know of to eat.'

The odd turn that came over me when I made my resolve to stick it out as above left its effects on me for an hour or so and for that time I scarce knew what I did; my brain trundled round in a way I could not control, turning out the oddest ideas. I recall I found five eggs in corners of the barn, three brown, two white, one very large, two quite small and none exactly the same size – I washed the muck and feathers off them in the bucket and put them in a row in front of me, each in its way a perfection of the geometry of life, and, as I say, no two exactly the same. I then fell into a reverie the matter of which was this – how to distribute them amongst the four of us fairly, for Marinetta had called to me they should be coddled in their shells, this being best for ladies in travail. Clearly the largest brown should go to one person, the two smallest – one white and one brown – to another; but these two shares would now both be bigger than the two remaining: moreover, one of these was speckled which might be thought to be not wholesome. And as I puzzled thus it came to me that Nature is all untidy and uneven, an awkward business to manage, and that Man has been lackadaisical and remiss in making Her properly organised, this no doubt on account of that part of us that remains unregenerately Natural.

For example, I thought, in this matter of eggs – it is surely not beyond our wit to train, cajole or constrain hens to lay regularly the number required instead of always one more or one less, and to lay them of a size and of a colour. Equally it is surely allowing a necessarily inconvenient and messy business as child birth to get too much on top of us when more important things, as battles, are toward: Surely, I thought, by manipulation or dosing with drugs, birth can be induced to occur at times, and places apt . . . yes, places too: it is an unwarrantable intrusion on the running of a proper household to have all upset by parturition, special buildings, on the same principle as Bedlams away from the rest, should be provided . . .

Here Marinetta enquired what I was at, so I set a pan to boil and my line of thought thus interrupted fell to musing again about the eggs, and how, being different sizes, they would not cook to the same point together. Eggs, and this wild phantasy I can scarce now credit, so absurd it seems to me as I write this at quiet peaceful time, not with my mind set off its balance by impending battle and geniture come together in awful unlikely junction, eggs I decided should be *graded* − according to colour and size. They could be *weighed* (this shows how far gone I was, for whoever heard of weighing an *egg*?) and weighed according to a rational scale thus − take a litre of water (a litre being the volume occupied by one tenth of a cube measuring one metre by one metre; a metre being one − or is it one tenth? − of one millionth of a line drawn from Barcelona to Dunkirk) and divide the litre into an hundred parts, or a thousand, and call these *grams* − a large egg I guessed would then weigh what, an hundred grams? Seventy? A small one fifty? Fifty-five? Yes, for accurate grading eggs would be classed on a scale of ten units, each unit covering five grams. Hens would be trained or constrained by diet and breeding to produce eggs as required according to this scale. Shopkeepers would sell them thus and minutely adjust their prices accordingly . . .

But at this moment the pan came to boil, Marinetta called again and asked what I was dreaming at, and far over to the West, five or six miles off, a cannonade began to roll like thunder in the hills. *The Battle of Vitoria* had started and *The Implementation of a Rational Scheme for the Classification of Eggs according to Colour and Avoirdupois* was thus postponed − *sine die*, to be sure.

2

Breakfast was finished, cleared away, and I did some chores, as emptying slops, then the sound of the battle coming no nearer I decided to venture out into the village to see what news there were, and how the Armies disposed, hoping thereby to arrive at a more accurate estimate of our chances of survival.

It was now a perfect morning; the first mists had been driven off, the sky was clear, the sun warm; yet following the cold and wretched weather of the two days previous the air was still cool and washed clear by the rain so all in all it was a day, Mid-Summer Day at that, on which it was a delight to be out. The cannon continued to roll away in the background but, as I say, no nearer, and so quickly does the Human Soul accommodate what is not immediately dangerous, however potentially so, I had soon forgot my initial fright at the sound, the more so since the earlier business in the streets had now ceased, the soldiers standing around in groups, smoking and gossiping, their arms piled.

Presently I came on a young Lieutenant standing by the Church which was in the small square where was the well I had already visited two or three times. I approached and jocularly addressed him thus in his own tongue: 'Good day, Sir. A fine day for a battle is it not?'

At which he took me for a French Civilian from the Park and answered that yes it was, and he made no doubt would see the beginning of the end of the *rosbifs* and the *godams* in Spain, and when I asked how this should be he kindly suggested I should step up the Church Tower with him, which was a good vantage point to study the whole field of battle from, and I should then see how the British were blundering into a trap. I should find it most instructive, he said, for it exemplified many of the arts of War he had but recently studied at the *Ecole Militaire*. He was not above seventeen and a fine, fresh-faced though earnest youngster, which accounts I suppose for his innocent readiness to accept me as one of his own kind on no better grounds than a few words of conventional greeting muttered in his tongue. Before the afternoon was out he had his head knocked in.

The tower was no great eminence at all, but even so the addition of some thirty feet to our stature opened up most of the country about to our eyes. The Lieutenant directed my gaze on a line a little South of due West to a point six miles off where the hills that blocked the West end of the Plain formed an angle with the wooded ridges that ran on the South side behind the twin towers of the Town.

'There,' he said, 'is where this river we stand on, called the Zadorra, debouches through a narrow gorge from the plain. There runs the Great Road and it is the only way by which the British can come in on us. I have seen the land,' and here he spoke with a certain youthful solemnness, 'and I think our Generals have chosen this spot very well indeed to stand in. Having come through the gorge the British will have to deploy beneath our guns in a restricted area. They will then have to come on at our lines up sloping ground. True they are in greater numbers than us, which is why today we fight on the defensive; but should they, because of this superiority of numbers, break our first line they will meet a second and then a third, all well established on hills and ridges, one after another, each with the river on one flank and the mountains on the other. No soldiers can carry out assaults on positions like these, one after the other. The result – either Milord Velington will call off the battle when he sees the strength of this position and withdraw (this is most likely for he is a cautious dog), or he will commit his men who will shortly break and then, being caught with only the narrow gorge to get out by, will be pinned against the Western mountains and destroyed in detail. Thus we shall at least hold our position and inflict heavy losses on the enemy, and in two days Clausel and Foy will be up with us which will give us the superiority in numbers, and the British will have to retreat pell-mell, or they will have been destroyed even before these reinforcements arrive.'

'So there is no danger for our armies or the baggage at all?' I asked.

'Oh none, none whatsoever.'

I looked about me, cocked my ear to the gunfire which I supposed was coming from the entrance to the gorge he spoke of, six miles off, and then saw flashes along the ridge to the left of it, along the Southern range of hills, and tiny puffs of white smoke blossoming above them, where they hung in the still and limpid air.

'There is then,' I asked, 'no possibility of the Enemy coming over the mountains and taking us in flank?'

'Oh no, none at all,' he assured me, 'the mountains are quite impassable to all but light troops. I see you have your eye on the ridge to the South – well I make no doubt that is naught but a demonstration on the part of the British, no serious attack can develop from that quarter.'

We always believe what we want to believe, and he said this despite the fact there were guns, a battery at least, banging away on the hills we spoke of.

'And what of our dispositions in this corner of the field?' I asked.

'*Eh bien*, you see this hill in front of us,' he had now turned to face North and was speaking of a lowish Down which neverthe-less rose steeply enough above us, a half mile off, 'round the left of it comes the high road from Bilbao, and up that we know is a divi-sion or so of Spanish, under their General Longa who does present a sort of threat to our flank, which is why we are here. However, our defence against this threat is very secure and also in depth as I shall explain. First, beyond the Down and across the road four brigades of foot and one of horse. If the Spanish come on in greater numbers than we expect, then these may fall back across the bridge here and at villages like this to the East and West. Now see what happens if the Spanish continue to come on,' and he turned me about so we faced South. Another ridge, lower than that to the North but considerable enough, ran roughly East and West on the other side of the river and shielded the Baggage Park from our view. It was lined with perhaps twenty or more guns, already unlimbered, their black muzzles pointing it seemed directly at us. I shuddered at the sight.

'The Spanish will have to come down the hill to the North to get to the river and will be caught in fire from that artillery; they will then have to force this village, finally cross the bridge, and all the time bombarded by those guns. It cannot be done. It cannot be done. No, have no fear, our flank and rear, which we stand on here, cannot be turned, the position is impregnable.'

'Suppose,' I hazarded, 'there is a British Army on the Bilbao road as well as a Spanish.'

He gave me a quick and serious look at this.

'There is a rumour to that effect,' he said, 'and that is why this position has been strengthened, we were in bivouac the other side of the town till late last night in reserve to the main Army. But it's not really possible, you know, not possible. They would have had to have made very considerable marches over very difficult ground, in rain, during the last two days to get there. No – we shall have only Spaniards to deal with today, and not many of those. I strongly doubt we'll see them here at all.'

At this I thanked him, and descended the Church tower very much cheered, for I believed most of what he said, especially that about the few allies to the North. After all, I knew very well where the rumour of a British Army in that direction came from and had even better reason for not giving it any credit at all than he had.

In the square three *vivandières* had arrived, women of the regiment with wine and bread. One of them had a small cask of brandy under her arm, and I bought a tot or two off her which raised my spirits up yet more, and a loaf of bread, which was white and would win Mistress Reaney's approval, and so went back to our cottage. Here I found Marinetta in a bustle – things had come on for Mistress Tweedy it appeared, more water was required, she had missed me and would have told me off had she time for it, though what it was all about I did not discover for she kept me away from the bedroom, indeed would not let me nearer than the stairhead, for all was now woman's business she said.

Things continued thus all morning – the sounds of battle five or six miles off rumbled on, but were scarcely audible in the stable

above the rustling of the chickens in the straw, Paqui's occasional
snort and Marinetta's feet on the boards above. Towards noon I
went out again in my own interest and spent a shilling with the
vivandières on wine in the empty cider bottle, a hard Béarnaise
sausage and more bread. With these, a repast I reckoned fit for a
King or Emperor, I fortified myself before composing myself for
an early *siesta*, but just as I had compacted a pillow from straw and
my red jacket and placed my head upon it, the sound of musketry,
perhaps a mile off, then shouts and a clatter of boots nearby, in the
street outside, brought me to my feet and to a chink in the door.
A bugle blew, more ran past on the cobbles, and at last I was sure
of what I feared: that the garrison of Gamarra Mayor, which had
been lounging about in the sun as much at its ease as I had been
in the cooler shades of my stable, was standing to arms and preparing to resist an assault.

3

It was not long coming, perhaps half an hour, but that half hour
the longest in my life I daresay, for while nothing happened the
signs that something was going to became by every minute more
certain. First the sounds of musketry and cannon, but now from
the East, and a general stir and bustle in the street outside marked
by more bugle calls and high shouts of command inflected to
express a newer urgency and even fear. Then suddenly the deep
and ominous roll of battery after battery let off and by this I
knew the guns the French Lieutenant had shown me to the South
were bombarding the slopes of the hill to the North, and no
enemy could be on those slopes for any reason other than to
assault our village, and now above the deeper roll of massed firing
half a mile off the sharper bang of the four-pounders set in the
gabions up on the other side of the square could be heard, adding
their mite of destruction to all the troops then advancing on us
were sustaining.

They would, I imagined, be coming on in open column of companies, and filling the gaps caused by grape and canister by moving into the centre where the colours would be, so with each salvo the lines became shorter and shorter. Perhaps the first company would break, reduced to half its original number, and fall in with the second coming up to it, but the effect of this would be no more than that of a missed step in the general advance. Now they must be within an hundred yards for the musketry from the village, until then sporadic, crashed out in a reverberating volley that stunned ears already numb, the attackers volleyed back, and before the defenders could reload the bayonets came down, the drums beat double, and on to and over the gabions the first man, and the line behind leaped, a young Colonel, pistol in one hand, sword in the other, hallooing to his men, 'Come on, you Villains, you Rogues, you thundering lousy Bastards, press home to the muzzle, to the very muzzle,' and this I heard or the like, for they were not Spaniards, but Red Coats all who were pouring into the square and driving all before them.

There was yet the second line of gabions and the second gun down in front of the bridge, and before the British could form it cracked, and cracked again, and a hail of grape whistled up the street it enfiladed, that is up our street, the missiles chipping the corners and sills and singing off into the air or ricocheting from side to side, and the line at the top of the street wavered then scattered, nor could it come together again before the gun was sponged, charged, rammed, pricked, loaded, and ready to fire again.

A frontal assault down this narrow street in face of this gun was not possible, but now in and out the side alleys the French were driven in by bayonet, sword and pistol, so soon the position at the head of the bridge was flanked, at which the gun was spiked and the last defenders of Gamarra Mayor scampered across to their lines on the other side of the Zadorra.

Which is to say an hundred or so on each side were variously torn apart by flying metal, hacked about by sword blades, stabbed through the guts, stomachs or lights with bayonets, and left much the worse for this treatment.

A brief lull now fell on the village in which only the screams of those whose bodies had been thus abused, and yet lived, could be heard, together with the squalling of a new-born infant, which, however, I scarcely marked, for a party of three red coats, assisting each other for none could have walked on their own, now came up the street and all lost balance and toppled right against our door, which I opened, and assisted him who was least hurt to pull in the other two, before all collapsed, moaning, and cursing, bleeding and vomiting up the black rum given them for courage, at my feet.

It was a mistake to open that door, for the consequence was that what should have been a haven of quiet in the midst of chaos suited for two young Ladies to lie up in whilst all around them were falling apart and dying, thus giving their darling sprouts a fair start in life, became a field hospital, which is to say a shambles, and a quickly crowded one at that. The lull aforesaid was soon dissipated in a new cannonade, this provoked by three platoons who came down our street, over the gabions and on to the bridge where they were swept apart – I mean limb from limb as well as man from man – by a storm of shot directed all on one small space from the batteries on the Down beyond. I doubt if any came back off the bridge unhurt, very few came back at all, but enough to fill up the rest of the space on the stable floor with more blood, bone, and offal.

What of these could talk now evinced a desire expressed with appropriate oaths in Scotch, Irish, Portuguese, and German, for water, for we require water on our going hence as much or more as on our coming hither, so I upped with my bucket and went off on the first of many short trips to the Well, and congratulated myself heartily that things were so much better arranged here than at Los Arapiles – there I tramped about the field seeking custom, here my clients came to me. On the first of these trips, and indeed on all that followed for he showed no desire to be up and away, I discovered my acquaintance of the morning, the sanguine French Lieutenant, who had lost half of his earnest good looks together with the back of his head.

As I returned from my first trip to the well the French began to bombard the village, as expected, but this turned out not so terrible after all – they had only field guns, no howitzers, nor were they sited any great height above us; the consequence was that only the houses near the river were much knocked about, and they were a shield for us. With one howitzer to drop shells from above our plight would have been serious indeed. Nevertheless an unlucky ball hit a gable or roof tree somewhere near and thus deflected dropped through the roof only a yard from Marinetta, or so I pieced together the incident from its aftermath, and this at last decided her to withdraw to the shambles below, notwithstanding there were no angels to carry her charges – which, by the by, now numbered three, Mistress Reaney having dropped a boy and both doing well.

Marinetta then was below stairs when I came back and hollering, cursing, blessing herself at the fright she'd had and at the sights now before her eyes so she was in a sort of fit that first I tried to shake her out of, but only had sense from her after emptying my bucket on her head, at which she backhanded me in my mouth and bruised my lip, but then calmed down enough to say what had happened. Fortunately I was able to enlist two brawny Scots who still had their limbs and some of their wits about them, they just passing on their way back to reform in the Square, and they came upstairs where they could scarce believe their eyes to see one woman just delivered and the other on the point, but they saw what was wanted and managed to carry both, or rather all three, down into the stable.

This, which had once been airy and even spacious, was now crowded: *item*, five fowl on the rafters who fluttered, squawked, and dropped on all below; *item*, one donkey, to wit Paqui, who munched on the hay and added her contributions to the litter on the floor; *item*, Violeta Reaney on the pillow I had made from my coat, her bodice undone, her infant sucking and a daft smile on her face – her eyes had lost their usual fire and she crooned continually, 'if only Reaney could see him, if only Reaney could see him'; *item*, a young Lieutenant who had lost one of his eyes and half his nose, and was complaining of it; *item*, a Corporal who held a swab a darker crimson than his coat over the hole in his midriff, and who spoke to us all thus, 'I don't think it's in my liver, I don't think it can be in my liver, but if it's not why else do I bleed so fast?'; *item*, two privates, one not much hurt, a broken wrist it looked like, and the other now dead; *item*, Flora Tweedy on the work-bench at the far end of the stable, her knees up, her legs apart, no modesty at all in either her posture or her speech which intermitted oaths with shouts; *item*, Marinetta, her normally black and glossy hair slipping down her back, revealing a bald patch the size of a palm beneath it, her shoulders and chest all wet, who stood above Mistress Tweedy and coaxed her to drink a mixture of laudanum and brandy from a flask; *item*, myself, none the worse really, and grateful for it, and not a little drunk on account of tots taken earlier, and the bottle of wine which I had almost finished, then back out into the smoking street to replace what I had so lavishly emptied on Marinetta.

This bedlam continued another hour or so, then Mistress Tweedy gave a great shout and in a gout of blood and water that spilled down the bench between her legs dropped, like Mistress Reaney before her, a fine boy which Marinetta hoisted up by the ankles and smacked into life. At this very moment a passing soldier who happened to glance in over my shoulder – I being just by the doorpost – turned pale and backed off, saying, 'Holy Mary, that's the second house in the street where there's new-born infants, this village breeds as quick as it kills,' which was manifest nonsense, he must have looked in the same door twice.

At about four o'clock I saw Captain Reaney and knew him straight, though unfamiliar out of his clerical disguise, on account of his fair skin and small size. He was lining up his men in the

Square – one Irish for each two Portuguese, all spic and span in brown with black shakoes, with brass bugle badges and Number Eight for their regiment. He saw me coming, and 'No, by Christ, I can't believe it, it's Joey,' he cried. And then went pale for the significance of my presence came home to him that if I was alive then Mistress Reaney might be so too. I told him this was indeed the case, and where to find her, and that he had an heir ready if he had a mind, like so many round him, to be killed.

'Oh the Deuce take it, Joey,' he cried, 'I well may be for I'm off now to cross that bridge,' and presently he marched them off, but he had a jolly swagger to his gait and as he went he gave me a wink. I was glad I had spoken to him. Whether he got off or not, I do not know, for I never saw him again, but I think he may have, for someone came and removed Mistress Reaney and her child when I was not there, as shortly I shall relate, and I like to think it was he.★

At about this time the noise of battle reached its height. To the West and only a mile or so off, the French made their last stand and massed near an hundred guns against the British who had as many or more, and together they made a din the like of which was never heard before and only equalled two years since at Waterloo. The ground the cottage stood on shook, wattle fell from the walls and dust from the rafters. The British by the by had done what everyone now knows, and the French thought impossible, that is had come down over the mountains and taken the Crahppos in the flank which they could not abide, and so gave way and eventually ran. All that's in the history books. By the time the battle was over, between five and six, I was in no shape to see what was toward on account of a head wound caused by a spent bullet which gave me a concussion, or rather a second bottle of wine I'd

★ According to Oman's *A History of the Peninsular War*, Vol. VI, quoted already, the official returns for the Eighth *Caçadores* after the battle of Vitoria were thirteen men killed, twenty-five wounded, no officers killed, two wounded: so it seems certain Captain Reaney survived.

come on, and was lying in the conduit of our house, where I remained till dusk came on. Marinetta found me there, gained her revenge by bringing me to with a bucket more of water, kicked me up on to my knees and then my feet, cursed me a good deal, till I managed to ask her what was the matter.

'Why you rogue, you villain,' she cried, 'Do you not remember you engaged most sincerely to take me back to Madame? Now see, I have your donkey here ready, my work is done, both sucking nicely, the afters come away clean, and it's time someone gave a thought for the midwife, but the story is always the same, she's always forgot when all is over,' and so on while I shook the wet out of my eyes and hair, gave her a lift up on to Paqui's back, and set our faces to the bridge.

Before we got even so far I wished I'd looked in to see how Mistress Tweedy and Mistress Reaney were, and by the time we were on it, had the courage to halt and say to Marinetta that I desired her to wait at the other end the bridge while I just ran back to say where I was going and on what errand, but she cursed me again, and asked what sort of man I was would leave an old woman out in the open amongst marauding armies, and I could be back in an hour in any case. Well, I was not back till morning the day following, for reasons I shall set down honestly, though they reflect little in the way of credit on me, and so I missed them, and never saw them again, though I searched up and down for them for weeks. But this is to get ahead of my tale.

CHAPTER XI

A Long Chapter Recording Amazing Scenes after Battle;
How a Villain suffered a Fate Deserved; and How Providence
put me in way of a Wet-Nurse, with other Matters too, of
almost equal Import.

I

'This,' said Patrick Coffey, 'this I am now in is a rare vision, a dream past the wit of man to say what dream it is.' He had his head in Brigid's lap, who would have cheerfully offered him greater comfort but he suffered from fatigue following a day marching, fighting, marching, fighting. 'The man who will offer to say what dream this is, is a patched fool. I shall get Joey Bosham to write a ballad of this dream, it shall be called Coffey's Dream . . .' but here Brigid shushed him with a crystal goblet she put to his lips, and he paused to quaff some of Madame's champagne.

'He has the lines off the t'eatricals Captain Branwater got up this Winter in Roger's Town,' Nolan explained, whose head lay on Dolores' bosom, his feet in Ishtar's lap.

'Indeed that's tru' Kevin, and never was the part so well portrayed our Captain said, and you were very competent in the part of Flute. Hark:

> *Sweet Moon I thank thee for thy sunny beams,*
> *I thank thee Moon for shining now so bright:*
> *For by thy gracious glittering golden gleams*
> *I trust to take of truest . . .* BRIGID *sight*

'. . . Give us a kiss then my Darling.'

Which she did, while the Moon thus apostrophised seemed to my fuddled gaze to swell and grow more round and bright and beautiful, for it hung like an orange in the purple forests of the night above us.

'Alberto,' said Madame, on whose shoulders my own head rested, 'how many bottles have we left?'

'Just half a dozen, Madame,' the little Minister in black replied.

'That is too few to be worth considering; I pray you uncork me one and another for our friends. I need consoling. Tomorrow will come soon enough and then we shall ponder what is to be done; now I could fancy being tipsy.'

Around us the pillaging of the Baggage Train, the most considerable booty ever won by an army on a battle-field, had subsided into restless bickering between roving gangs of drunks who staggered about in the fitful dark and light of the Moon dripping napoleons and doubloons from their pockets, carrying sacks on their backs that clanged and clanked with church plate, and in one or two instances still trying to smash their way through hasps and bolts, locks and chains, at treasures not yet uncased.

This was nothing to the riot that had been under way when Marinetta, Paqui and I arrived in the Park: then the first waggons to try the Pamplona road had just stuck, that part of the Convoy that had begun to move behind them had piled upon them – all this at the Eastern end, at the West the first British horse were skirmishing about, and in the middle the looting had begun, and not by the Allies at all, but by French soldiers broken from their ranks and fleeing, and by the servants and lacqueys, mule-drivers and coachmen in the pay of the French. Through all this we had contrived to make our way, though despairing often with men and women mad with fear or greed milling about, cattle panicked rearing and plunging, and the noise of battle only a mile or so off – while on either side the trickle of French breaking grew with terrible quickness into a torrent as all realised the jig was up and the cry *Sauve qui Peut* rose on all sides. Through all this, I say, we

pushed and shoved until at last after passing Rubén in his smart
coach, this time with a pistol in each hand, staring whitely out at
the riot around him, and as yet untouched, we came again to
where Madame's four coaches had been (for the one where I had
supped the night before was only part of her equipage) and found
them hardly moved at all, save one, and that an enclosed cart,
locked and framed like a strong chest with all her cash and the
most valuable objects saved from her life as Madame of a Superior
Bordello in it. This had gone entire, taken not by English, Irish,
Portuguese, nor even French, but by the Catalan Coachman who
drove it, abetted by Lady Secret Rose who was half Catalan herself and who it now seemed certain had been in league with the
coachman for just such an opportunity. 'The Bitch even took my
keys at point of pistol,' Madame complained once the fit of sobbing and cursing and wringing her hands had subsided, but she
was now much calmer and facing her loss with stoicism, as above.

Into all this, and about half an hour after Marinetta, Paqui, and
me, had come Coffey and Nolan, and some others of the
Connaughts, strolling by merely gaping at the sights as if at a fair
in Cork or Wexford, Coffey eating an early apple which may
have been all the loot he took that day, all openly at any rate, but
I think he had hid some doubloons either about his person or
where he could return to find them, for when I came up with
him again a month later at Sorauren, he boasted he had got off
very well at Vitoria where others had been forced to part with
their thievings into the common purse and many flogged as well.
As I say, he and Nolan came by singing their jaunty song:

> I'm really much more willing
> To make myself a killing
> Living off the pickings of the Ladies of the Town . . .

at a most opportune moment for three louts from Tyneside, big
coarse lads with hands like hams and boots like fiddle-cases were
about to force their way into the open coach, desiring to plunder

the ladies of their jewellery and maybe worse (though our ladies would cheerfully have gone on their backs to save their gew-gaws) and I, recognising first their song then my pair of old friends, hallooed above the mêlée, at which Coffey chucked his core and – 'Why Kev, if it's not our old mucker Joey come back from the dead and in trouble with some boggers from the Sixty-Eighth,' he said, and came on in.

The upshot was the Geordies were seen off with cracked pates and bloody noses, Nolan and Coffey welcomed by Madame and the three remaining girls, and had stayed with us since, supping champagne, fondling and fondled with the girls and answering further unwelcome callers on our behalf. Satisfied she was now safe from further harm with these friends Marinetta now took herself off to the coach behind, and aided by a flask of Armagnac, her favourite tipple, soon passed out into an unshakeable slumber, the consequence of her labours and the frights she'd had.

So there we all were, and presently: 'It was a fine battle,' said Coffey, finding he had no more to say to the Moon, 'a fine battle.'

'It was a fine battle, Patrick,' said Kevin, 'a fray with a Geordie always has its own particular flavour, I've noticed it before.'

'Y'fool, I was referring to the Battle.'

'Y'were indeed, I onnerstan' y' now Patrick, you was referring to the Battle.'

'D'ye recall,' went on Coffey, 'how auld Tom Picton answered that pretty bhoy come down from Atty?'

'Not exactly,' said Kevin, 'you was nearer to the both of them than I was.'

'Well, he was already in a rage, and he in his top hat to keep the sun out of his eyes, for we had been stuck in front of the river an hour or more . . .'

'More, more, two at least.'

'. . . and "Damn it, Lord Wellington must have forgotten us," he said.'

'Worse than that, Patrick, 'twas not "damn it" he said.'

'Kev, let me put you in mind of the ladies amongst us.'

'Y'right Patrick quite right – "Damn it" was his very words.'

'Then this pretty bhoy comes up to him on his horse and asks where Lord Dalhousie and the Seventh was, and that 'twas the Seventh was to attack the bridge in our front. So auld Tom says "Tell Lord Wellington that in less than ten minutes I and the Third will take yon bridge and let who wills support us, then Come on ye rascals, come on ye fighting villains," he says, or words to that effect, and to cut a short tale shorter, for there was not much to it after that but volley, load, volley, charge, in with the bayonet, load, volley and charge until here we are. 'Twas a fine battle, a famous victory as the song says.'

And he knocked back a bumper of champagne, wiped his mouth, and then contrived to lean forward out of Brigid's bosom a little while Dolores filled his goblet, the better to hear what Madame now said.

'Mr Coffey,' she asked, 'I take it Boney is now well beat and done for?'

'Quite done for, Madame, our gentlemen expect to be in Paris by Christmas if not before, and they'll take us along with them they say. There'll be fine larks then, I promise you.'

'Paris,' said Dolores, and heaved a sigh of ecstasy that lifted her ebony breasts into the moonlight, 'Madame, would we not do well in Paris?'

'Ay Dolly, we would an that contriving minx had not got off with our chinks: for as you know a proper establishment requires a proper outlay. But it's a thought – a thought indeed; a short season only it would be, but imagine it – Russians, Prussians, Austrians, British, the Bourbons returned, in three months we could make what took three years in Salamanca, ay me, ah well.' A thought now occurred to her. 'Señor Alberto,' she said, turning to the ex-Minister, 'surely you have a bit put by, a sum you could invest for a quick return?'

'No Madame, I'm afraid not. My fortunes are entirely bound up with King Pepe's, and you can see what has happened to them,' the little man gestured with his goblet at the scene around us, some drops of his champagne falling on a huge painting just then being carried by four Riflemen who were singing gross words to the tune of *Bladon Races* – it figured a very large and buxom woman standing on a crescent Moon, and turning soulful eyes to Heaven, while angels, or rather cupids, swooped about her.

'Murillo's *Immaculate Conception*,' said Ishtar with some interest, raising her eyes from her book, which I now saw was verse and in English. 'We saw it in Madrid.'

'I recollect it,' said Madame, 'and that woman is as immaculate as I am I thought then, and think so now. Moreover, you said she has a look of me about her, but I can't see it. What a shame, Alberto, an hundred thousand francs would have been sufficient: let me see – shift your head you booby – (this to me for now she required fingers for her sums) or three thousand *Louis*, for no doubt it will be Louis once more. Or do I mean thirty thousand?'

The factor of ten I thought, for I was far gone, dizzy and sometimes drifting off to sleep, but warm too, with the cosy excitement I always felt when embraced by this Aunt/Mother of mine.

'After Paris,' said Ishtar, 'London would seem to indicate itself.'

'How's that, Girl?'

'There is much wealth there, and there will be more with the wars done: and if I had money I should put it in steam carts or steam ships, not a house of pleasure.'

'Hmm. Since we have no money it's not worth arguing the toss; but I see no chance of a well-run bordello ever failing, while steam carts on rails are a fashion only, I'm sure.'

'Yon daft Prigg was always on about these steam engines; do you mind Corporal Prigg then, Kevin?' asked Coffey.

'Aye, I mind Prigg, the daft bogger. Picking up the ball and running. Said he was ahead of his time, daft bogger.'

'One should try to move with the times,' said Ishtar, a touch reprovingly, 'this is, after all, the Nineteenth Century.'

'For my part,' said Brigid, 'I find machines unnatural. I like things natural.'

'So do I, my Lovely,' said Coffey, 'give us another kiss.'

Two more large paintings went by. The riflemen were now singing *The Ball of Killiemuir*. Madame suddenly sat up straight again so my head rolled sideways just as I was dozing off.

'Holy Mary,' she cried, 'Zeppo, I pray you look at that picture.'

I did, pulling myself up and blinking. Lit by a flambeau and the moon the painting in question was fairly easy to discern. It depicted in the foreground a large clay water jar with a vagrant friar dressed in a torn brown robe and white shirt holding the handle as if about to lift and pour from it into a fine drinking glass. This he held in his other hand by the base, the top of the stem being supported by the fingers of a young lad of about ten or eleven who had brought it to be filled. The whole very cunningly and smoothly painted and the persons and objects lit by a sharp light as if from a high window in a dark room.

But 'twas not the excellence of the painter's art had brought Madame so wide awake and intent on the picture, but the face of the vagrant, to which she now directed my attention after first calling to the riflemen to hold the picture steady the while, which, in good humour, they did.

'Is not that the very livingest likeness of your poor dear Father?' she now went on.

'Uncle or Father,' I muttered, and I'm afraid I was a touch surly.

The glance she threw me was suddenly alert, then softened again as she returned to the painting. 'Don't be silly, he was a Father to you in thought and deed and that is all that is material. But is this not his very image?'

I looked at the face more closely and I suppose there was a sort of similarity in the sad wisdom of the eyes, in the resigned but still suffering set of the mouth: for the rest this man had a heavy, solid look about him, a weather-scorched peasant look, that was quite unlike, though as I said as much I felt I had but recently met his living counterpart but could not, and still cannot, recall where.

'Zeppo, you did not know your Father when he was young; and only remember him as a wasted up old book-worm. At all events I am sure you were much like yon boy when you were of an age; I should like to think you were, though I never saw you after you was six.'

The boy was dark, as I am, and with a slight podginess in his face, though large-eyed, and I suppose I might have looked like that then. At all events it's how I think of little *Lazarillo* the eponymous hero of the one book I have from my Father's library, which sits on my table now, and was carried in my pocket at Vitoria.

'I wish,' said Madame, 'that meddling stoat had not stole every stiver we have, I should have happily have given those boys whatever they wish for it,' and with a sigh she waved them on.

''Tis not much of a painting,' said Ishtar, '*chiaroscuro* is now not much rated by people of taste.'

However, I was touched by the tear that gleamed in the corner of Madame's eye, the sister of the diamond chips in her high comb, that flinked in the moonlight like glow-worms, so I was almost moved to offer her her ring, so she could barter for the painting. But while the offer was still unborn on my lips she threw off her dumps and called on Alberto to open the last bottles and fill up our goblets.

Presently she sent Ishtar for wraps and cloaks from the coach where Marinetta slept for she said a dew was coming on and soon had all arranged about us and over us, and thus folded up together we severally dozed off, and surely never carriage held so mixed and motley a crew being three ladies of pleasure with their Mistress or Bawd, two Irish soldiers, one Government Minister (Retired), and . . . how shall I describe myself? Let who will try it – it has taken me all these memoirs to attempt it.

The Moon sank, and was veiled by envious clouds, the noise of riot and debauch, of drunkenness and thieving died away, first a mist came up and then with the first touch of greyness not long after it, for it was the Shortest Night after the Longest Day, a thin drizzle began to fall on our faces – all else was covered – fall out of the darkness like a blessing on the battlefield.

★

However, all was not yet done in that place that weighed with me, for an half hour or so later, that is after the Moon was set, with the Dawn coming up stronger, though very dull with low cloud, mists and warm rain, I woke with a start and this time on account of a lamp, dim not dazzling, held above our heads. Because he who held it was behind it I could not discern his face, but I heard his gasp and an oath, then: 'Little *Busné* Lord from Helmantica – is it really you?'

With cold dread on me I answered that it was I.

'Then your friend the flame-headed *sungaló* (traitor) must be near as well.'

I said nothing, but now the light swung away and down so for a second I thought he was gone but then felt the warmth of tainted breath on my forehead, a hand wrapped in a cloak on my face, so my cry was prevented, and the cold prick of steel in my neck.

'Sing for me, Little Lord, or I shall cut your throat; the Evil One is near, is he not?'

Before I could answer, and I know not how I should have answered, truly I do not, I heard a noise as it might be a carriage door opened and shut some way up from us and then a low whistle; the presence that held me, and was about to kill me I'm sure, melted away as if it had never been there at all, was just a dream brought on by drunkenness and the horrors of the day before.

Coffey stirred, coughed, flung out an arm, so that Dolores who now lay with him cuddled him in closer and soothed him, and all was quiet and my heart beat a little less fast, the sweat on my brow mingled with the rain and dispersed, and I was almost ready indeed to believe I had dreamed. Then a sudden cry – high, swiftly interrupted so the note fell to a bubbling whimper that faded, and all, as it were, on one breath – had me starting up again in the darkness so the fur-trimmed cloak Madame and I shared fell away from my shoulders and a strangled cry rose to my lips too.

At this she stirred, my Aunt/Mother, and her white arm curled up and about my neck, pulling me down to her bosom again and then rearranging the cloak about us so once more all was the soft animal caress of fur and silk, and warm velvety darkness, and fragrance, save for the whisper of rain about my ears, and in spite of the dreadful fright I had had I almost slept. But the light by seconds strengthened into damp greyness and presently my Aunt/Mother's fingers that first soothed my shoulder, then my neck and chest, so I almost swooned with the pleasure of it, fastened on the ring she had given me, and all these kept me waking.

We lay thus for some minutes and neither of us stirred, though I felt, I knew she was awake as well, though her eyes closed, for by now I could see her eyelids, so lined and papery beneath the violet paint she affected, and the tiny drops of misty rain like pearls on her lashes. Presently I contrived to inch my hand to the clasp of the chain and undo it, and thus obtained my release.

Now it was time to give my thoughts leave to dwell again on what I had tried to put from my mind the moment I had first climbed into the carriage at my Aunt/Mother's strong insistence, namely how fared Mistresses Tweedy and Reaney, and their infant boys; for though I knew the battle to be won, the village in British hands, and Captain Reaney near and still alive when I left, I felt I should go back to see that all was well and as it should be.

And it was well for the Darling Boy who has since been all my care that I did.

2

Madame stirred: one hand, the nails painted red, a little claw-like and the skin wrinkled, came out to pull the cloak about her, as I went; the other remained within clasping the ring – which I felt better to be done with, it had done me no good, though charitably offered – and so I set off, lowering myself down to the churned and dewy grass below. But I had yet a friend to find, one I would not so easily be parted from, and that my faithful Paqui, and it took some stumbling about that bizarre and garish field to find her.

Everywhere were coaches unwheeled or tipped or stuck in ditches, their cargoes and luggage spilled and strewed, and under the drizzle in the grassy mud the finest things took on a sad and tawdry look as if it was all so much lumber, the leavings of a travelling circus that had packed up and gone elsewhere taking what it valued but dumping what did not signify. Thus the finest silks shot through with gold thread, watered in shifting blues or reds look drab when spattered with mud; a gold chalice that a horse has trodden in is as woe-begone as a dinted kettle; chipped crystal has less worth than a whole jug, a crushed violin than a penny flute.

There were statues from churches, Christs, Virgins and Saints who had suffered in the night a second martyrdom – an ungilded stub of wood where a well-carved hand had once held the tools of their torture bearing sharper witness of man's barbarity than the ecstatic and vision-blurred pain expressed by their holy faces; there were paintings in heavy gilded frames like those carried past us the night before, and paintings torn from their stretchers and rolled up; there were scientific instruments as microscopes and telescopes – here a surgical case of teak lined with purple velvet its fine knives, tongs and probes scattered about where a disappointed thief had thrown them; there a map-maker's kit of fine-turned measuring wheel, dividers and rule similarly cast on the ground; and books, libraries and libraries of books, some small and handy with fine print, others huge and leather-bound with characters inked on vellum that now blotched and ran where the rain fell. There were too, and especially near the periphery, the impedimenta of fleeing soldiers knapsacks, bayonets, swords and muskets strewn in the grass, some already spotted with bright rust; there were coats and shakoes and a banner – a tricolour fringed with gold tassles, with an eagle on the flag-pole, and a Roman numeral sewn in gold to the panel of white in the centre, but the numbers part unstitched almost as if the bearer, in a last moment of failing pride had tried to rip them off before throwing the thing away;

there were even coins – but the gold and silver well-clipped which bore witness to the wealth: so much that the looters had been choosy and spilled away what was not new minted or milled. Well, I picked up a few of these, but the futility weighed heavy on me as I did – for though a fortune lay about me I had means to filch what might buy survival for a month, not a life-time of ease: and that, I suppose was the case of most of who came thence with their pockets full.

I scouted about thus in a widening circle from Madame's coaches, always with my eyes open for Paqui, yet not even glancing towards that small but smartly trimmed up chariot of Rubén's that lay on its side now an hundred yards off: but even so I could not avoid an occasional as it were accidental glimpse between the carts and carriages and thus saw at one moment an outstretched hand in the grass beside it, then a leg, and finally his head, twisted awkwardly on one side as if he were a broken doll, the long flame hair harsh against a pallor yet more ivory like than ever before, the scar I'd given him a paltry thing beside the gash in his throat. It came to me that he had had real gold, a strong box stuffed with the gains of six years of devilry in that coach, but I could not face going near enough to see if it remained – and surely if his own bravoes had not robbed him before the gypsies came, then the latter, who were perhaps somewhere still about, and I did not want to see them, had gone off with his loot. And for all the thieving and smashing, rapine and destruction whose ruins I was walking through, Rubén's was the only body I saw in the Baggage Park at Vitoria, though plenty later where the fighting had been.

At length I came on Paqui, and it was as well I did, for with every moment passing more of my kind moved about me – grey-faced, wide-eyed as consciousness of the new dawn and memory of what had gone before returned; and while thoroughbreds and glossy mules had been there for the taking in the night, and a moke might be spurned, there were plenty now stirring – from Bishops to Irish drummer boys, from Generals' wives to the drabs that follow the camp, from King Joseph's Judges to King George's Gaol-Birds, who would, when they looked about them, be glad to find a donkey. Well, as I say, I came upon her grazing on a clump of fresh grass with one trim black hoof dragging in a vast tapestry that depicted Kings and Queens of long ago hawking and hunting and a neat heap of her glossy dung, still steaming, on the edge of a portrait of a dull-looking school-masterly sort of person with glasses and an old ruff who was described a poet in the inscription. I bent over with the odour of Paquita's offering in my nostrils and one of Fernando's proverbs came back to me, dear Fernando – *Más caga un buey que cien golondrinas*, one ox shits more than an hundred swallows, which unworthy thought lightened my heart almost as if I had spiritually performed the deed that Paquita had materially done before me, so it was with a sort of smile I fetched up her head with her bridle, gave her floppy ears a tug, and pulled myself up and into her saddle: '*Arre, Burrita! Arre, Paquita!*' I cried and kicked her going, so we were soon jogging down those streets of ruined cars, watched by the grey and ravaged faces of the waking robbed and robbers – thieves all, for nothing there was fairly gained to start with.

Yet my way back to the village threw up one last chance encounter to be recorded – in spite of the fact that I had had the niceness to dismount and walk on the far side of Paqui to avoid it. For as I reached the road, which was raised a little above the meadow, who should be coming along it on his small bay mare, leading a mule with his baggage but Captain Branwater, and the reason why I got down, and as it were hid, was that I knew if he recognised me he must, for duty would compel it, stop, and question me at least, which I foresaw would delay him, and indeed delay him for some considerable time if I was to explain in full what has taken the last one hundred pages and more of these memoirs, that is why I had not reported to him at Divisional Head Quarters in Roger's Town the previous November, as he had ordered when spying me on the road with the Baggage; all of which might inconvenience him to no purpose.

But spot me again he did, though almost past me, when he drew rein and half turning called after me: 'Joey! Joey Bosham, come out from there and show yourself.'

So I came round and stood by his mule which had halted too. For a space he looked down at me and hemmed, then: 'Now, Joey. Where shall we start?' and he tapped his crop on his boot and bit his lip. 'How about whose donkey is that you were riding, until you saw me coming? That will be as good a place to begin as any.'

Well, this was a vexing question, for I feared he would·not wish to hear all the ins and outs of how Mistress Reaney's Father, Don Jorge Martín, since shot by the French, had put the moke in my care to carry his daughter to Ciudad and so on and so forth, so the best answer which was as near to the truth as could be simply arrived at was to say, as I did, 'Captain Reaney's, Sir.'

'And what regiment, pray, is Captain Reaney?'

'Eighth *Caçadores*, Sir; they lie in yonder village, over the bridge, having been much mauled in the battle.'

'And why are you now leading this Captain's cattle at this early hour to his village and *from* the French Baggage Park?'

'It's a long story, Sir.'

Hoping he would tell me to be about my business rather than keep him there listening to my tales I now looked out across the sodden plain where a heavy mist lay in the hollows, which yet did not deter the big black crows that could scarcely heave their gorged frames up into the air, but hopped and flapped from one corpse to the next.

'No doubt, Joey. And no doubt it will take in, in its meandering way, why you are not wearing your regimental coat. Nevertheless I must put it to you, Joey, your situation is awfully like that of a deserter and a thief.'

A dizziness came over me and I put my hand on Captain Branwater's trunk, the one with moleskin lid and wicker frame, that always went with him and was now strapped across the back of the mule. This dizziness was, I believe, the consequence of all the privations of the previous days, and not least the near starvation and too much intoxicating liquor in the preceding twenty-four hours.

But I shook the spell off and told the truth as briskly as I could. 'Mistress Reaney was yesterday brought to bed of a child, Sir, a fine boy. I was sent to fetch a midwife, who, her duties now fulfilled and there being no further need for her, I have just seen back to her home. Mistress Reaney also has my coat which I rolled up for her for a pillow which she lacked.'

'Oh My Sainted Grand-Mother, what a rogue you are, Joey,' and my Friend now roared with laughter and in earnest smacked his boot with his crop so his mare shifted about a bit at the noise, 'Why, that is so ridiculous a tale, Joey, it must have some truth in it for it could never be invented. Well, get back to your Captain Reaney and ask him to be so good as to send me a ticket vouching for you this time or I'll have the Judge Advocate General's staff after you like the pack of bloodhounds they are, and it will all end in the hanging matter as I make no doubt it should.' And with that he was done and clicking his tongue had his mare in a trot with mule and moleskin and wicker trunk bouncing behind him.

Many times since, when in his and Mistress Branwater's service here in Pau, we have chuckled over this incident, and on occasion, when he was especially genial, I have ribbed him in turn, asking him what he was up to in that Dawn jogging towards that Park with his trunk behind him – 'Tell me, James,' I have said, 'what pickings did you load into that wicker chest when my back was turned?' Though the truth is almost less creditable, and he blushed to own it, that in the *mêlée* of the evening before he had lost Sir Thomas Picton's staff which he served with and now jogged about to find them.

At first there seemed no-one in the village but the dead, and most of these about the bridge where we could scarce pick our way across them without treading on them, so thickly did they lie; but when a door opened high up the street, quite near if not next to

the cottage I had left the Ladies in, and that Brobdingnagian obe-
sity who had frighted me before appeared – the hugest and ugliest
woman in the world, six feet in all dimensions and so almost a
third as big as me again, clutching her rags and gowns and shawls
about her, and waddling, rolling, stumbling her whale-like way up
to the little square. Surprised I was to see her, but relieved now I
had seen her to be reminded of her so she would not come on me
so unexpected again, yet as she disappeared from view she went
out of my mind again for my ears now detected the high caterwauling of an infant, which spurred me on to our cottage door.

Sure enough a baby was there, but – and this is the greatest
mystery of my life, one which I have spent all my days trying to
solve – one baby was all. No Mistress Reaney, no Mistress Tweedy,
no Captain Reaney, no wounded – just one dead soldier on the
floor of the stable, but laid out decently now beneath a coat and a
blanket, and one new-born infant boy, wrapped in a soldier's red
coat, and placed in the manger, where now he squawled as if his
tiny lungs would burst.

Clearly he was hungry, and that being the first consideration all
others were pushed to the back of my mind; first I tethered Paqui,
away from the manger, and then went above stairs as quick as may
be – but finding the rooms there not only empty too, but all
tidied up so all was exactly as it had been when first we came
there, save for two gold guineas left on the table in the first room,
I was forced to wonder as I searched for milk, on just what had
happened. And neither then, nor since, nor now have I been able
to fathom it. That Mistress Tweedy and Mistress Reaney were
able to put all straight in their condition is not to be believed –
that they knew they were going and directed it, is possible;
but that argues a planned and unhurried departure – and how
could that be when one of them had actually left her new-born
child behind?

Whose squalling continued, and spurred me on to greater
efforts to satisfy its needs, and at last in the pantry I came on an
earthenware jar we had overlooked before, which contained a

half-pint of milk, which, through the cooling action of the terra-
cotta, was, while cheesy on the tongue, not quite turned – though
it must have been there two days at least. How to introduce this
life-supporting liquid where it was needed was now the problem.
Something temporary with a teapot suggested itself – but teapots
are not part of the furniture of Biscayan households nor even kettles with spouts. The mewling below now discovered a frenzy I
should not have thought possible in an infant so new and I began
to feel a desperation, even a despair as to how to shush it and as I
did the meaning of those two gold guineas came to me – the
Mother, whether Mistress Tweedy or Reaney, had left them to
hire what was now so clearly needed – a wet-nurse; so I scooped
them up and made for the stairhead again, thinking now that
what I must do was gather up the infant, remount Paqui and
make for the Town as quickly as I could and hire one there, and at
that very moment what I must consider to be the most wonderful miracle of my life, God-Sent for sure, occurred.   ·

The squalling stopped.

The silence that fell like balm on the house was not complete – first my ear picked up the clop of Paqui's hooves on the
flags, and her snuffle as she stretched for hay, then another sound,
a sort of cooing and crooning, low and chuckling, that, if it had
not been such a loving noise, might have frightened me, since I
could not begin to guess its origin. Thus, with a mild sort of trepidation I began to descend the stair and as I did the gurgling I had
heard was cut off by a gasp, followed by a harsh croak of fear, and
the infant began to bawl again. I descended further and backing
away from me as I came into view I thus discovered that land-
lodged Leviathan I had last seen heading up to the square, and in
her arms was the Boy, still wrapped in his red coat, but most marvellous of all was this – the woman had pulled back her shawls and
cloaks to bare the most mountainous breast in the World, a monstrous rolling lolloping blubbery lardy thing, the size of the udder
of a Béarnaise Cow, which are huge and give several gallons of
milk a day – but this udder I now beheld had only one teat; but,

that a huge and cow-like one, orangy-red, and, unbelievably, unmistakeably leaking milk, and this, even as she backed away from me croaking with fear, as above, she pushed as it were without thinking back into the Baby's mouth, which was really too small to accommodate it, and could only manage with difficulty, and so the squalling was shushed again.

But not my Lady Corpulence, who continued to croak, but with a high pleading note that signified fear and need, I make no doubt, so I came no nearer to her but held out the two gold guineas in my palm towards her at which she first fell silent, then her eyes narrowed, and finally she returned her gaze to the infant lost in the massive pillows of her mottled bosom, and she began again the crooning gurgling chortling noise I'd heard before.

So here, God-sent, as above, was our wet-nurse come most nicely when required and a cart-load more of questions with her, almost as perplexing as those pertaining to the whereabouts of either of the Ladies, the Infant's Mother: most impenetrable of which was – how came this Gargantua in milk?

Well, it's not a question I have yet found the answer to, for, with all her deformities, the poor woman is struck dumb, yet she can understand and signify denial and acquiescence and simple needs by signs, and over the years – for she still lives nearby to Pau and now is housekeeper to the *curé* of Bizanos where I still visit and take Arthur along too to see her, whom, big though he is and long grown beyond the original need he had of her which went from nursing to fostering, she still takes delight in and dotes on – over the years, I say, I believe she has more or less confirmed my first thoughts on the matter – *videlicet*: in spite of, perhaps even because of her monstrous size and ugliness she had sometime before, a year perhaps, who knows? been victim of a cruel and japing rape, French Grenadiers being no doubt the criminals, for who else would be big and strong enough? – had calved an ogre that had not lived, yet come into milk and remained so since, and no doubt made a living too, as she did with me, as nurse to orphaned babies or those whose mothers lacked her exuberant glut of galactic fluid. This and other questions relating to *Pilar* (for that, I believe is her name – María Pilar after Our Lady of Zaragossa – at all events I called her that after a day or two of her acquaintance when she pointed to a statue of Our Lady thus and then to herself) may yet be answered quite soon, for the Curé aforesaid seems to be in the way of teaching her to read and write; indeed, she has improved in other ways too, being much less fat and ugly, though still of course over two yards high.

Still, of some interest though these speculations were and are, there remained and persist still others of more moment – namely, whose was the Infant? and, What to do with him? The answer to the second being dependent on the first, and as to the first I reasoned thus and thus: while there was no reason I could guess at for either Lady to abandon their so recently borne offspring, there was *less* reason for Mistress Reaney: *item* – she was married; *item* – her husband, her child's Father, had no doubt come upon her shortly after I left; *item* – even if he had not and she was at last a widow, she had money and family. Mistress Tweedy had none of these advantages and it seemed to me just possible that some unforeseen and unguessable event had intervened to make her choose to separate from the Reaneys and then leave her child. For instance it could be she had decided out of a sort of pride, and she was a proud woman, to shift for herself. Or, and this I hardly liked or dared to think, but she had shown herself most loving to me, she had insisted on waiting in the house for me, while duty had called the Reaneys away, and then herself been forced to leave – why? perhaps hunger had overtaken her, and she had gone out for food and suffered some mishap. Yes, the more I thought on these lines the more certain it seemed to me that the Boy was Flora's, and the fact he was wrapped in a red coat, just like hers, with the yellow regimentals of the Connaughts on it, added a sort of certainty to my speculations.

What to do then? If I had thought the baby to be Mistress Reaney's the obvious thing would have been to seek out where the Fifth Division had moved to, and find Captain Reaney; but if something in the way of what I have suggested was the truth then the best thing was to stay fast as long as possible: whatever errand Mistress Tweedy was on might be done within an hour, or even two or three, whatever ill may have befallen might yet at least allow her to send back news – for instance, supposing she had fainted by the way (a not unlikely event so soon after parturition) might she not have been discovered and removed to an hospital in the town? Might it not be a matter even of a day or two before she got word sent back to this village she had left her Child there?

In the event, we – that is Pilar, the Boy, and I – remained at Gamarra Mayor another three weeks; and no word or sign of Mistress Tweedy (nor of the Reaneys either, for that matter) came to us at all. The inhabitants returned – before Noon all were back from Vitoria where they had sheltered – and treated us kindly enough, as long as I paid for our lodgings which were near the bridge, and during this period I had the Boy Christened. I chose the names, and if there is presumption in this I hope I may be forgiven, *Arthur* and *Victor* for reasons not unconnected with his birth; so he is Arthur Victor Bosham, a fine name for a fine lad for he is a fine lad, and big for his age – though not the name he should have.

By the end of three weeks the money I had, the remains of the guineas given me by Mr Curtis for my Uncle/Father's microscope, what I had picked up in the Baggage Park, and the two guineas left, I still suppose, by Mistress Tweedy, though how she came by them I cannot pretend to guess, was half spent (Pilar was a prodigious eater), and seeing things could not continue thus much longer, a new course had to be decided on.

Since Arthur's Mother must be presumed unable or unwilling to care for him (I must believe not able; Captain Branwater says not willing, for he heard news of her at third or fourth hand some years later, that she was well provided for and lived first at the Bath and later at Waterford in Ireland – but I cannot believe this, Flora would never leave her child so), it seemed to me I should now take steps to seek out his Father, who, for all the weal of nations was his burden, might yet spare a thought and a guinea or two for the consequence of the solace freely given him by a too-liberal girl; and so we set off, the four of us, for Paqui came too, though now I rode on her, Pilar being too heavy for the little moke, in search of the Peer.

3

It was ever His Lordship's practice to be elusive – we had already had experience of that chasing him up from Ciudad to Salamanca, to Toro, to Burgos, and so at last to Vitoria, and in the next two weeks he ran true to form. The first stage was simple enough – the French had run to Pampeluna and the Allies had followed; some of the former remained in Pampeluna which was well-fortified, and some of the latter sat down outside to keep them there till a siege train could be brought up or the besieged grew hungry and gave in. But the main French Armies continued their flight across the Pyrenees which his Lordship declined, for reasons of policy, to cross straightway, and so the Allies were scattered in a long line from Pampeluna to San Sebastián on the Atlantic coast (which was also fortified and remained in French hands) and most of them up at the heads of passes. These I supposed to be impenetrable to a very large woman, a small mule, a very small baby and myself for I too found their slopes too much for my legs and my stomach, for I loath to be high. Moreover, as above, no-one we asked seemed to know where the General Head Quarters was in all this wild country, though most thought they were somewhere on a river called the Bidassoa.

This river rises in the watershed some eight leagues above Pampeluna and then flows North, though circuitously, through grand gorges and between high peaks to empty itself on the very angle 'twixt France and Spain; and so it was towards this watershed I directed my tiny convoy, having spent a day or so refreshing ourselves in the environs of Villalba where the besiegers of Pampeluna, who were mostly Spanish, had their cantonments, and this was on the Twenty-Fifth of July; and we were a scant league up the road, just beyond a village called Sorauren, when we heard the rumbling of heavy furniture moved in an upstairs room that experience has taught me is gunfire – but still far off. This caused us to hasten, for I could not but believe this meant a battle, and a battle would not be won by the French, and presently all would be flooding down into the plain about Bayonne, and we should never catch his Lordship; yet the road was difficult and steep and wearisome, especially towards nightfall, and so we rested up that night only a further three or four leagues on, in a shepherd's hut on the Pass known as the *Puerto de Velate*, and it was as well we were no further on, else we should surely have been taken by the French.

At Dawn next day the gunfire started early, and as we descended the North side of the Pass, which was yet steeper and more tortuous in its bends than the South, we caught glimpses of columns winding up towards us. By nine they were close enough for me to be sure their uniforms were predominantly red and brown; and soon there were further signs as Aides and Messengers storming up on blown horses, then carts with wounded, that we were indeed not pursuing the pursuers but making our way in the face of what was surely a retreat, and from the speed the main column came winding up through the rocks and firs from meadows and rivers below, could well be a rout. So at eleven o'clock I halted, turned us round, and set our faces back up the slopes for the Pass we had left. At this Pilar stuck, and would not budge, planting her enormous mass on a boulder, setting her arms akimbo, and shaking her head so all her chins and cheeks variously and severally wobbled which would have made me laugh had I not spied French Chasseurs scouting along the rear of the Allied Column, the end of which was now in sight about two leagues below us. Paqui began to browse on the sweet mountain grass, little Atty yelled, and Pili unloosed her great udders which presently cascaded into full view, almost to where her waist would be an she had one, as she always did if the little lordling cried. I pleaded and cajoled for an half hour at least but to no avail, for it was that long and more before my charges had satisfied all their needs which on Pili's part included a loaf of bread, a whole Pampeluna sausage, and a can of ewe's milk I'd bought off the shepherd.

The consequence was that although once across the pass again the way was all down hill, we were still a league short of Sorauren at nightfall, most of the British Army had marched past us, and only a rearguard and pickets lay between us and the French. Yet with nightfall Pili stuck again, was adamant (if something so soft can be so described) to stick the night out — she never would move at all in the dark, and thus they slept out the night of the Twenty-Sixth, while I sweated and chafed, and this time in a stable in a village called Ostiz.

Nor would they be up betimes in the morning. Before she would move Pili must needs feed the brat again, and break her own fast on a cheese and half a dozen eggs, and counting up my last handful of coin before we set off, I said to myself if we don't come up with his Lordship soon and get something on account for support of his Bastard's Nurse we shall be in a pretty way indeed. And the oddity was, the case was the other way about, a matter of his Lordship coming up on us, rather than us on him.

The league between Ostiz and Sorauren had me as much afraid as I have ever been in all these trials and horrors and so forth, for all was bustle about us, up and down the road and on the hills which were high and steep but grassy, and especially to the East of the road, where all the signs were a battle would shortly begin, for columns were massing by regiments facing each other across a steep-sided valley, each army on its own high crest, and I could see that only by pushing on as quick as may be would we end up in the British and Allied lines ahead of us before the thing started. Indeed as we came out of the South side of the village of Sorauren, with it lacking about fifteen minutes of eleven o'clock, we found ourselves amongst a company or so of Portuguese who were pulling back up a track which deviated off the road and over the shoulder of the Down, and thus into the main British position; and these were the very last rear-guards of the Allies, a skirmishing line of light troops, and as we climbed above the village we could see the French *voltigeurs* skirmishing down towards its North-Eastern corner, a scant half mile off, if so much.

You may be sure I now urged my charges on with all the wit and strength I could spare from keeping my own legs going – for the track was very steep, and flinty too, too steep for Paqui to manage with me on her back, yet I could not but mark the splendour of the sights around us. Behind us and stretching to the East a long high ridge covered with grass and bushes supported battalions in blue that marched with drums, fifes and bugles and colours uncased – tricolours all – to their positions, and out in front, a long cannon shot only from the British line, their staff – distinguishable by white plumes blowing in the breeze, by the quality of their horse, and by the maps they perused and the glasses they peered at us through – Clausel, d'Erlon, and Reille, with Marshal Soult himself in their midst, or so the History before me says.

Meanwhile ahead along the facing ridge and behind it, and we could see this now for we had breasted the low rise at last that took us into the British position, the lines of brown and red stretched to the skyline, also with bands playing and the Jacks out, and Generals Byng and Anson and Lowry-Cole and Sir Thomas Picton – but no Lord Wellington, for he was still up North towards San Sebastián, I'd heard it said about us, and if we didn't watch out we'd be beat again without him, beat as we were yesterday and the day before, the men said, and looked glum at it.

Well, no doubt we were a comickal sight – Pili waddling up that white track holding the baby; Paqui, stoickal as ever, head down, ears back, stumbling at the flints; and me running from one to other, first pulling at the ass's head, then round the back to push at Pili's monstrous bum, and many a grim-faced Portuguese about us cracked the dourness of their faces at the sight: but my first thought was, I must confess, that cheers and wild glee were a touch misplaced, for that is what now broke out about us as we toiled over that shoulder, huzzas all round and hats off to cheer and 'Douro, Douro, Douro,' rolled out from all the Portuguese in line about us, and 'Douro, Douro, Douro,' rolled on the cry into the lines beyond us.

Bewildered beyond anything I straightened up to peer at those weathered faces, grinning white teeth flashing, some were even embracing their neighbours as though the battle was already won instead of nearly lost, and then I turned and looked down the track we'd climbed back to the village of Sorauren a mile below, shook the sweat from my eyes, and looked again.

A solitary horseman was coming up behind us but where we had sweated and laboured, it seemed his horse had wings – the silhouette from a distance already familiar, the short frock-coat, the small plumeless cocked hat, nearer the great Roman nose, the high-arched brows, and nearer still the strong hands on the rein, the firm set of the mouth that did not smile much, but smiled a little then, as reaching the crest, five yards from us, he reined up in an easy little pirouette and briefly doffed his hat – as much at the French across the way as at us.

'Douro, Douro, Douro,' cried the Portuguese.

'Viva el Velintón y Viva la Nación,' cheered the Spanish.

'By Jasus – it's Atty,' I heard a voice nearby, 'auld Nosey himself, the bogger that licks the French . . .'

And with all this tumult about us my eye strayed to the dried grass by the chalky track where I marked mauve-tinted scabious, sage, and yellow trefoil, and a cinnamon-coloured butterfly with small black spots hovering and flitting above the flowers,

AFTERWORD

With that unsatisfactory comma Joseph's Memoir ends, which is a pity, I suppose. As a writer and reader of thrillers I like tidy ends – most people do, I think. I like to be able to guess how the principal characters, those that survive, are likely to go on; above all I hate mysteries unsolved. Still, on his very first page Joseph warned us: 'life in its entirety, and life is not often nice or neat', he promised.

Yet, he has left questions unanswered – particularly concerning the two episodes in his life he is most ashamed of: his rescue from mutilation leading to his incorporation in the British Army, and the death of his father. As far as the first is concerned it is clear the initial account (at the beginning of Volume Two), which describes pursuit and castration at the hands of a Polish Sergeant is out and out fiction, though borrowing from anecdotes later recounted at secondhand; then in Chapter IV of Volume Three he makes a real effort to get it right, declares he is not romanticizing, but leaves us uncertain as to the injuries he received, though earlier during his account of Prigg's misadventures, he seems to suggest that he has been castrated, and that Flora Tweedy thinks he has. However, against this there is a third version, reported more or less consistently by Branwater, the Gypsy Count, and Flora, a version that asserts that Joseph was not rescued but ransomed unhurt by Branwater, who at the time believed he was saving an English drummer-boy.

Why then the earlier versions? No doubt the Freudians will have their answer – but on a practical level I would suggest that Joseph first claimed he had been castrated to support his defence on a charge of seducing one of Madame Hugue's pupils (see Chapter I of Volume Three); then later he might have used the fiction, or contemplated using it, as a basis for denying paternity of Arthur Victor.

As far as the death of his father is concerned he comes clean in the end of course, but again it seems he can only bear to write of it in parenthesis while actually dealing with something else; yet I think it might not be too much to say that this moment of truth telling in an aside is a sort of climax, if not to the memoir itself then the *writing* of the memoir – it is almost as if the whole monstrous book has been heading to this point where he can at last face and record the worst he knows of himself.

As for the rest, well of course Joseph's references to Pau and the Branwaters give us an inkling of the next ten years of his life (though we have no idea of *how* he got to Pau) – we know he was an usher in a girls' academy, that he fell in with, and out with the Branwaters, and then, from that comma, written I suppose in 1824, a blank, a complete silence.

Perhaps something could be discovered. I don't know. I am not a historian, I've no training in searching through archives, my French is shaky, and I am not at ease with officialdom. Lacking these disabilities I might have dug something out of the Béarnaise records, but I'm afraid I did not even make the effort.

What I did do was go over the English cemetry with a fine tooth comb – and that's a story in itself, with its Generals who died the day after the twenty-fifth anniversary of Waterloo (what sort of a party was that?); its consumptives dying at 18 or 20 after only six months in a climate as wet as the West coast of Ireland; and from 1860 its Americans with megalithic tombstones – but no Boshams.

So much for Pau. While and since preparing Joseph's memoirs for publication I have read widely but unsystematically round the period and have stumbled on the following snippets which might be of interest.

Patrick Curtis became Archbishop of Armagh and Primate of Ireland. He lived to be over ninety, and quarrelled with the Duke over Catholic Emancipation, though he owed his elevation in part to the Duke's recommendation.

Julián Sánchez, *el Charro*, was unjustly accused of liberalism by Ferdinand, after the latter's Restoration. Don Julián died in poverty and obscurity as a result in 1832.

The University of Salamanca did not begin to recover from the depradations of the War until well into the second half of the nineteenth century. The same could be said of the whole of Iberia.

Ferdinand invited the Duke to keep Velasquez's *Waterseller of Seville*, and *Portrait of the Poet Quevedo*. Both now hang in Apsley House. Murillo painted more than one *Immaculate Conception*; the one especially admired by Marshal Soult, which may be the one mentioned in the memoirs, is safely back in the Prado.

I am grateful to a musicologist friend, who wishes to remain anonymous, for tentatively identifying Mr Curtis's first piece of music as Beethoven's Piano Sonata No. 21 in C, Op. 53, *The Waldstein*; the second, played in Volume Three, he thinks may be the first two movements of No. 26 in E Flat, Op. 81a, *Les Adieux*.

Finally, may I say I should be delighted to hear from anyone who stumbles across anything which sheds light on what happened to, *inter alia*, Fernando, Mistress Tweedy, the Reaneys, Coffey, Nolan, Madame La Granace, not to mention Joey Bosham himself.

J.R.

(Salamanca, Southampton, Pau, Lyndhurst, 1974–1978)

Now you can order superb titles directly from Abacus

☐	The Last English King	Julian Rathbone	£6.99
☐	Every Man for Himself	Beryl Bainbridge	£6.99
☐	Master Georgie	Beryl Bainbridge	£6.99
☐	How to Murder a Man	Carlo Gebler	£6.99
☐	Hannibal	Ross Leckie	£6.99
☐	Scipio	Ross Leckie	£6.99

Please allow for postage and packing: **Free UK delivery.**
Europe; add 25% of retail price; Rest of World; 45% of retail price.

To order any of the above or any other Abacus titles, please call our credit card orderline or fill in this coupon and send/fax it to:

Abacus, 250 Western Avenue, London, W3 6XZ, UK.
Fax 0181 324 5678   Telephone 0181 324 5517

☐ I enclose a UK bank cheque made payable to Abacus for £ ....

☐ Please charge £.............. to my Access, Visa, Delta, Switch Card No.

☐☐☐☐☐☐☐☐☐☐☐☐☐☐☐☐☐☐☐

Expiry Date ☐☐☐☐   Switch Issue No. ☐☐

NAME (Block letters please) ....

ADDRESS ....

....

....

Postcode ....Telephone ....

Signature ....

Please allow 28 days for delivery within the UK. Offer subject to price and availability.

Please do not send any further mailings from companies carefully selected by Abacus ☐

British Qualifications 2017